DREAMWORKS
HOW TO TRAIN YOUR
DRAGON

ALSO FROM JOE BOOKS

DreamWorks Trolls Cinestory Comic
DreamWorks Kung Fu Panda 3 Cinestory Comic
Disney 101 Dalmatians Cinestory Comic
Disney•Pixar Comics Treasury
Disney Big Hero 6 Cinestory Comic
Disney•Pixar Inside Out Cinestory Comic
Disney Gravity Falls Cinestory Comic Volume One
Disney Gravity Falls Cinestory Comic Volume Two
Disney Gravity Falls Cinestory Comic Volume Three
Disney•Pixar The Good Dinosaur Cinestory Comic
Disney Zootopia Cinestory Comic
Disney Star vs the Forces of Evil Cinestory Comic

DREAMWORKS
HOW TO TRAIN YOUR
DRAGON

CINESTORY COMIC

JOE BOOKS

How to Train Your Dragon

Published simultaneously in the United States and Canada by Joe Books Ltd,
489 College Street, Suite 203, Toronto, Ontario, M6G 1A5.

www.joebooks.com

First Joe Books edition: July 2018

Print ISBN: 978-1-77275-455-1
ePub ISBN: 978-1-77275-464-3
Kindle ISBN: 978-1-77275-932-7

Library and Archives Canada Cataloguing in Publication information is available upon request.

Adapted by Steven J. Bright.

Printed and bound in Canada
1 3 5 7 9 10 8 6 4 2

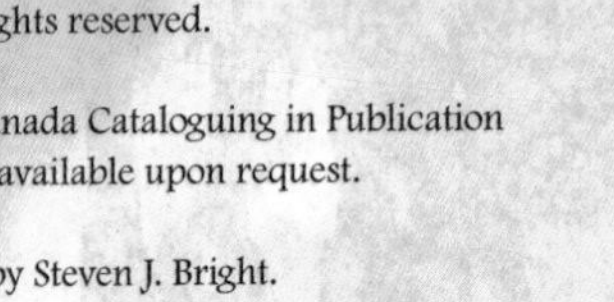

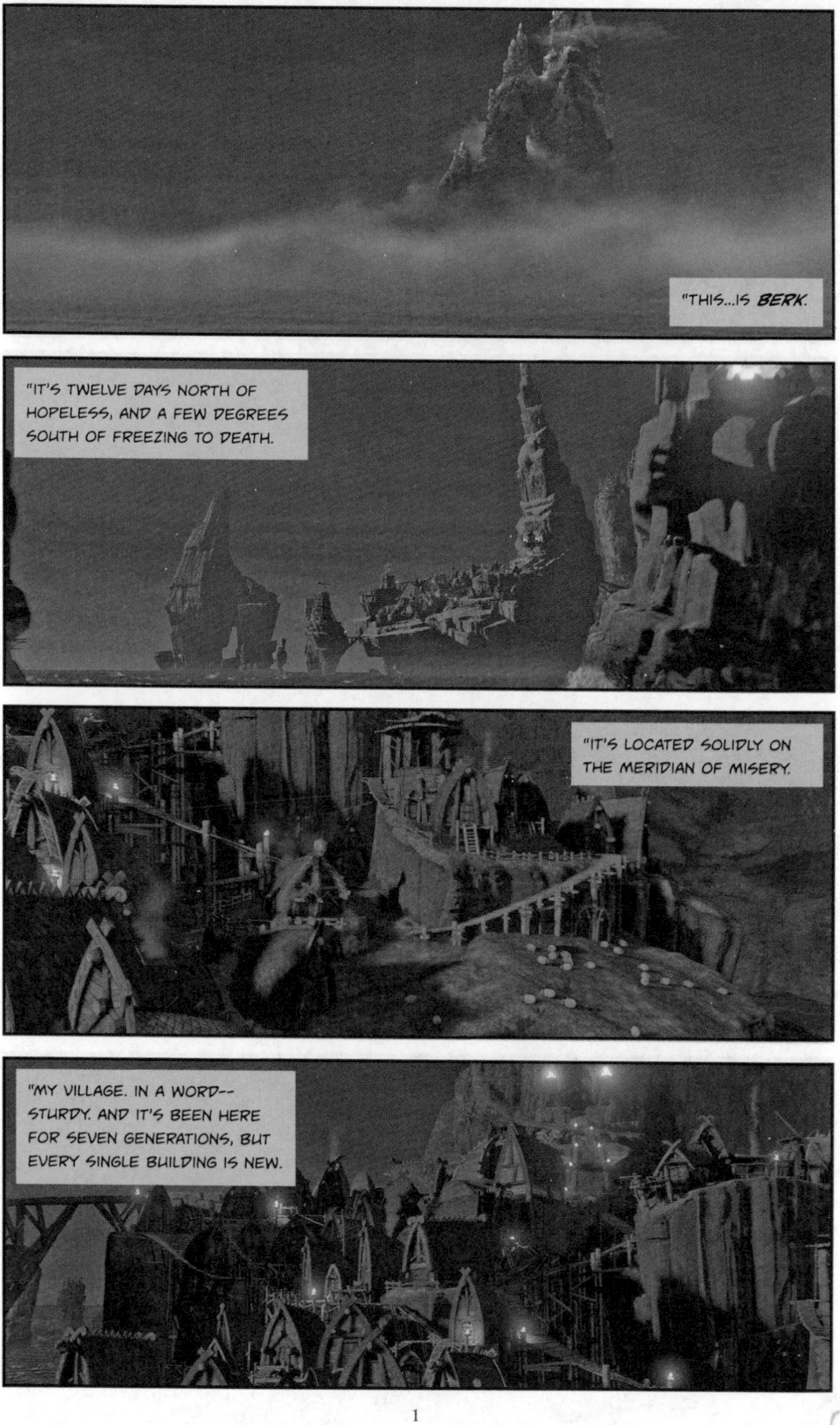
"THIS...IS BERK.
"IT'S TWELVE DAYS NORTH OF HOPELESS, AND A FEW DEGREES SOUTH OF FREEZING TO DEATH.
"IT'S LOCATED SOLIDLY ON THE MERIDIAN OF MISERY.
"MY VILLAGE. IN A WORD-- STURDY. AND IT'S BEEN HERE FOR SEVEN GENERATIONS, BUT EVERY SINGLE BUILDING IS NEW.

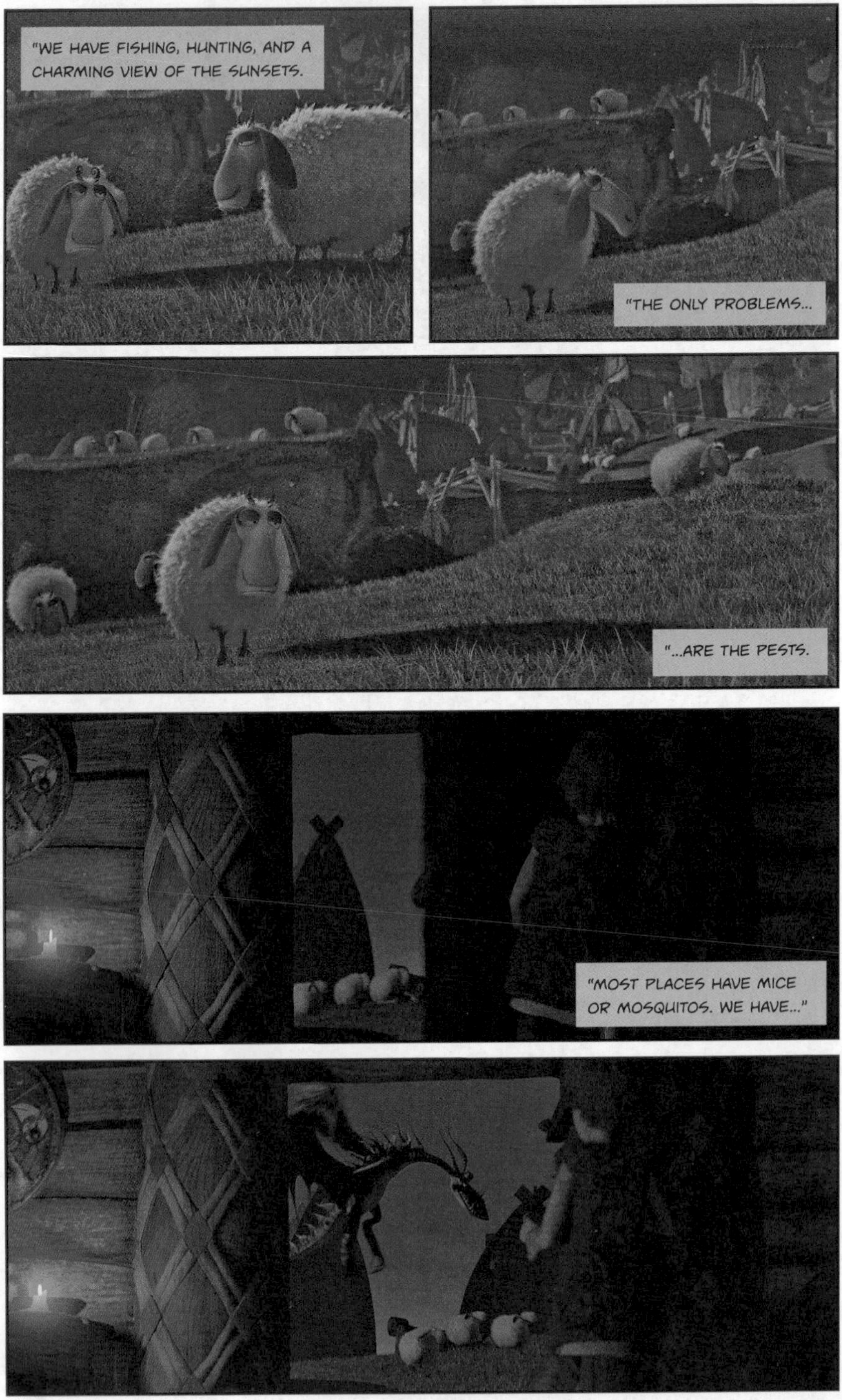
"WE HAVE FISHING, HUNTING, AND A CHARMING VIEW OF THE SUNSETS.
"THE ONLY PROBLEMS...
"...ARE THE PESTS.
"MOST PLACES HAVE MICE OR MOSQUITOS. WE HAVE..."

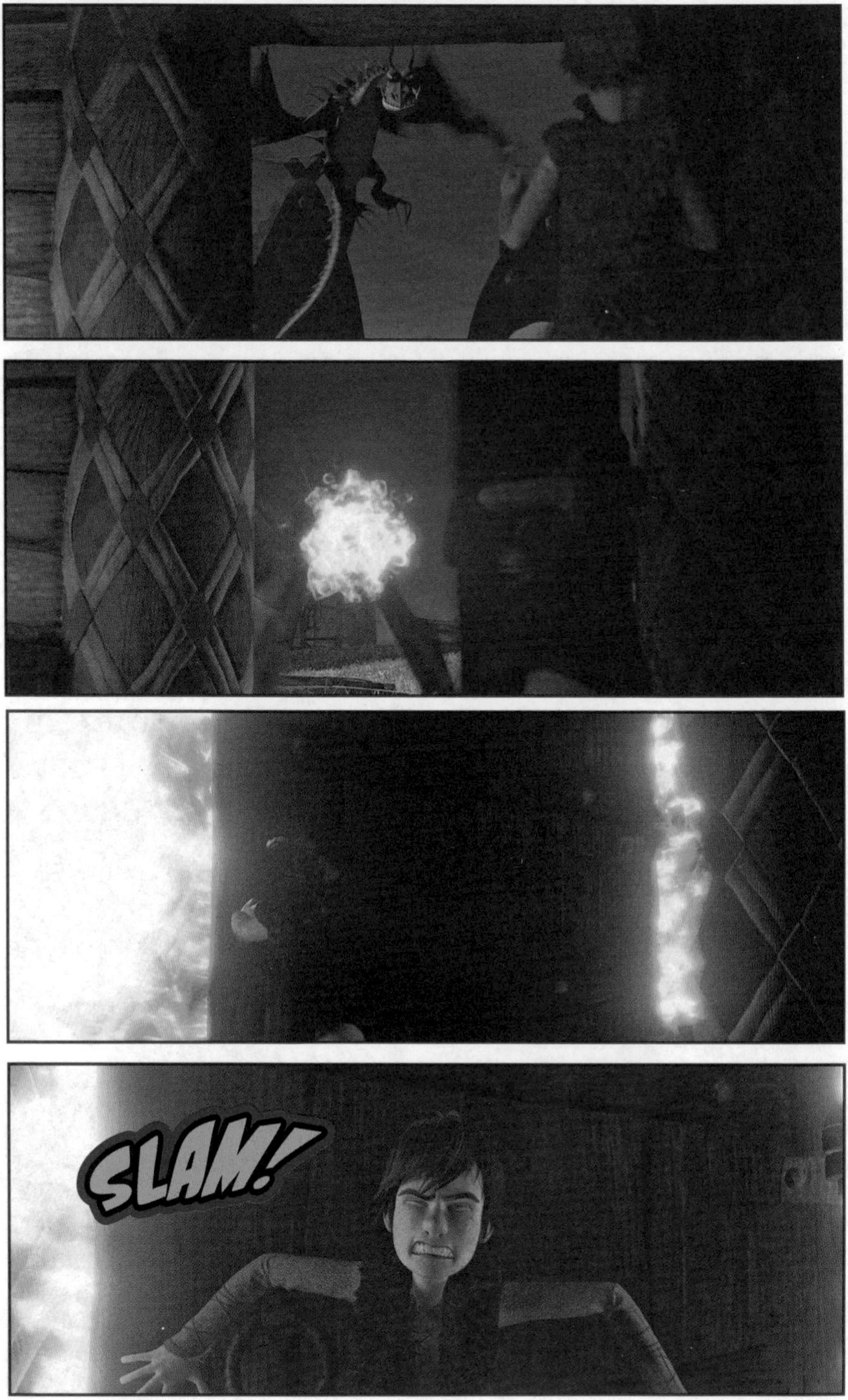
SLAM!

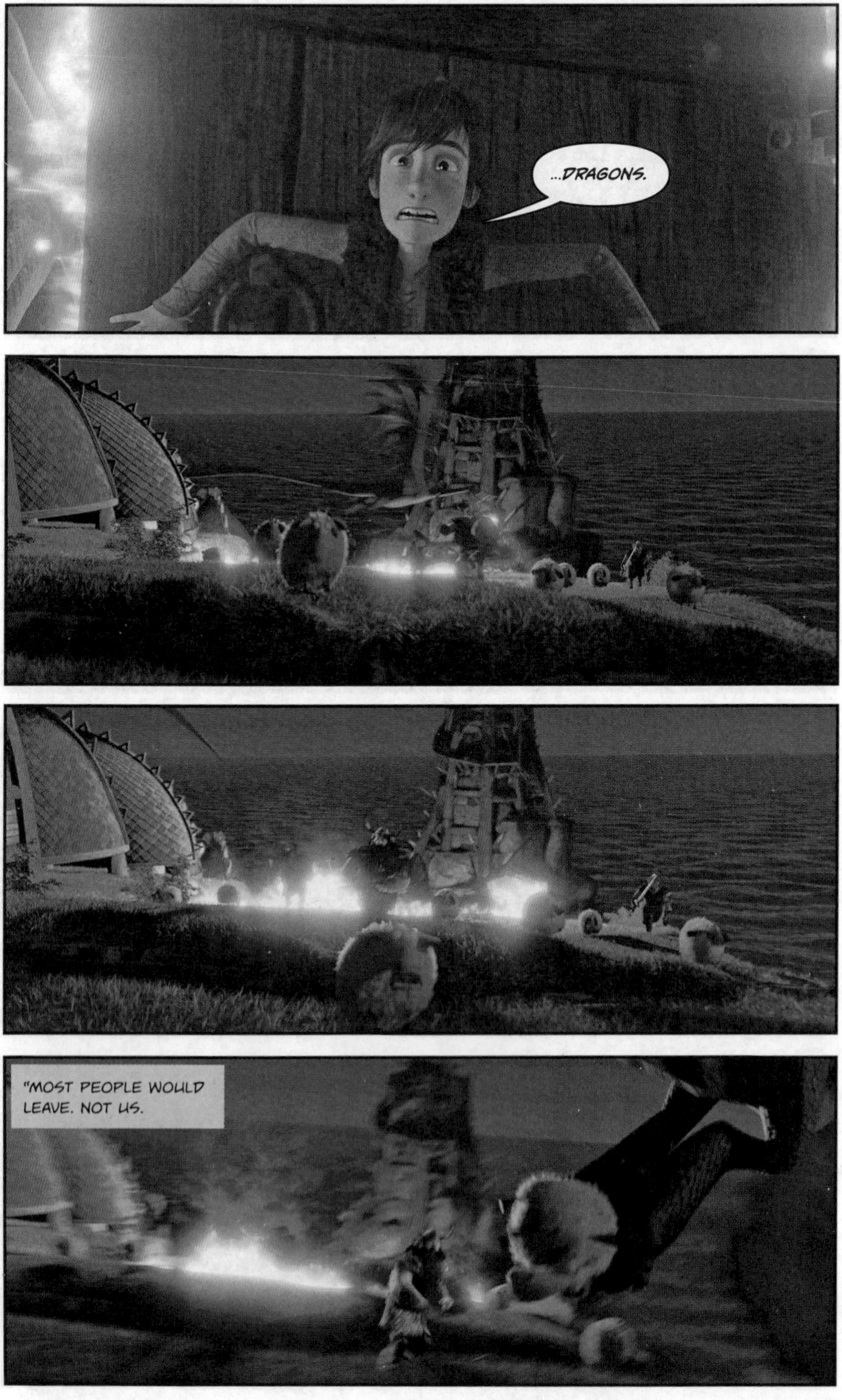
...DRAGONS.
"MOST PEOPLE WOULD LEAVE. NOT US.

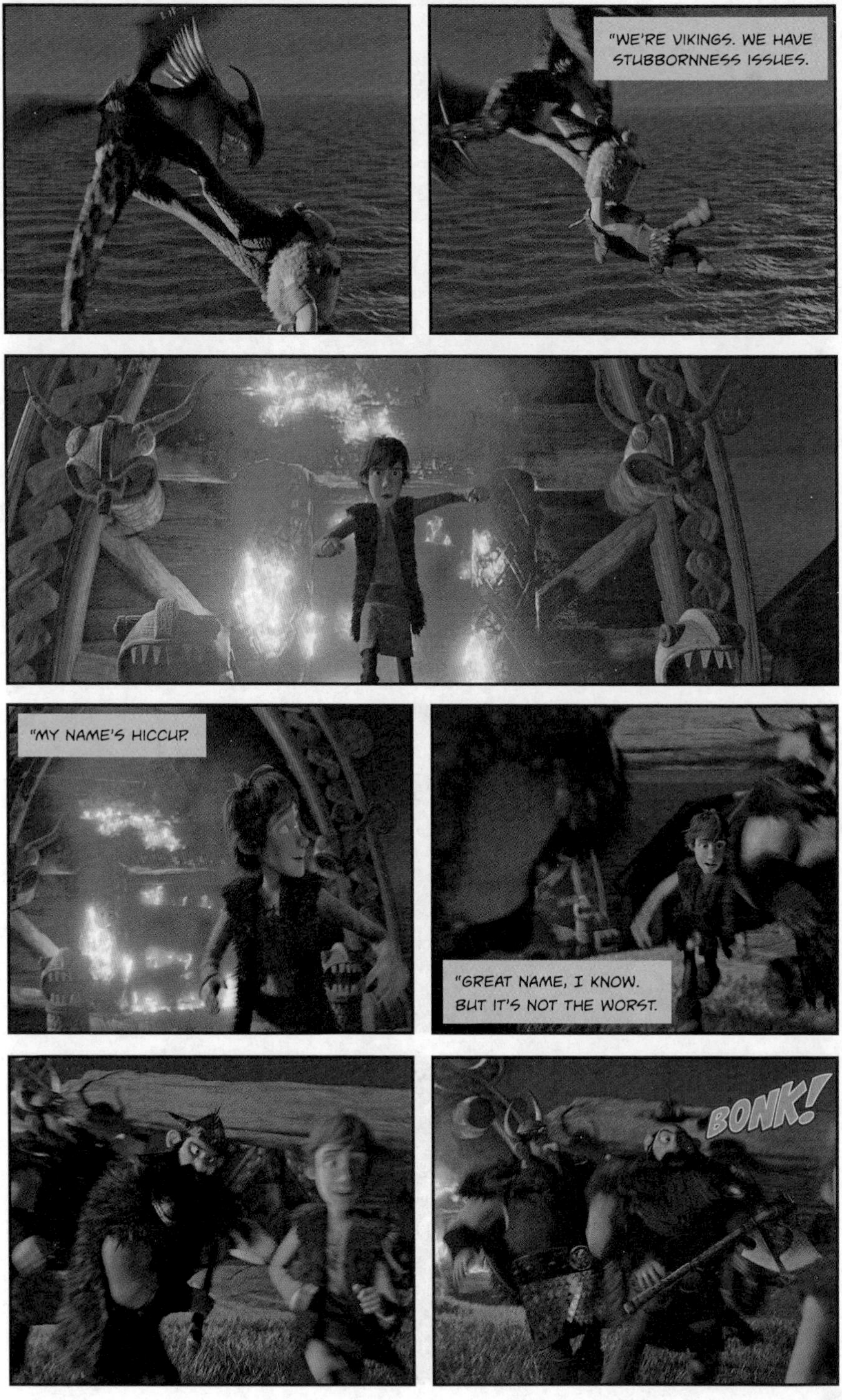
"WE'RE VIKINGS. WE HAVE STUBBORNNESS ISSUES.
"MY NAME'S HICCUP.
"GREAT NAME, I KNOW. BUT IT'S NOT THE WORST.
BONK!

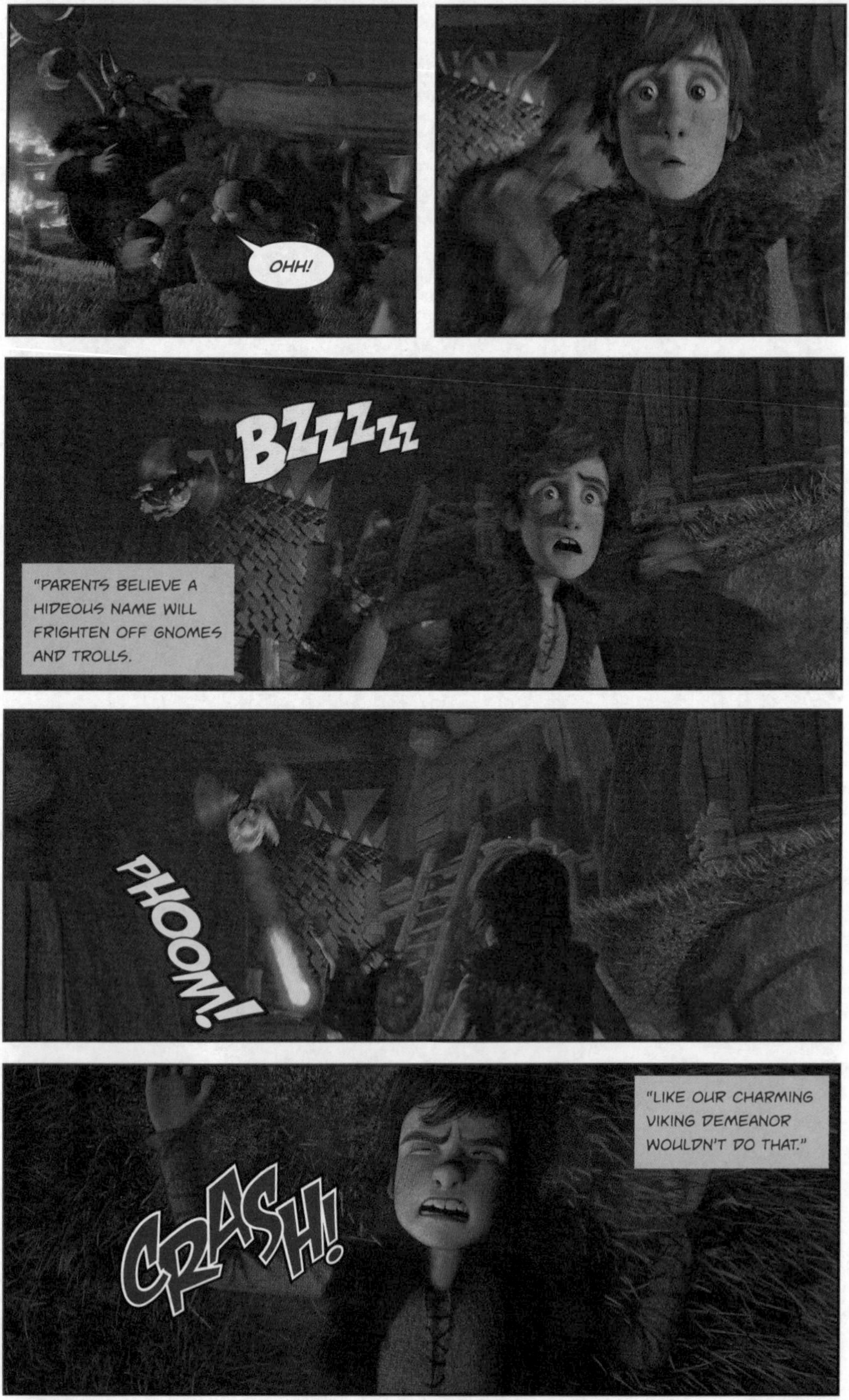
OHH!
BZZZZZ
"PARENTS BELIEVE A HIDEOUS NAME WILL FRIGHTEN OFF GNOMES AND TROLLS.
PHOOM!
CRASH!
"LIKE OUR CHARMING VIKING DEMEANOR WOULDN'T DO THAT."

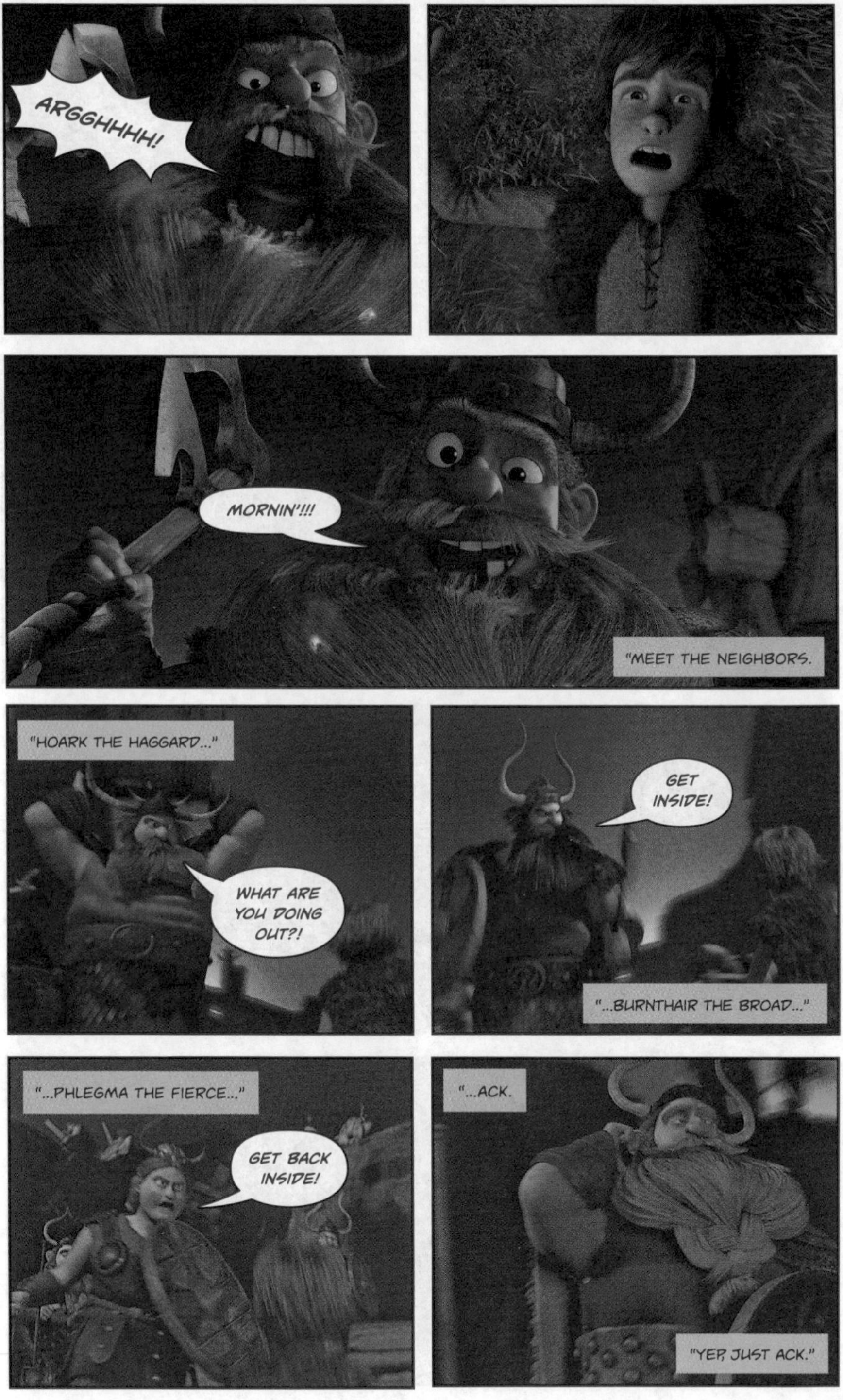
ARGGHHHH!
MORNIN'!!!
"MEET THE NEIGHBORS.
"HOARK THE HAGGARD..."
WHAT ARE YOU DOING OUT?!
GET INSIDE!
"...BURNTHAIR THE BROAD..."
"...PHLEGMA THE FIERCE..."
GET BACK INSIDE!
"...ACK.
"YEP, JUST ACK."

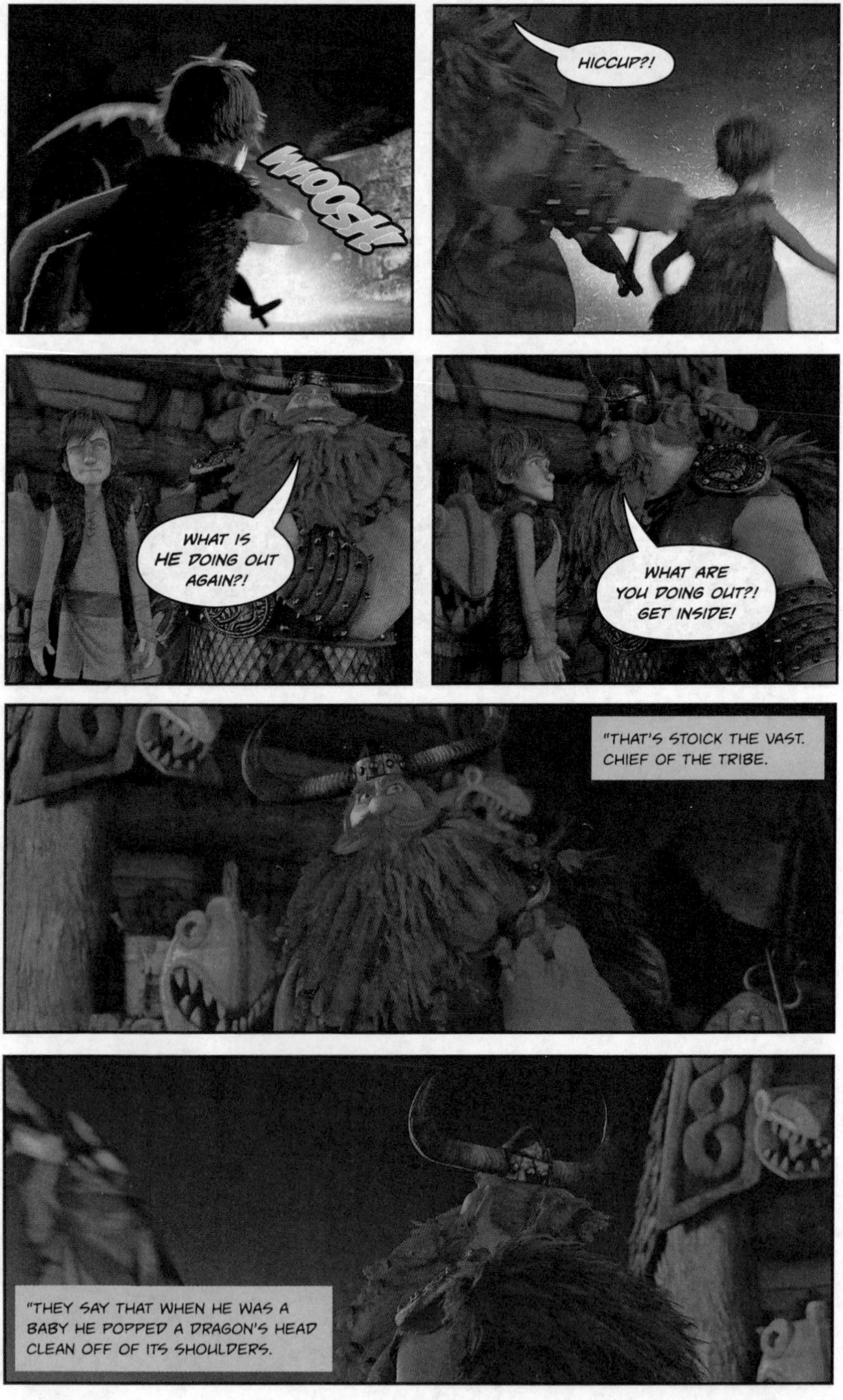
WHOOSH!
HICCUP?!
WHAT IS HE DOING OUT AGAIN?!
WHAT ARE YOU DOING OUT?! GET INSIDE!
"THAT'S STOICK THE VAST. CHIEF OF THE TRIBE.
"THEY SAY THAT WHEN HE WAS A BABY HE POPPED A DRAGON'S HEAD CLEAN OFF OF ITS SHOULDERS.

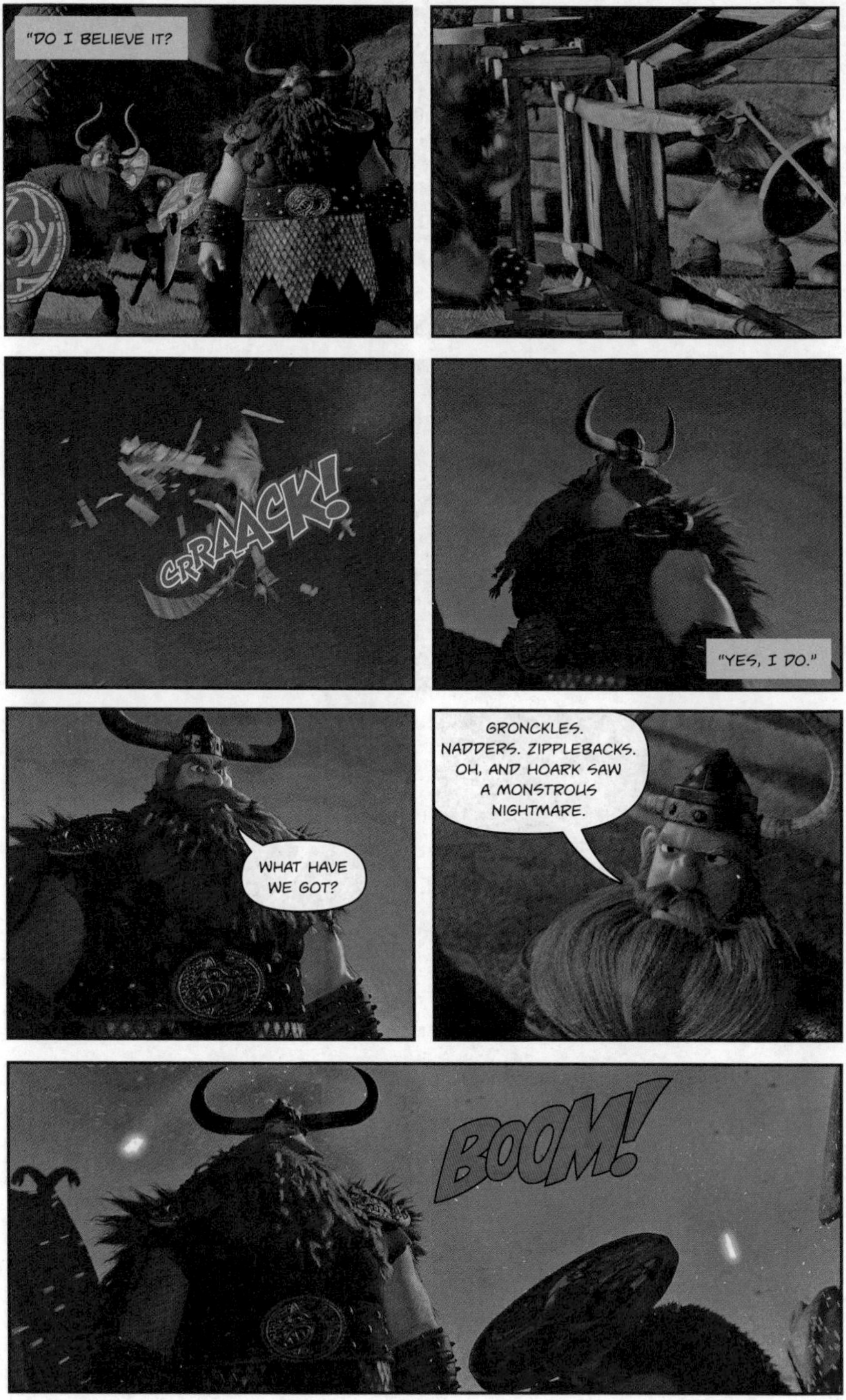
"DO I BELIEVE IT?
CRRAACK!
"YES, I DO."
WHAT HAVE WE GOT?
GRONCKLES. NADDERS. ZIPPLEBACKS. OH, AND HOARK SAW A MONSTROUS NIGHTMARE.
BOOM!

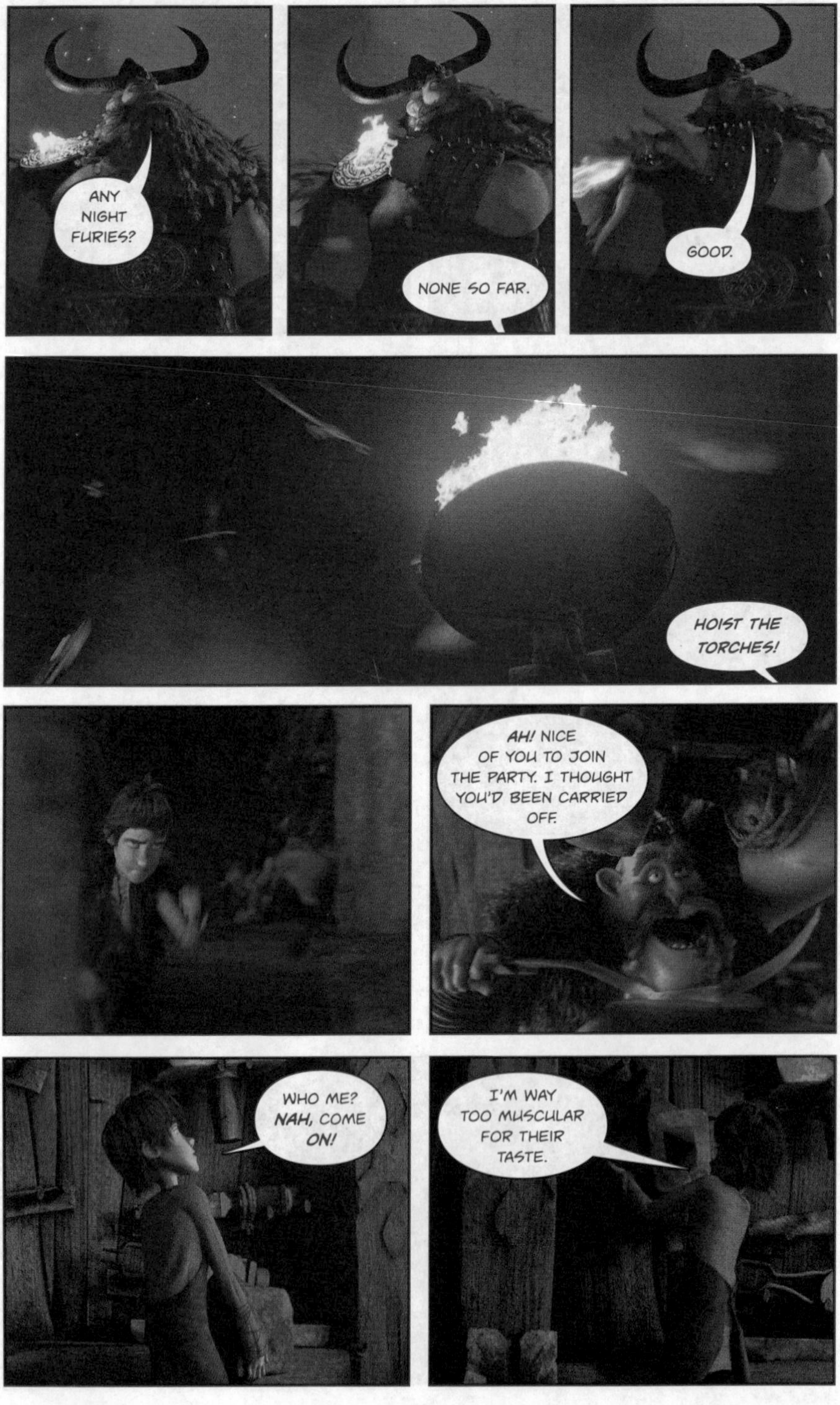
ANY NIGHT FURIES?
NONE SO FAR.
GOOD.
HOIST THE TORCHES!
AH! NICE OF YOU TO JOIN THE PARTY. I THOUGHT YOU'D BEEN CARRIED OFF.
WHO ME? NAH, COME ON!
I'M WAY TOO MUSCULAR FOR THEIR TASTE.

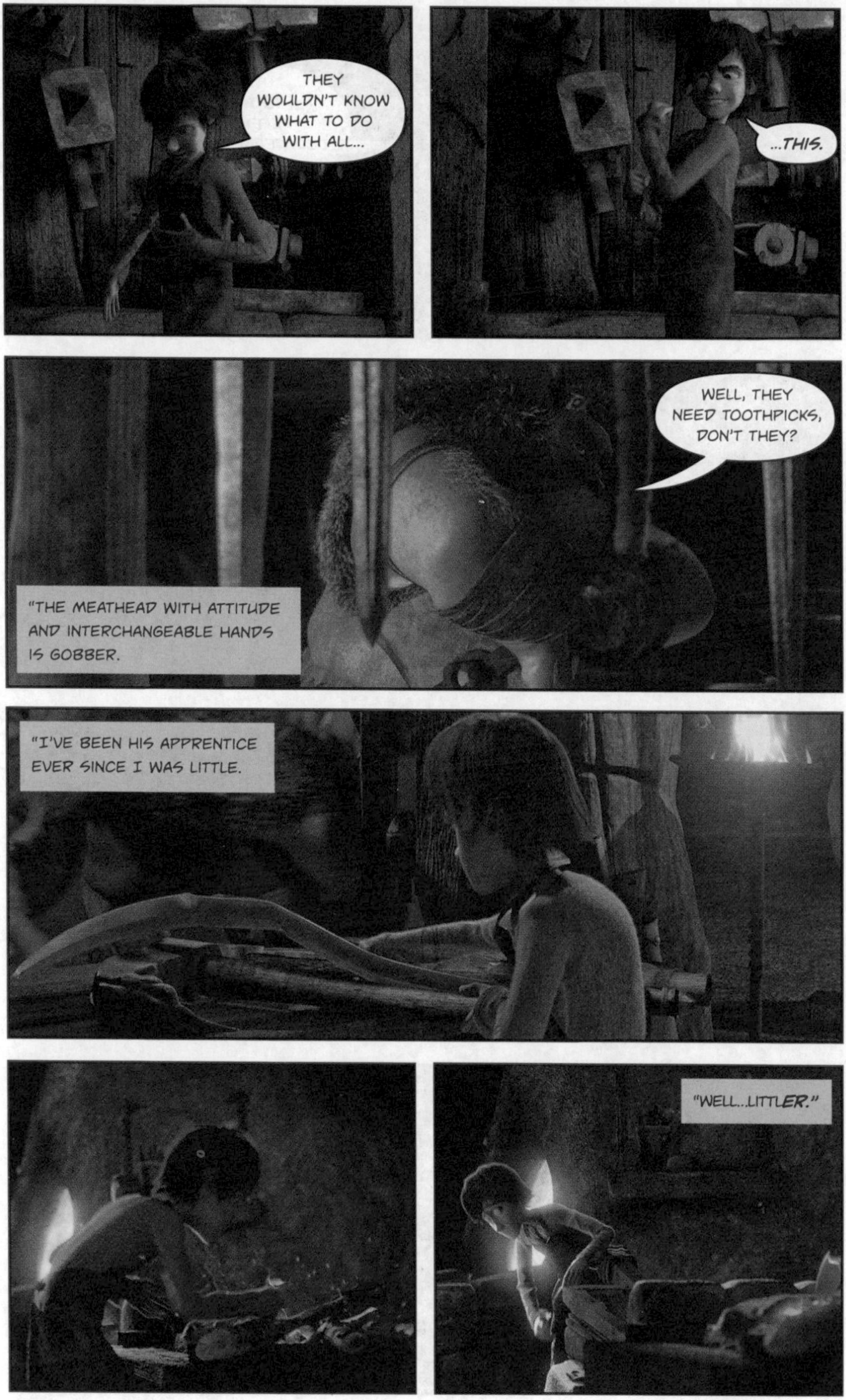
THEY WOULDN'T KNOW WHAT TO DO WITH ALL...
...THIS.
WELL, THEY NEED TOOTHPICKS, DON'T THEY?
"THE MEATHEAD WITH ATTITUDE AND INTERCHANGEABLE HANDS IS GOBBER.
"I'VE BEEN HIS APPRENTICE EVER SINCE I WAS LITTLE.
"WELL...LITTLER."

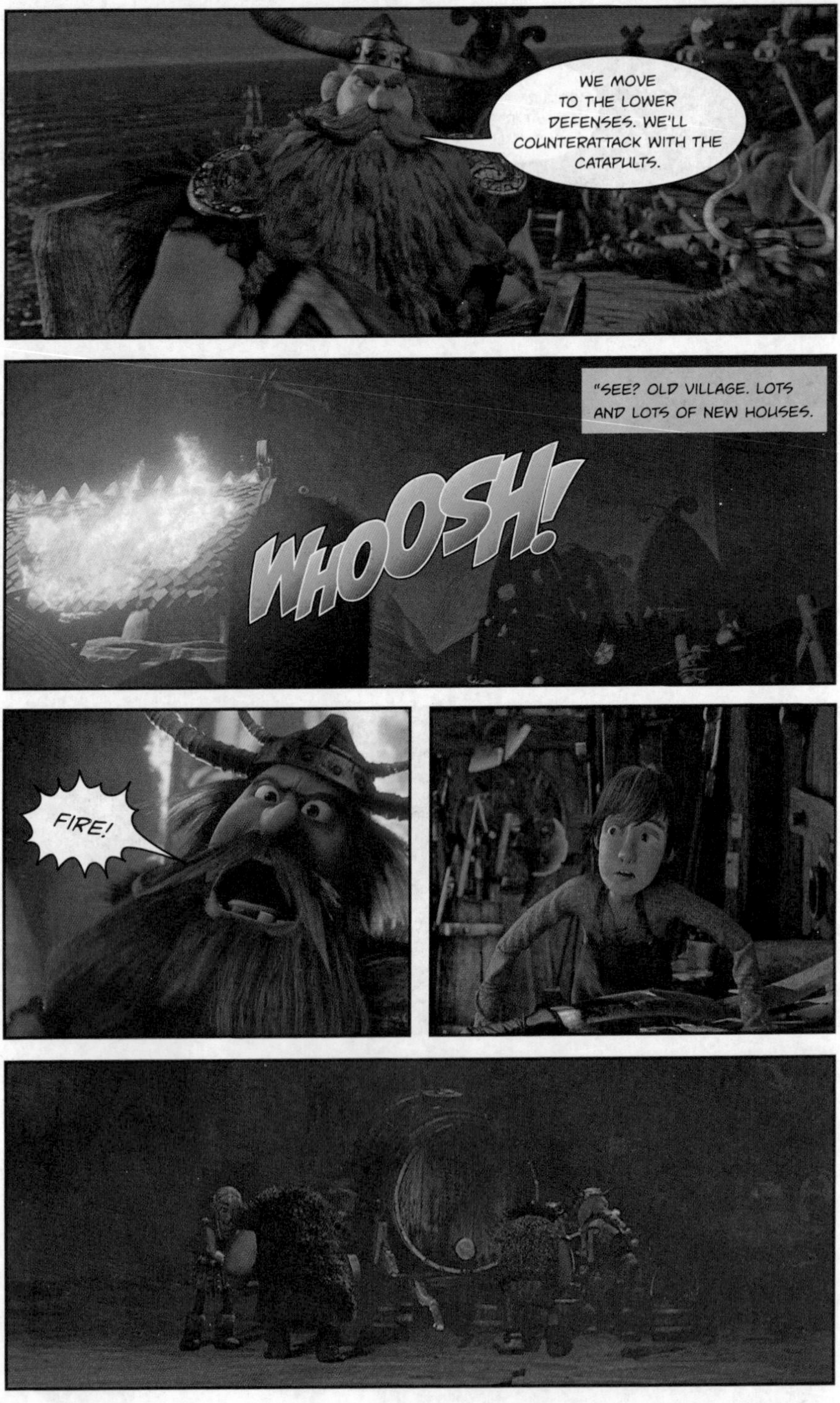
WE MOVE TO THE LOWER DEFENSES. WE'LL COUNTERATTACK WITH THE CATAPULTS.
"SEE? OLD VILLAGE. LOTS AND LOTS OF NEW HOUSES.
WHOOSH!
FIRE!

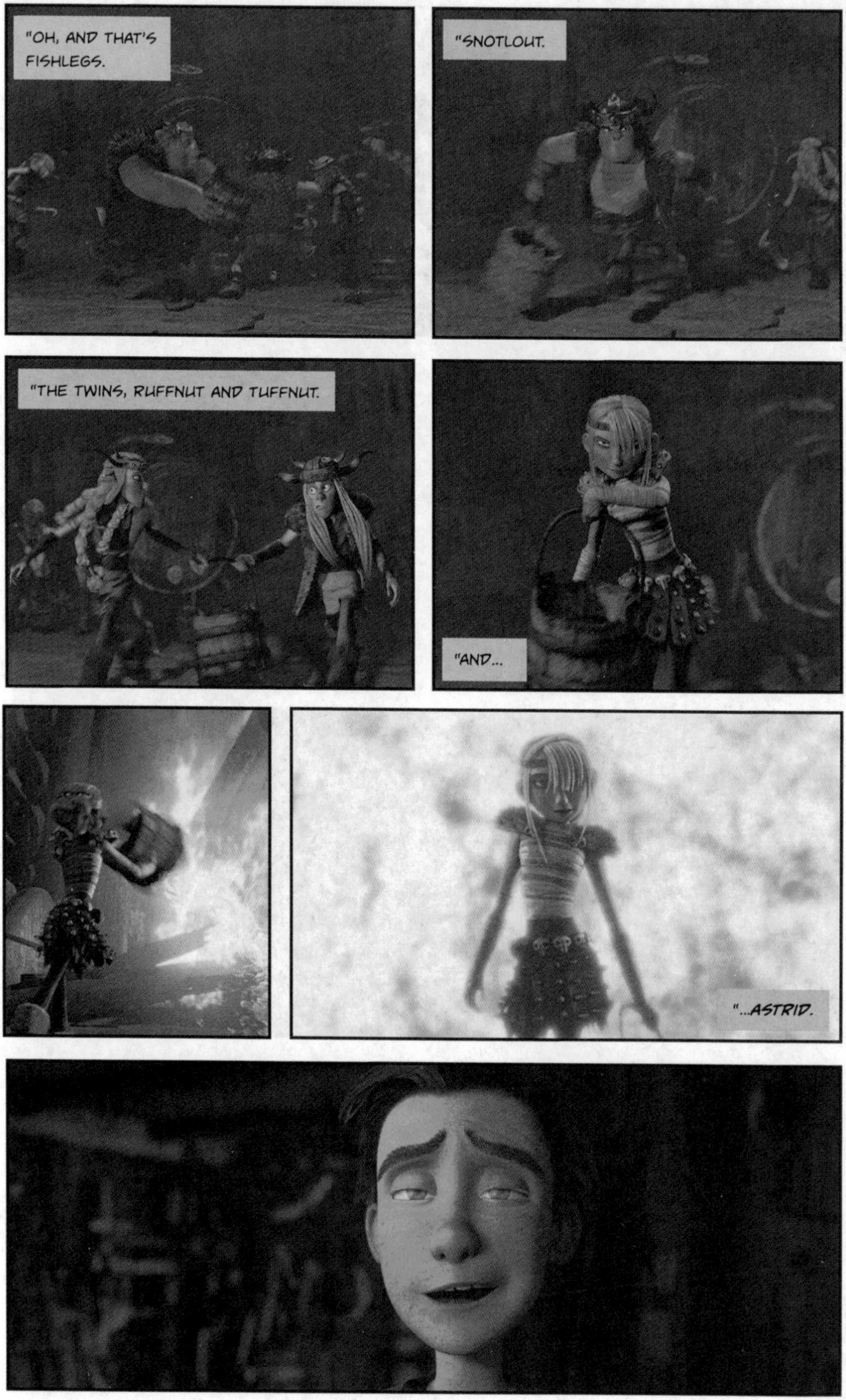
"OH, AND THAT'S FISHLEGS.
"SNOTLOUT.
"THE TWINS, RUFFNUT AND TUFFNUT.
"AND...
"...ASTRID.

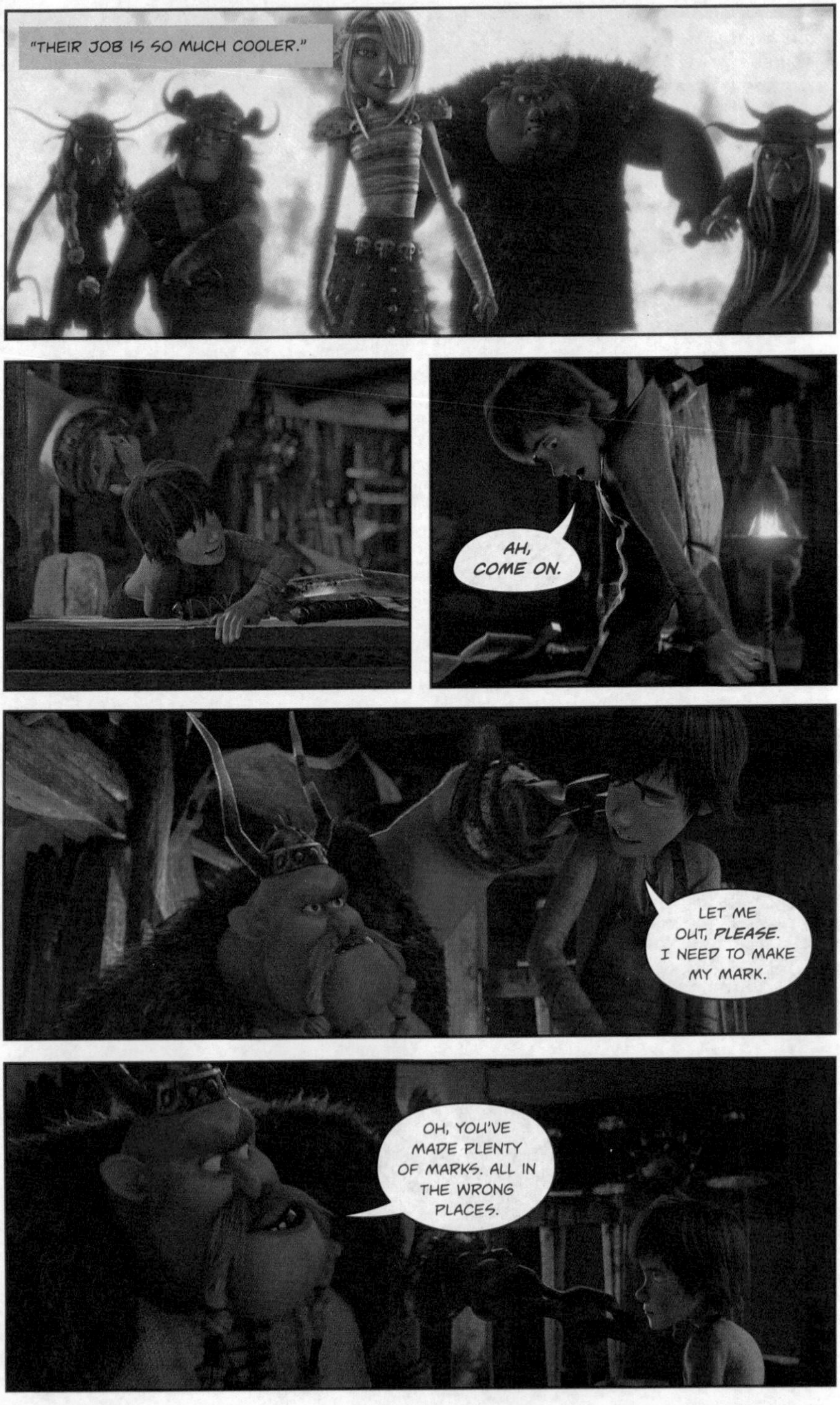
"THEIR JOB IS SO MUCH COOLER."
AH, COME ON.
LET ME OUT, PLEASE. I NEED TO MAKE MY MARK.
OH, YOU'VE MADE PLENTY OF MARKS. ALL IN THE WRONG PLACES.

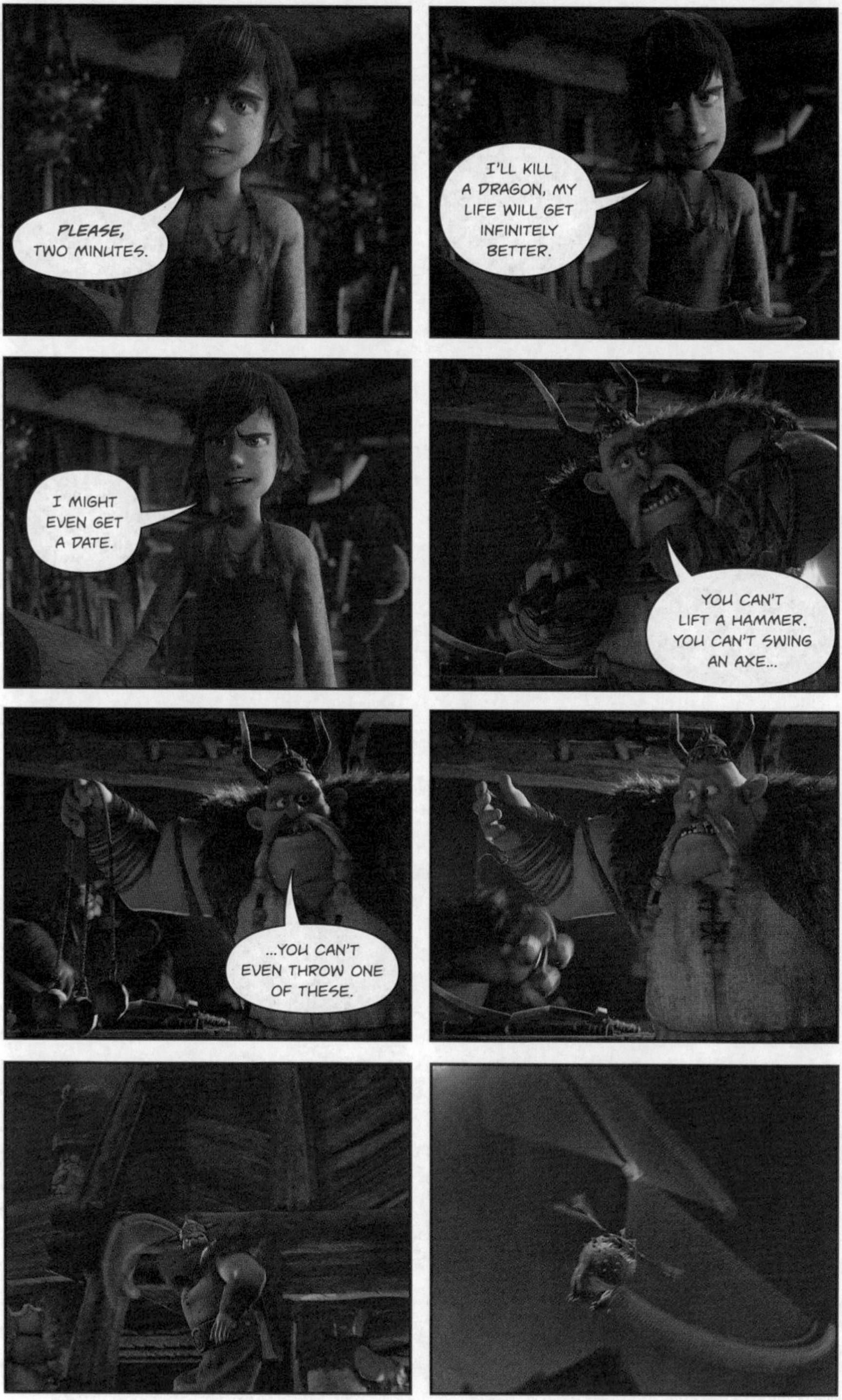
PLEASE, TWO MINUTES.
I'LL KILL A DRAGON, MY LIFE WILL GET INFINITELY BETTER.
I MIGHT EVEN GET A DATE.
YOU CAN'T LIFT A HAMMER. YOU CAN'T SWING AN AXE...
...YOU CAN'T EVEN THROW ONE OF THESE.

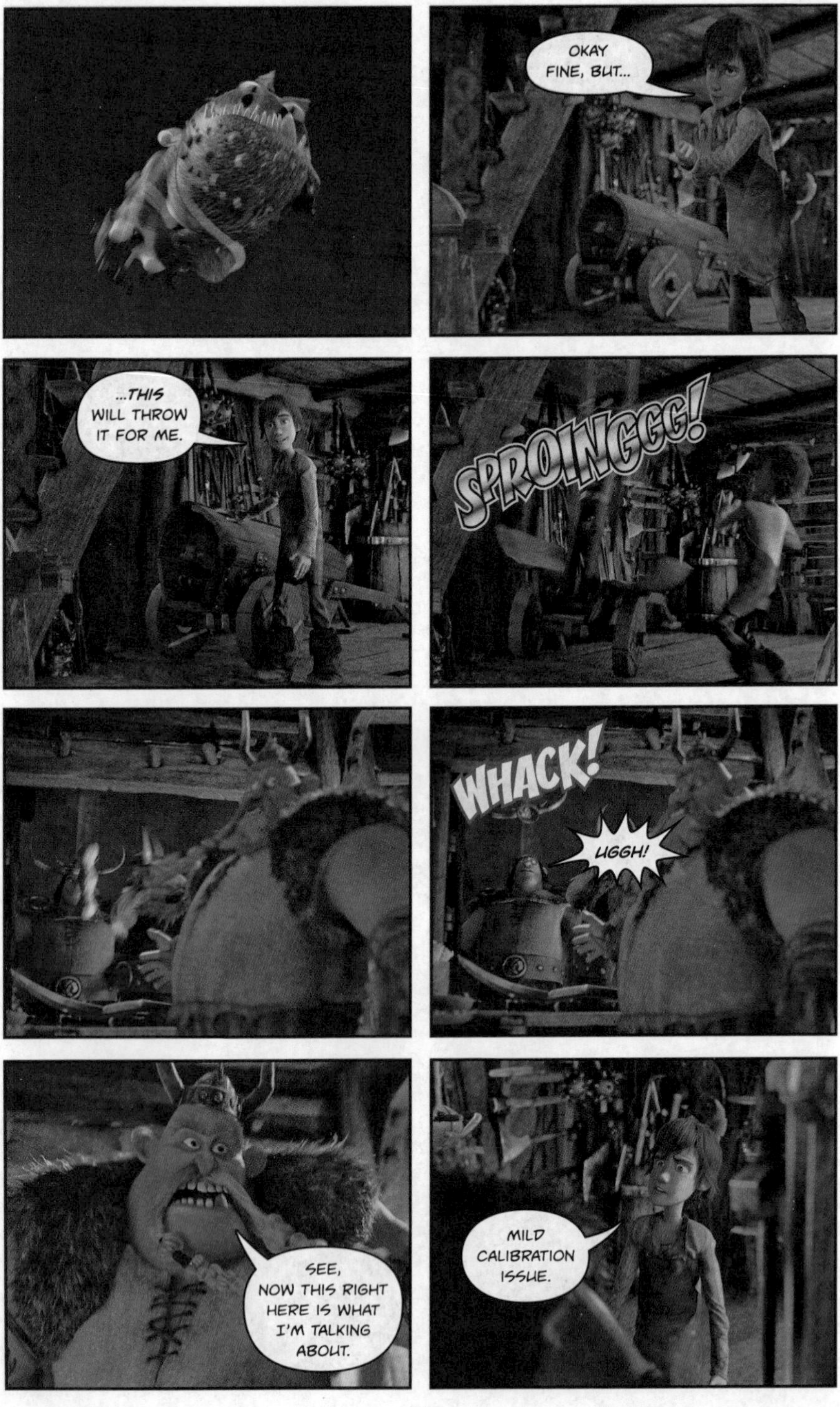
OKAY FINE, BUT...
...THIS WILL THROW IT FOR ME.
SPROINGGG!
WHACK!
UGGH!
SEE, NOW THIS RIGHT HERE IS WHAT I'M TALKING ABOUT.
MILD CALIBRATION ISSUE.

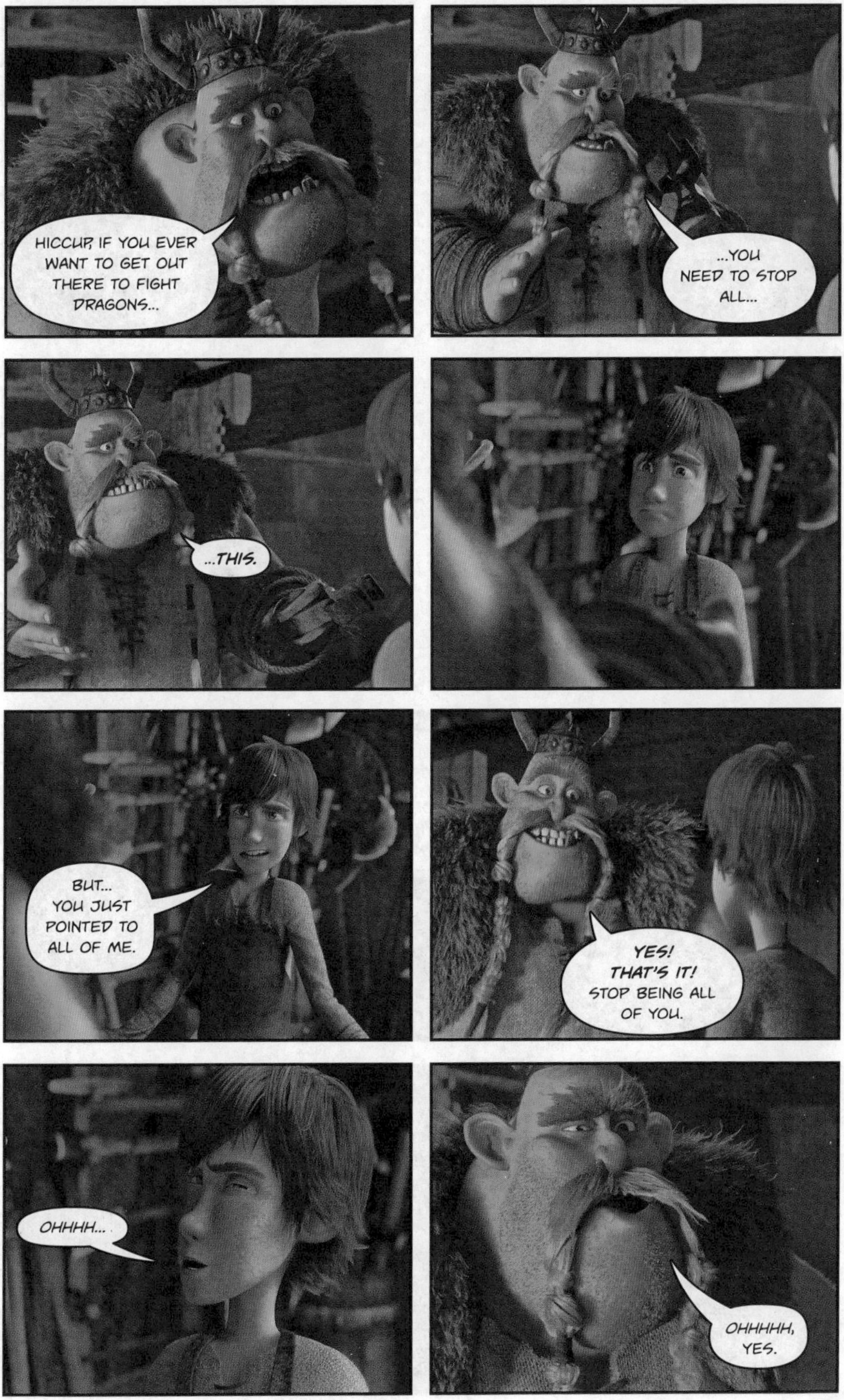
HICCUP, IF YOU EVER WANT TO GET OUT THERE TO FIGHT DRAGONS...
...YOU NEED TO STOP ALL...
...THIS.
BUT... YOU JUST POINTED TO ALL OF ME.
YES! THAT'S IT! STOP BEING ALL OF YOU.
OHHHH...
OHHHHH, YES.

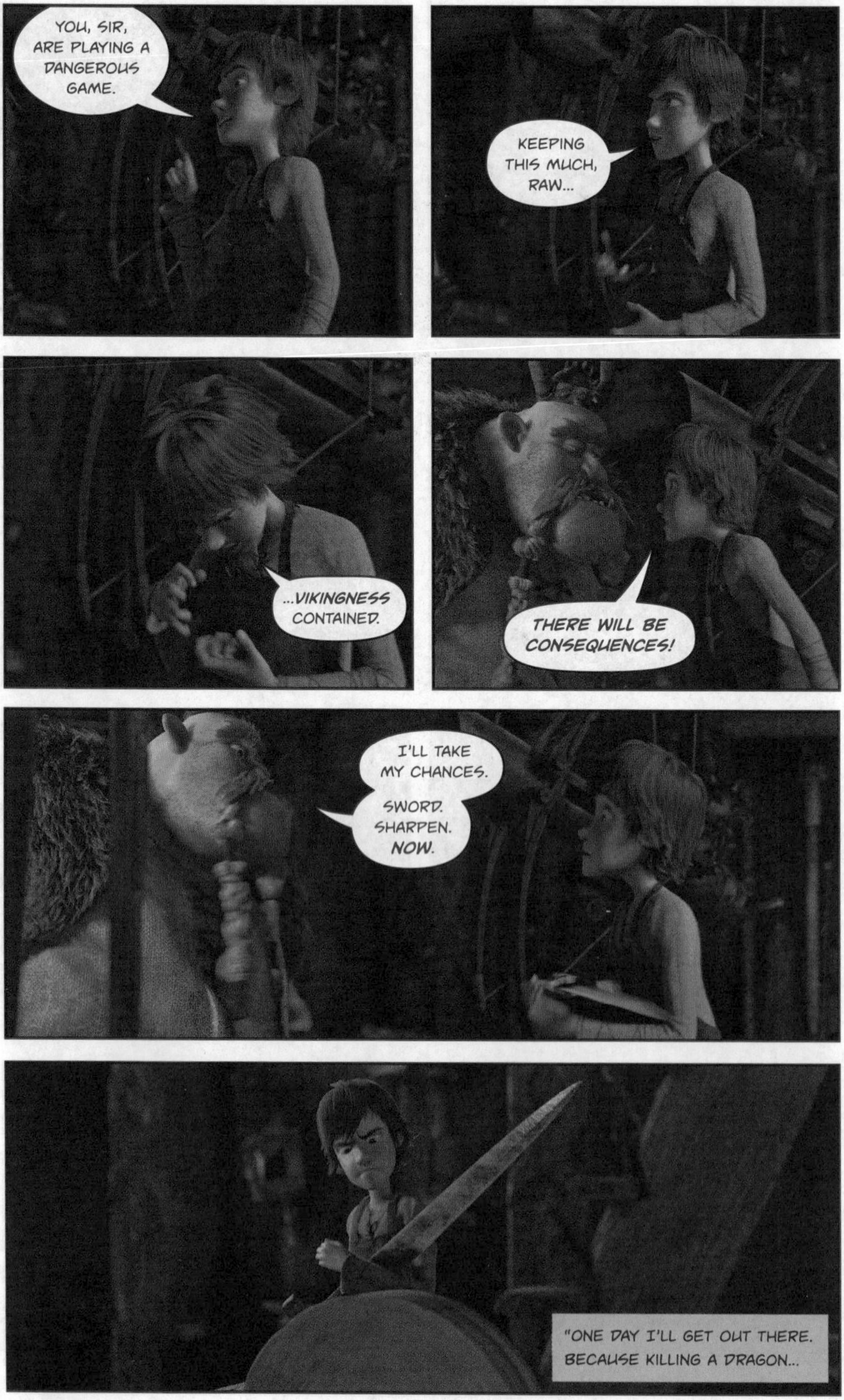
YOU, SIR, ARE PLAYING A DANGEROUS GAME.
KEEPING THIS MUCH, RAW...
...VIKINGNESS CONTAINED.
THERE WILL BE CONSEQUENCES!
I'LL TAKE MY CHANCES.
SWORD. SHARPEN. NOW.
"ONE DAY I'LL GET OUT THERE. BECAUSE KILLING A DRAGON...

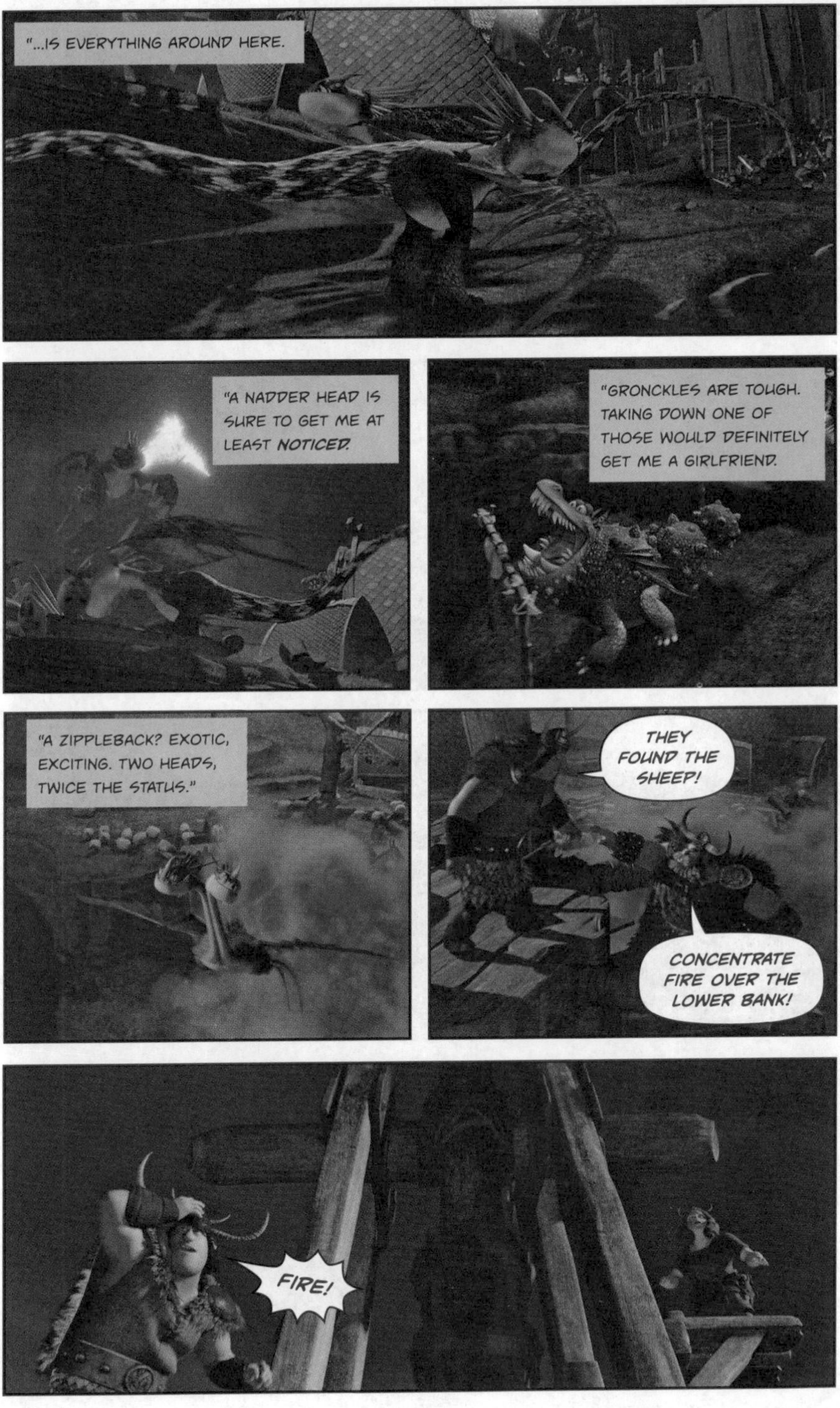
"...IS EVERYTHING AROUND HERE.
"A NADDER HEAD IS SURE TO GET ME AT LEAST *NOTICED*.
"GRONCKLES ARE TOUGH. TAKING DOWN ONE OF THOSE WOULD DEFINITELY GET ME A GIRLFRIEND.
"A ZIPPLEBACK? EXOTIC, EXCITING. TWO HEADS, TWICE THE STATUS."
THEY FOUND THE SHEEP!
CONCENTRATE FIRE OVER THE LOWER BANK!
FIRE!

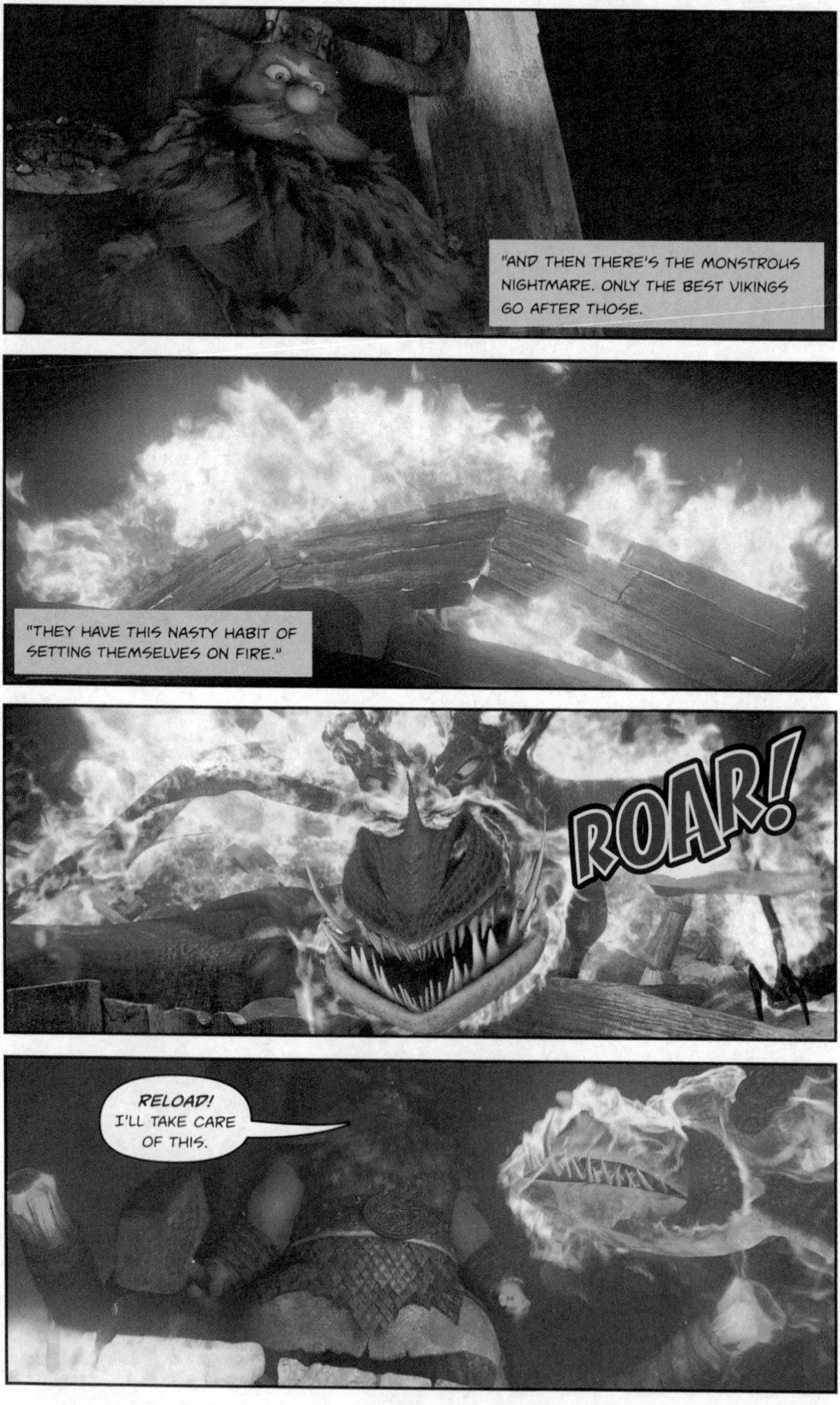
"AND THEN THERE'S THE MONSTROUS NIGHTMARE. ONLY THE BEST VIKINGS GO AFTER THOSE.
"THEY HAVE THIS NASTY HABIT OF SETTING THEMSELVES ON FIRE."
ROAR!
RELOAD! I'LL TAKE CARE OF THIS.

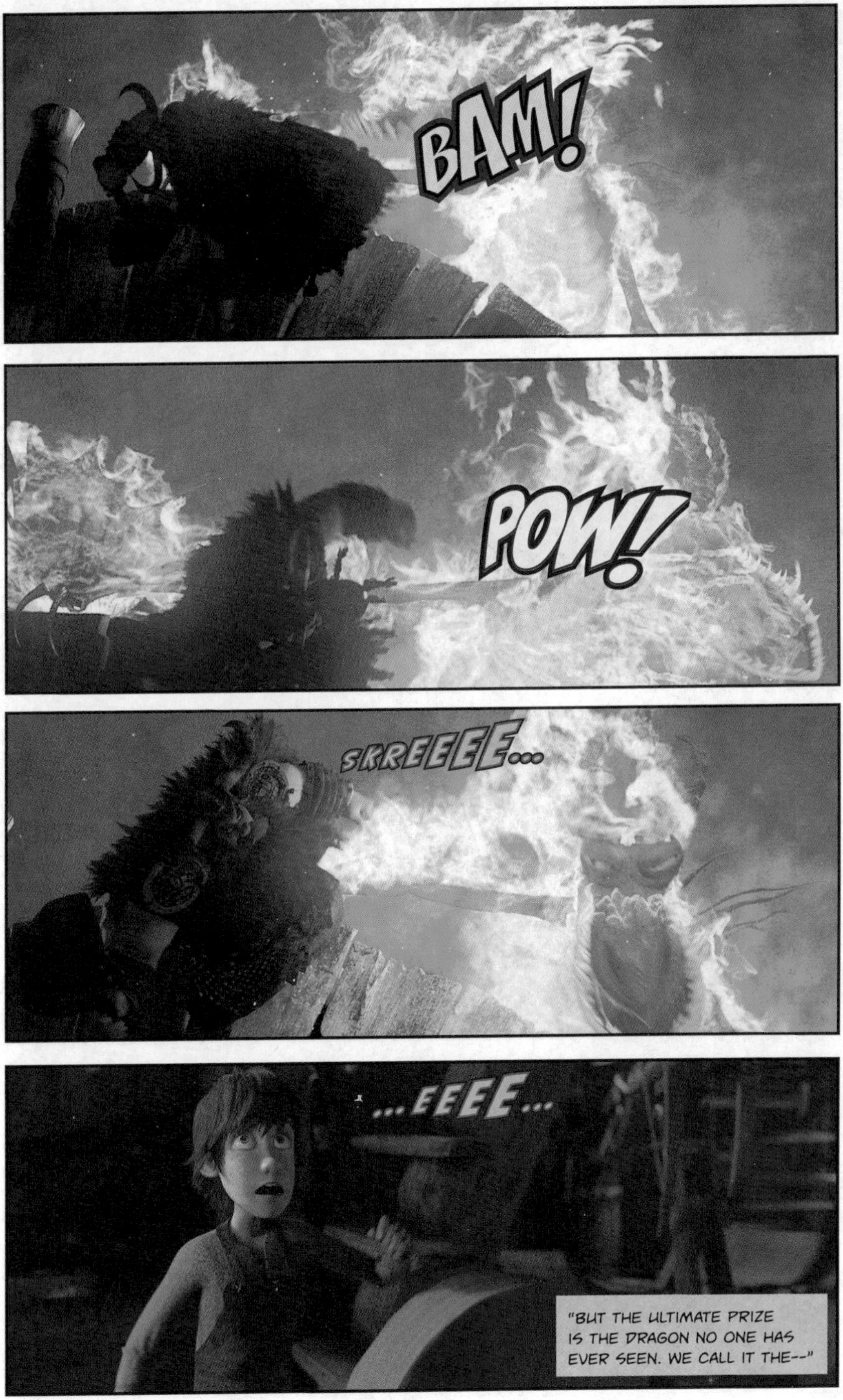
BAM!
POW!
SKREEEEE...
...EEEE...
"BUT THE ULTIMATE PRIZE IS THE DRAGON NO ONE HAS EVER SEEN. WE CALL IT THE--"

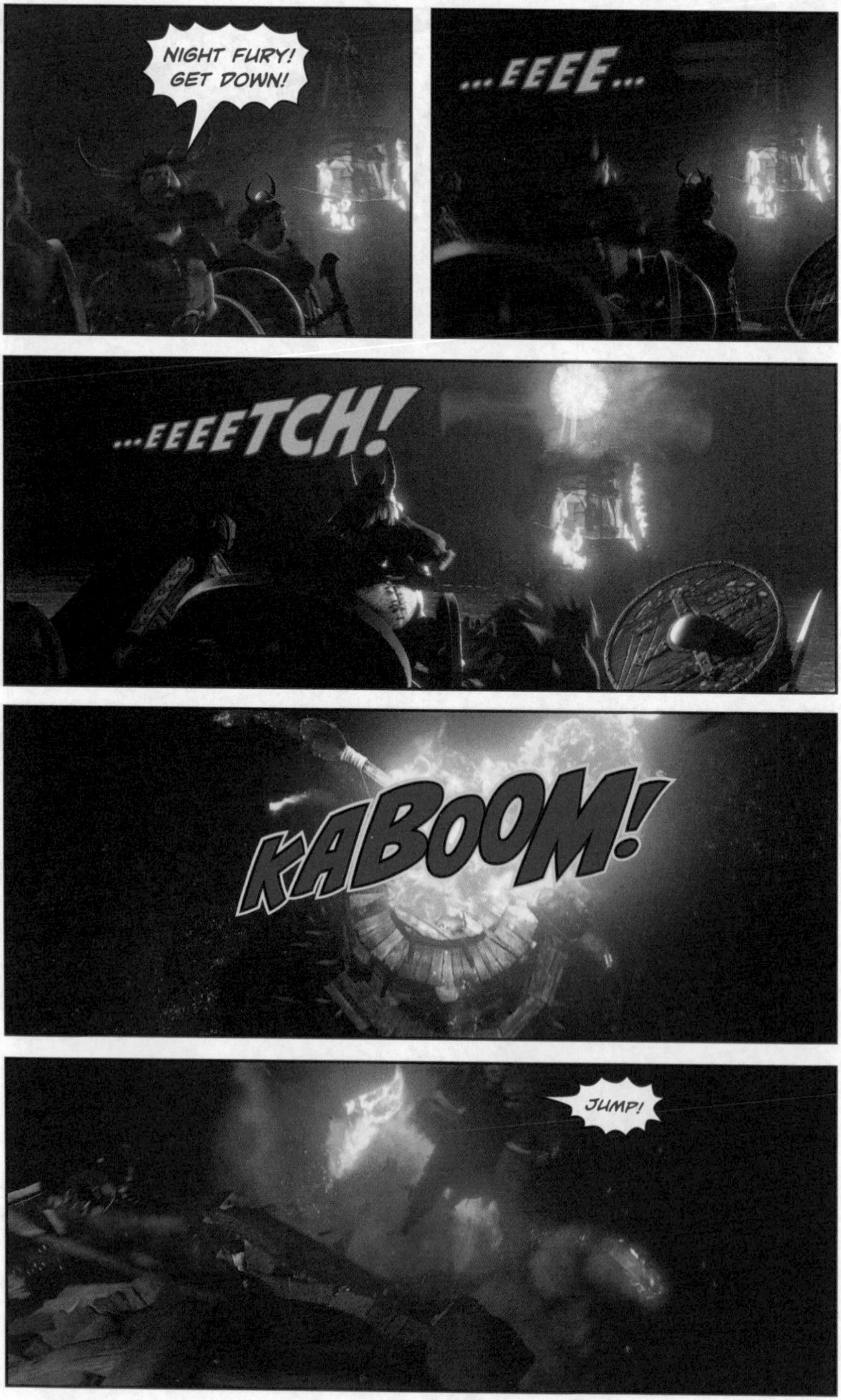
NIGHT FURY! GET DOWN!
...EEEE...
...EEEETCH!
KABOOM!
JUMP!

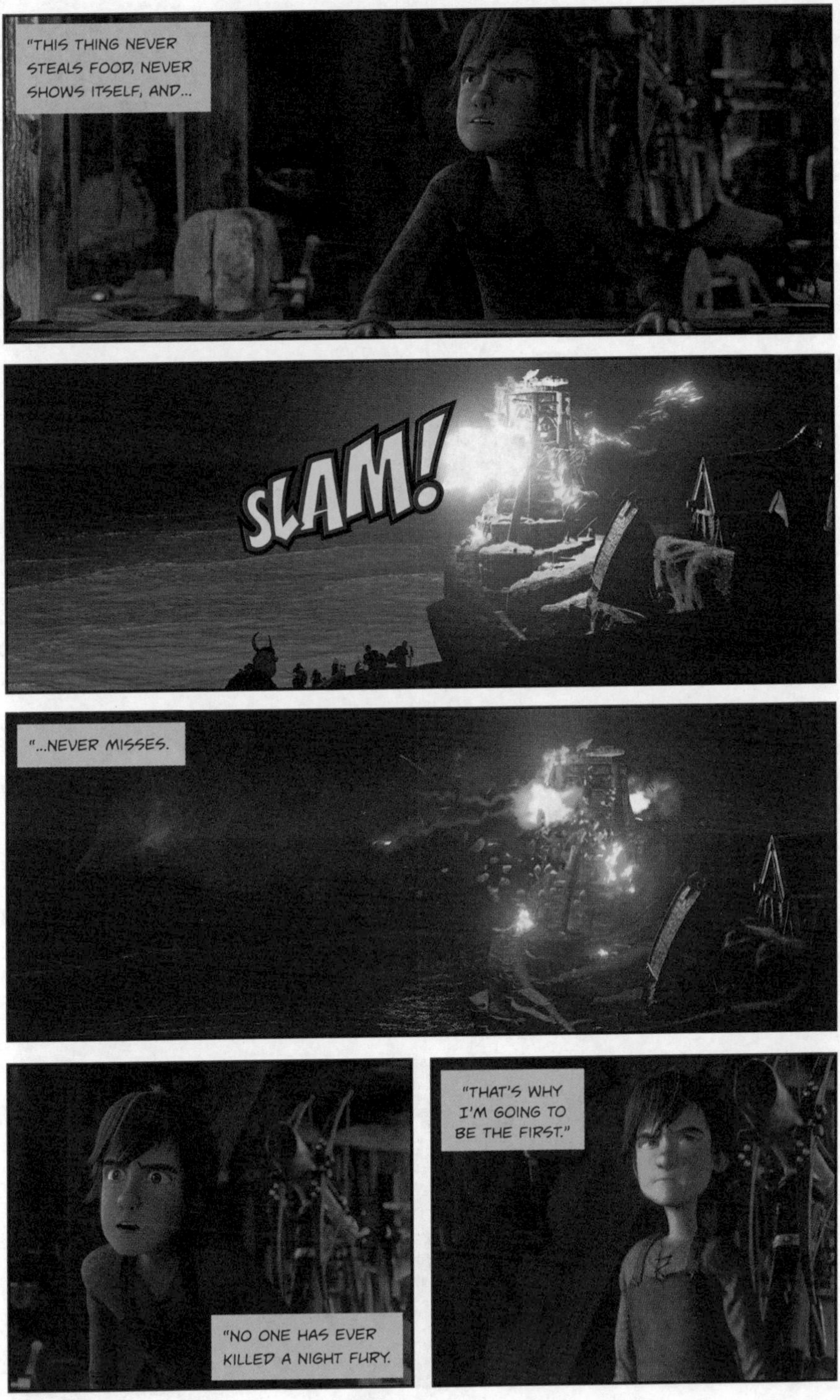
"THIS THING NEVER STEALS FOOD, NEVER SHOWS ITSELF, AND...
SLAM!
"...NEVER MISSES.
"NO ONE HAS EVER KILLED A NIGHT FURY.
"THAT'S WHY I'M GOING TO BE THE FIRST."

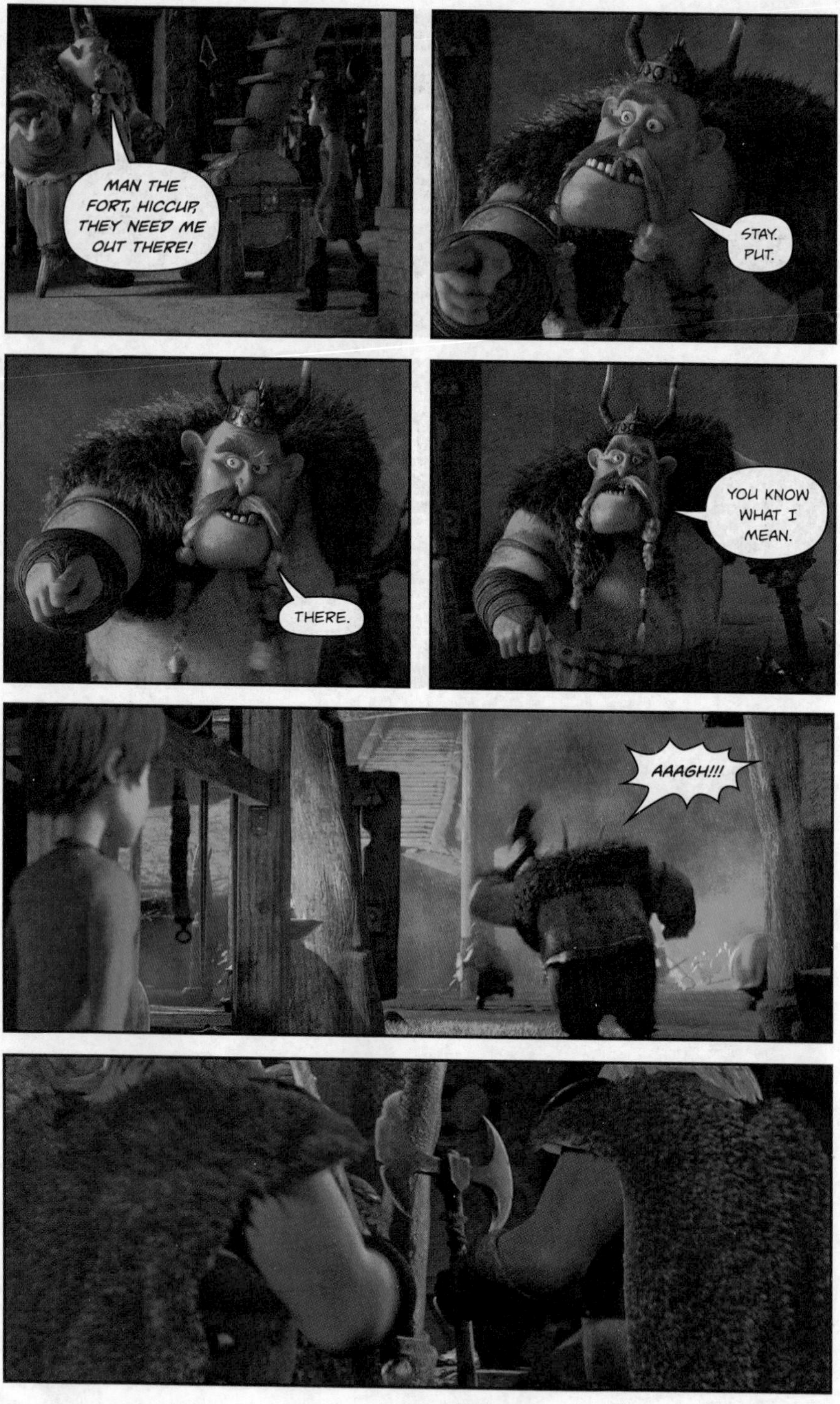
MAN THE FORT, HICCUP, THEY NEED ME OUT THERE!
STAY. PUT.
THERE.
YOU KNOW WHAT I MEAN.
AAAGH!!!

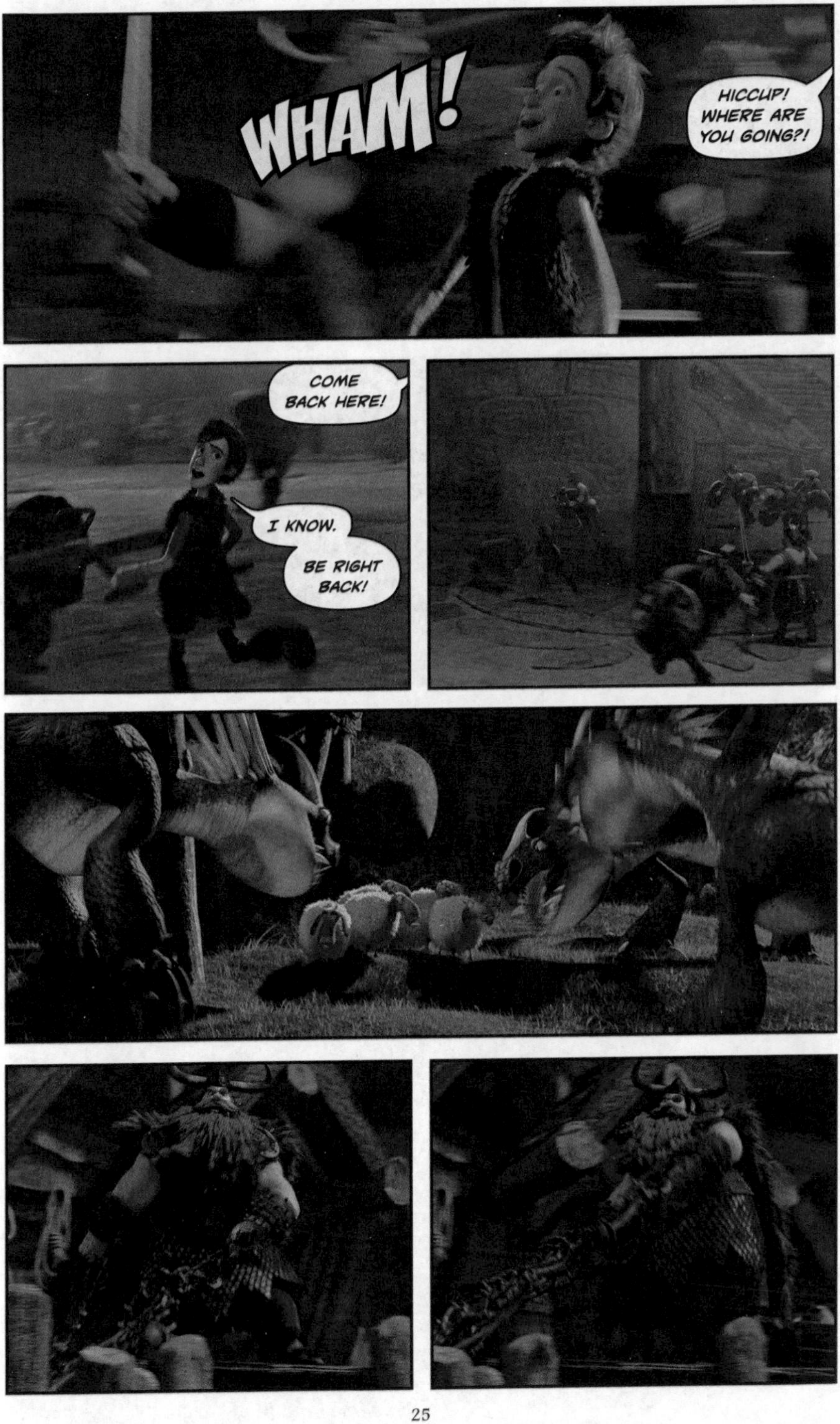
WHAM!
HICCUP! WHERE ARE YOU GOING?!
COME BACK HERE!
I KNOW.
BE RIGHT BACK!

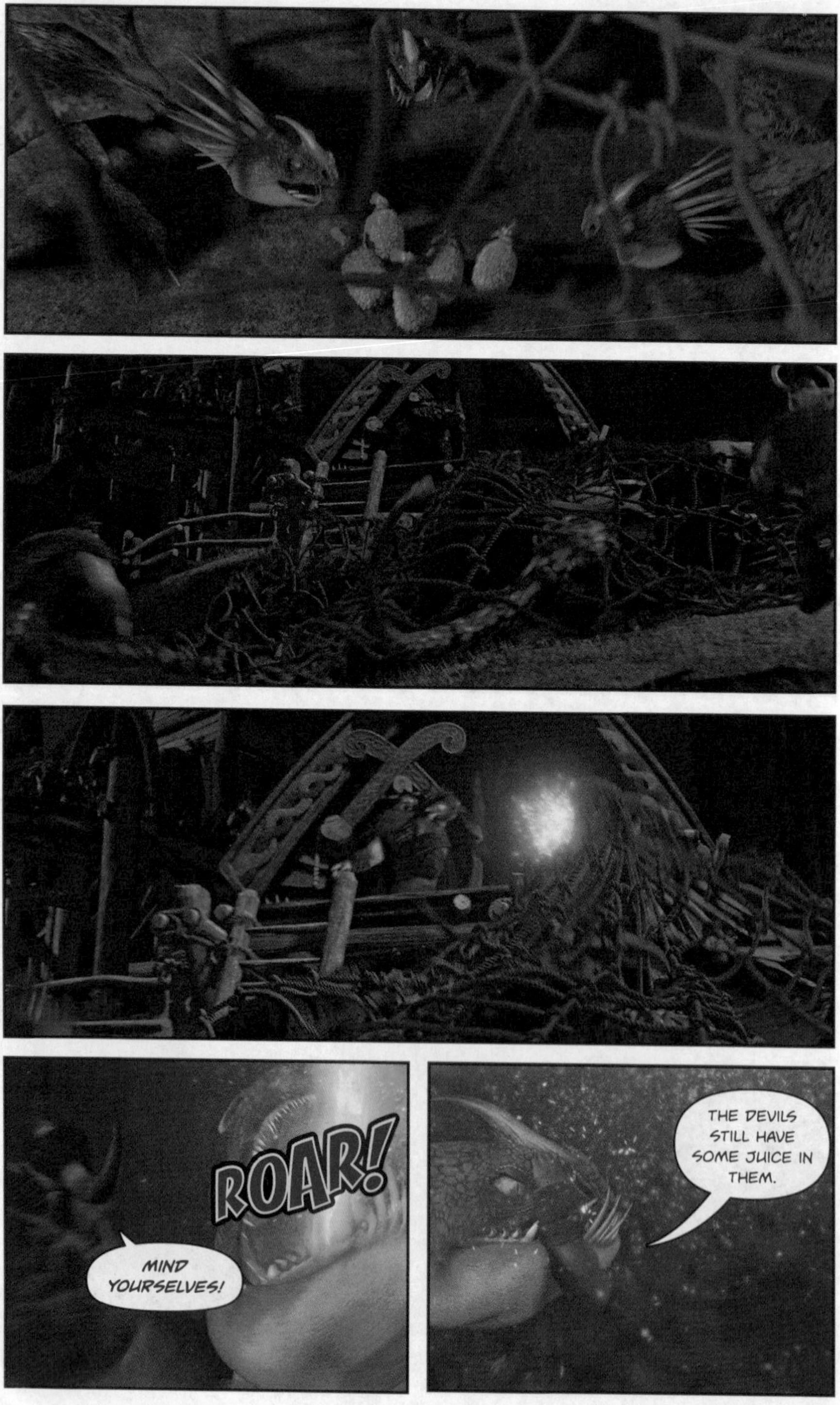
ROAR!
MIND YOURSELVES!
THE DEVILS STILL HAVE SOME JUICE IN THEM.

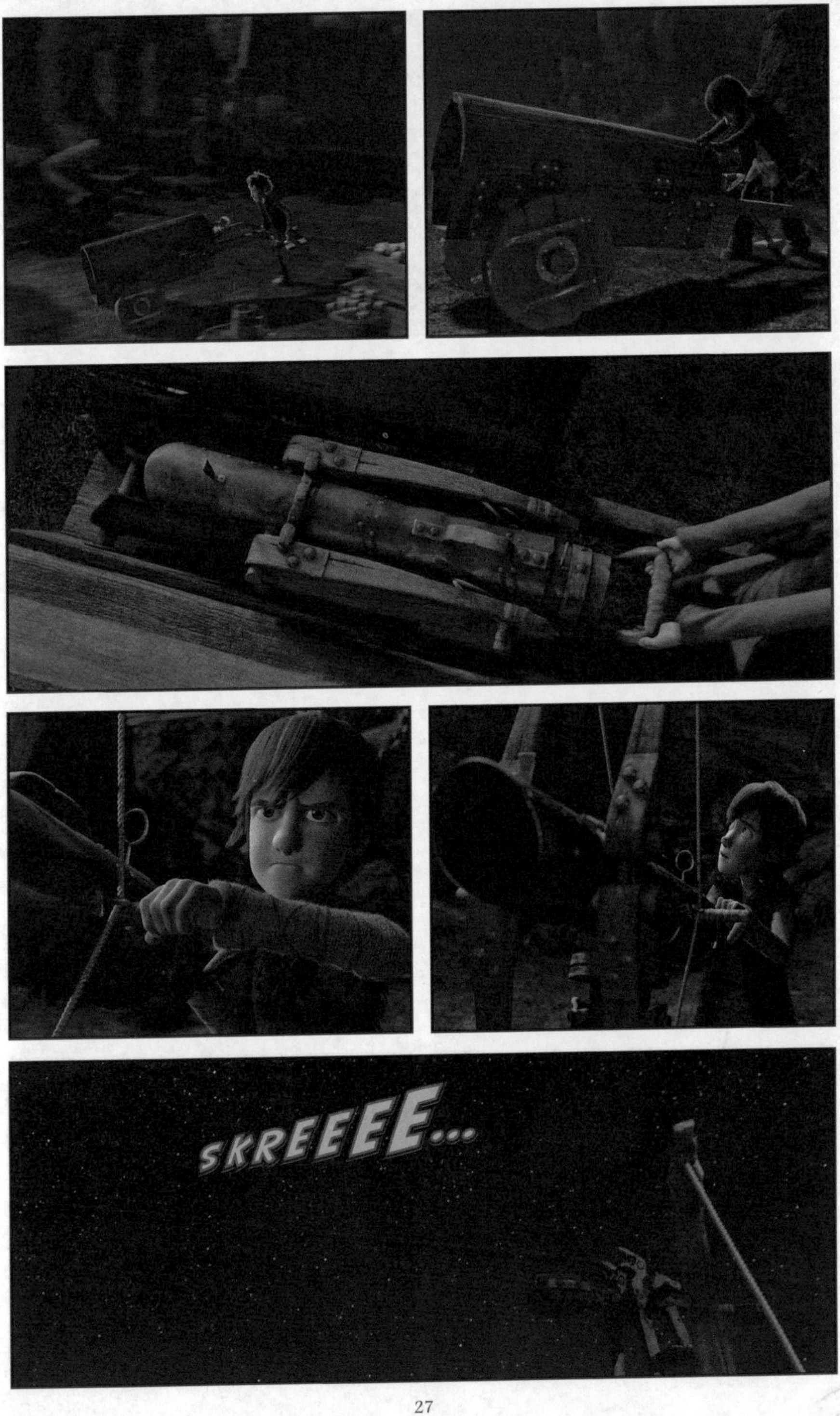
SKREEEE...

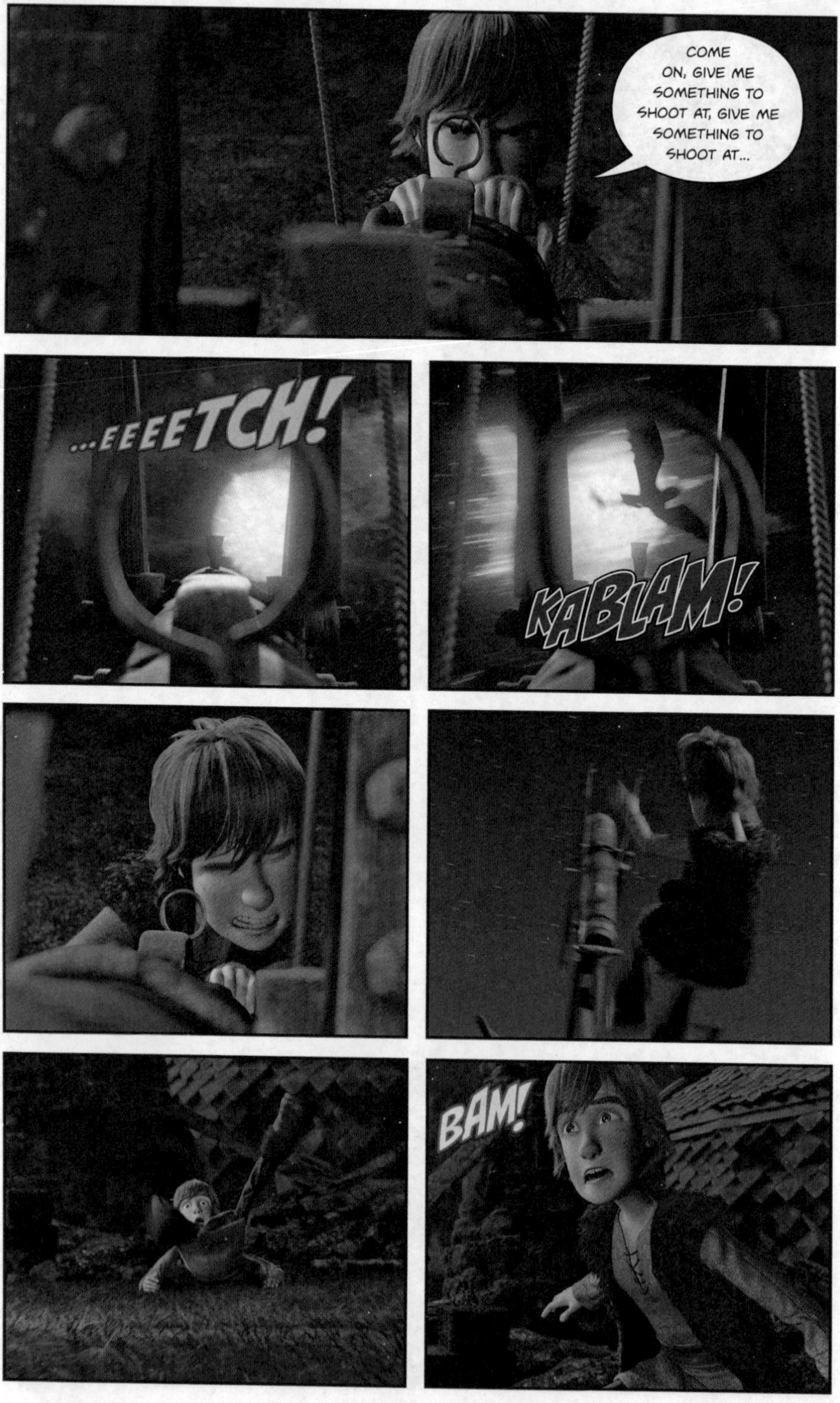
COME ON, GIVE ME SOMETHING TO SHOOT AT, GIVE ME SOMETHING TO SHOOT AT...
...EEEETCH!
KABLAM!
BAM!

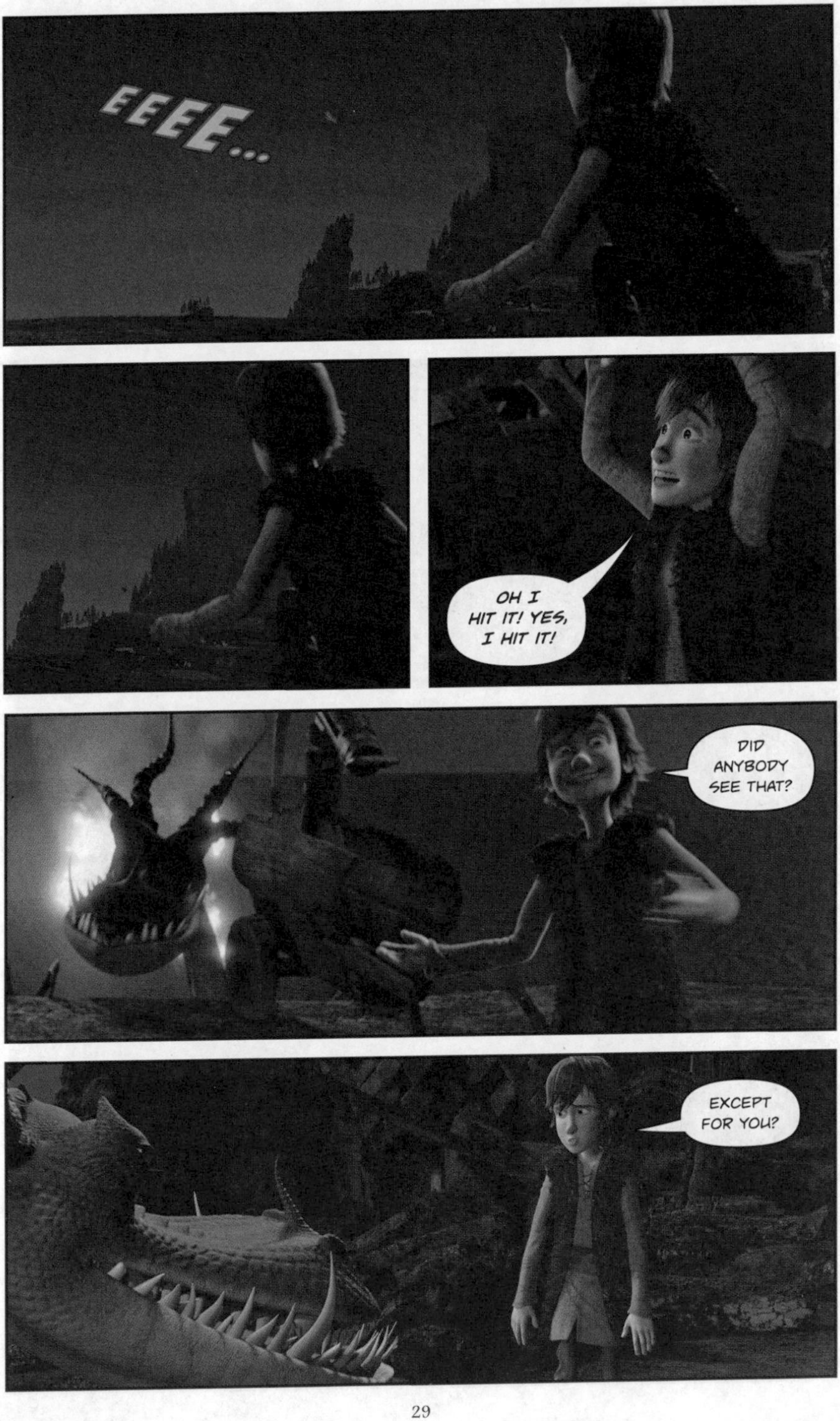
EEEE...
OH I HIT IT! YES, I HIT IT!
DID ANYBODY SEE THAT?
EXCEPT FOR YOU?

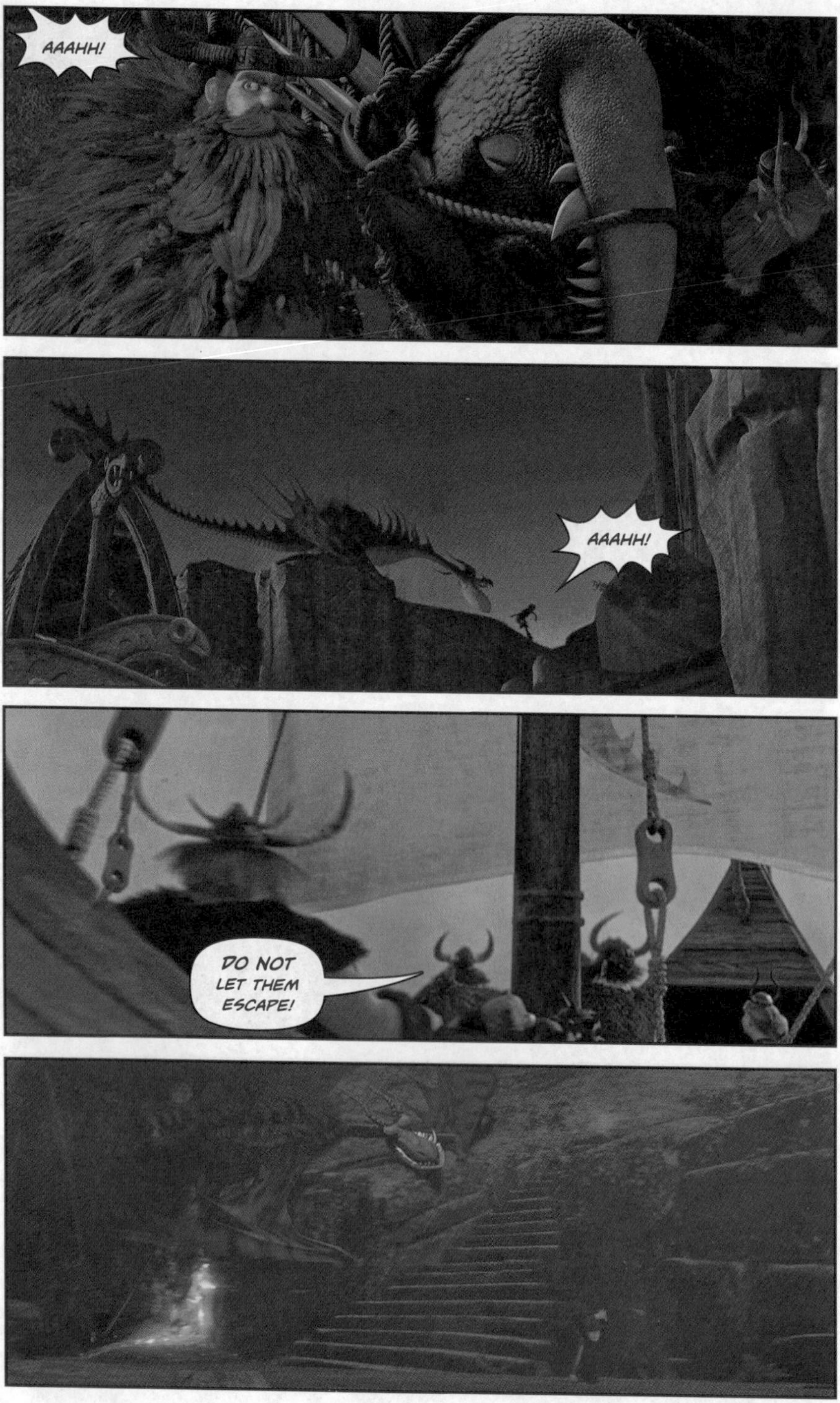
AAAHH!
AAAHH!
DO NOT LET THEM ESCAPE!

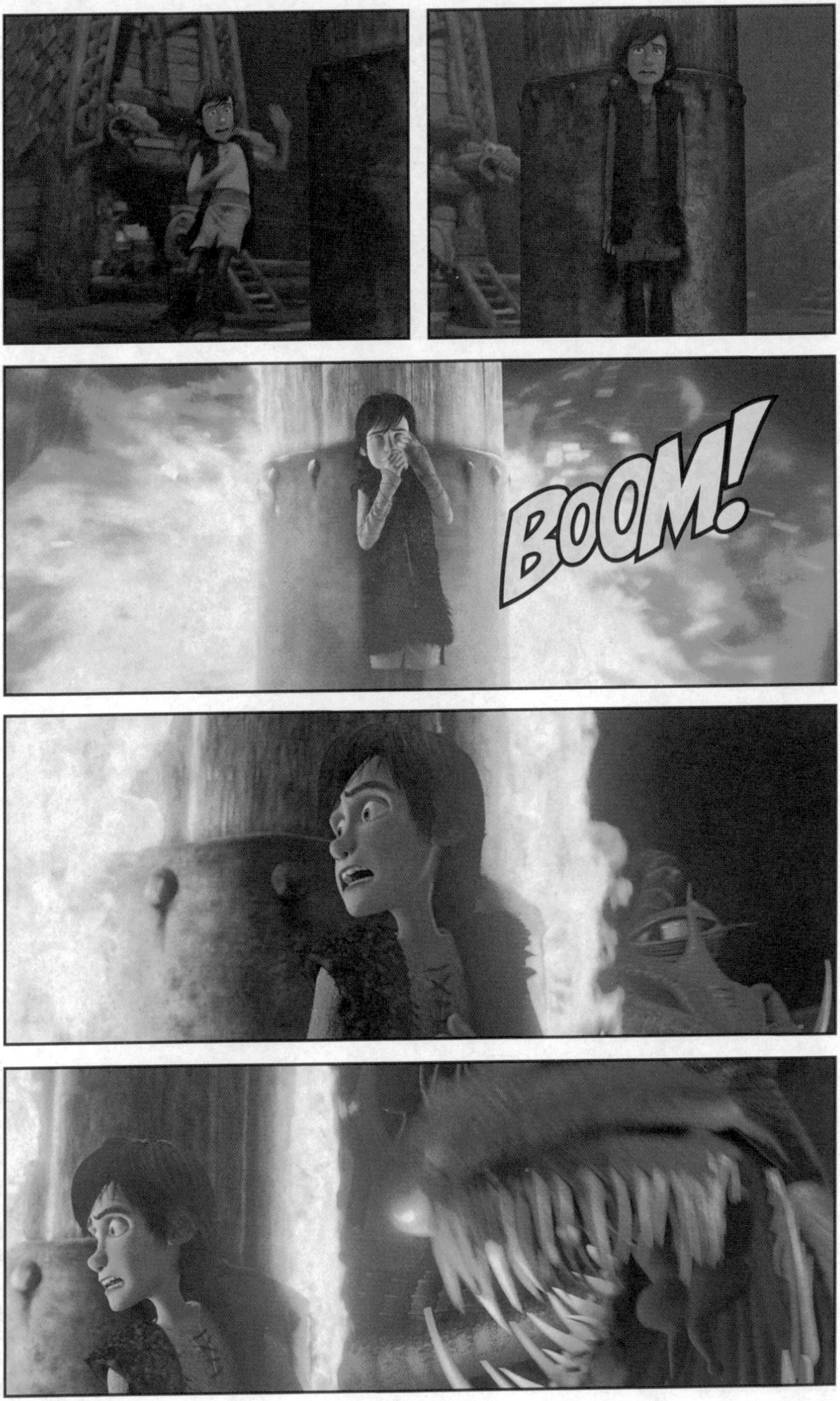
BOOM!

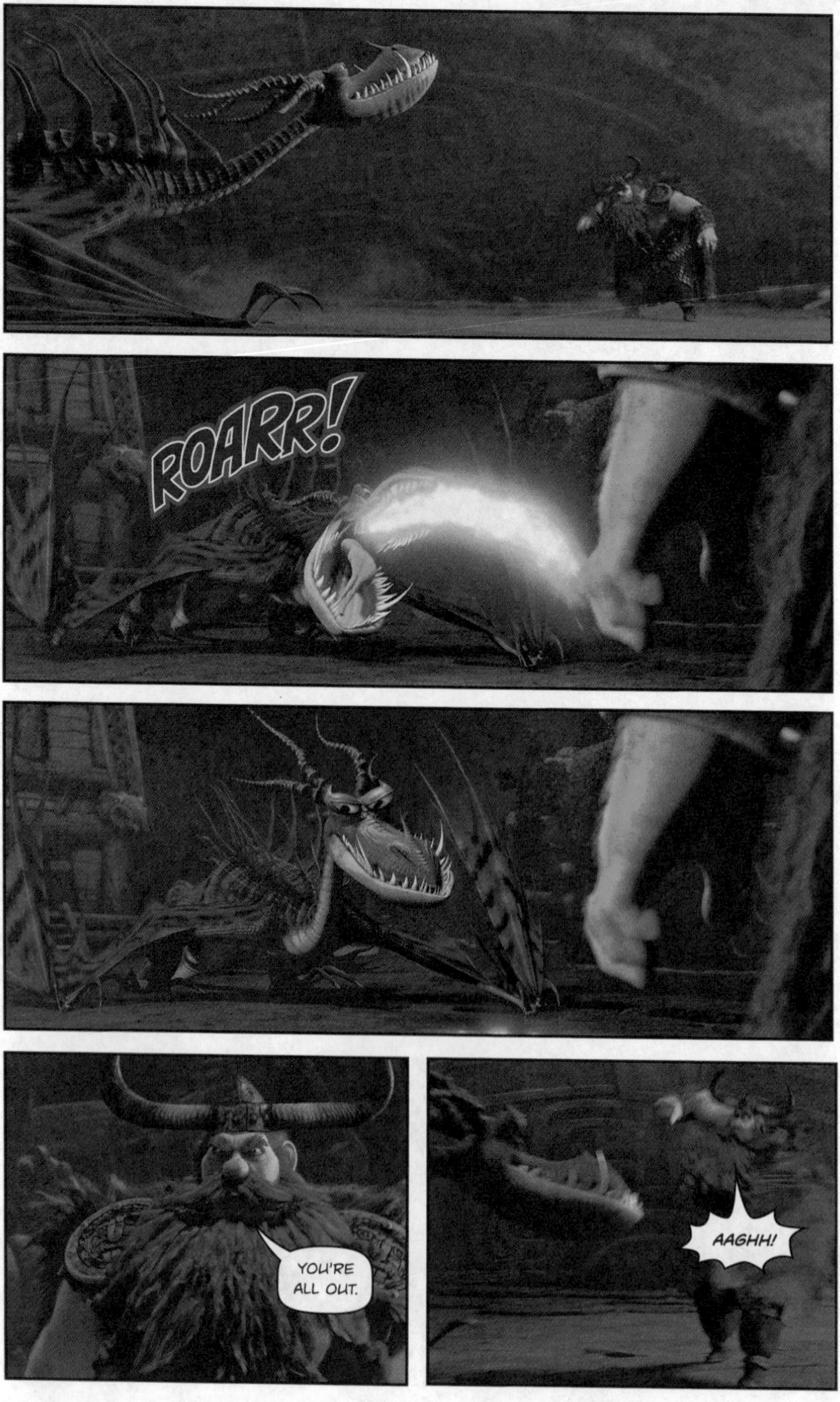
ROARR!
YOU'RE ALL OUT.
AAGHH!

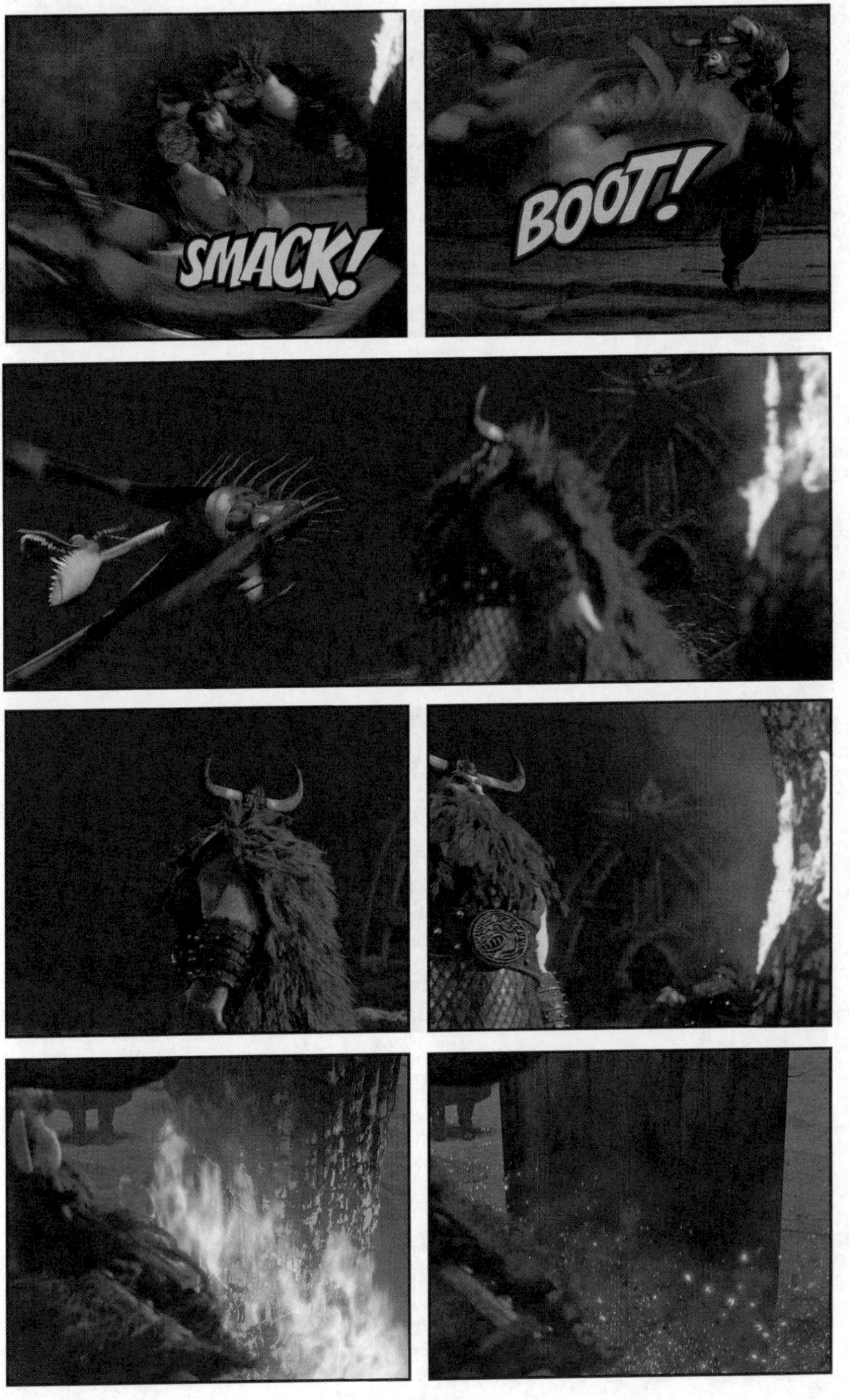
SMACK!
BOOT!

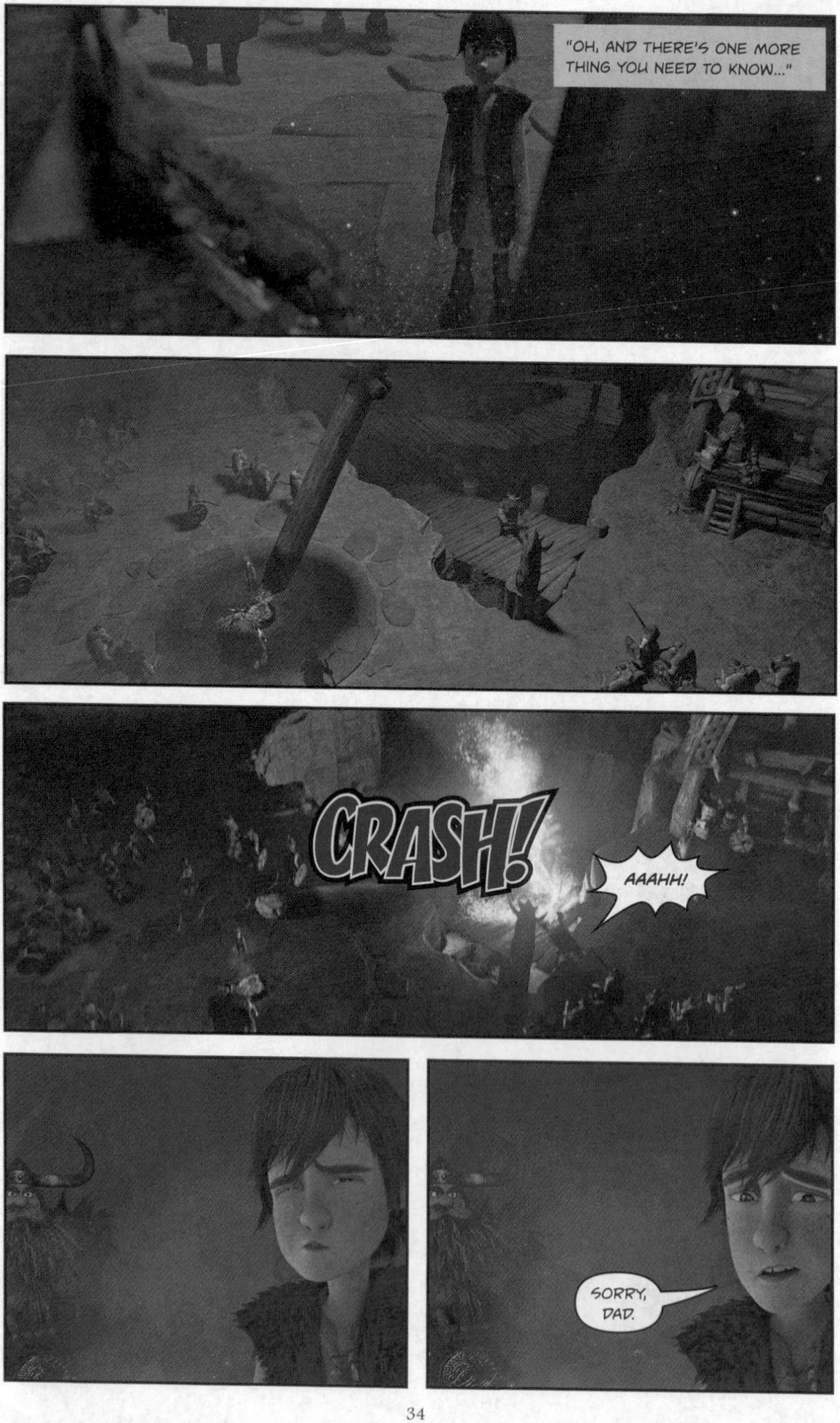
"OH, AND THERE'S ONE MORE THING YOU NEED TO KNOW..."
CRASH!
AAAHH!
SORRY, DAD.

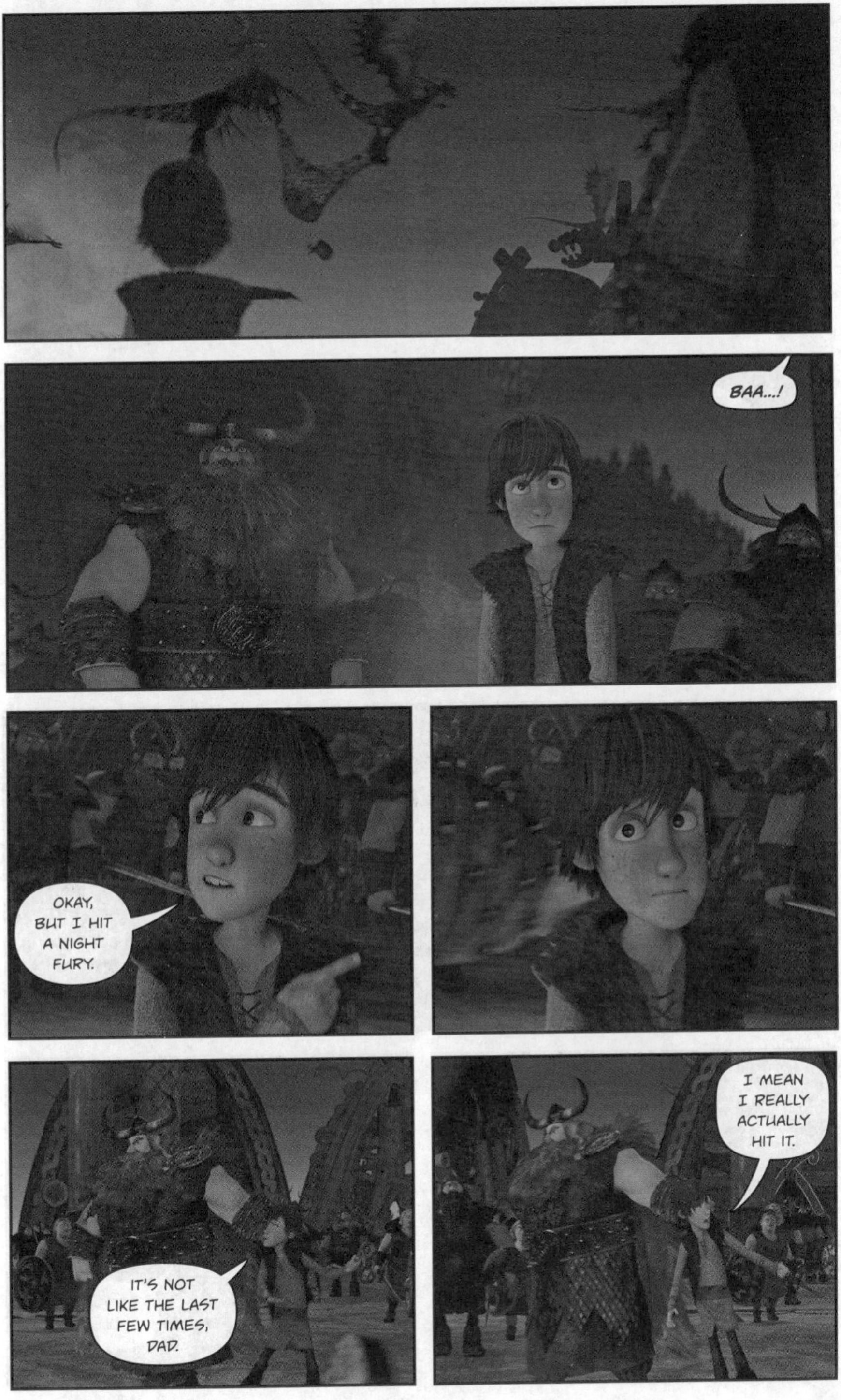
BAA...!
OKAY, BUT I HIT A NIGHT FURY.
IT'S NOT LIKE THE LAST FEW TIMES, DAD.
I MEAN I REALLY ACTUALLY HIT IT.

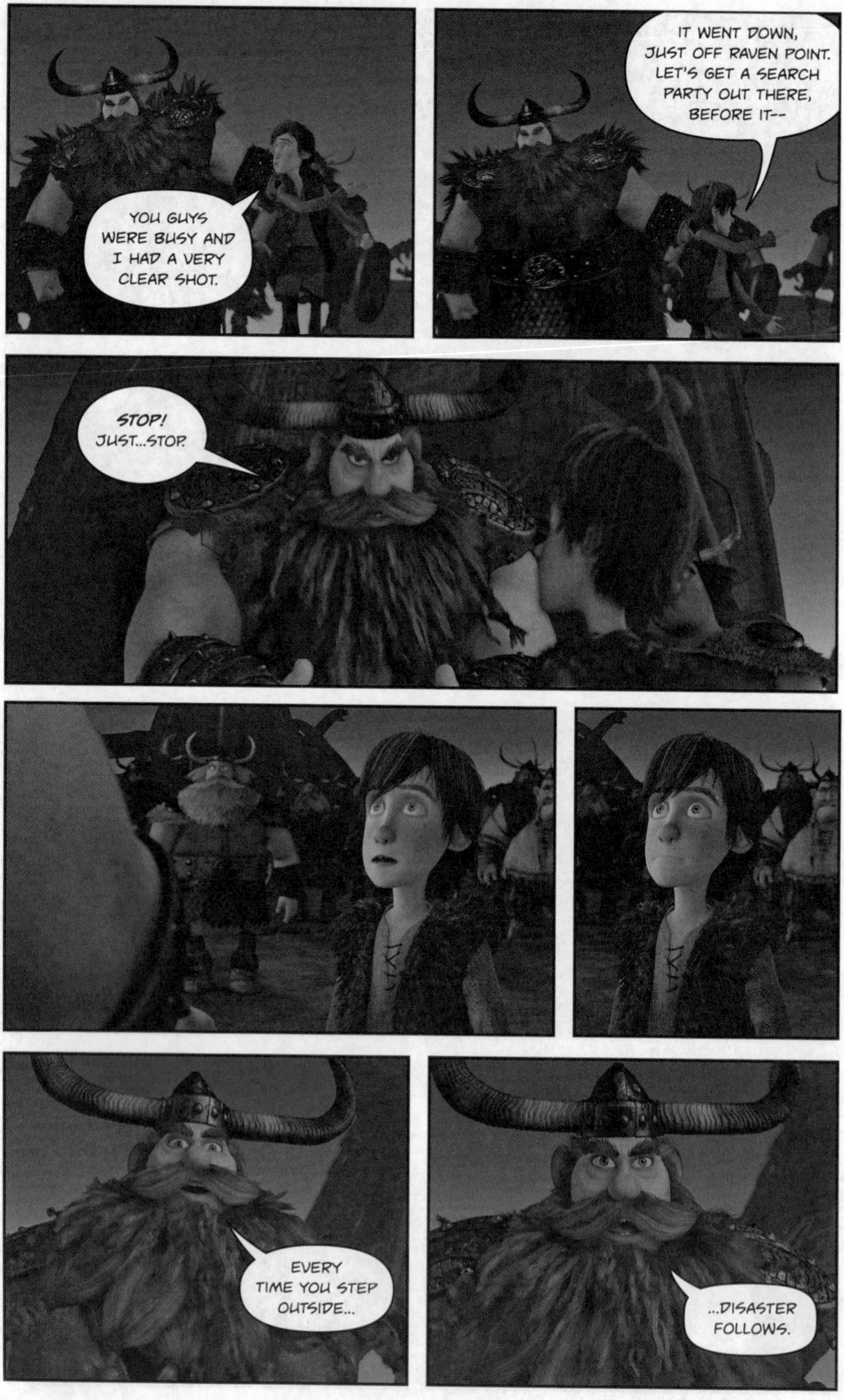
YOU GUYS WERE BUSY AND I HAD A VERY CLEAR SHOT.
IT WENT DOWN, JUST OFF RAVEN POINT. LET'S GET A SEARCH PARTY OUT THERE, BEFORE IT--
STOP! JUST...STOP.
EVERY TIME YOU STEP OUTSIDE...
...DISASTER FOLLOWS.

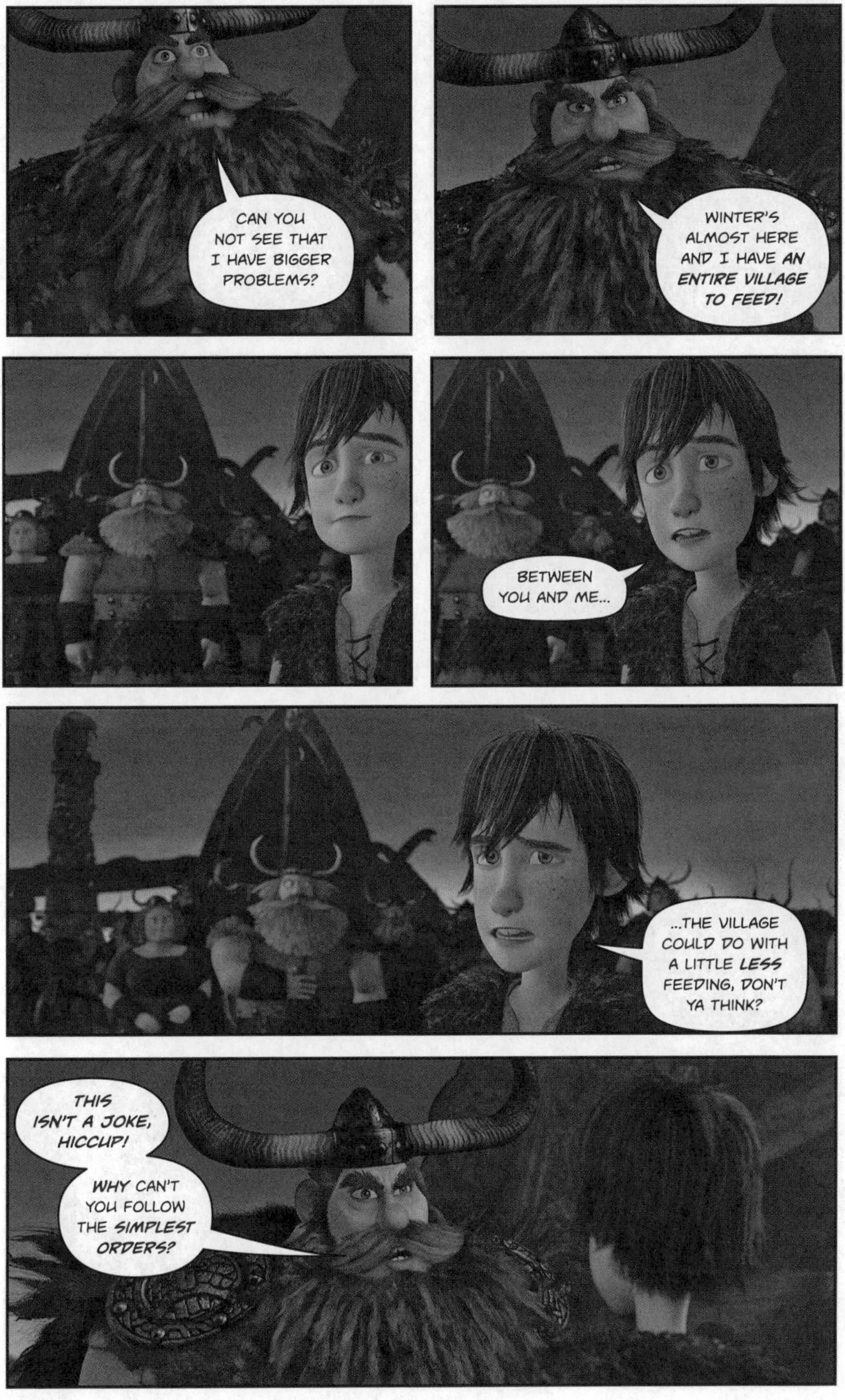
CAN YOU NOT SEE THAT I HAVE BIGGER PROBLEMS?
WINTER'S ALMOST HERE AND I HAVE AN ENTIRE VILLAGE TO FEED!
BETWEEN YOU AND ME...
...THE VILLAGE COULD DO WITH A LITTLE LESS FEEDING, DON'T YA THINK?
THIS ISN'T A JOKE, HICCUP!
WHY CAN'T YOU FOLLOW THE SIMPLEST ORDERS?

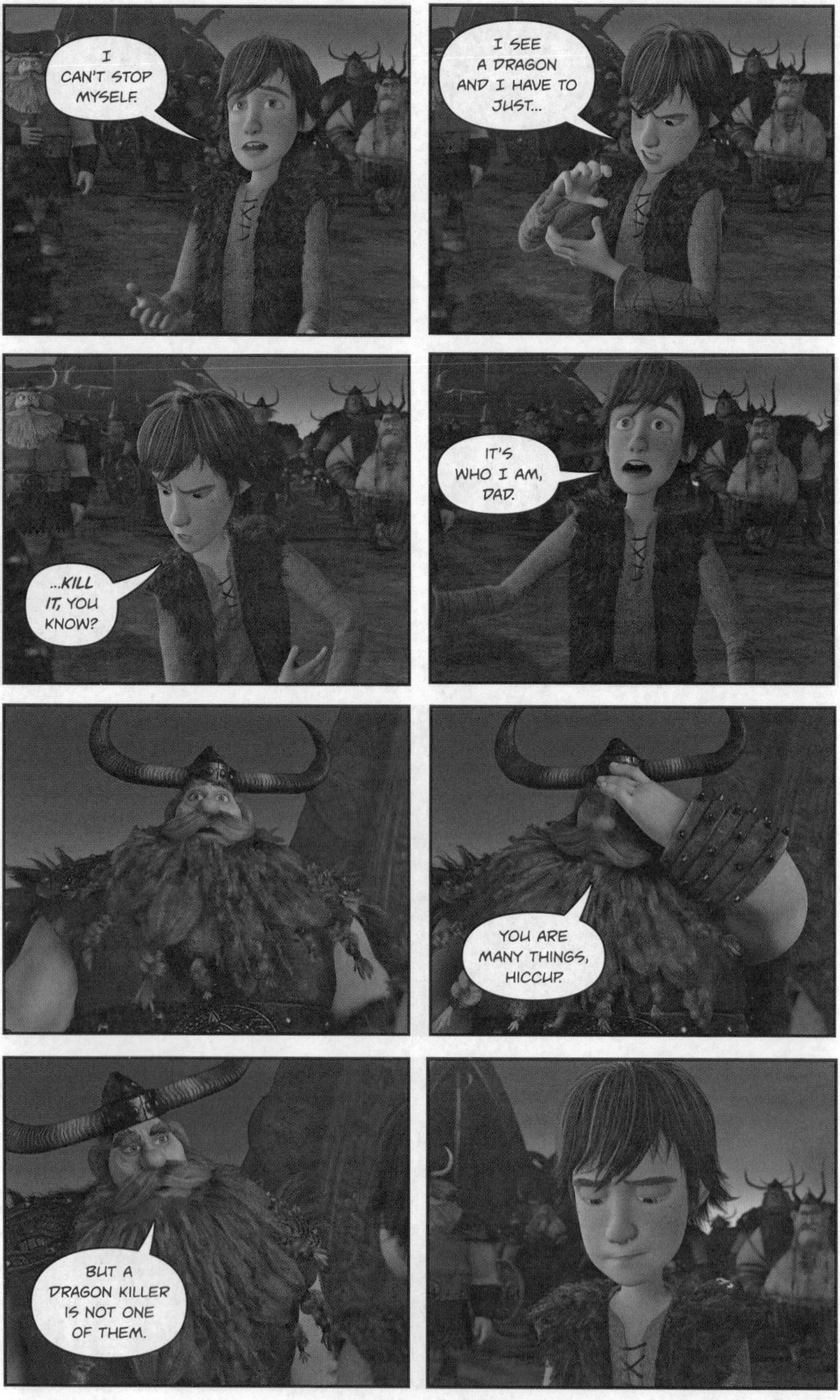
I CAN'T STOP MYSELF.
I SEE A DRAGON AND I HAVE TO JUST...
...KILL IT, YOU KNOW?
IT'S WHO I AM, DAD.
YOU ARE MANY THINGS, HICCUP.
BUT A DRAGON KILLER IS NOT ONE OF THEM.

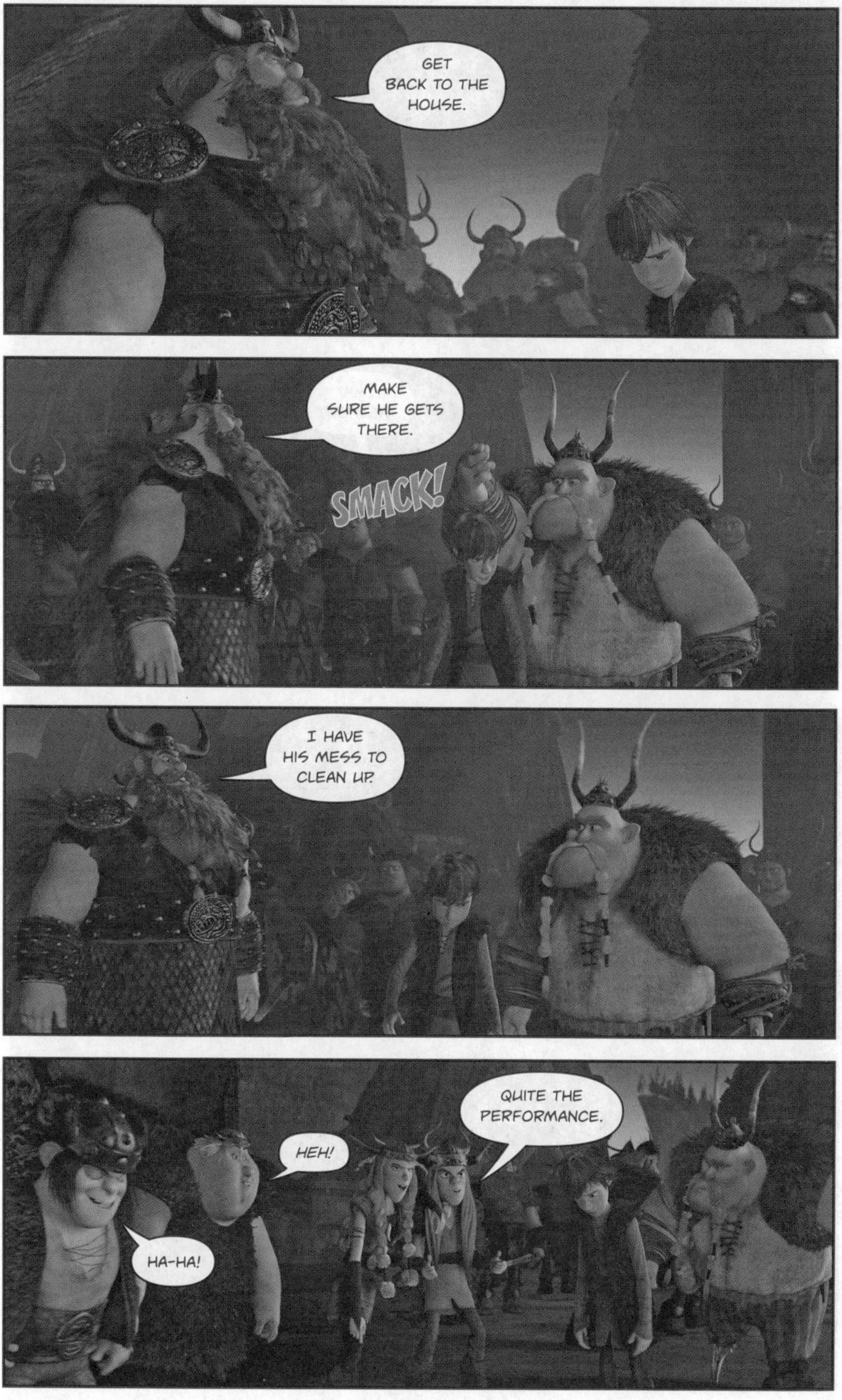
GET BACK TO THE HOUSE.
MAKE SURE HE GETS THERE.
SMACK!
I HAVE HIS MESS TO CLEAN UP.
HA-HA!
HEH!
QUITE THE PERFORMANCE.

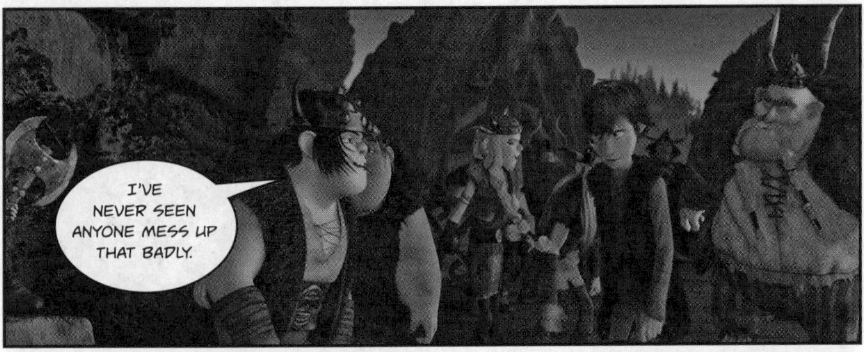
I'VE NEVER SEEN ANYONE MESS UP THAT BADLY.

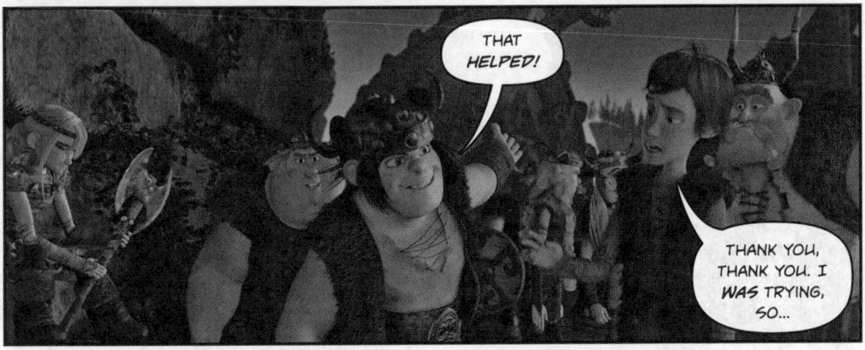
THAT HELPED!
THANK YOU, THANK YOU. I WAS TRYING, SO...

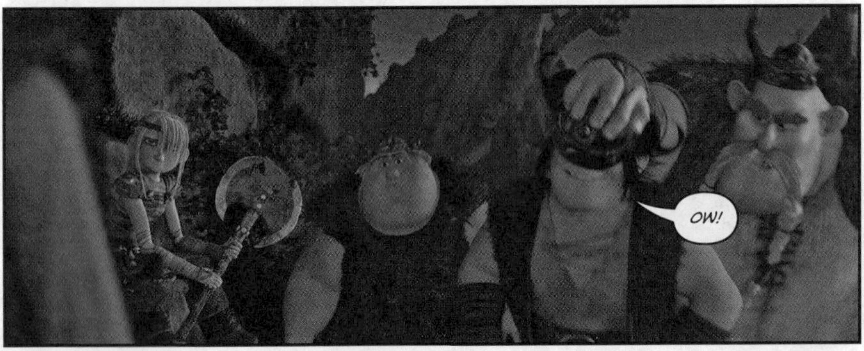
OW!

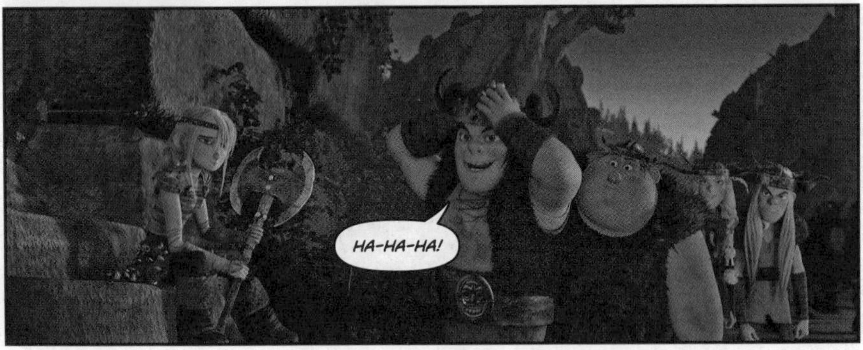
HA-HA-HA!

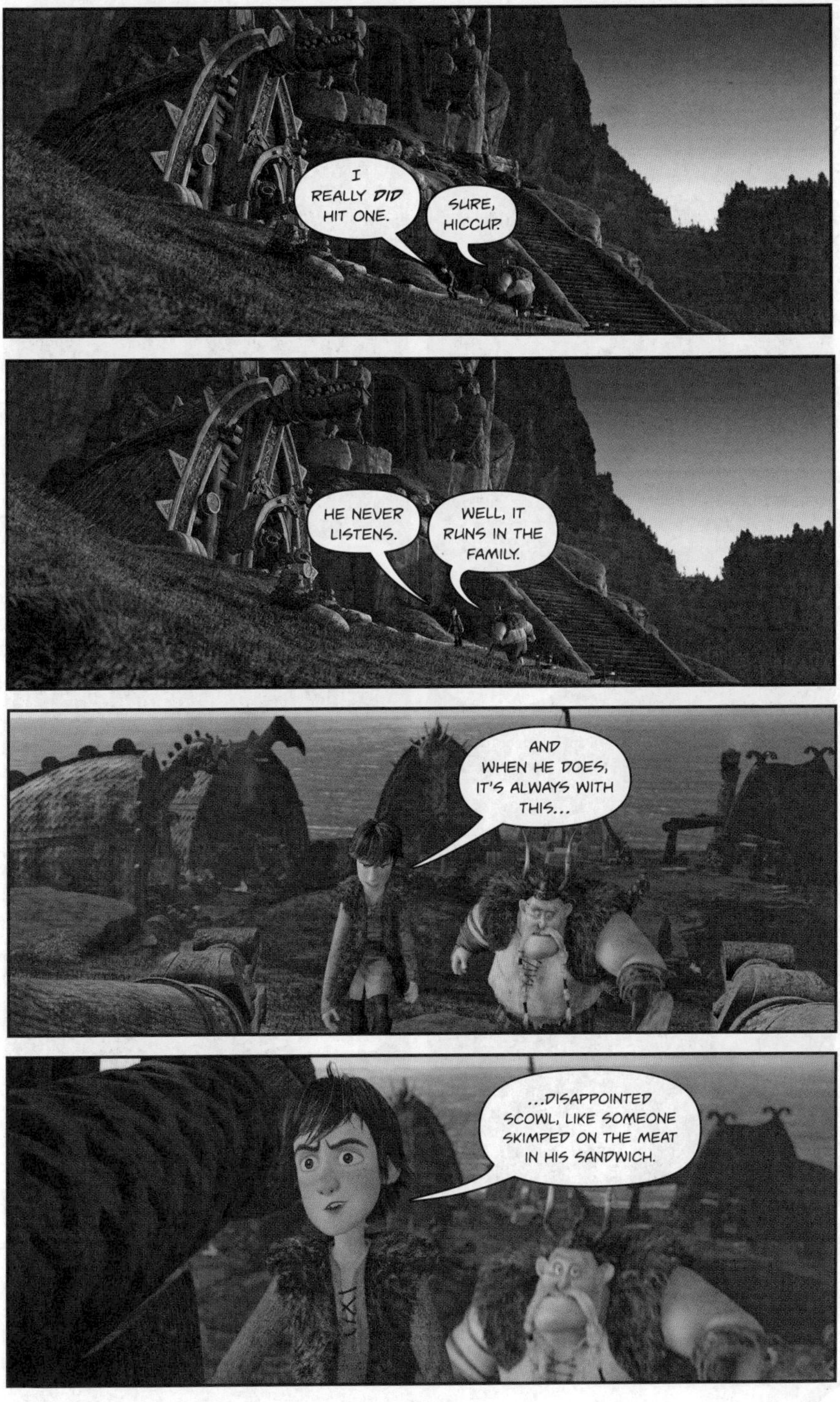
I REALLY DID HIT ONE.
SURE, HICCUP.
HE NEVER LISTENS.
WELL, IT RUNS IN THE FAMILY.
AND WHEN HE DOES, IT'S ALWAYS WITH THIS...
...DISAPPOINTED SCOWL, LIKE SOMEONE SKIMPED ON THE MEAT IN HIS SANDWICH.

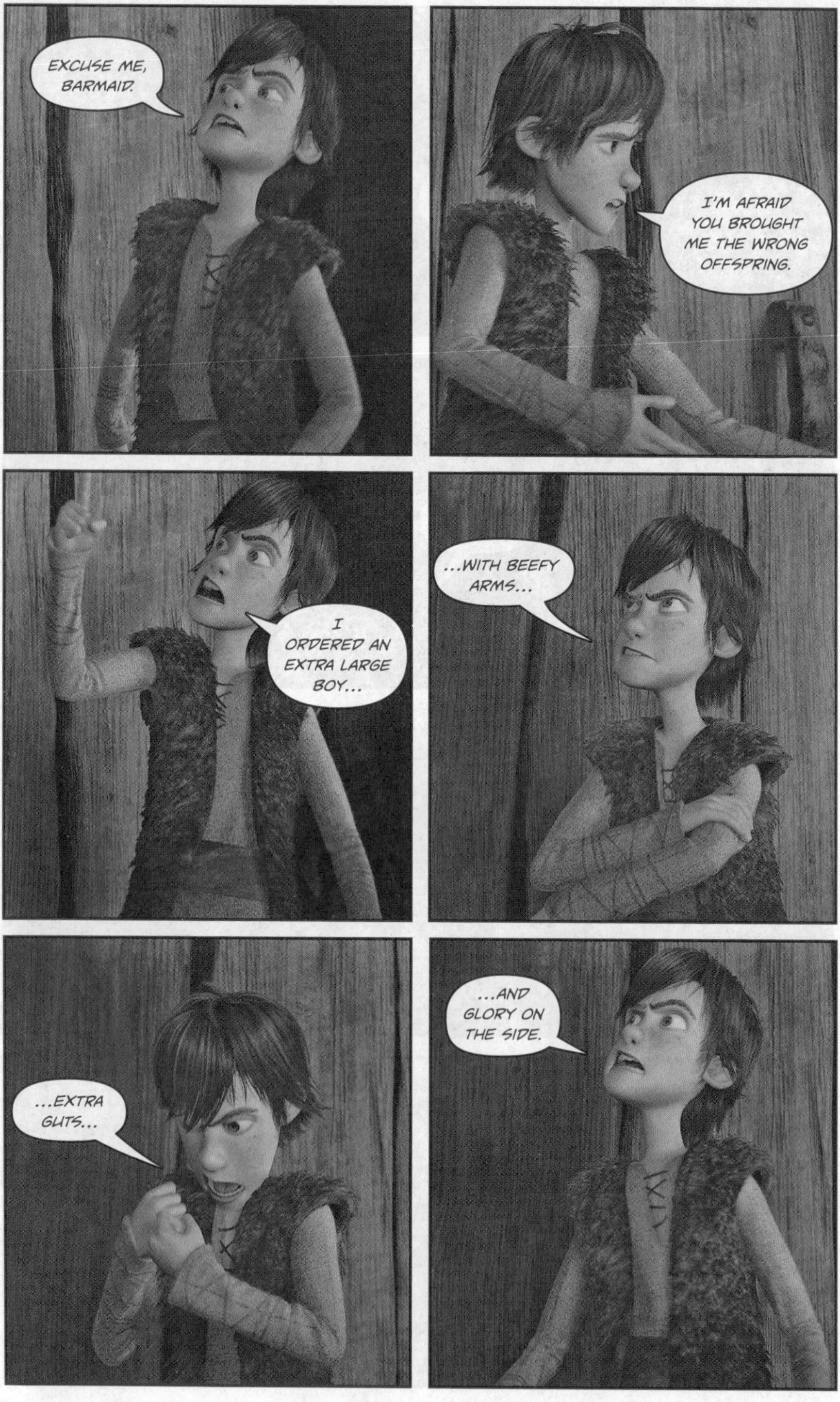
EXCUSE ME, BARMAID.
I'M AFRAID YOU BROUGHT ME THE WRONG OFFSPRING.
I ORDERED AN EXTRA LARGE BOY...
...WITH BEEFY ARMS...
...EXTRA GUTS...
...AND GLORY ON THE SIDE.

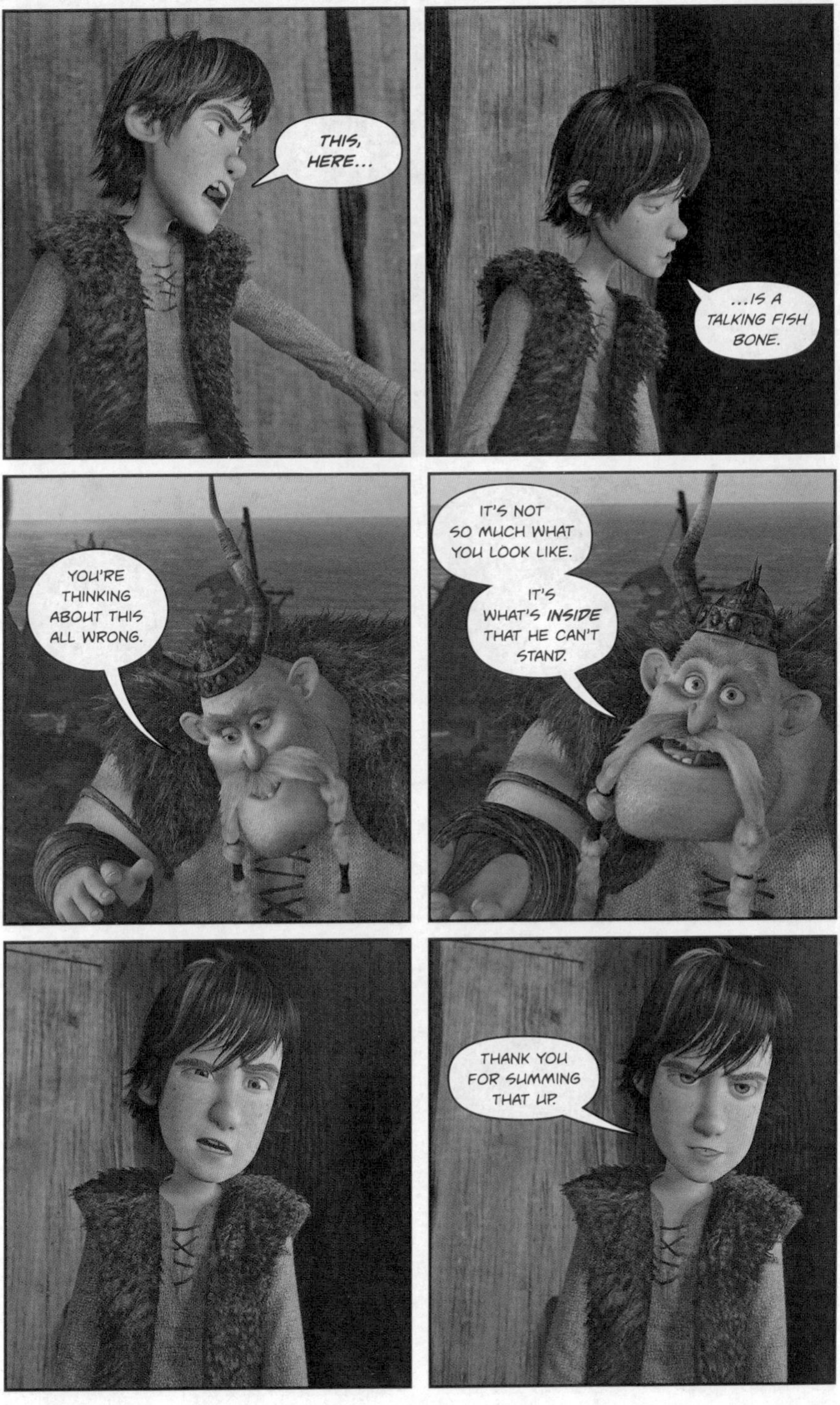
THIS, HERE...
...IS A TALKING FISH BONE.
YOU'RE THINKING ABOUT THIS ALL WRONG.
IT'S NOT SO MUCH WHAT YOU LOOK LIKE.
IT'S WHAT'S *INSIDE* THAT HE CAN'T STAND.
THANK YOU FOR SUMMING THAT UP.

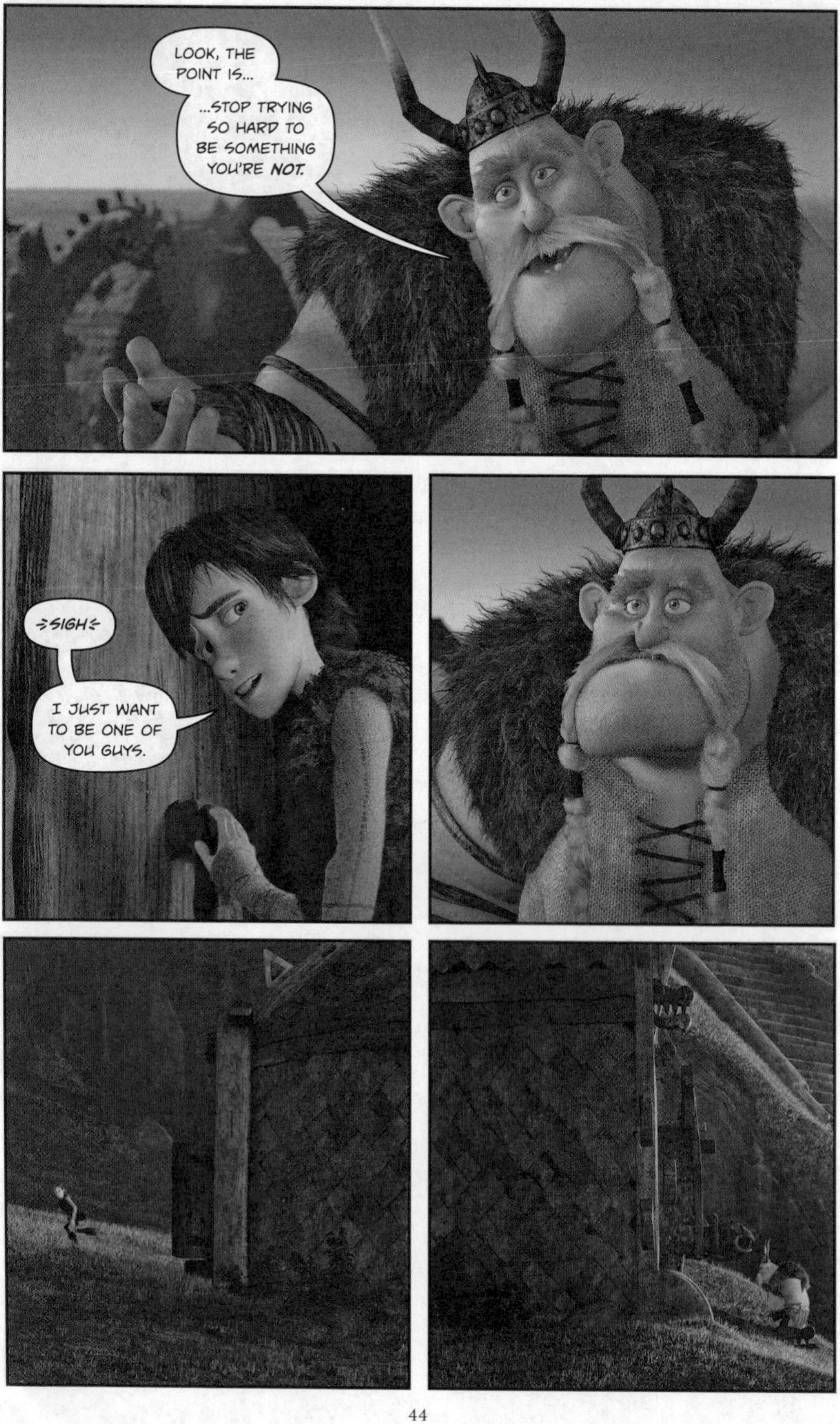
LOOK, THE POINT IS...
...STOP TRYING SO HARD TO BE SOMETHING YOU'RE NOT.
SIGH
I JUST WANT TO BE ONE OF YOU GUYS.

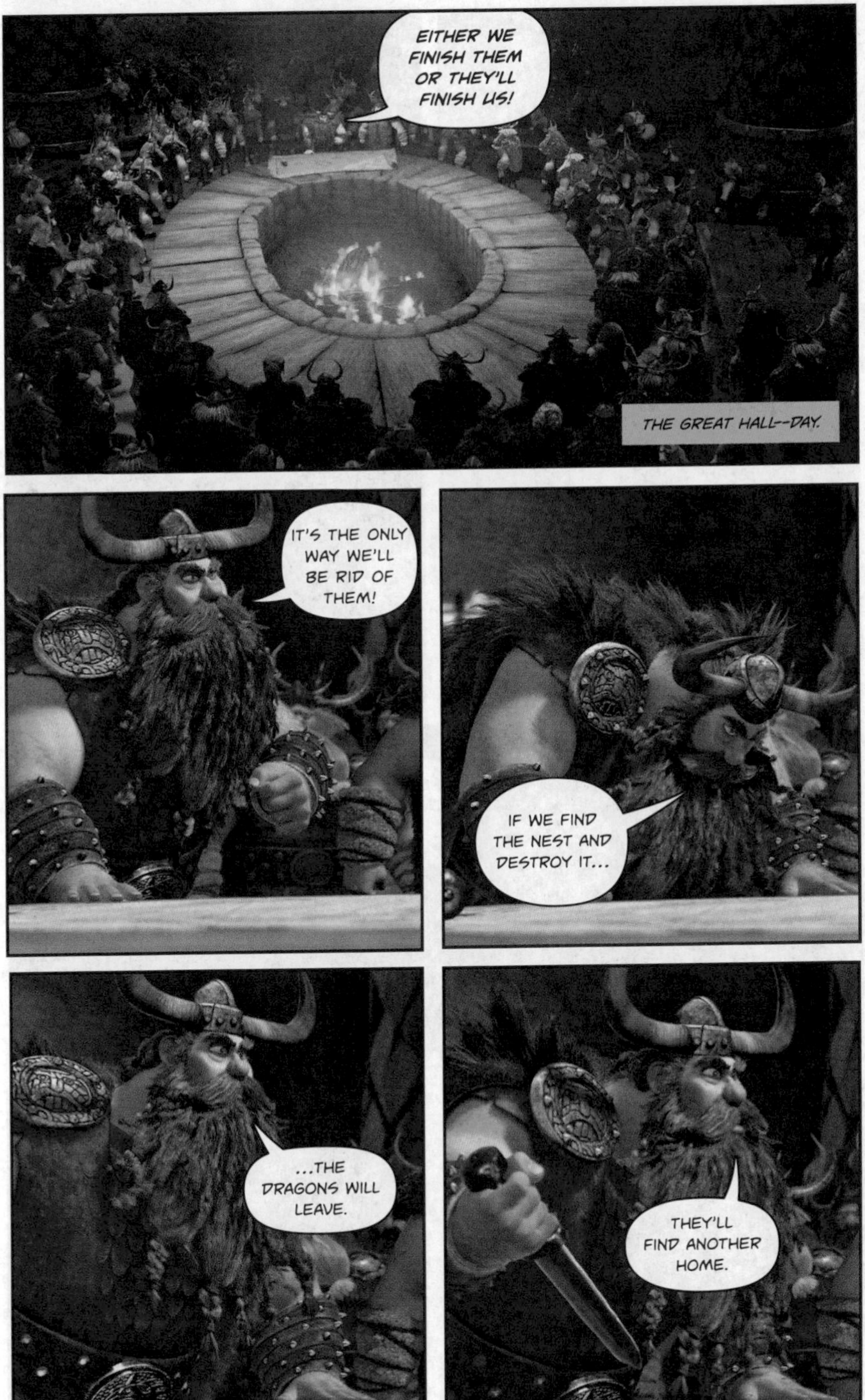
EITHER WE FINISH THEM OR THEY'LL FINISH US!
THE GREAT HALL--DAY.
IT'S THE ONLY WAY WE'LL BE RID OF THEM!
IF WE FIND THE NEST AND DESTROY IT...
...THE DRAGONS WILL LEAVE.
THEY'LL FIND ANOTHER HOME.

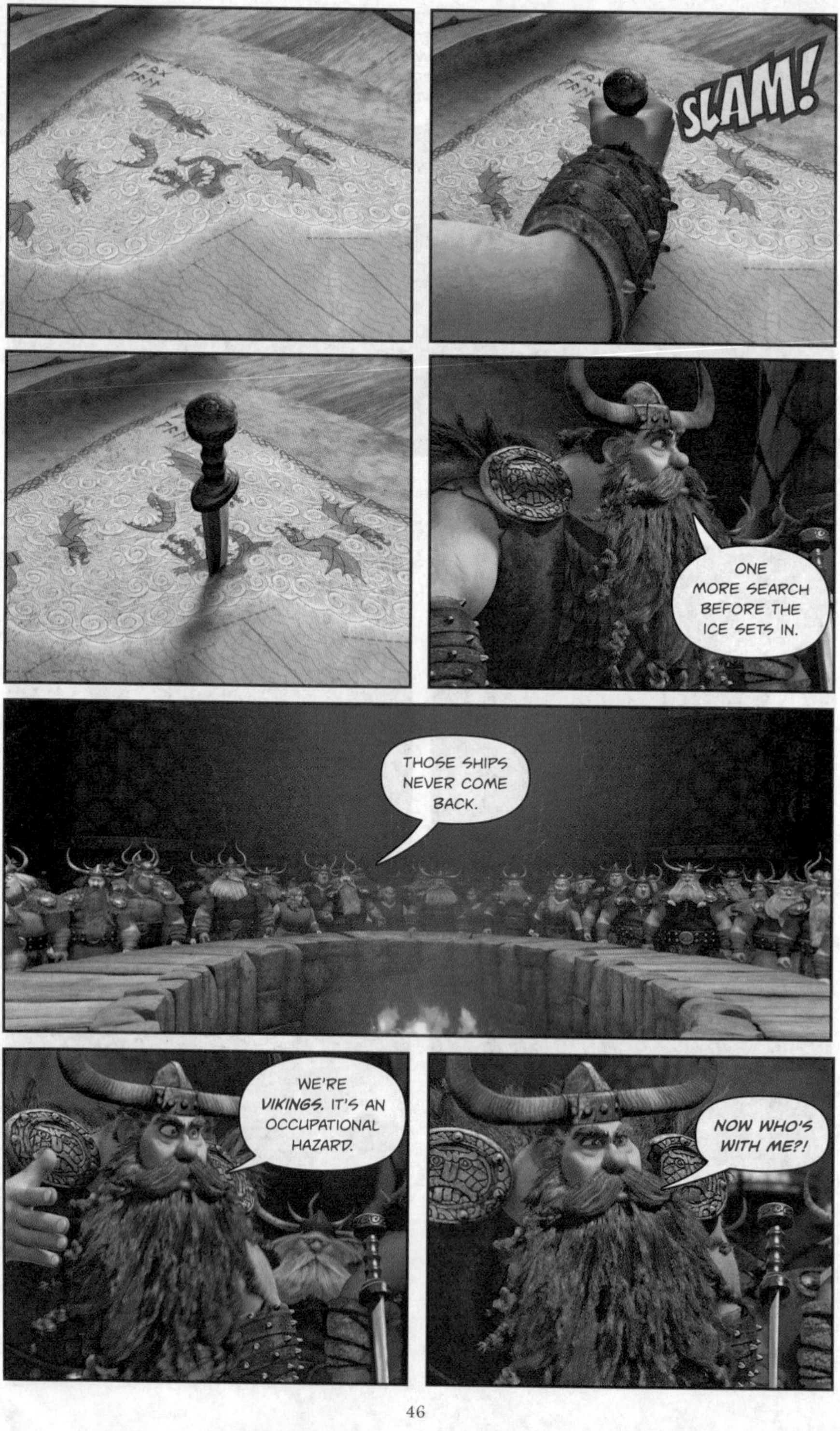
SLAM!
ONE MORE SEARCH BEFORE THE ICE SETS IN.
THOSE SHIPS NEVER COME BACK.
WE'RE *VIKINGS.* IT'S AN OCCUPATIONAL HAZARD.
NOW WHO'S WITH ME?!

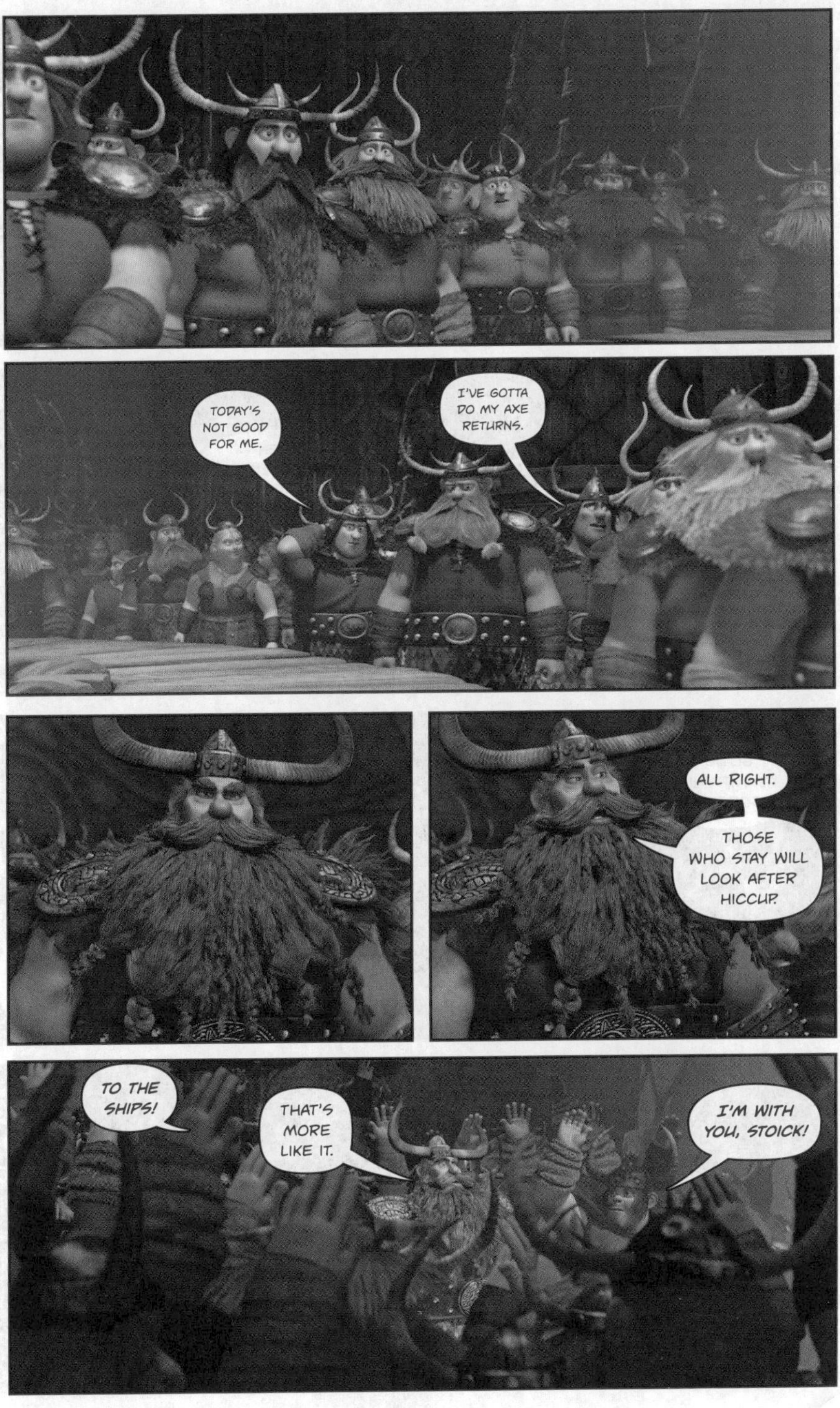
TODAY'S NOT GOOD FOR ME.
I'VE GOTTA DO MY AXE RETURNS.
ALL RIGHT.
THOSE WHO STAY WILL LOOK AFTER HICCUP.
TO THE SHIPS!
THAT'S MORE LIKE IT.
I'M WITH YOU, STOICK!

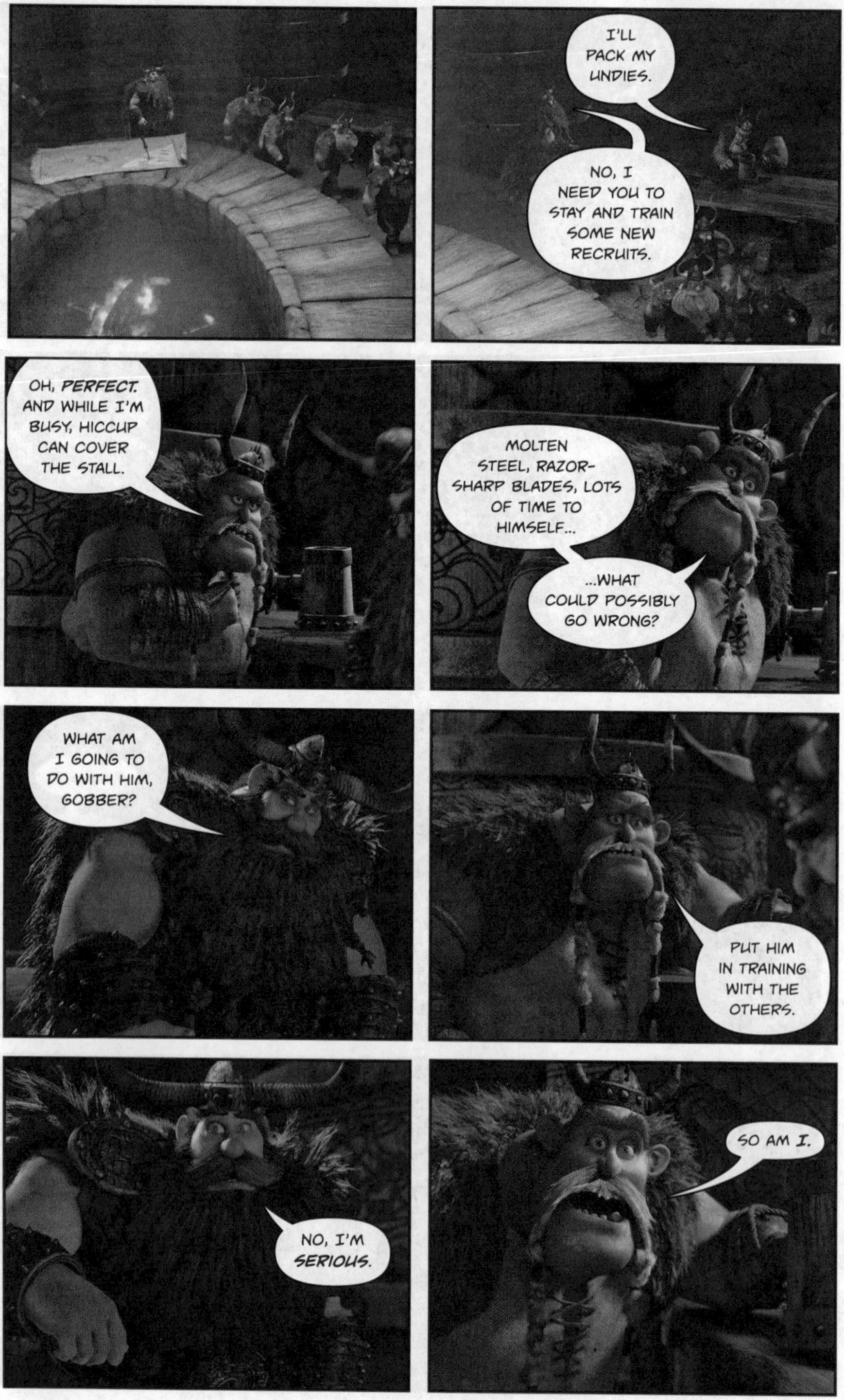
I'LL PACK MY UNDIES.
NO, I NEED YOU TO STAY AND TRAIN SOME NEW RECRUITS.
OH, *PERFECT.* AND WHILE I'M BUSY, HICCUP CAN COVER THE STALL.
MOLTEN STEEL, RAZOR-SHARP BLADES, LOTS OF TIME TO HIMSELF...
...WHAT COULD POSSIBLY GO WRONG?
WHAT AM I GOING TO DO WITH HIM, GOBBER?
PUT HIM IN TRAINING WITH THE OTHERS.
NO, I'M *SERIOUS.*
SO AM *I.*

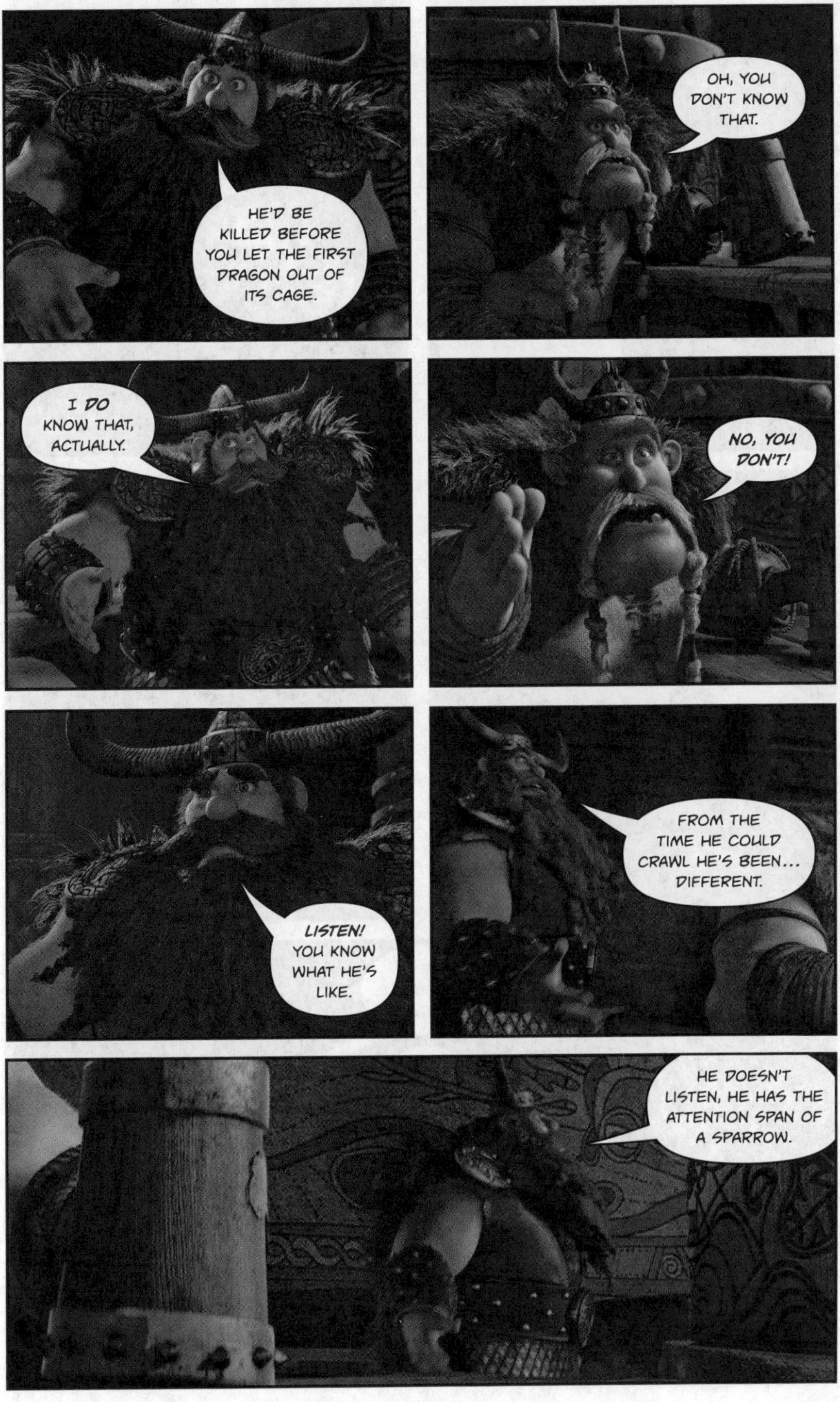
HE'D BE KILLED BEFORE YOU LET THE FIRST DRAGON OUT OF ITS CAGE.
OH, YOU DON'T KNOW THAT.
I DO KNOW THAT, ACTUALLY.
NO, YOU DON'T!
LISTEN! YOU KNOW WHAT HE'S LIKE.
FROM THE TIME HE COULD CRAWL HE'S BEEN... DIFFERENT.
HE DOESN'T LISTEN, HE HAS THE ATTENTION SPAN OF A SPARROW.

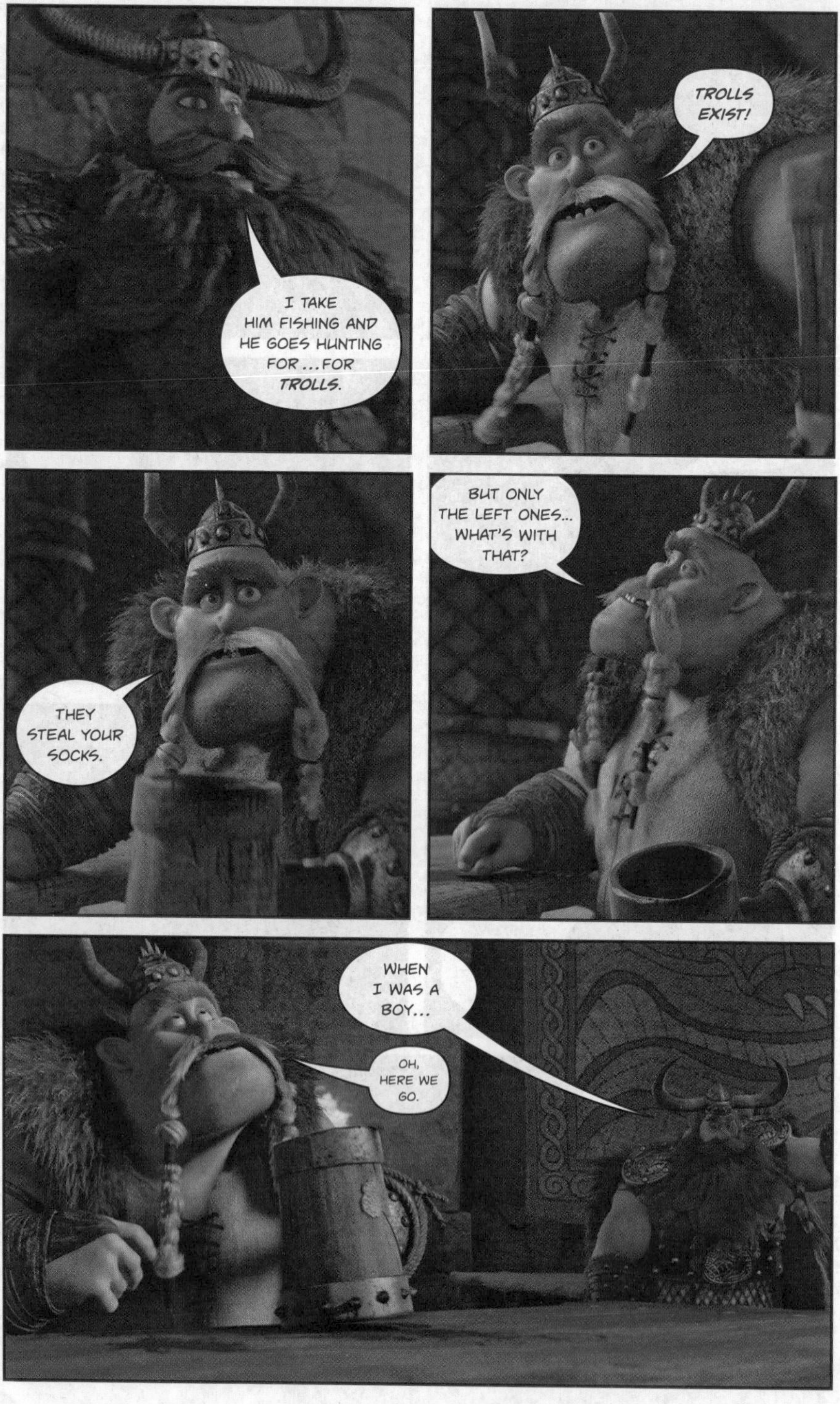
I TAKE HIM FISHING AND HE GOES HUNTING FOR...FOR *TROLLS.*
TROLLS EXIST!
THEY STEAL YOUR SOCKS.
BUT ONLY THE LEFT ONES... WHAT'S WITH THAT?
WHEN I WAS A BOY...
OH, HERE WE GO.

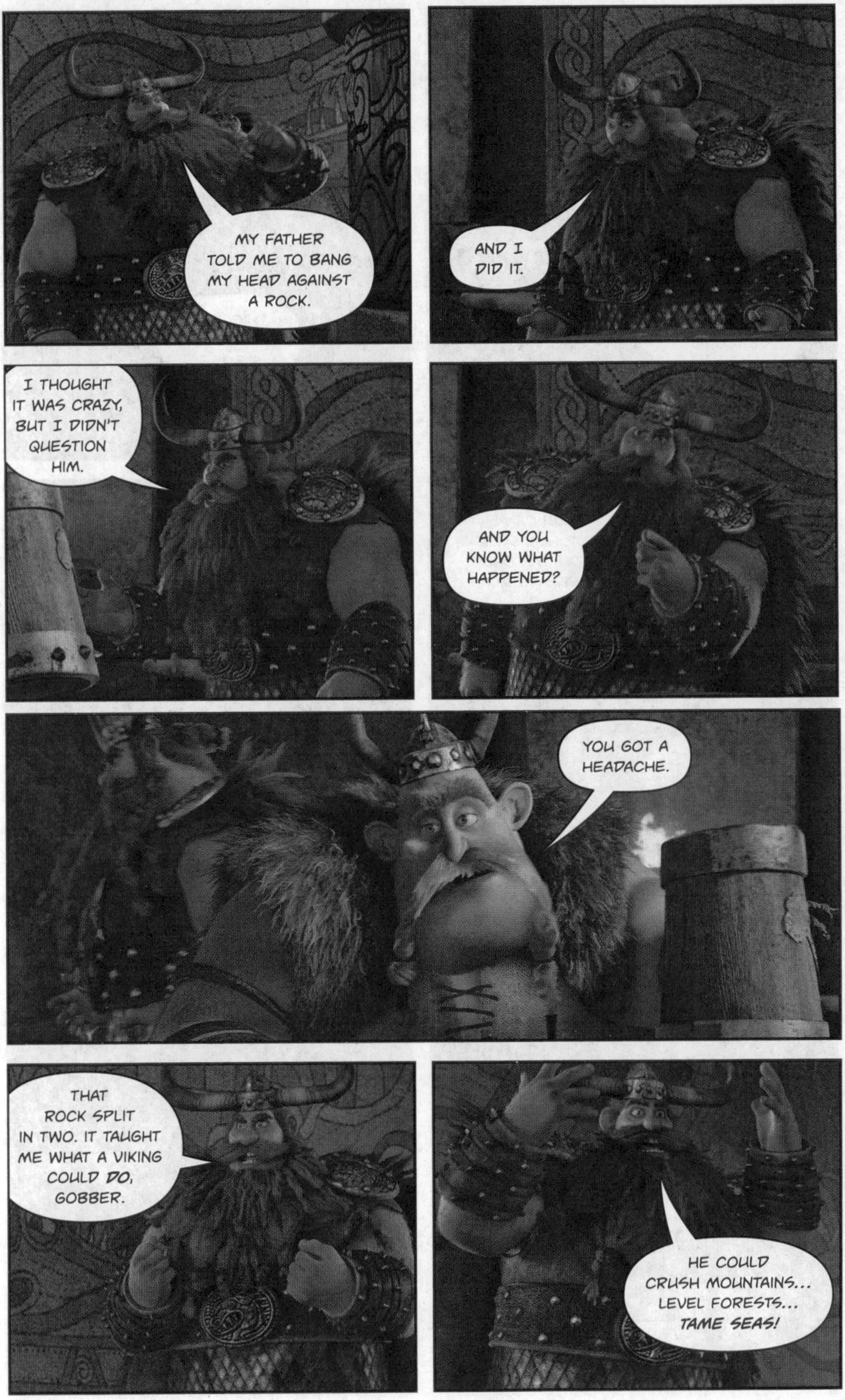
MY FATHER TOLD ME TO BANG MY HEAD AGAINST A ROCK.
AND I DID IT.
I THOUGHT IT WAS CRAZY, BUT I DIDN'T QUESTION HIM.
AND YOU KNOW WHAT HAPPENED?
YOU GOT A HEADACHE.
THAT ROCK SPLIT IN TWO. IT TAUGHT ME WHAT A VIKING COULD *DO*, GOBBER.
HE COULD CRUSH MOUNTAINS... LEVEL FORESTS... *TAME SEAS!*

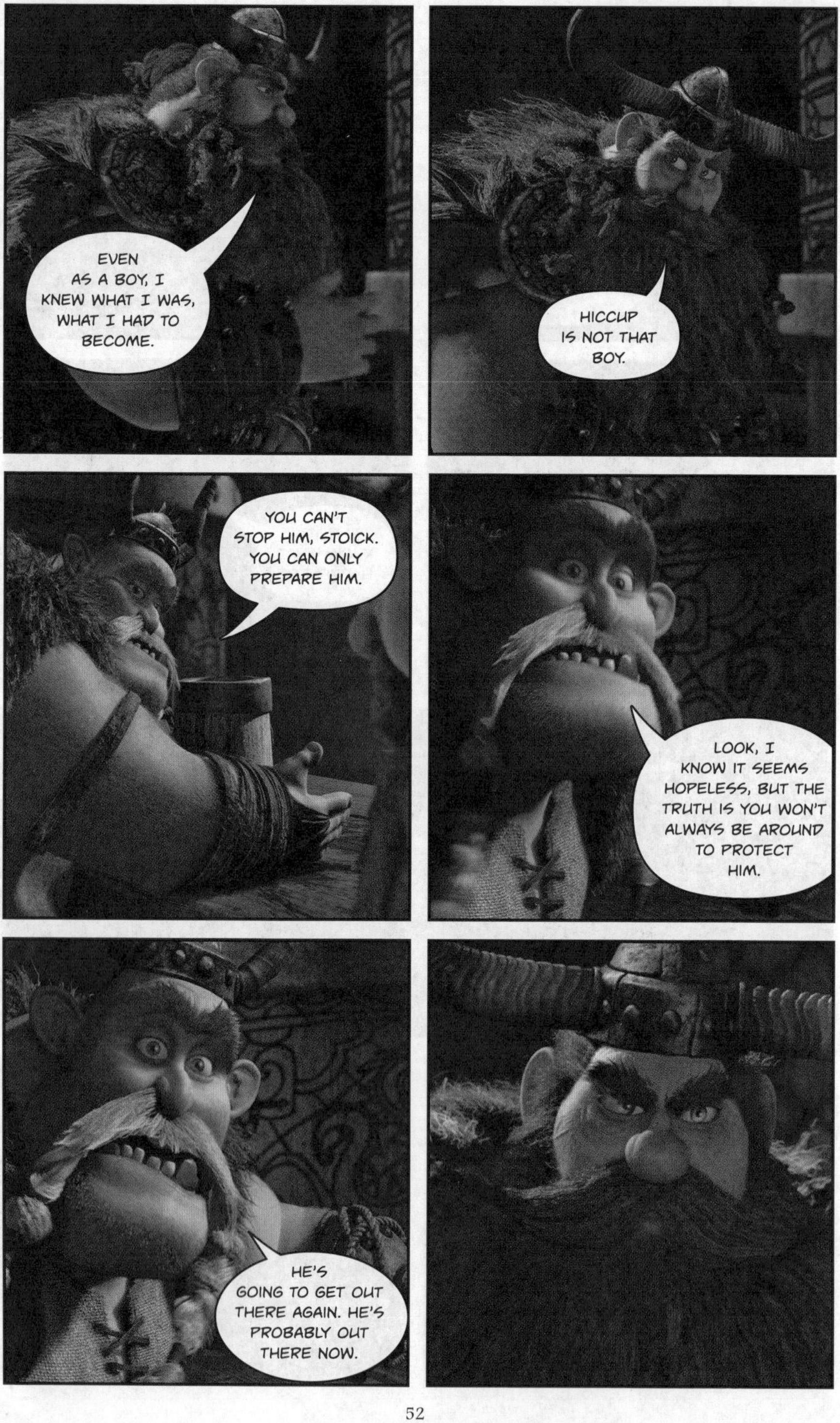
EVEN AS A BOY, I KNEW WHAT I WAS, WHAT I HAD TO BECOME.
HICCUP IS NOT THAT BOY.
YOU CAN'T STOP HIM, STOICK. YOU CAN ONLY PREPARE HIM.
LOOK, I KNOW IT SEEMS HOPELESS, BUT THE TRUTH IS YOU WON'T ALWAYS BE AROUND TO PROTECT HIM.
HE'S GOING TO GET OUT THERE AGAIN. HE'S PROBABLY OUT THERE NOW.

THE FOREST.

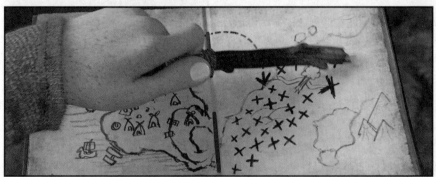

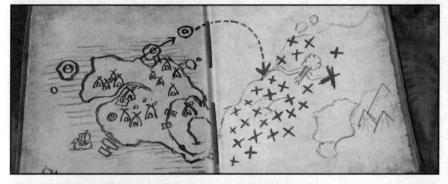

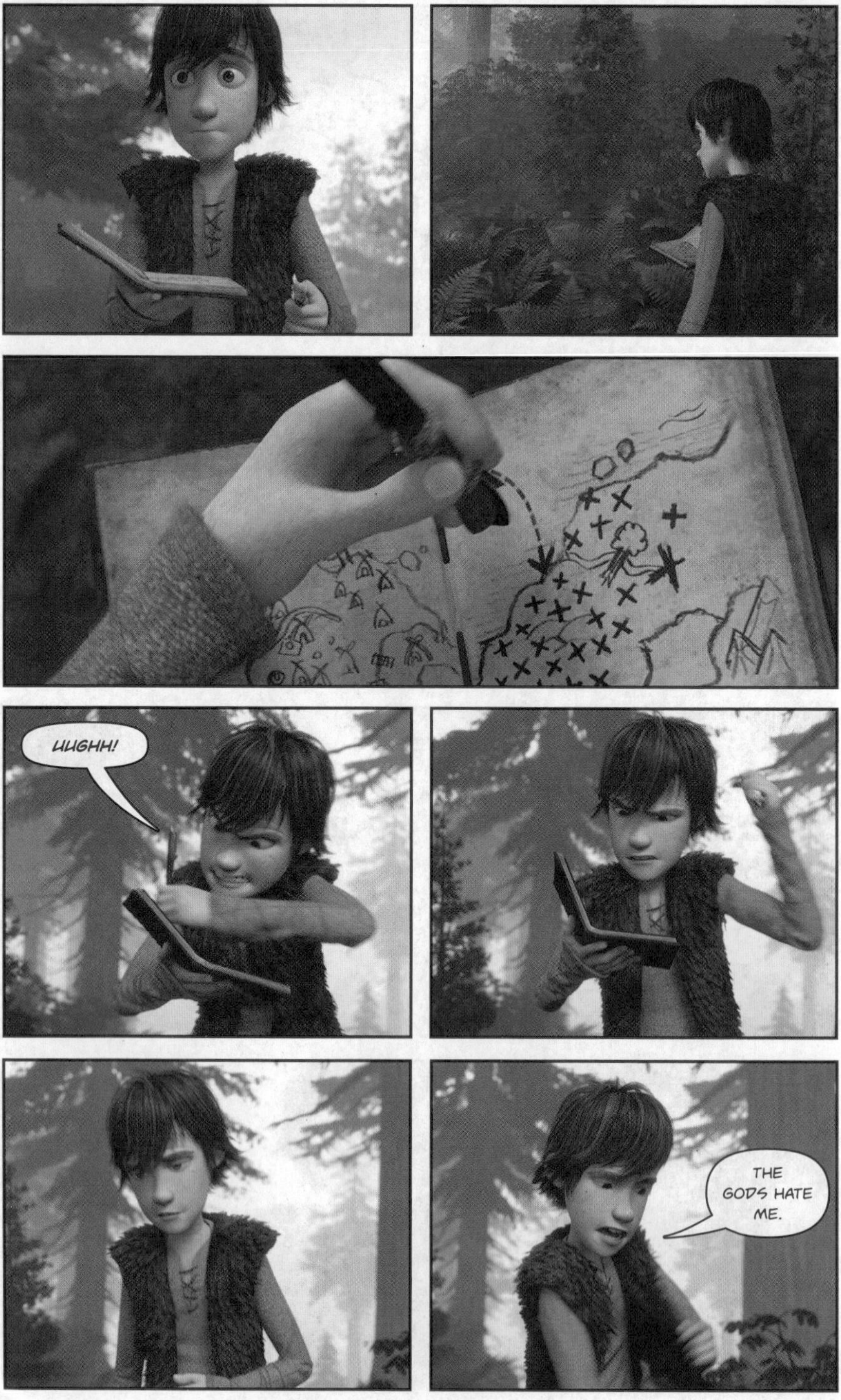
UUGHH!
THE GODS HATE ME.

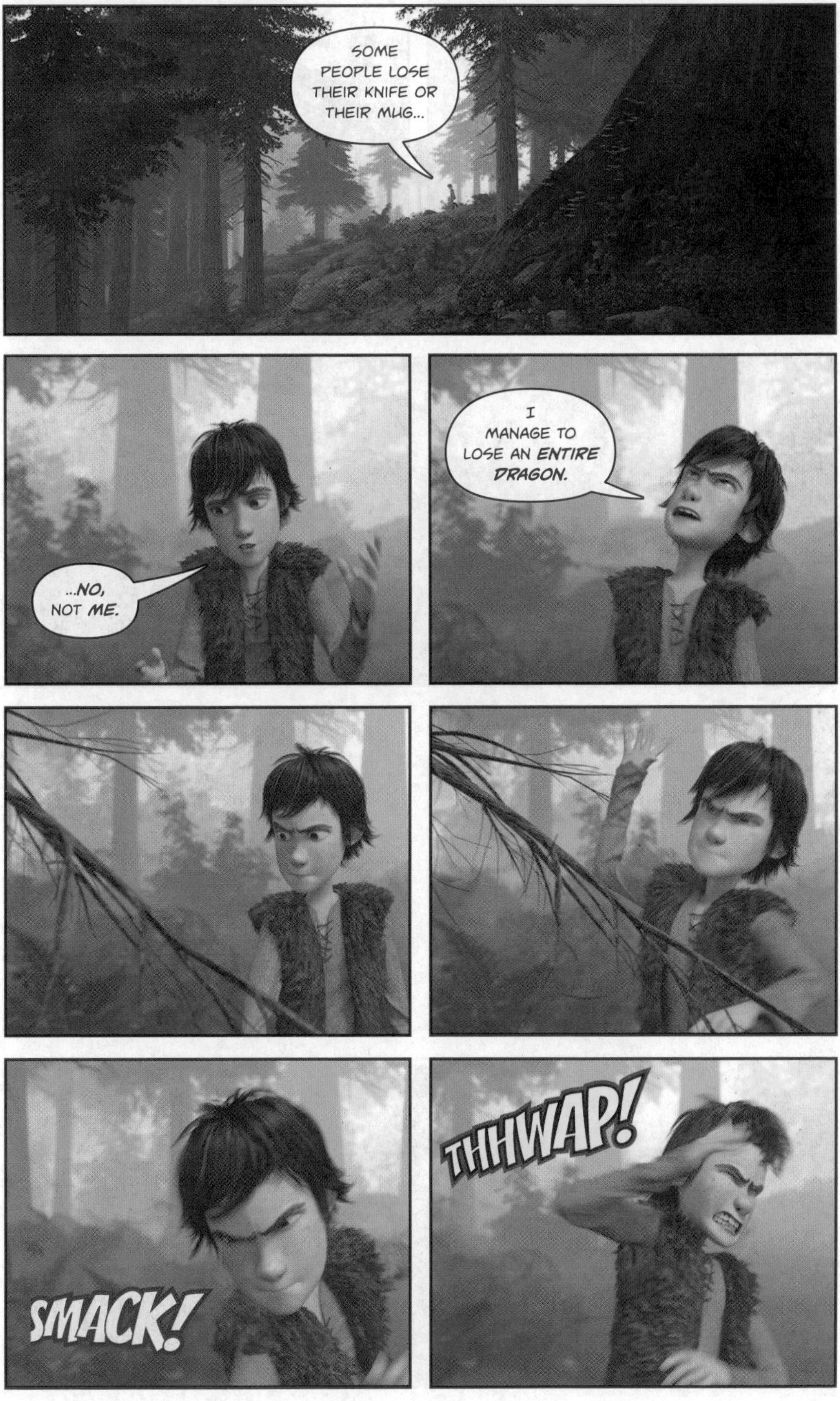
SOME PEOPLE LOSE THEIR KNIFE OR THEIR MUG...
...NO, NOT *ME*.
I MANAGE TO LOSE AN *ENTIRE DRAGON*.
SMACK!
THHWAP!

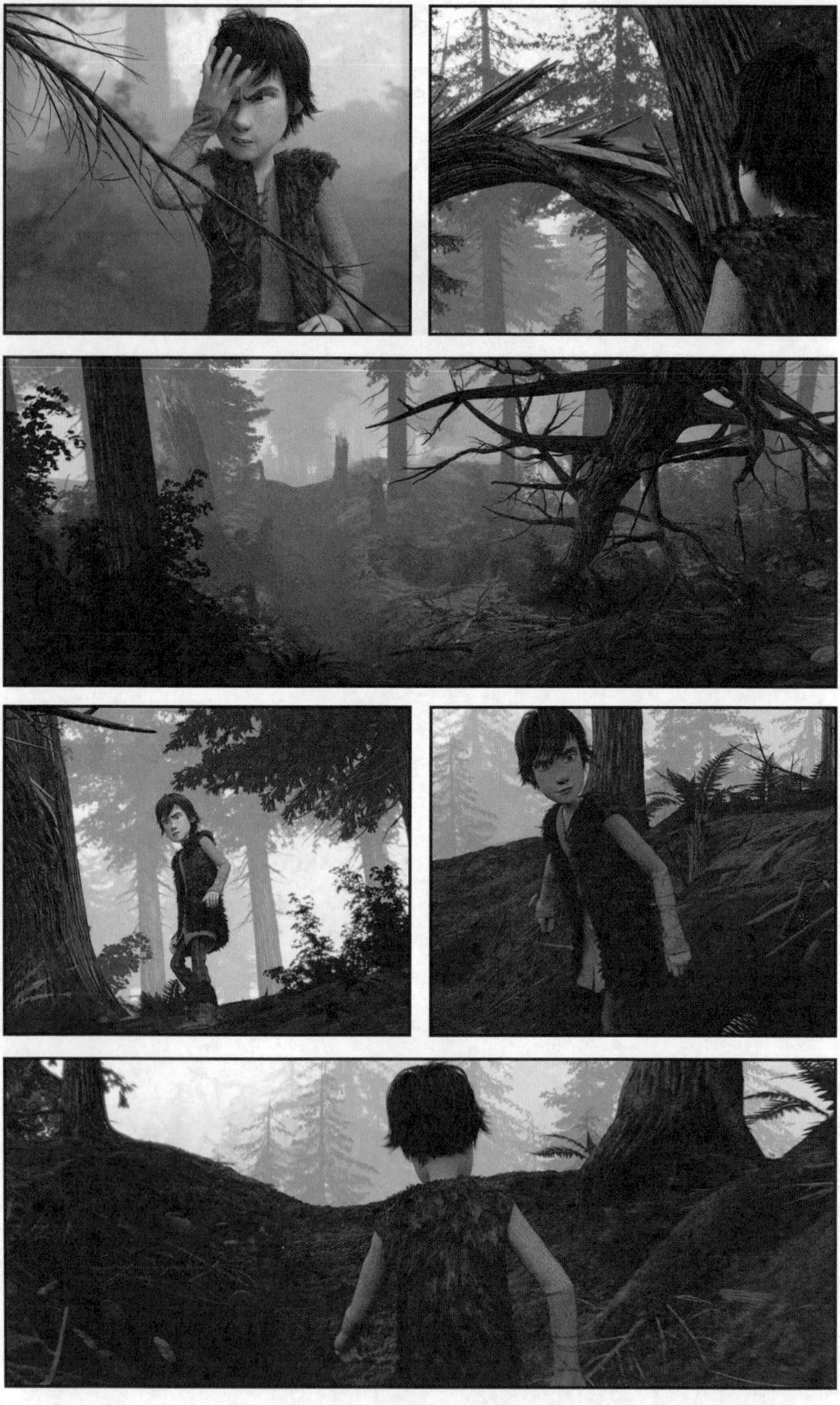

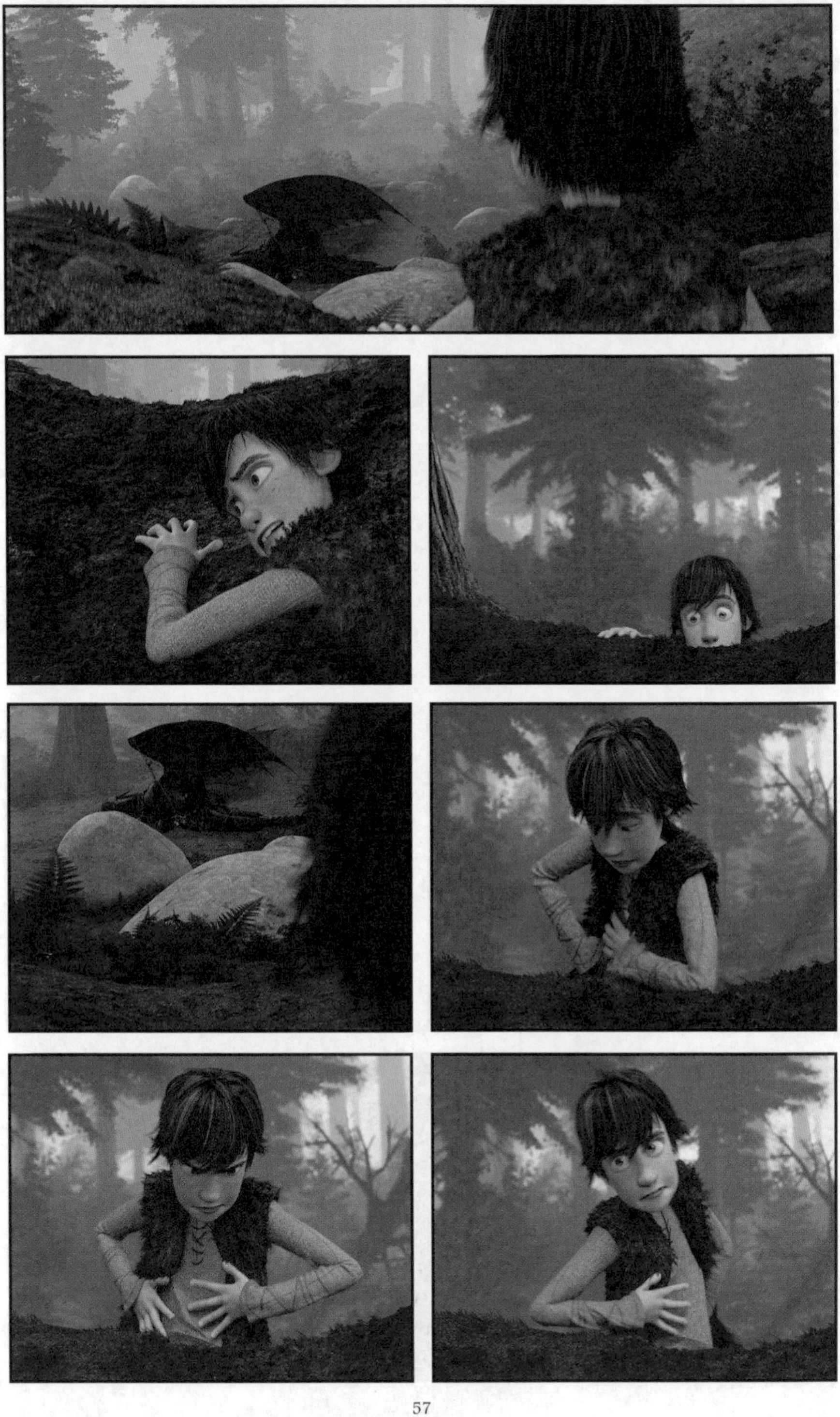

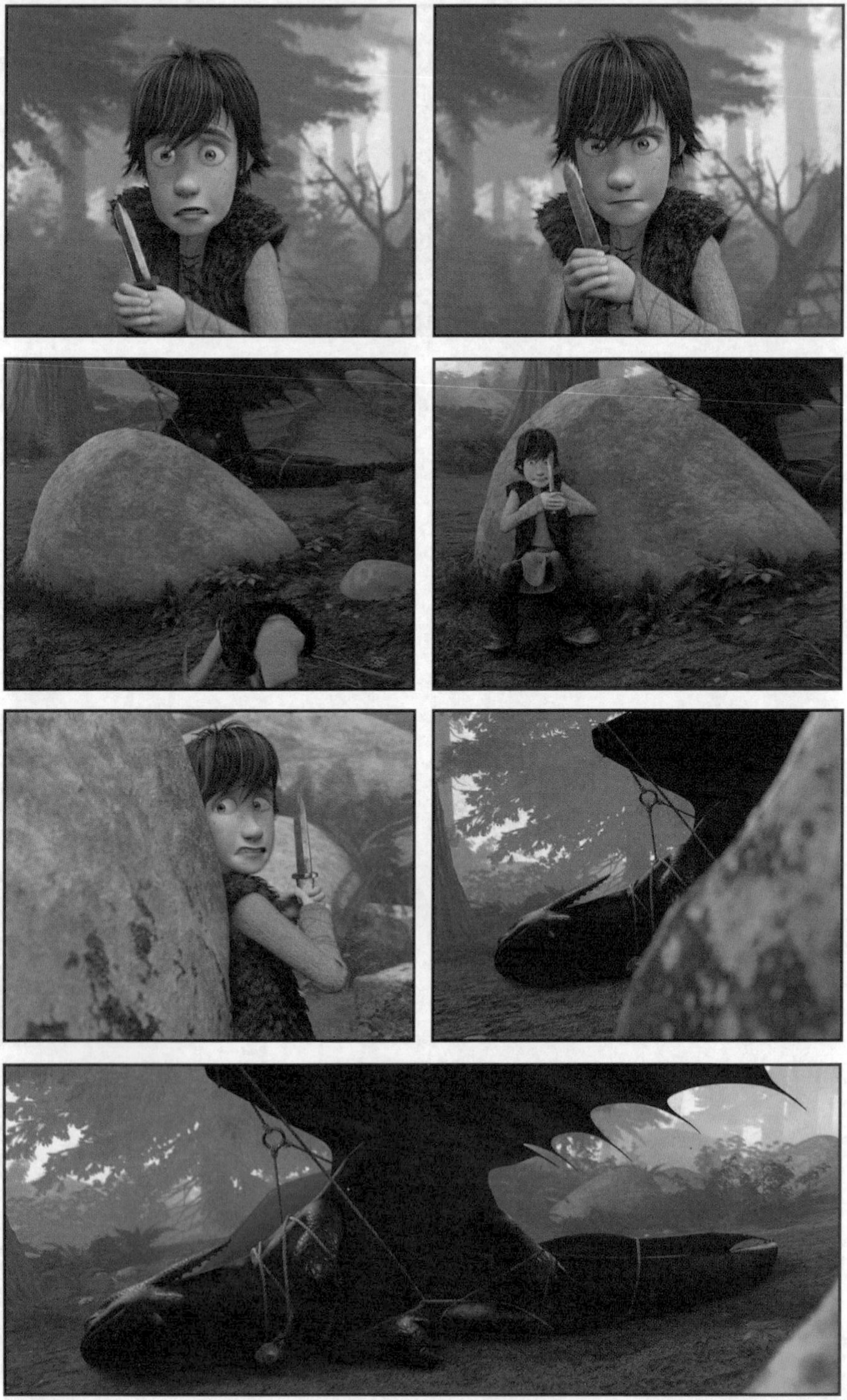

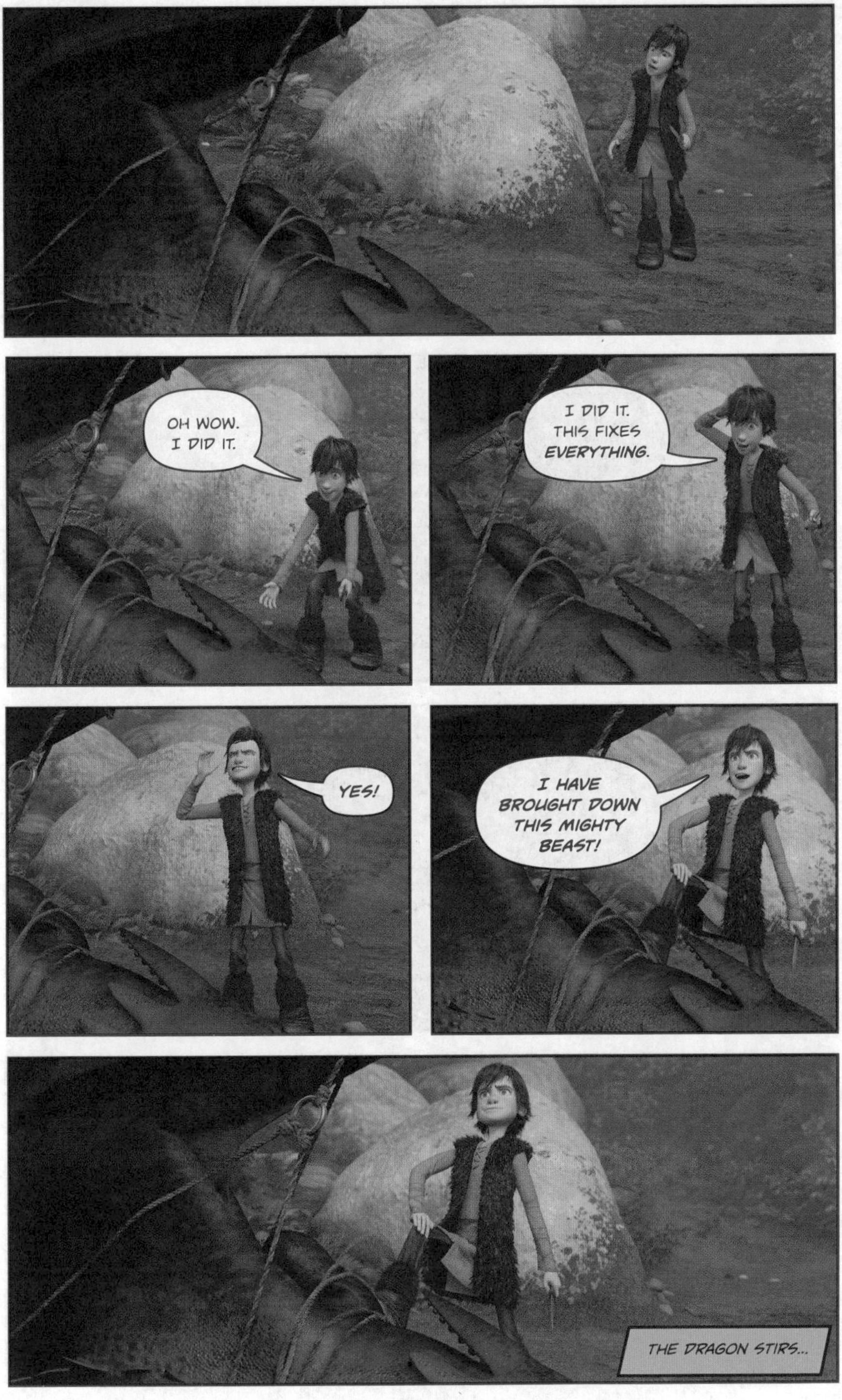
OH WOW.
I DID IT.
I DID IT.
THIS FIXES
EVERYTHING.
YES!
I HAVE
BROUGHT DOWN
THIS MIGHTY
BEAST!
THE DRAGON STIRS...

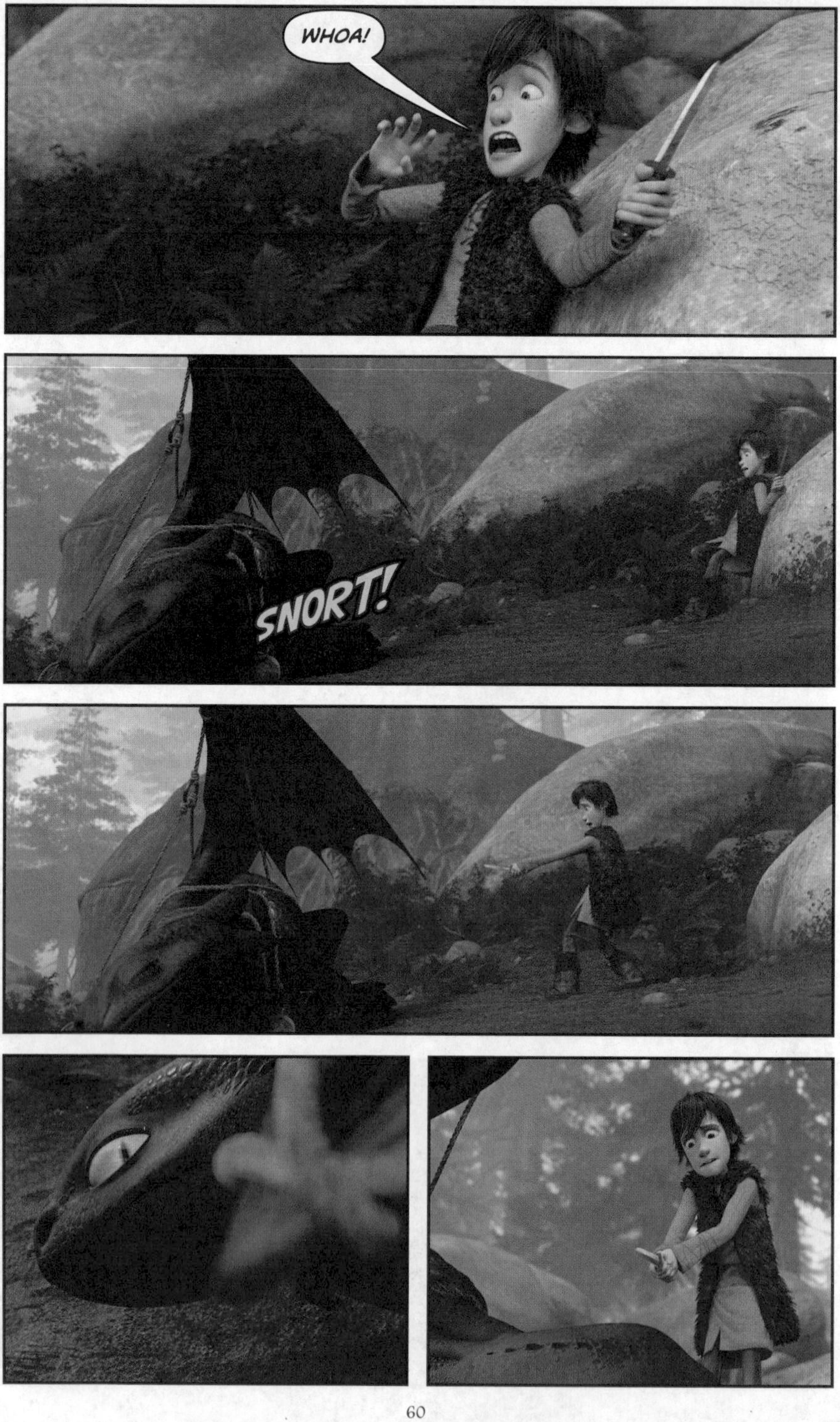
WHOA!
SNORT!

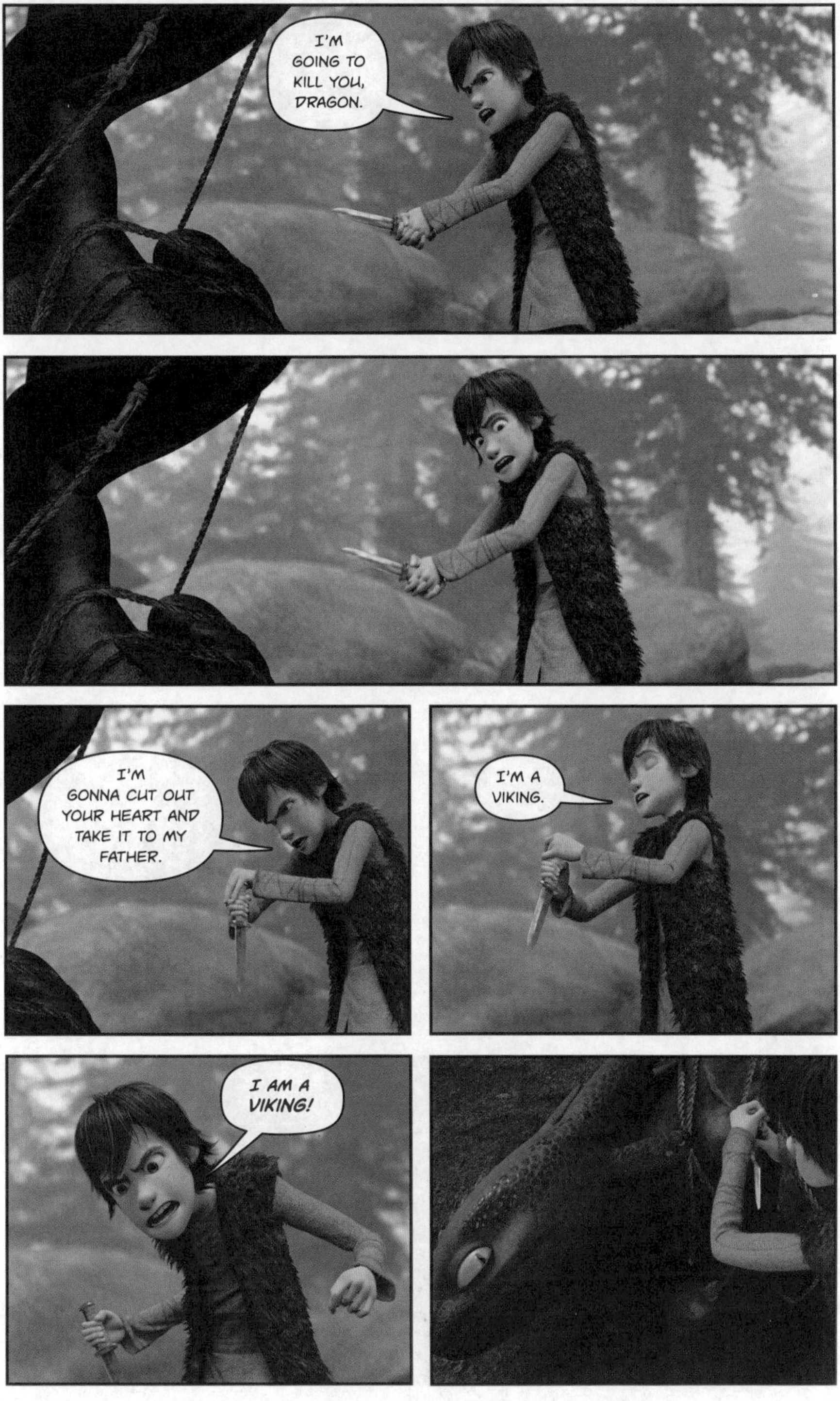
I'M GOING TO KILL YOU, DRAGON.
I'M GONNA CUT OUT YOUR HEART AND TAKE IT TO MY FATHER.
I'M A VIKING.
I AM A VIKING!

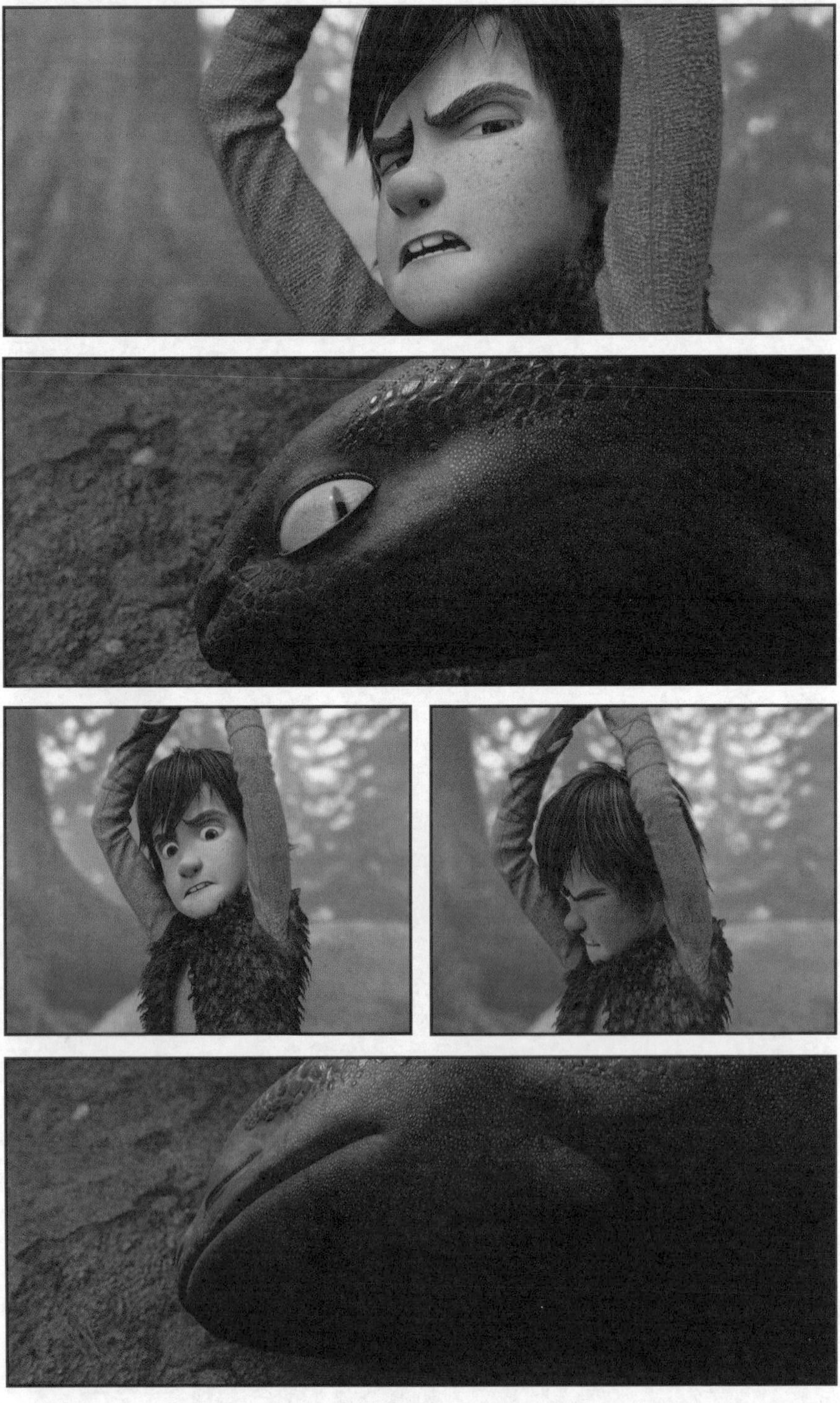

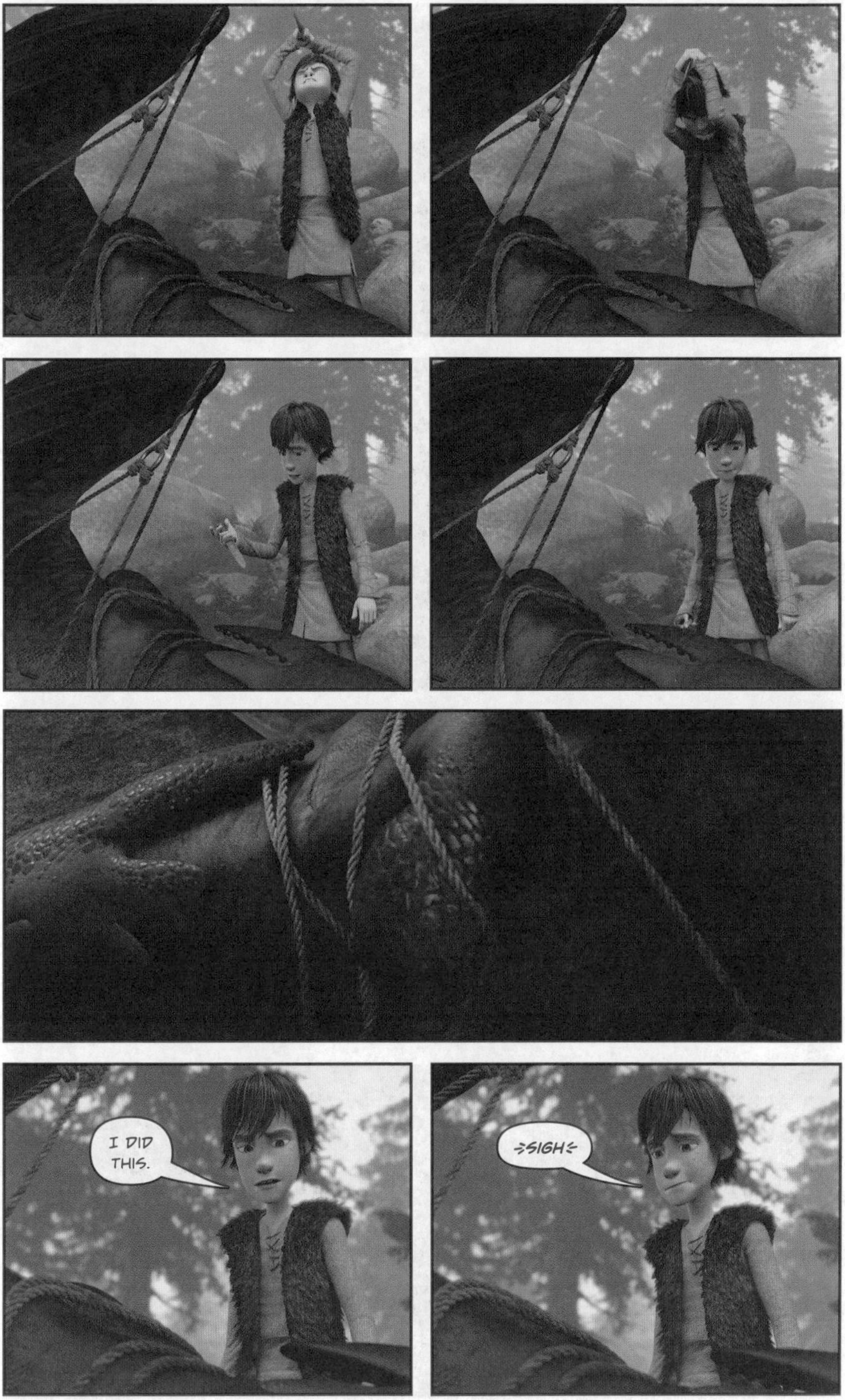
I DID THIS.
SIGH

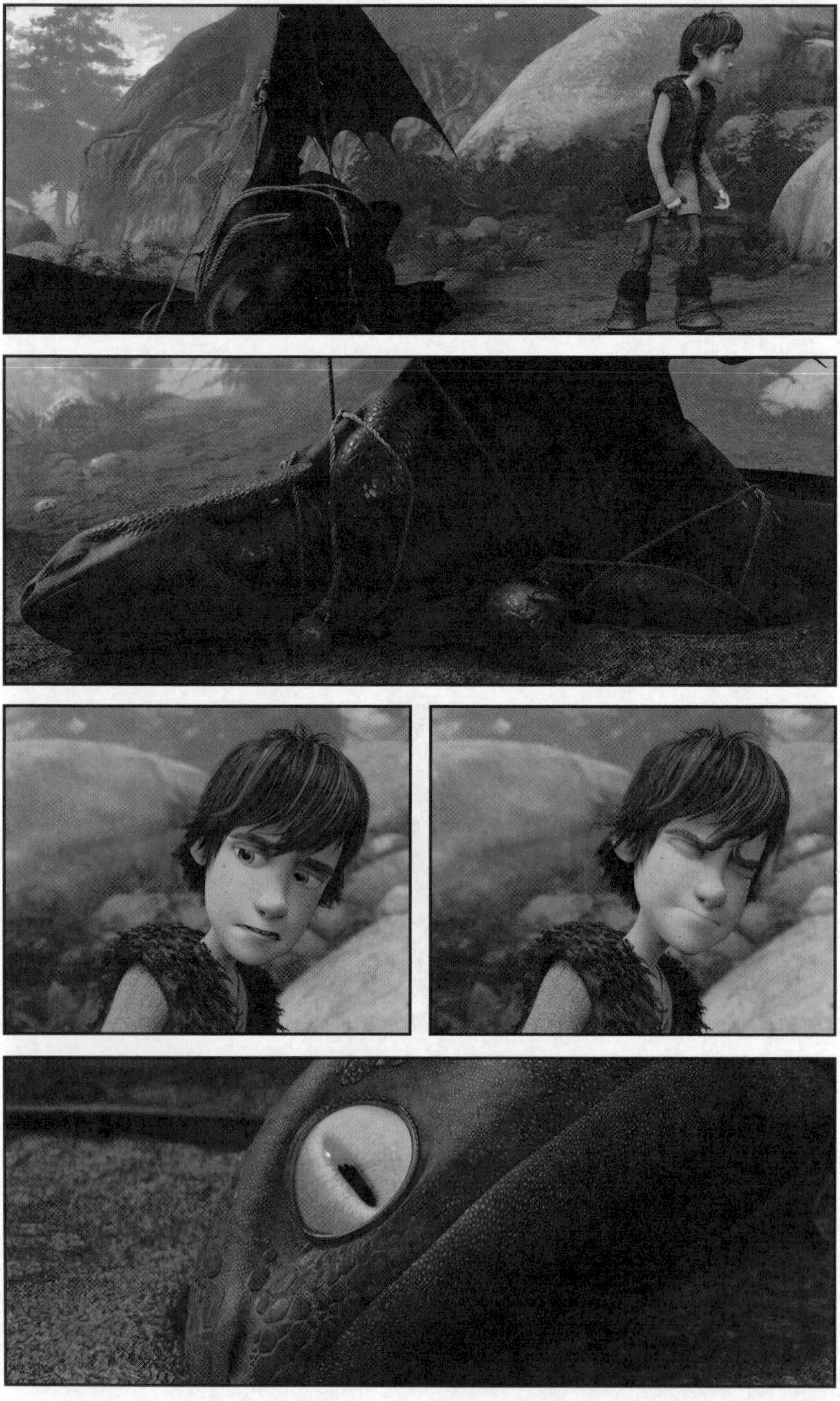

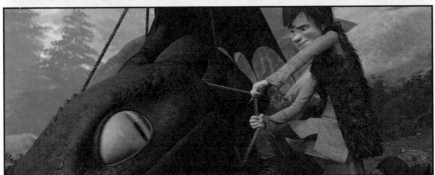

FREED, THE DRAGON POUNCES!

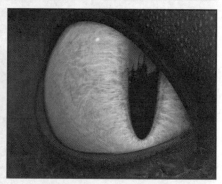

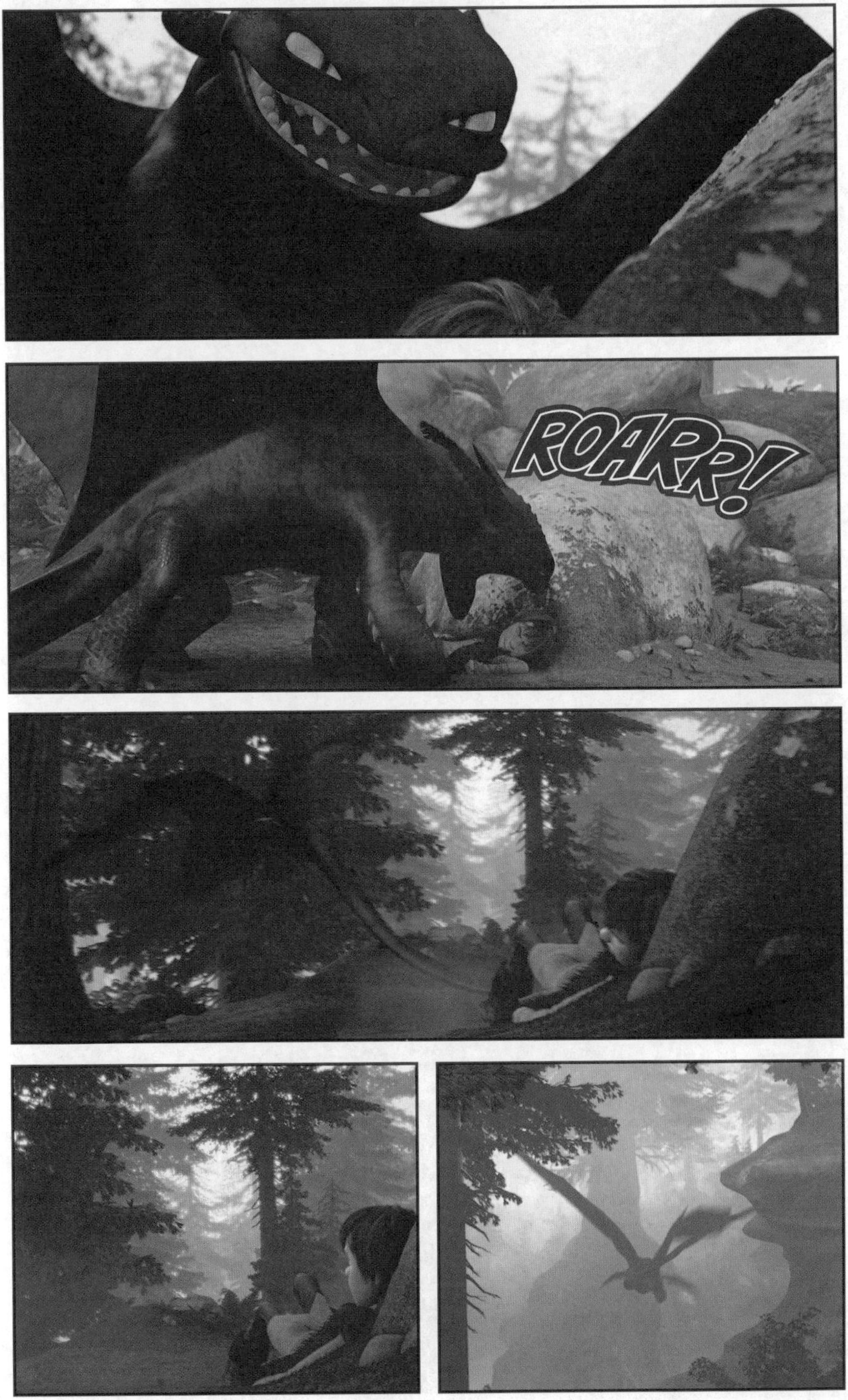
ROARR!

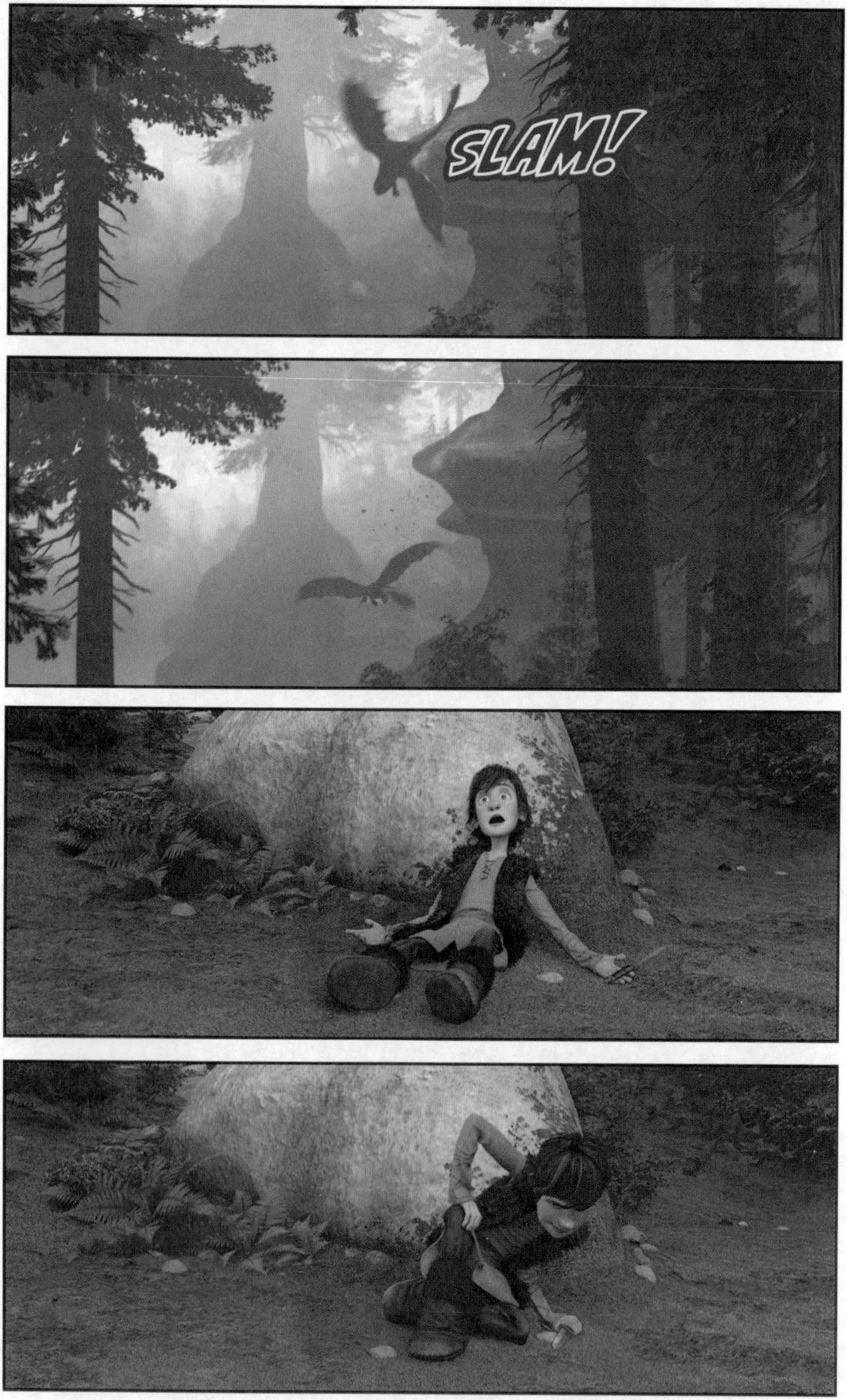
SLAM!

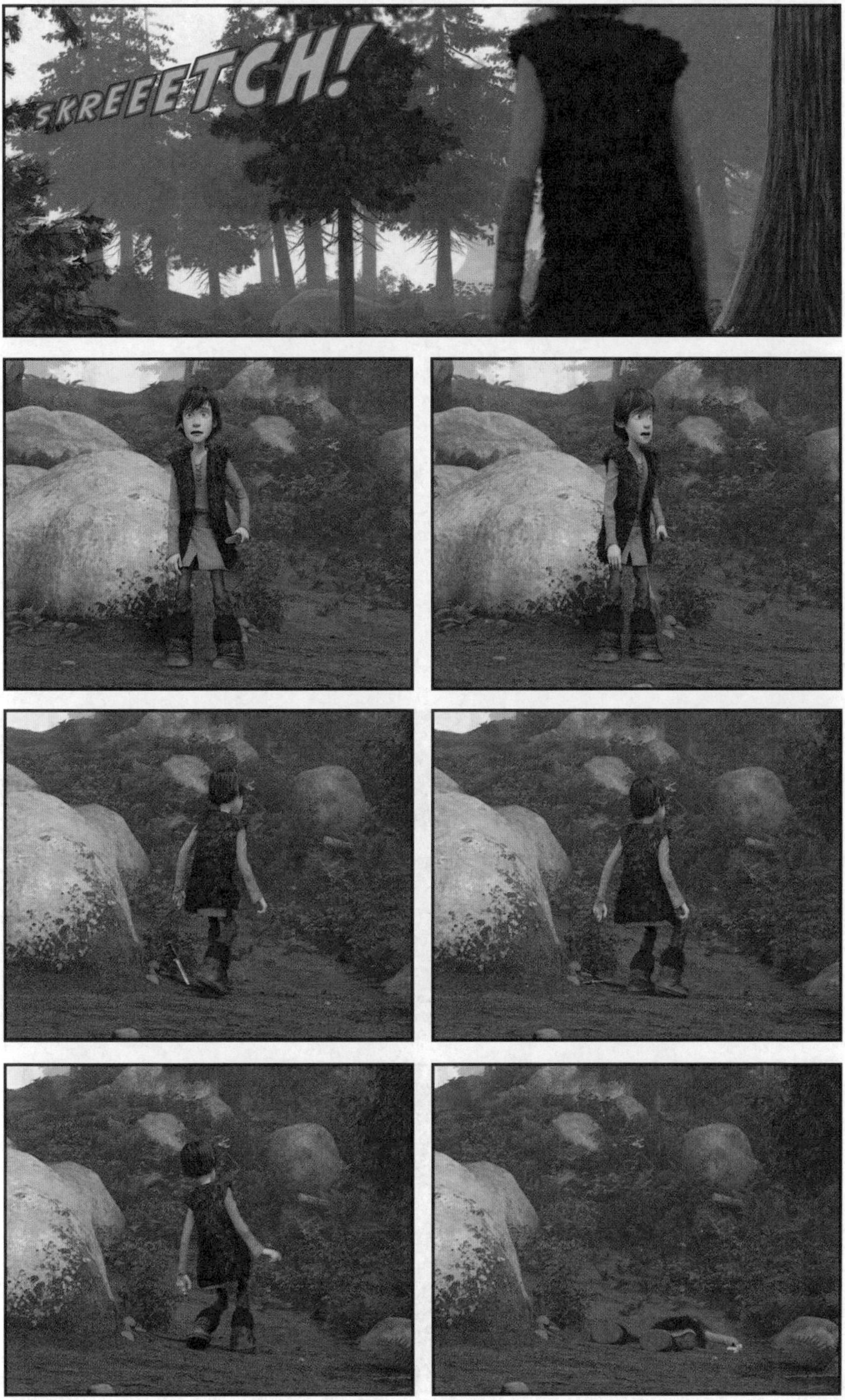
SKREEETCH!

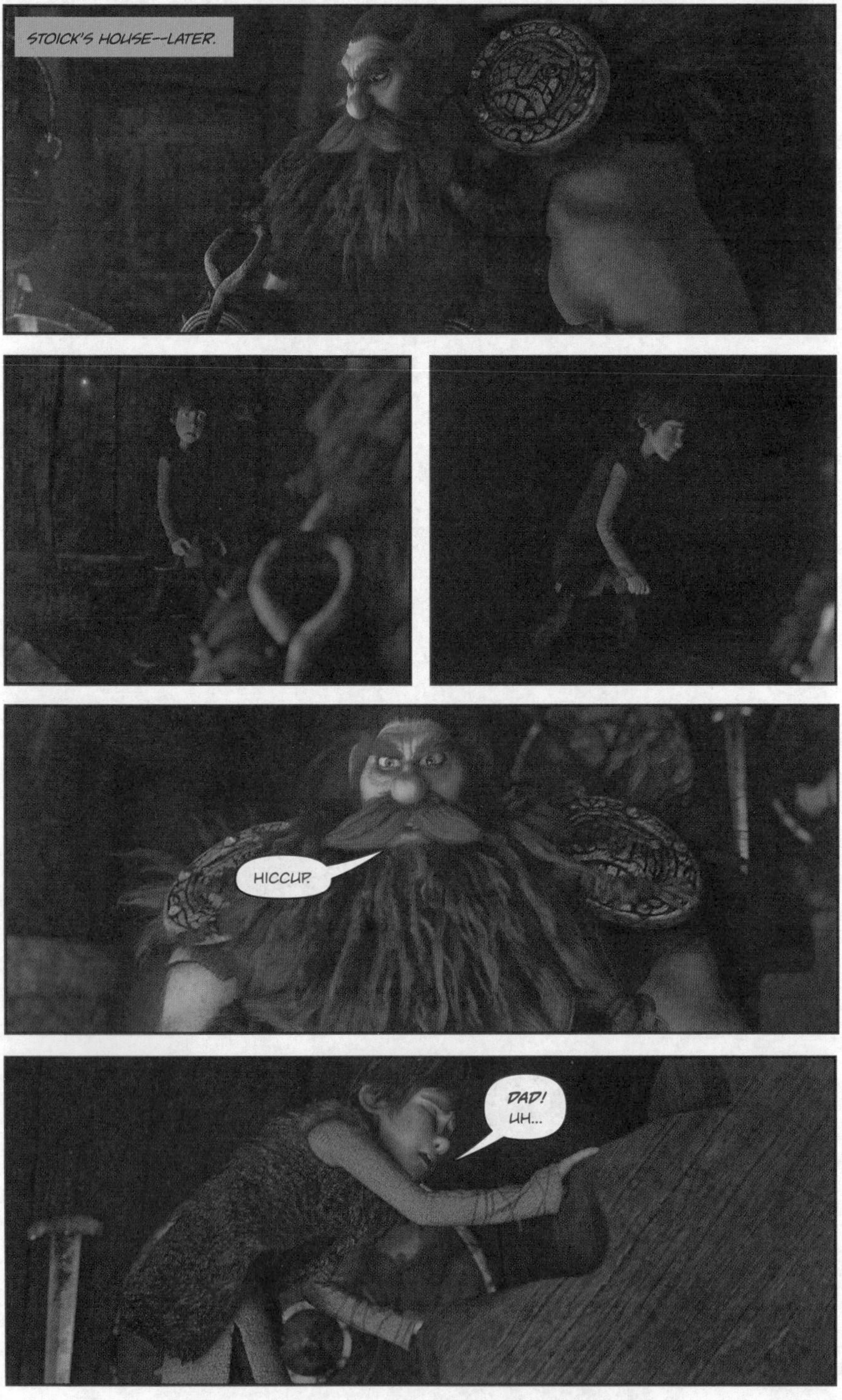
STOICK'S HOUSE--LATER.
HICCUP.
DAD! UH...

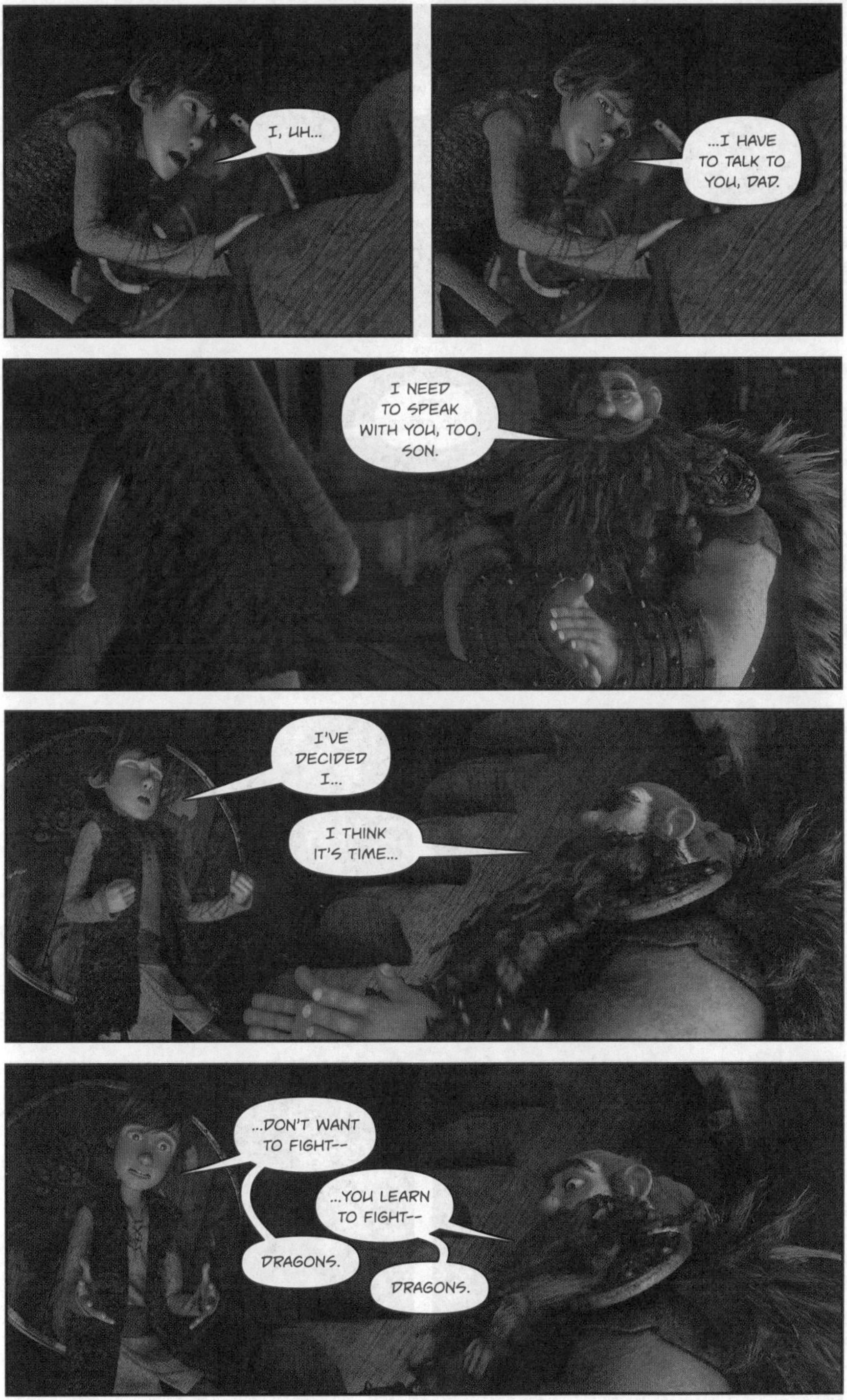
I, UH...
...I HAVE TO TALK TO YOU, DAD.
I NEED TO SPEAK WITH YOU, TOO, SON.
I'VE DECIDED I...
I THINK IT'S TIME...
...DON'T WANT TO FIGHT--
DRAGONS.
...YOU LEARN TO FIGHT--
DRAGONS.

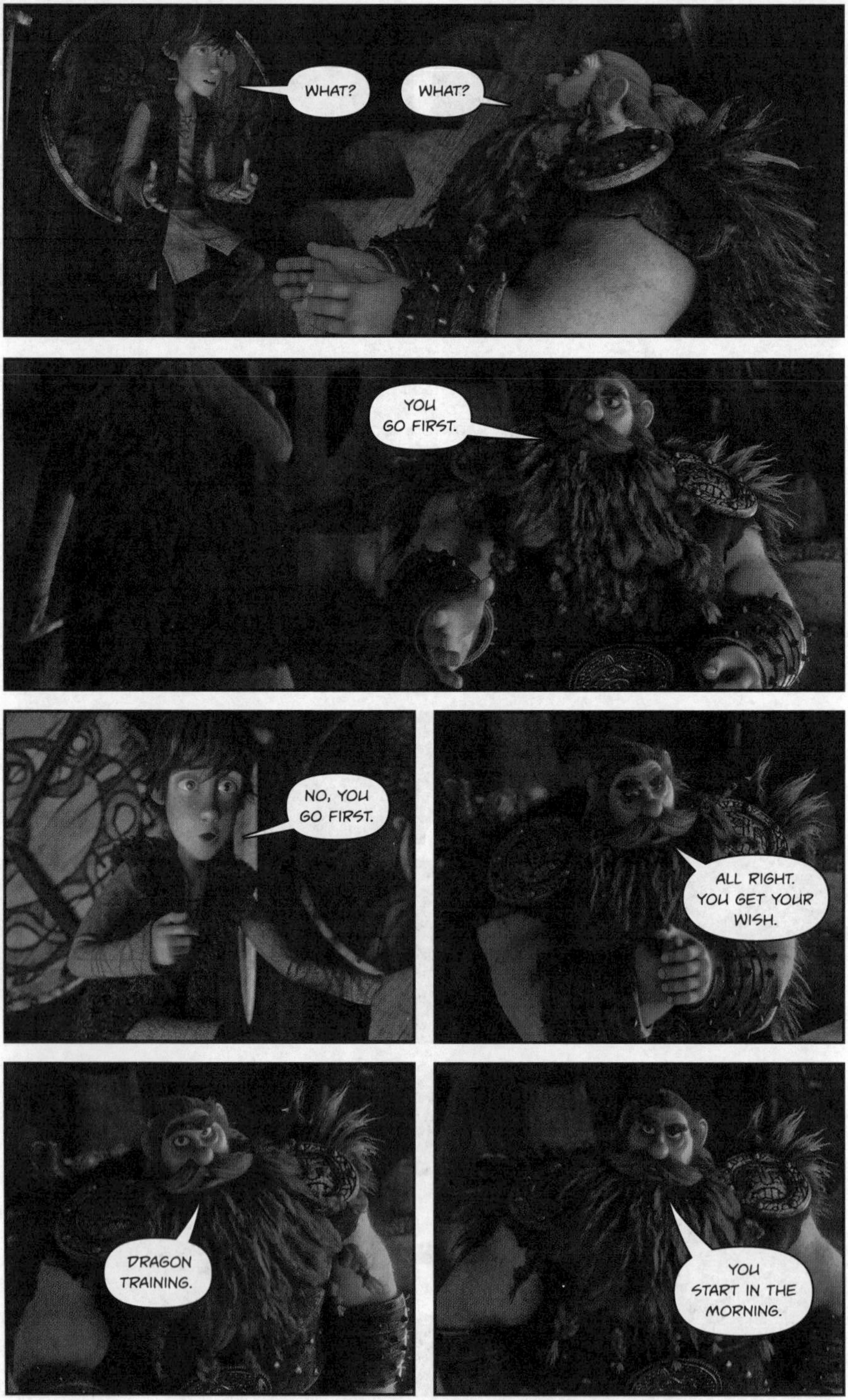
WHAT?
WHAT?
YOU GO FIRST.
NO, YOU GO FIRST.
ALL RIGHT. YOU GET YOUR WISH.
DRAGON TRAINING.
YOU START IN THE MORNING.

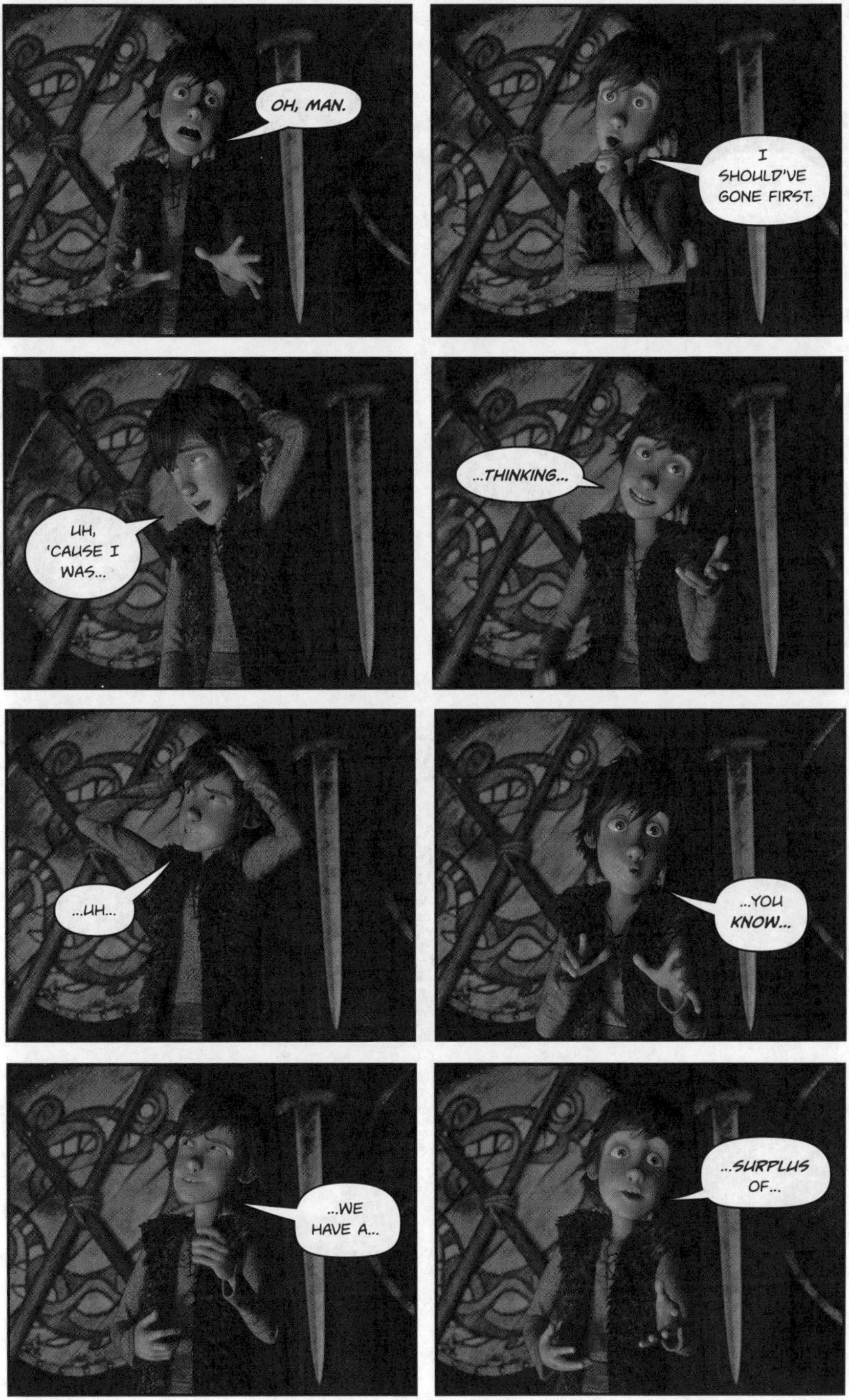
OH, MAN.
I SHOULD'VE GONE FIRST.
UH, 'CAUSE I WAS...
...THINKING...
...UH...
...YOU KNOW...
...WE HAVE A...
...SURPLUS OF...

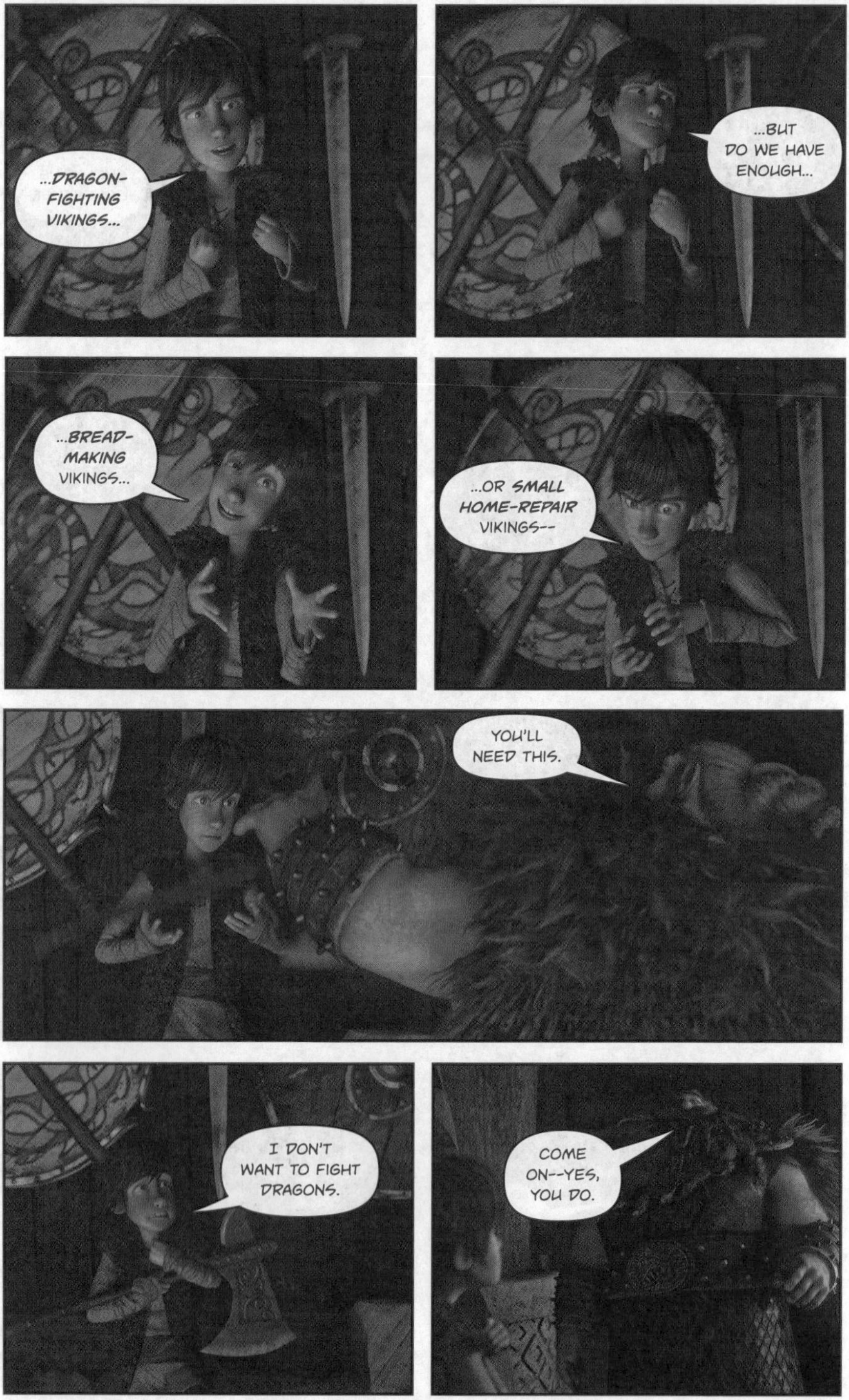
...DRAGON-FIGHTING VIKINGS...
...BUT DO WE HAVE ENOUGH...
...BREAD-MAKING VIKINGS...
...OR SMALL HOME-REPAIR VIKINGS--
YOU'LL NEED THIS.
I DON'T WANT TO FIGHT DRAGONS.
COME ON--YES, YOU DO.

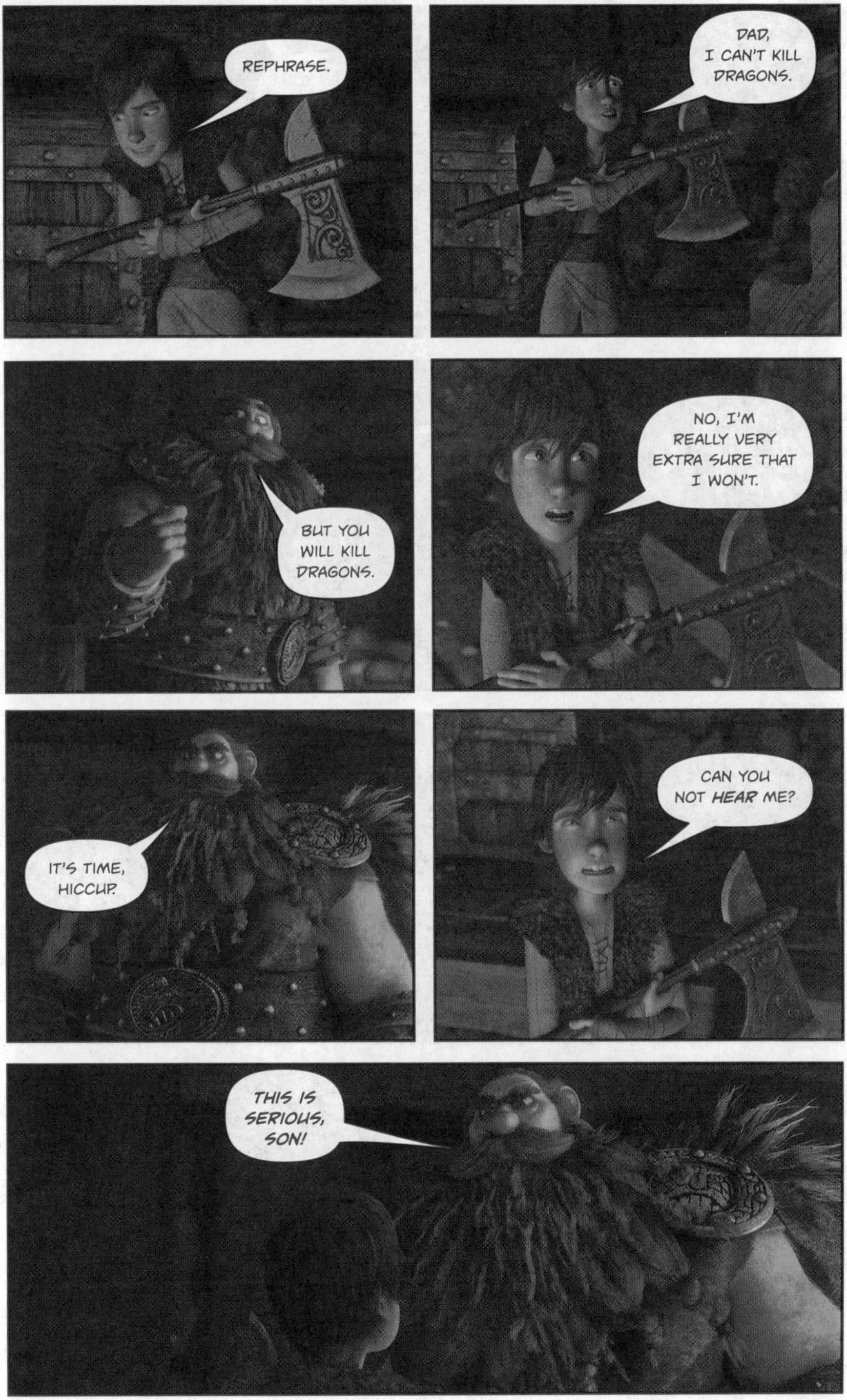
REPHRASE.
DAD, I CAN'T KILL DRAGONS.
BUT YOU WILL KILL DRAGONS.
NO, I'M REALLY VERY EXTRA SURE THAT I WON'T.
IT'S TIME, HICCUP.
CAN YOU NOT *HEAR* ME?
THIS IS SERIOUS, SON!

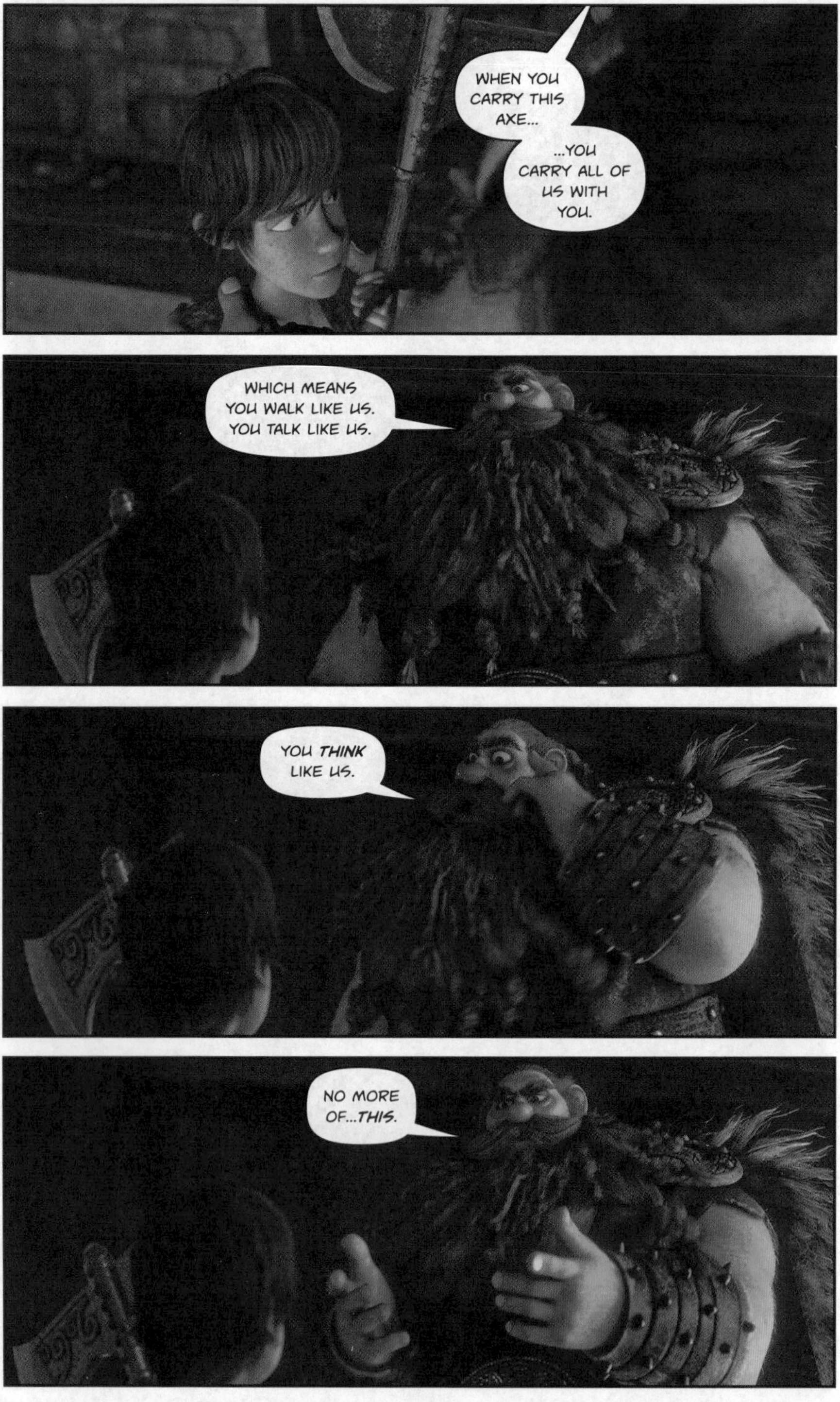
WHEN YOU CARRY THIS AXE...
...YOU CARRY ALL OF US WITH YOU.
WHICH MEANS YOU WALK LIKE US. YOU TALK LIKE US.
YOU *THINK* LIKE US.
NO MORE OF...*THIS*.

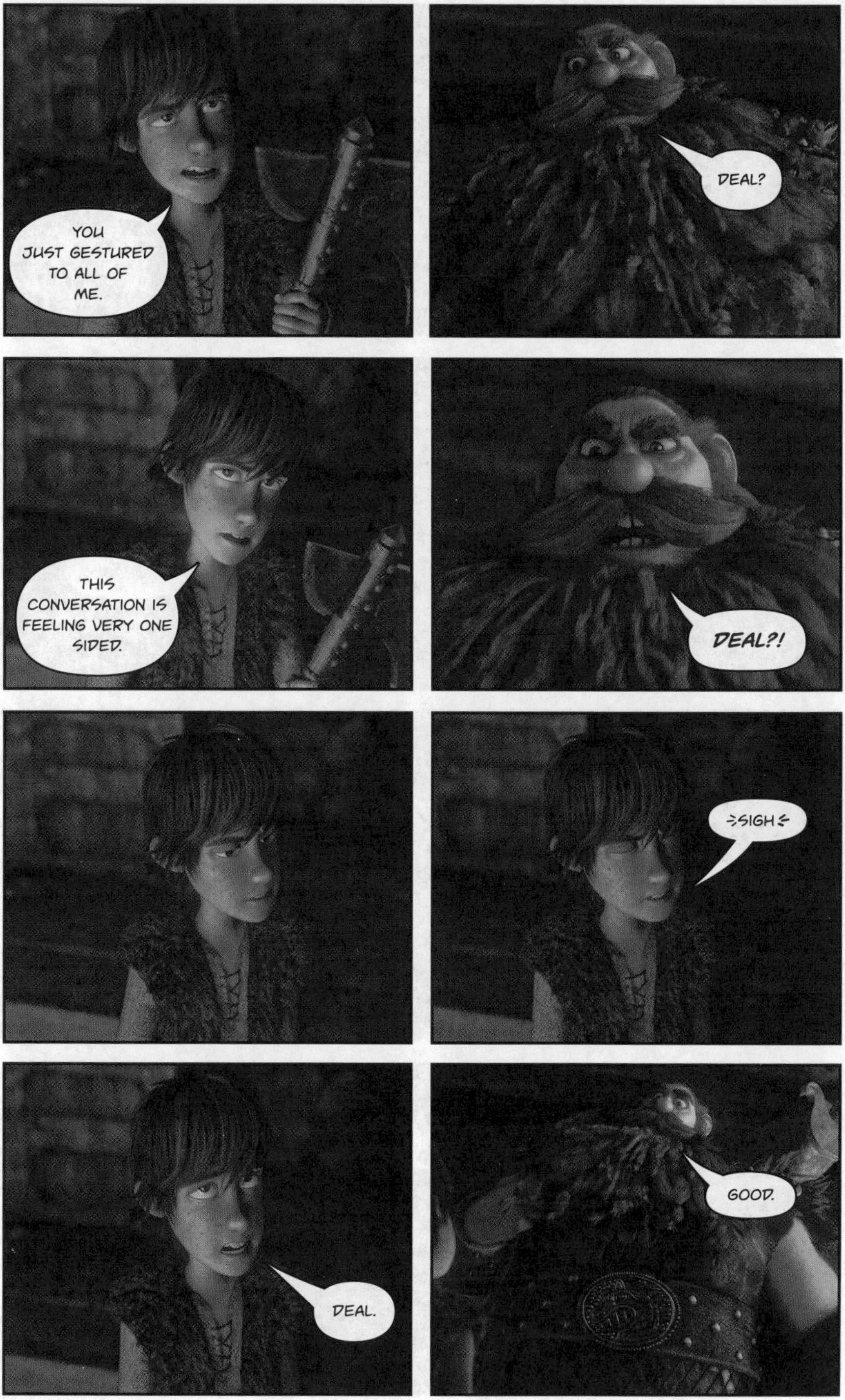
YOU JUST GESTURED TO ALL OF ME.
DEAL?
THIS CONVERSATION IS FEELING VERY ONE SIDED.
DEAL?!
SIGH
DEAL.
GOOD.

TRAIN HARD.

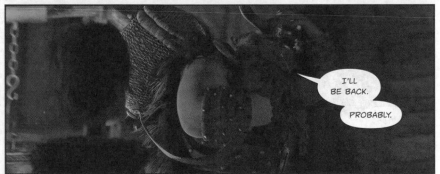

I'LL BE BACK.

PROBABLY.

AND I'LL BE HERE.

MAYBE.

SLAM!

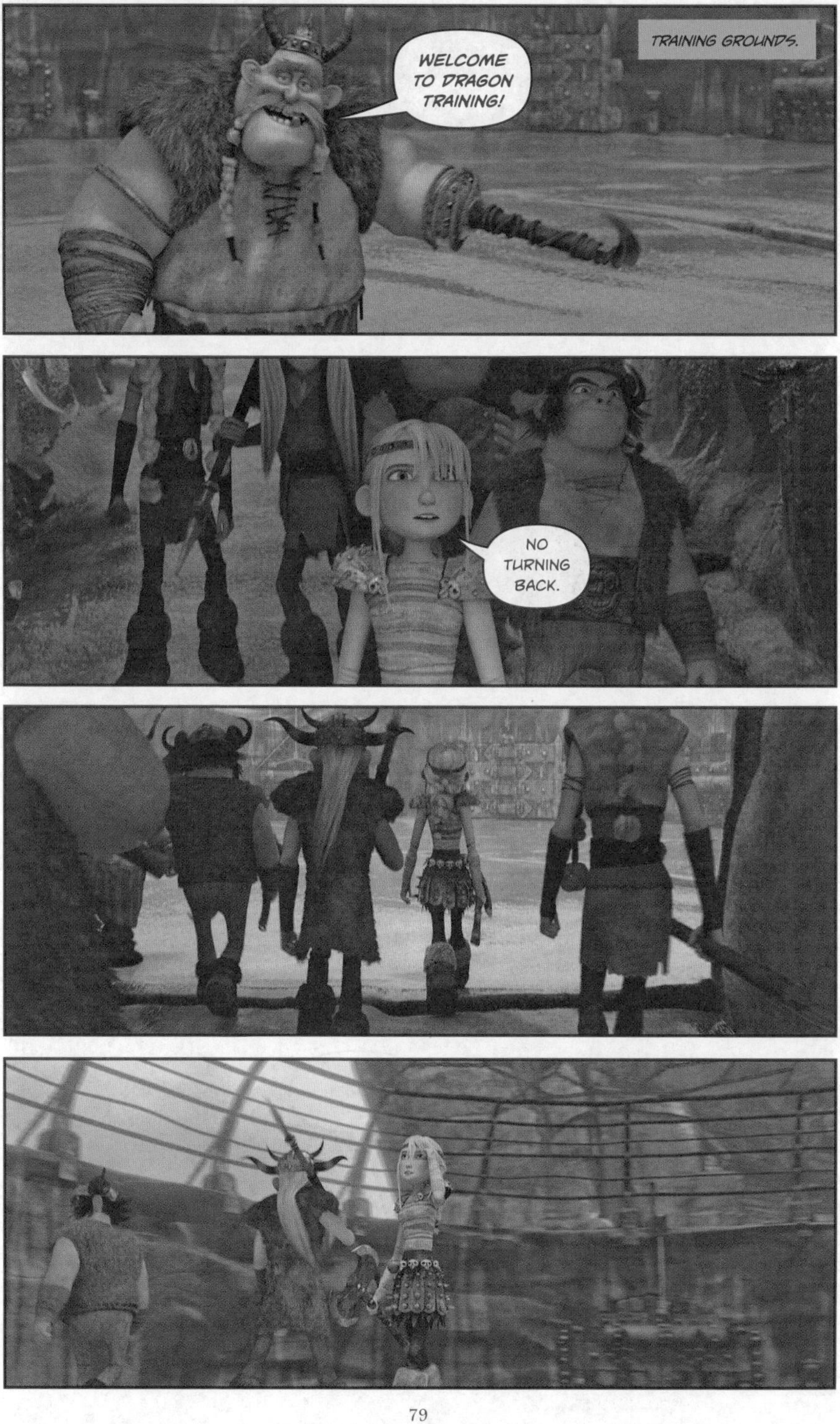
TRAINING GROUNDS.
WELCOME TO DRAGON TRAINING!
NO TURNING BACK.

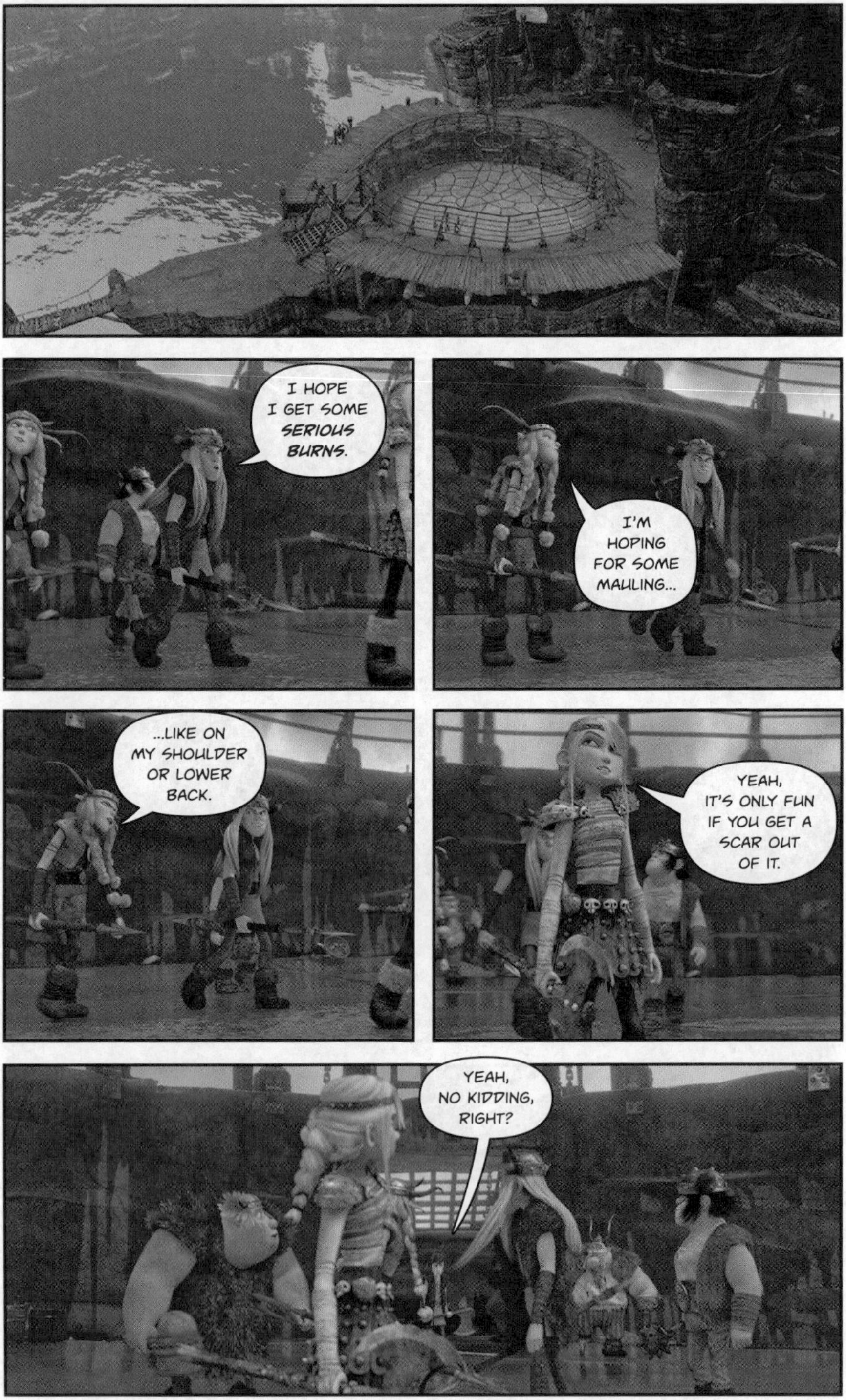
I HOPE I GET SOME SERIOUS BURNS.
I'M HOPING FOR SOME MAULING...
...LIKE ON MY SHOULDER OR LOWER BACK.
YEAH, IT'S ONLY FUN IF YOU GET A SCAR OUT OF IT.
YEAH, NO KIDDING, RIGHT?

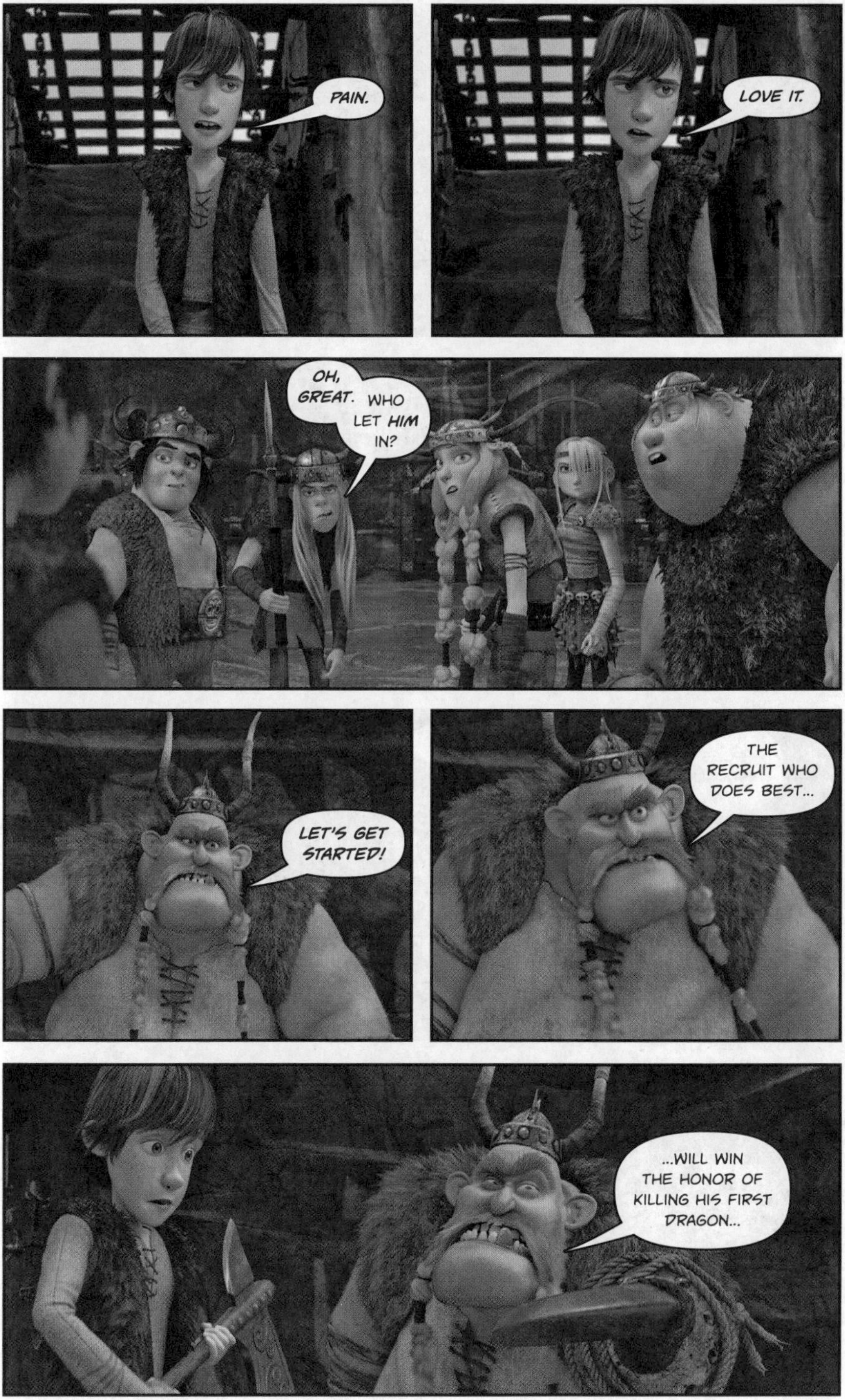
PAIN.
LOVE IT.
OH, GREAT. WHO LET HIM IN?
LET'S GET STARTED!
THE RECRUIT WHO DOES BEST...
...WILL WIN THE HONOR OF KILLING HIS FIRST DRAGON...

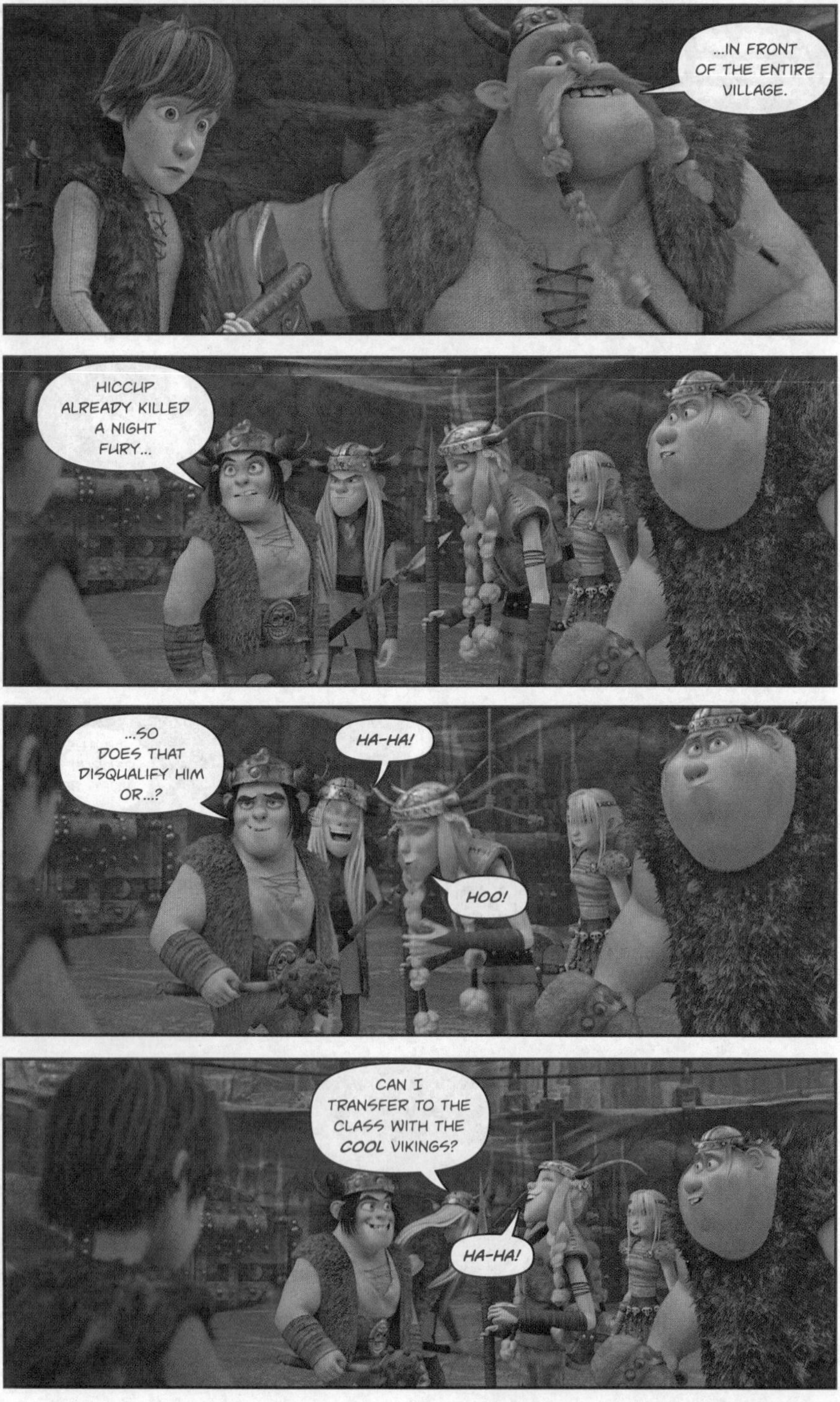
...IN FRONT OF THE ENTIRE VILLAGE.
HICCUP ALREADY KILLED A NIGHT FURY...
...SO DOES THAT DISQUALIFY HIM OR...?
HA-HA!
HOO!
CAN I TRANSFER TO THE CLASS WITH THE *COOL* VIKINGS?
HA-HA!

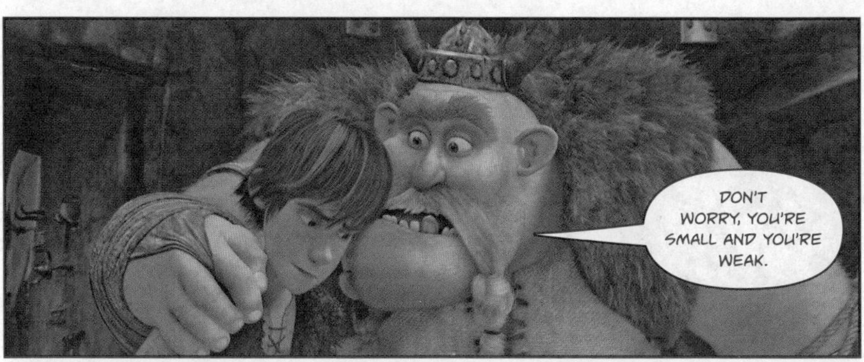
DON'T WORRY, YOU'RE SMALL AND YOU'RE WEAK.

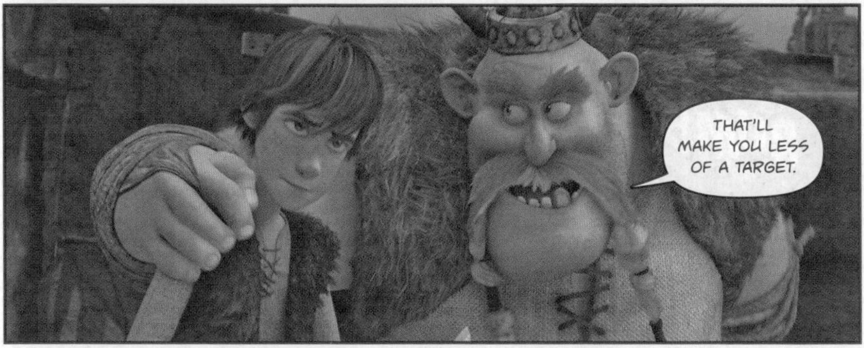
THAT'LL MAKE YOU LESS OF A TARGET.

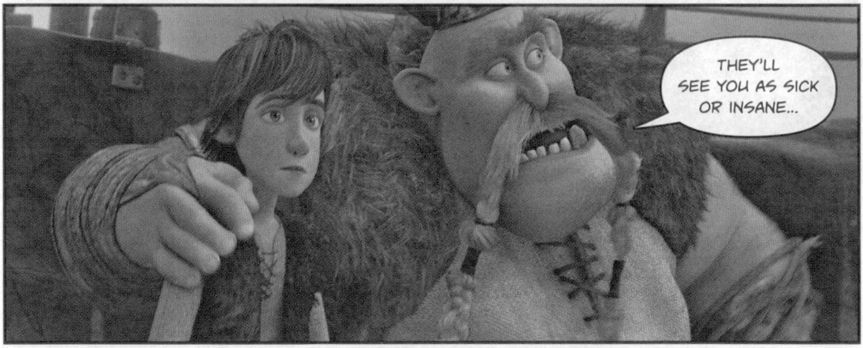
THEY'LL SEE YOU AS SICK OR INSANE...

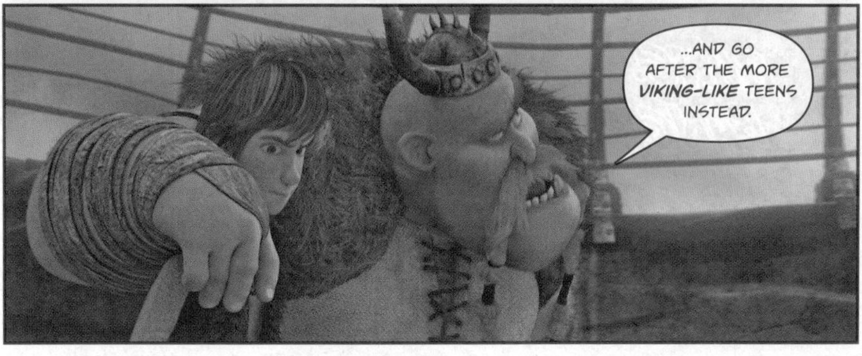
...AND GO AFTER THE MORE ***VIKING-LIKE*** TEENS INSTEAD.

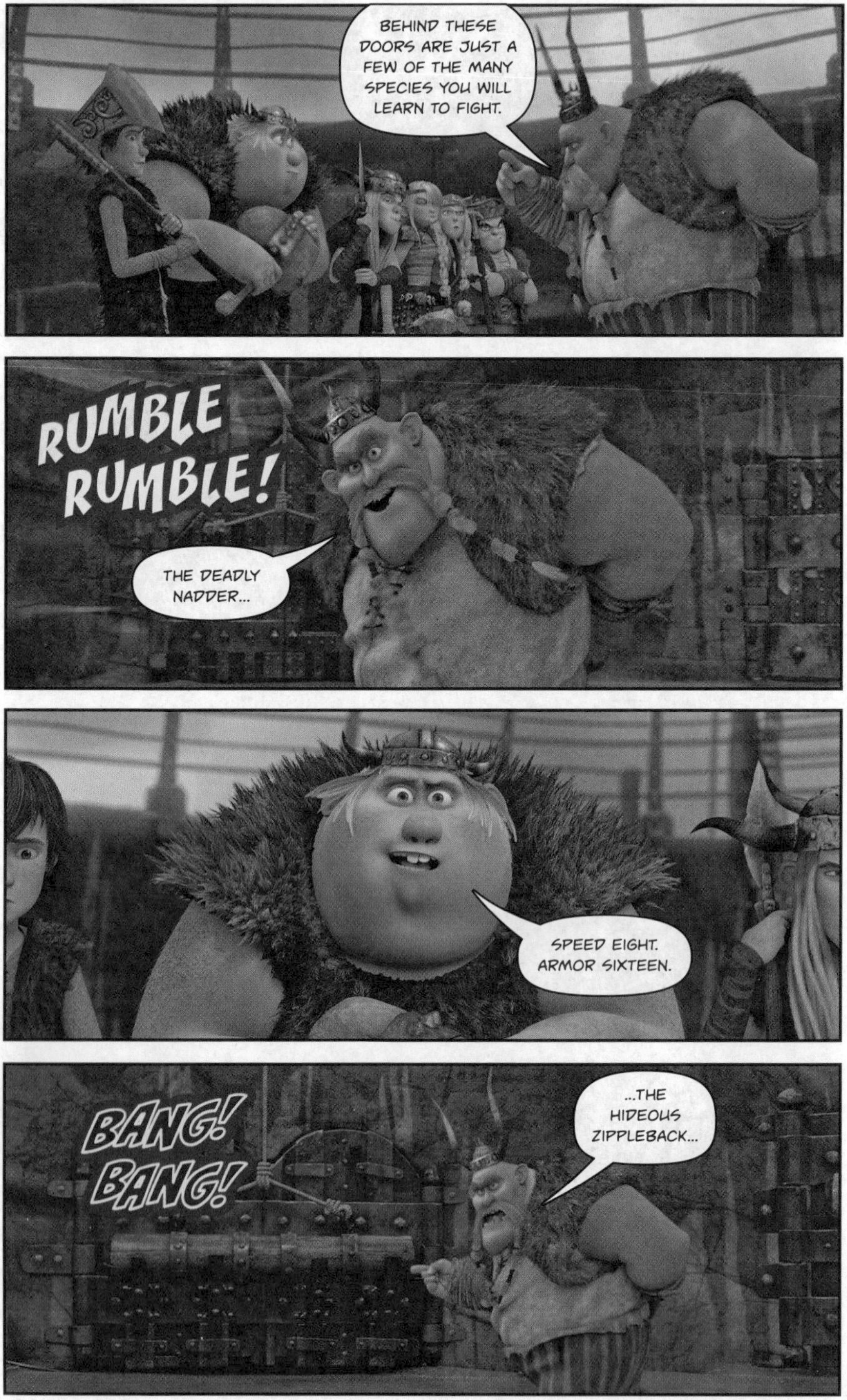
BEHIND THESE DOORS ARE JUST A FEW OF THE MANY SPECIES YOU WILL LEARN TO FIGHT.
RUMBLE RUMBLE!
THE DEADLY NADDER...
SPEED EIGHT. ARMOR SIXTEEN.
BANG! BANG!
...THE HIDEOUS ZIPPLEBACK...

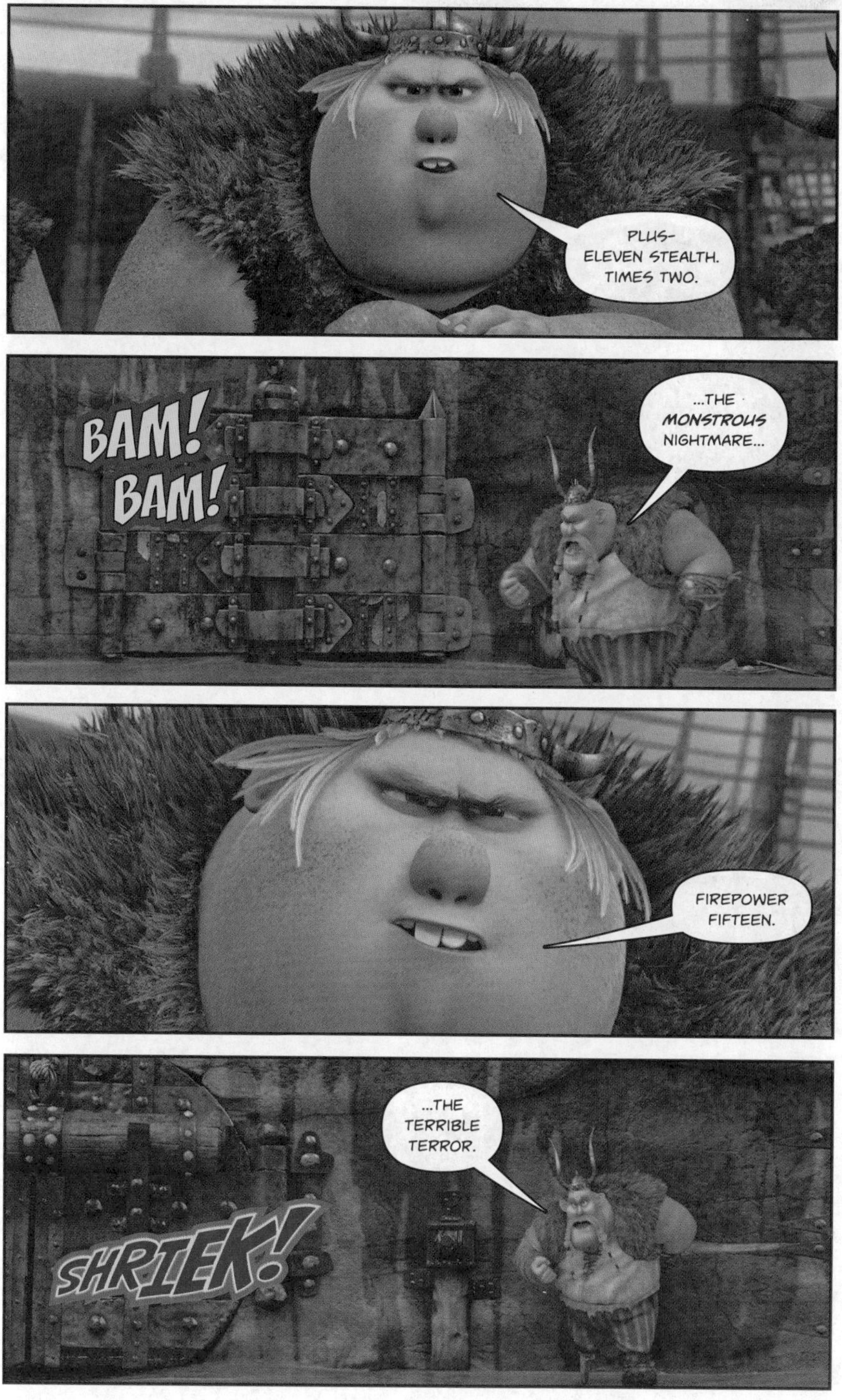
PLUS-
ELEVEN STEALTH.
TIMES TWO.
BAM! BAM!
...THE MONSTROUS NIGHTMARE...
FIREPOWER FIFTEEN.
...THE TERRIBLE TERROR.
SHRIEK!

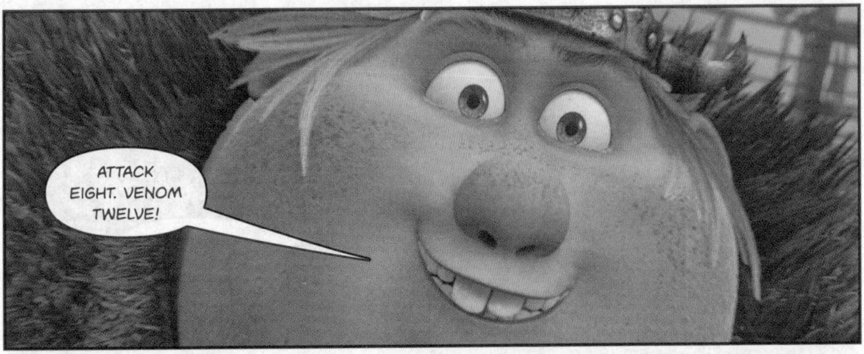
ATTACK EIGHT. VENOM TWELVE!

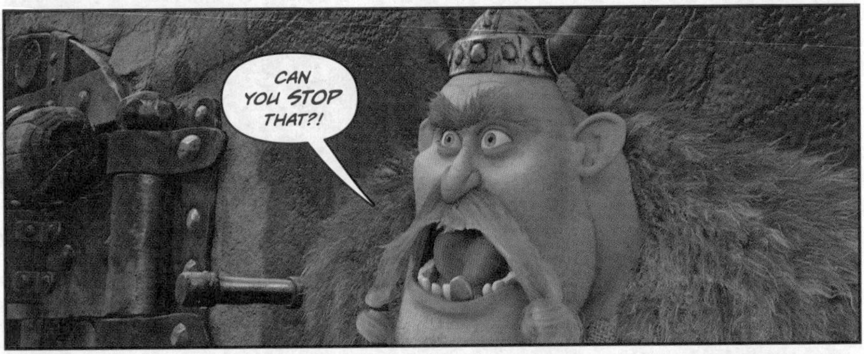
CAN YOU STOP THAT?!

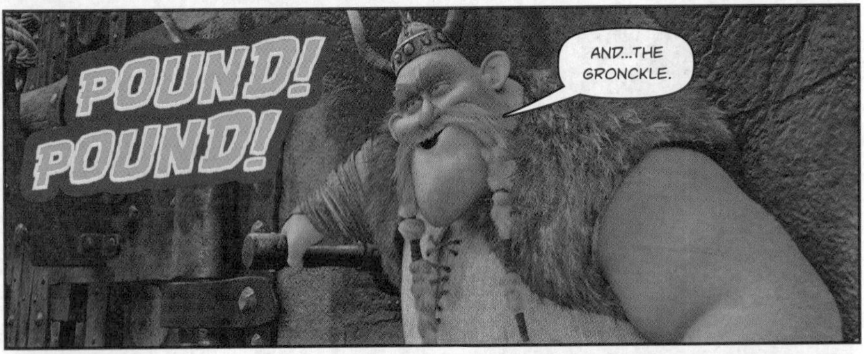
POUND! POUND!
AND...THE GRONCKLE.

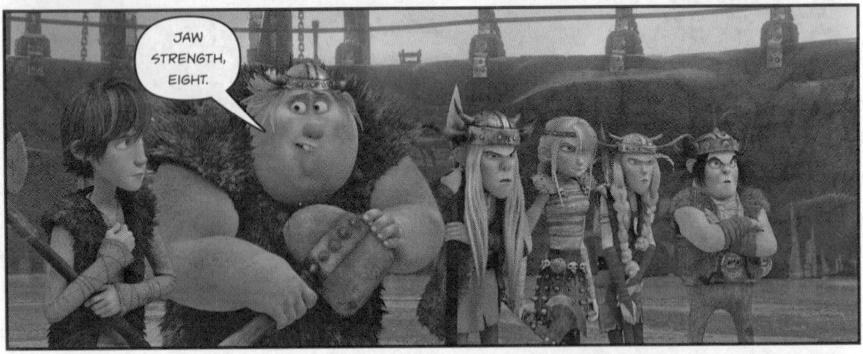
JAW STRENGTH, EIGHT.

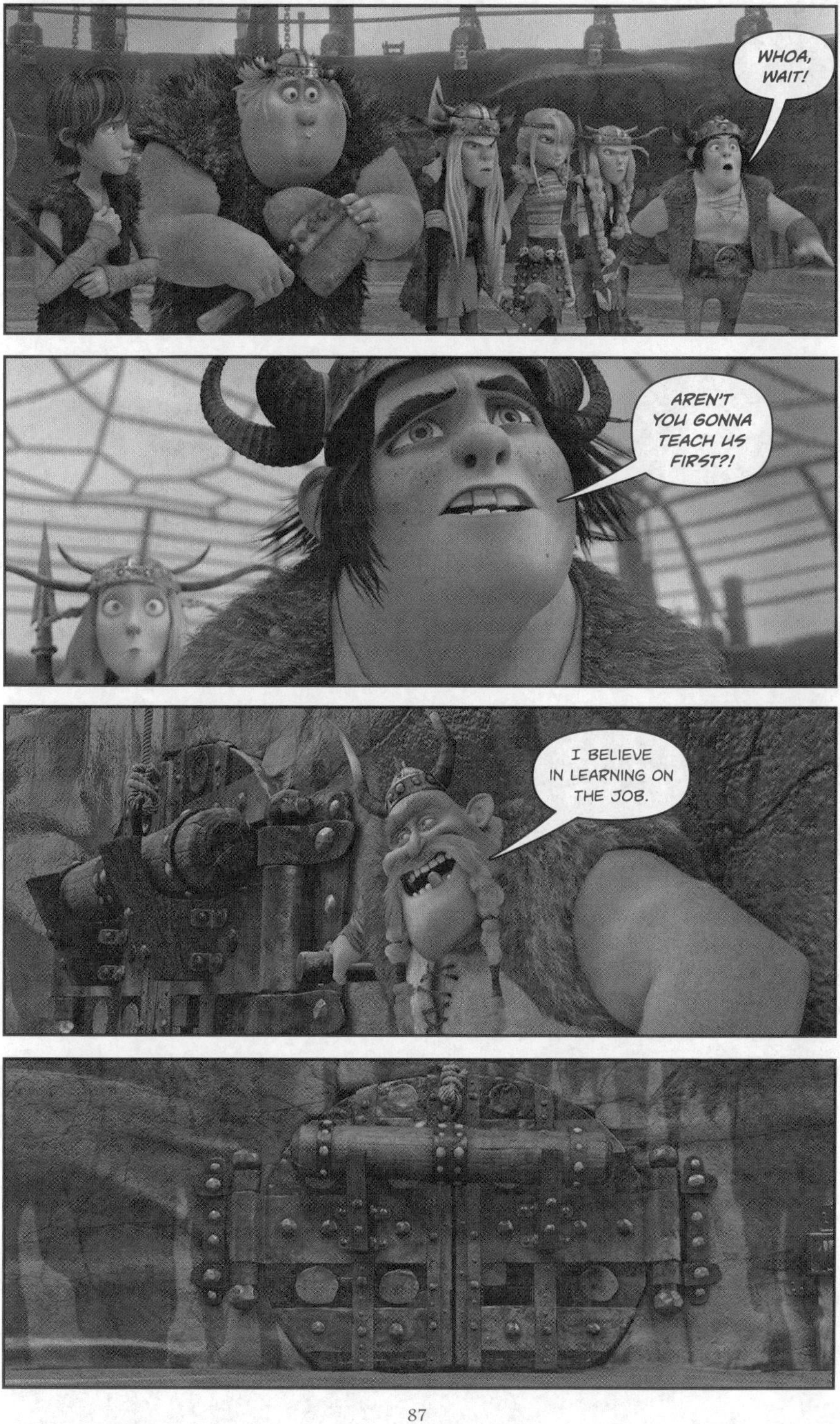
WHOA, WAIT!
AREN'T YOU GONNA TEACH US FIRST?!
I BELIEVE IN LEARNING ON THE JOB.

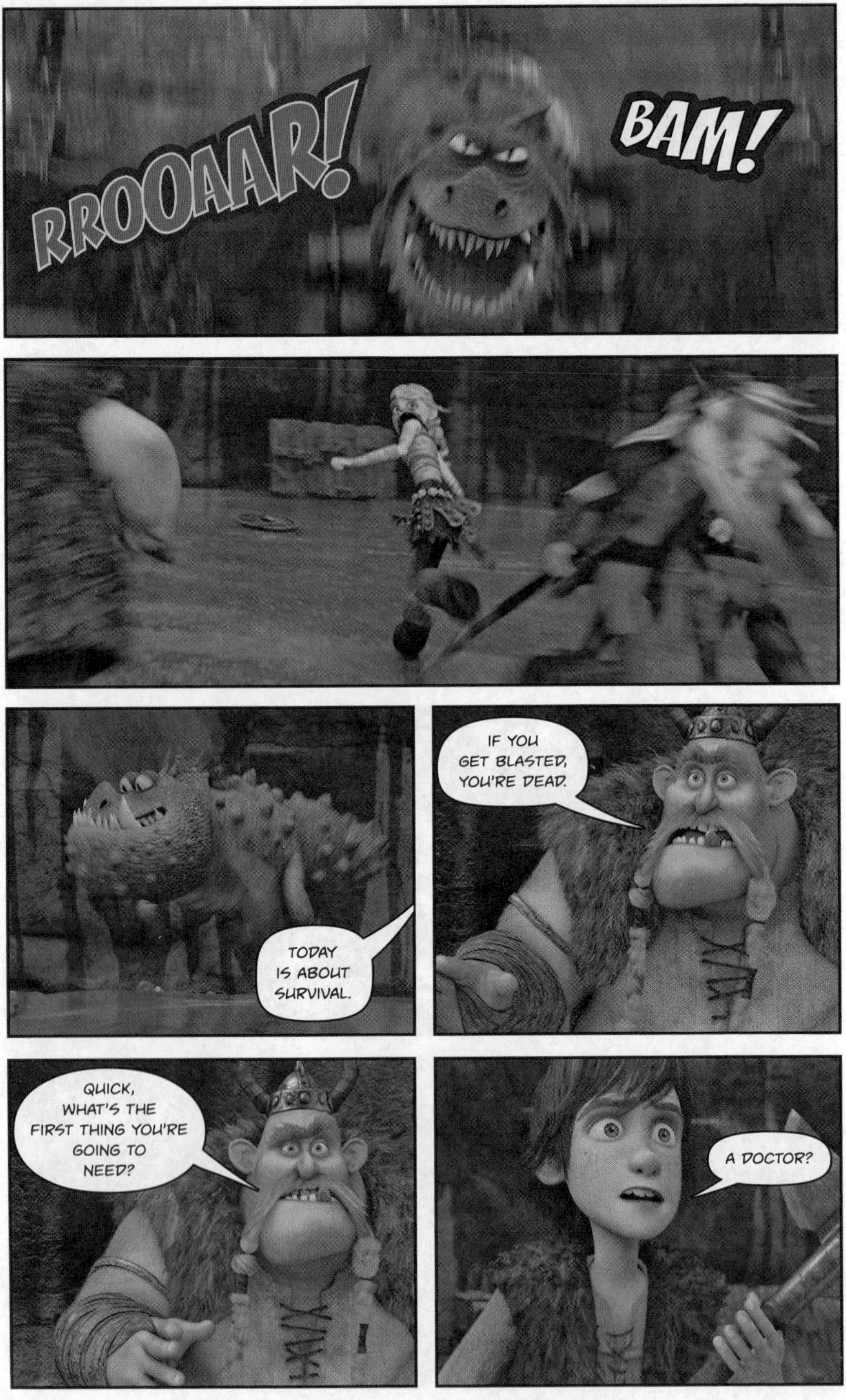

RROOAAR!
BAM!
TODAY IS ABOUT SURVIVAL.
IF YOU GET BLASTED, YOU'RE DEAD.
QUICK, WHAT'S THE FIRST THING YOU'RE GOING TO NEED?
A DOCTOR?

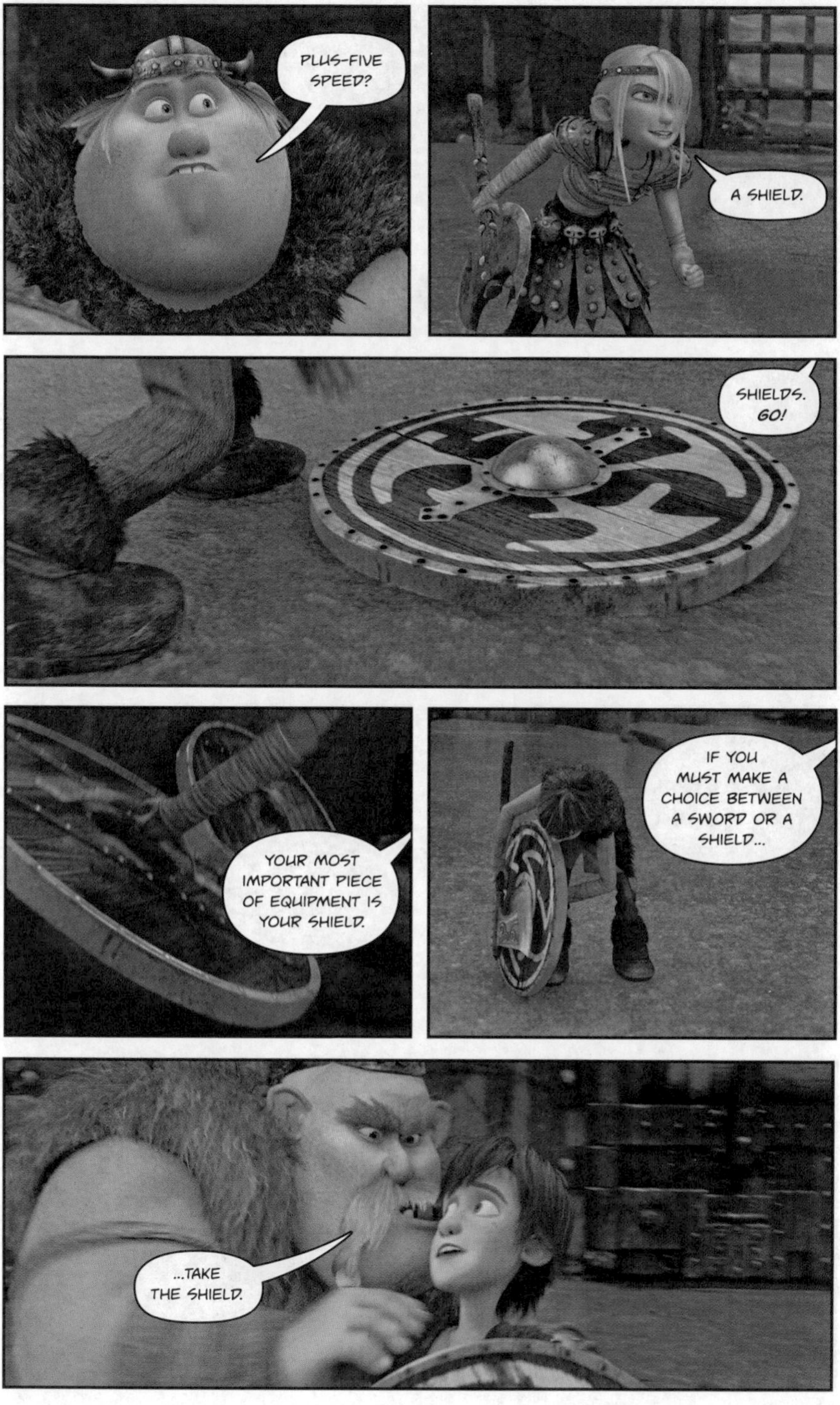
PLUS-FIVE SPEED?
A SHIELD.
SHIELDS. GO!
YOUR MOST IMPORTANT PIECE OF EQUIPMENT IS YOUR SHIELD.
IF YOU MUST MAKE A CHOICE BETWEEN A SWORD OR A SHIELD...
...TAKE THE SHIELD.

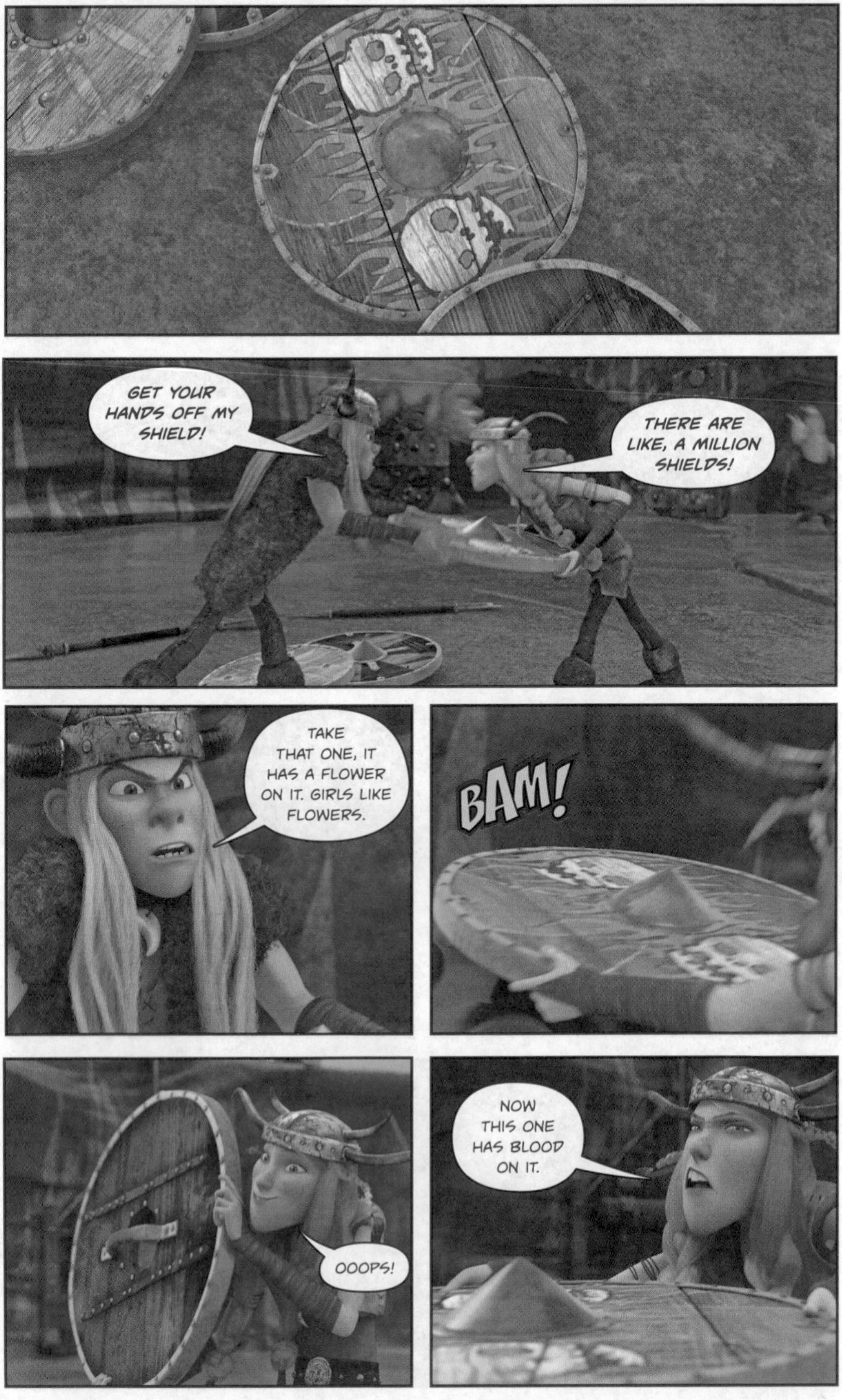
GET YOUR HANDS OFF MY SHIELD!
THERE ARE LIKE, A MILLION SHIELDS!
TAKE THAT ONE, IT HAS A FLOWER ON IT. GIRLS LIKE FLOWERS.
BAM!
OOOPS!
NOW THIS ONE HAS BLOOD ON IT.

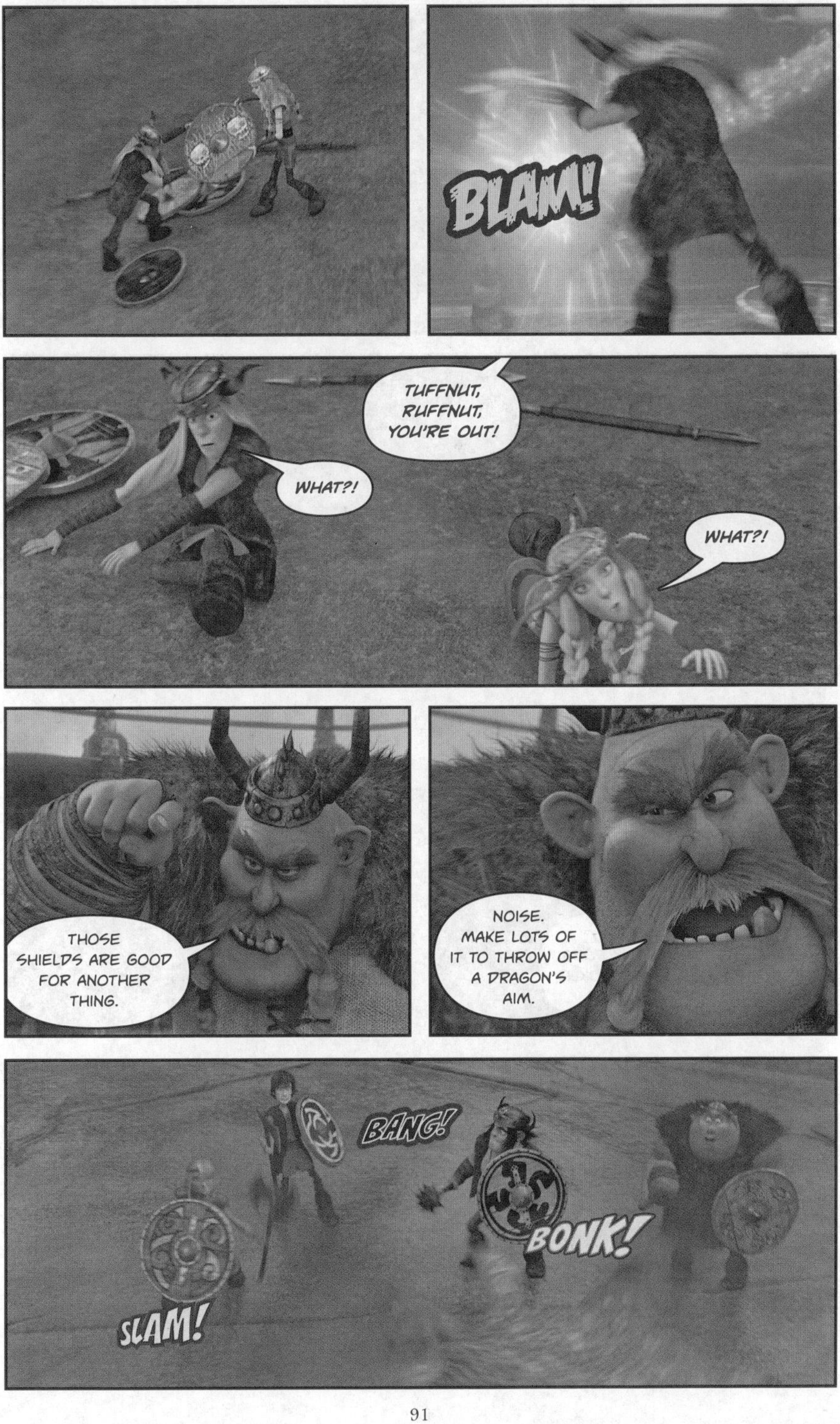
BLAM!
TUFFNUT, RUFFNUT, YOU'RE OUT!
WHAT?!
WHAT?!
THOSE SHIELDS ARE GOOD FOR ANOTHER THING.
NOISE. MAKE LOTS OF IT TO THROW OFF A DRAGON'S AIM.
BANG!
BONK!
SLAM!

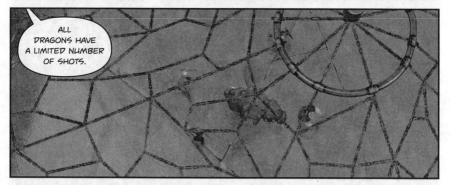

ALL DRAGONS HAVE A LIMITED NUMBER OF SHOTS.

HOW MANY DOES A GRONCKLE HAVE?

FIVE.

NO, SIX!

CORRECT, SIX. THAT'S ONE FOR EACH OF YOU!

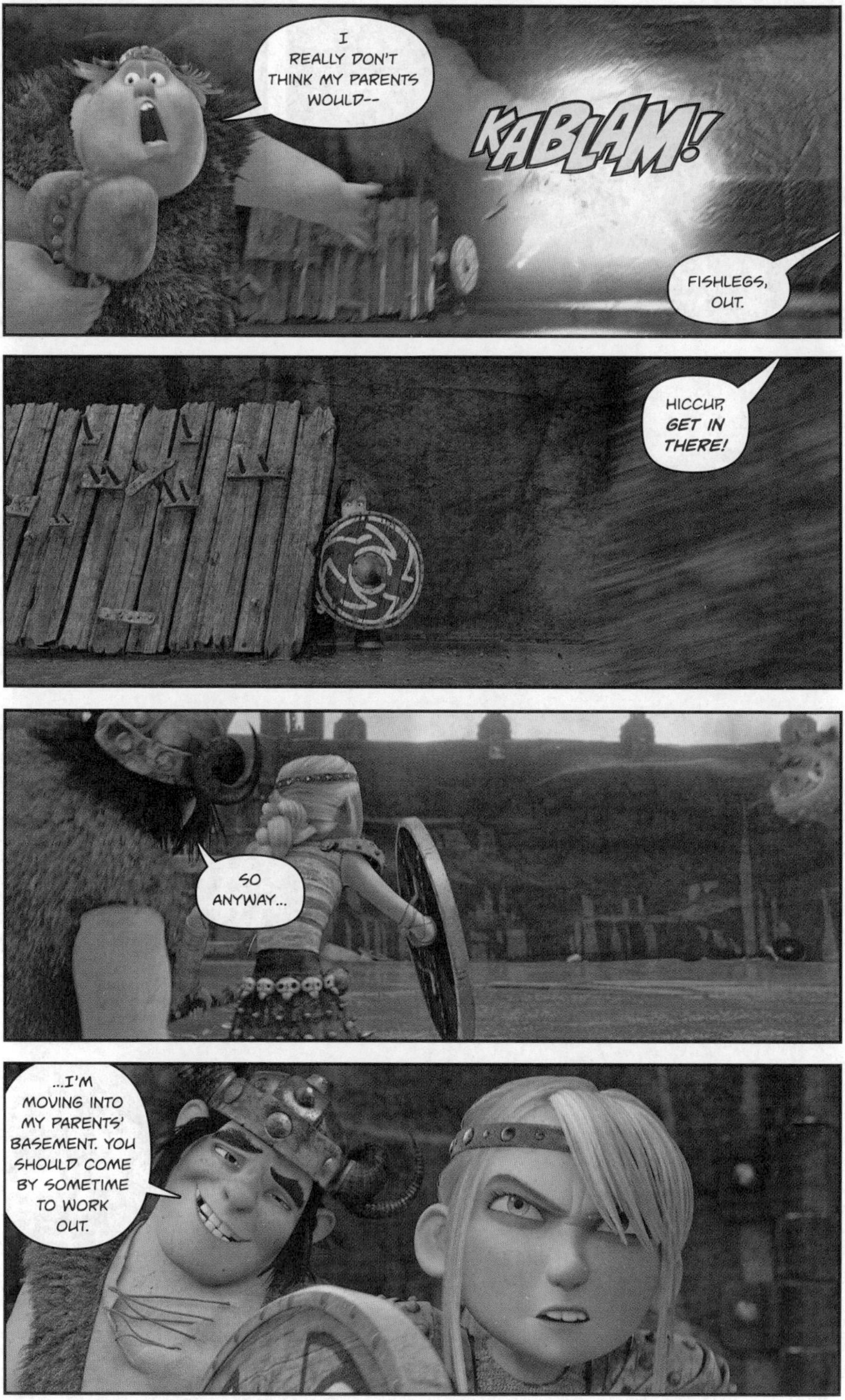
I REALLY DON'T THINK MY PARENTS WOULD--
KABLAM!
FISHLEGS, OUT.
HICCUP, GET IN THERE!
SO ANYWAY...
...I'M MOVING INTO MY PARENTS' BASEMENT. YOU SHOULD COME BY SOMETIME TO WORK OUT.

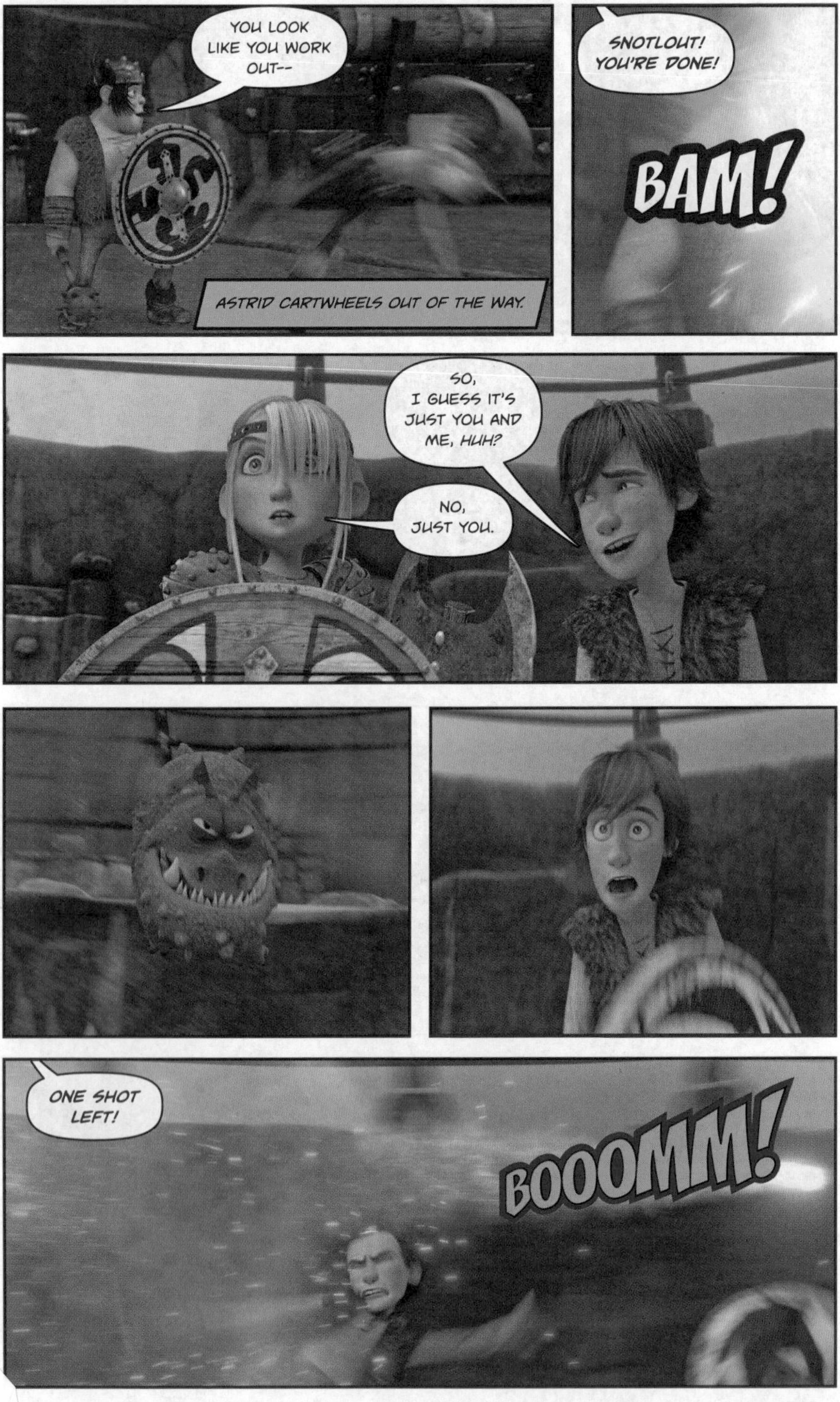
YOU LOOK LIKE YOU WORK OUT--
ASTRID CARTWHEELS OUT OF THE WAY.
SNOTLOUT! YOU'RE DONE!
BAM!
SO, I GUESS IT'S JUST YOU AND ME, HUH?
NO, JUST YOU.
ONE SHOT LEFT!
BOOOMM!

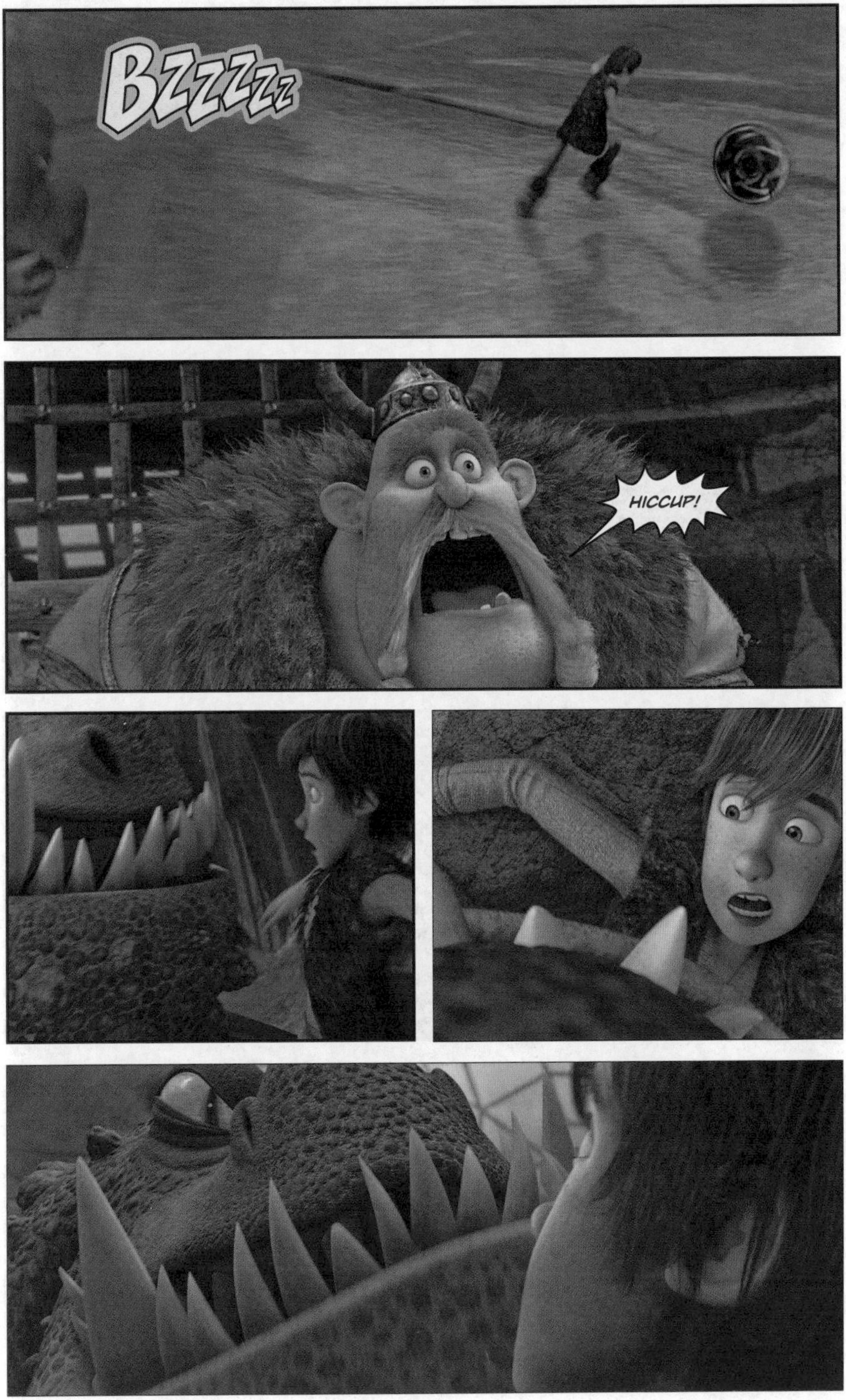
BZZZZZ
HICCUP!

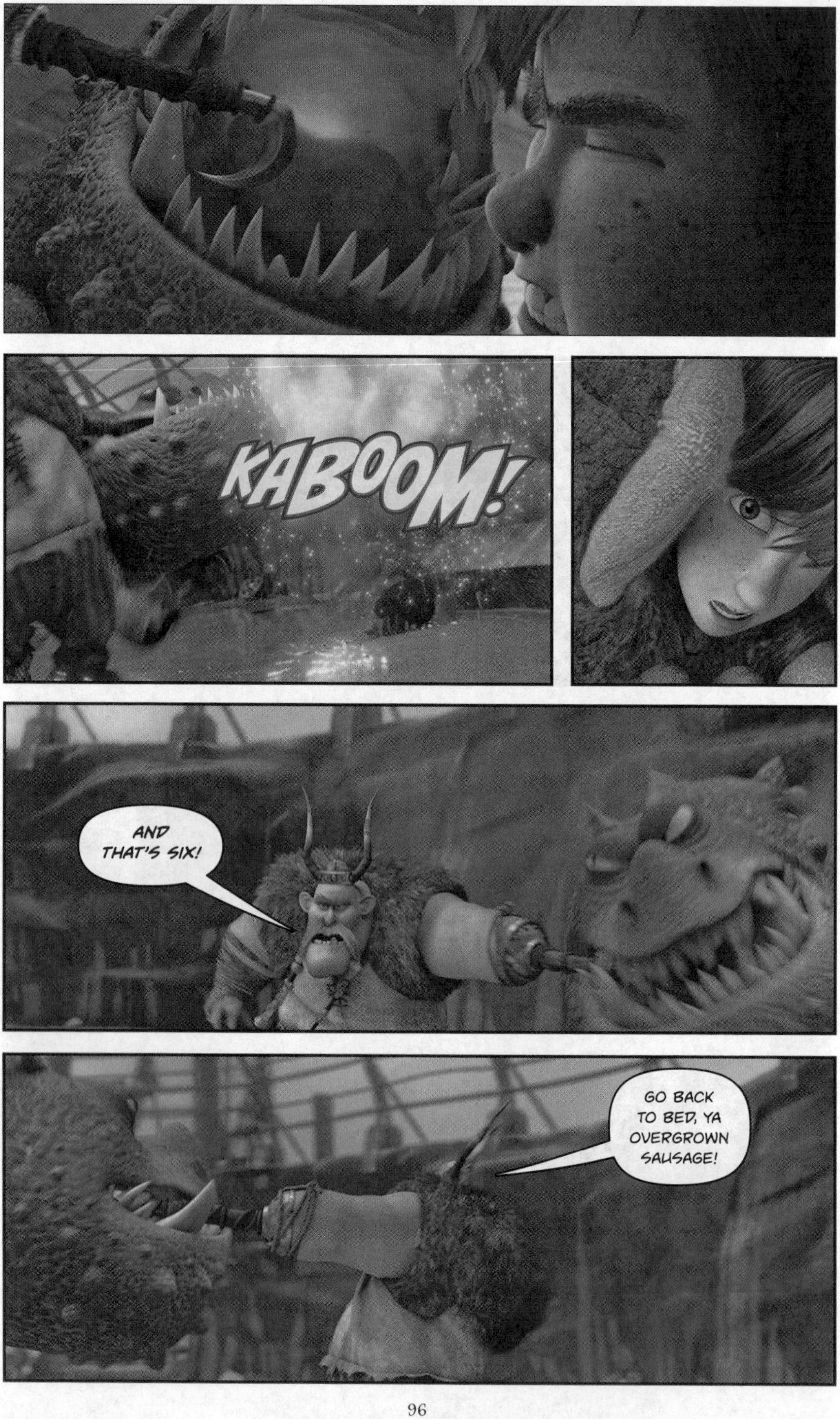
KABOOM!
AND THAT'S SIX!
GO BACK TO BED, YA OVERGROWN SAUSAGE!

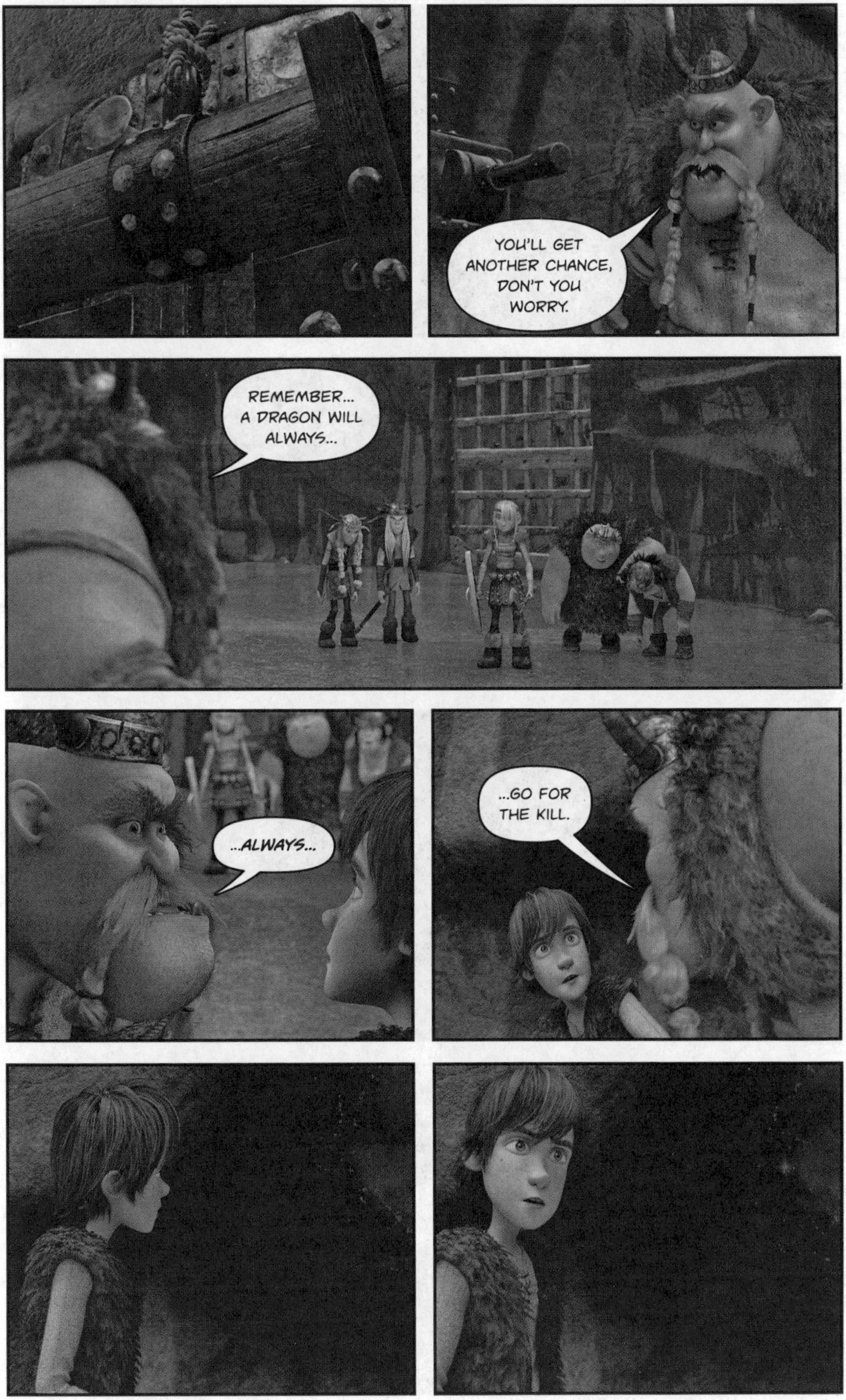
YOU'LL GET ANOTHER CHANCE, DON'T YOU WORRY.
REMEMBER... A DRAGON WILL ALWAYS...
...ALWAYS...
...GO FOR THE KILL.

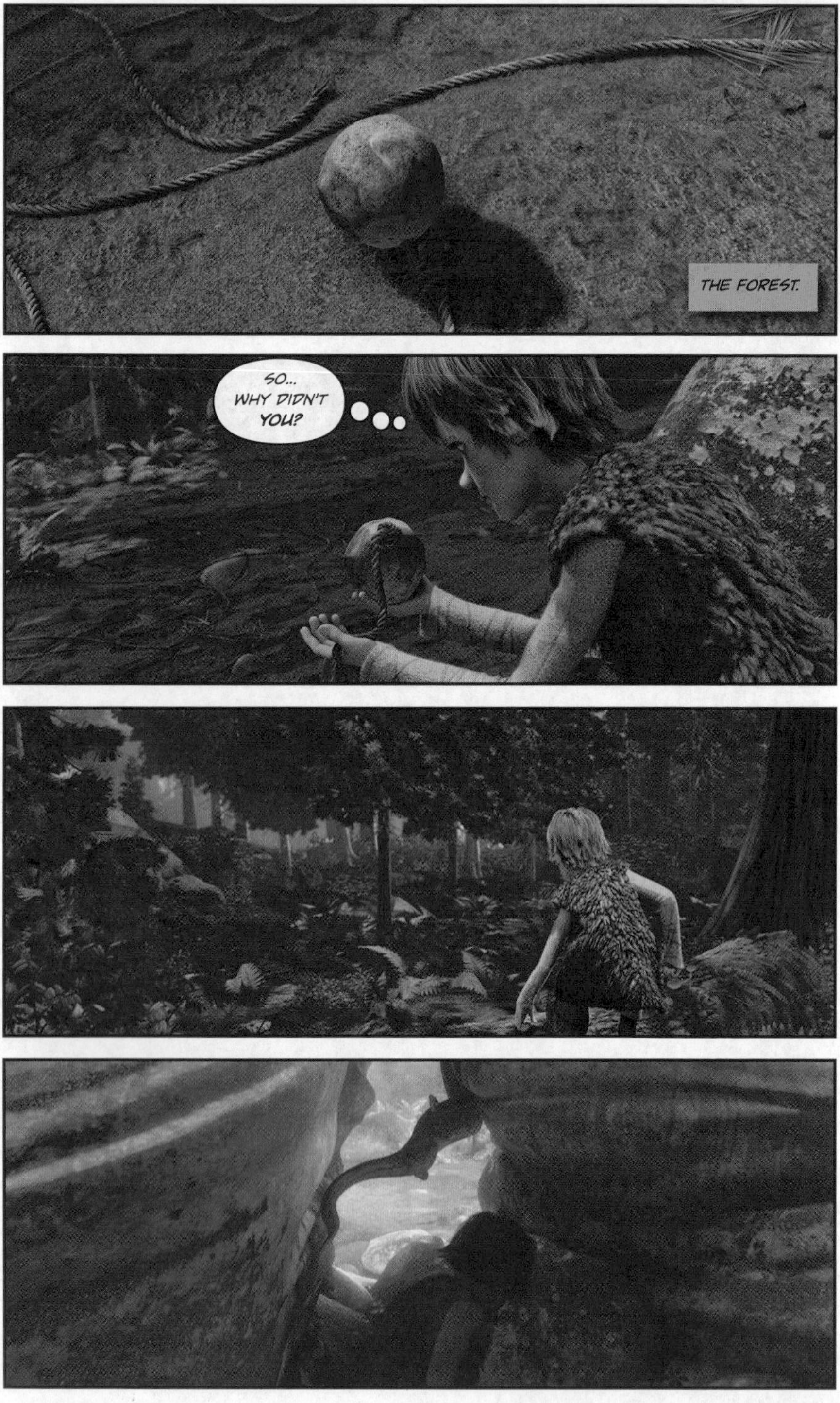
THE FOREST.
SO... WHY DIDN'T YOU?

WELL THIS WAS STUPID.

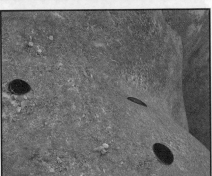

BANG!

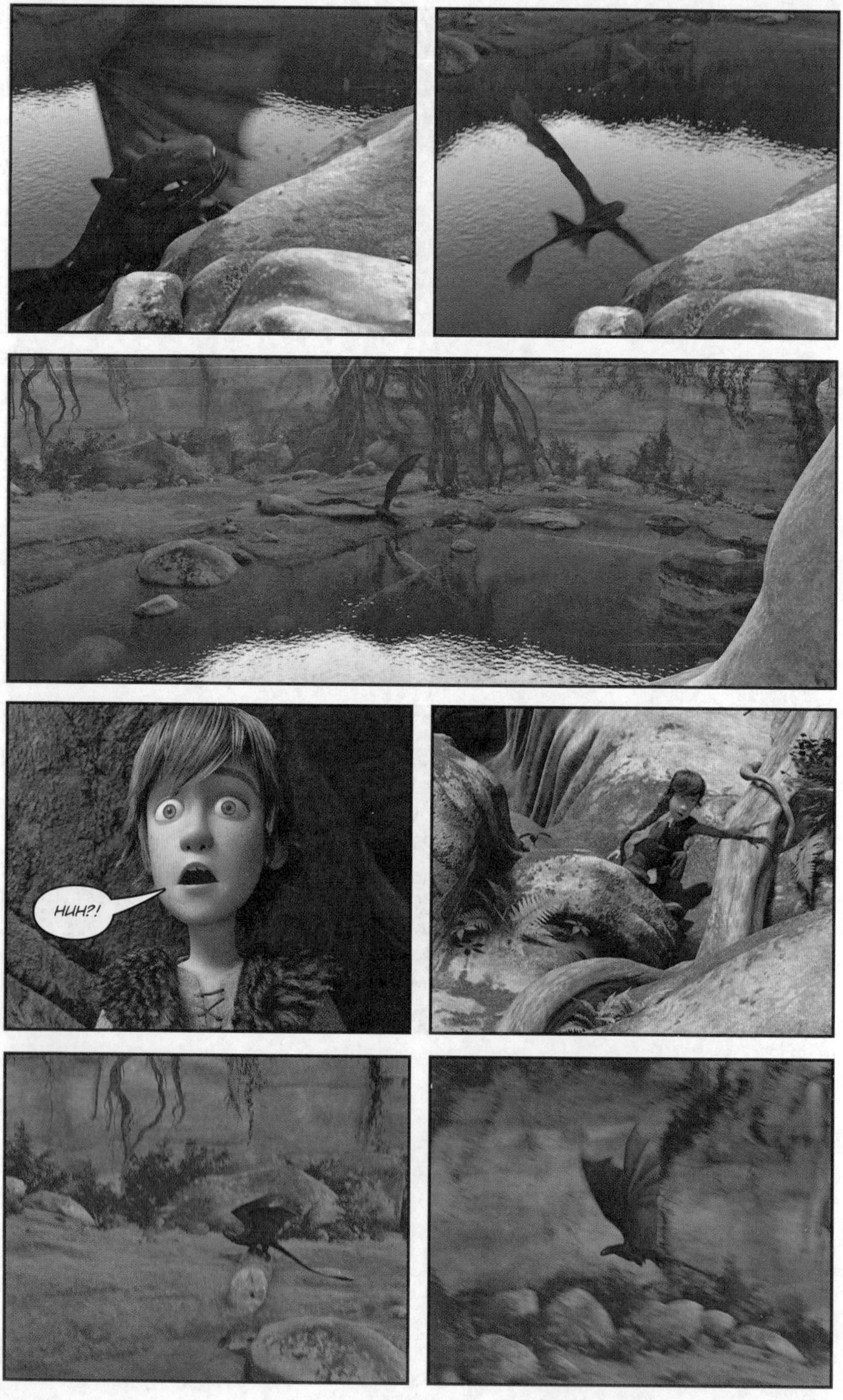
HUH?!

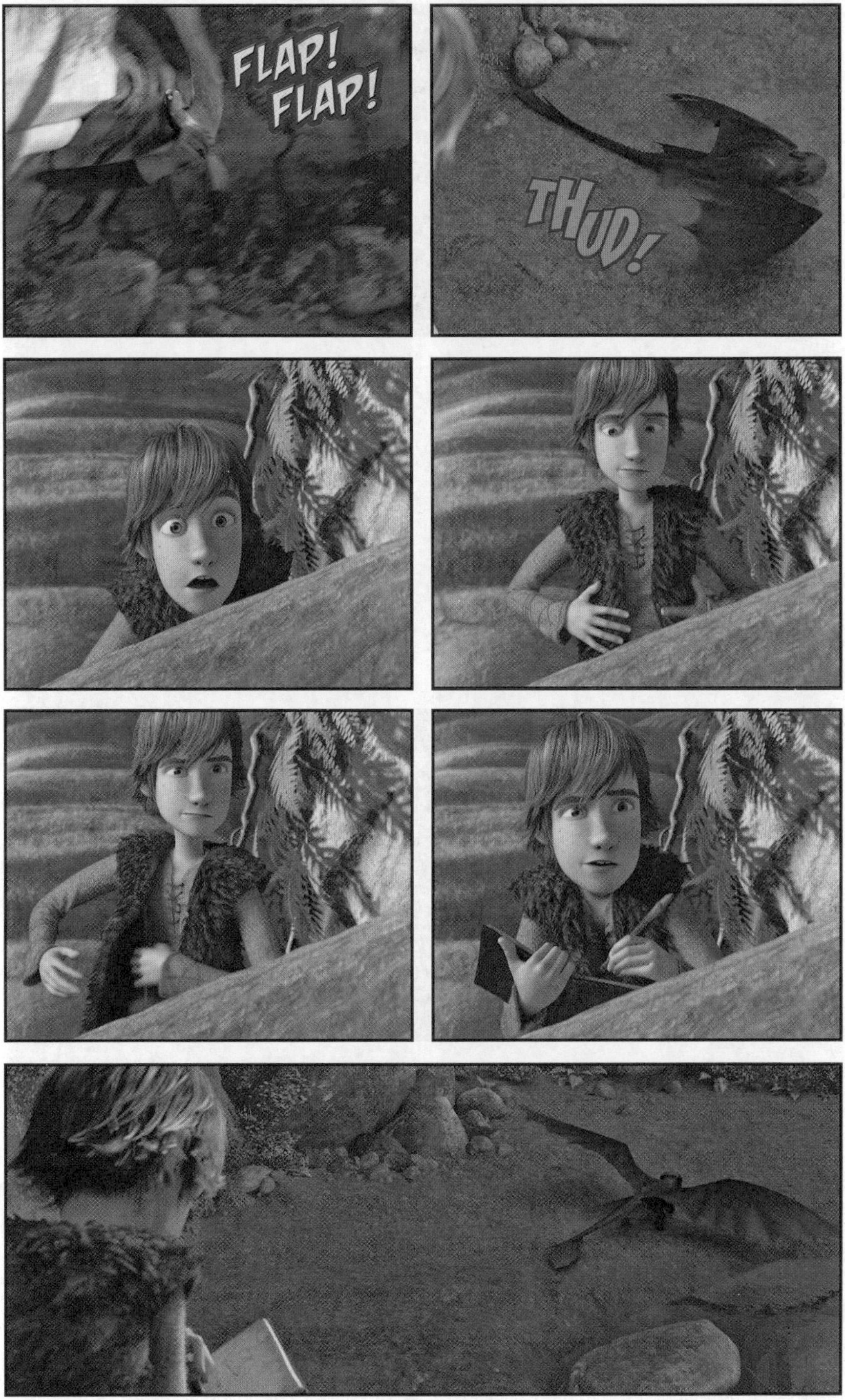
FLAP!
FLAP!
THUD!

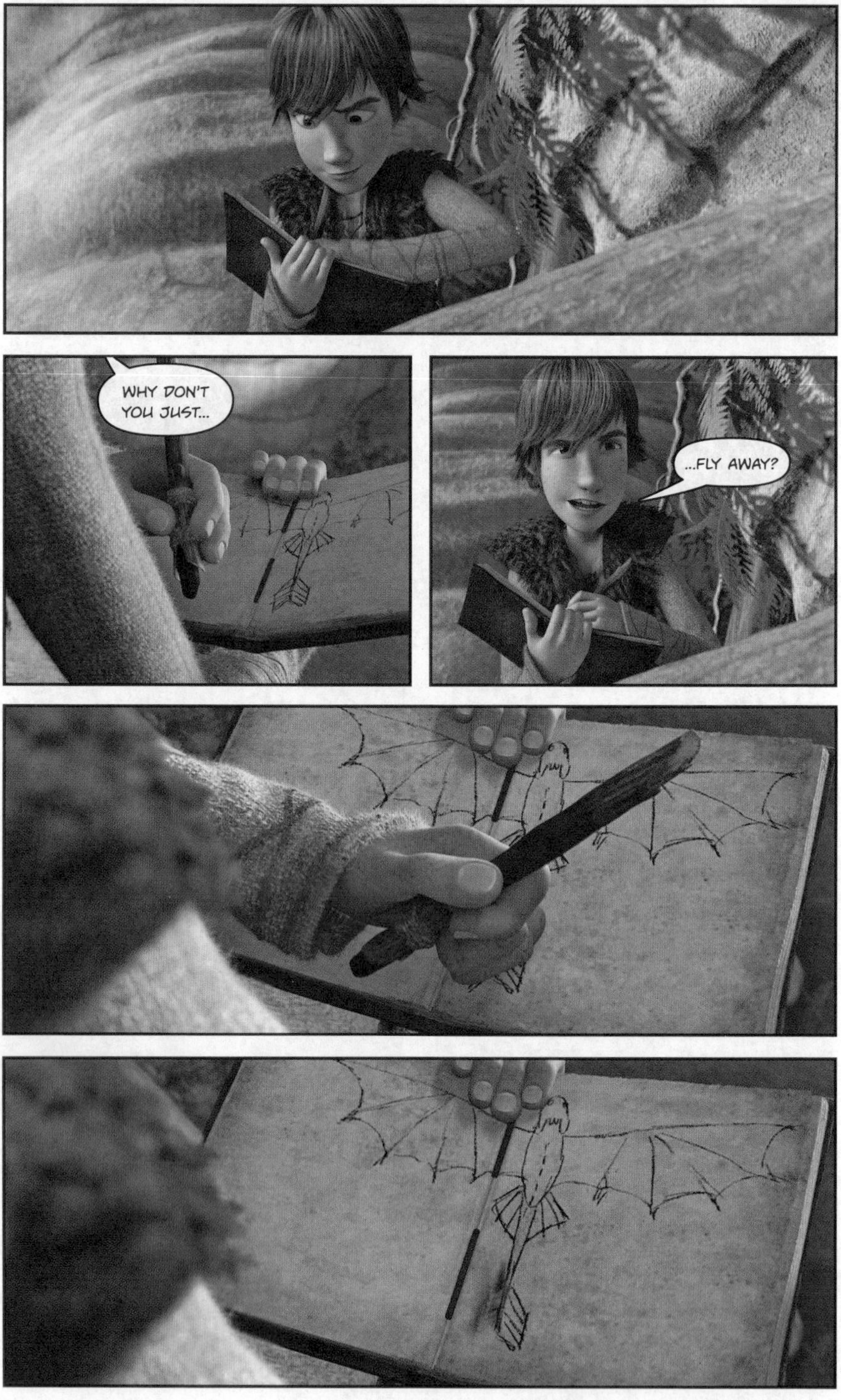
WHY DON'T YOU JUST...
...FLY AWAY?

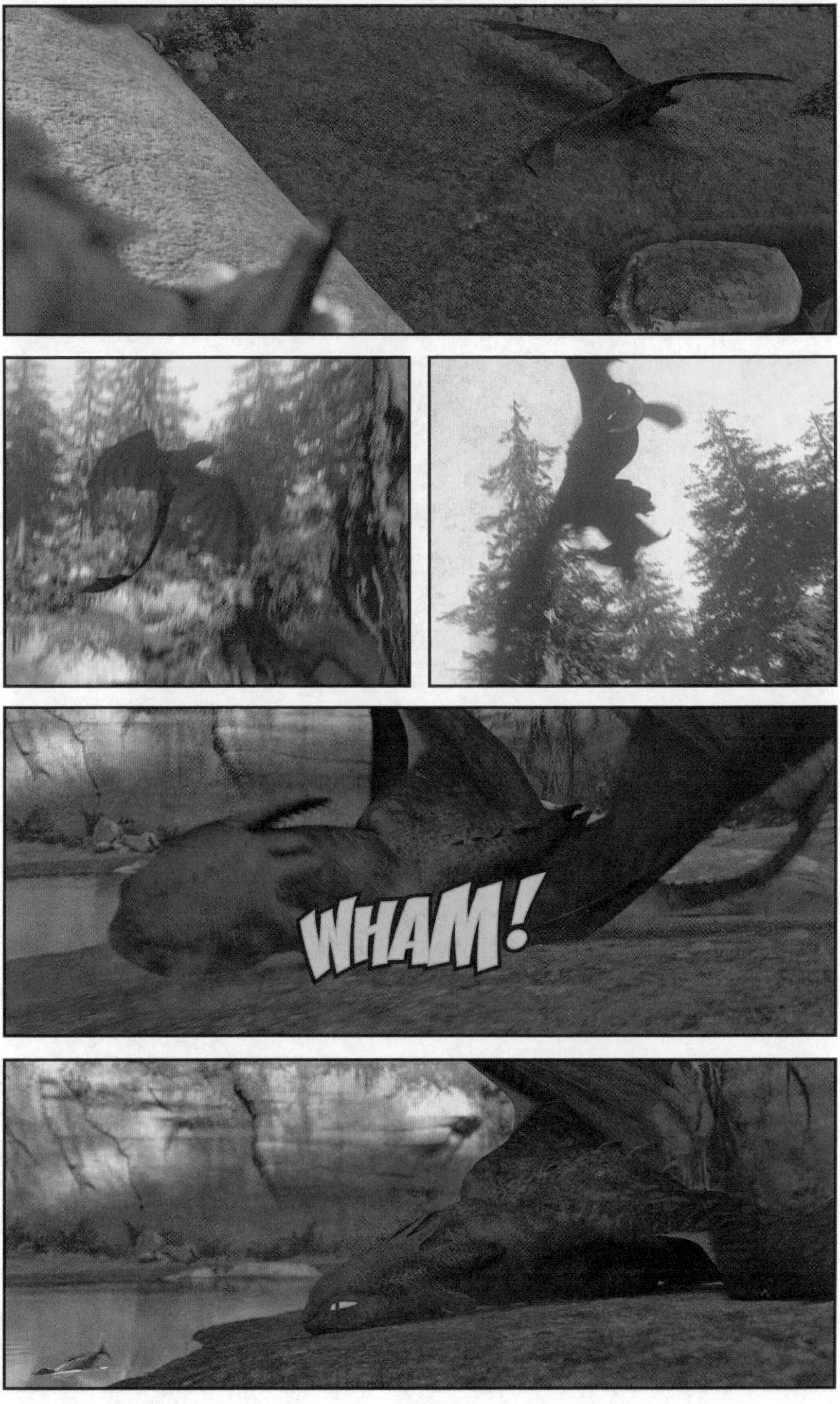
WHAM!

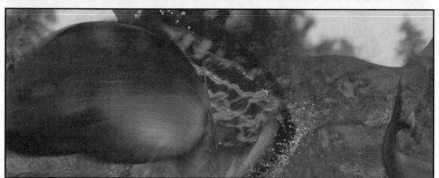

WHOOSH!

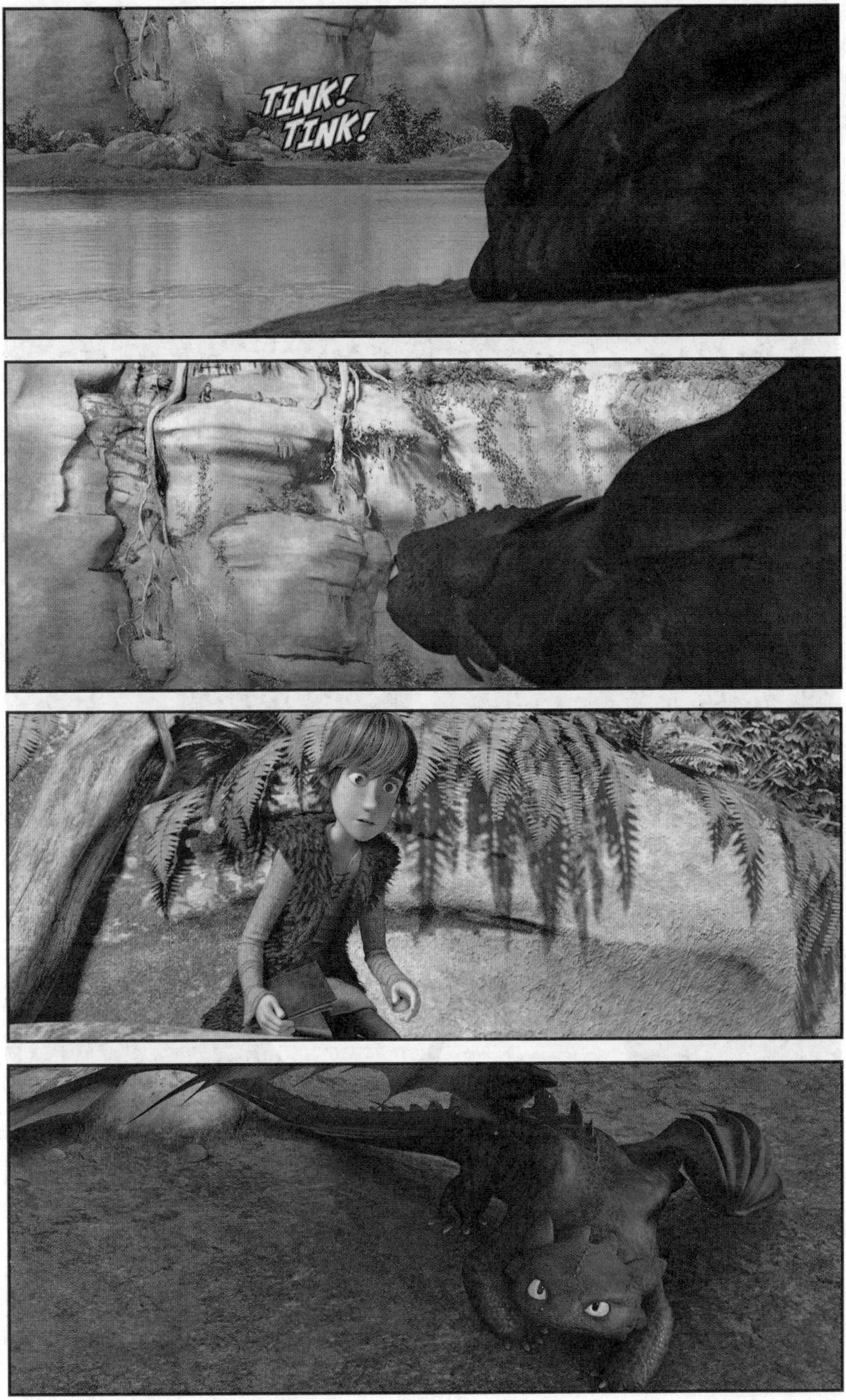
TINK!
TINK!

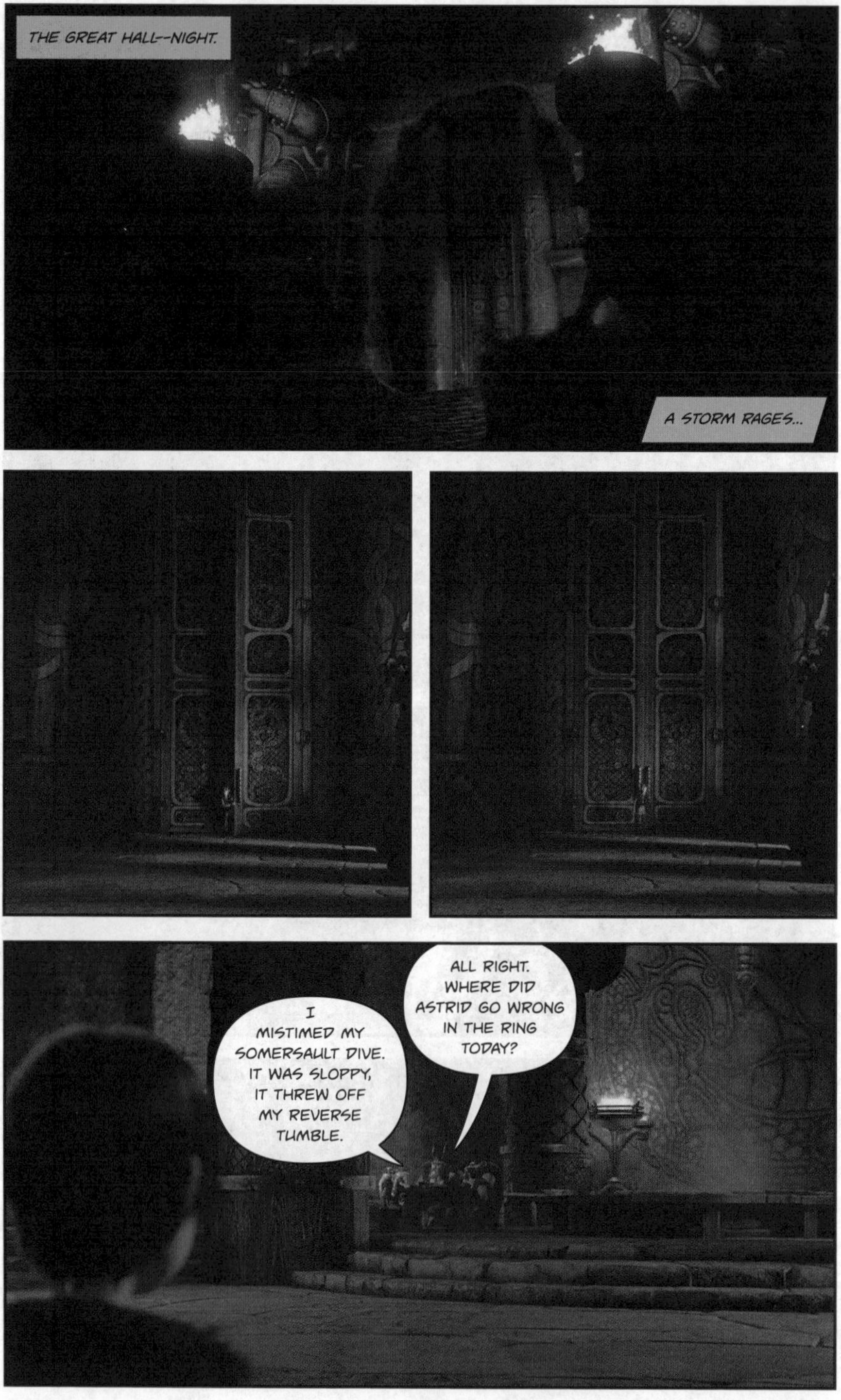
THE GREAT HALL--NIGHT.
A STORM RAGES...
ALL RIGHT. WHERE DID ASTRID GO WRONG IN THE RING TODAY?
I MISTIMED MY SOMERSAULT DIVE. IT WAS SLOPPY, IT THREW OFF MY REVERSE TUMBLE.

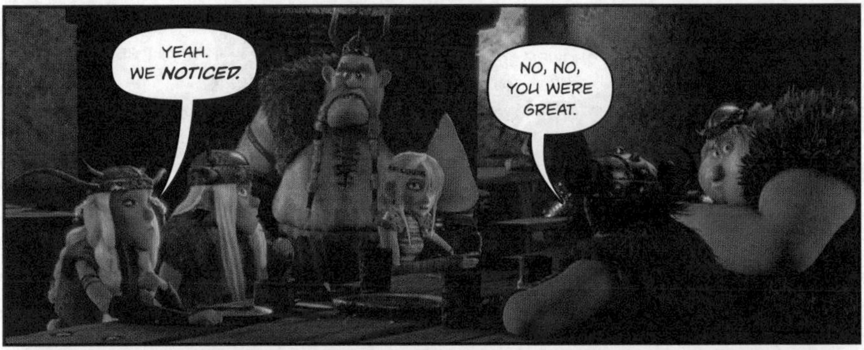
YEAH. WE NOTICED.
NO, NO, YOU WERE GREAT.

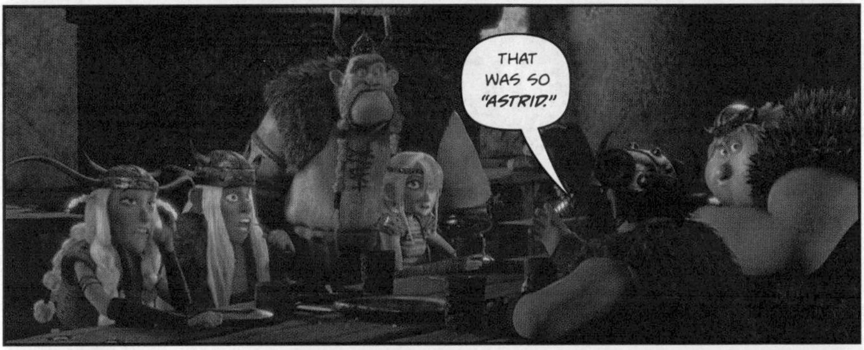
THAT WAS SO "ASTRID."

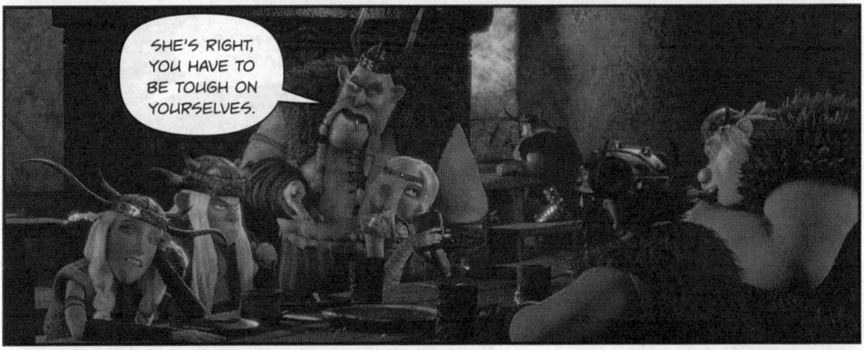
SHE'S RIGHT, YOU HAVE TO BE TOUGH ON YOURSELVES.

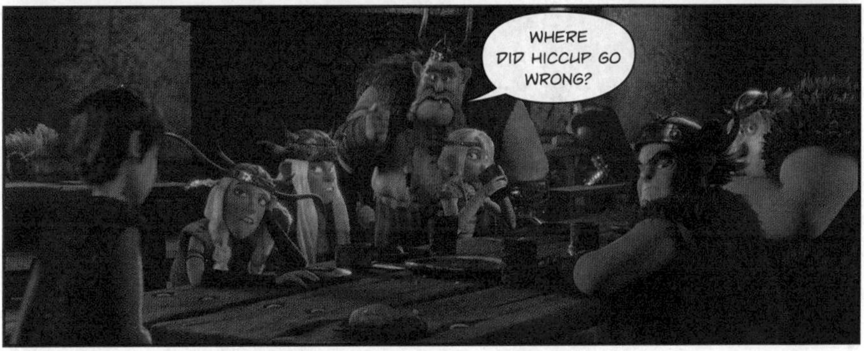
WHERE DID HICCUP GO WRONG?

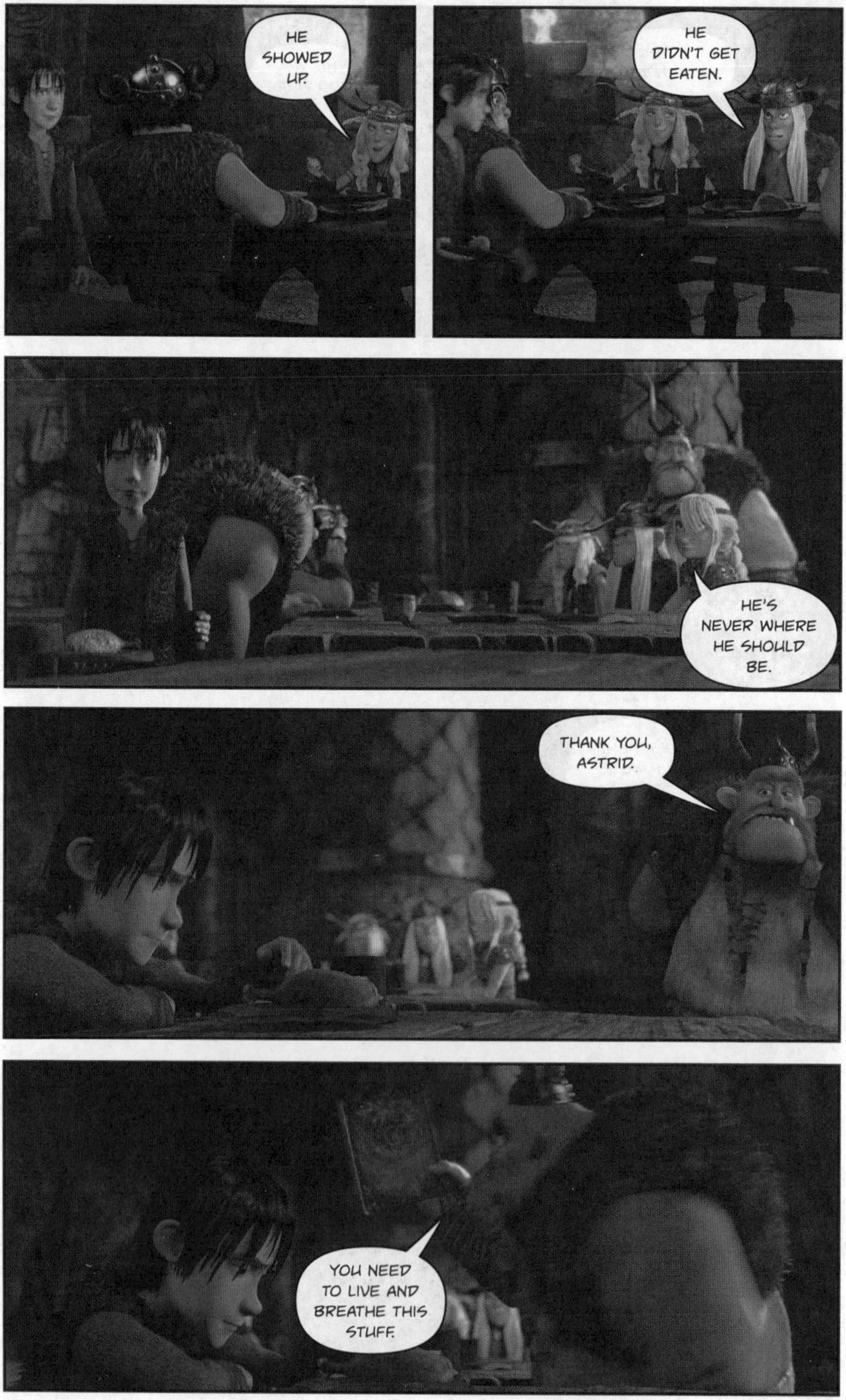
HE SHOWED UP.
HE DIDN'T GET EATEN.
HE'S NEVER WHERE HE SHOULD BE.
THANK YOU, ASTRID.
YOU NEED TO LIVE AND BREATHE THIS STUFF.

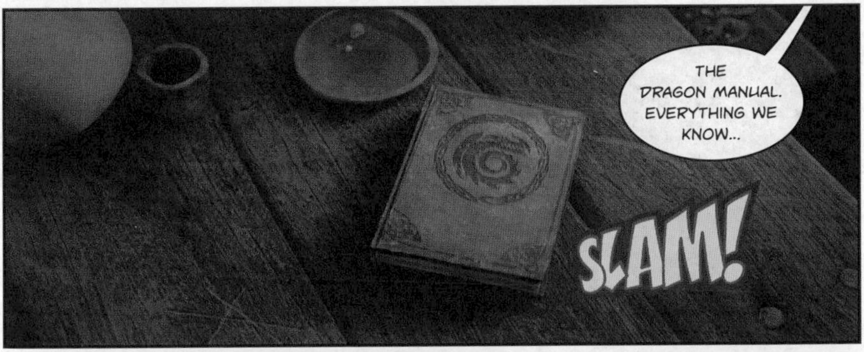
THE DRAGON MANUAL. EVERYTHING WE KNOW...
SLAM!

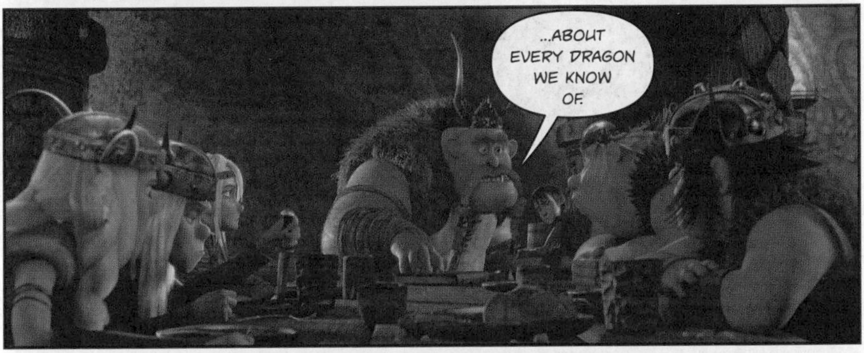
...ABOUT EVERY DRAGON WE KNOW OF.

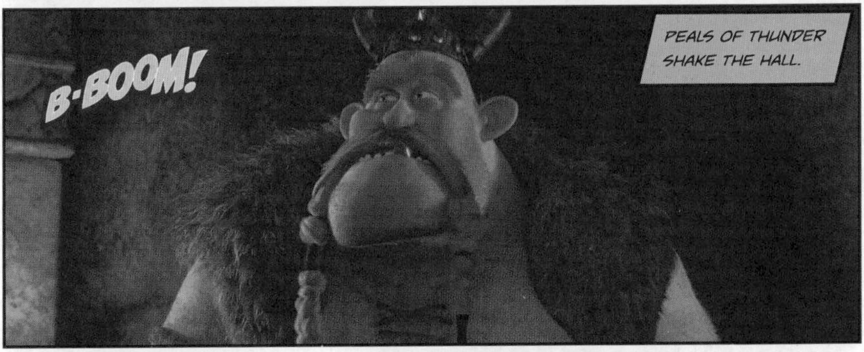
B-BOOM!
PEALS OF THUNDER SHAKE THE HALL.

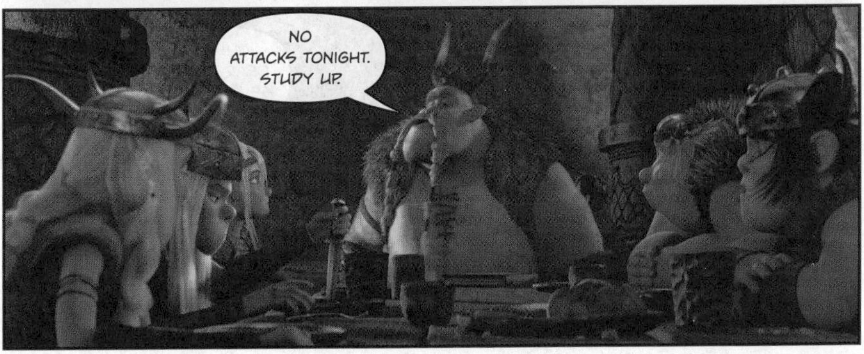
NO ATTACKS TONIGHT. STUDY UP.

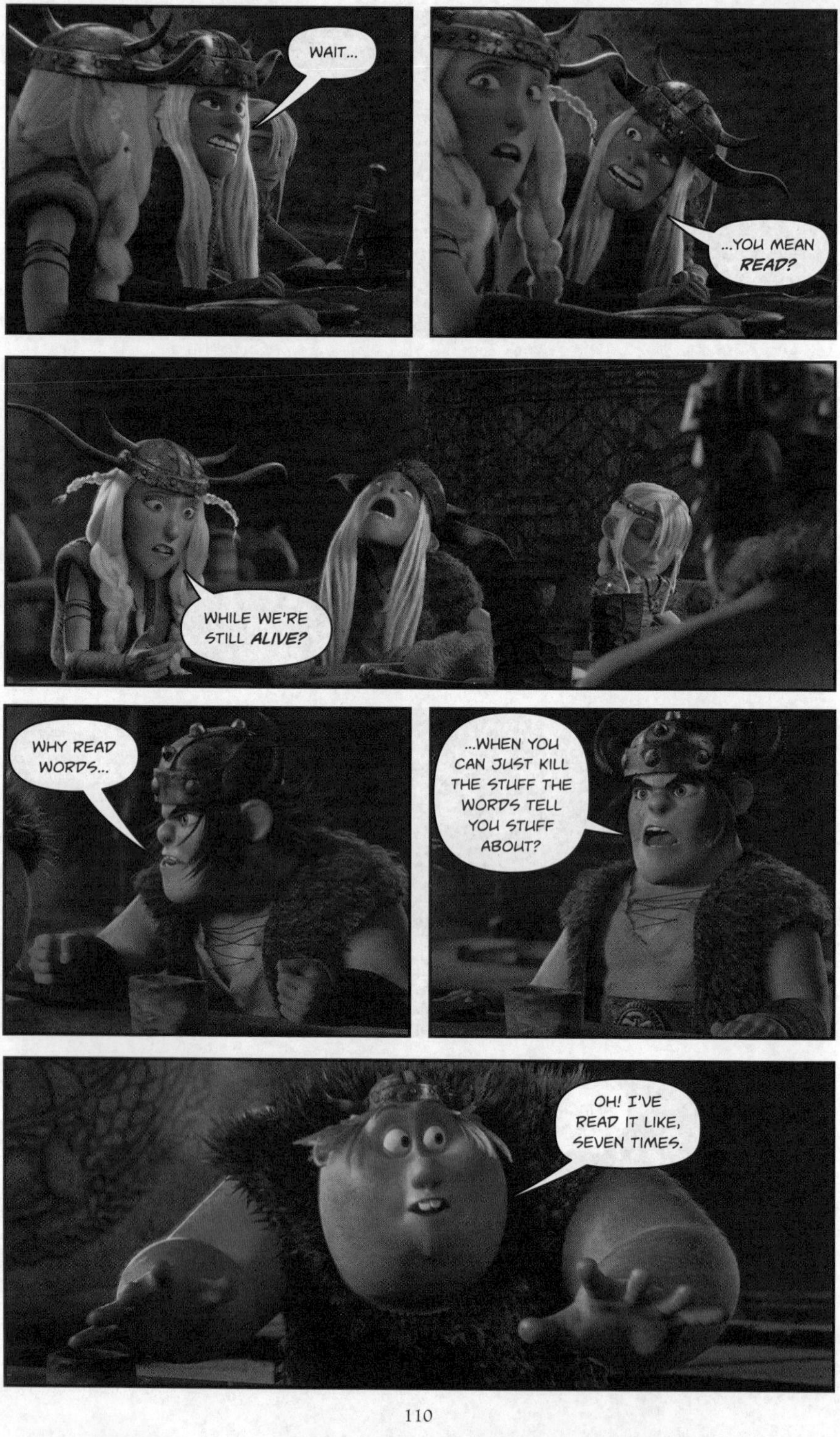
WAIT...
...YOU MEAN READ?
WHILE WE'RE STILL ALIVE?
WHY READ WORDS...
...WHEN YOU CAN JUST KILL THE STUFF THE WORDS TELL YOU STUFF ABOUT?
OH! I'VE READ IT LIKE, SEVEN TIMES.

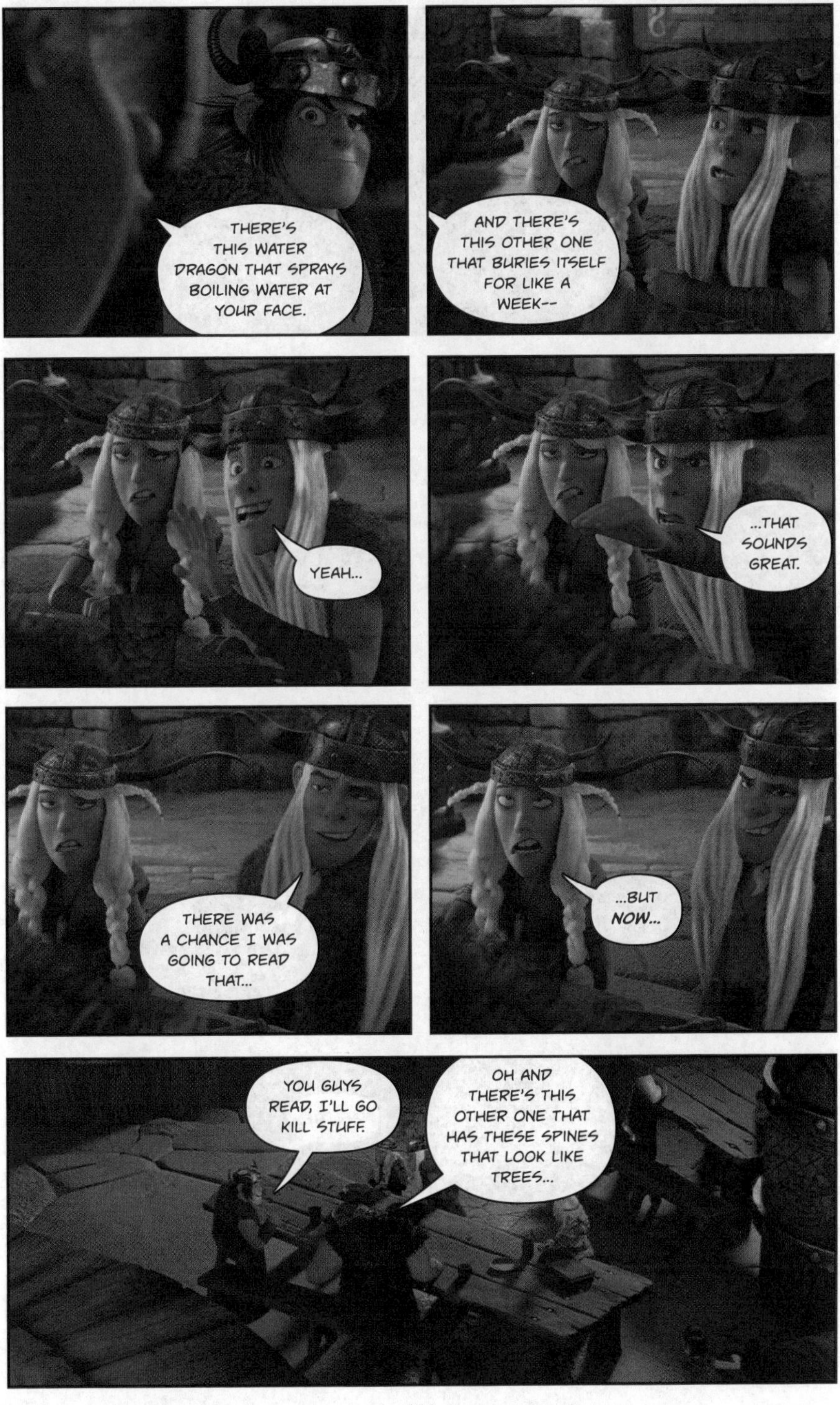
THERE'S THIS WATER DRAGON THAT SPRAYS BOILING WATER AT YOUR FACE.
AND THERE'S THIS OTHER ONE THAT BURIES ITSELF FOR LIKE A WEEK--
YEAH...
...THAT SOUNDS GREAT.
THERE WAS A CHANCE I WAS GOING TO READ THAT...
...BUT NOW...
YOU GUYS READ, I'LL GO KILL STUFF.
OH AND THERE'S THIS OTHER ONE THAT HAS THESE SPINES THAT LOOK LIKE TREES...

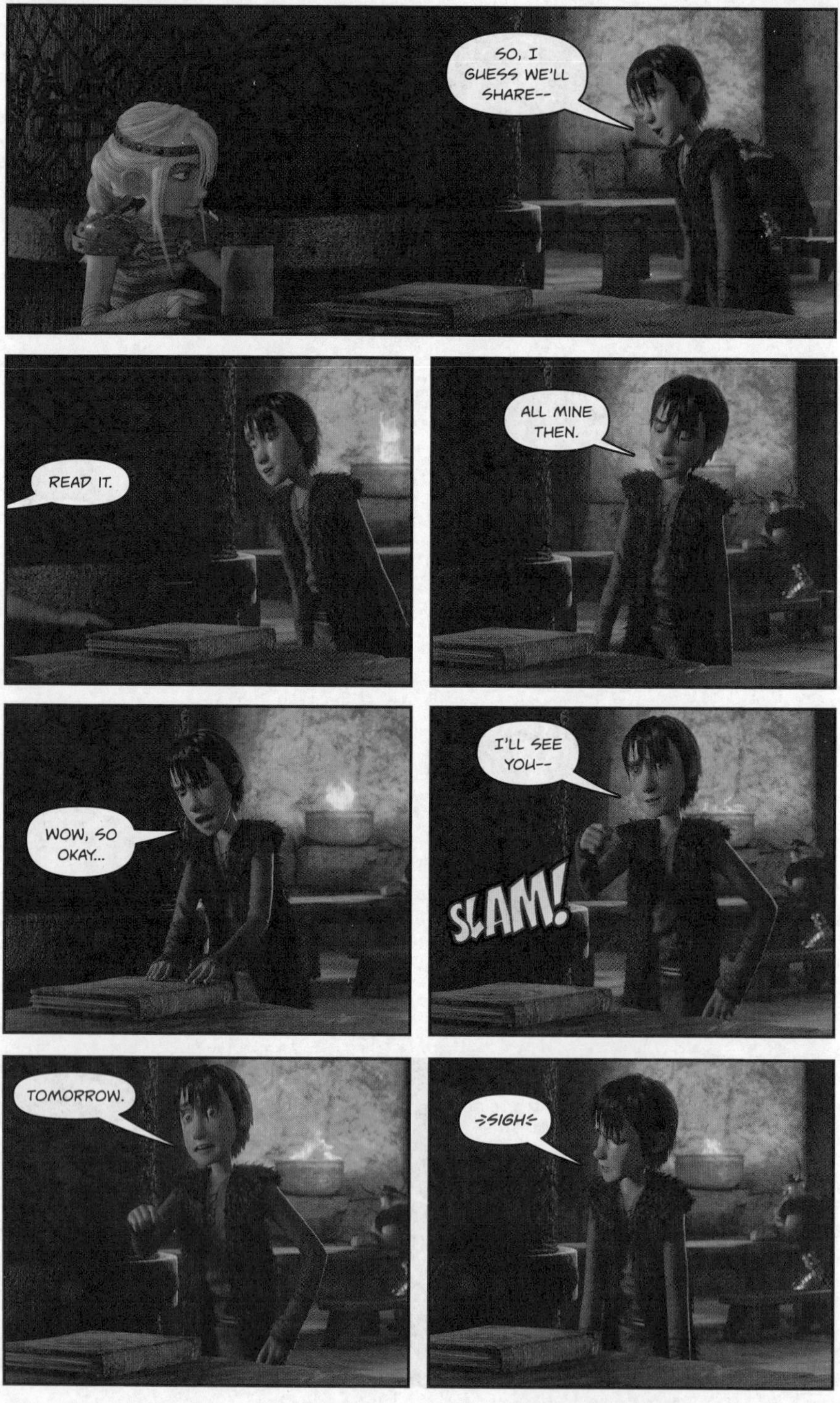
SO, I GUESS WE'LL SHARE--
READ IT.
ALL MINE THEN.
WOW, SO OKAY...
I'LL SEE YOU--
SLAM!
TOMORROW.
=SIGH=

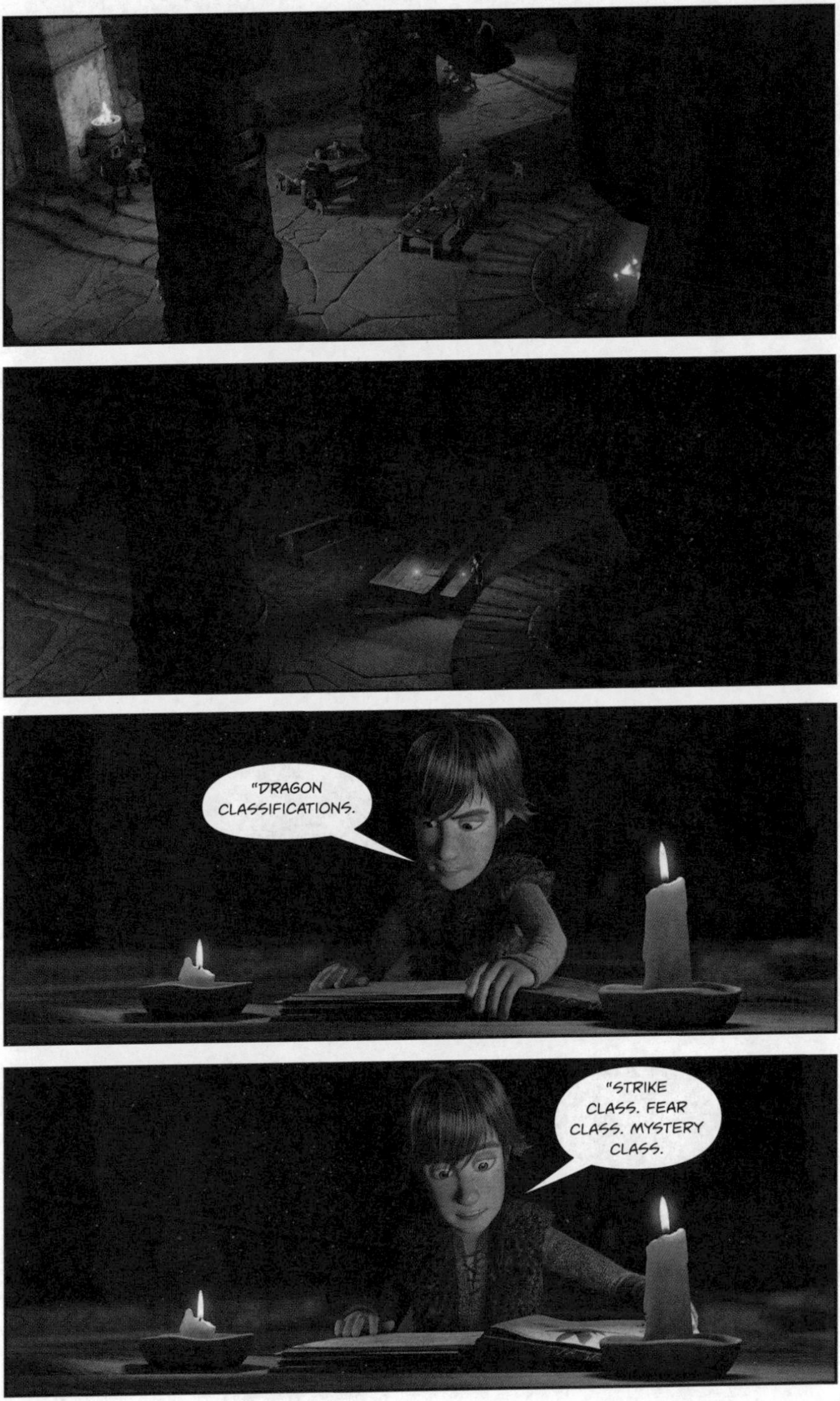
"DRAGON CLASSIFICATIONS.
"STRIKE CLASS. FEAR CLASS. MYSTERY CLASS.

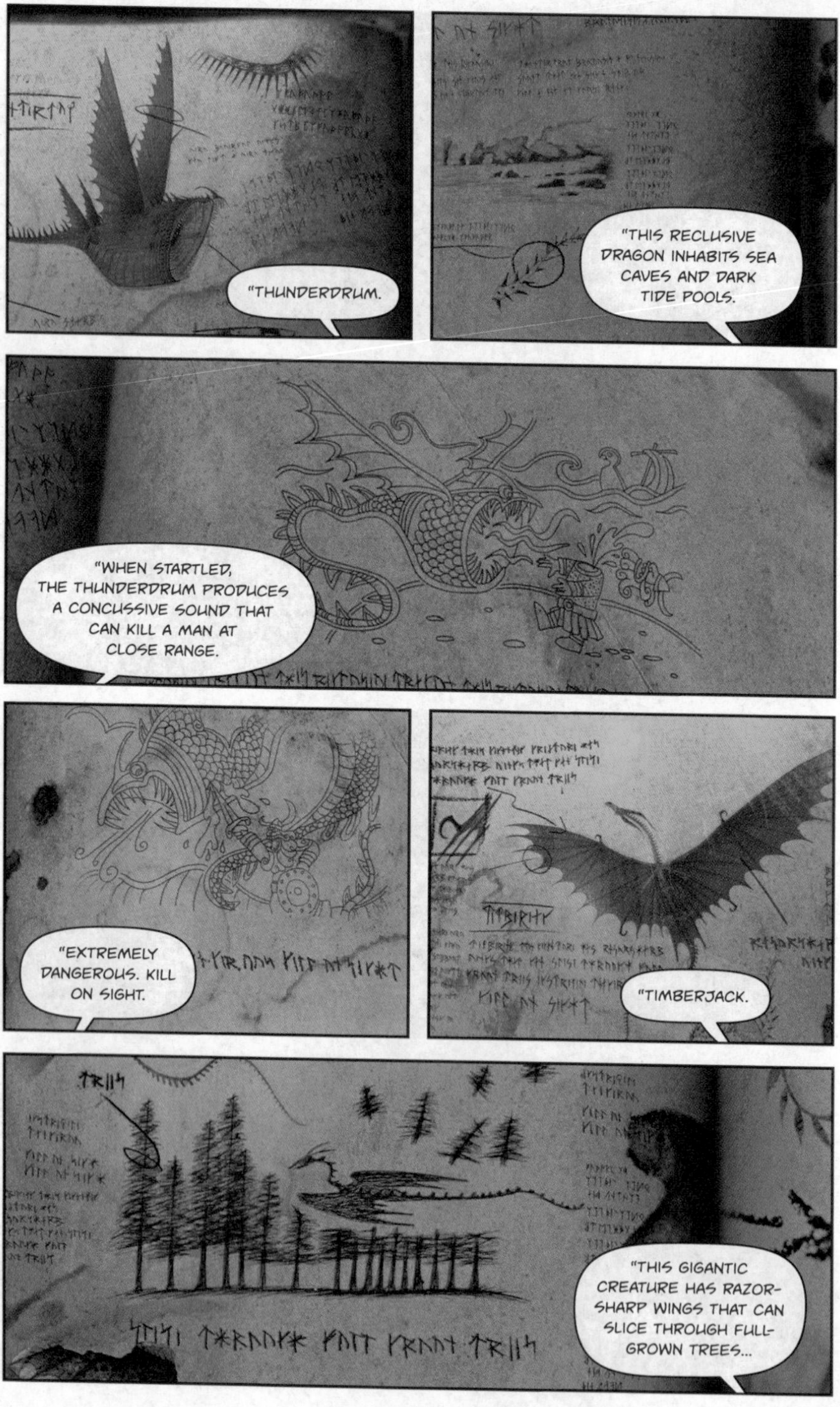
"THUNDERDRUM.
"THIS RECLUSIVE DRAGON INHABITS SEA CAVES AND DARK TIDE POOLS.
"WHEN STARTLED, THE THUNDERDRUM PRODUCES A CONCUSSIVE SOUND THAT CAN KILL A MAN AT CLOSE RANGE.
"EXTREMELY DANGEROUS. KILL ON SIGHT.
"TIMBERJACK.
"THIS GIGANTIC CREATURE HAS RAZOR-SHARP WINGS THAT CAN SLICE THROUGH FULL-GROWN TREES...

"EXTREMELY DANGEROUS. KILL ON SIGHT.

"SCAULDRON.

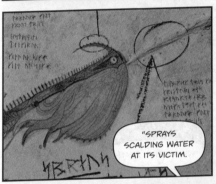

"SPRAYS SCALDING WATER AT ITS VICTIM.

"EXTREMELY DANGEROUS.

CRA-AACK!

"CHANGEWING.

EVEN NEWLY HATCHED DRAGONS CAN SPRAY ACID. KILL ON SIGHT.

"GRONCKLE.

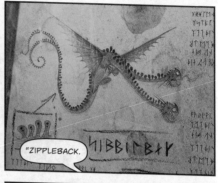

"ZIPPLEBACK.

"THE SKRILL.

"WHISPERING DEATH.

"BURNS ITS VICTIMS. BURIES ITS VICTIMS. CHOKES ITS VICTIMS.

"TURNS ITS VICTIMS INSIDE OUT.

"EXTREMELY DANGEROUS.

116

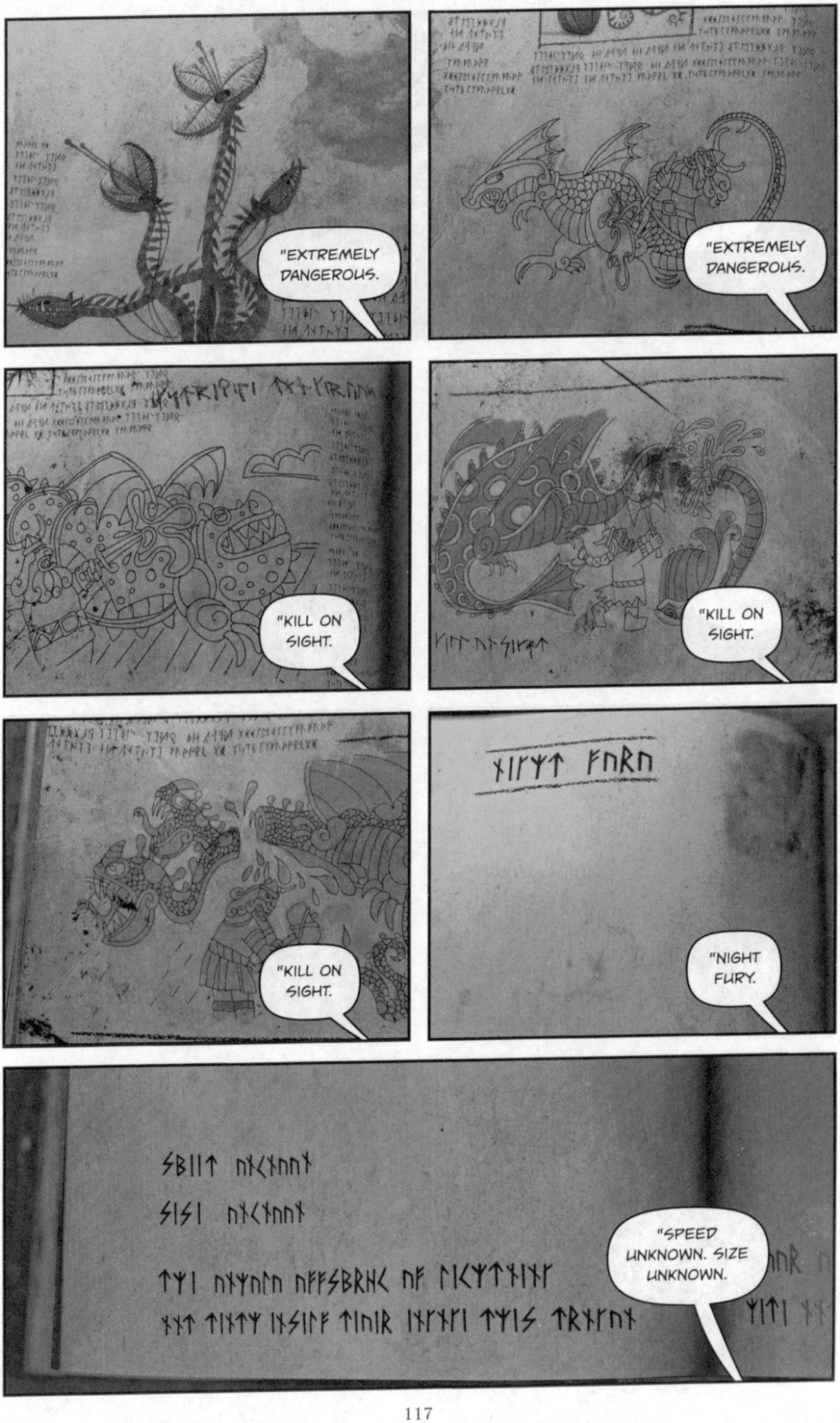
"EXTREMELY DANGEROUS.
"EXTREMELY DANGEROUS.
"KILL ON SIGHT.
"KILL ON SIGHT.
"KILL ON SIGHT.
"NIGHT FURY.
"SPEED UNKNOWN. SIZE UNKNOWN.

"THE UNHOLY OFFSPRING OF LIGHTNING AND DEATH ITSELF.

"NEVER ENGAGE THIS DRAGON.

"YOUR ONLY CHANCE... HIDE AND PRAY...

ᚢᚢᚢᚱ ᚾᛁᚠᚾ ᚱᛁᛁᛁᛋᛁ
ᛁᛁᛏᛁ ᛁᛁᛏ ᛒᛁᛁᛁ ᛁᛏ ᛏ

"...IT DOES NOT FIND YOU."

ᚾᛁᛋ ᛁᚾᛏ ᚠᛁᛁᛏ ᚢᚢᚢ

ᛁᛁᛁᛁᛏ ᚠᚢᚱᚾ

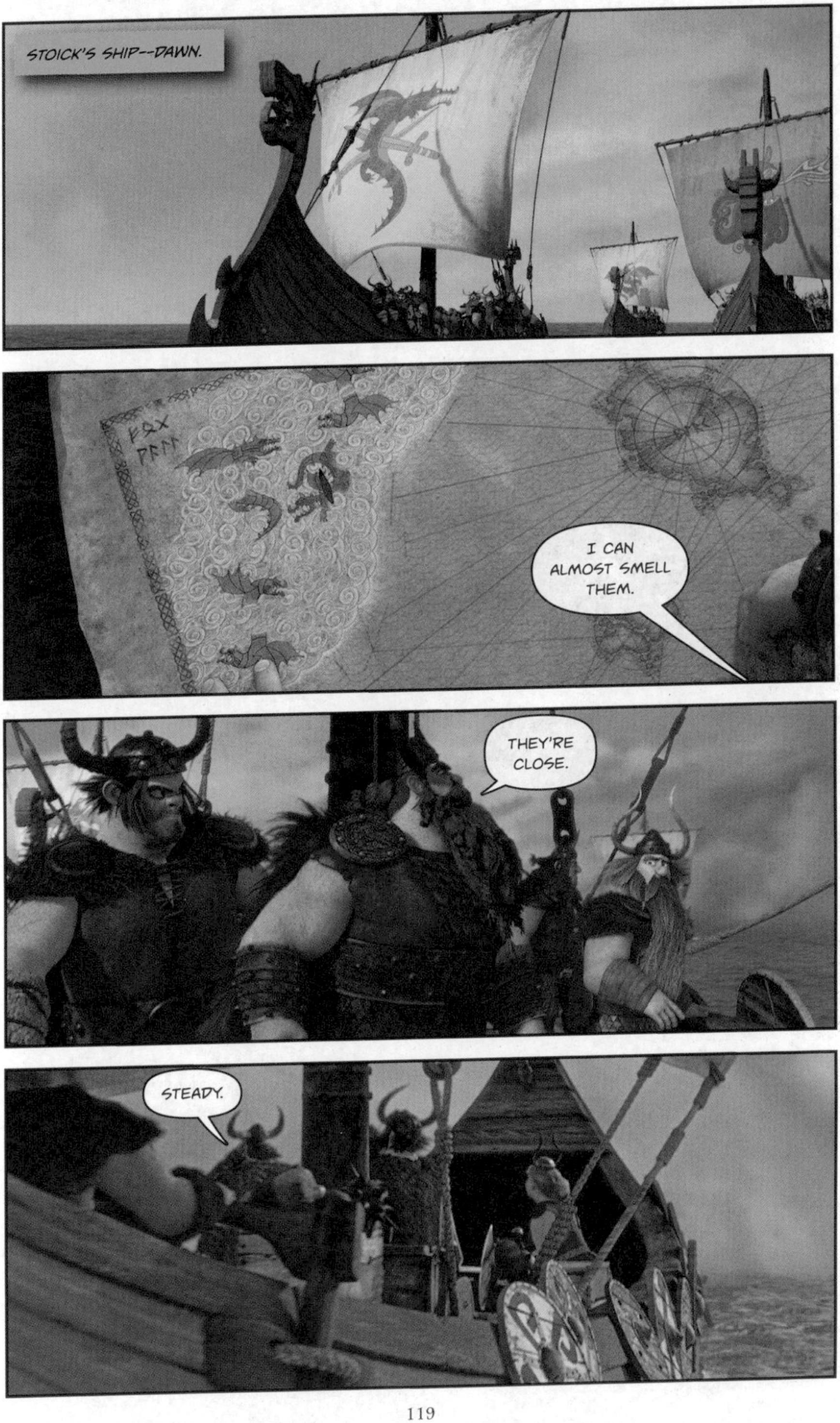
STOICK'S SHIP--DAWN.
I CAN ALMOST SMELL THEM.
THEY'RE CLOSE.
STEADY.

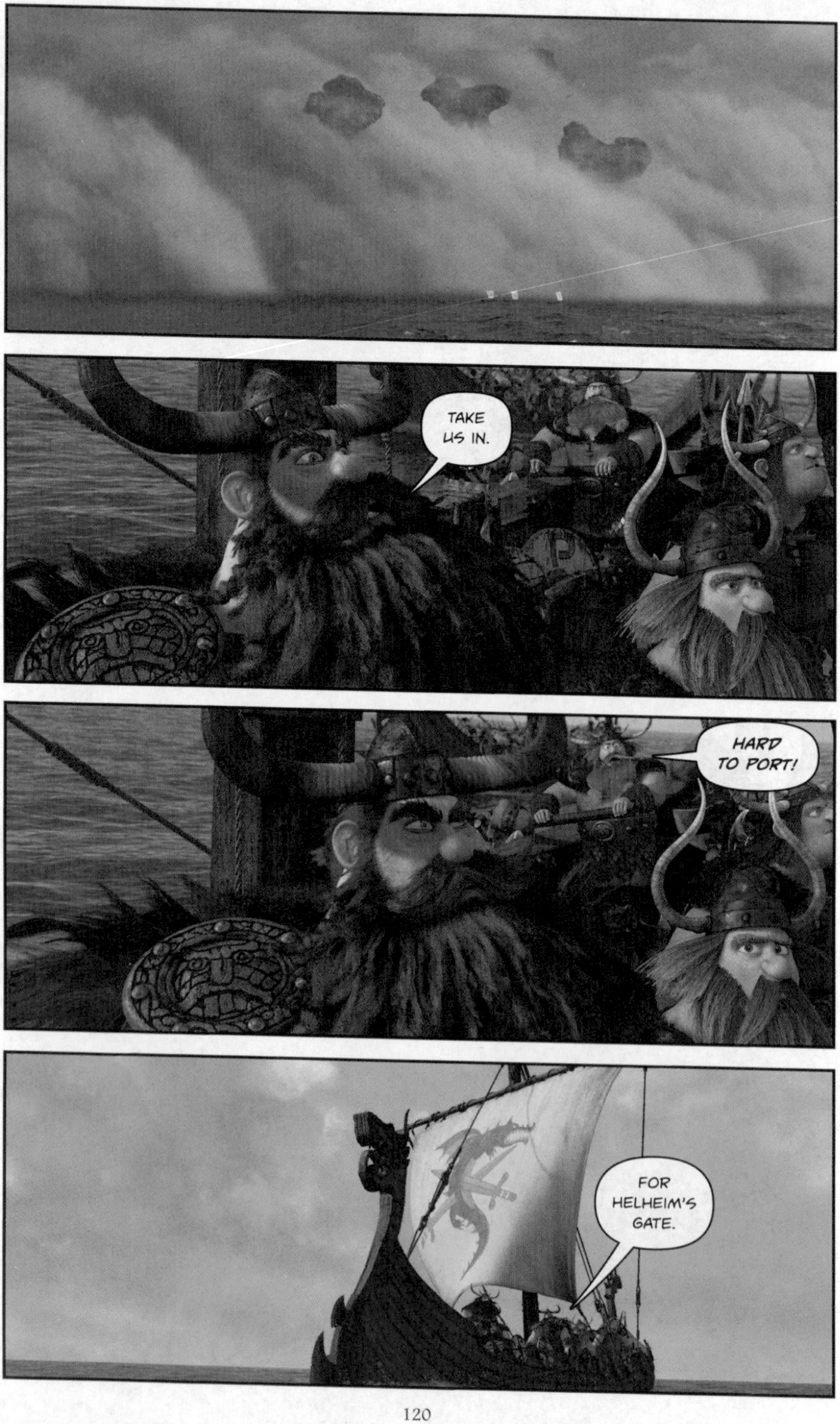
TAKE US IN.
HARD TO PORT!
FOR HELHEIM'S GATE.

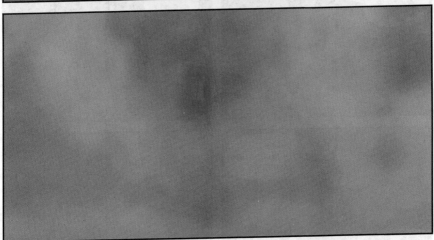

SHRIEK!

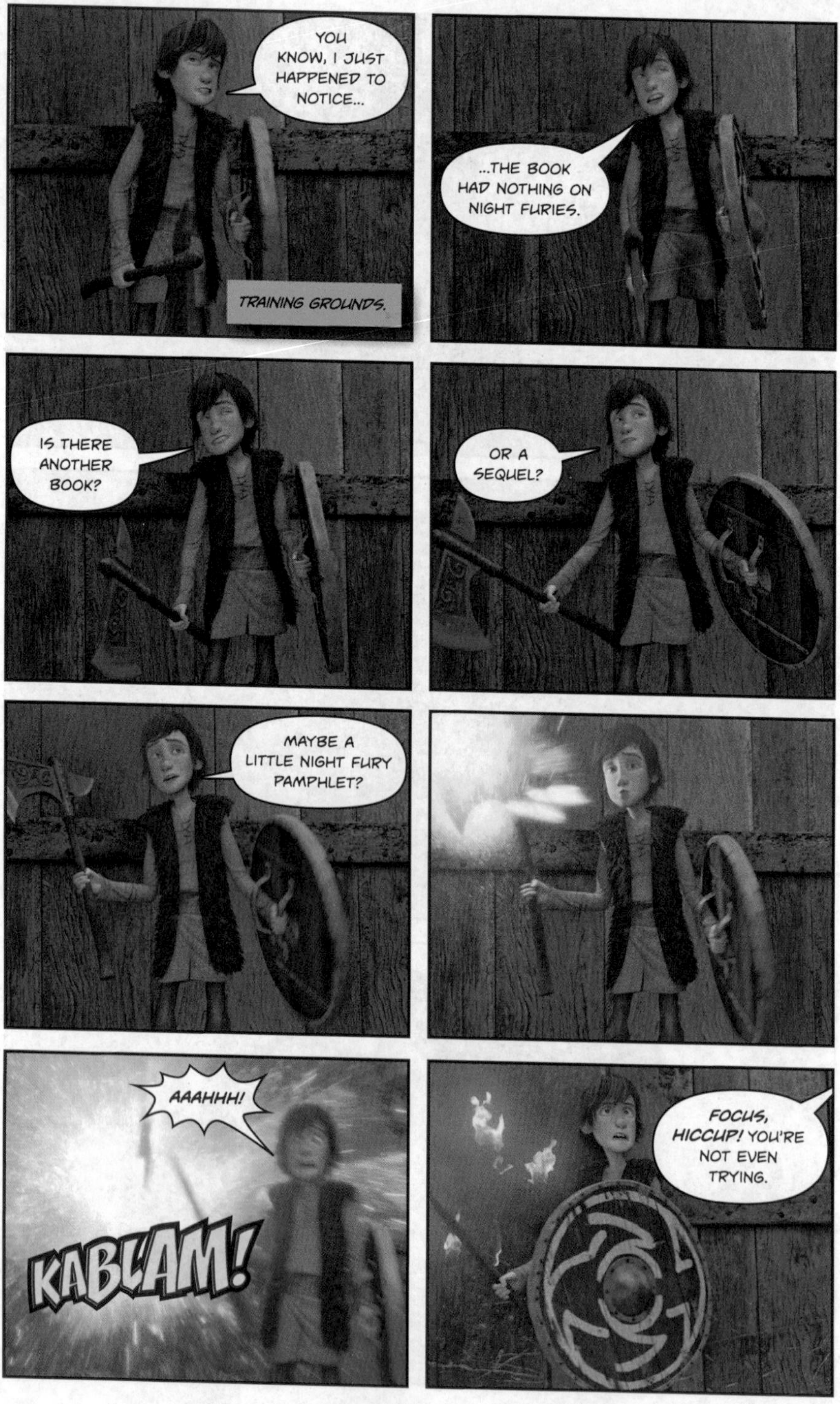
YOU KNOW, I JUST HAPPENED TO NOTICE...
TRAINING GROUNDS.
...THE BOOK HAD NOTHING ON NIGHT FURIES.
IS THERE ANOTHER BOOK?
OR A SEQUEL?
MAYBE A LITTLE NIGHT FURY PAMPHLET?
AAAHHH!
KABLAM!
FOCUS, HICCUP! YOU'RE NOT EVEN TRYING.

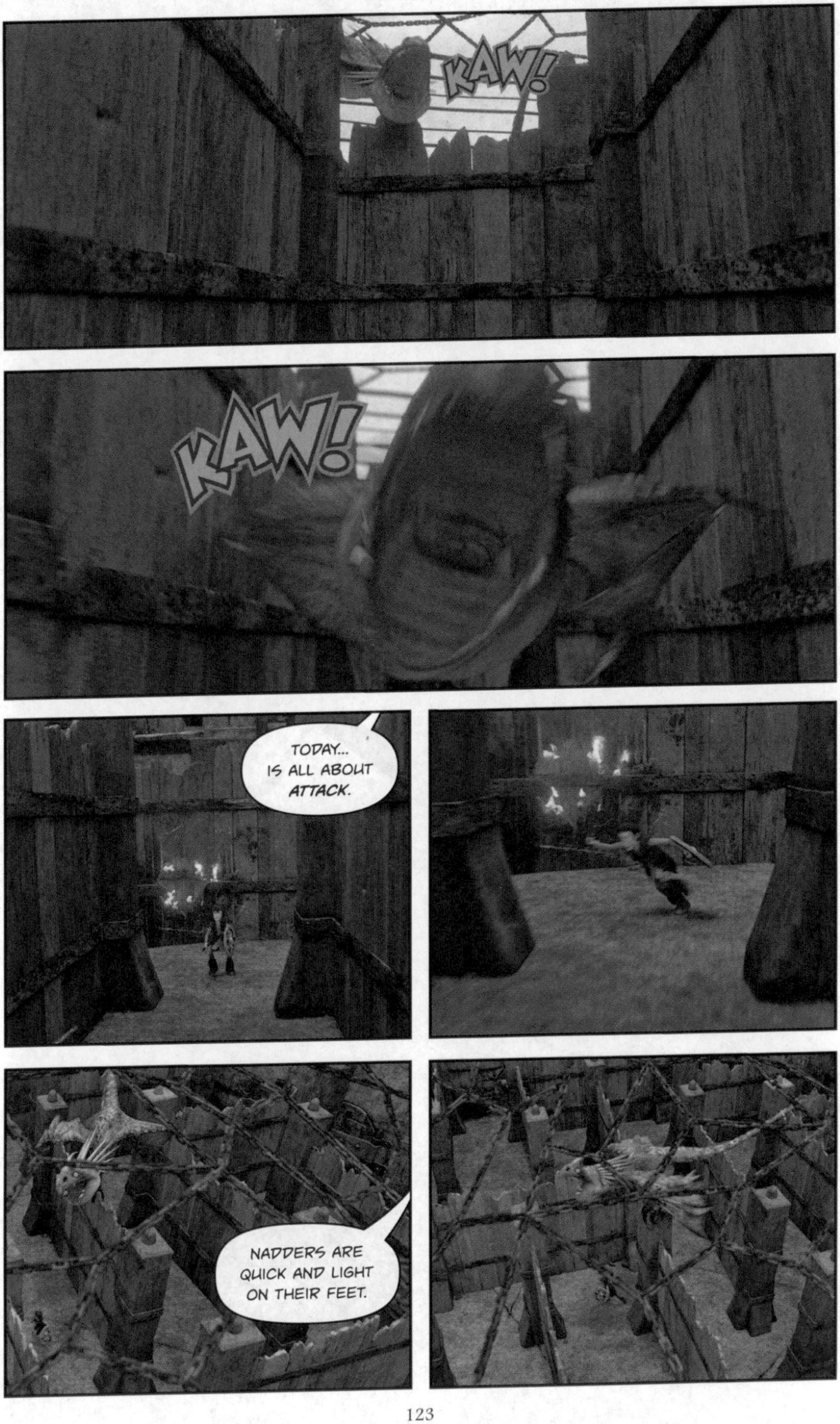
KAW!
KAW!
TODAY... IS ALL ABOUT ATTACK.
NADDERS ARE QUICK AND LIGHT ON THEIR FEET.

YOUR JOB IS TO BE QUICKER AND LIGHTER.

KAW!

I'M REALLY BEGINNING TO QUESTION YOUR TEACHING METHODS!

AAAGH!!!

LOOK FOR ITS BLIND SPOT. EVERY DRAGON HAS ONE.

FIND IT, HIDE IN IT, AND STRIKE.

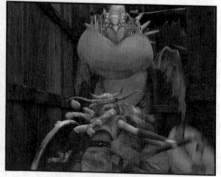

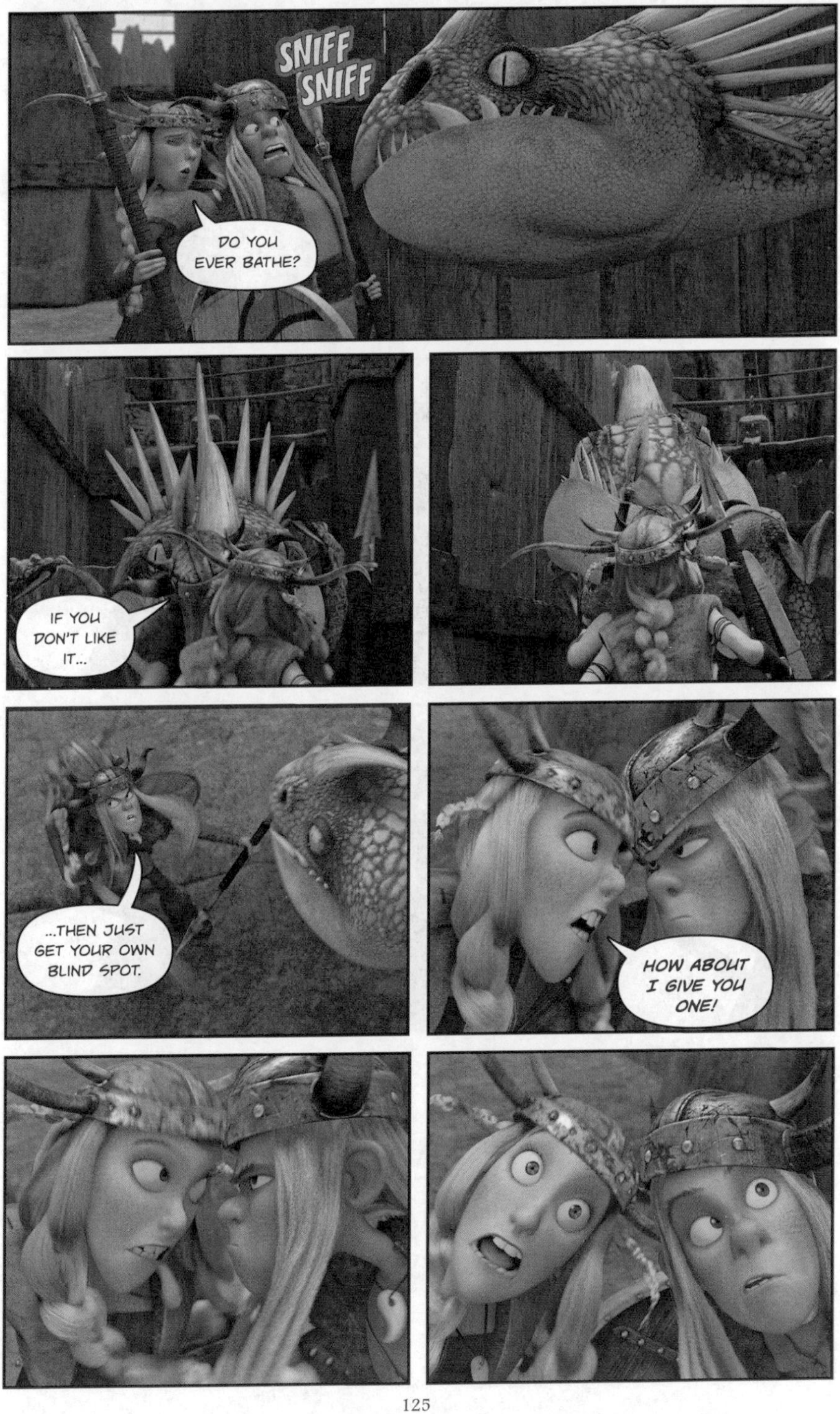
SNIFF SNIFF
DO YOU EVER BATHE?
IF YOU DON'T LIKE IT...
...THEN JUST GET YOUR OWN BLIND SPOT.
HOW ABOUT I GIVE YOU ONE!

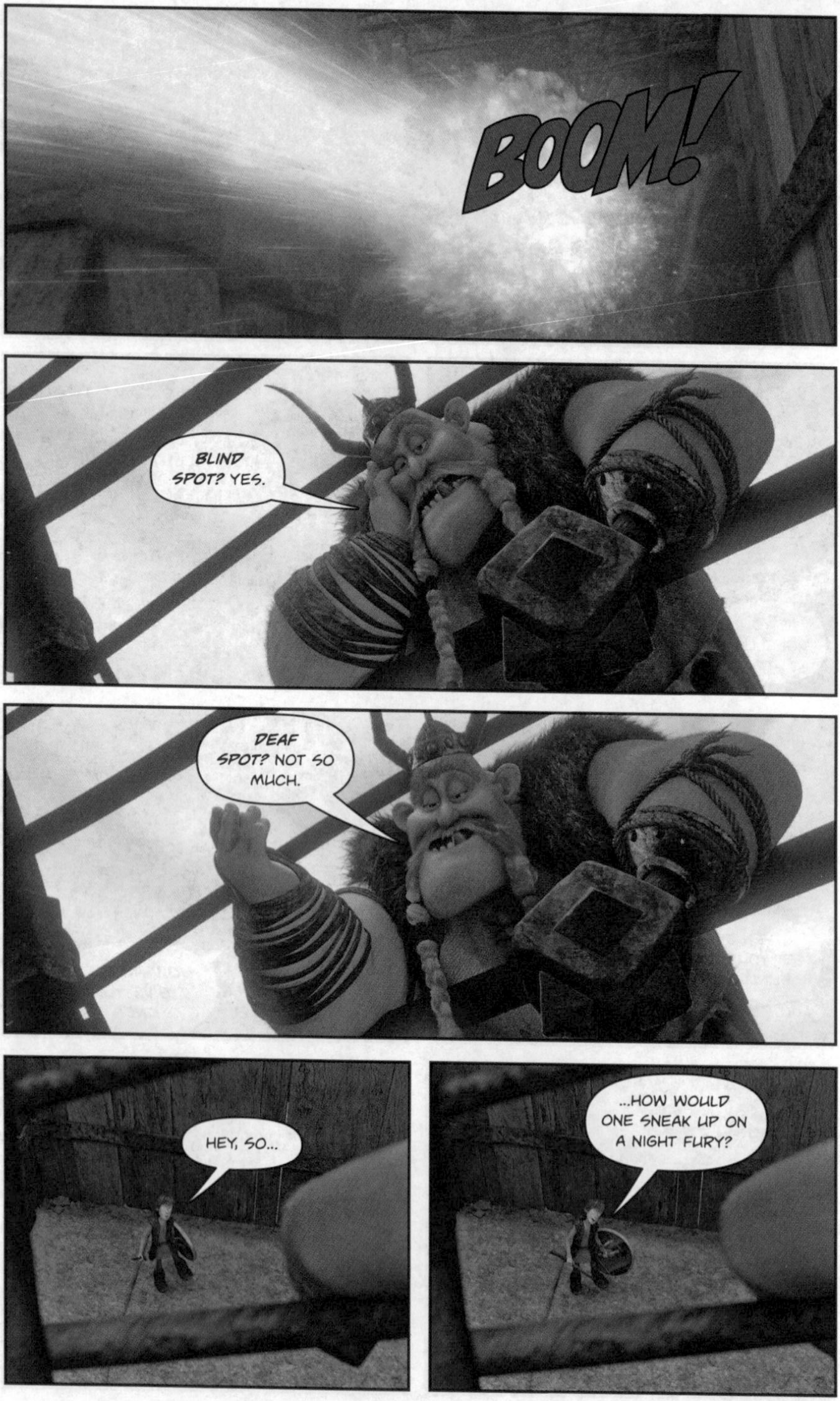
BOOM!
BLIND SPOT? YES.
DEAF SPOT? NOT SO MUCH.
HEY, SO...
...HOW WOULD ONE SNEAK UP ON A NIGHT FURY?

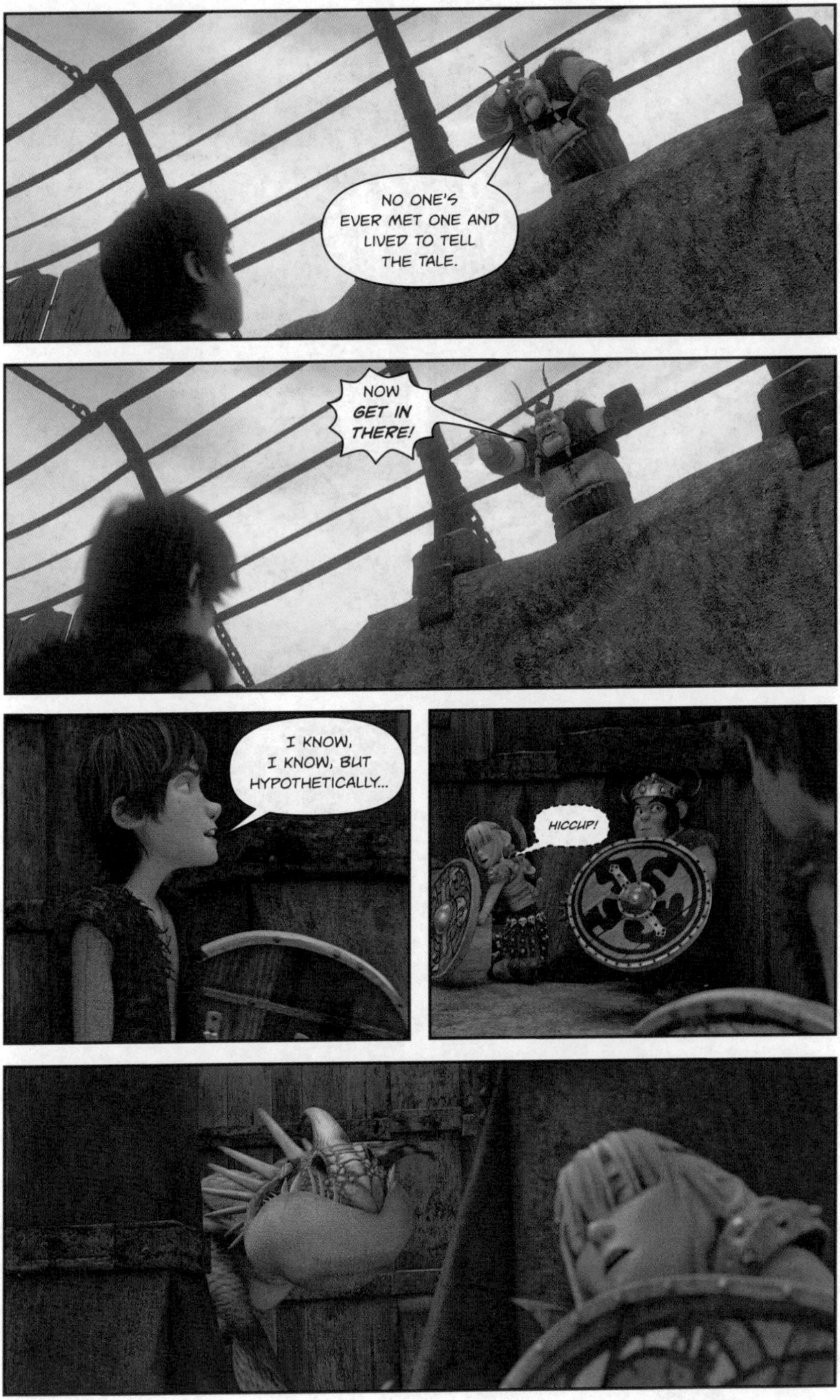

NO ONE'S EVER MET ONE AND LIVED TO TELL THE TALE.
NOW GET IN THERE!
I KNOW, I KNOW, BUT HYPOTHETICALLY...
HICCUP!

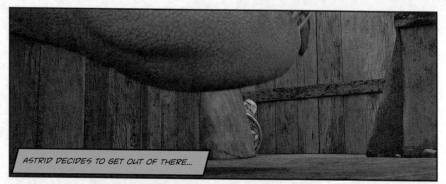
ASTRID DECIDES TO GET OUT OF THERE...

...AND SOMERSAULTS AWAY.

THE OTHERS FOLLOW...

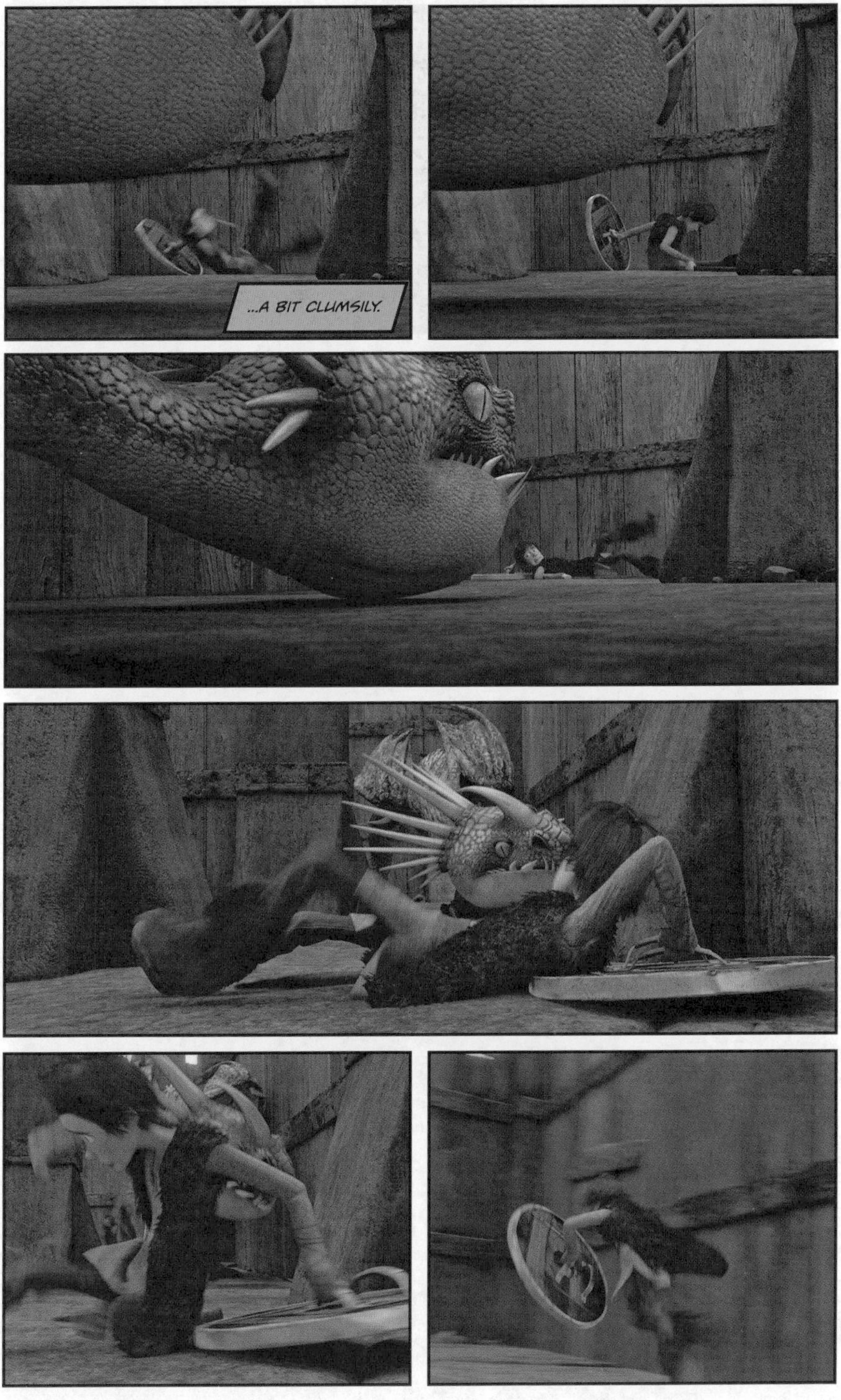
...A BIT CLUMSILY.

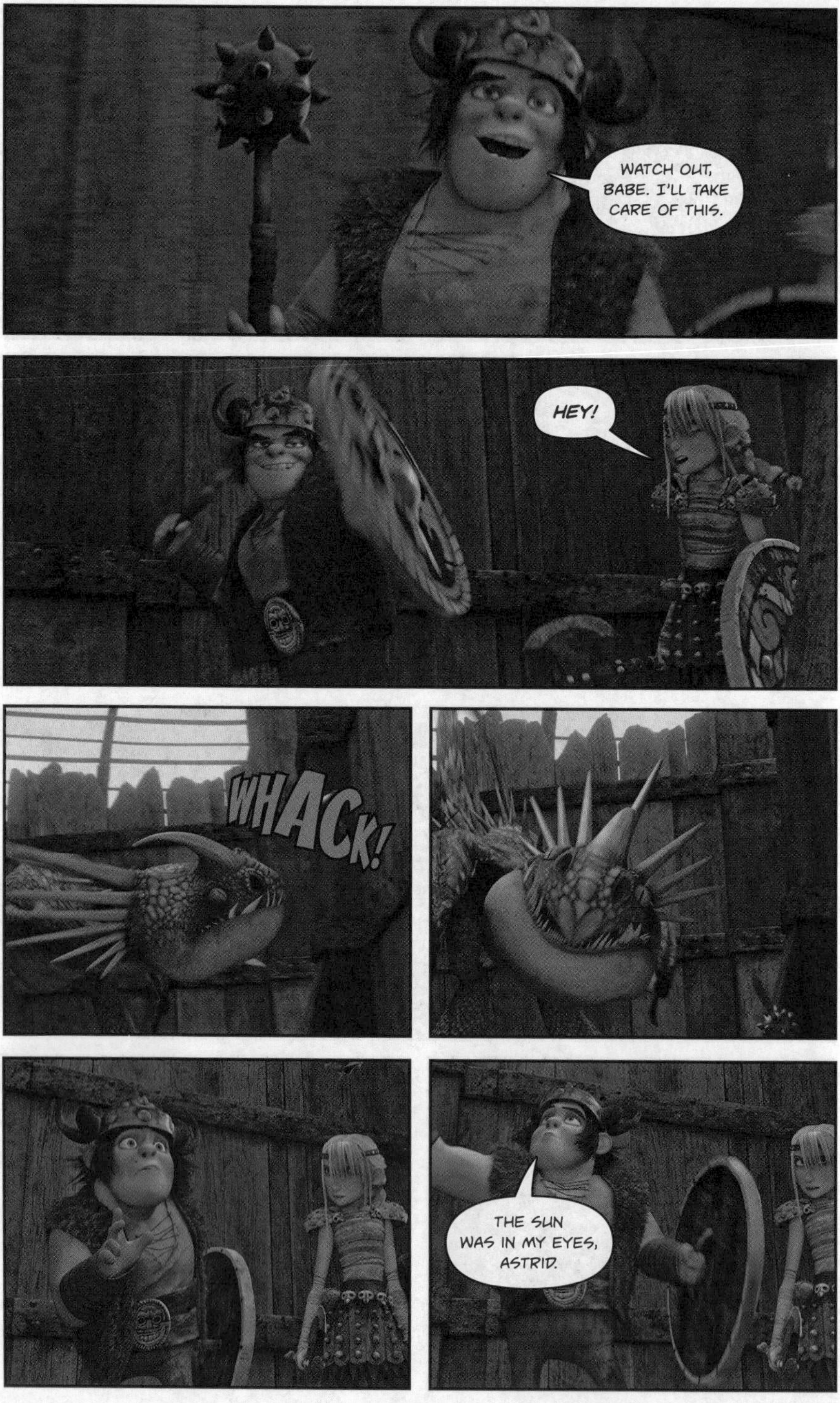
WATCH OUT, BABE. I'LL TAKE CARE OF THIS.
HEY!
WHACK!
THE SUN WAS IN MY EYES, ASTRID.

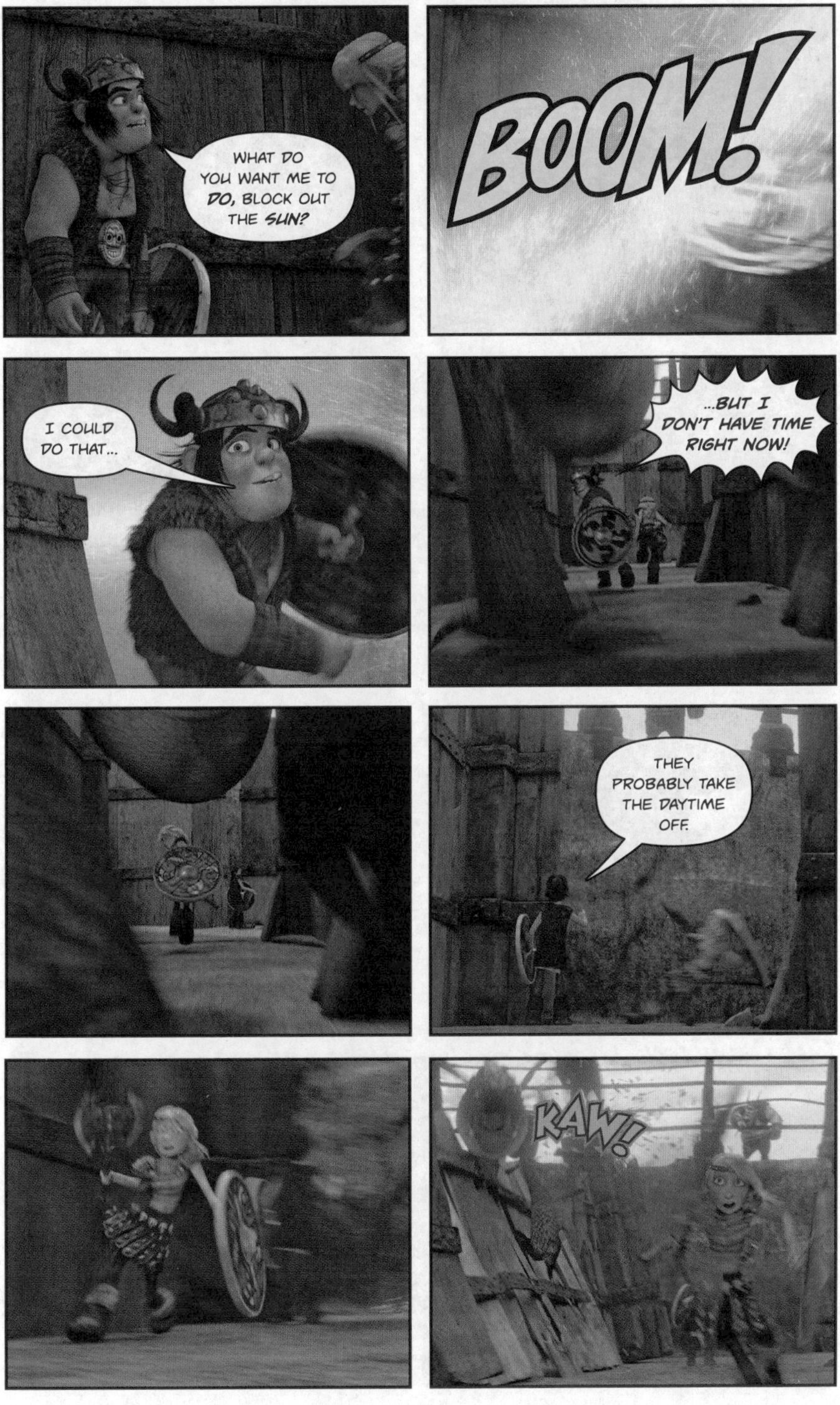
WHAT DO YOU WANT ME TO DO, BLOCK OUT THE SUN?
BOOM!
I COULD DO THAT...
...BUT I DON'T HAVE TIME RIGHT NOW!
THEY PROBABLY TAKE THE DAYTIME OFF.
KAW!

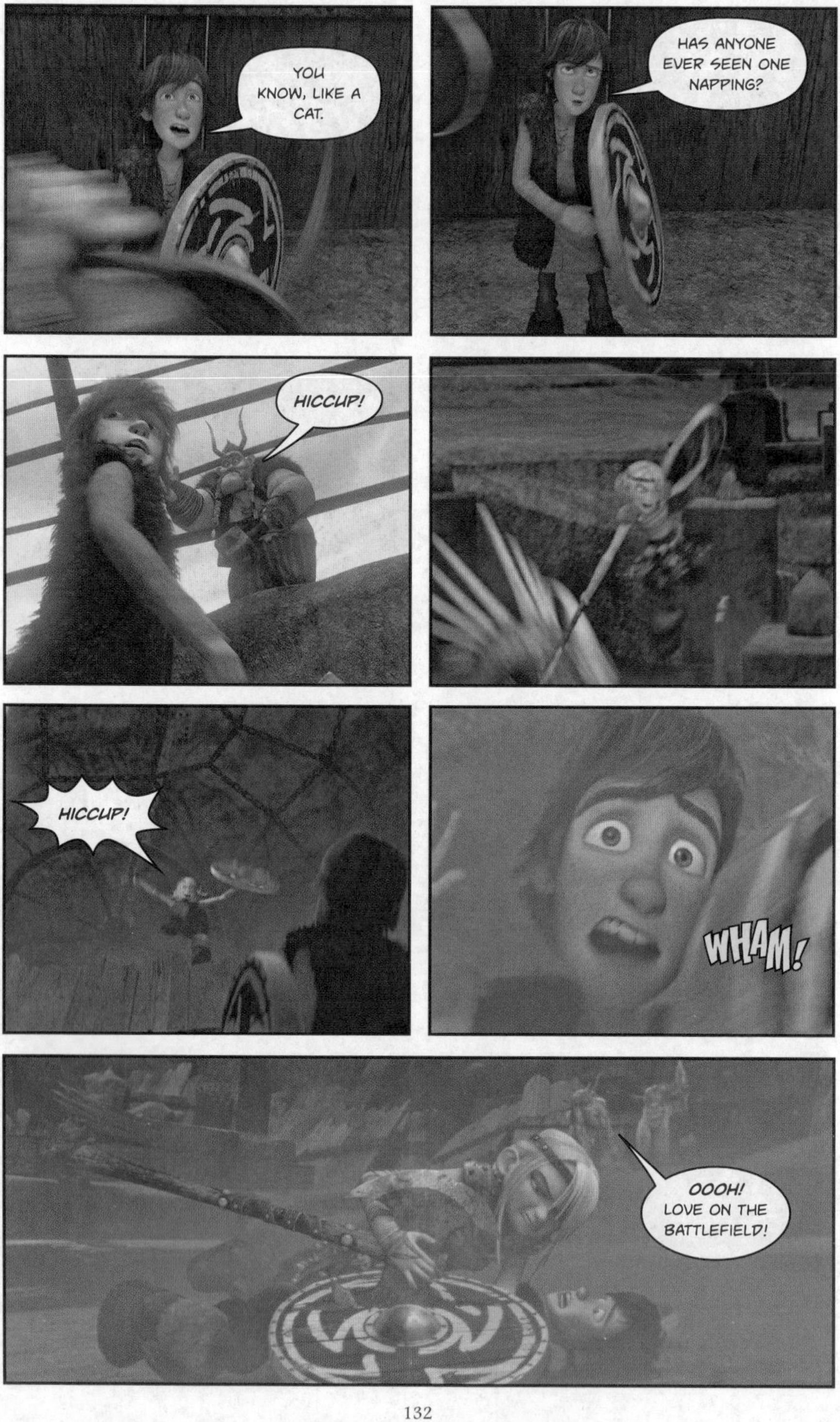
YOU KNOW, LIKE A CAT.
HAS ANYONE EVER SEEN ONE NAPPING?
HICCUP!
HICCUP!
WHAM!
OOOH! LOVE ON THE BATTLEFIELD!

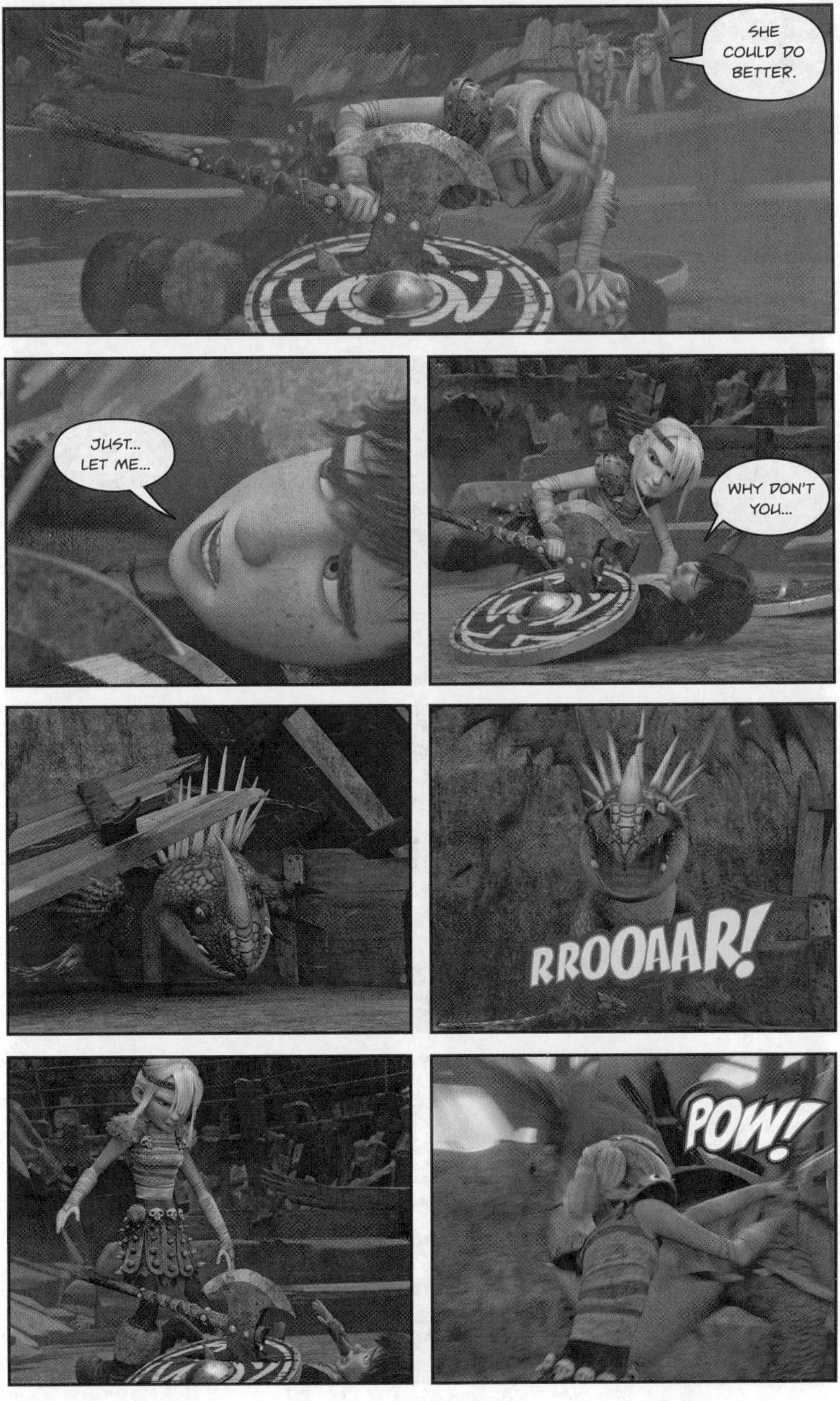
SHE COULD DO BETTER.
JUST... LET ME...
WHY DON'T YOU...
RROOAAR!
POW!

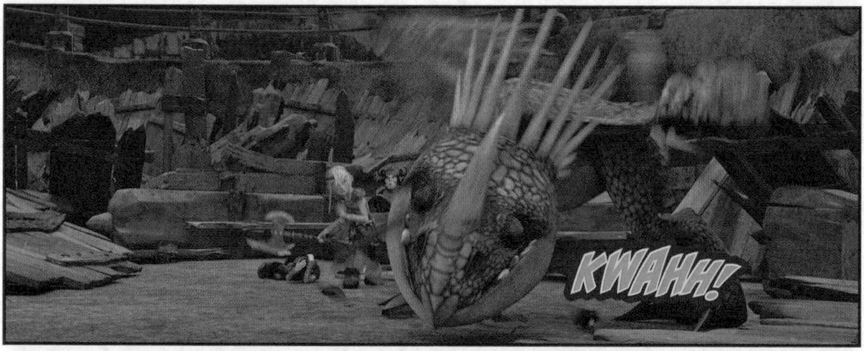
KWAHH!

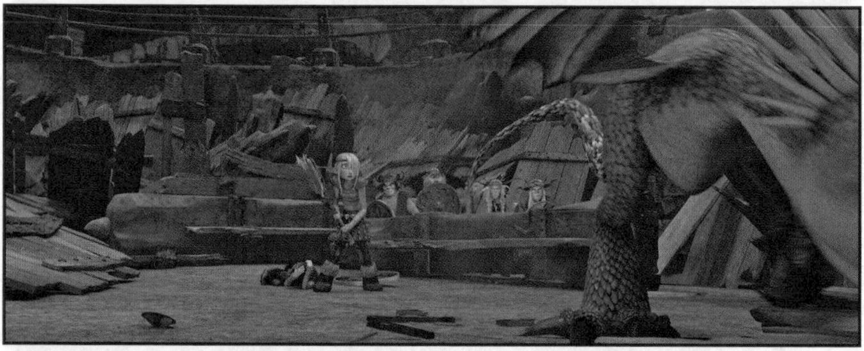

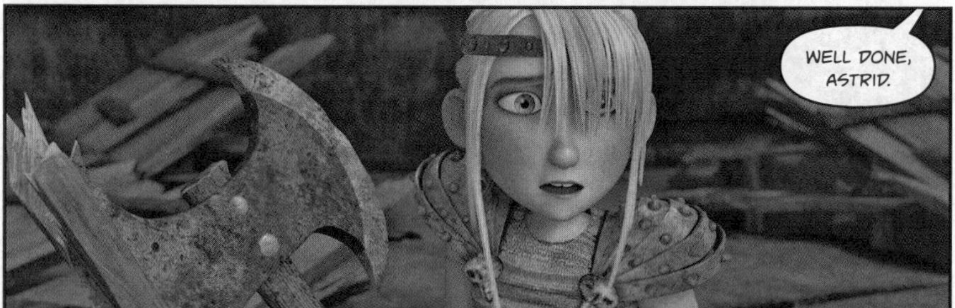
WELL DONE, ASTRID.

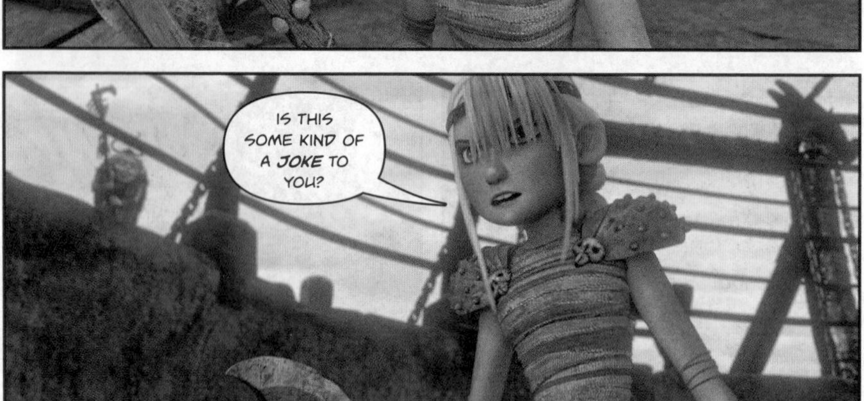
IS THIS SOME KIND OF A *JOKE* TO YOU?

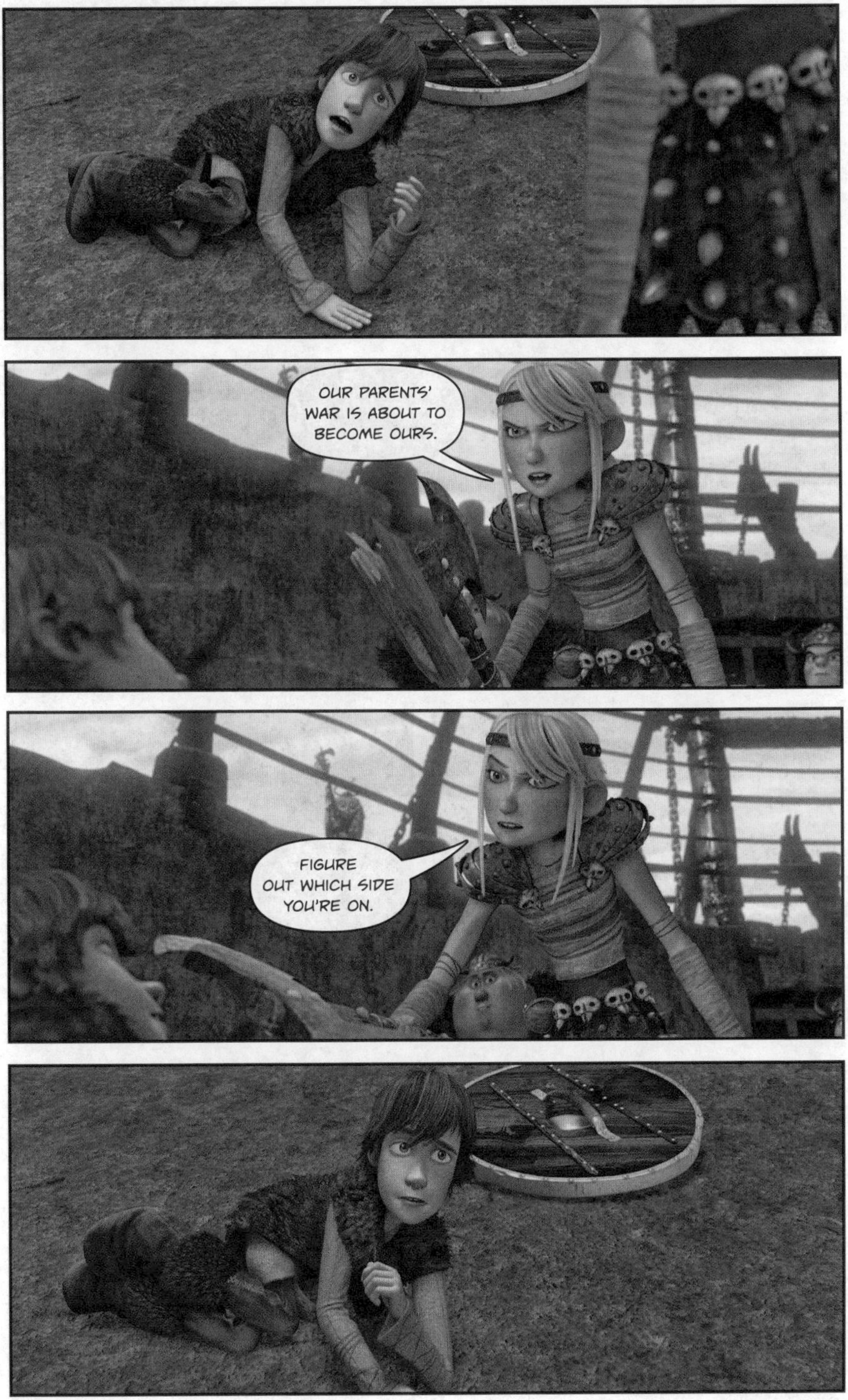
OUR PARENTS' WAR IS ABOUT TO BECOME OURS.
FIGURE OUT WHICH SIDE YOU'RE ON.

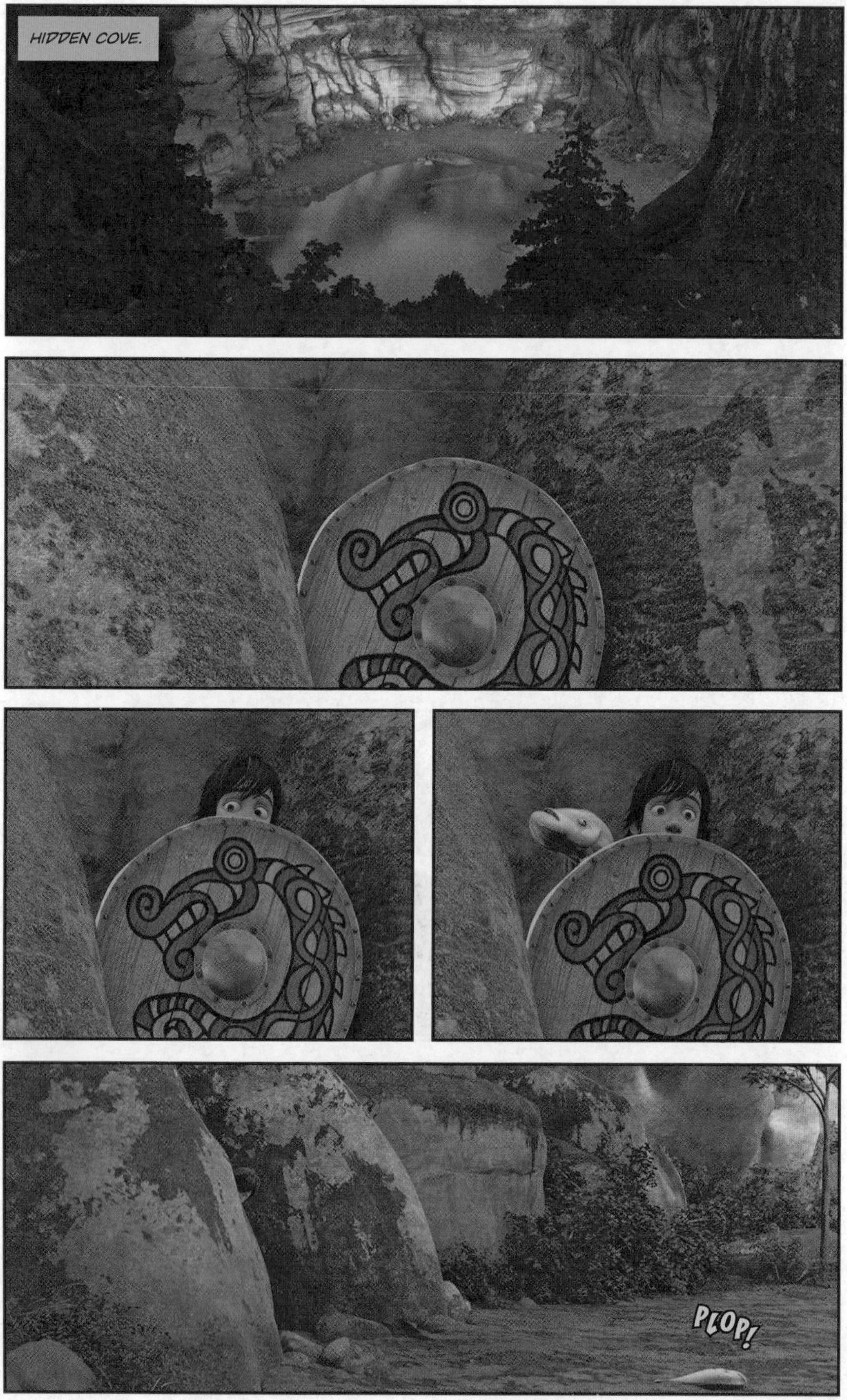
HIDDEN COVE.
PLOP!

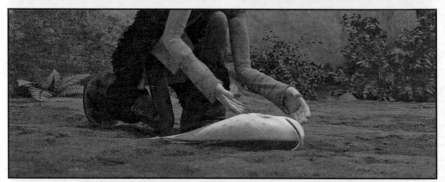

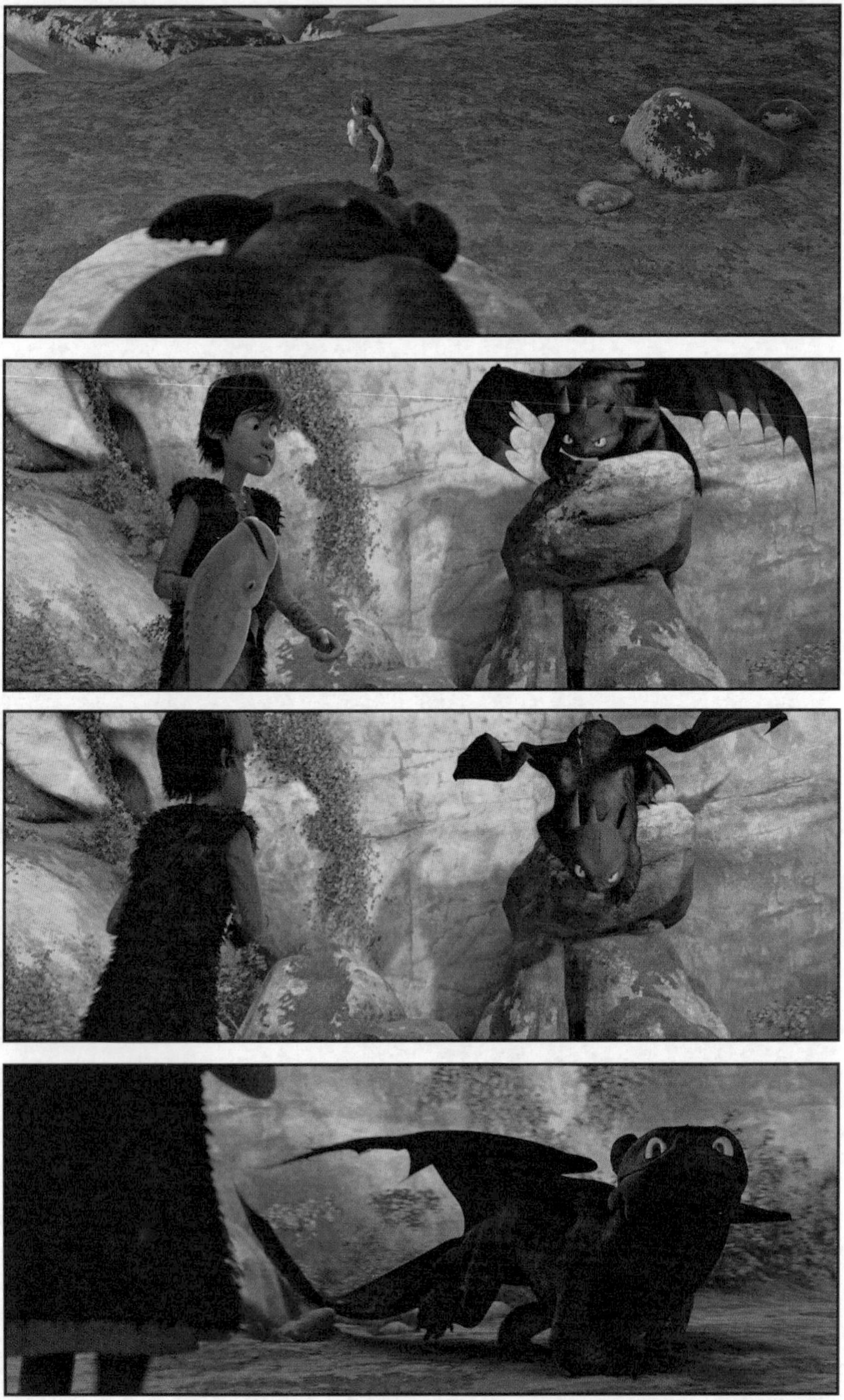

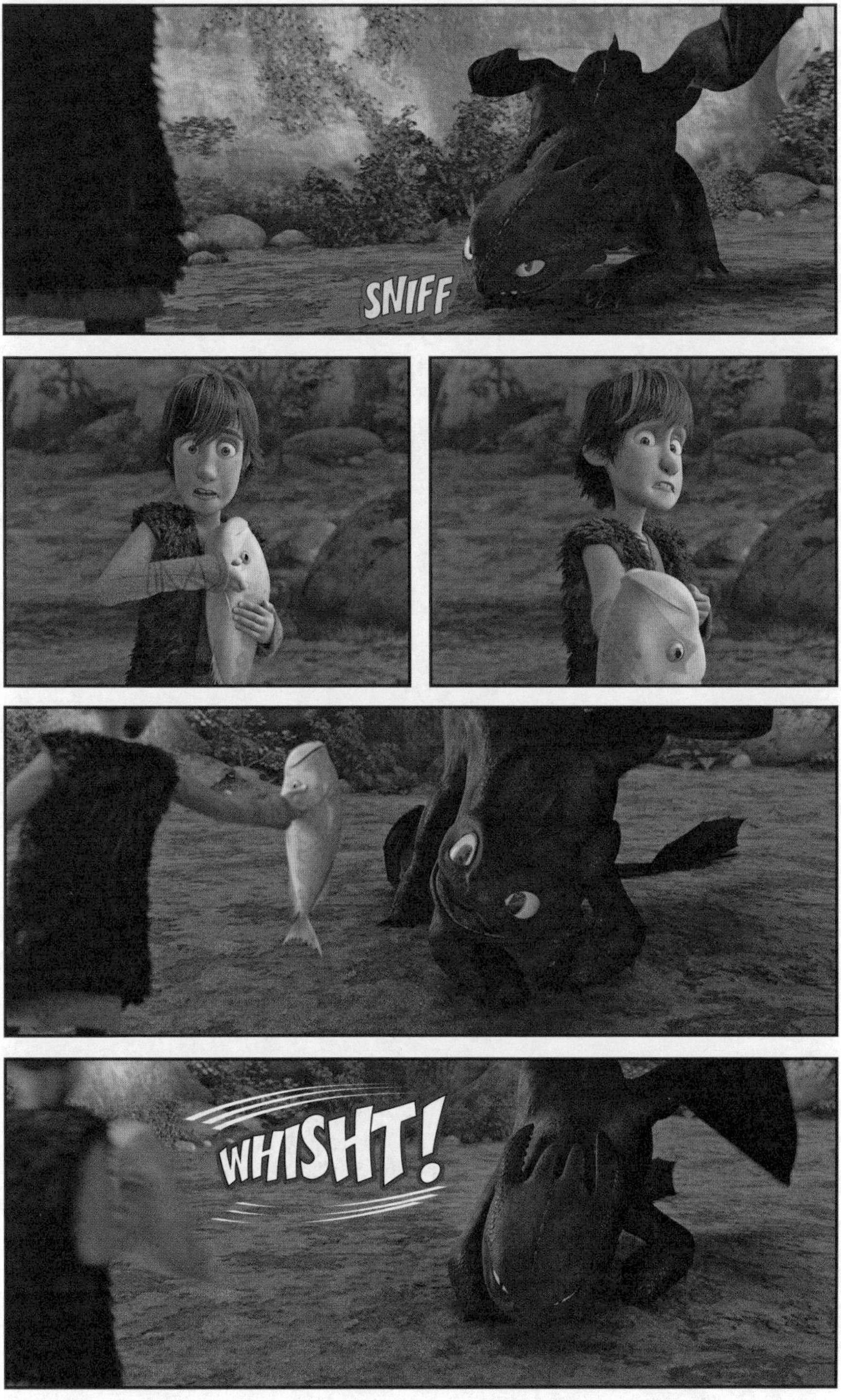
SNIFF
WHISHT!

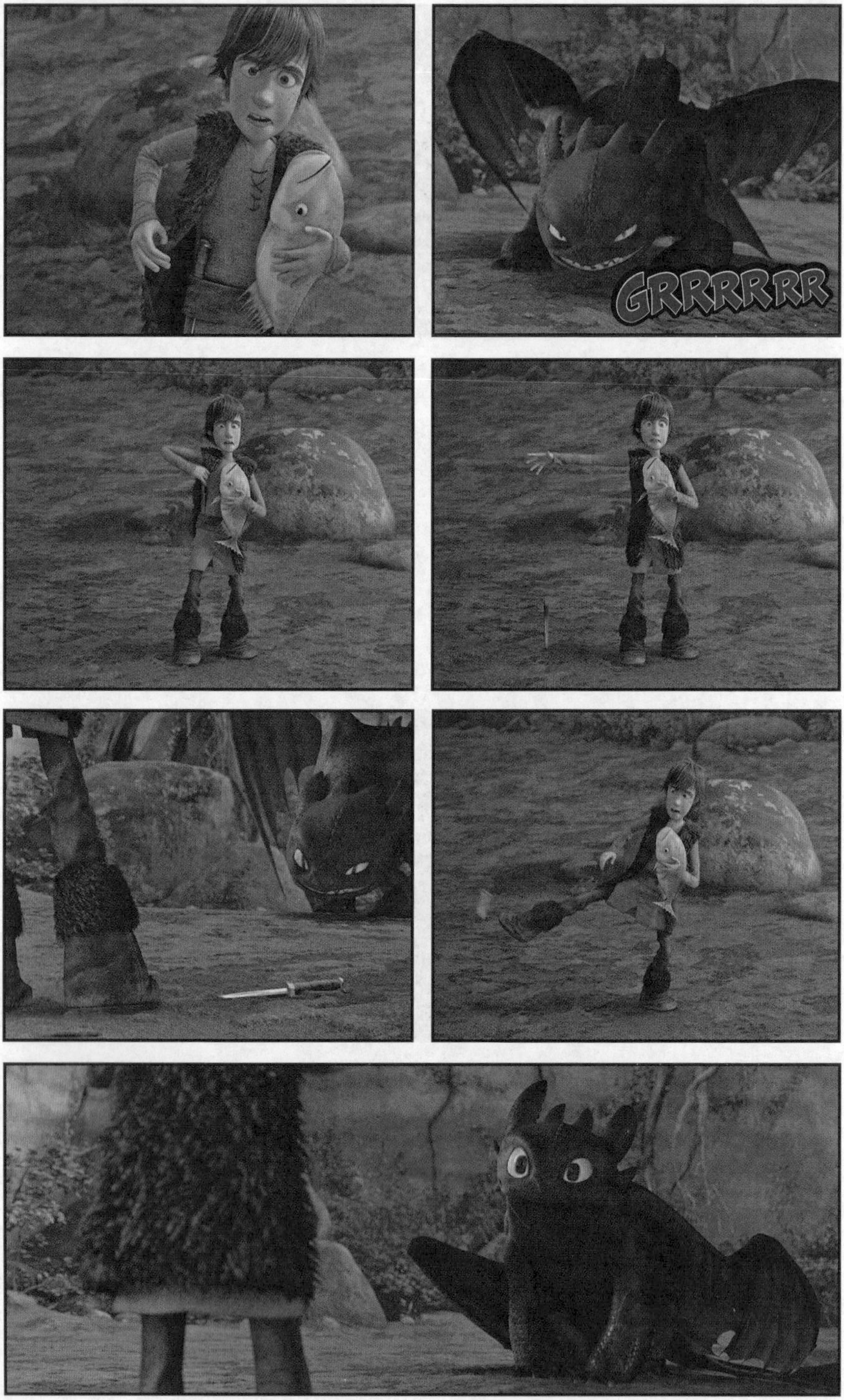
GRRRRRR

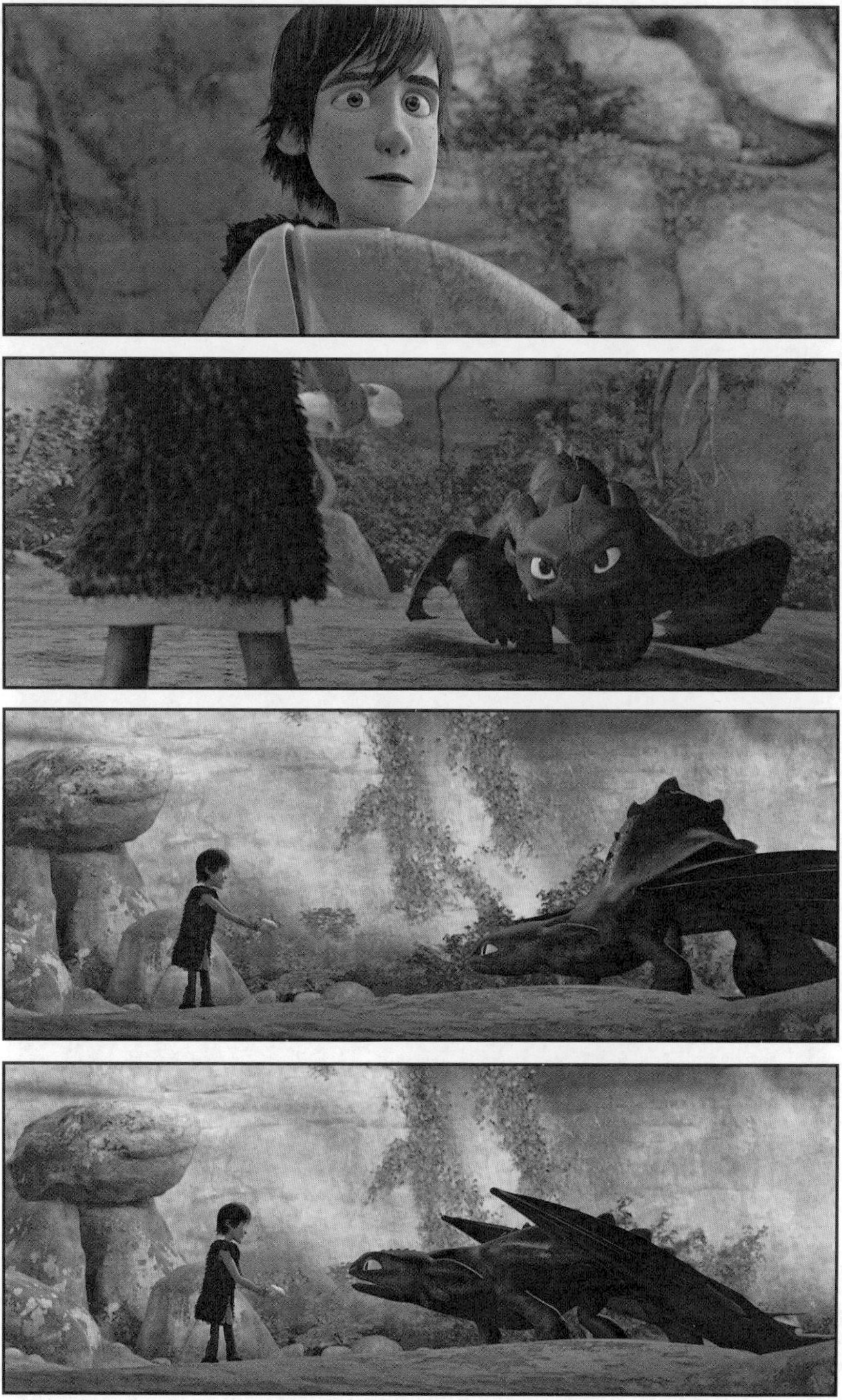

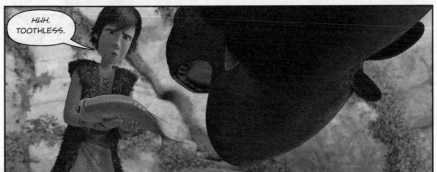

HUH.
TOOTHLESS.

I COULD'VE
SWORN YOU
HAD...

SPROING!

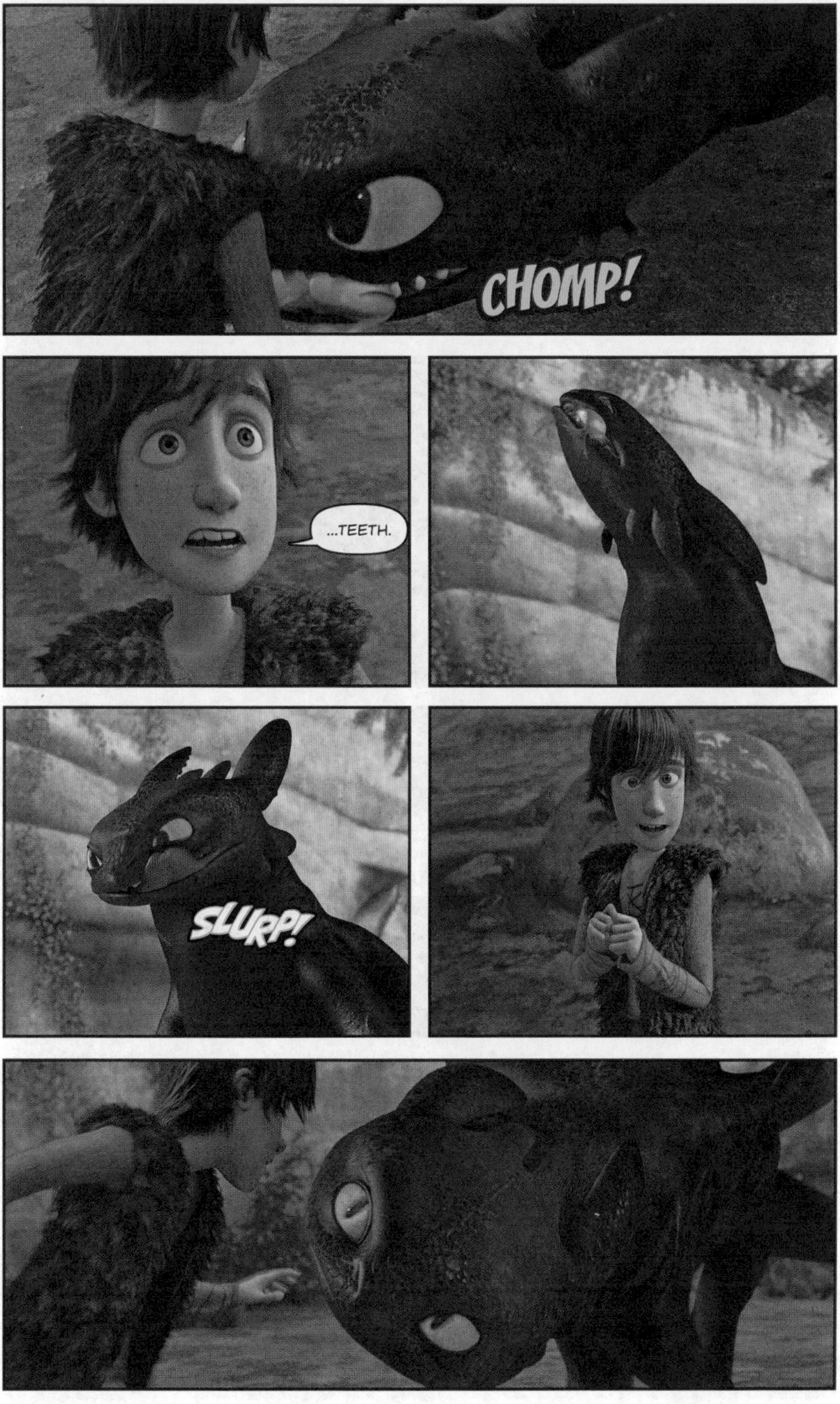
CHOMP!
...TEETH.
SLURP!

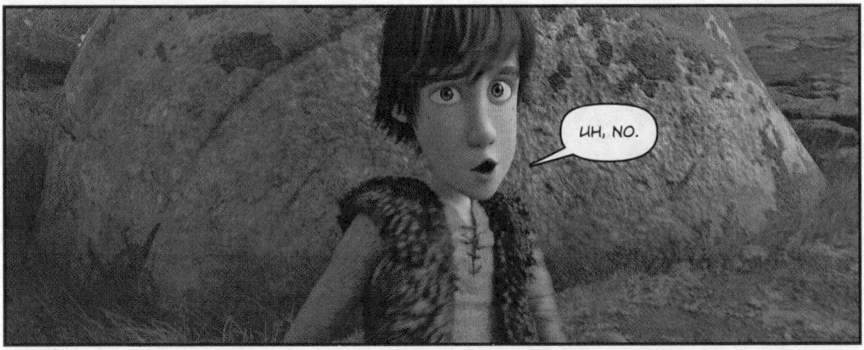
UH, NO.

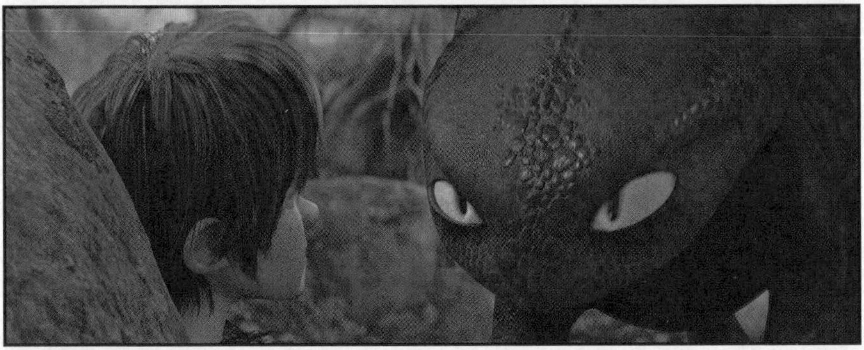

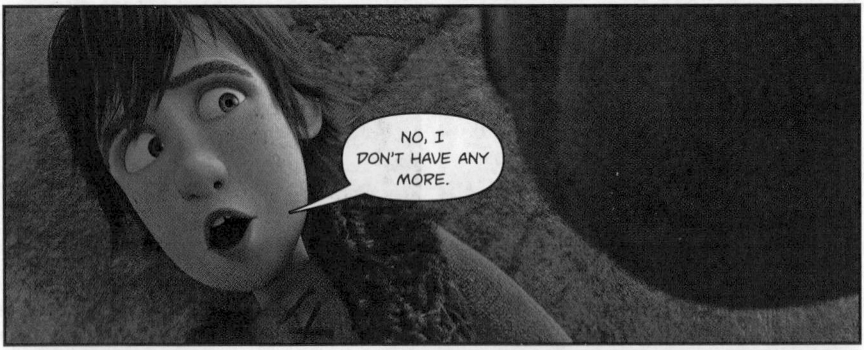
NO, I DON'T HAVE ANY MORE.

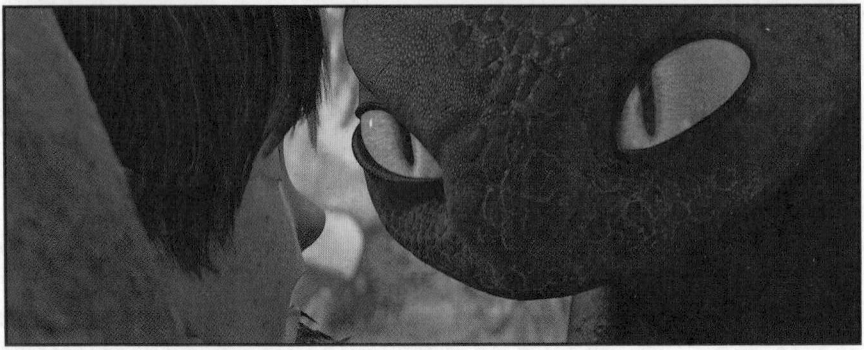

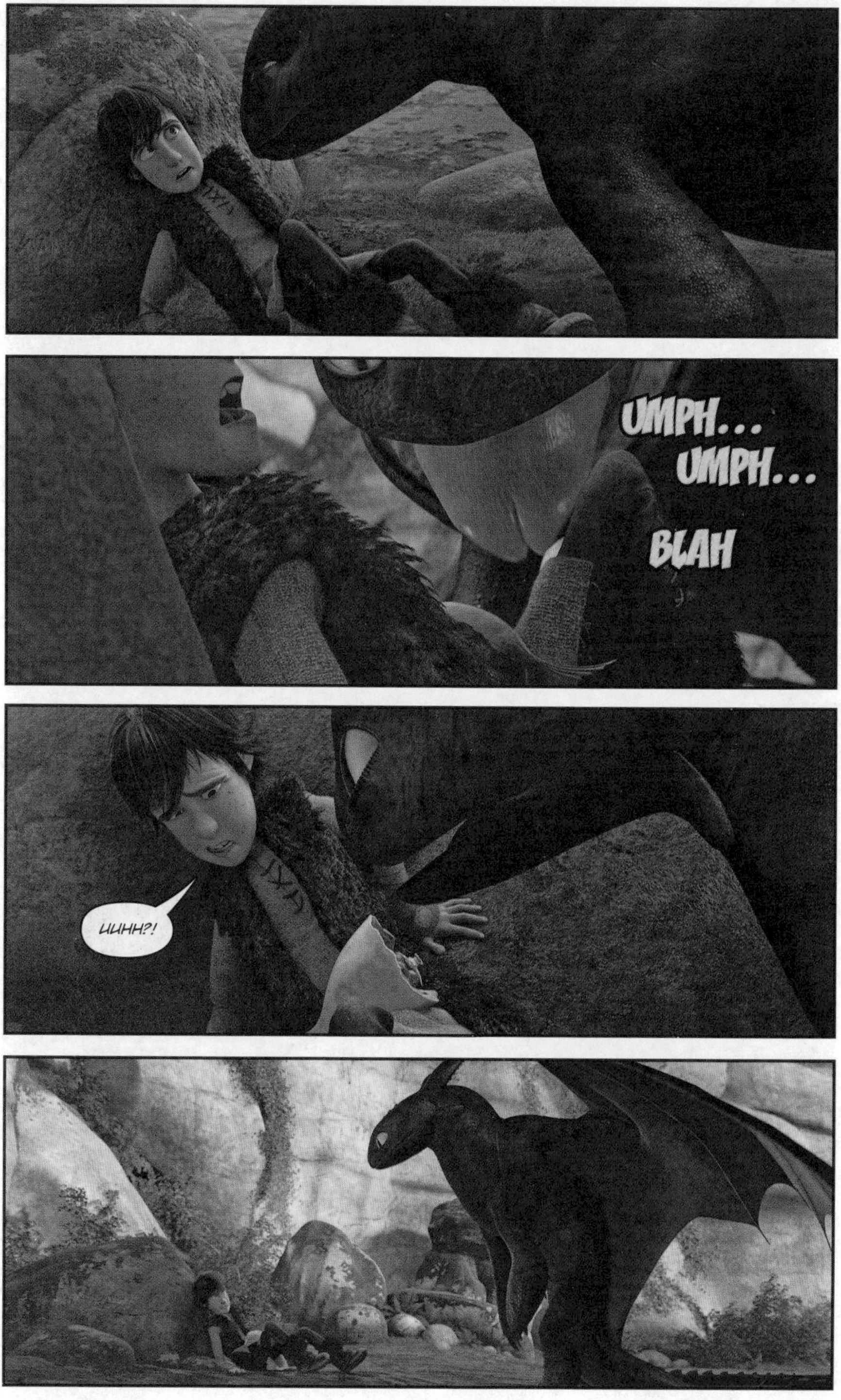
UMPH...
UMPH...
BLAH
UUHH?!

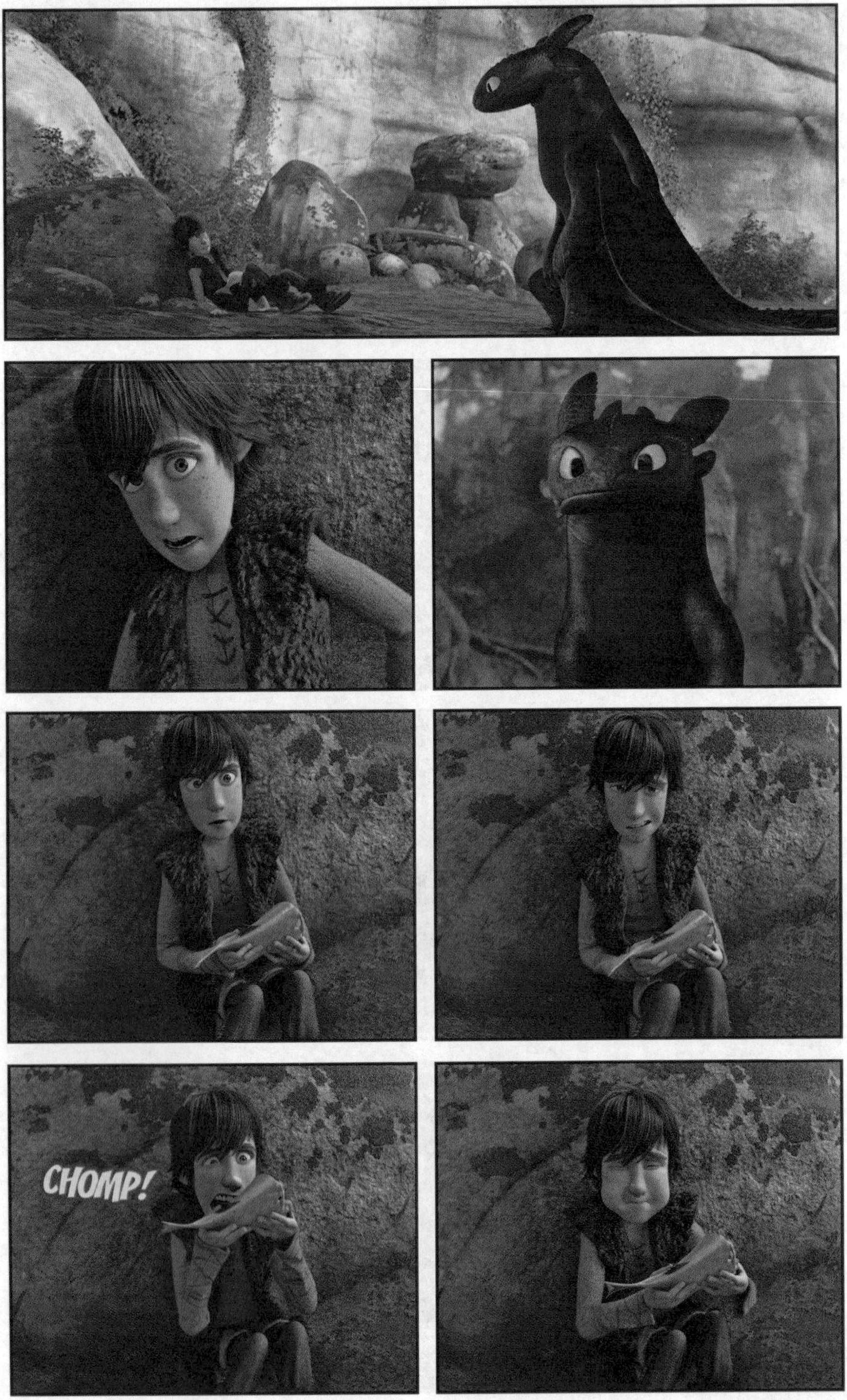
CHOMP!

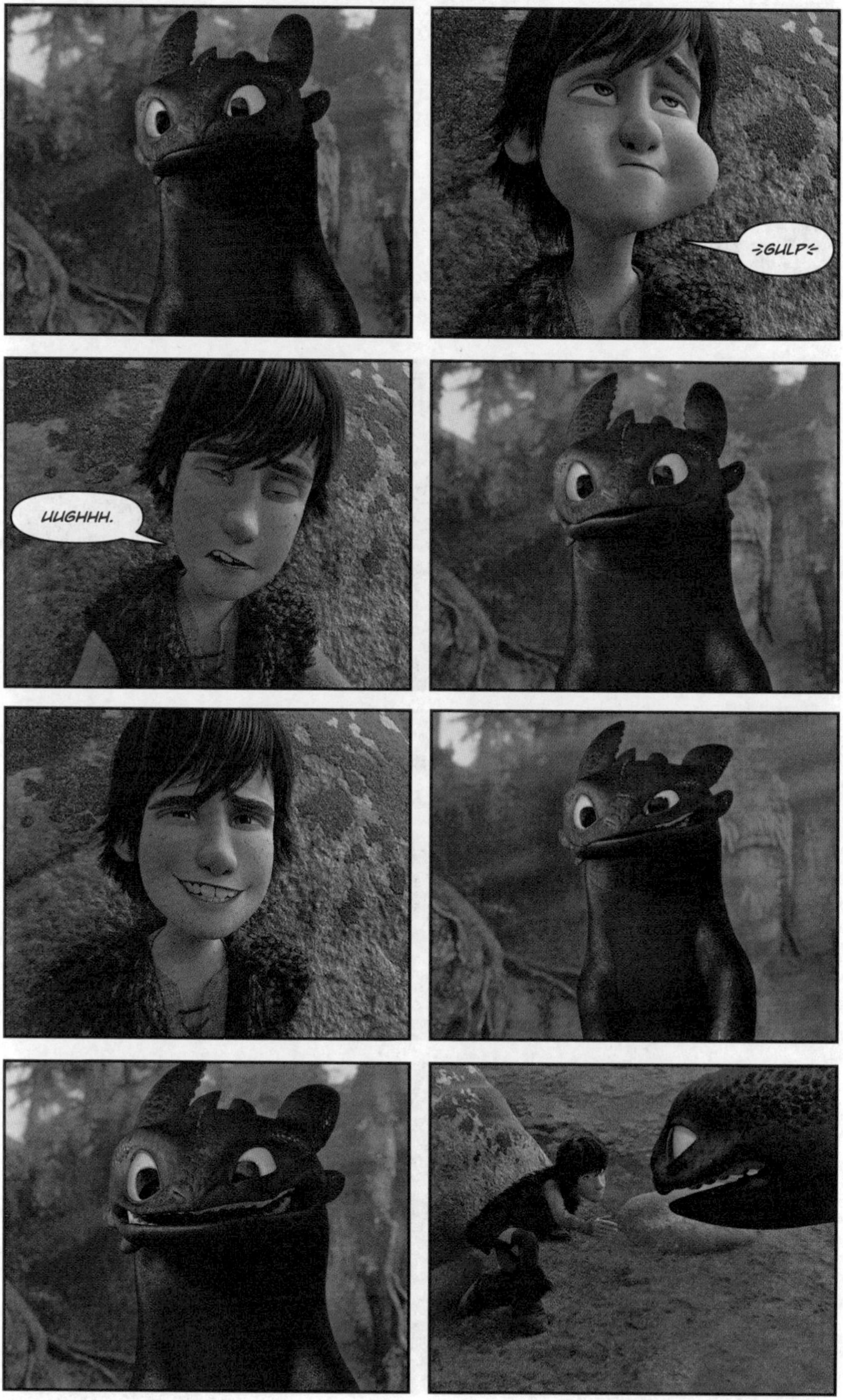
GULP
UUGHHH.

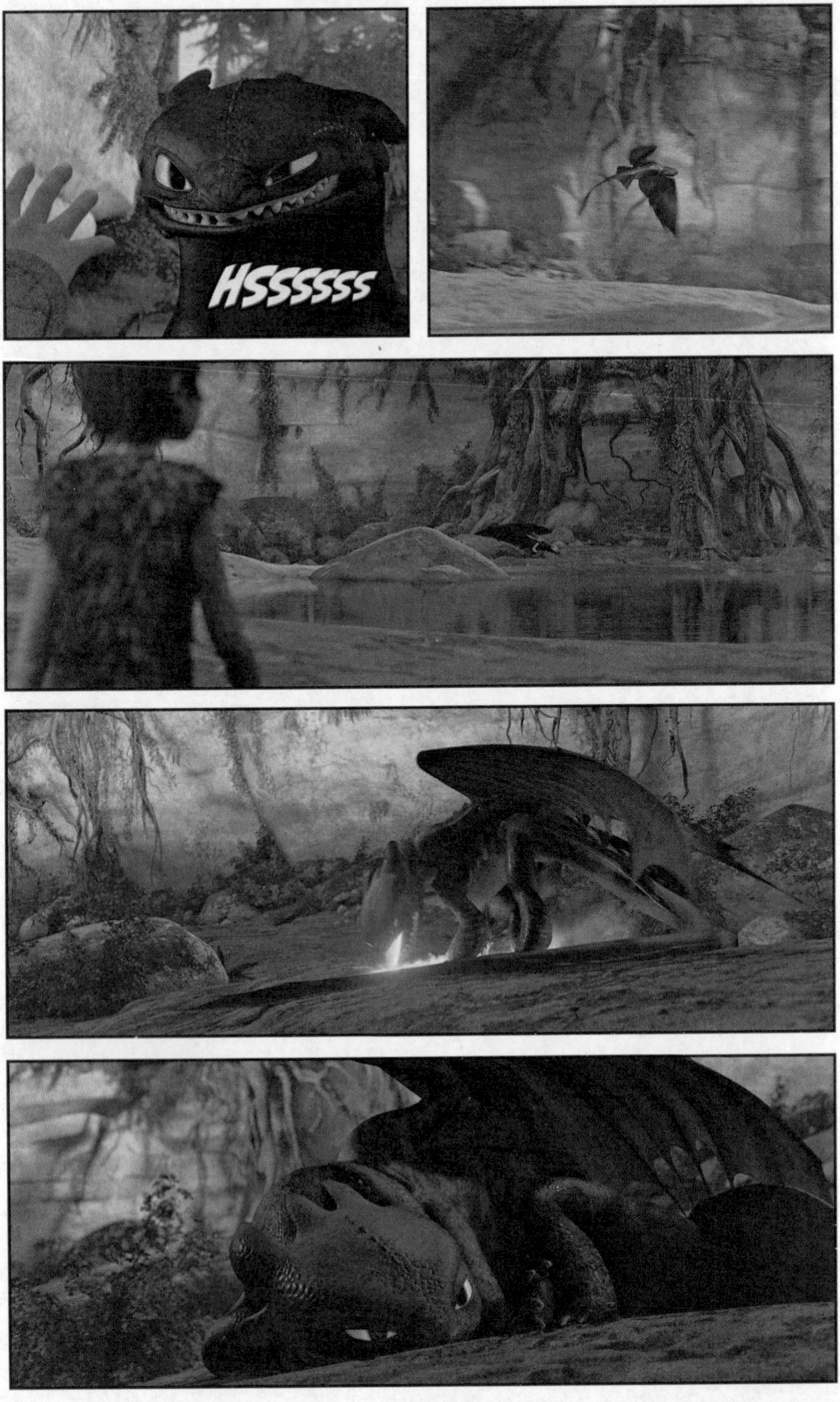
HSSSSSS

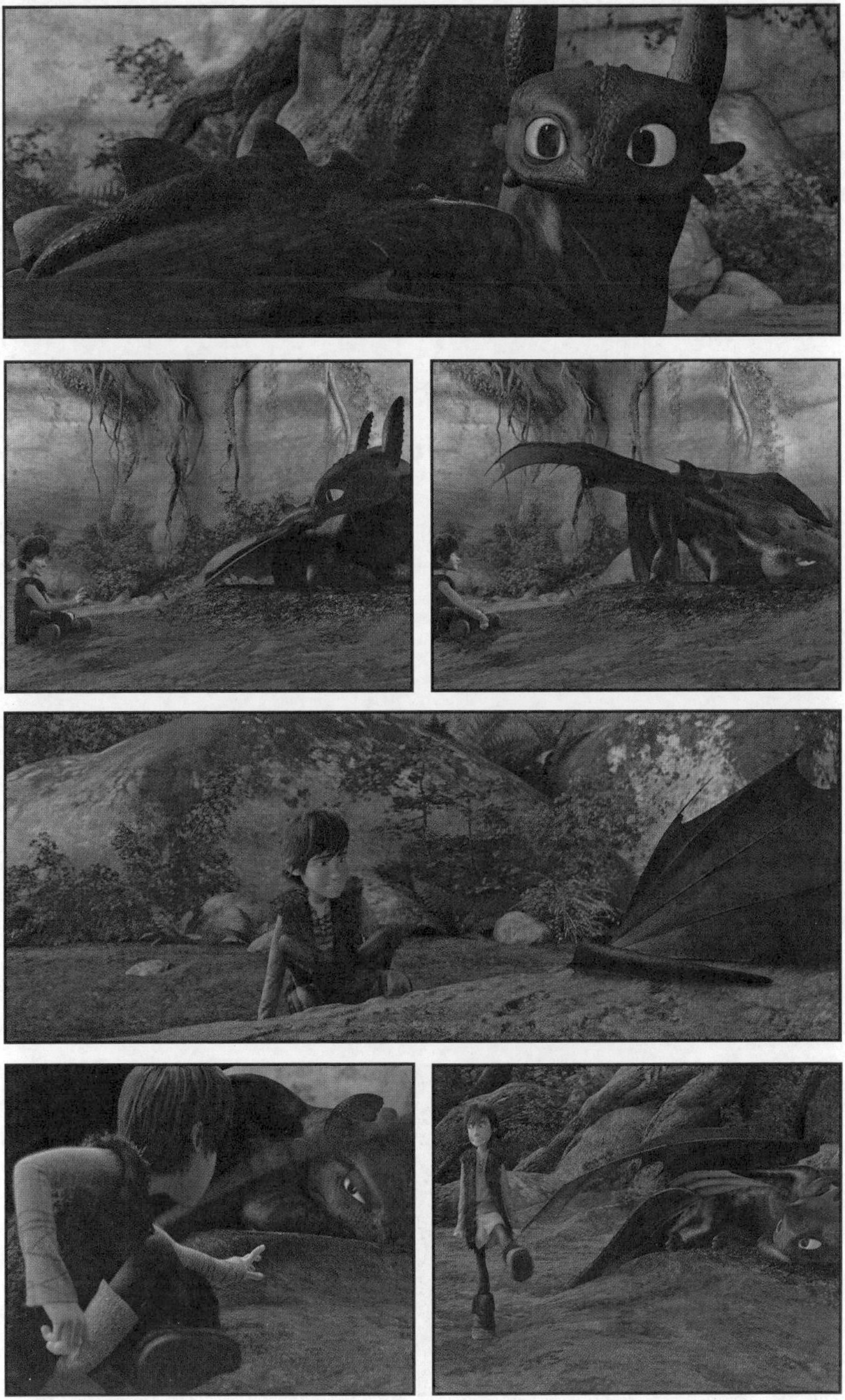

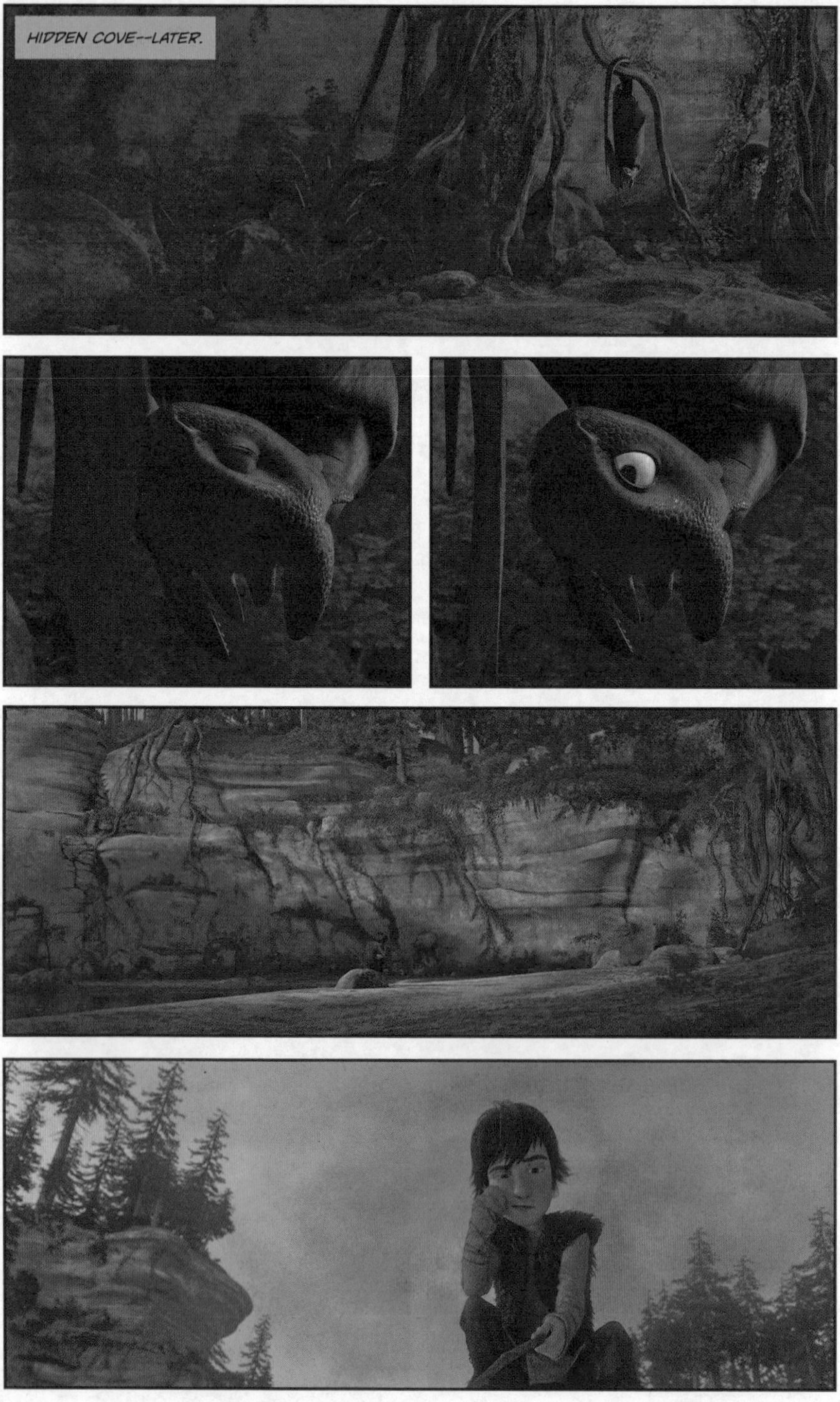
HIDDEN COVE--LATER.

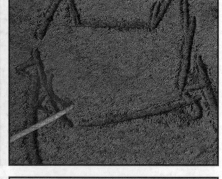

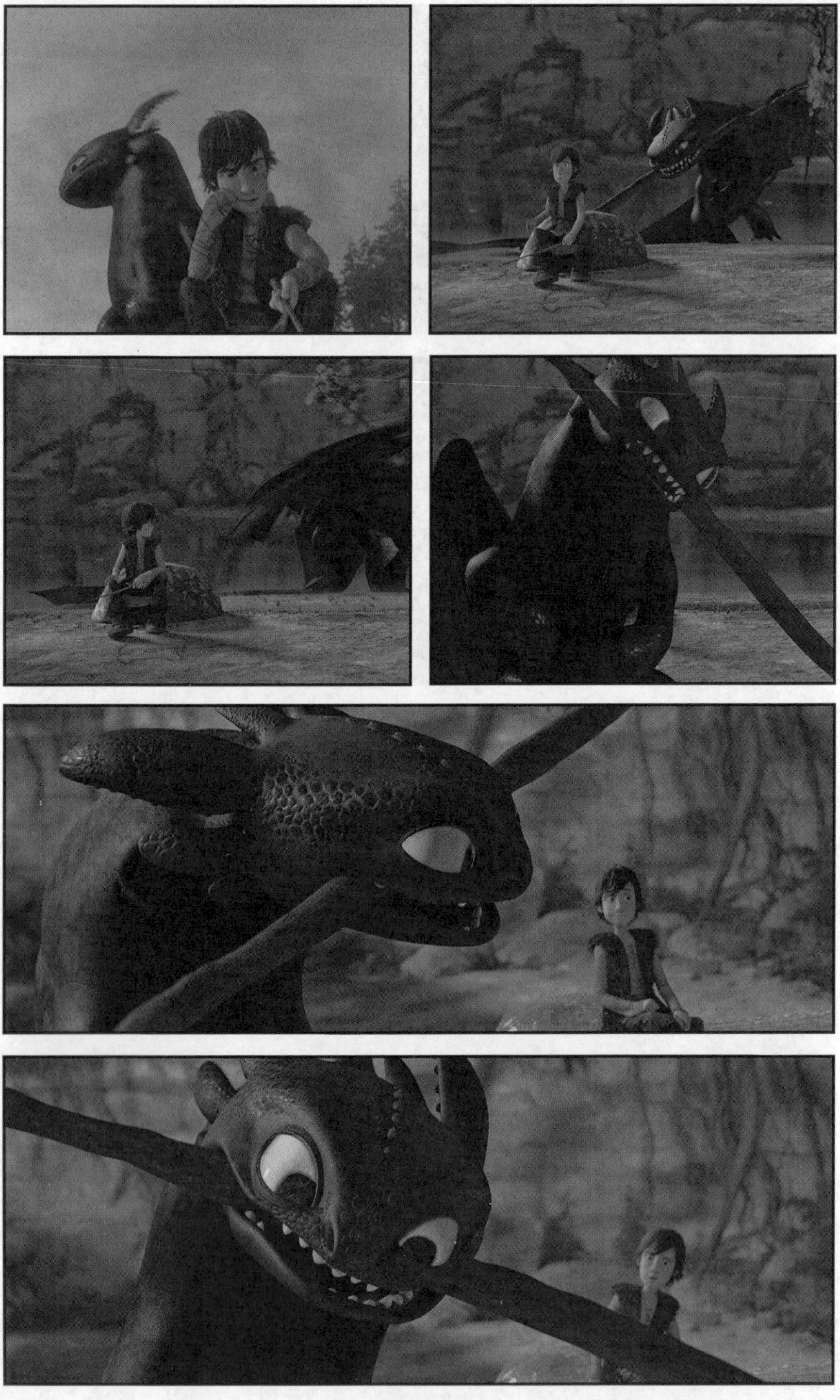

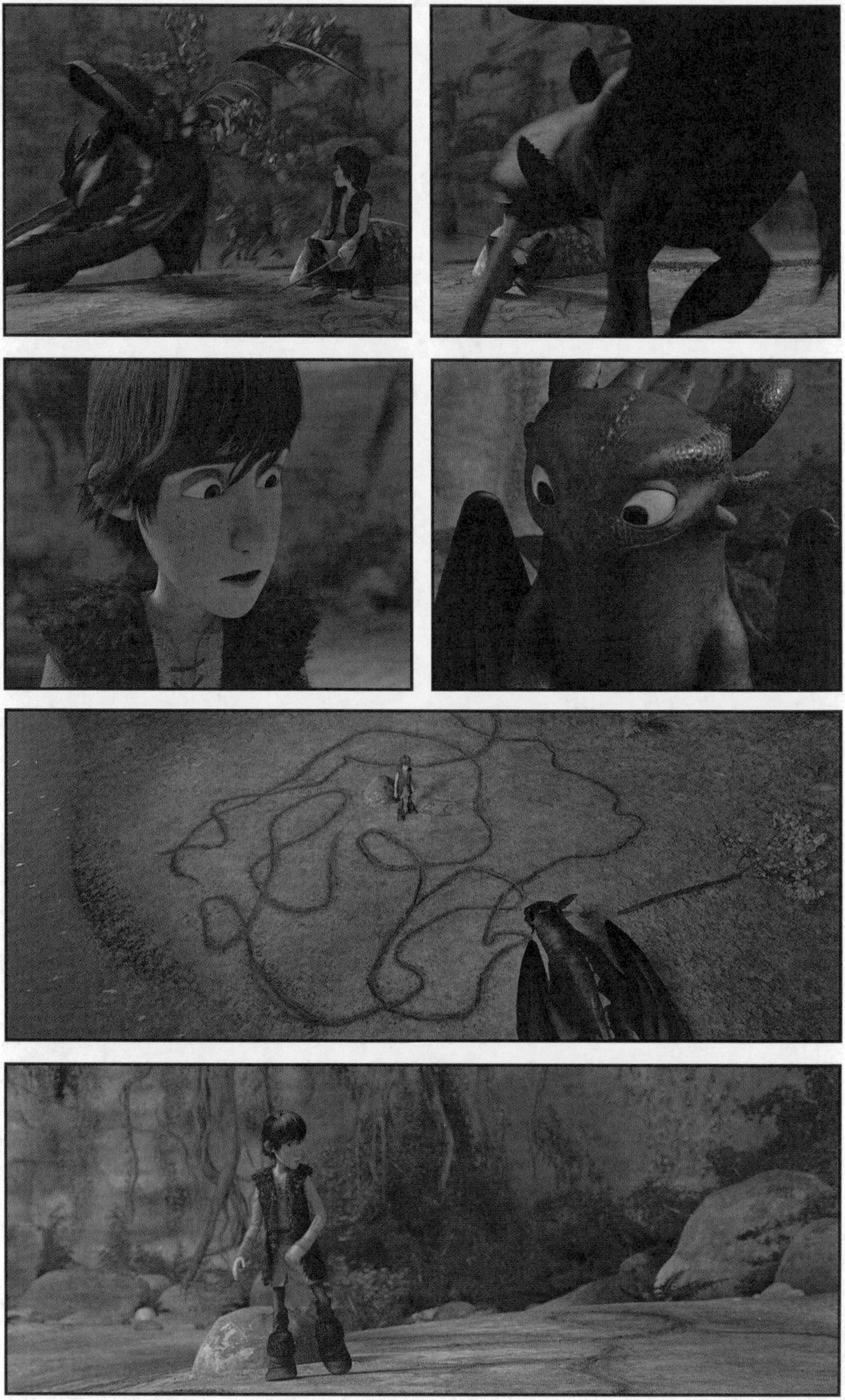

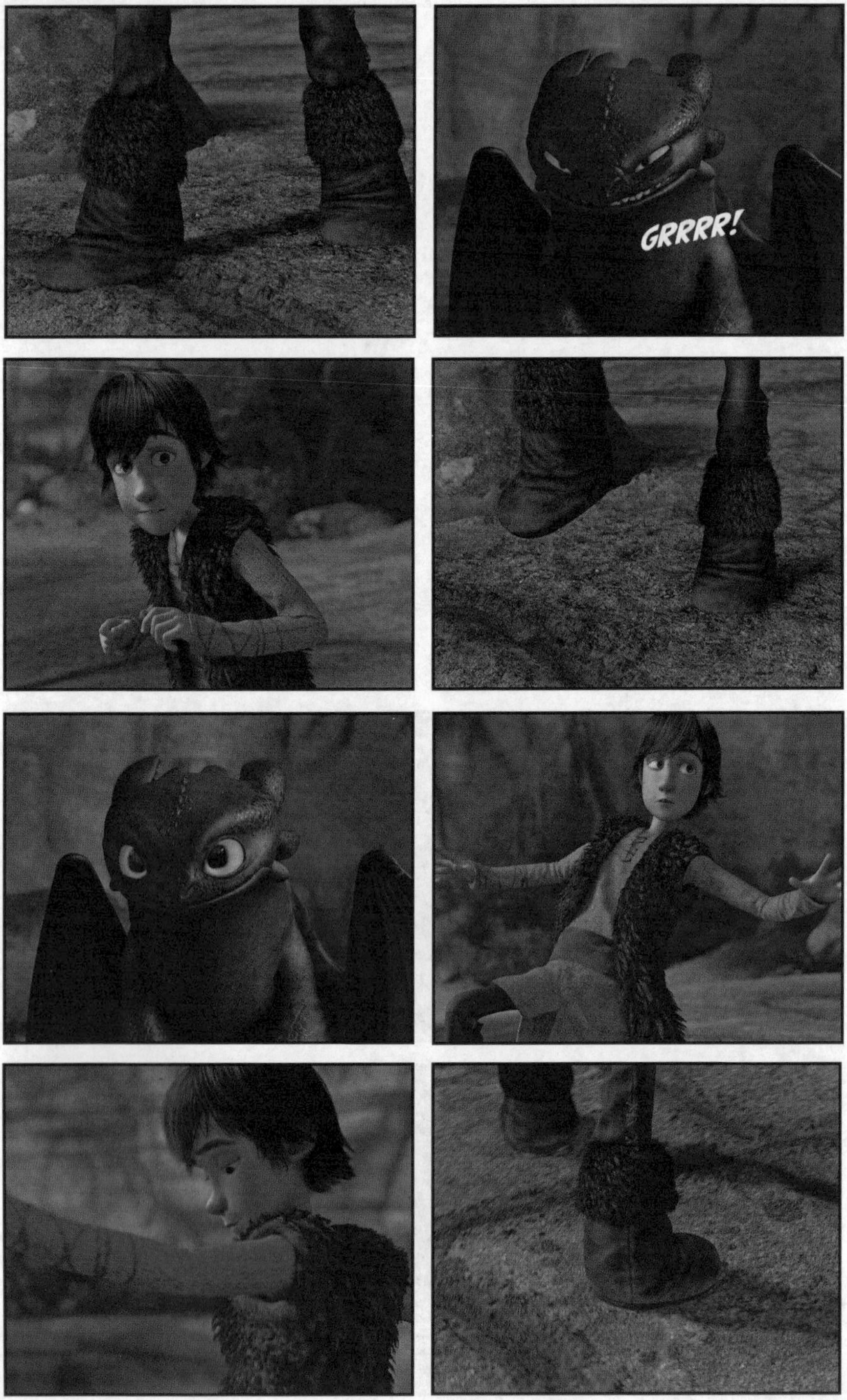
GRRRR!

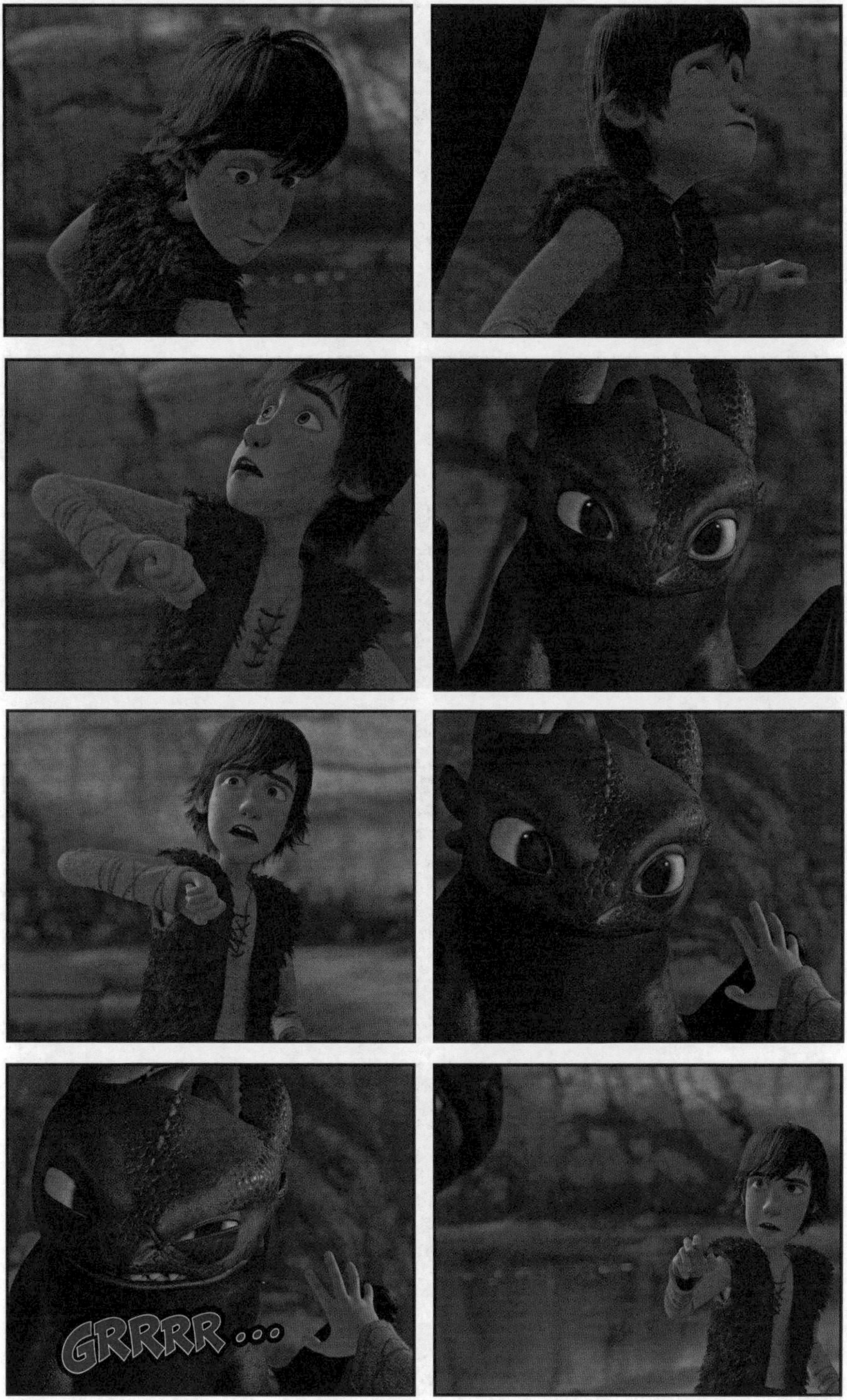
GRRRR ...

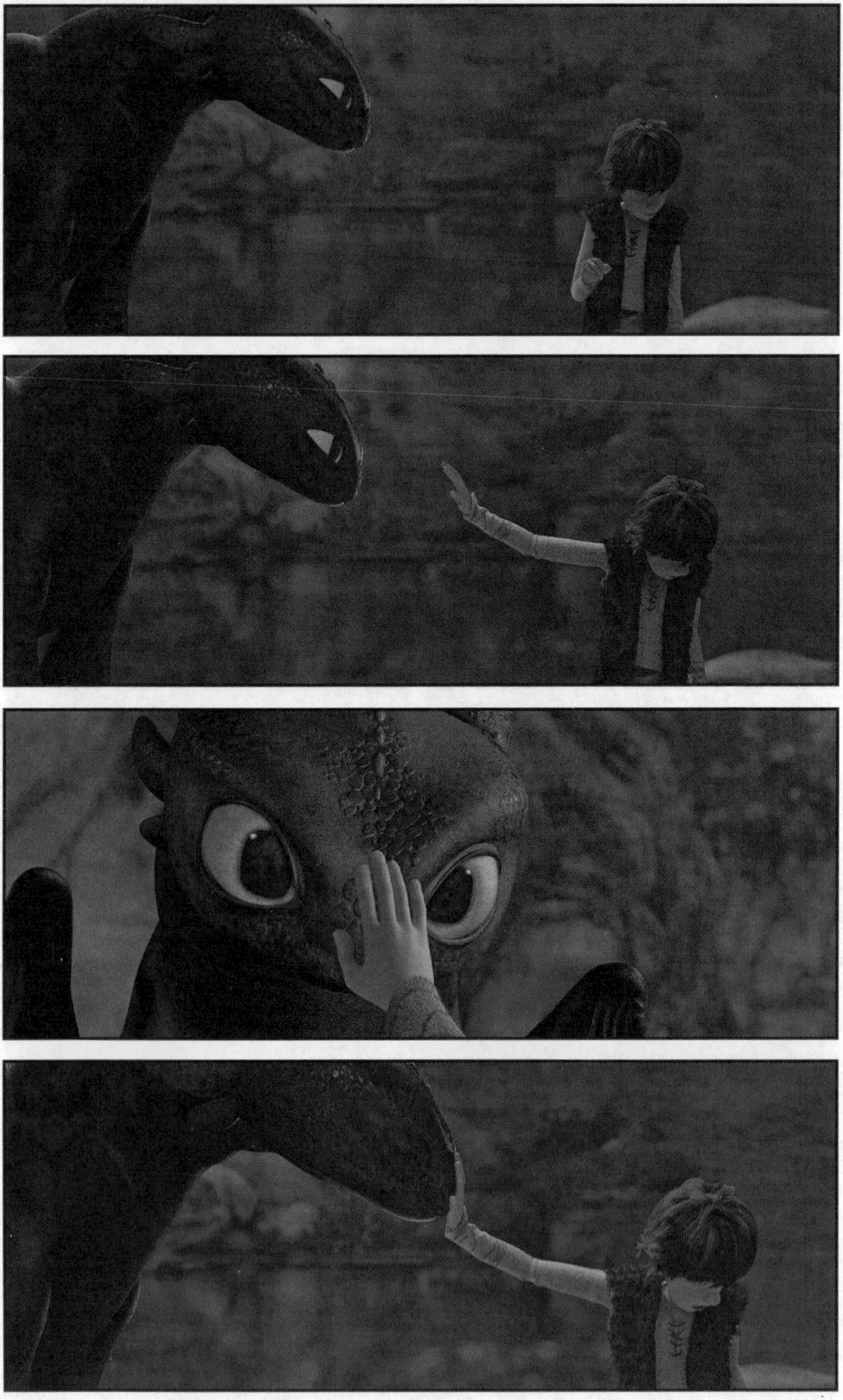

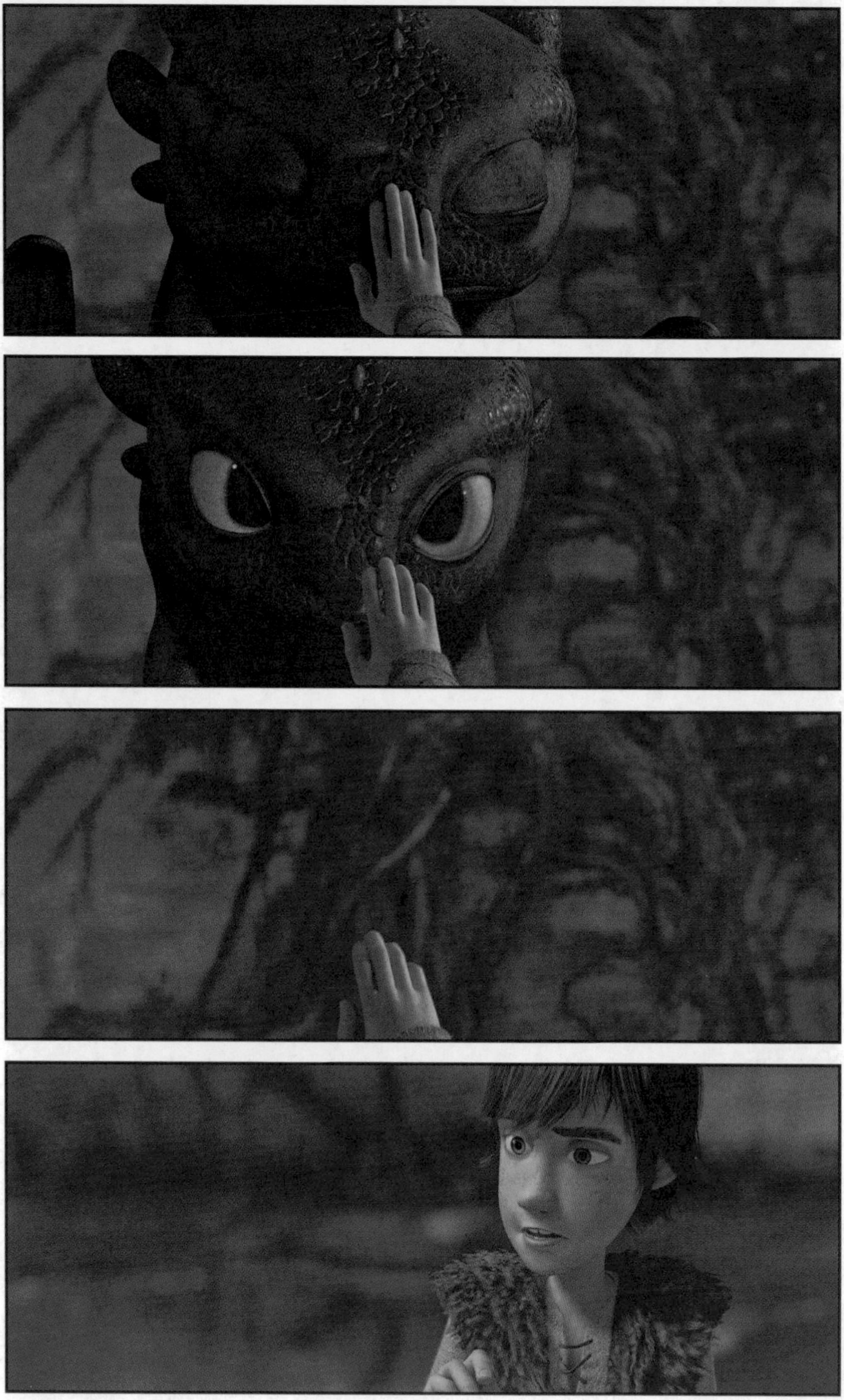

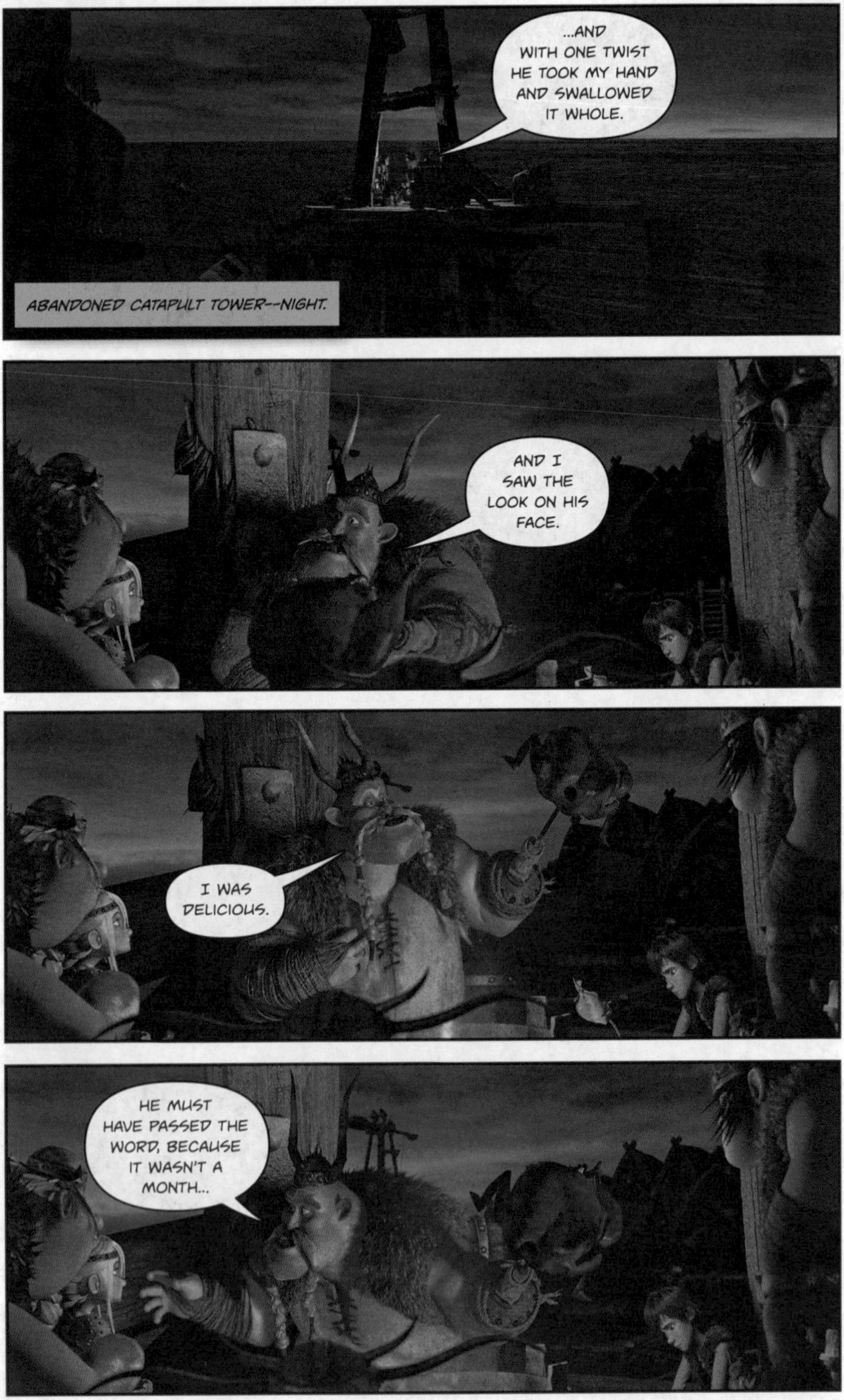
...AND WITH ONE TWIST HE TOOK MY HAND AND SWALLOWED IT WHOLE.
ABANDONED CATAPULT TOWER--NIGHT.
AND I SAW THE LOOK ON HIS FACE.
I WAS DELICIOUS.
HE MUST HAVE PASSED THE WORD, BECAUSE IT WASN'T A MONTH...

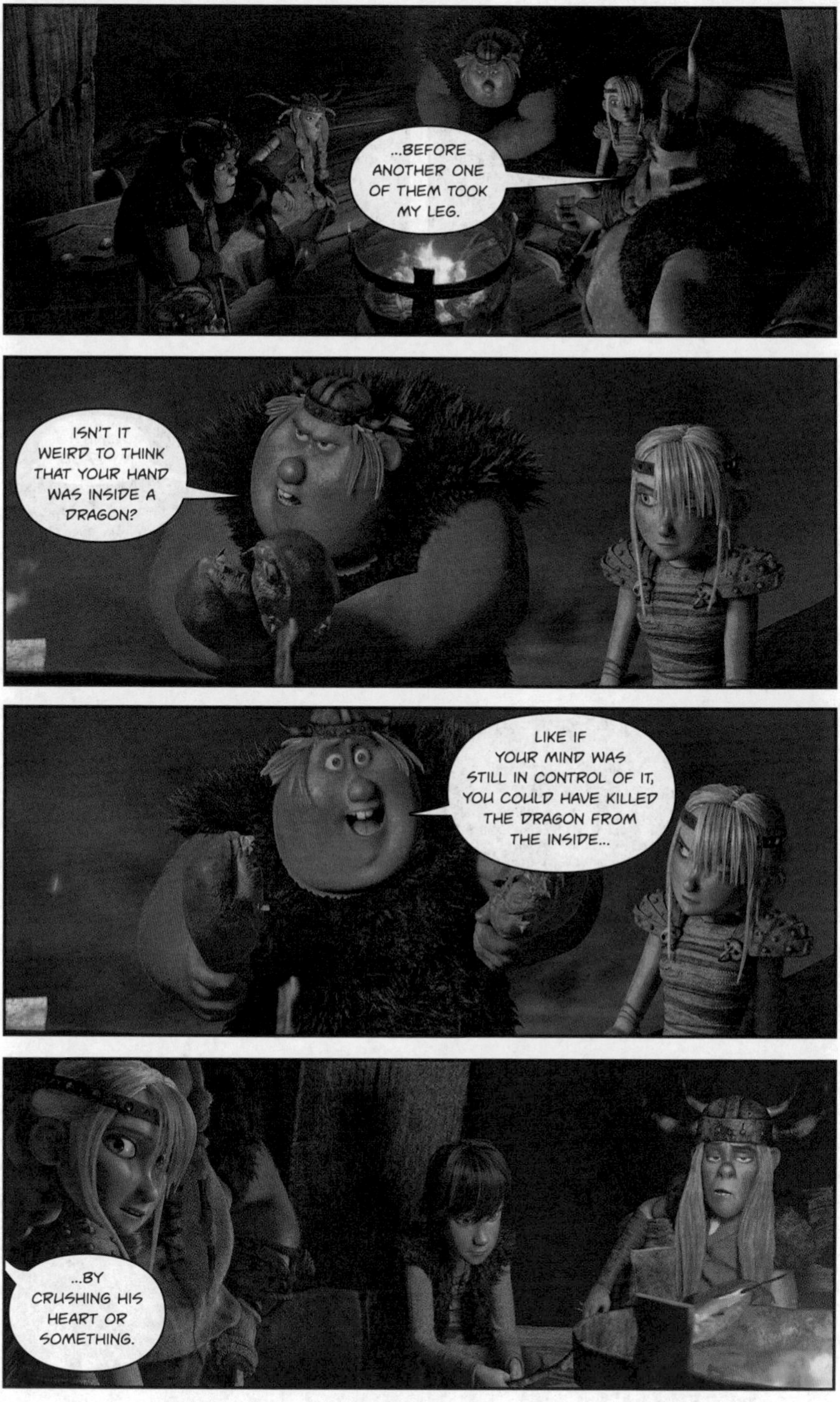
...BEFORE ANOTHER ONE OF THEM TOOK MY LEG.
ISN'T IT WEIRD TO THINK THAT YOUR HAND WAS INSIDE A DRAGON?
LIKE IF YOUR MIND WAS STILL IN CONTROL OF IT, YOU COULD HAVE KILLED THE DRAGON FROM THE INSIDE...
...BY CRUSHING HIS HEART OR SOMETHING.

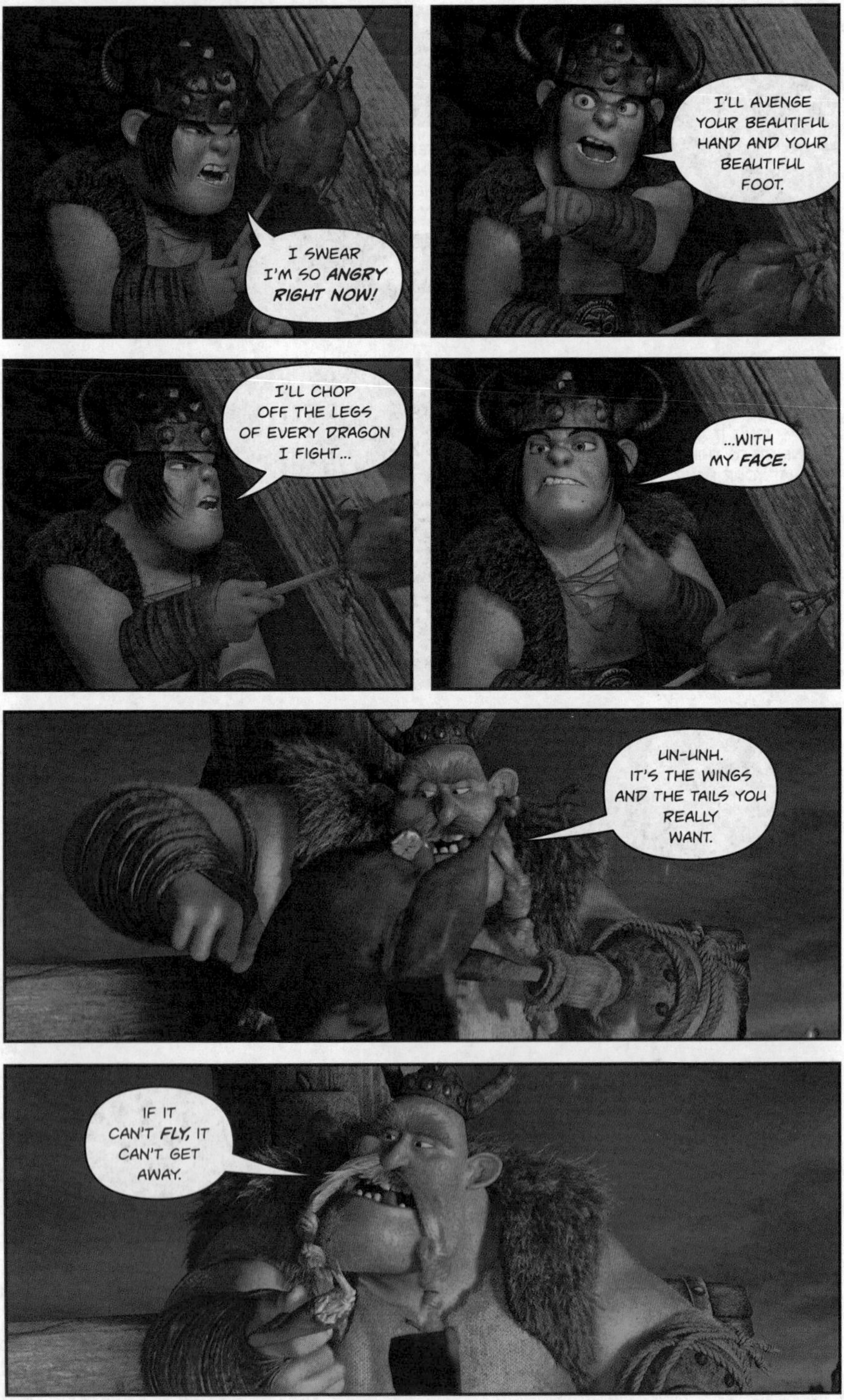
I SWEAR I'M SO ANGRY RIGHT NOW!
I'LL AVENGE YOUR BEAUTIFUL HAND AND YOUR BEAUTIFUL FOOT.
I'LL CHOP OFF THE LEGS OF EVERY DRAGON I FIGHT...
...WITH MY FACE.
UN-UNH. IT'S THE WINGS AND THE TAILS YOU REALLY WANT.
IF IT CAN'T FLY, IT CAN'T GET AWAY.

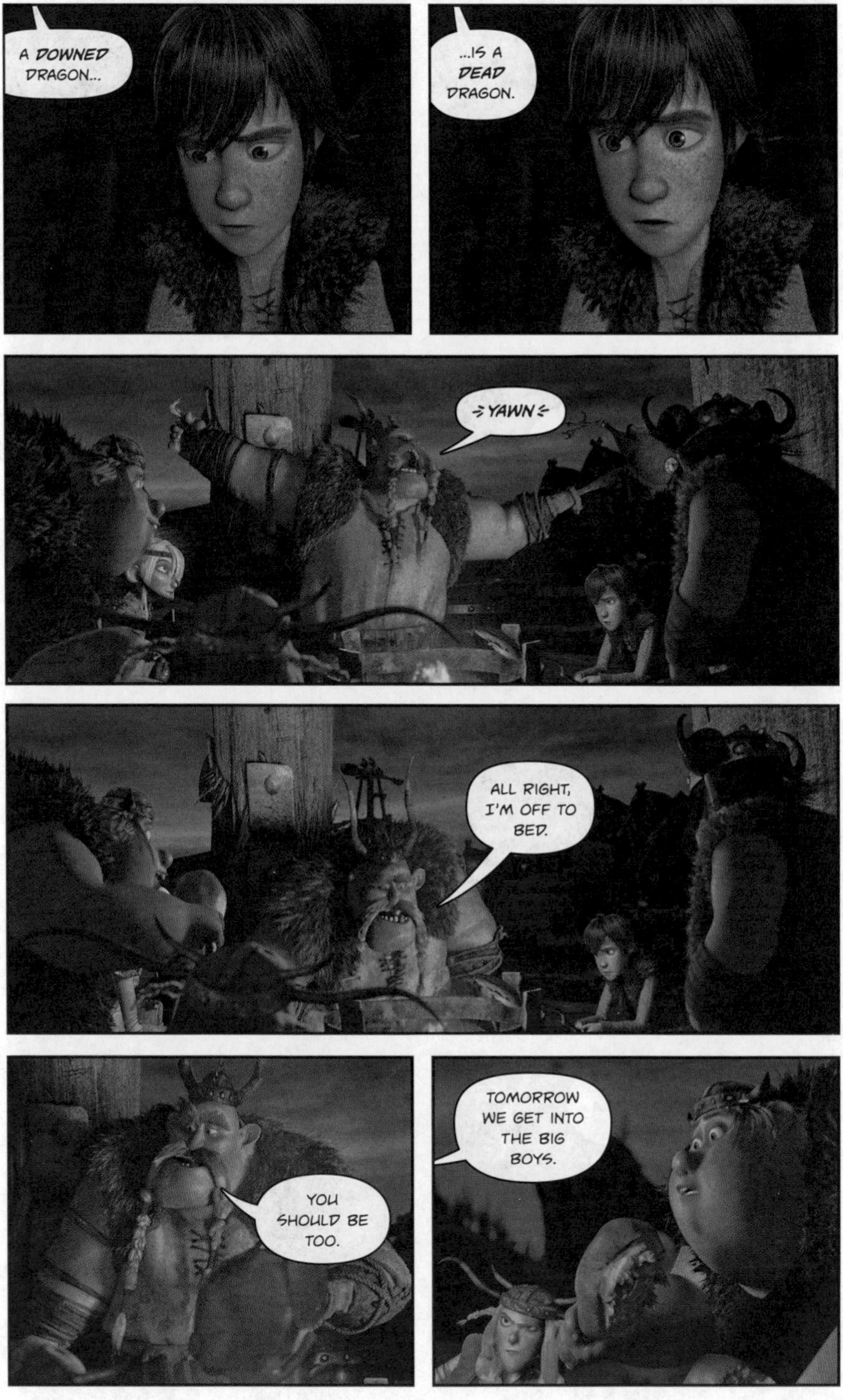
A DOWNED DRAGON...
...IS A DEAD DRAGON.
YAWN
ALL RIGHT, I'M OFF TO BED.
YOU SHOULD BE TOO.
TOMORROW WE GET INTO THE BIG BOYS.

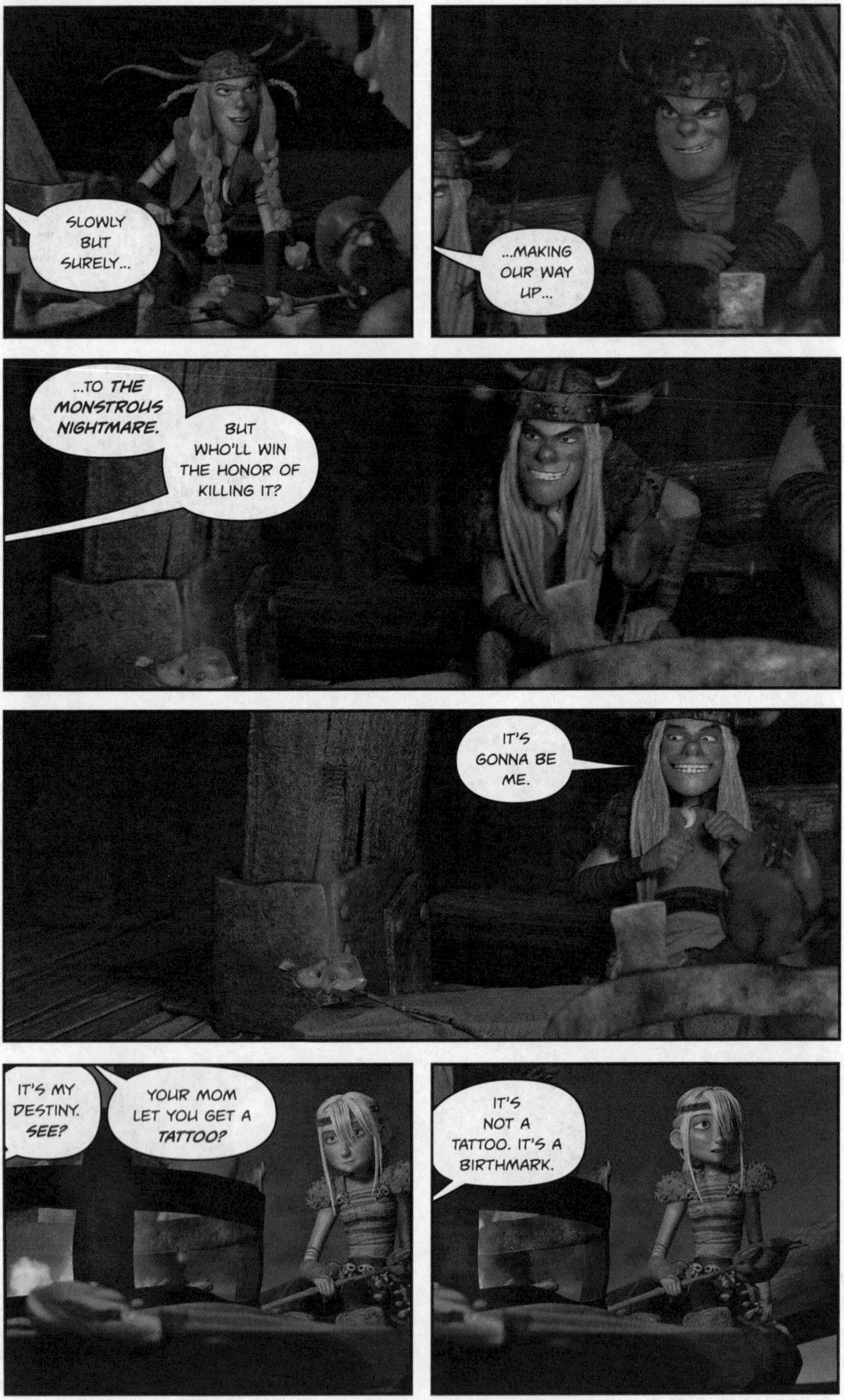
SLOWLY BUT SURELY...
...MAKING OUR WAY UP...
...TO THE MONSTROUS NIGHTMARE.
BUT WHO'LL WIN THE HONOR OF KILLING IT?
IT'S GONNA BE ME.
IT'S MY DESTINY. SEE?
YOUR MOM LET YOU GET A TATTOO?
IT'S NOT A TATTOO. IT'S A BIRTHMARK.

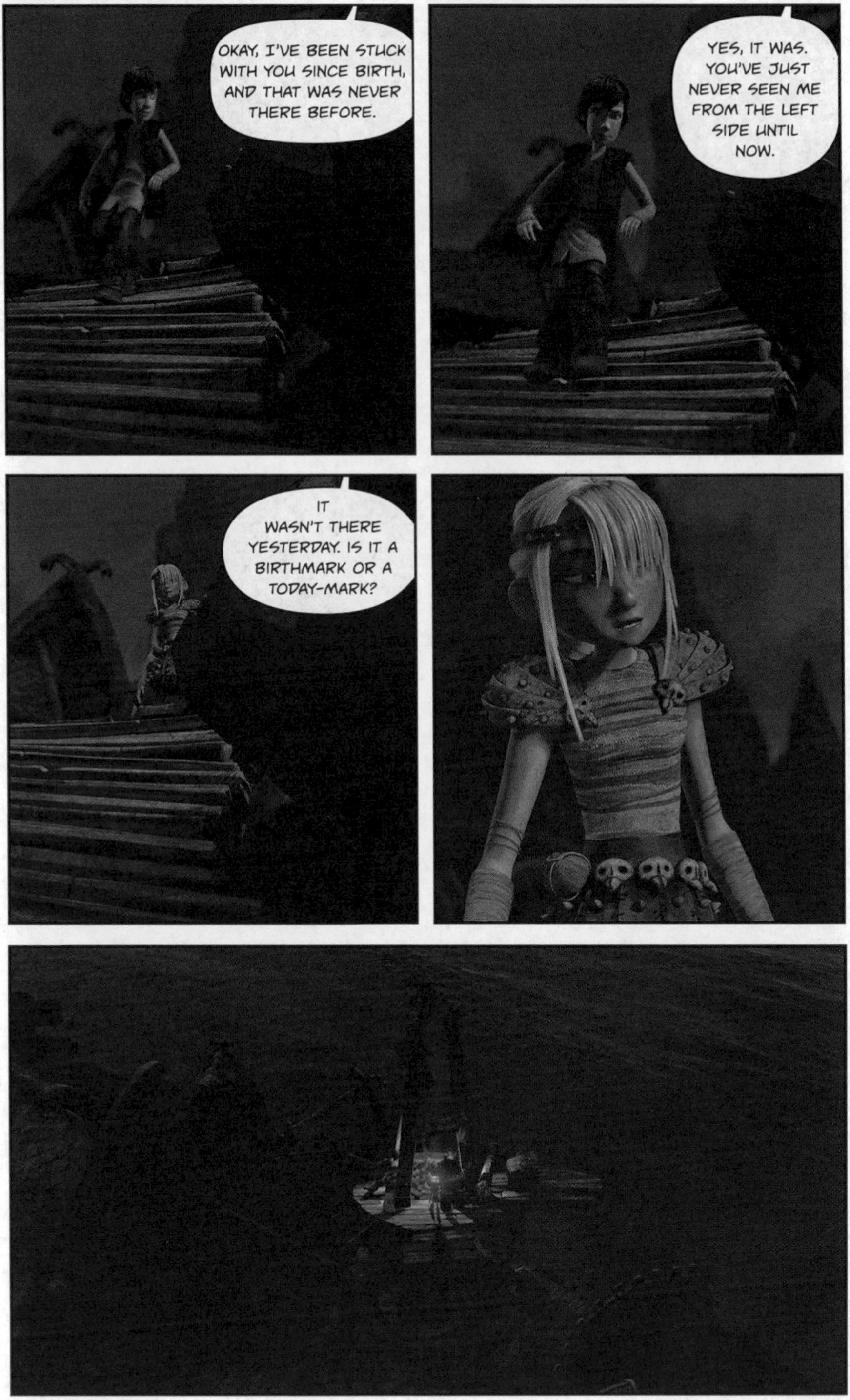
OKAY, I'VE BEEN STUCK WITH YOU SINCE BIRTH, AND THAT WAS NEVER THERE BEFORE.
YES, IT WAS. YOU'VE JUST NEVER SEEN ME FROM THE LEFT SIDE UNTIL NOW.
IT WASN'T THERE YESTERDAY. IS IT A BIRTHMARK OR A TODAY-MARK?

BLACKSMITH STALL--LATER.

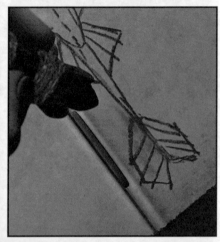

WHOOSH... WHOOSH

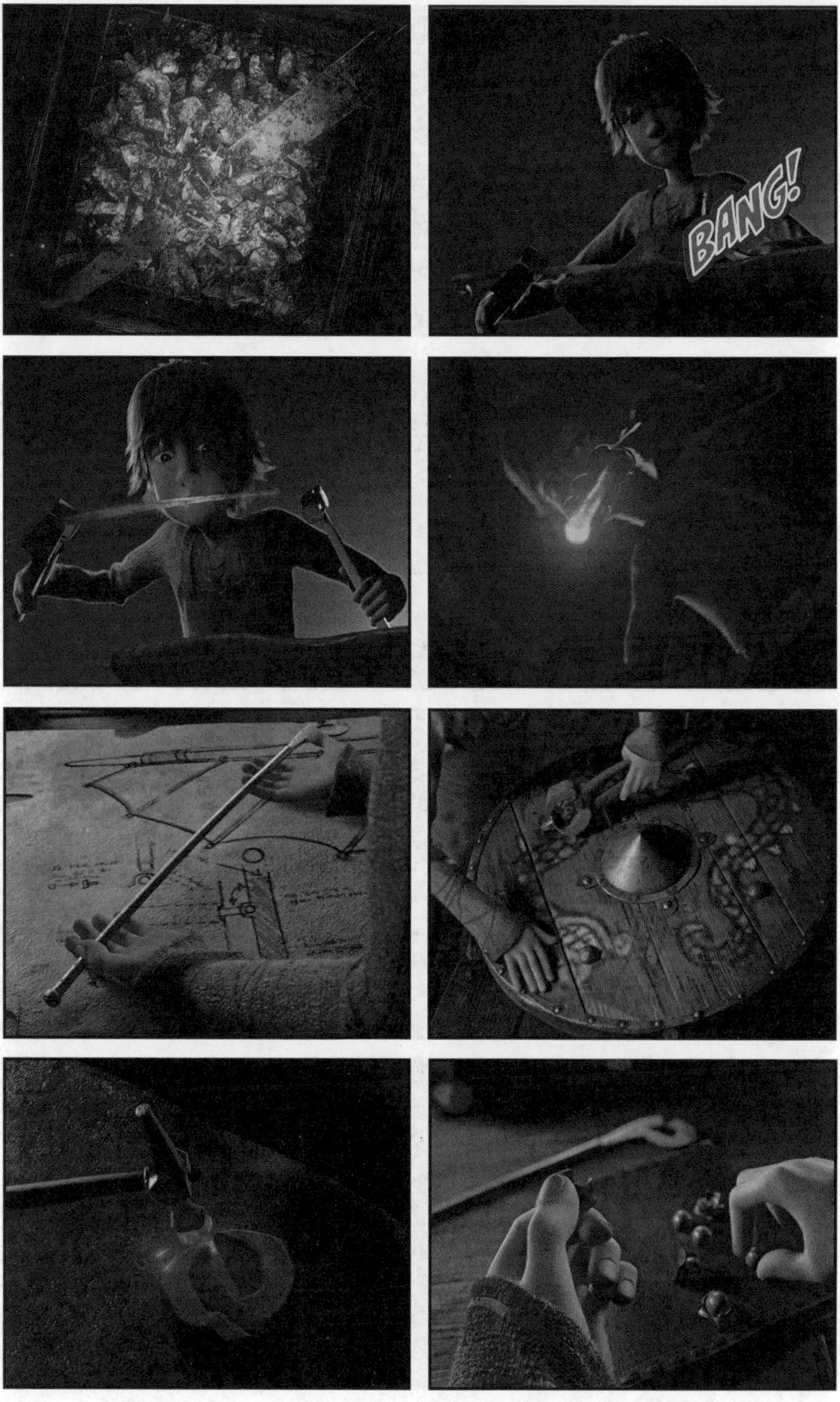
BANG!

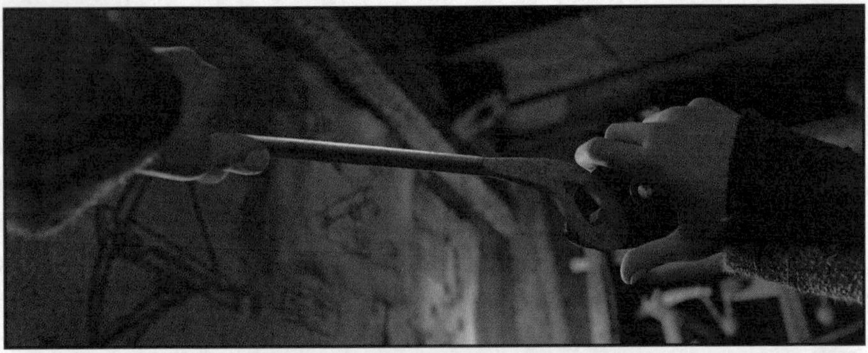
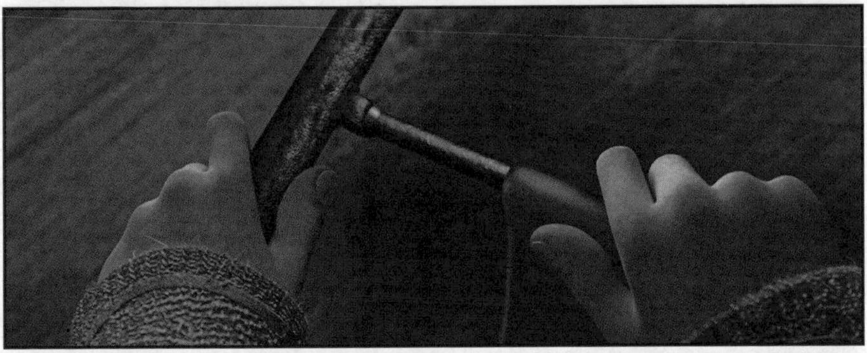
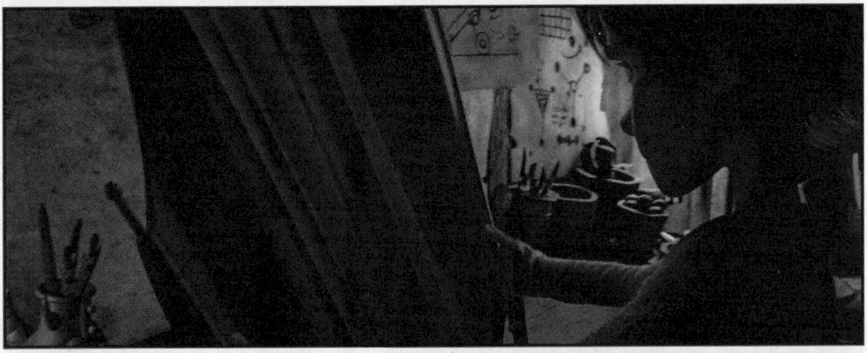
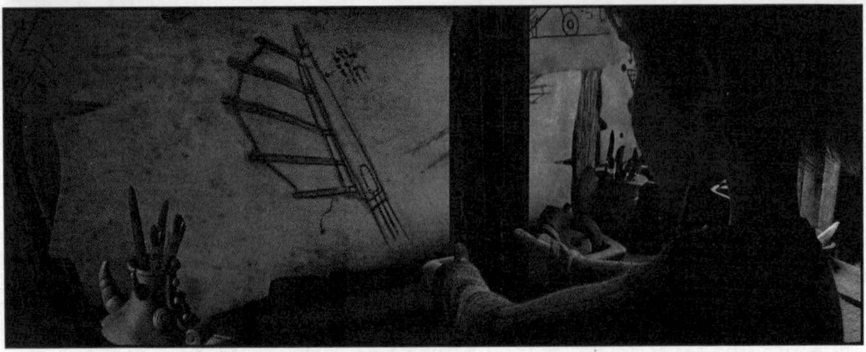

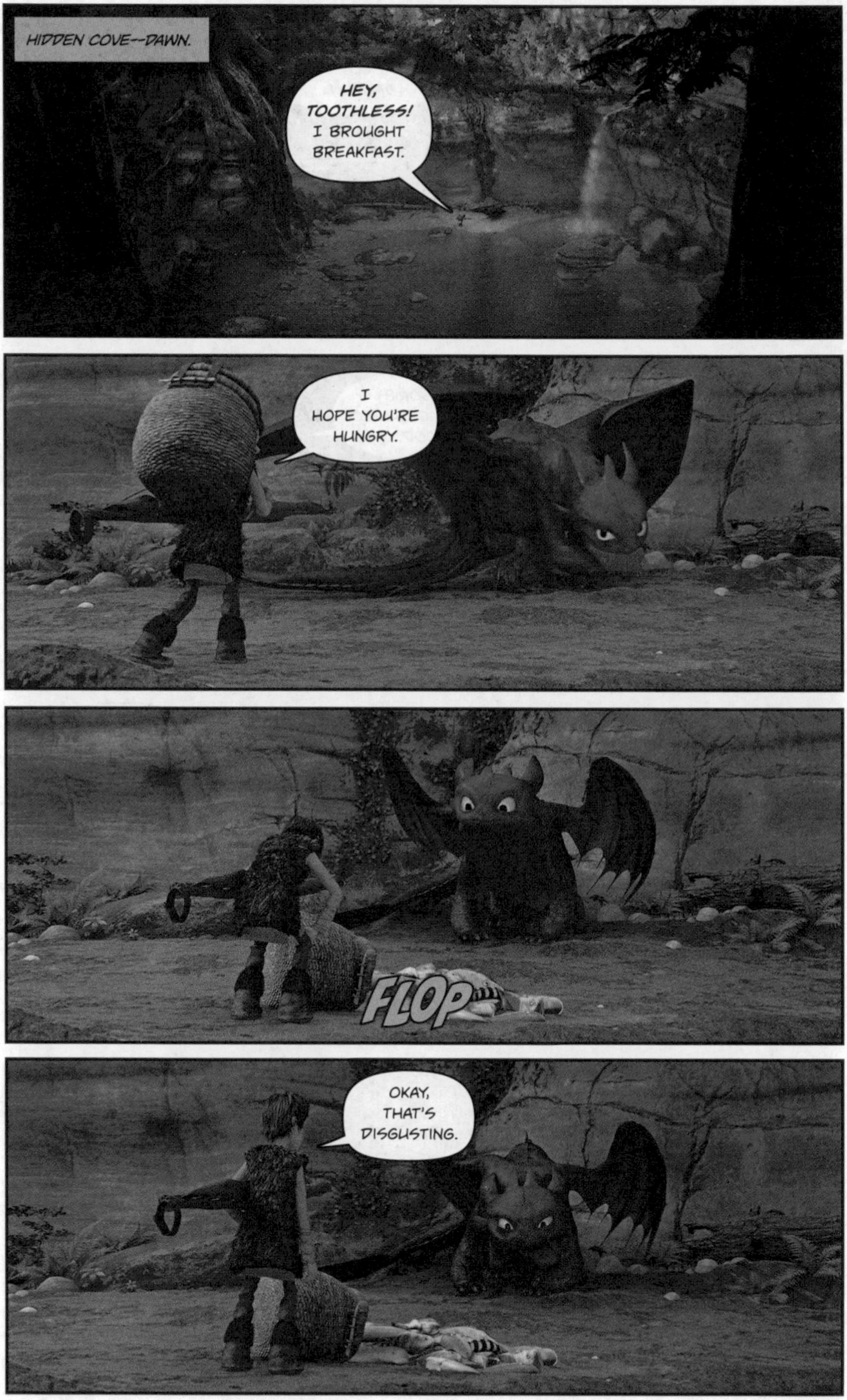
HIDDEN COVE--DAWN.
HEY, TOOTHLESS! I BROUGHT BREAKFAST.
I HOPE YOU'RE HUNGRY.
FLOP
OKAY, THAT'S DISGUSTING.

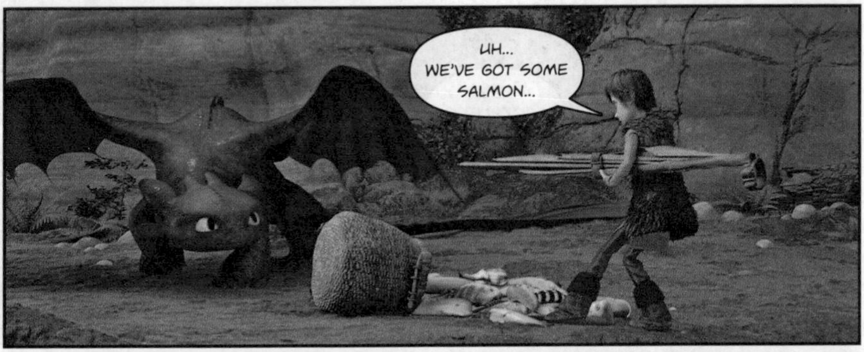
UH...
WE'VE GOT SOME SALMON...

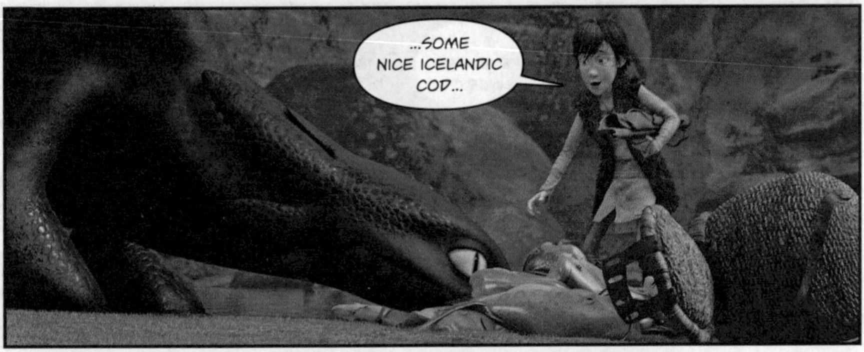
...SOME NICE ICELANDIC COD...

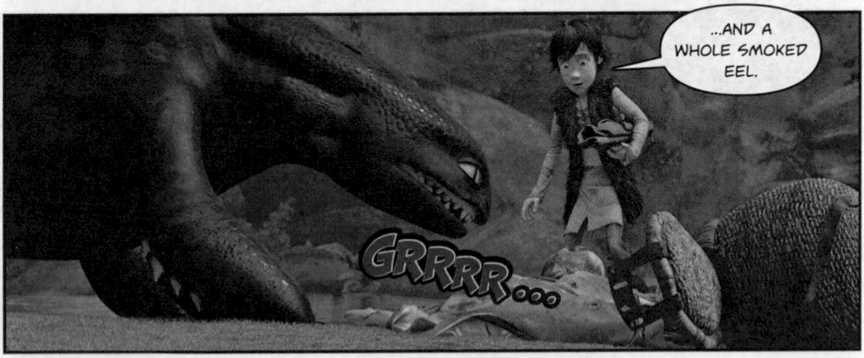
...AND A WHOLE SMOKED EEL.
GRRRR...

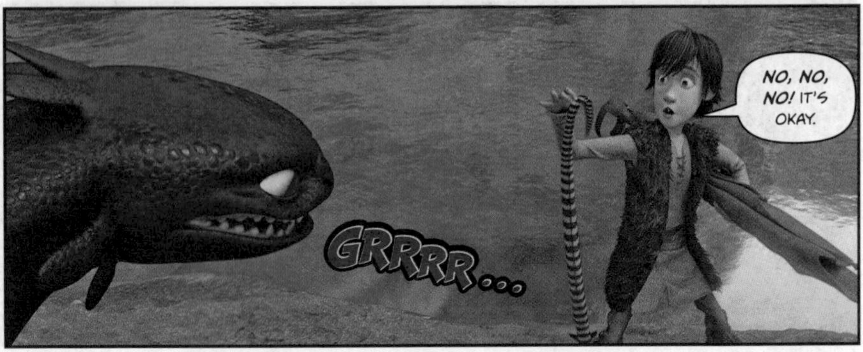
GRRRR...
NO, NO, NO! IT'S OKAY.

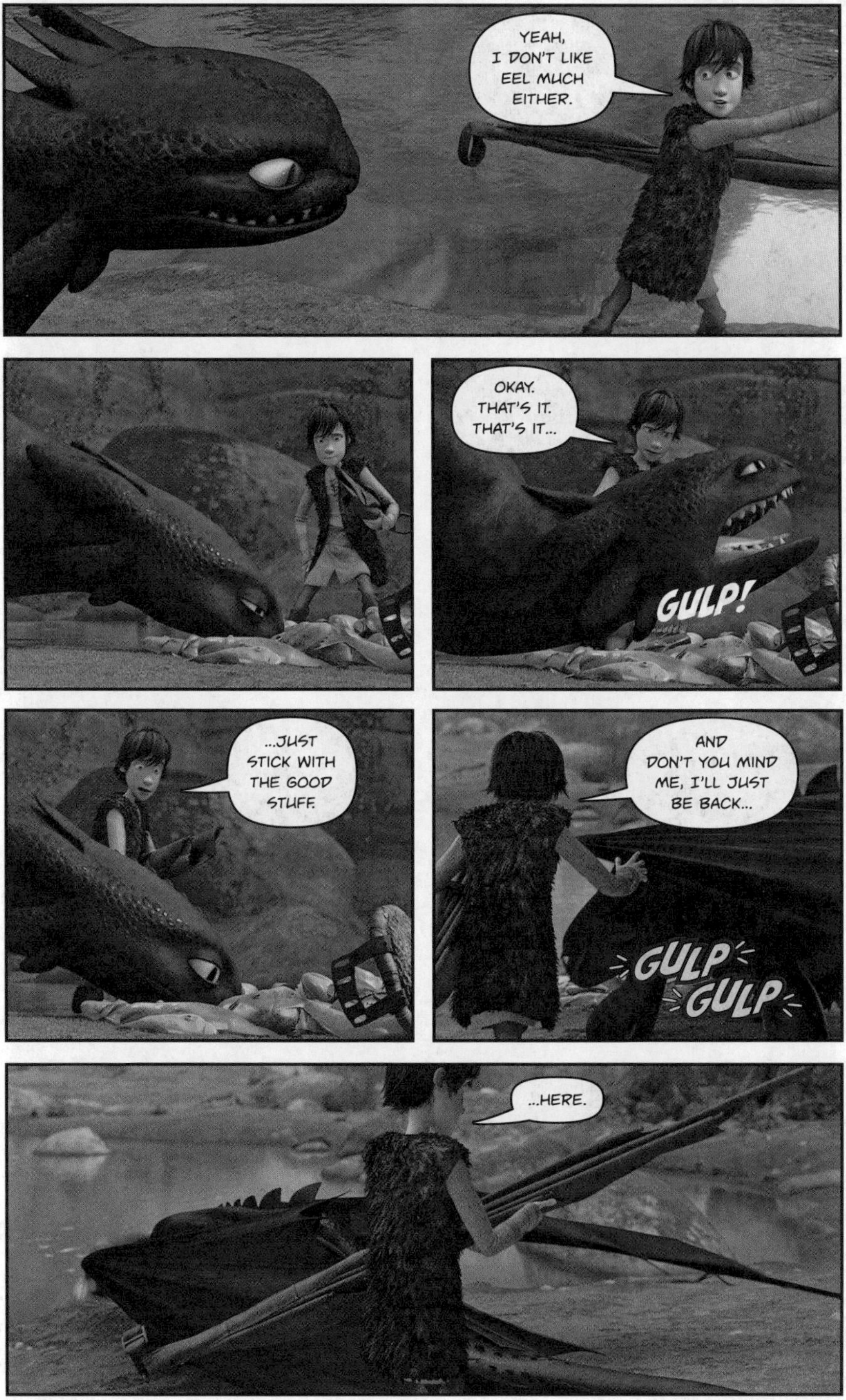
YEAH, I DON'T LIKE EEL MUCH EITHER.
OKAY. THAT'S IT. THAT'S IT...
GULP!
...JUST STICK WITH THE GOOD STUFF.
AND DON'T YOU MIND ME, I'LL JUST BE BACK...
GULP
GULP
...HERE.

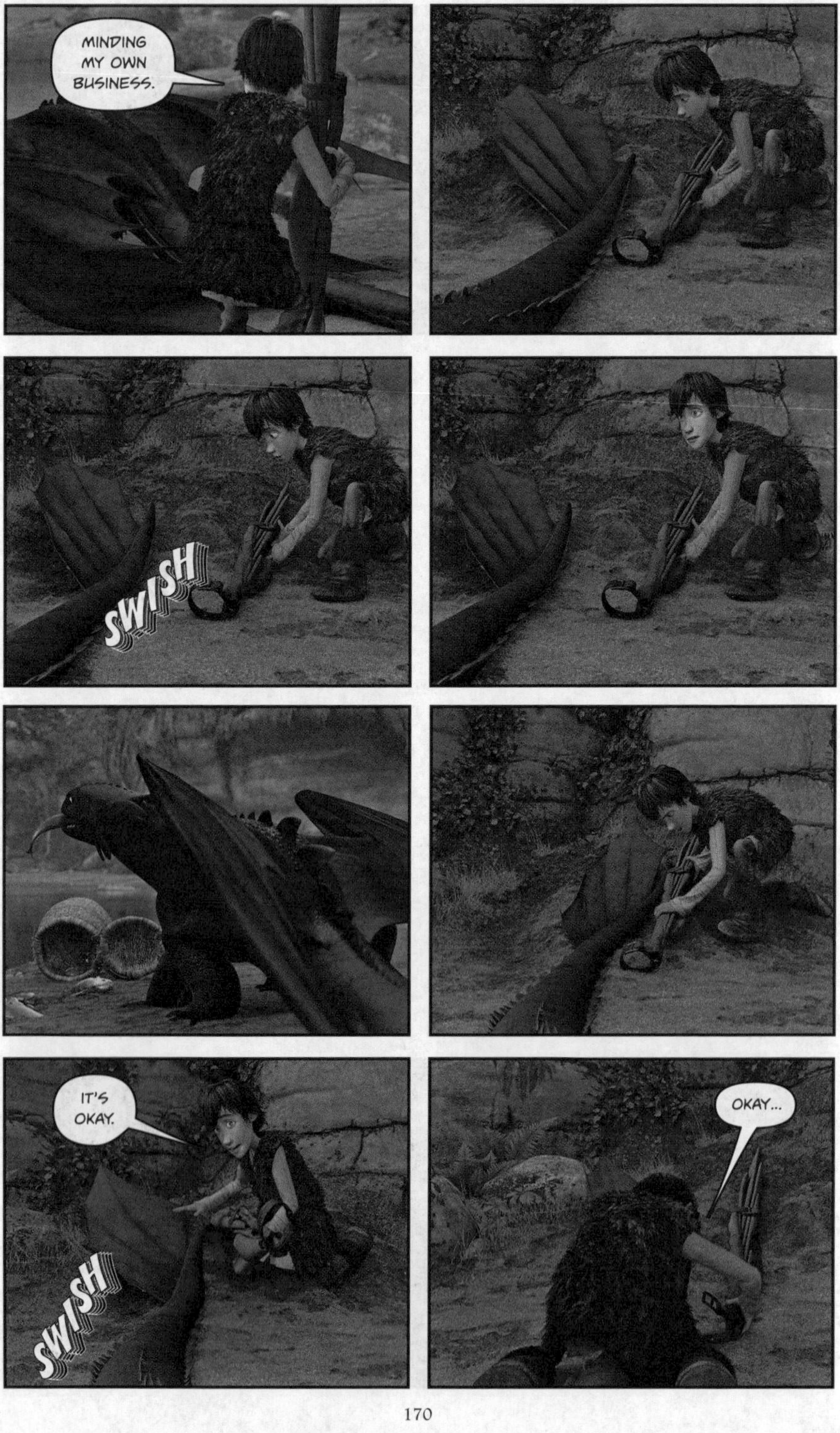
MINDING MY OWN BUSINESS.
SWISH
IT'S OKAY.
SWISH
OKAY...

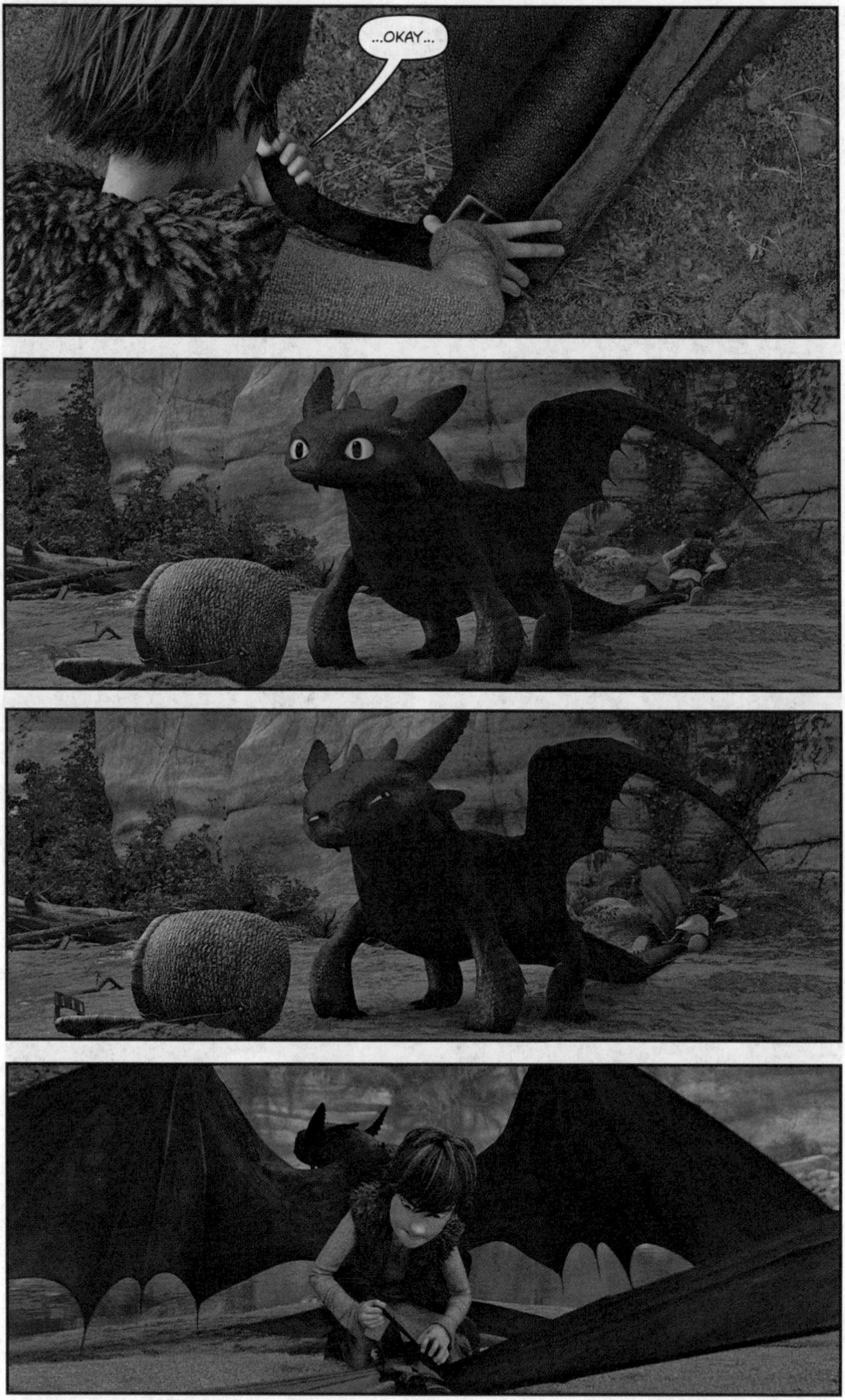
...OKAY...

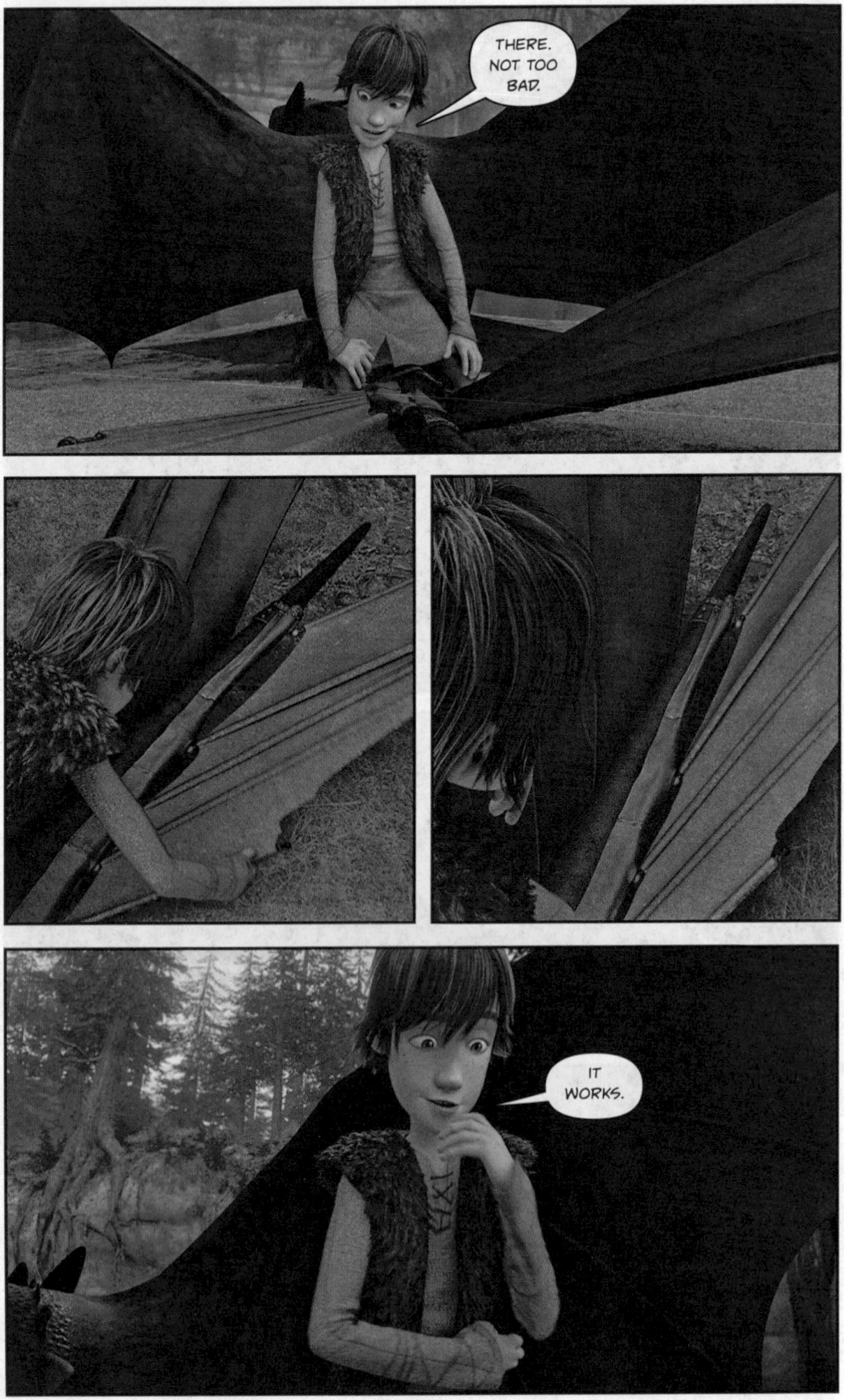
THERE. NOT TOO BAD.
IT WORKS.

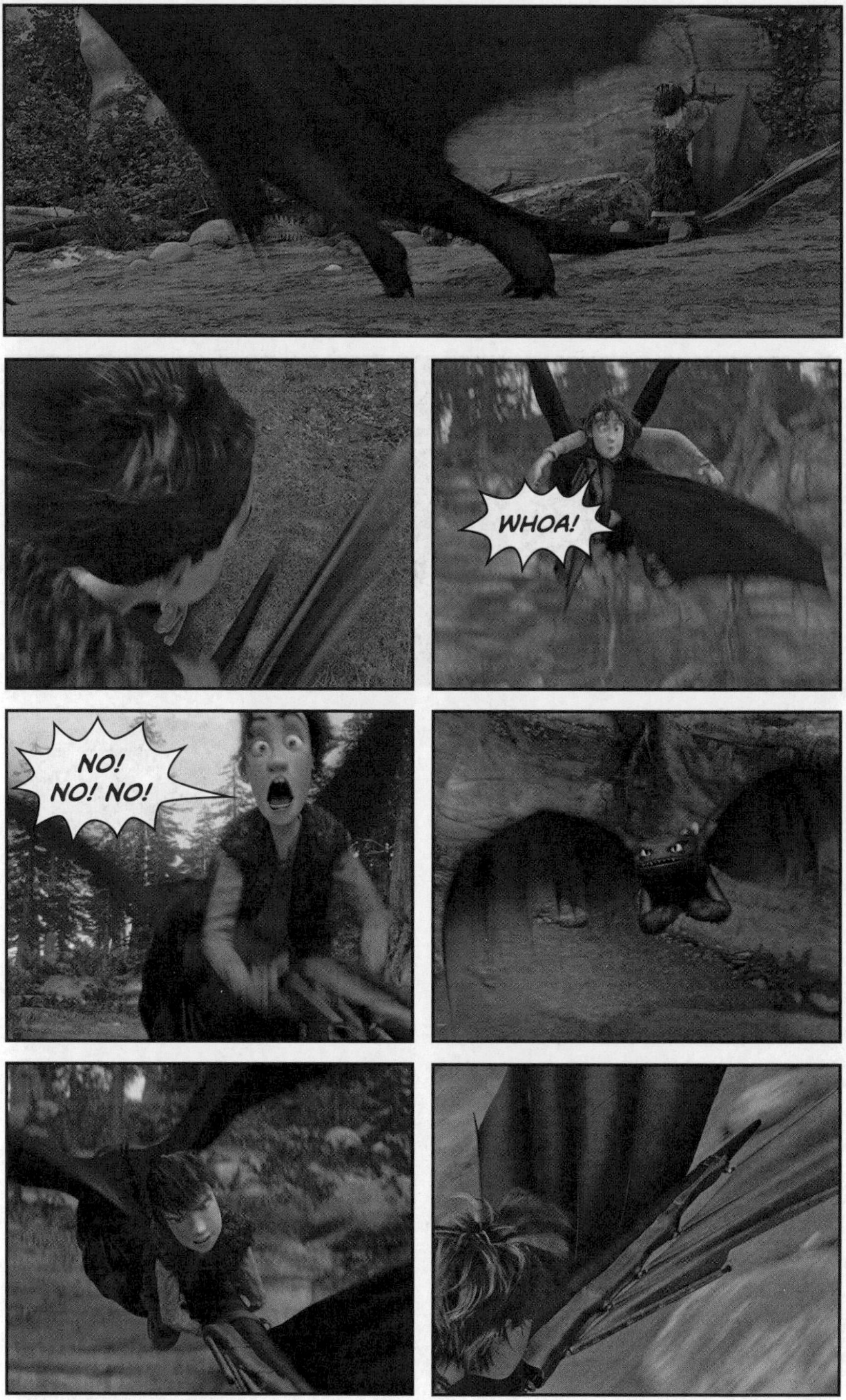
WHOA!
NO! NO! NO!

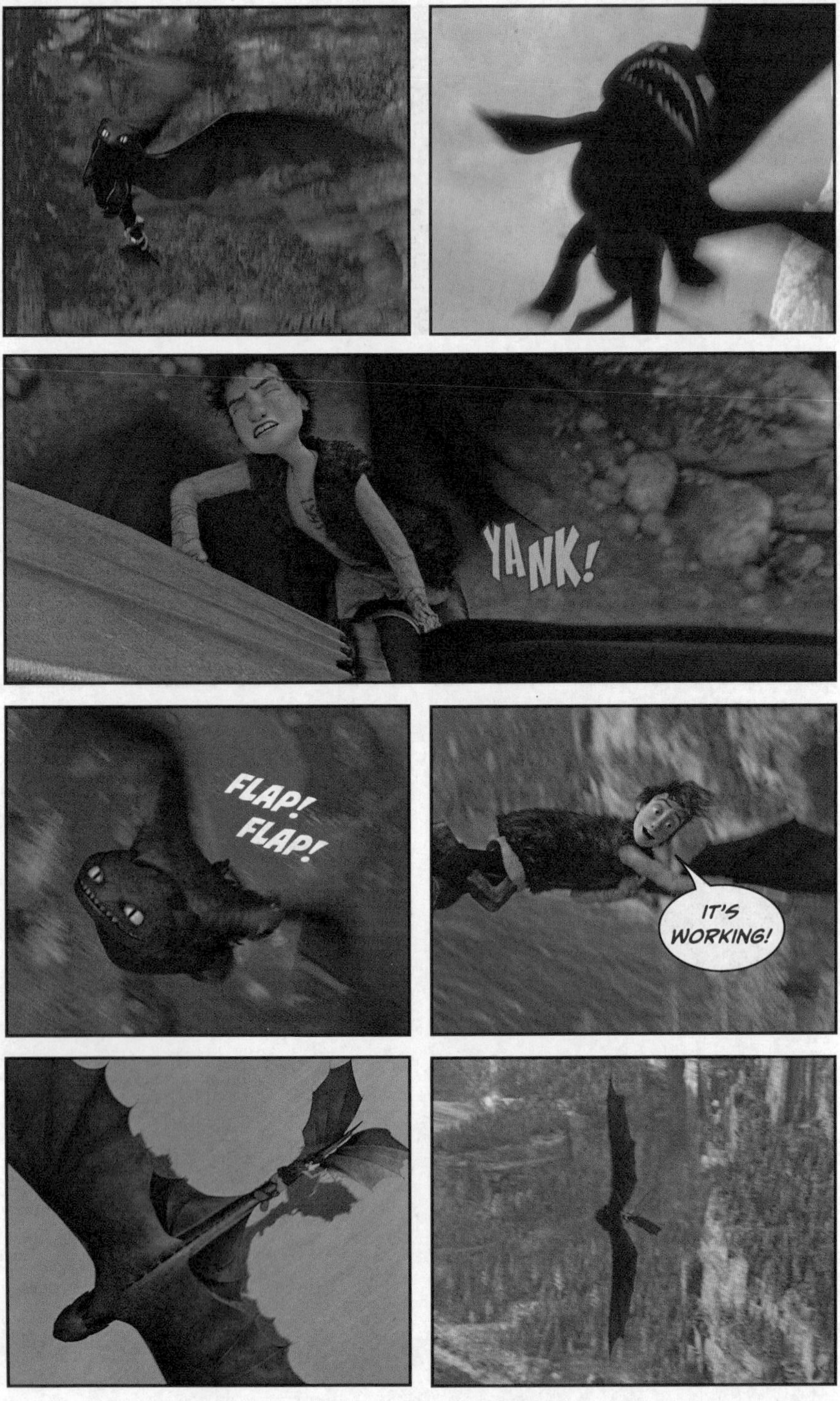
YANK!
FLAP!
FLAP!
IT'S WORKING!

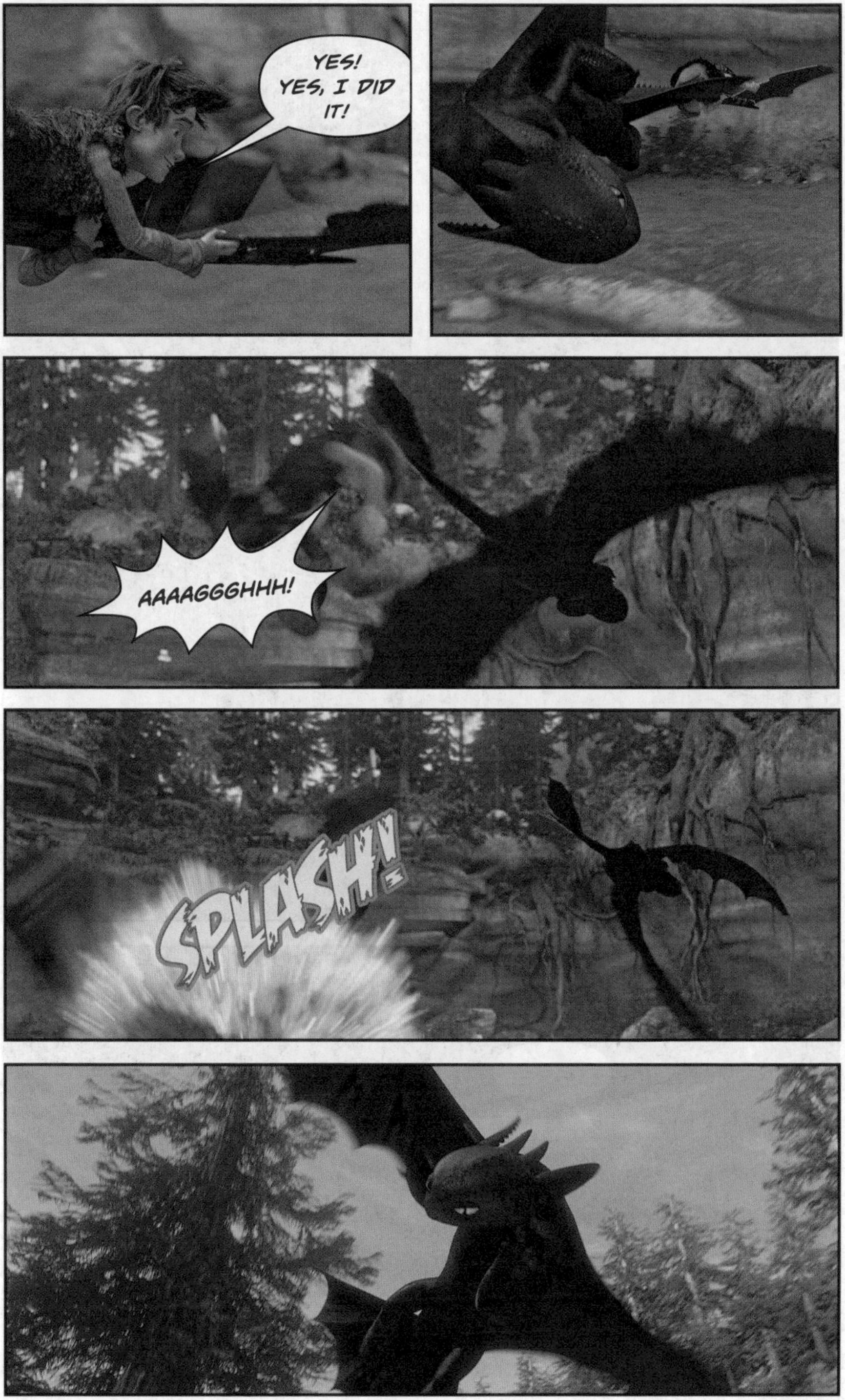
YES! YES, I DID IT!
AAAAGGGHHH!
SPLASH!

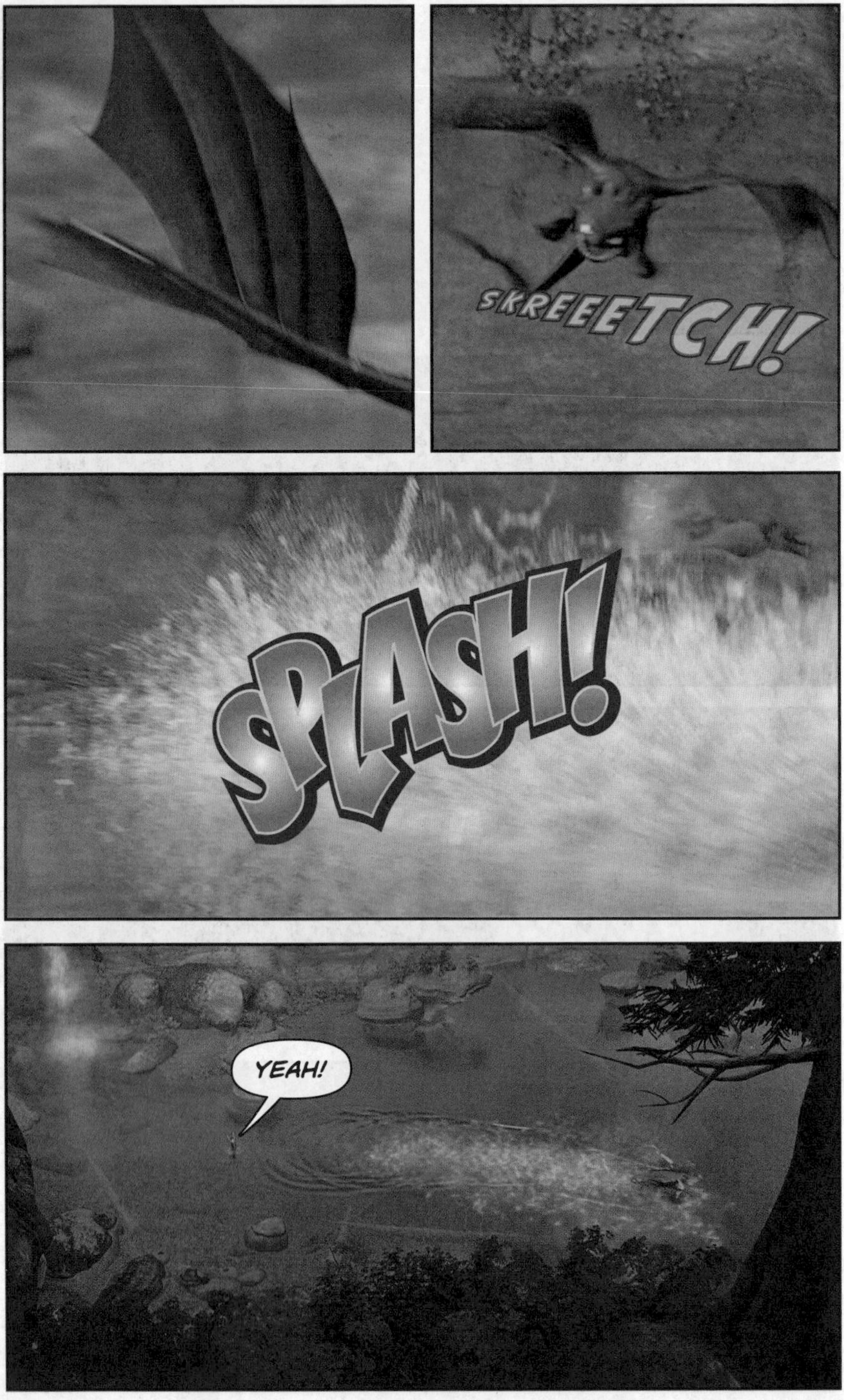
SKREEETCH!
SPLASH!
YEAH!

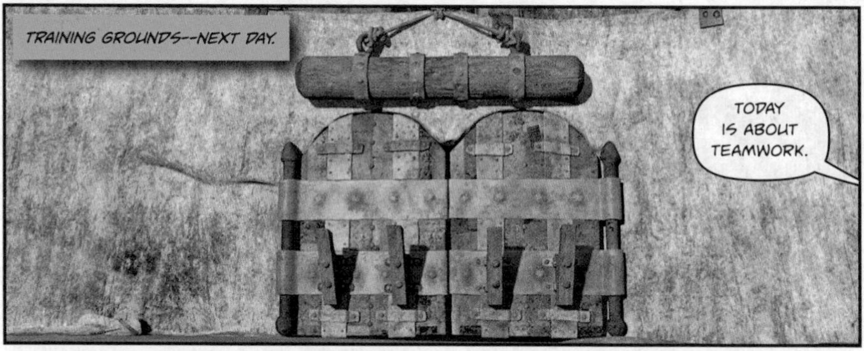
TRAINING GROUNDS--NEXT DAY.
TODAY IS ABOUT TEAMWORK.

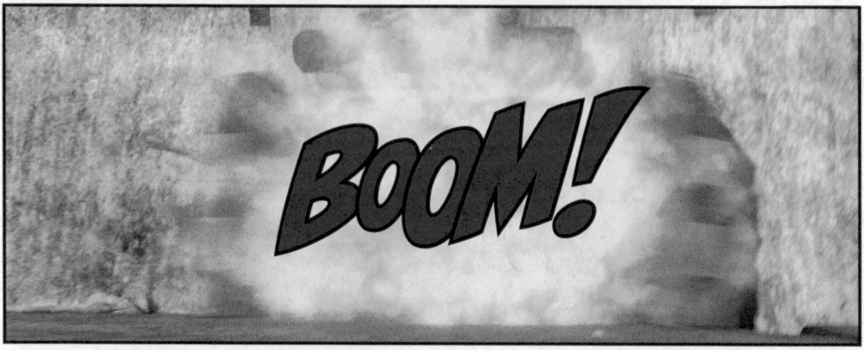
BOOM!

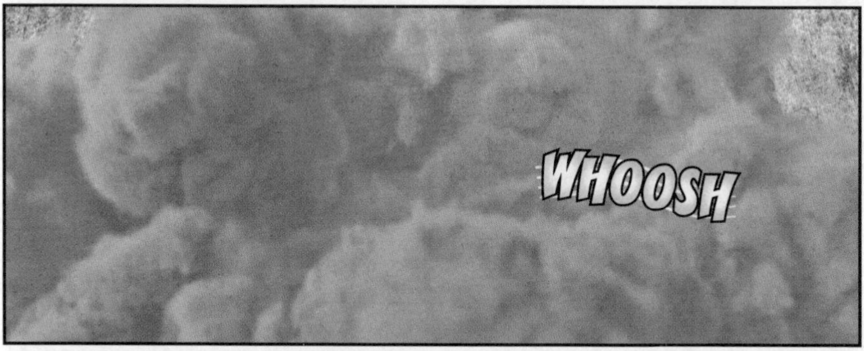
WHOOSH

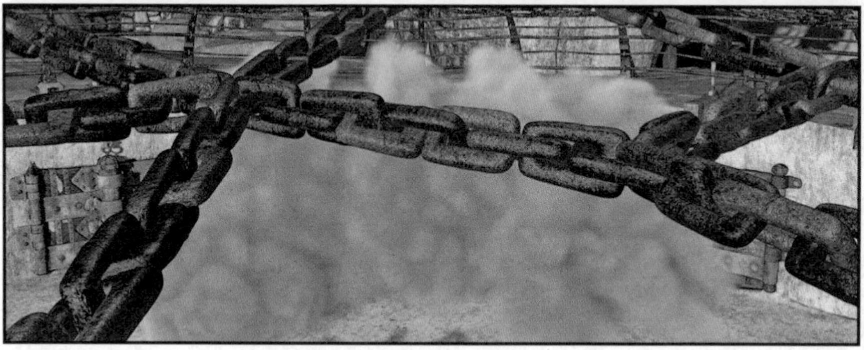

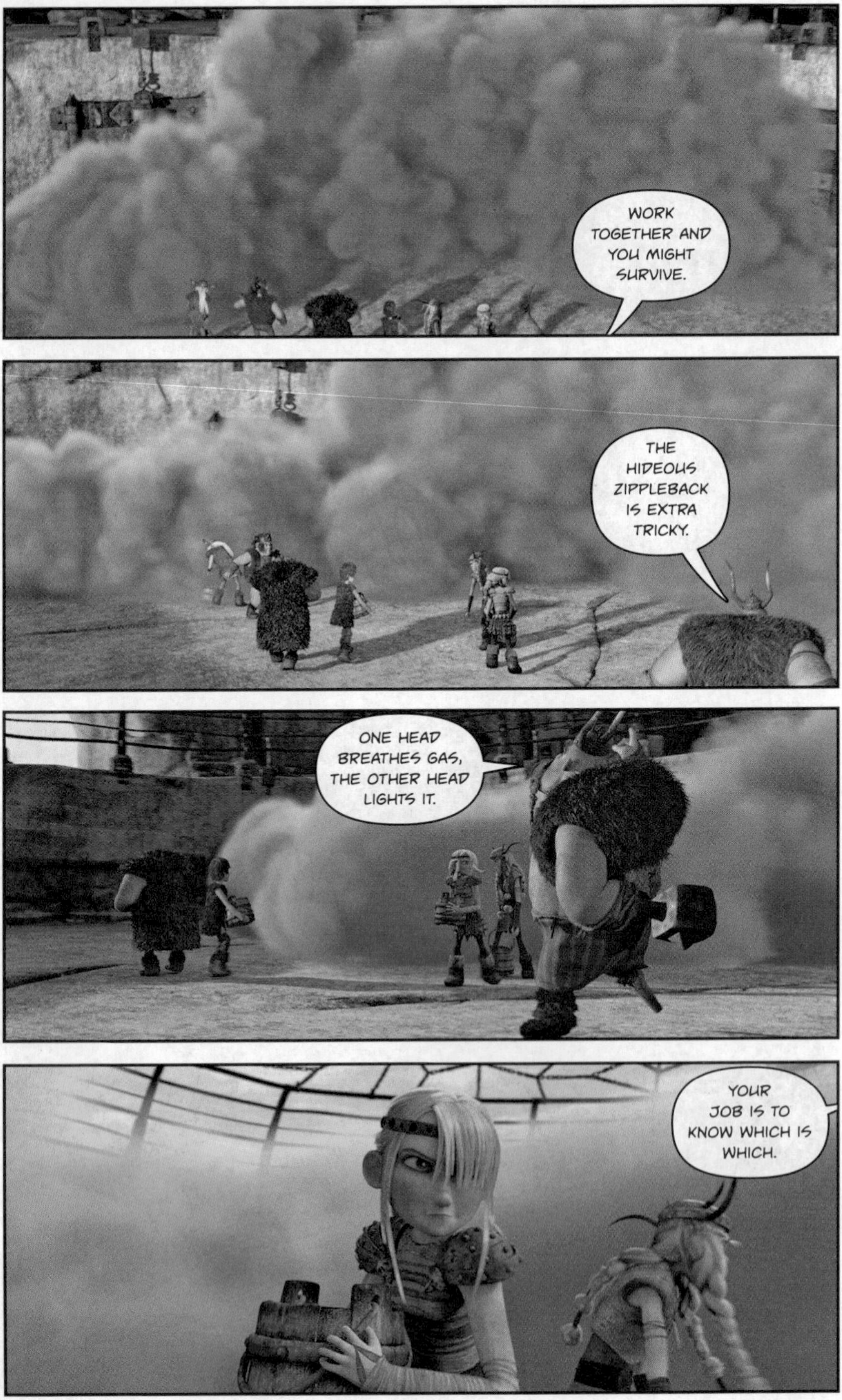
WORK TOGETHER AND YOU MIGHT SURVIVE.
THE HIDEOUS ZIPPLEBACK IS EXTRA TRICKY.
ONE HEAD BREATHES GAS, THE OTHER HEAD LIGHTS IT.
YOUR JOB IS TO KNOW WHICH IS WHICH.

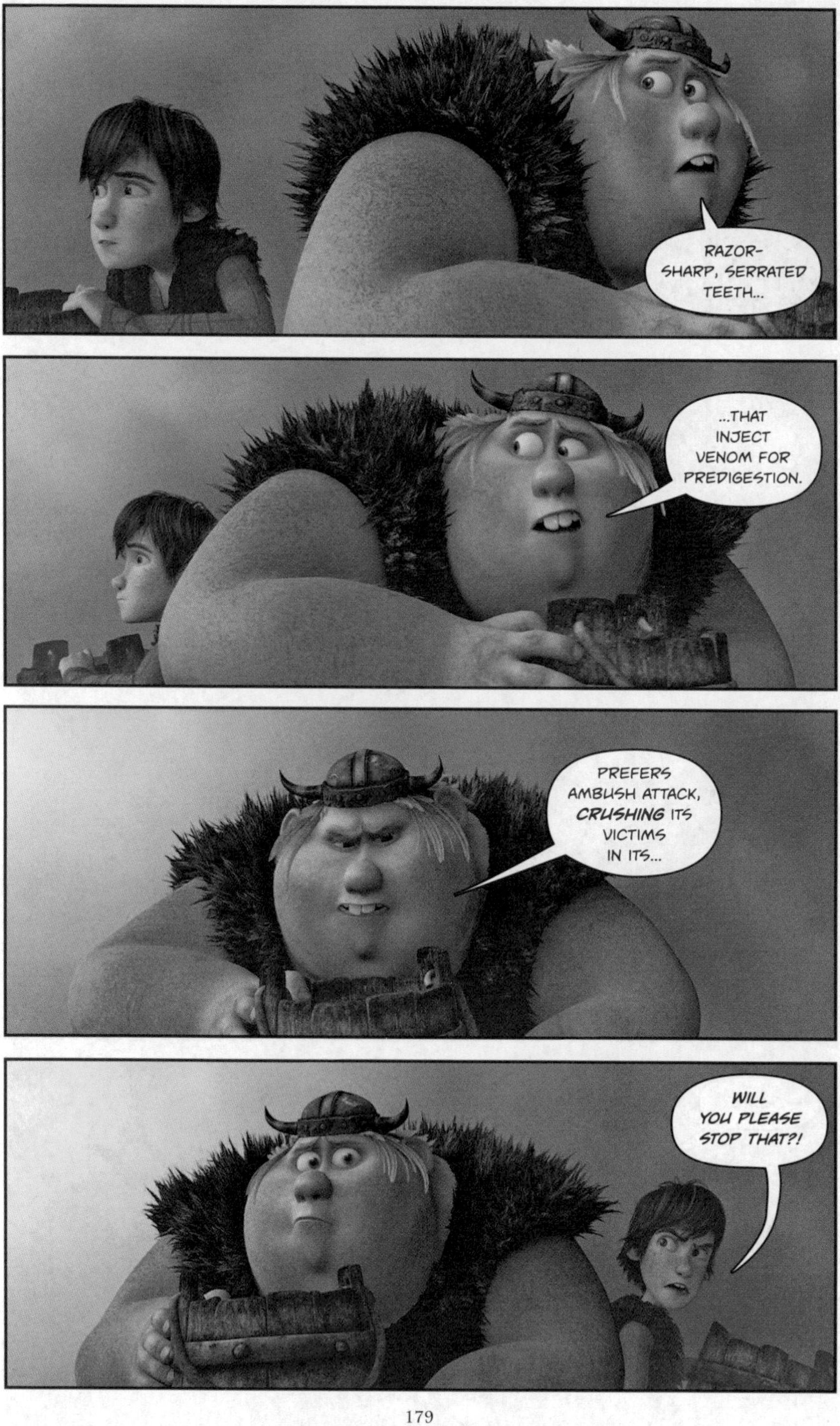
RAZOR-SHARP, SERRATED TEETH...
...THAT INJECT VENOM FOR PREDIGESTION.
PREFERS AMBUSH ATTACK, CRUSHING ITS VICTIMS IN ITS...
WILL YOU PLEASE STOP THAT?!

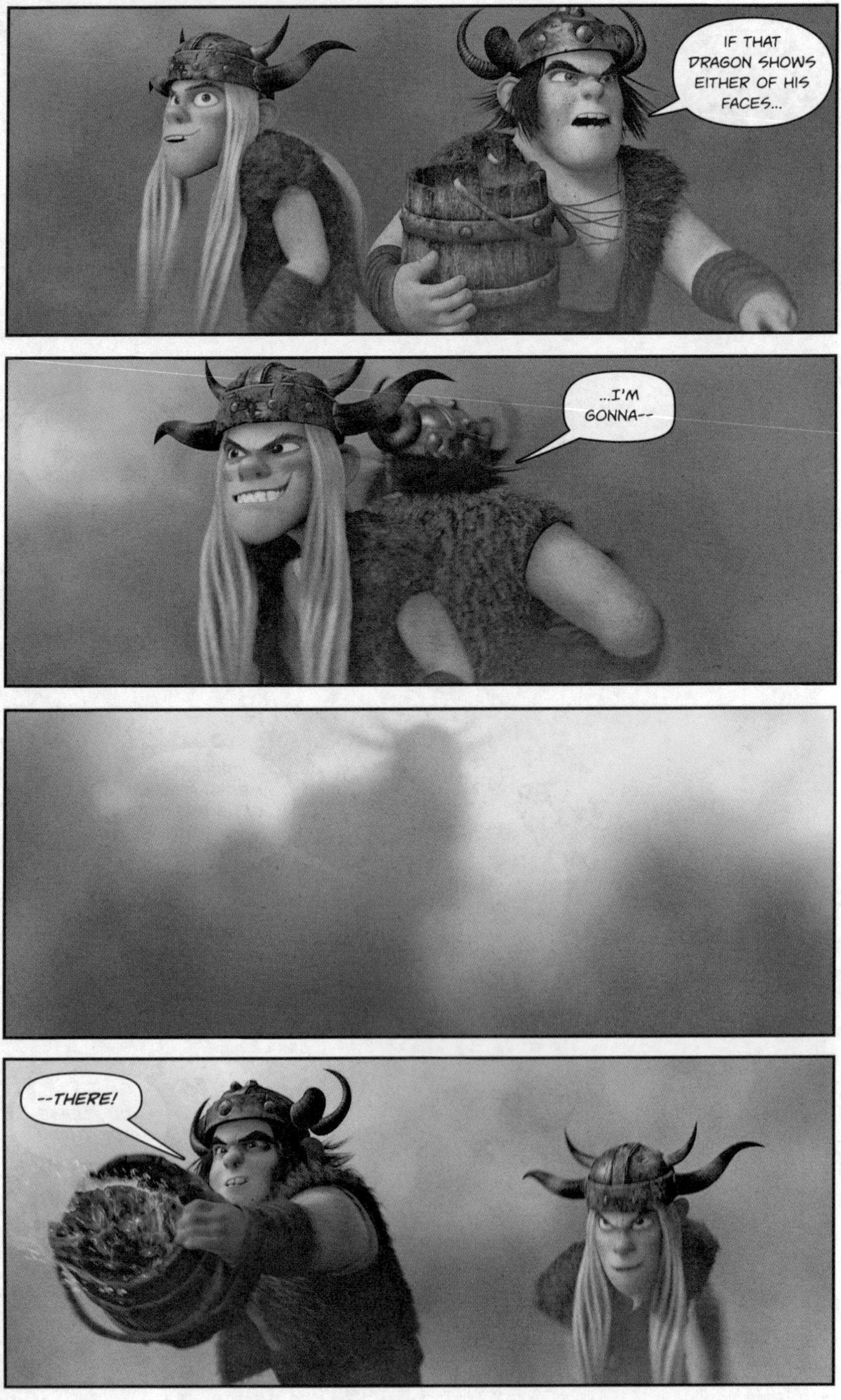
IF THAT DRAGON SHOWS EITHER OF HIS FACES...
...I'M GONNA--
--THERE!

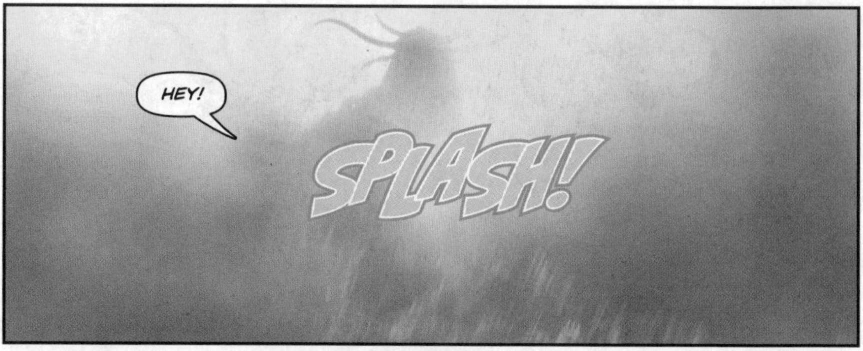
HEY!
SPLASH!

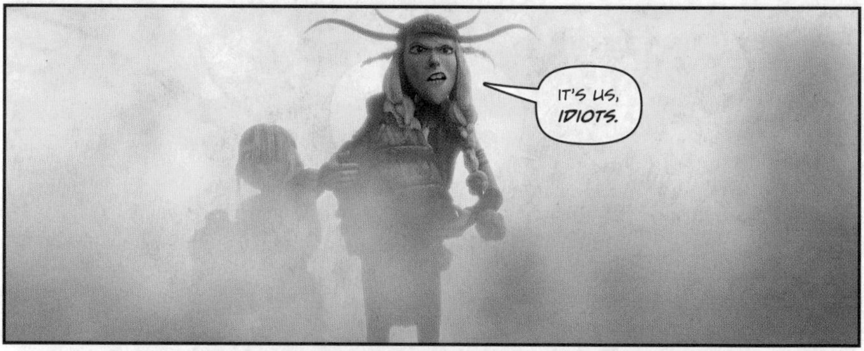
IT'S US, IDIOTS.

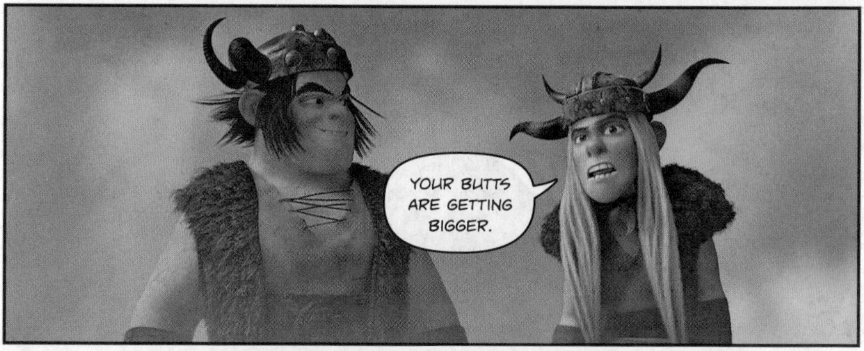
YOUR BUTTS ARE GETTING BIGGER.

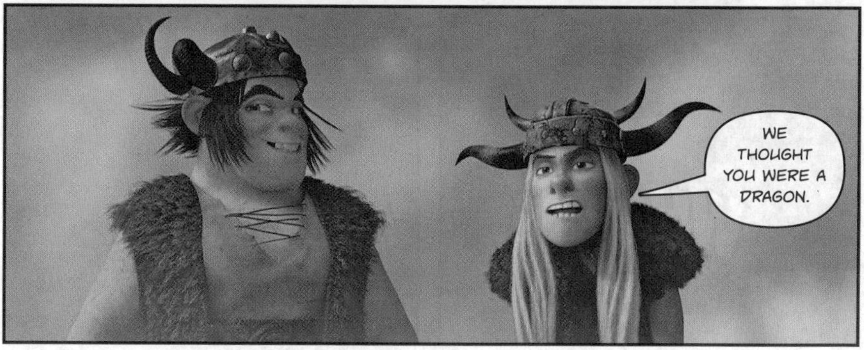
WE THOUGHT YOU WERE A DRAGON.

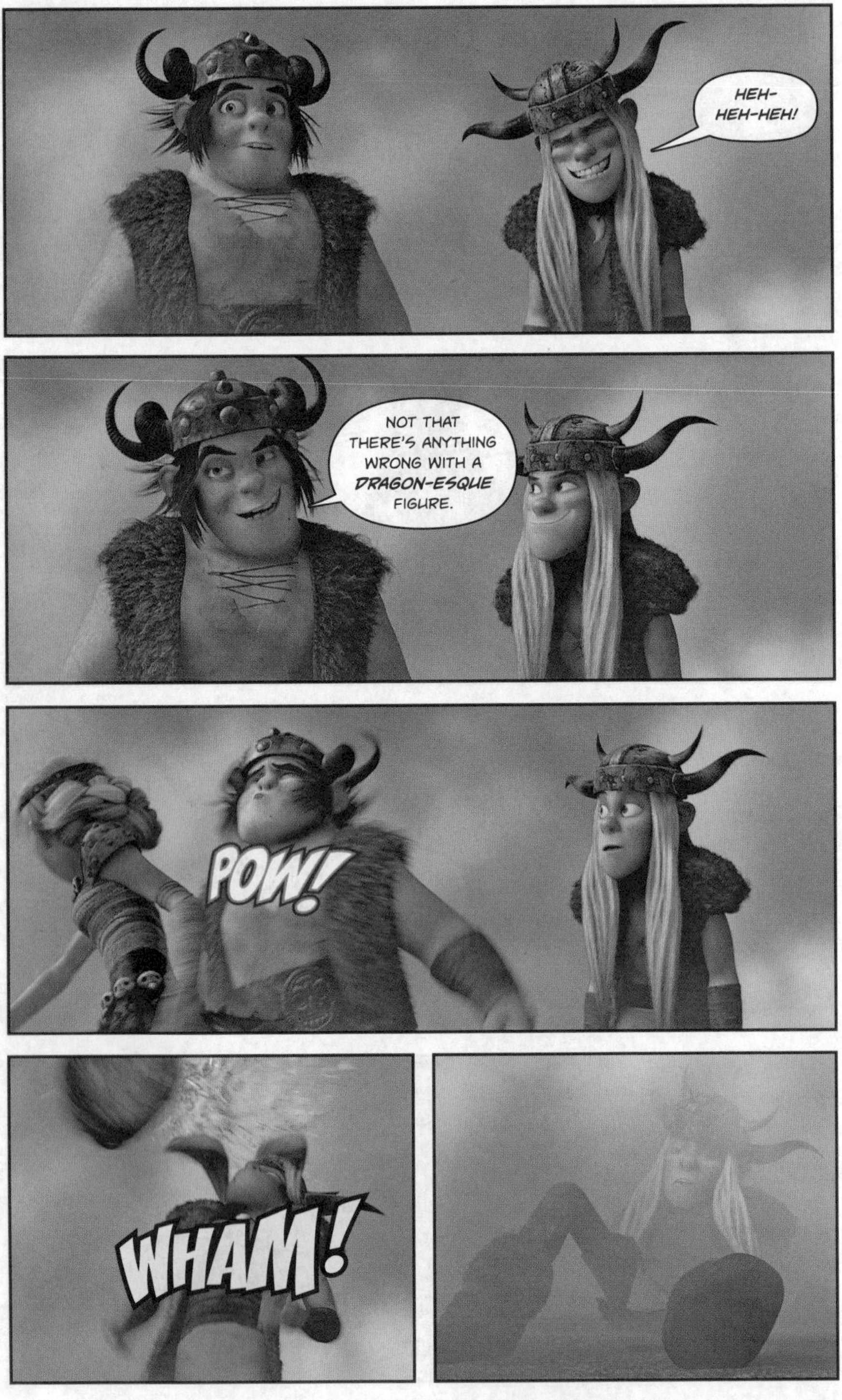
HEH-
HEH-HEH!
NOT THAT THERE'S ANYTHING WRONG WITH A DRAGON-ESQUE FIGURE.
POW!
WHAM!

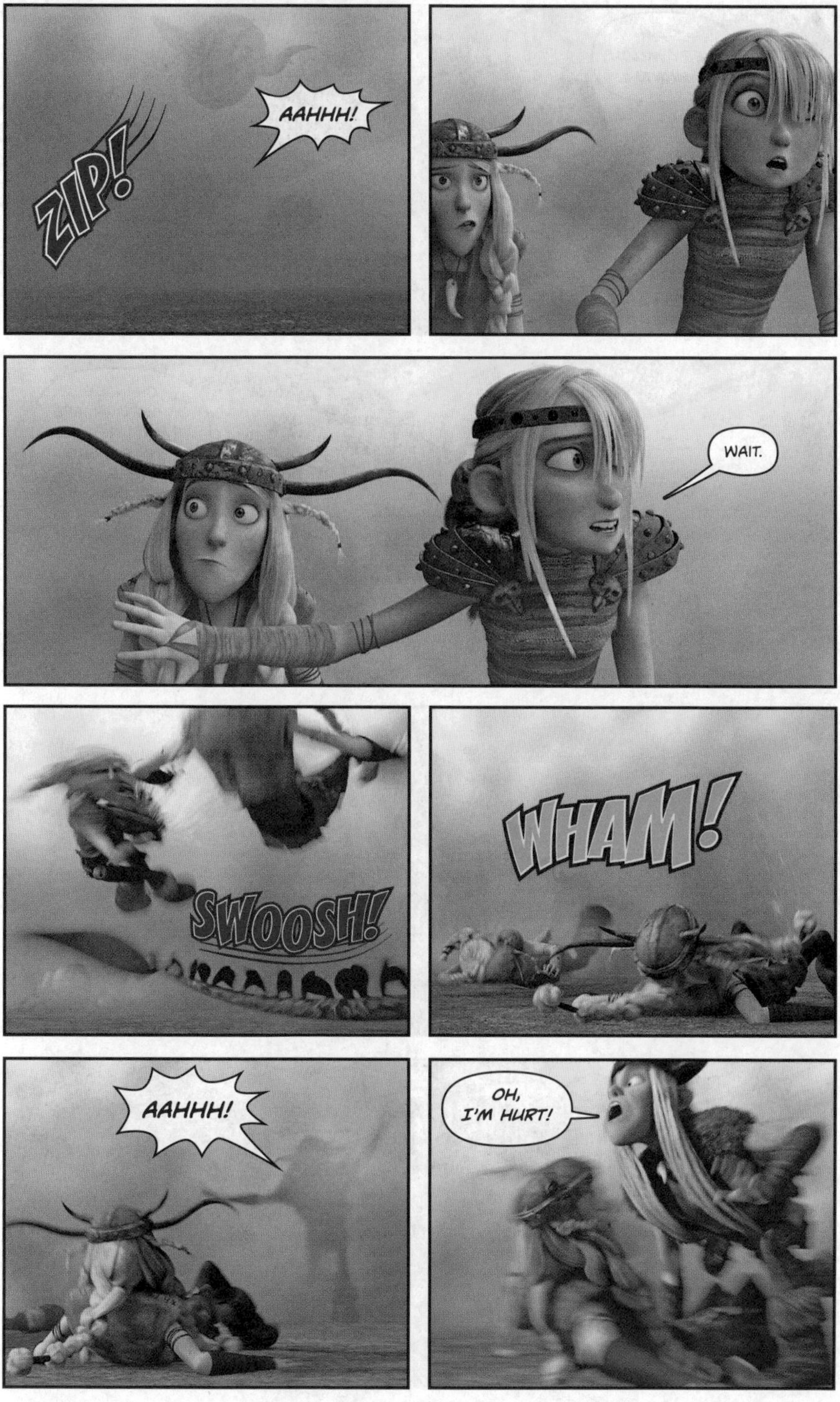
ZIP!
AAHHH!
WAIT.
SWOOSH!
WHAM!
AAHHH!
OH, I'M HURT!

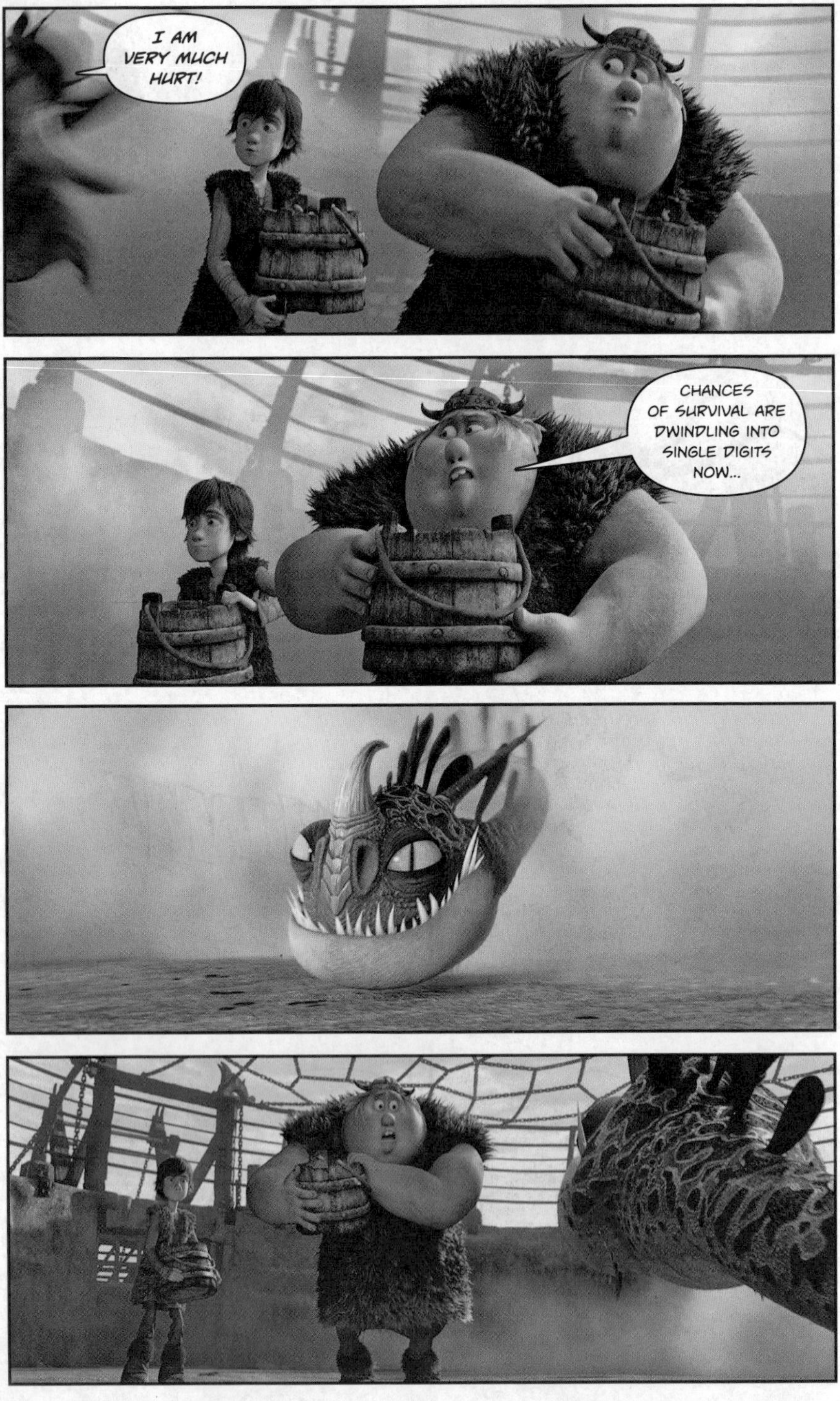
I AM VERY MUCH HURT!
CHANCES OF SURVIVAL ARE DWINDLING INTO SINGLE DIGITS NOW...

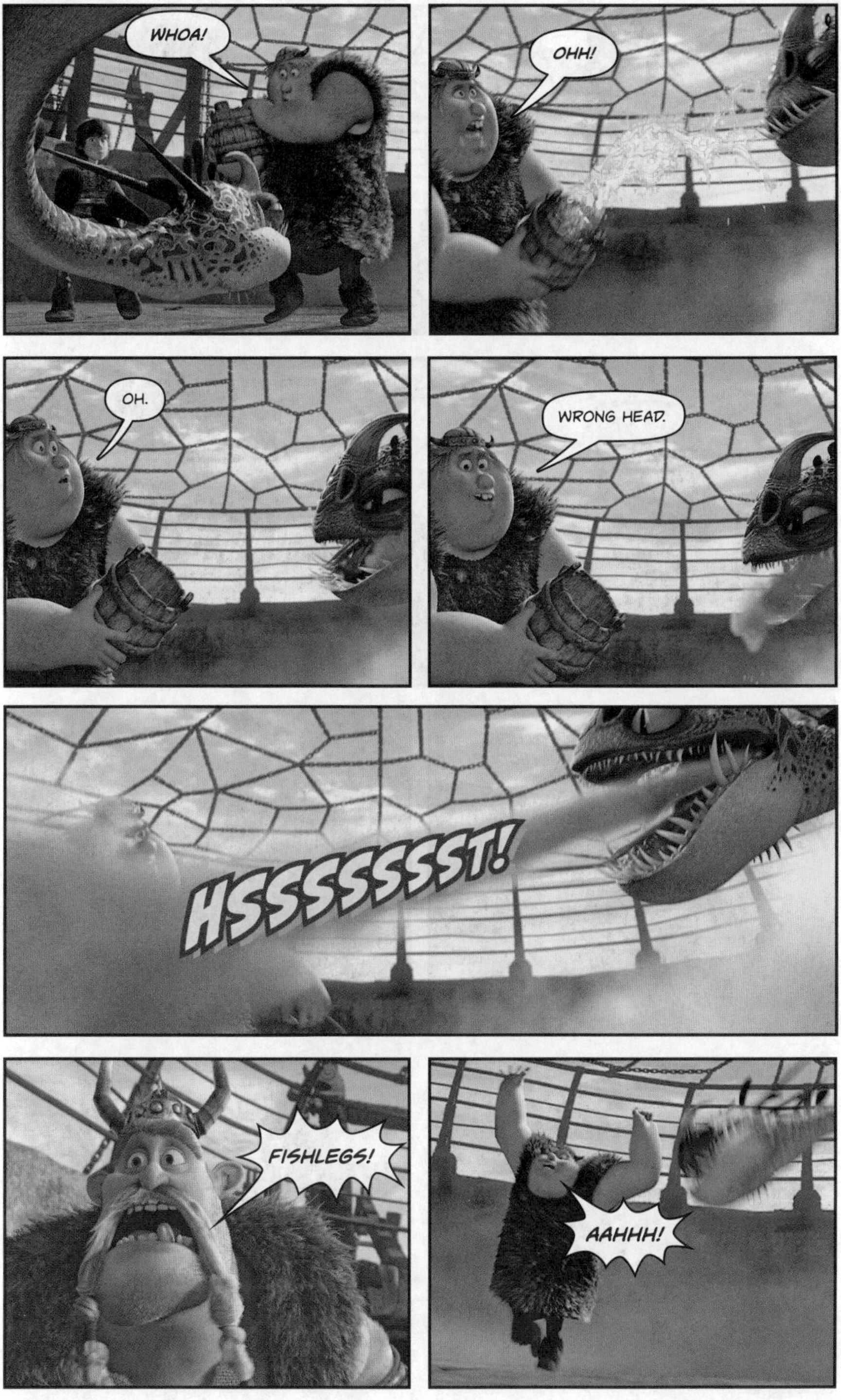
WHOA!
OHH!
OH.
WRONG HEAD.
HSSSSSST!
FISHLEGS!
AAHHH!

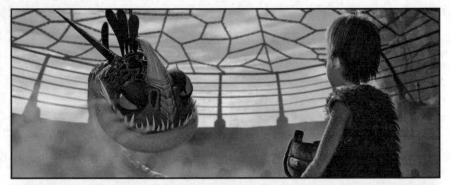

NOW, HICCUP!

SPLAT!

OH, COME ON!

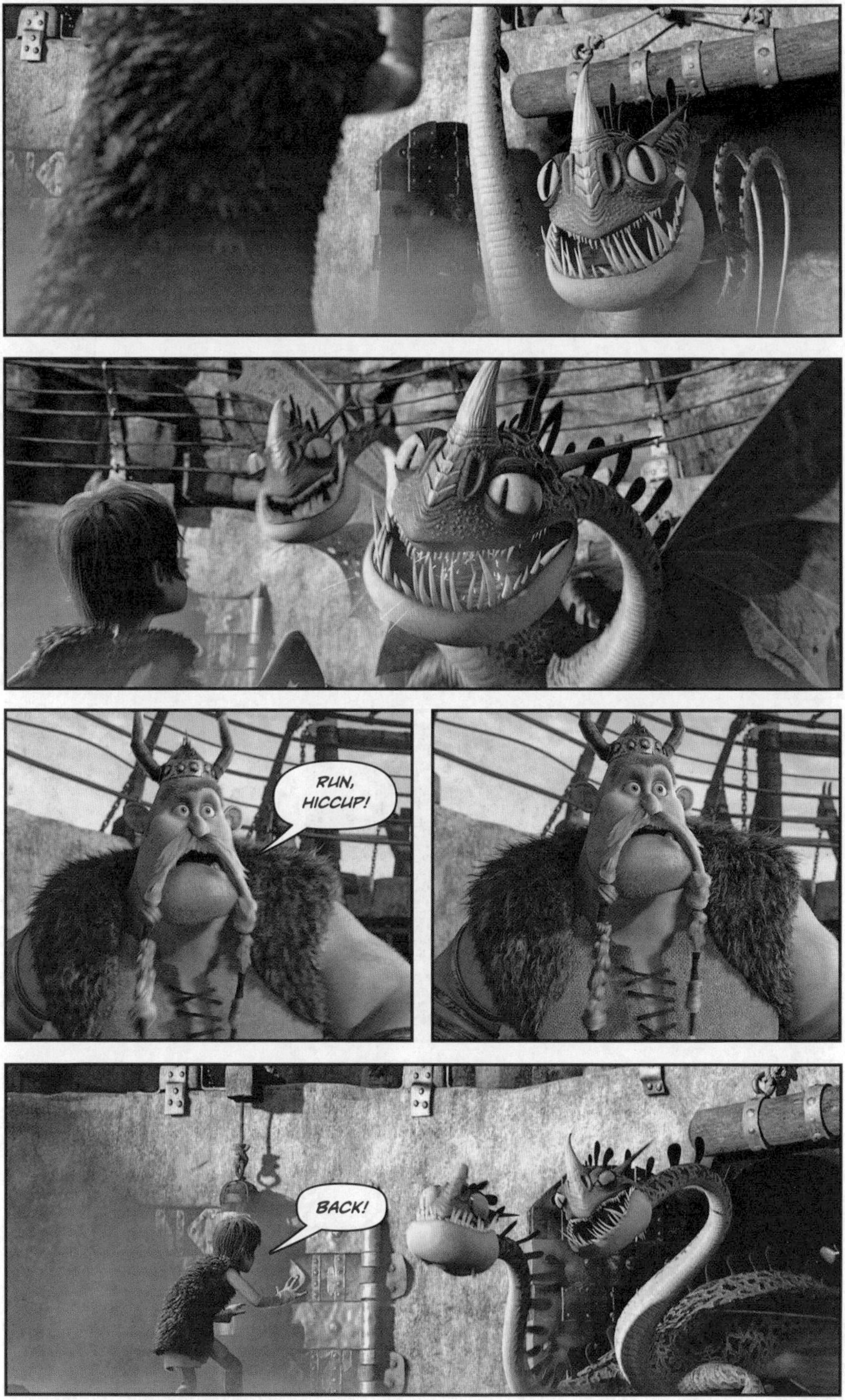
RUN, HICCUP!
BACK!

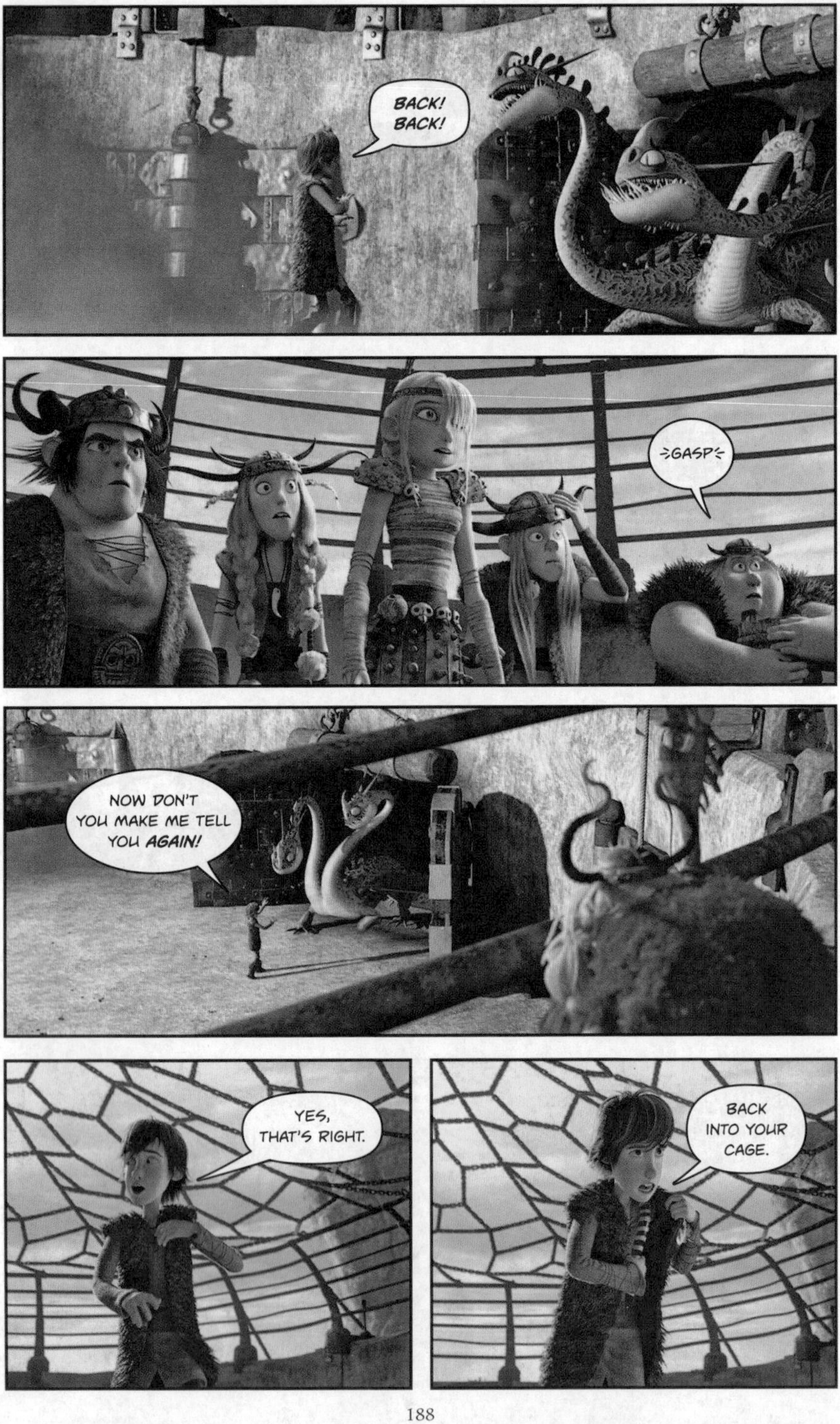

BACK! BACK!
GASP
NOW DON'T YOU MAKE ME TELL YOU AGAIN!
YES, THAT'S RIGHT.
BACK INTO YOUR CAGE.

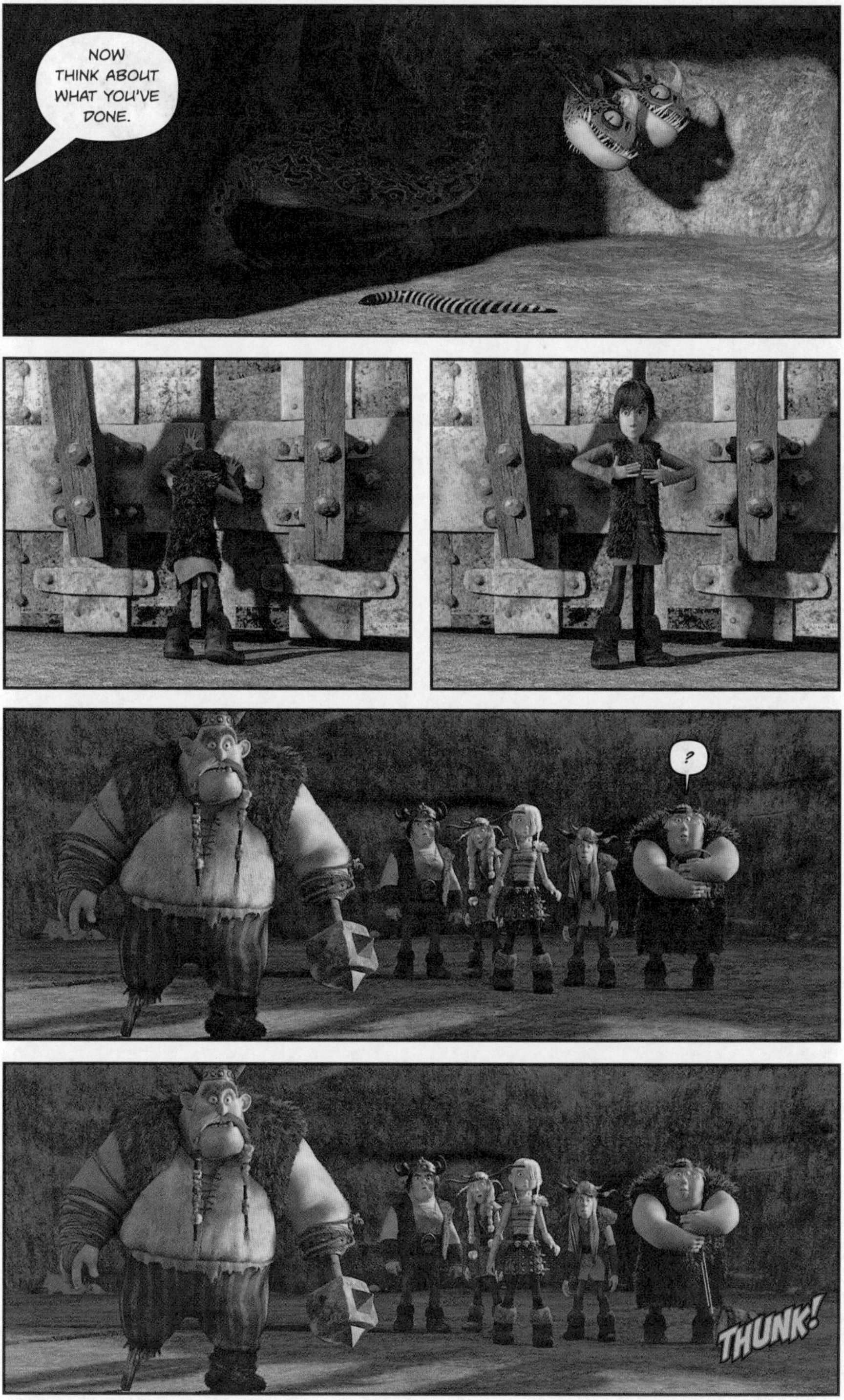
NOW THINK ABOUT WHAT YOU'VE DONE.
?
THUNK!

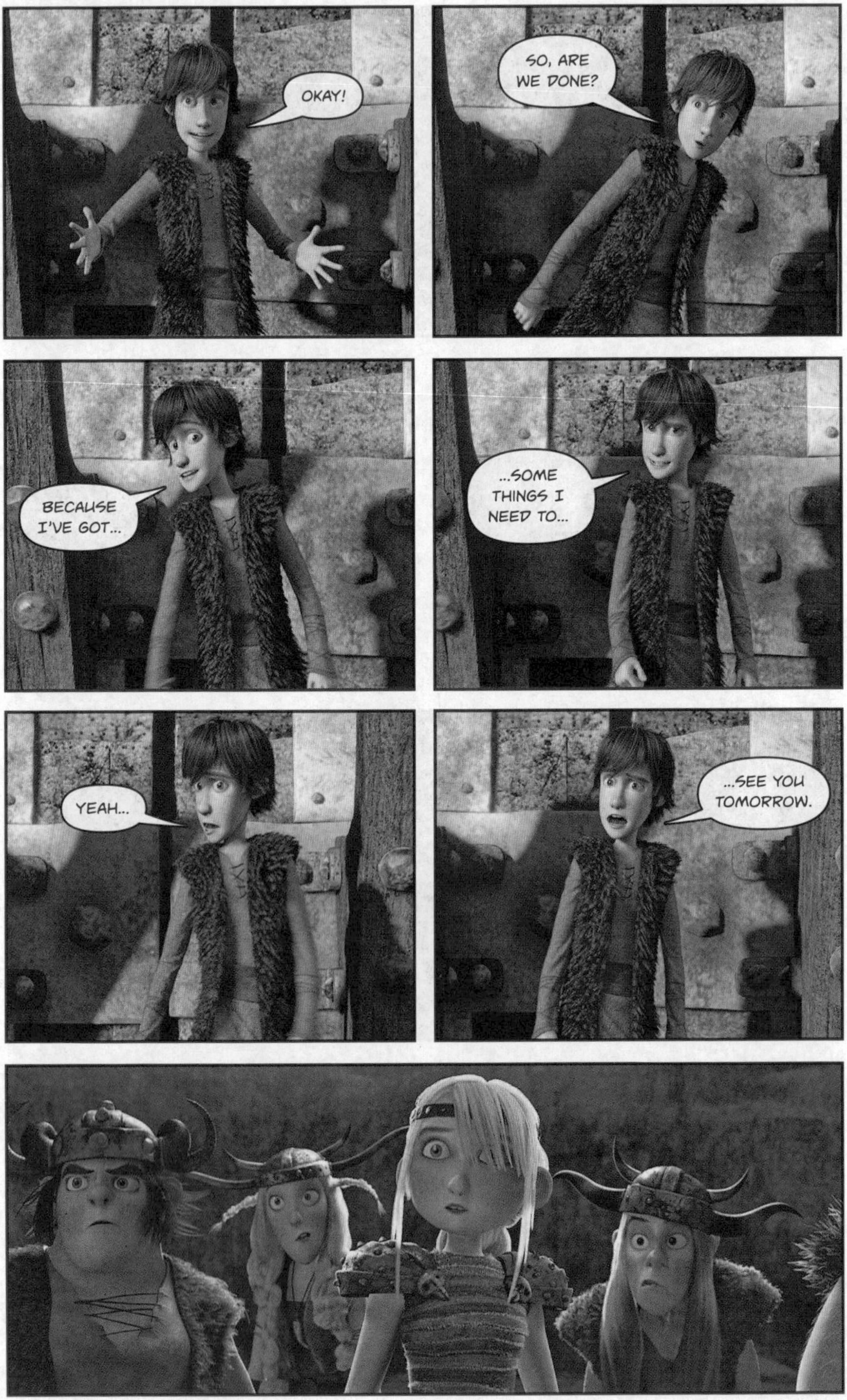
OKAY!
SO, ARE WE DONE?
BECAUSE I'VE GOT...
...SOME THINGS I NEED TO...
YEAH...
...SEE YOU TOMORROW.

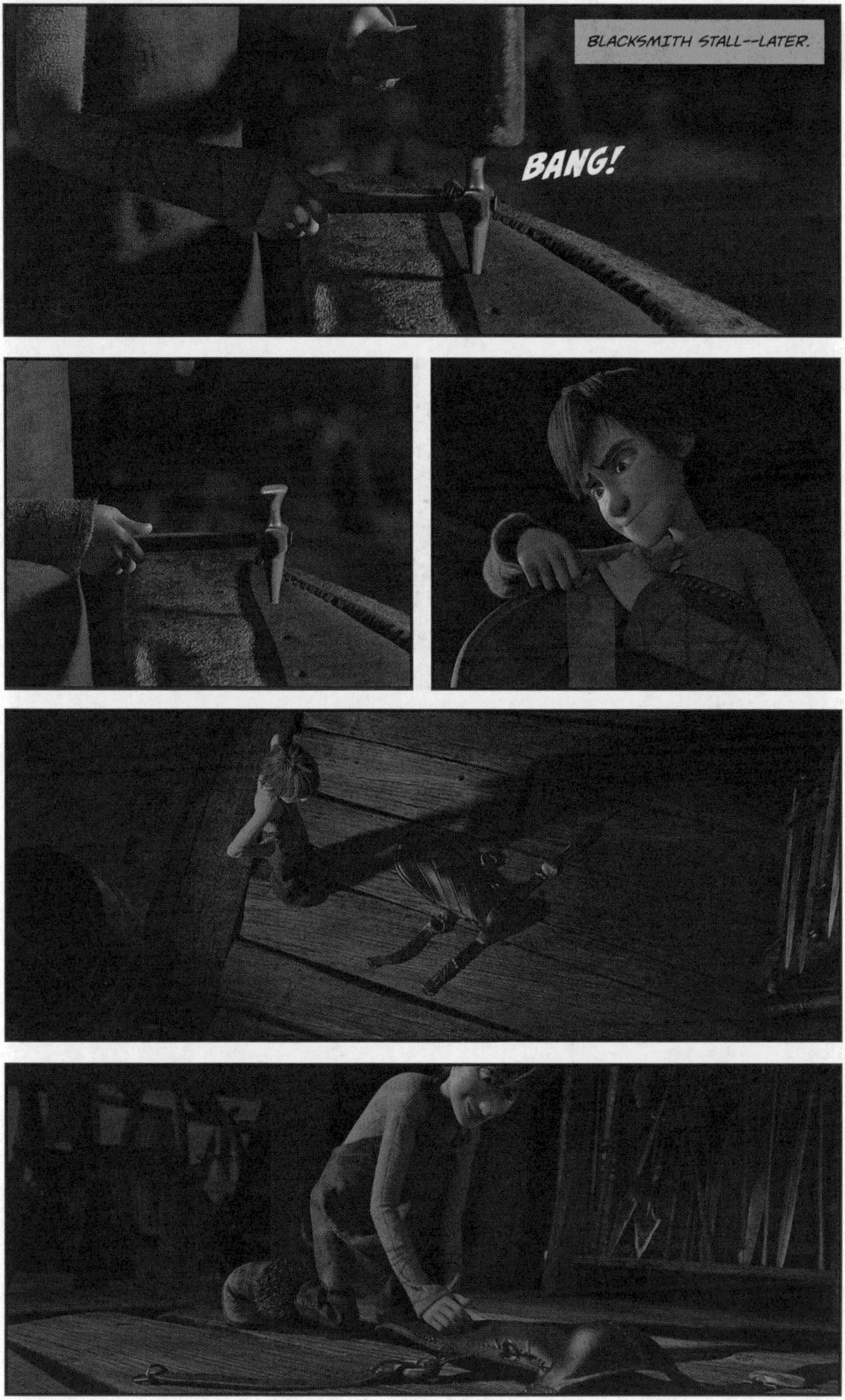
BLACKSMITH STALL--LATER.
BANG!

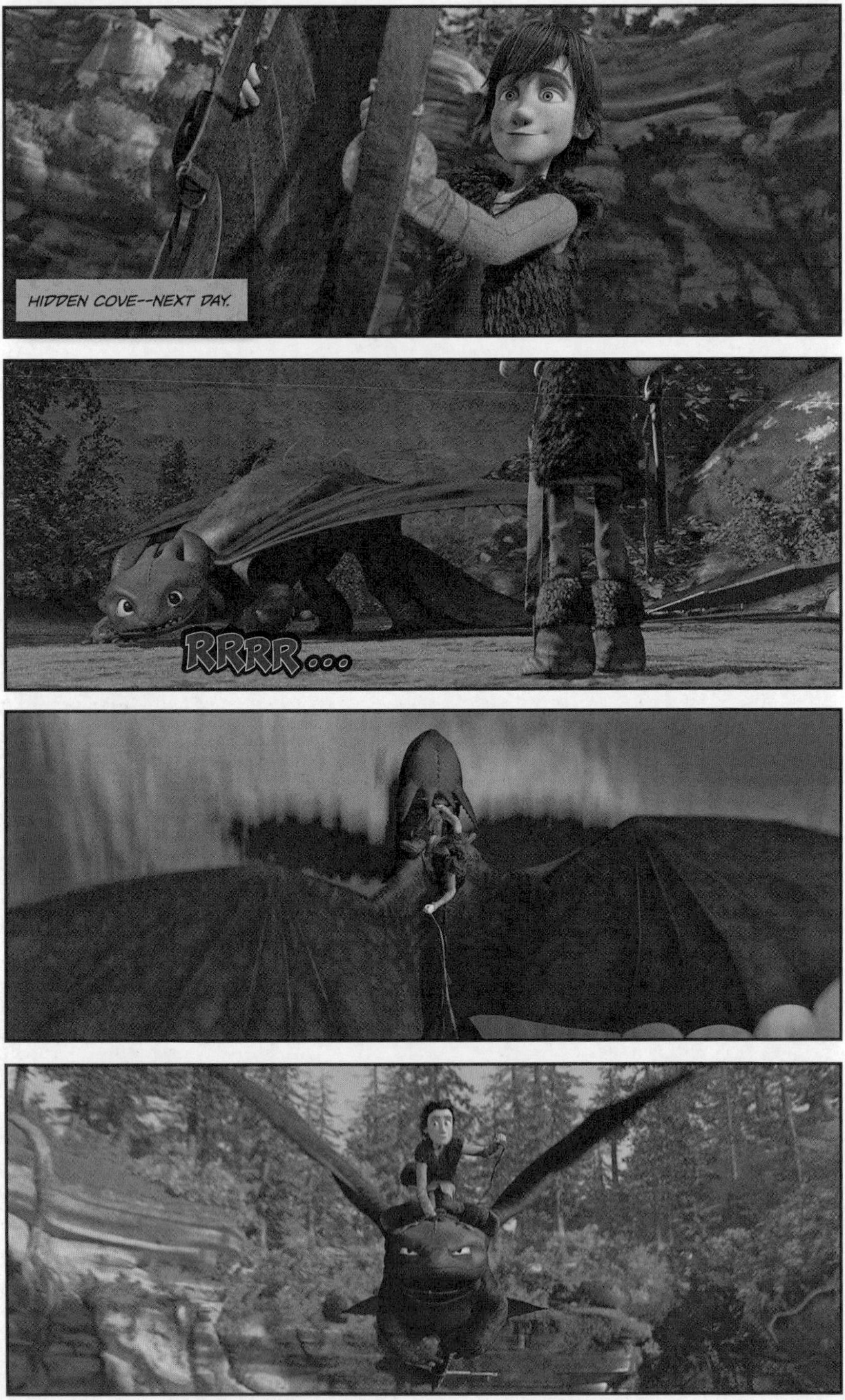
HIDDEN COVE--NEXT DAY.
RRRR...

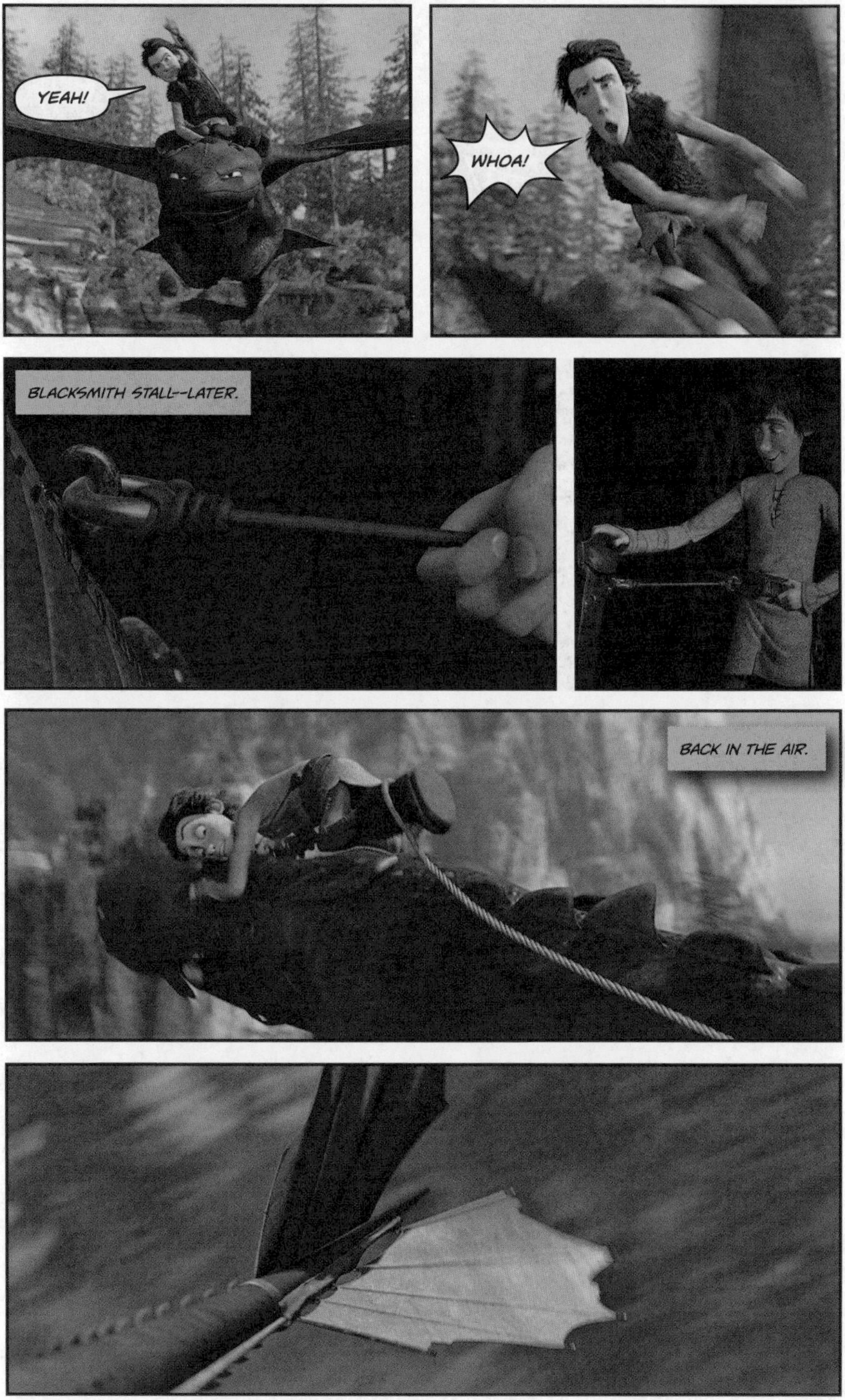
YEAH!
WHOA!
BLACKSMITH STALL--LATER.
BACK IN THE AIR.

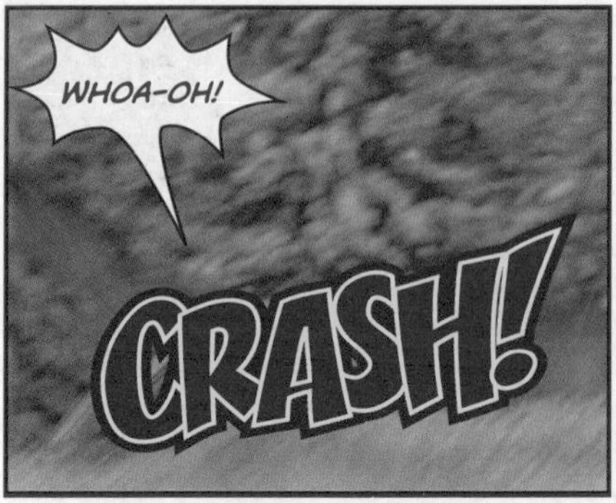
WHOA-OH!
CRASH!

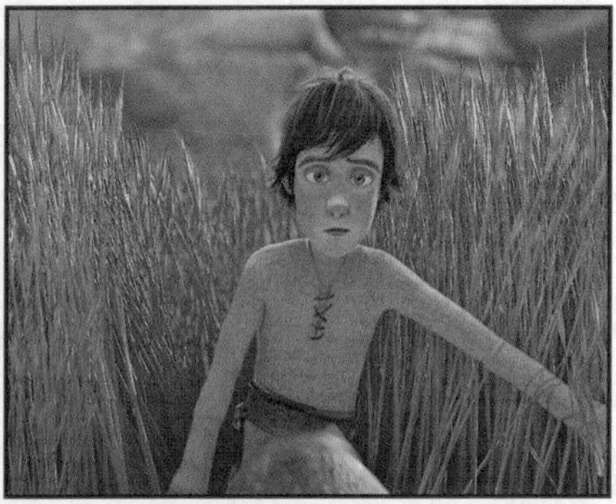

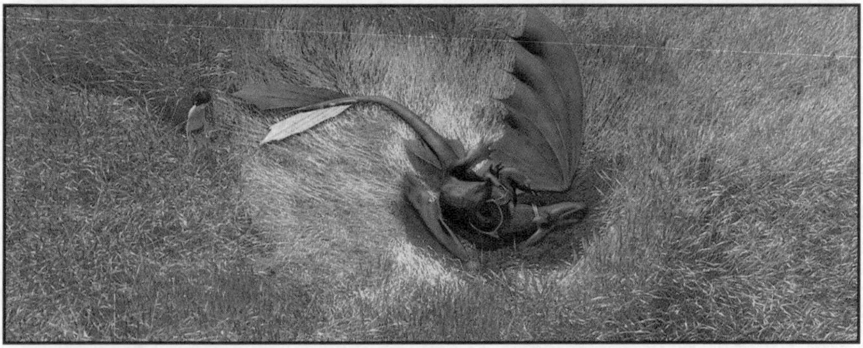

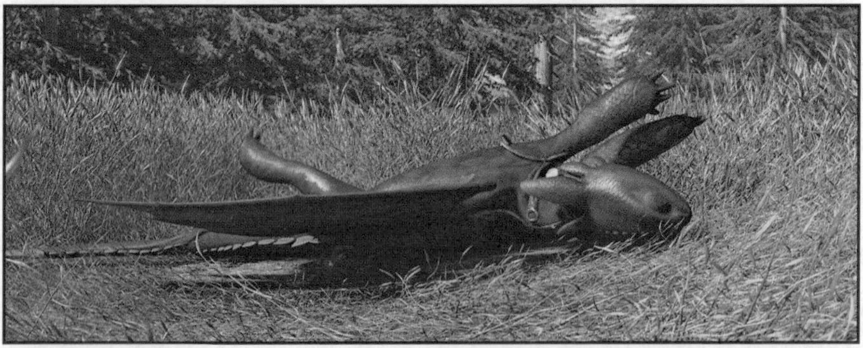

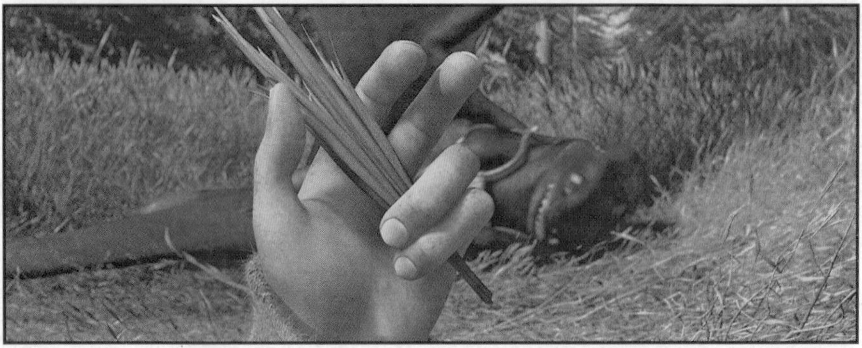

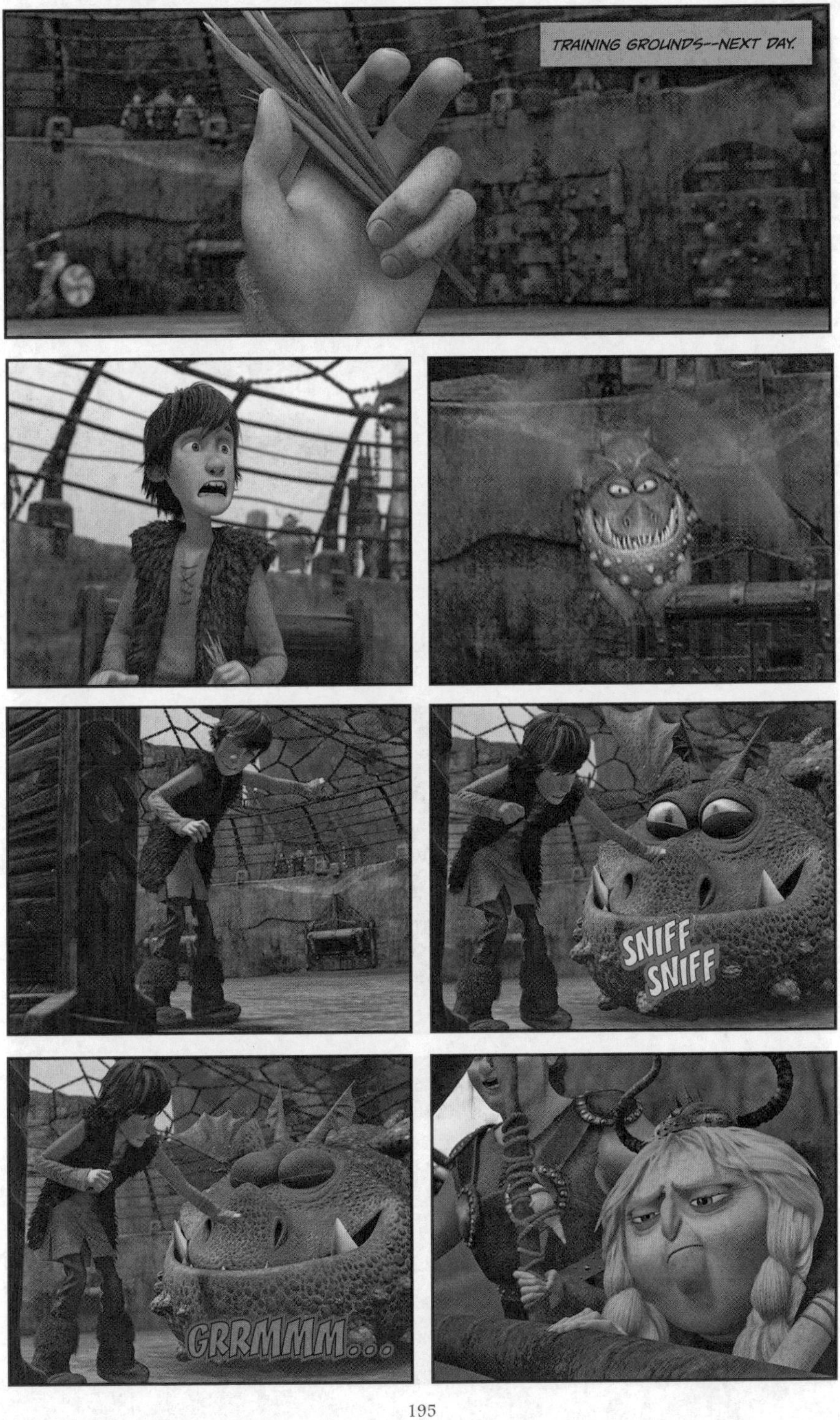
TRAINING GROUNDS--NEXT DAY.
SNIFF
SNIFF
GRRMMM...

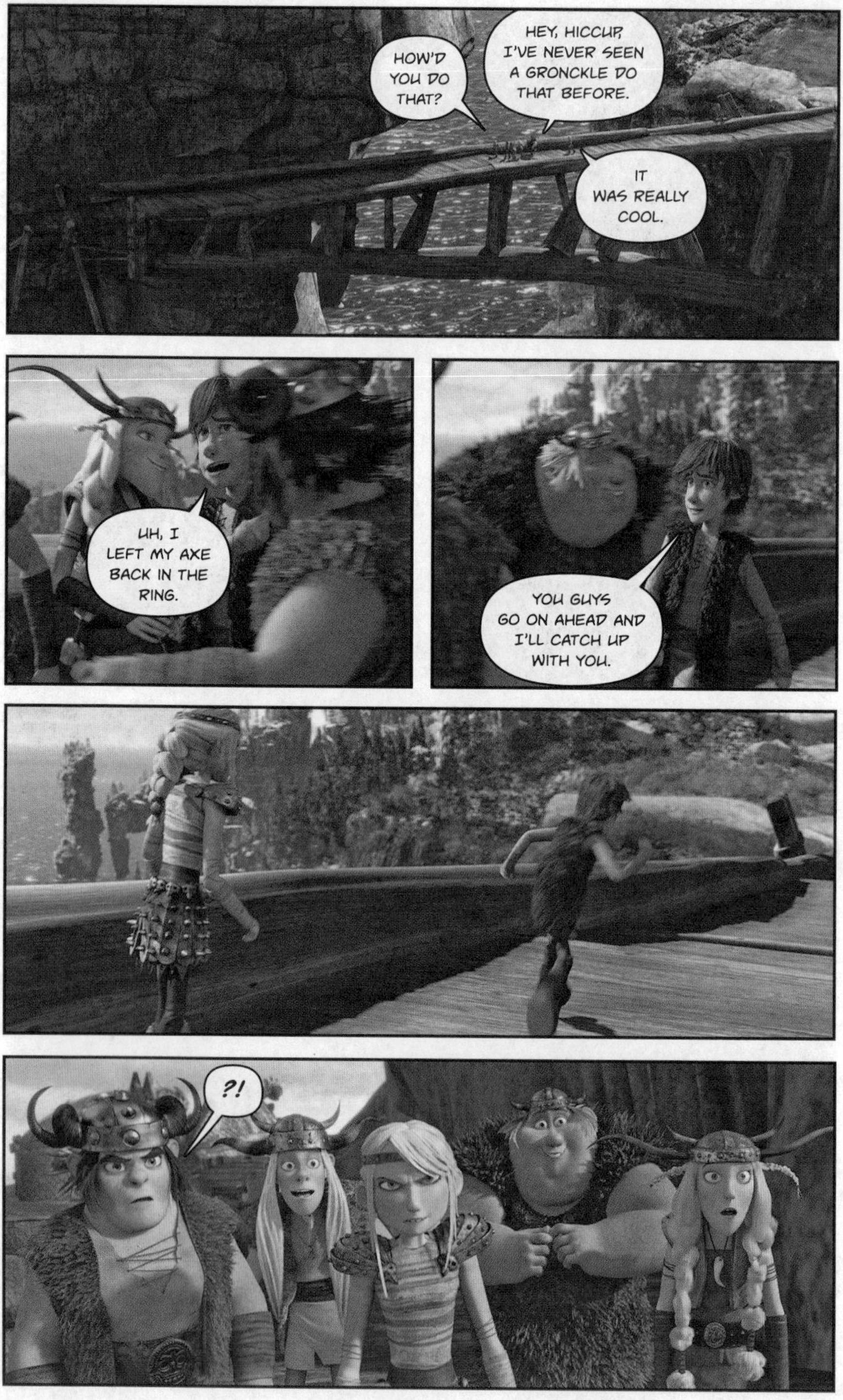
HOW'D YOU DO THAT?
HEY, HICCUP, I'VE NEVER SEEN A GRONCKLE DO THAT BEFORE.
IT WAS REALLY COOL.
UH, I LEFT MY AXE BACK IN THE RING.
YOU GUYS GO ON AHEAD AND I'LL CATCH UP WITH YOU.
?!

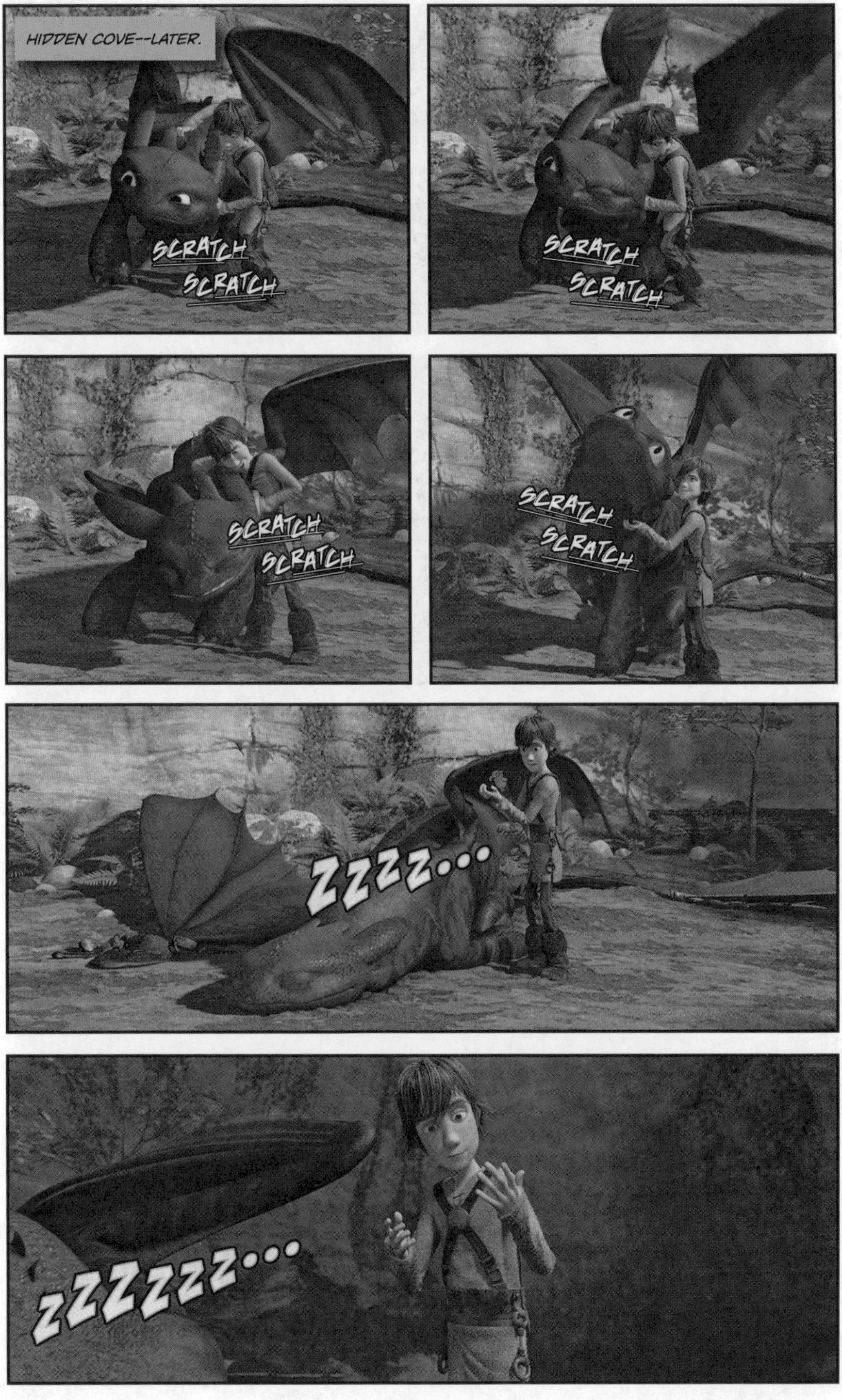
HIDDEN COVE--LATER.
SCRATCH
SCRATCH
SCRATCH
SCRATCH
SCRATCH
SCRATCH
SCRATCH
SCRATCH
ZZZZ...
zZZZZZ...

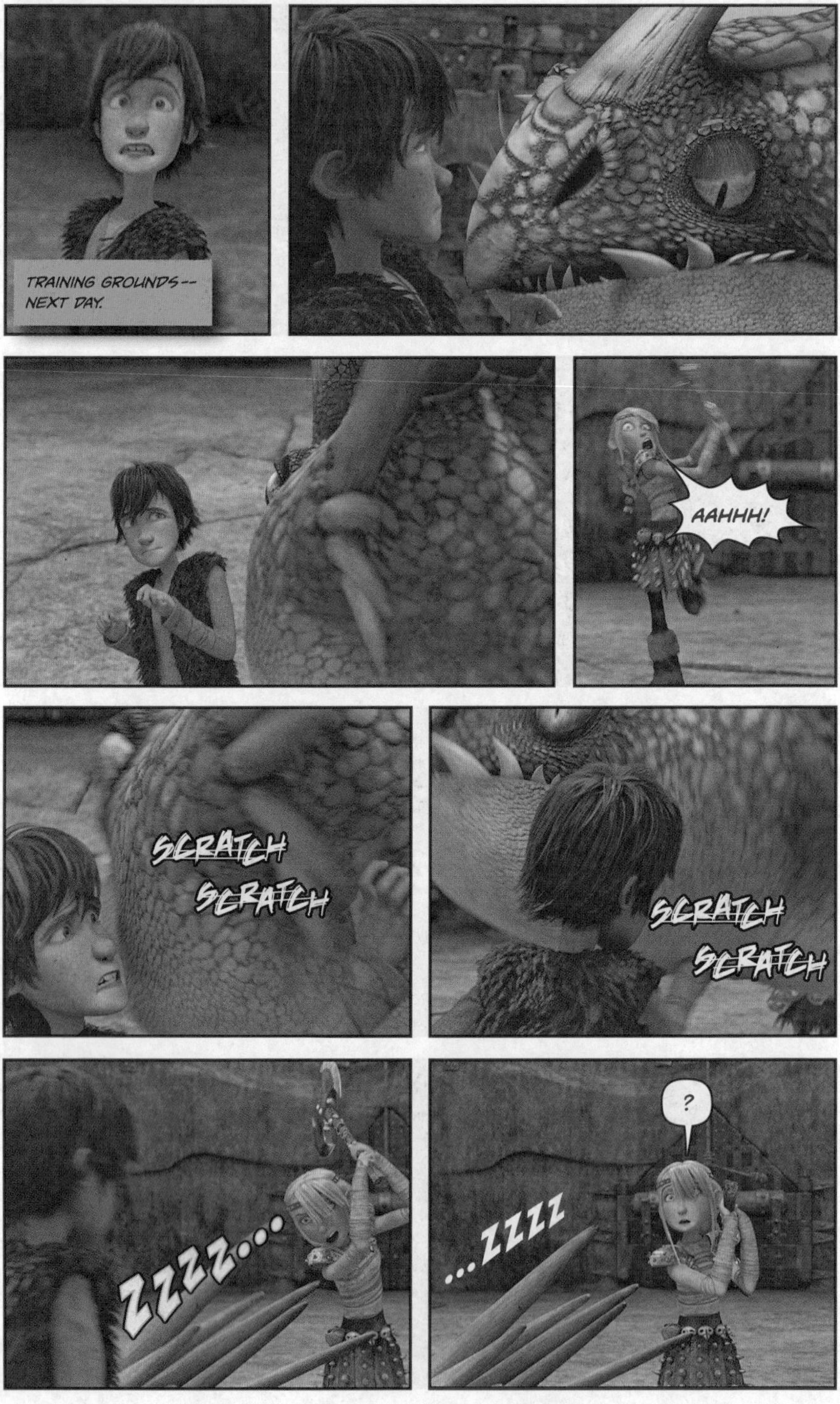
TRAINING GROUNDS--
NEXT DAY.
AAHHH!
SCRATCH
SCRATCH
SCRATCH
SCRATCH
ZZZZ...
...ZZZZ
?

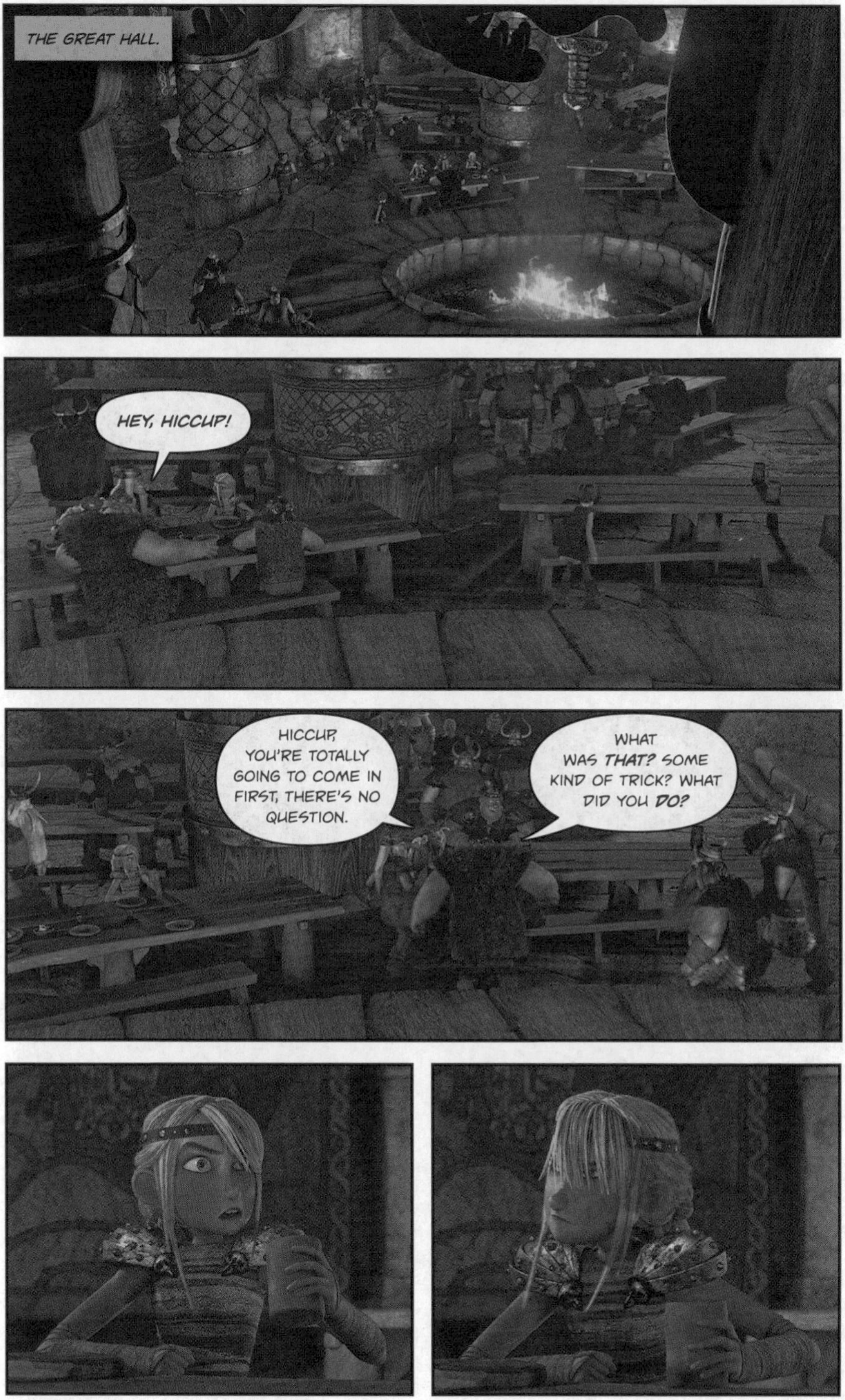
THE GREAT HALL.
HEY, HICCUP!
HICCUP, YOU'RE TOTALLY GOING TO COME IN FIRST, THERE'S NO QUESTION.
WHAT WAS *THAT?* SOME KIND OF TRICK? WHAT DID YOU *DO?*

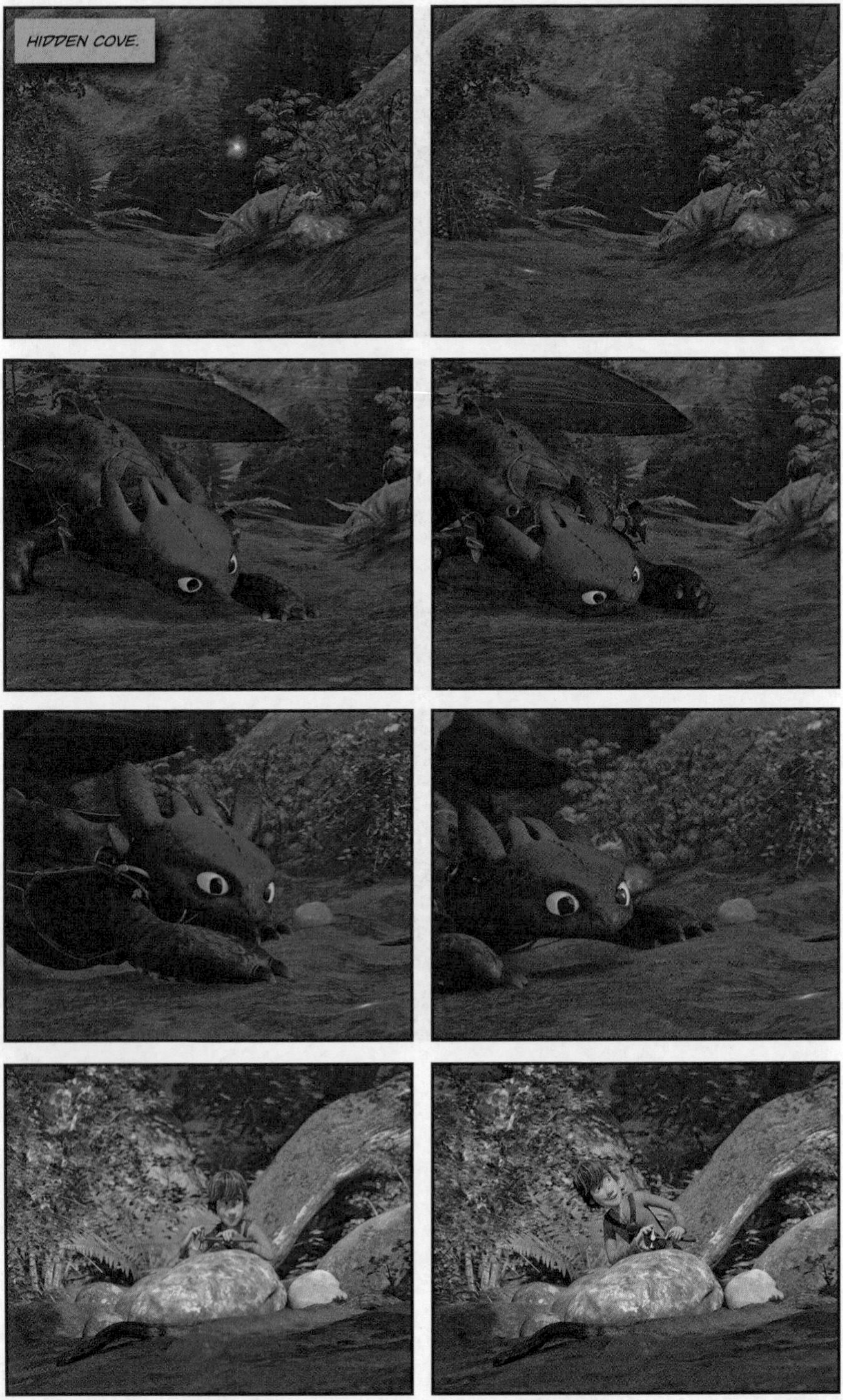
HIDDEN COVE.

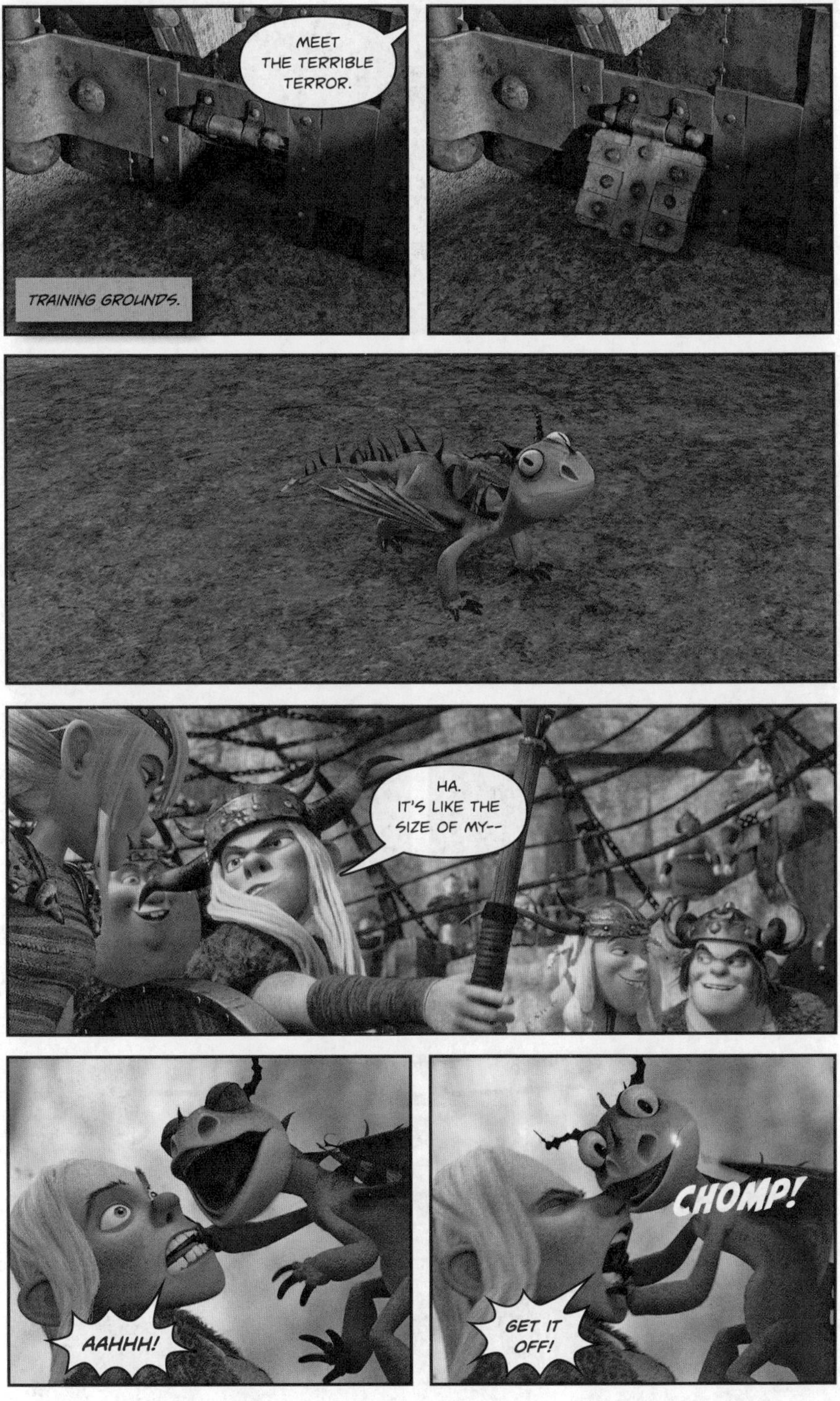
MEET THE TERRIBLE TERROR.
TRAINING GROUNDS.
HA. IT'S LIKE THE SIZE OF MY--
AAHHH!
CHOMP!
GET IT OFF!

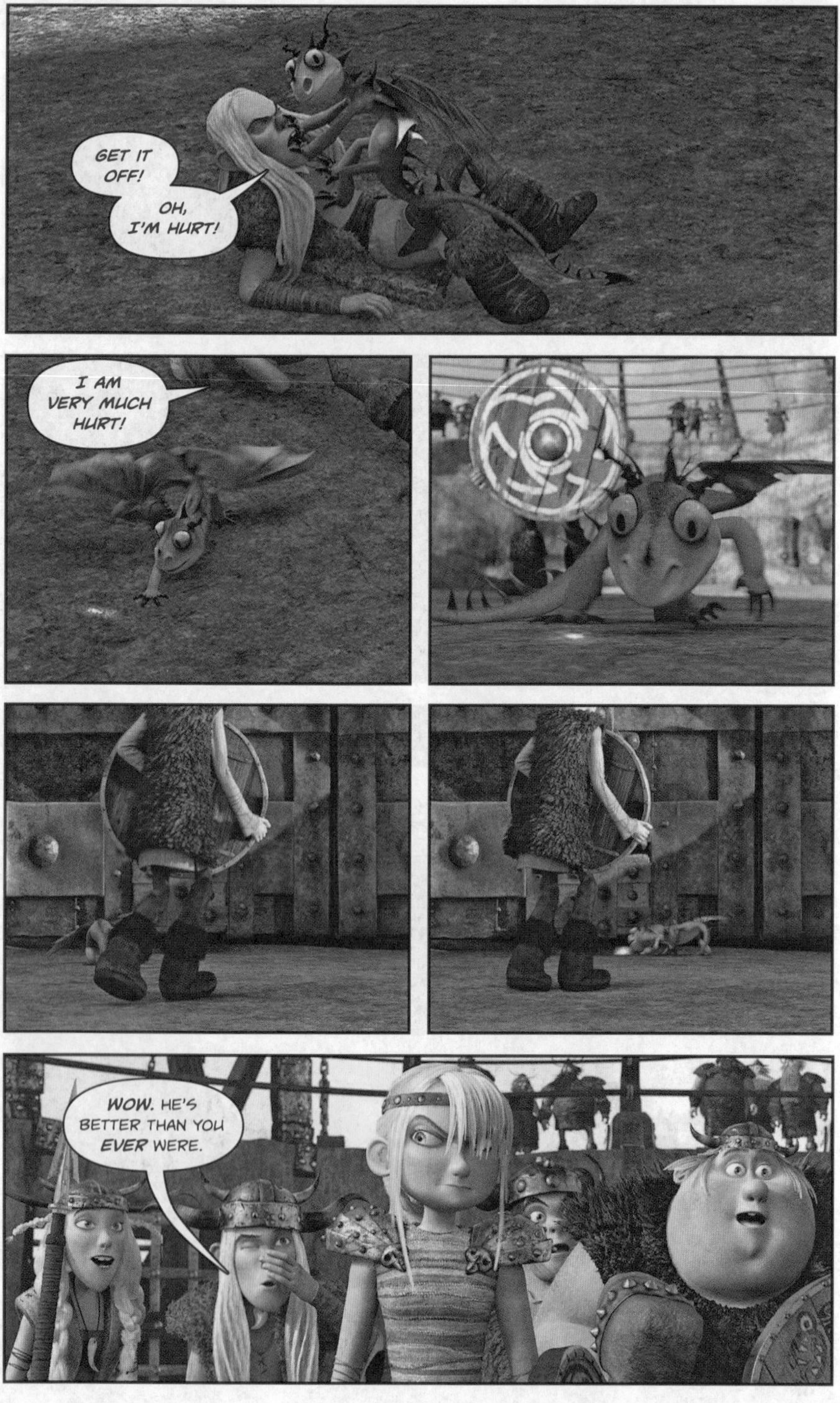
GET IT OFF!
OH, I'M HURT!
I AM VERY MUCH HURT!
WOW. HE'S BETTER THAN YOU EVER WERE.

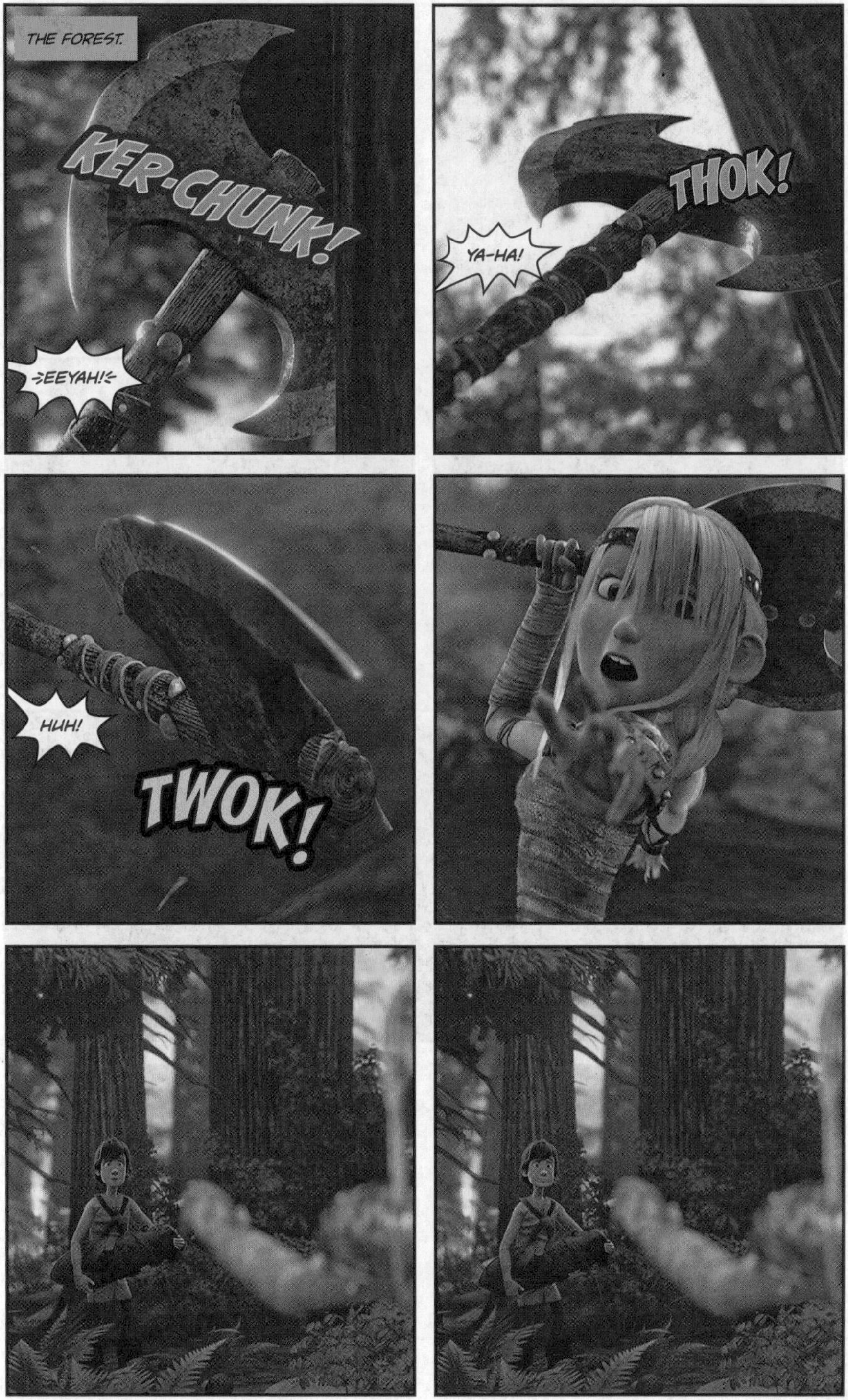
THE FOREST.
KER-CHUNK!
EEYAH!
THOK!
YA-HA!
HUH!
TWOK!

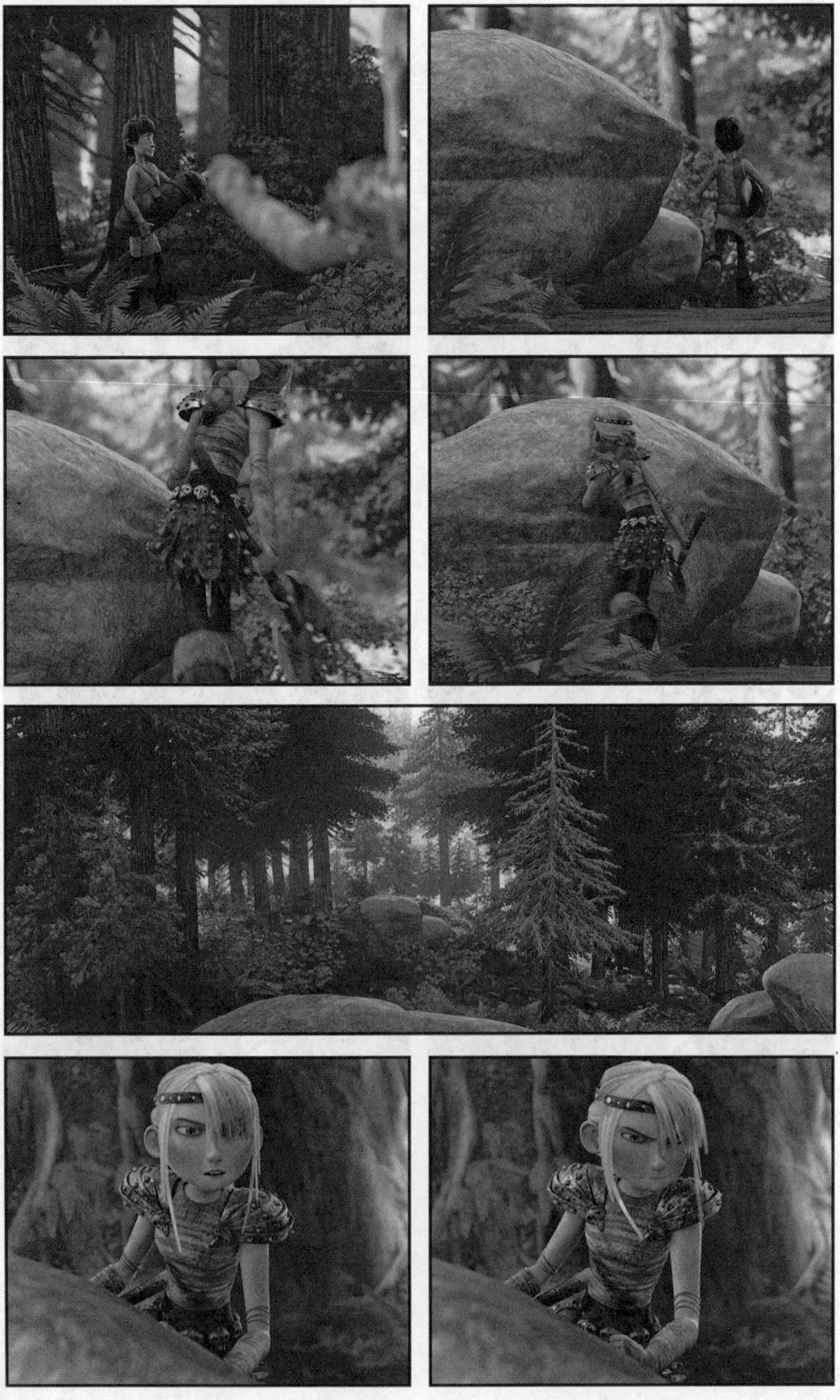

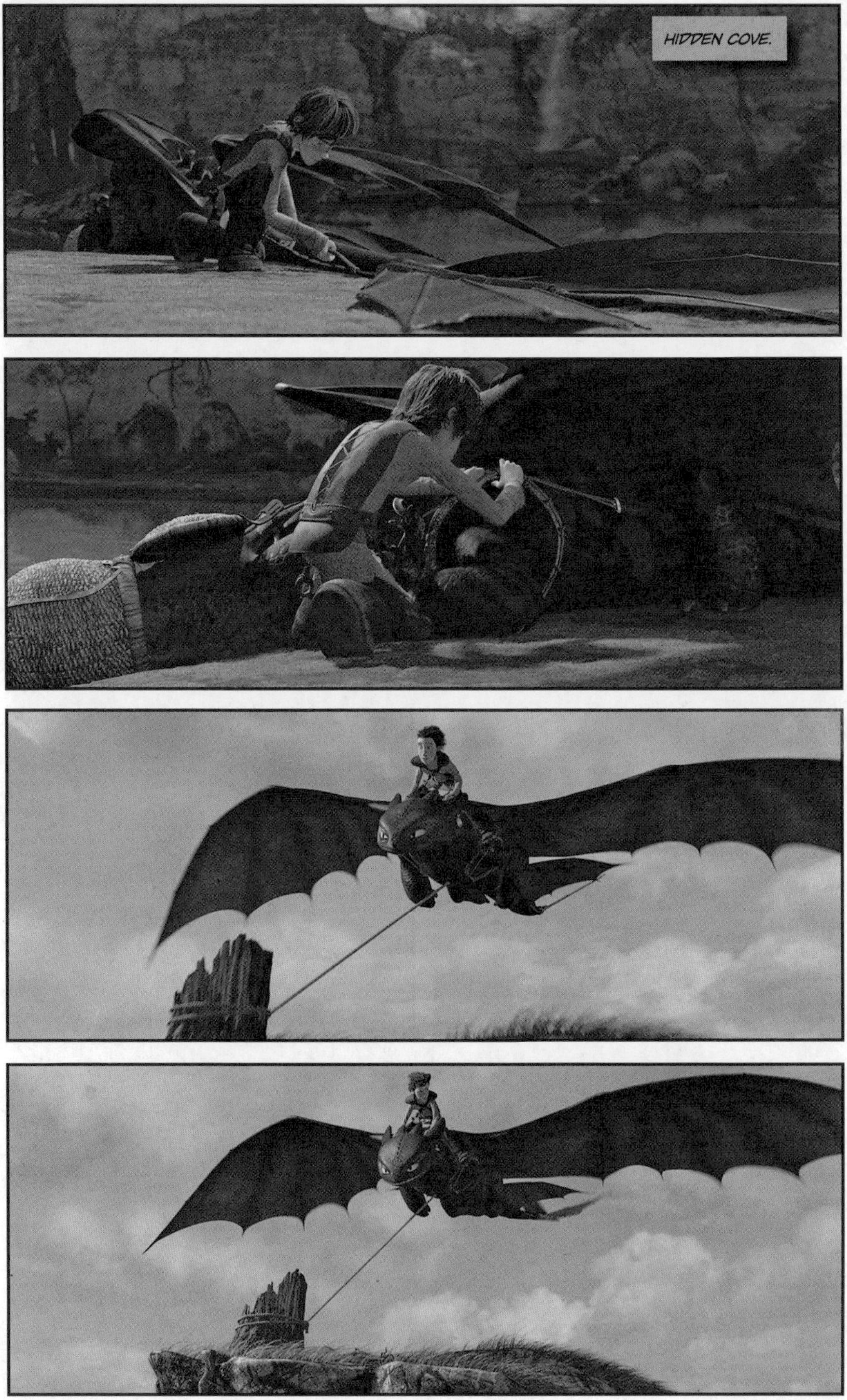
HIDDEN COVE.

CLICK!

THWAP!

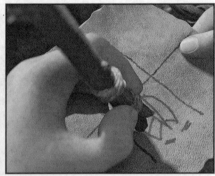

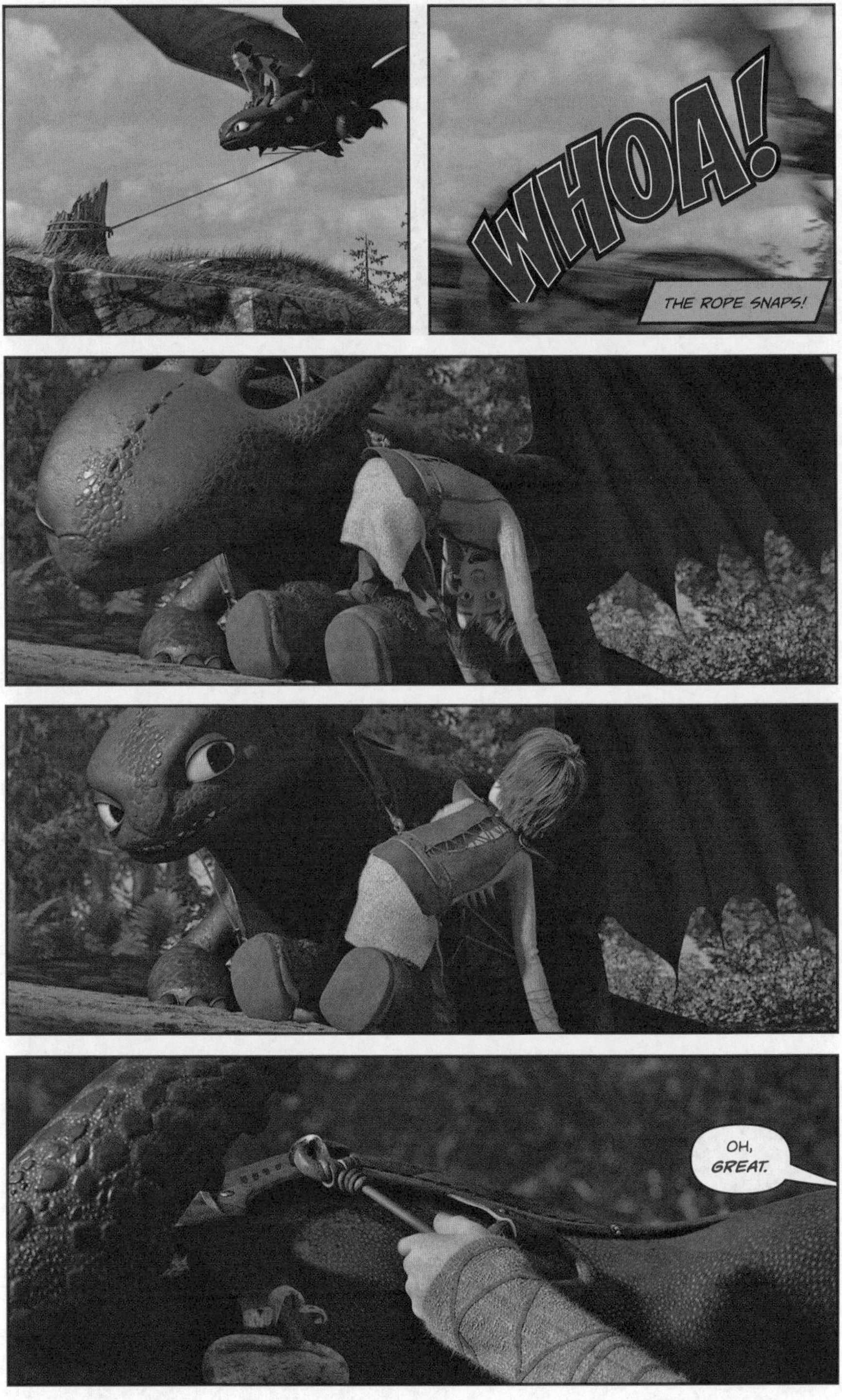
WHOA!
THE ROPE SNAPS!
OH, GREAT.

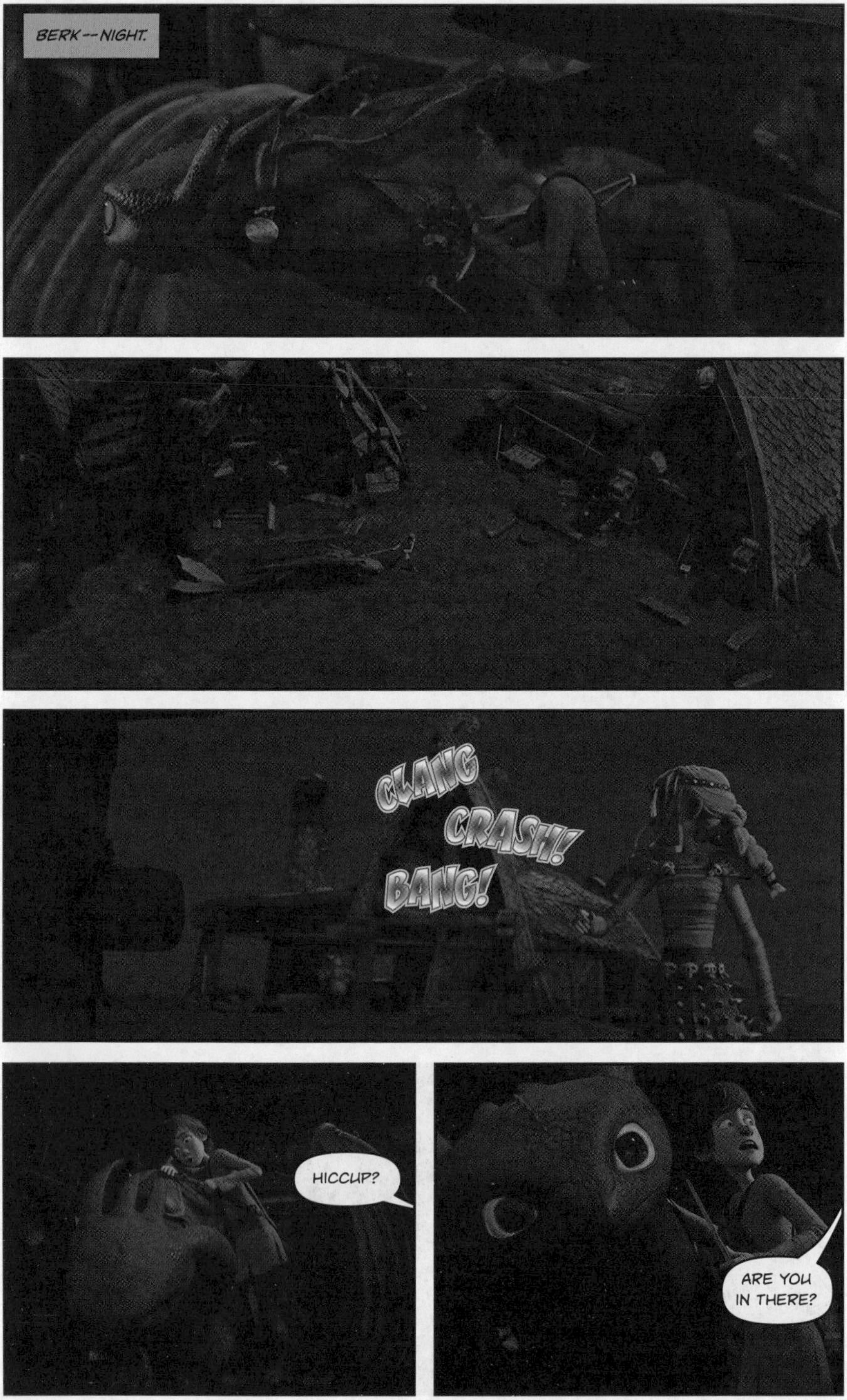
BERK--NIGHT.
CLANG
CRASH!
BANG!
HICCUP?
ARE YOU
IN THERE?

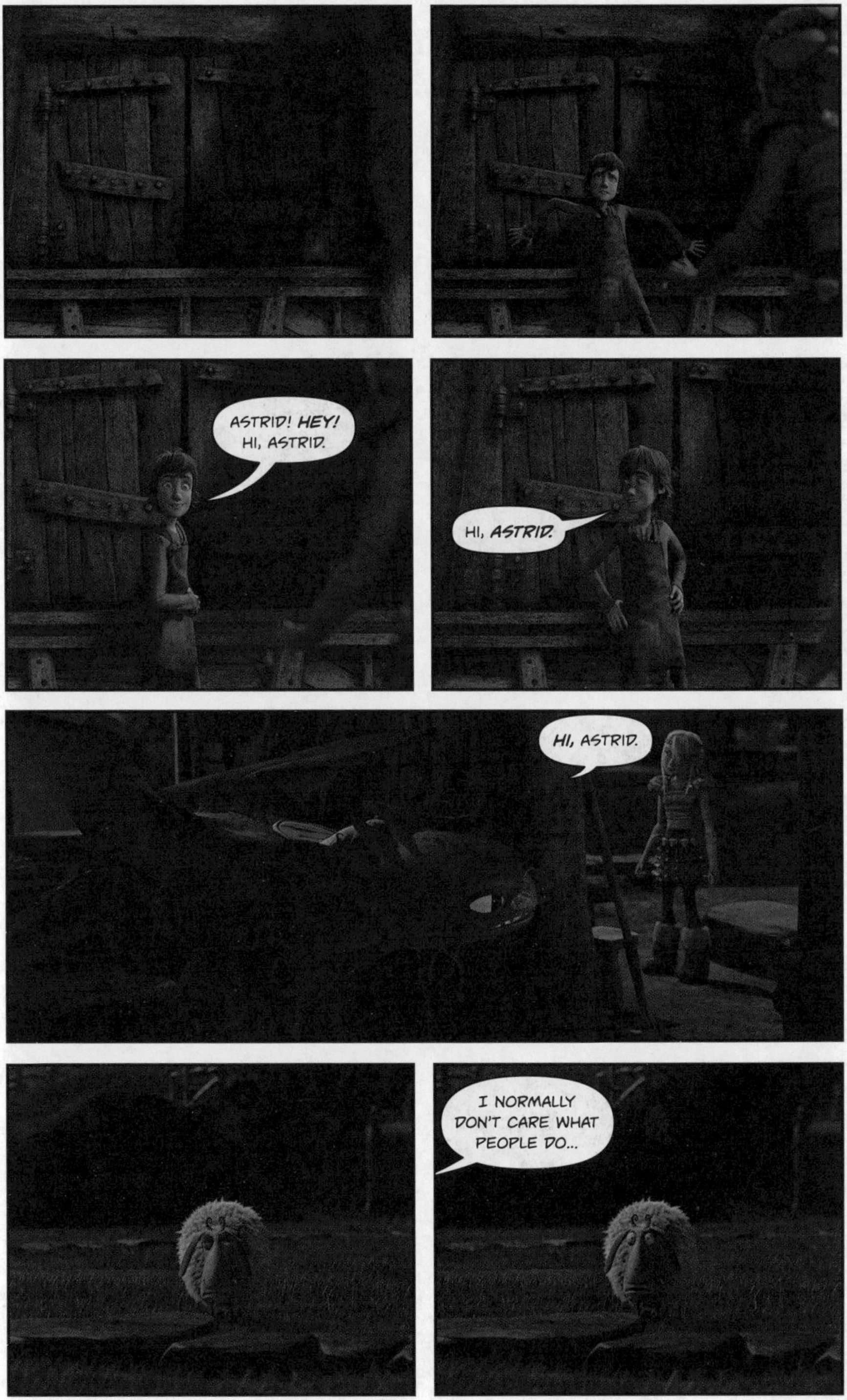
ASTRID! HEY! HI, ASTRID.
HI, ASTRID.
HI, ASTRID.
I NORMALLY DON'T CARE WHAT PEOPLE DO...

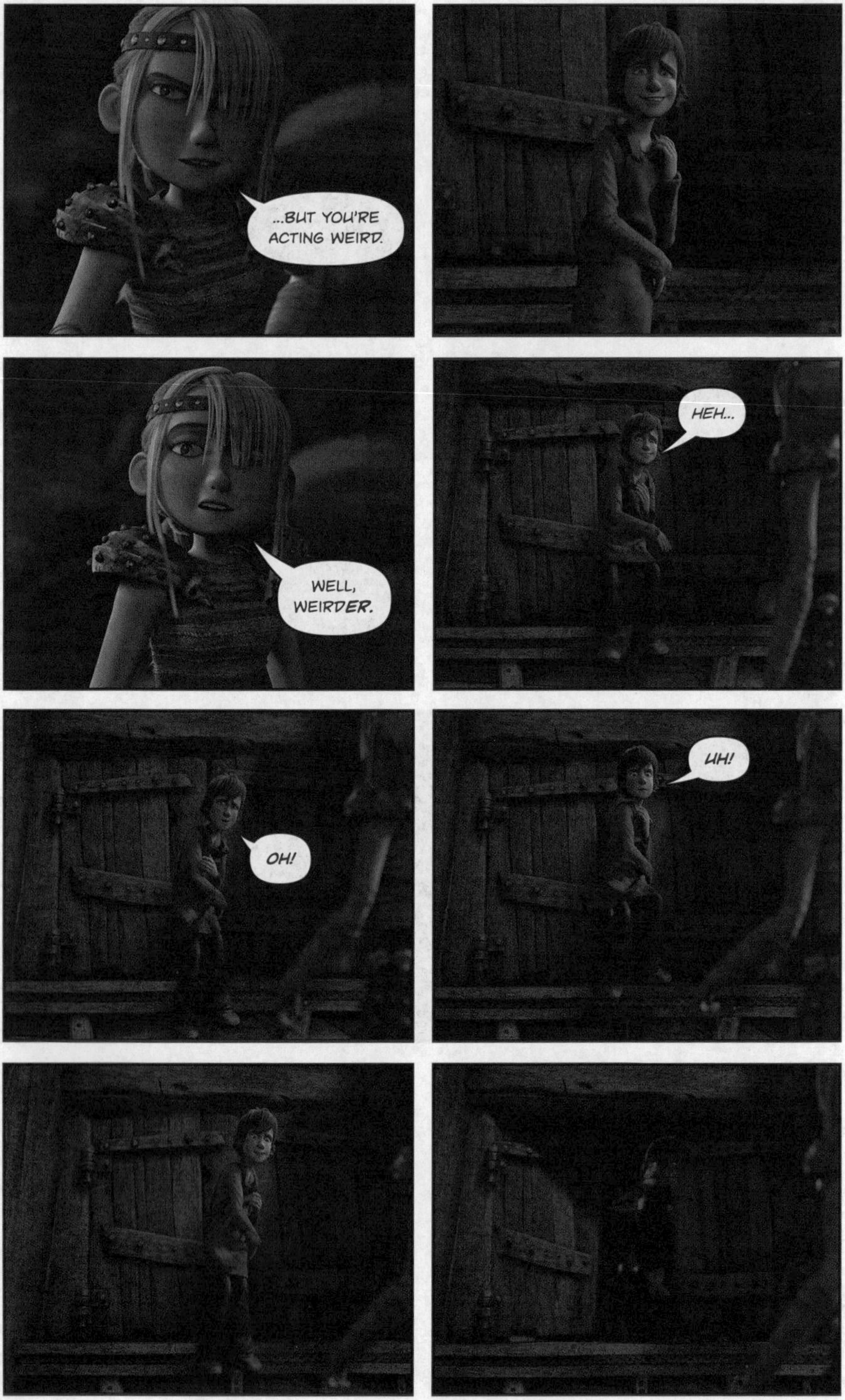
...BUT YOU'RE ACTING WEIRD.
WELL, WEIRDER.
HEH...
OH!
UH!

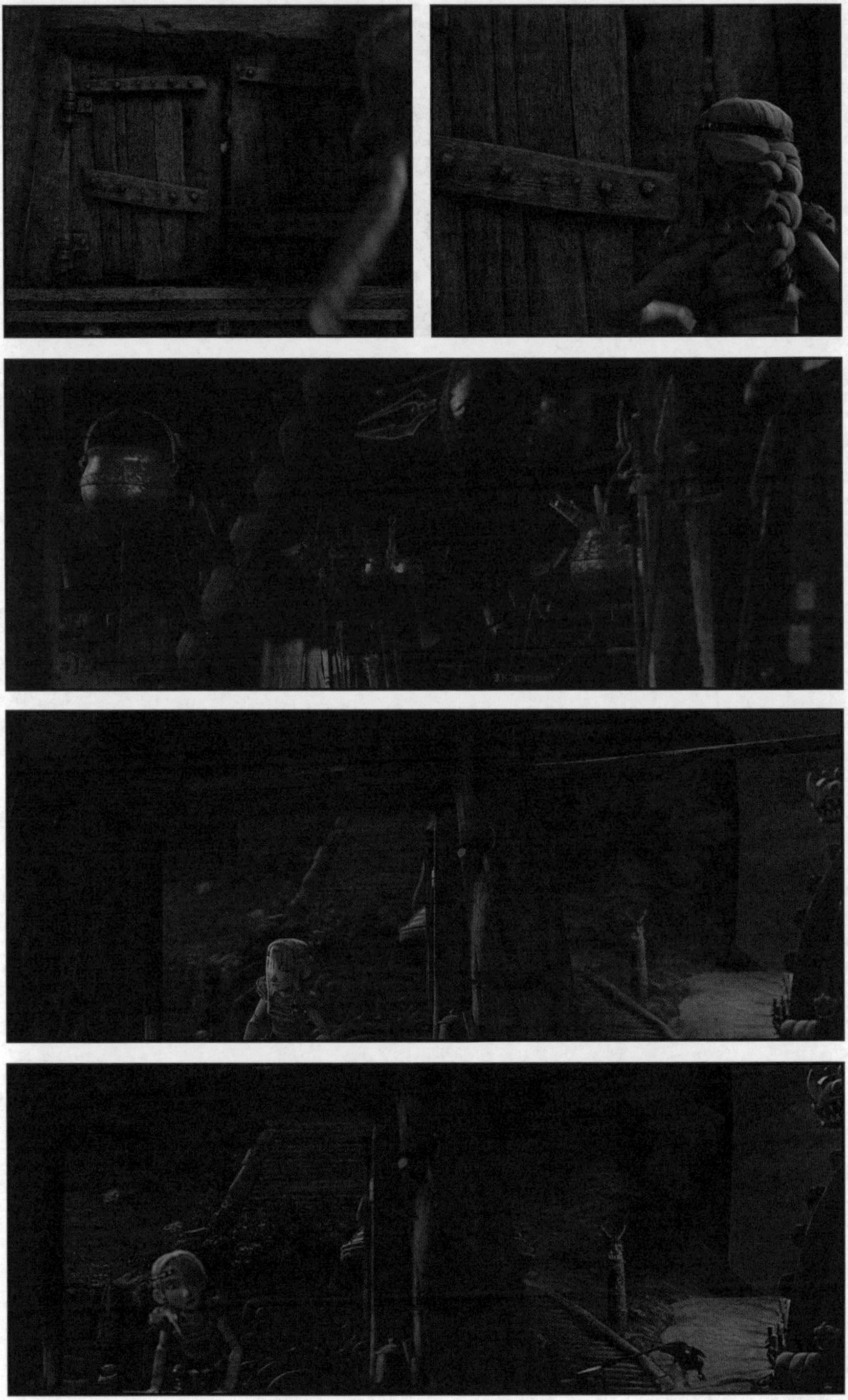

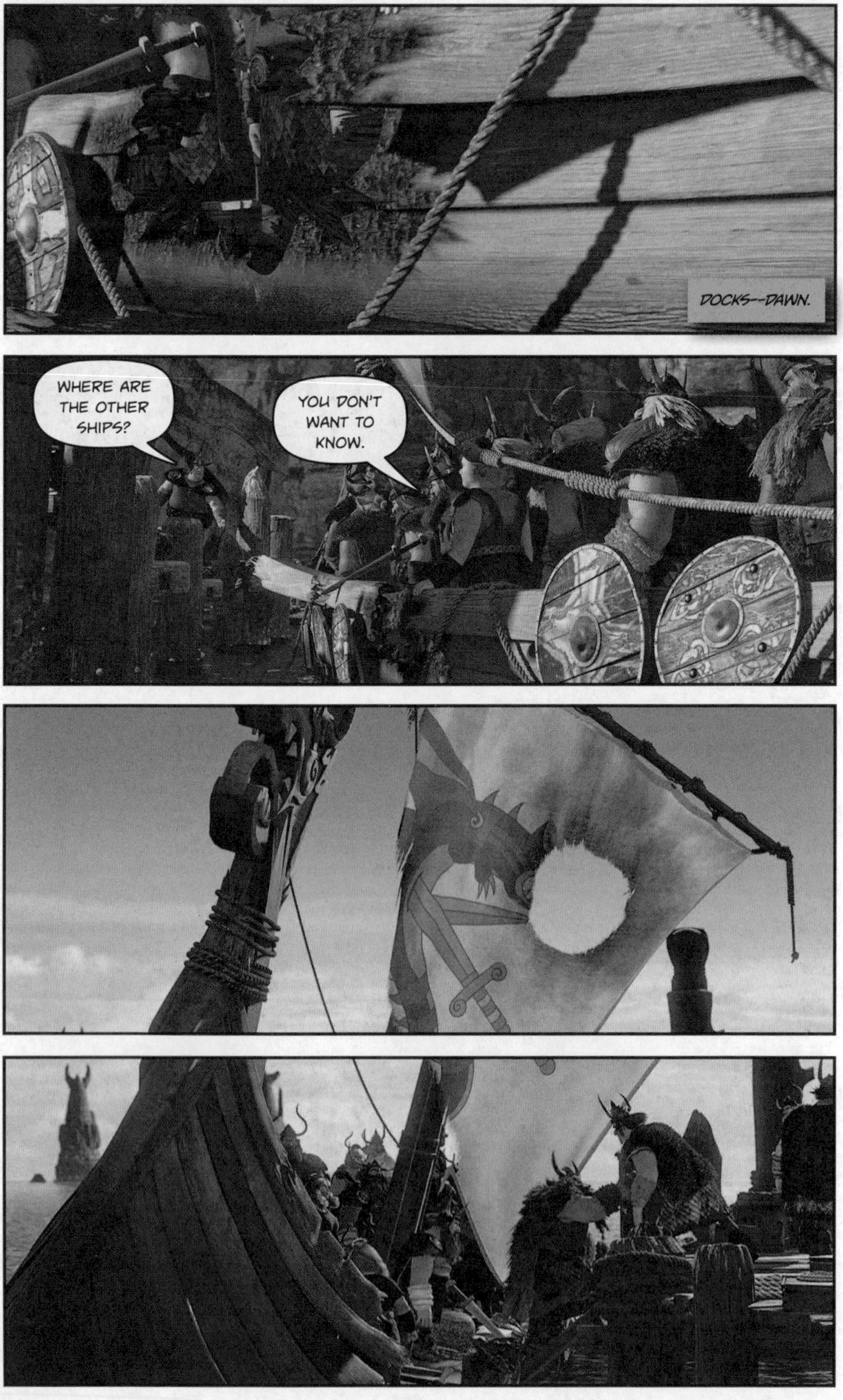
DOCKS--DAWN.
WHERE ARE THE OTHER SHIPS?
YOU DON'T WANT TO KNOW.

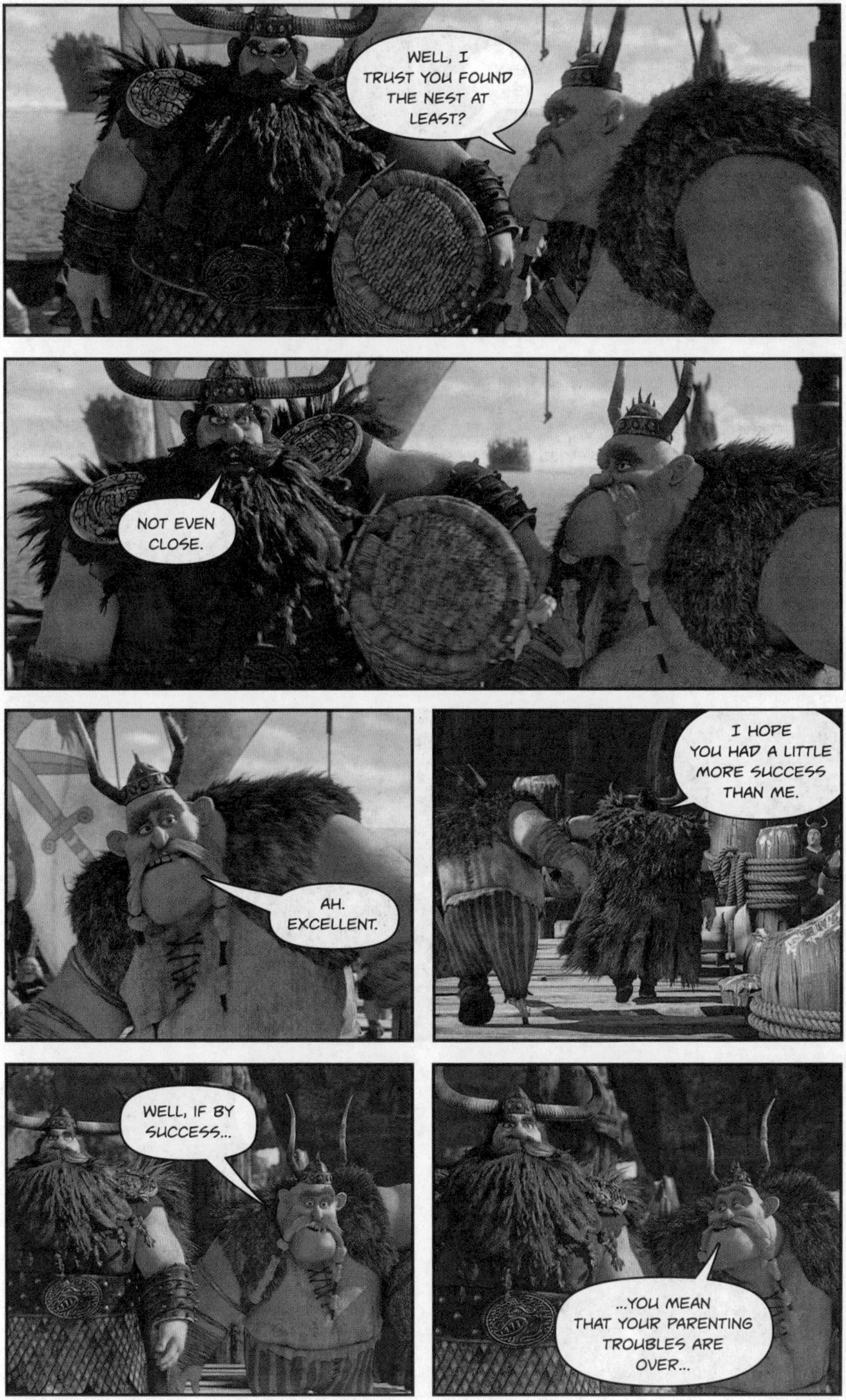
WELL, I TRUST YOU FOUND THE NEST AT LEAST?
NOT EVEN CLOSE.
AH. EXCELLENT.
I HOPE YOU HAD A LITTLE MORE SUCCESS THAN ME.
WELL, IF BY SUCCESS...
...YOU MEAN THAT YOUR PARENTING TROUBLES ARE OVER...

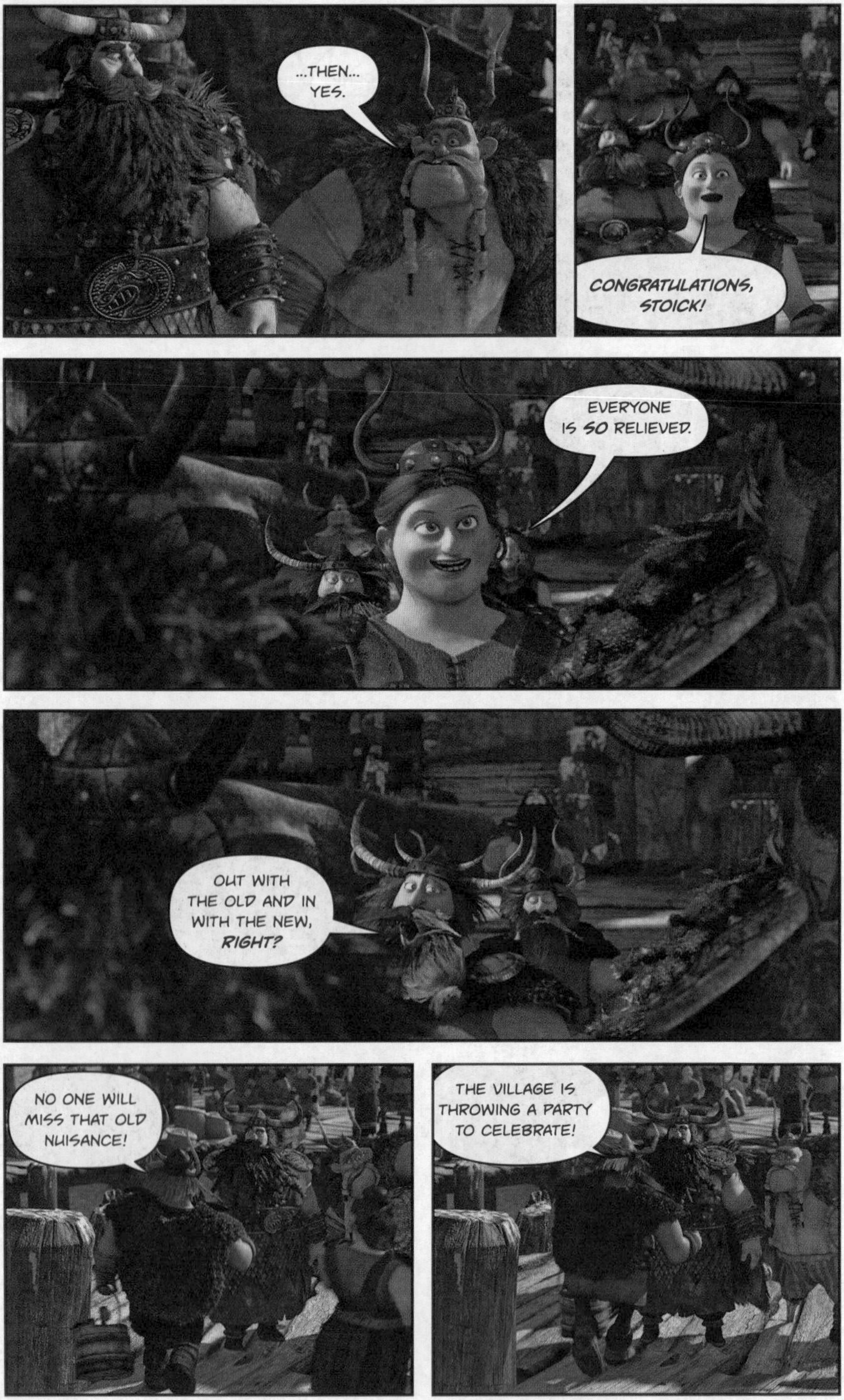
...THEN... YES.
CONGRATULATIONS, STOICK!
EVERYONE IS SO RELIEVED.
OUT WITH THE OLD AND IN WITH THE NEW, RIGHT?
NO ONE WILL MISS THAT OLD NUISANCE!
THE VILLAGE IS THROWING A PARTY TO CELEBRATE!

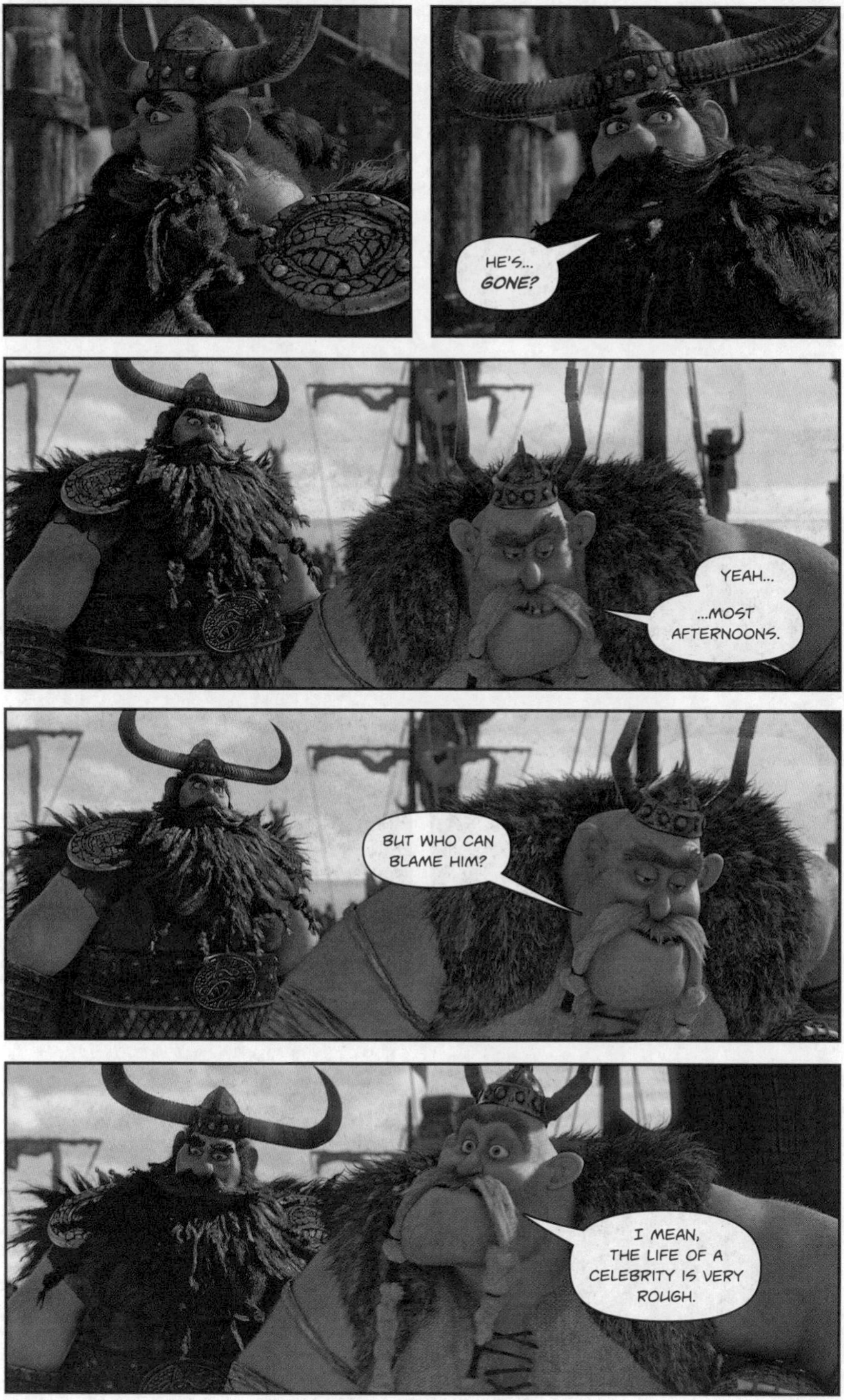
HE'S... GONE?
YEAH...
...MOST AFTERNOONS.
BUT WHO CAN BLAME HIM?
I MEAN, THE LIFE OF A CELEBRITY IS VERY ROUGH.

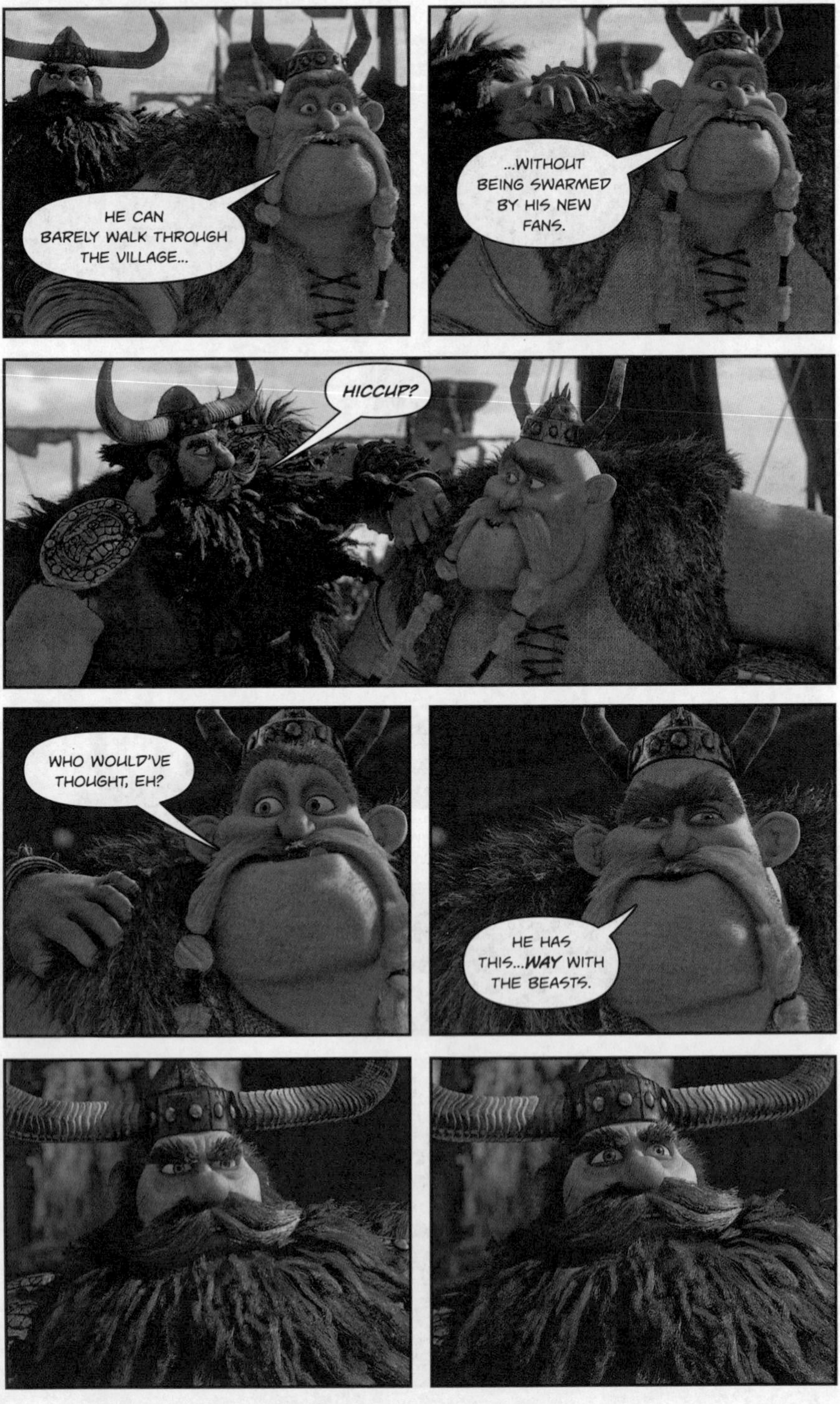
HE CAN BARELY WALK THROUGH THE VILLAGE...
...WITHOUT BEING SWARMED BY HIS NEW FANS.
HICCUP?
WHO WOULD'VE THOUGHT, EH?
HE HAS THIS...WAY WITH THE BEASTS.

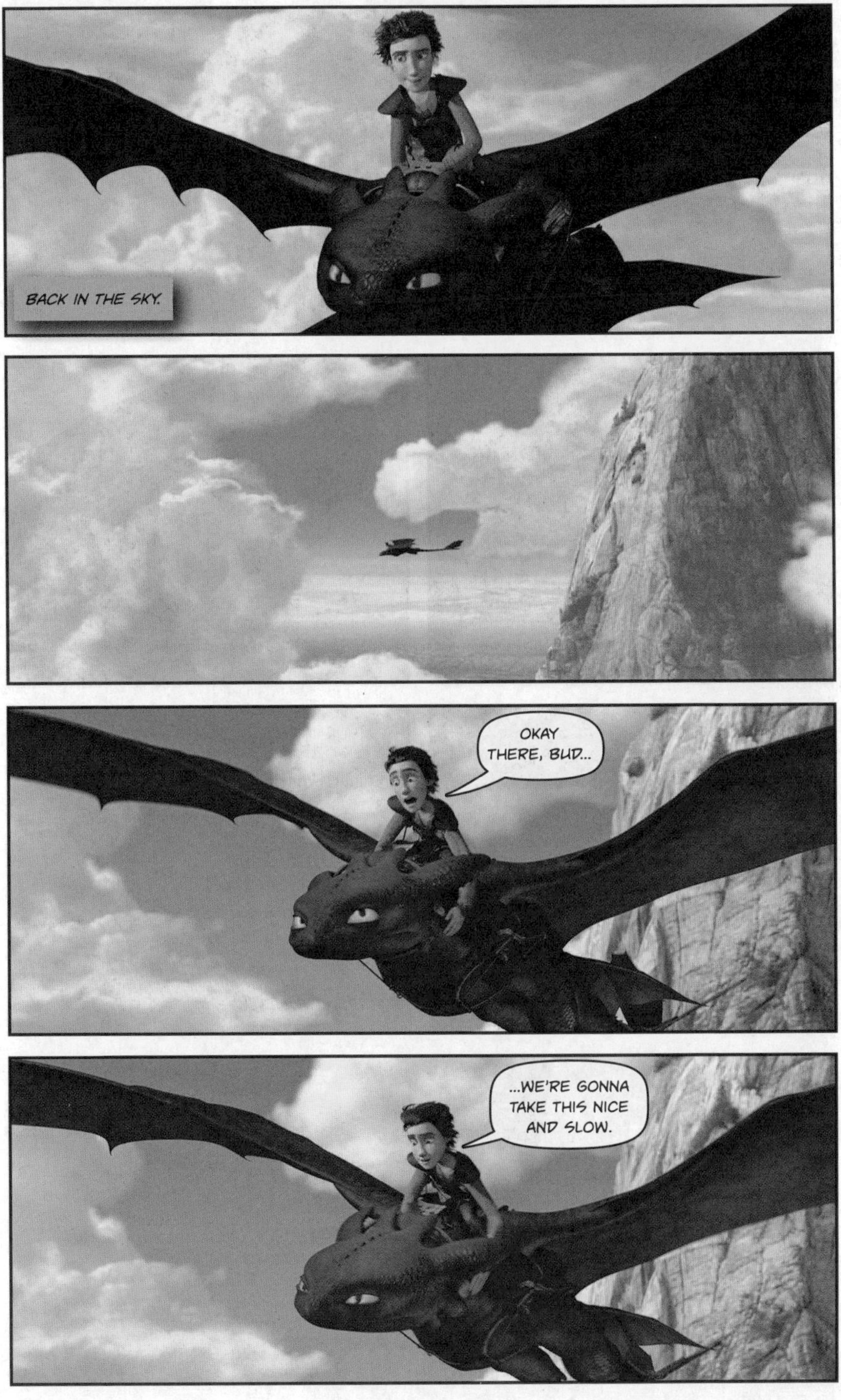
BACK IN THE SKY.
OKAY THERE, BUD...
...WE'RE GONNA TAKE THIS NICE AND SLOW.

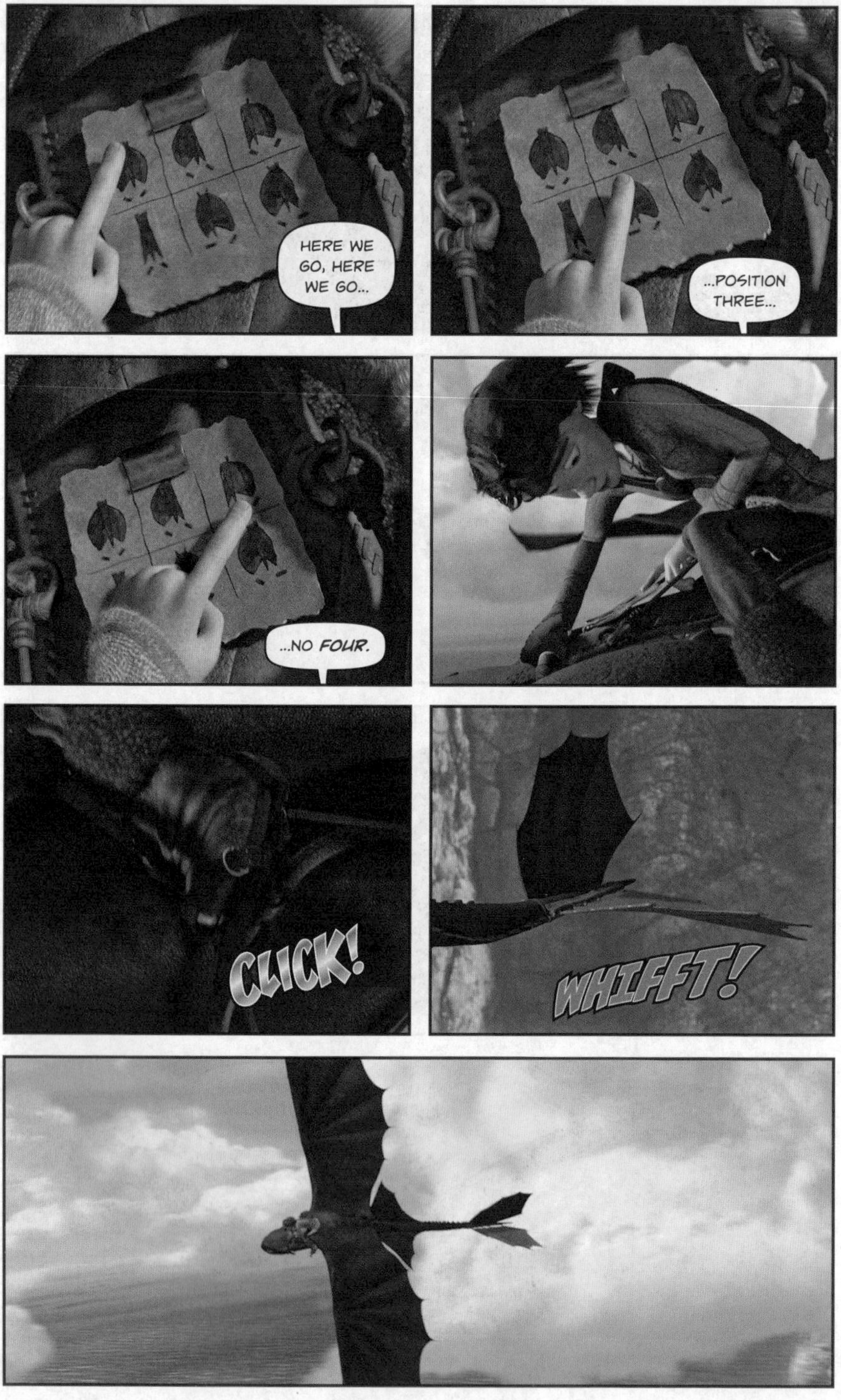
HERE WE GO, HERE WE GO...
...POSITION THREE...
...NO FOUR.
CLICK!
WHIFFT!

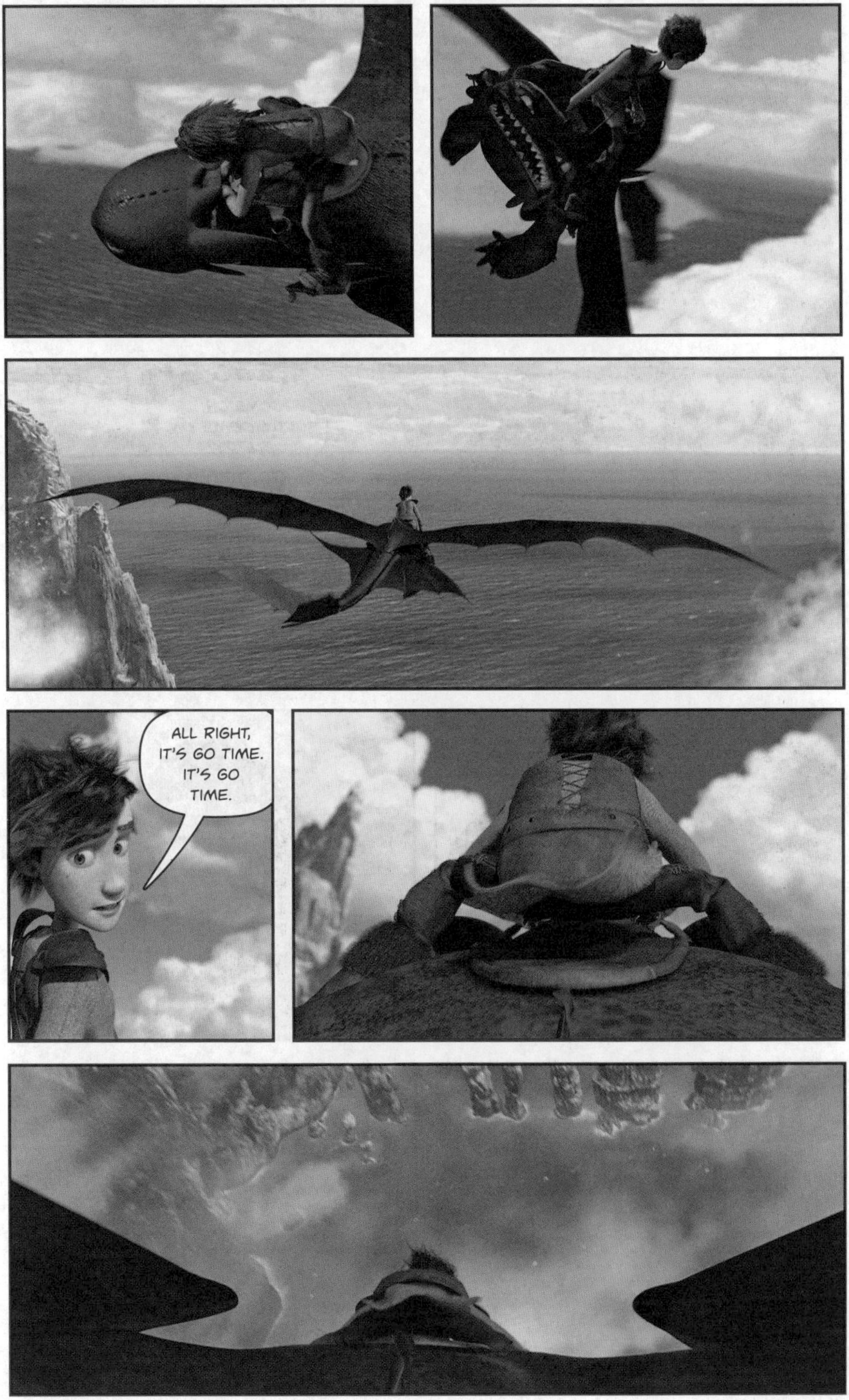
ALL RIGHT, IT'S GO TIME. IT'S GO TIME.

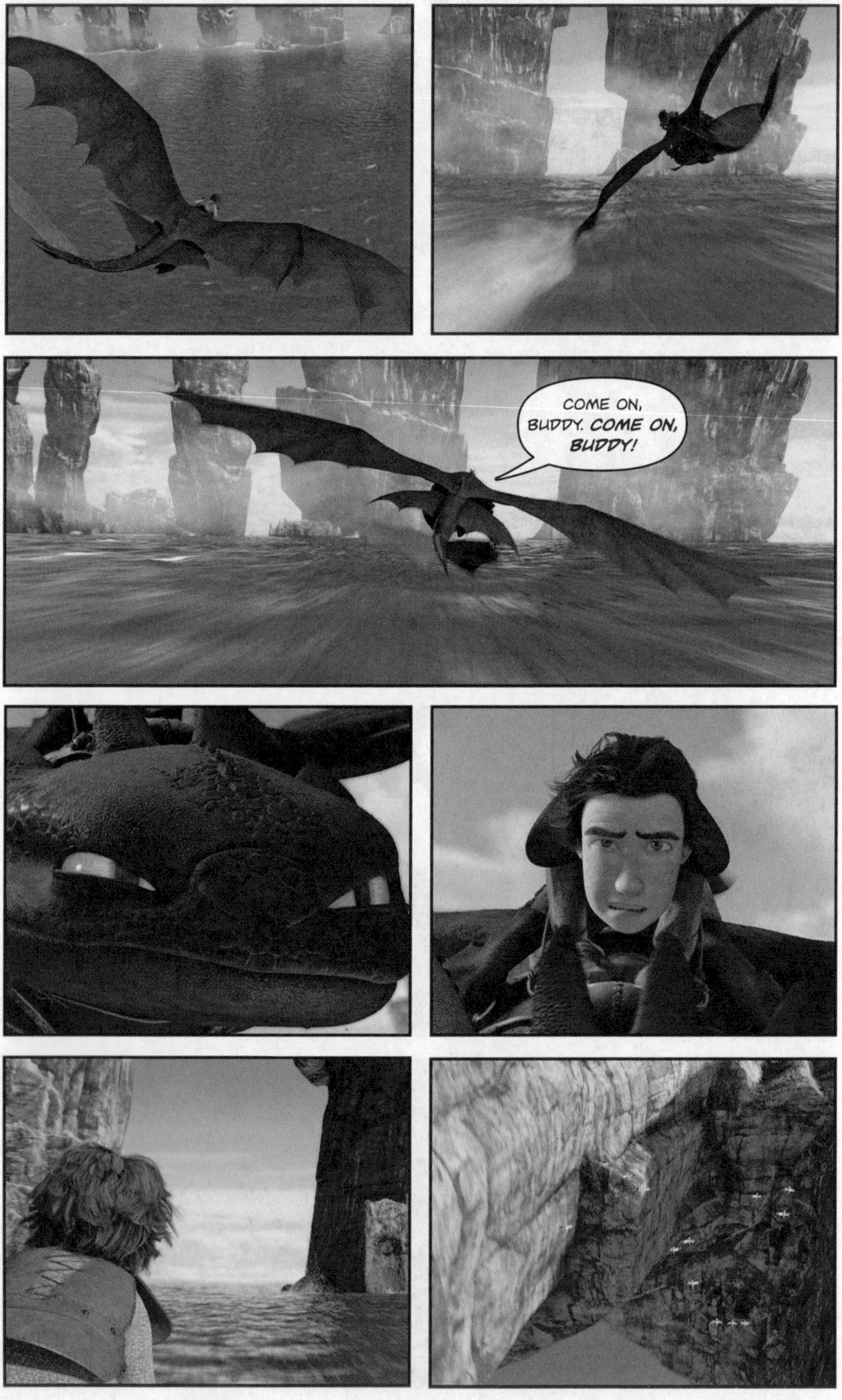
COME ON, BUDDY. COME ON, BUDDY!

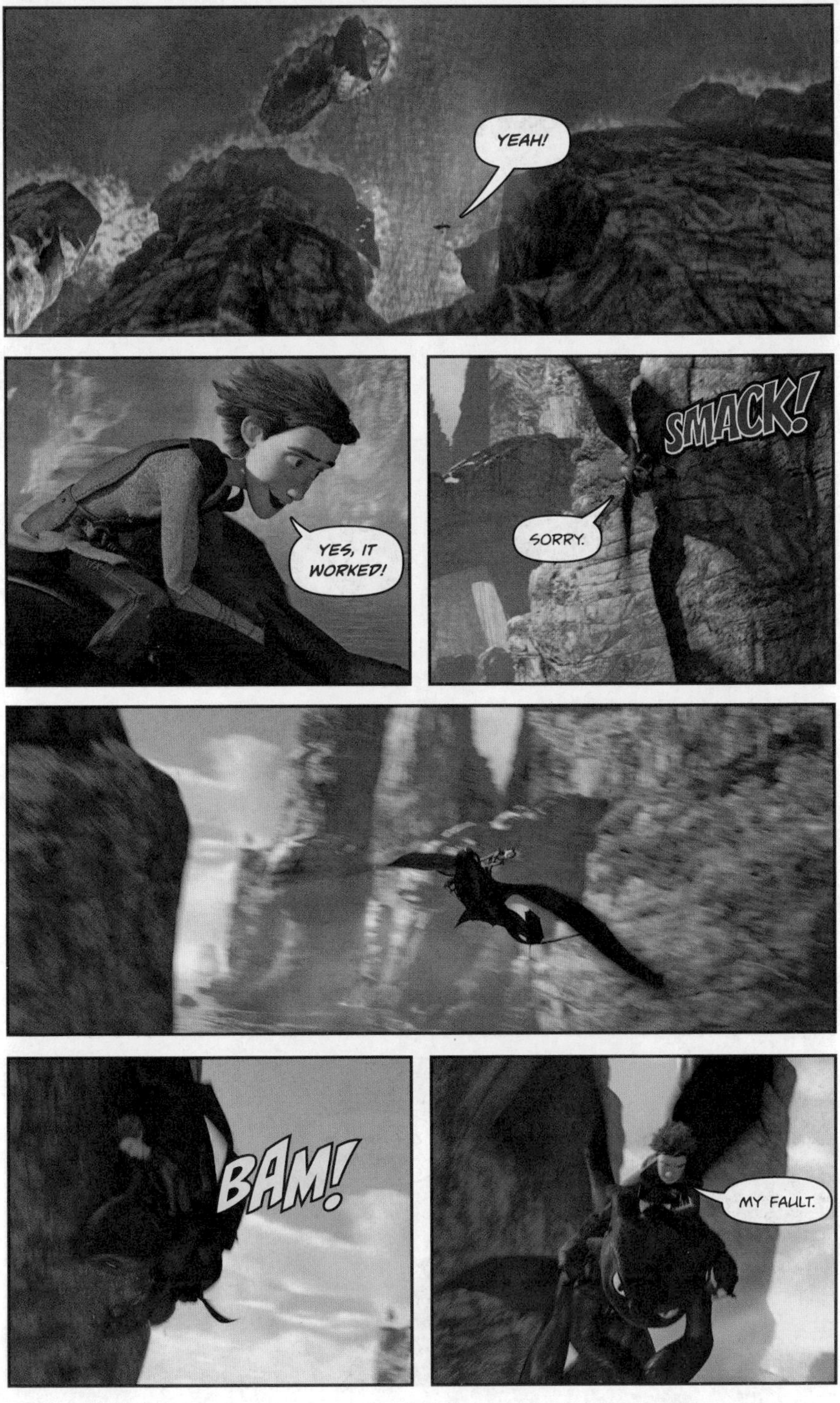
YEAH!
YES, IT WORKED!
SMACK!
SORRY.
BAM!
MY FAULT.

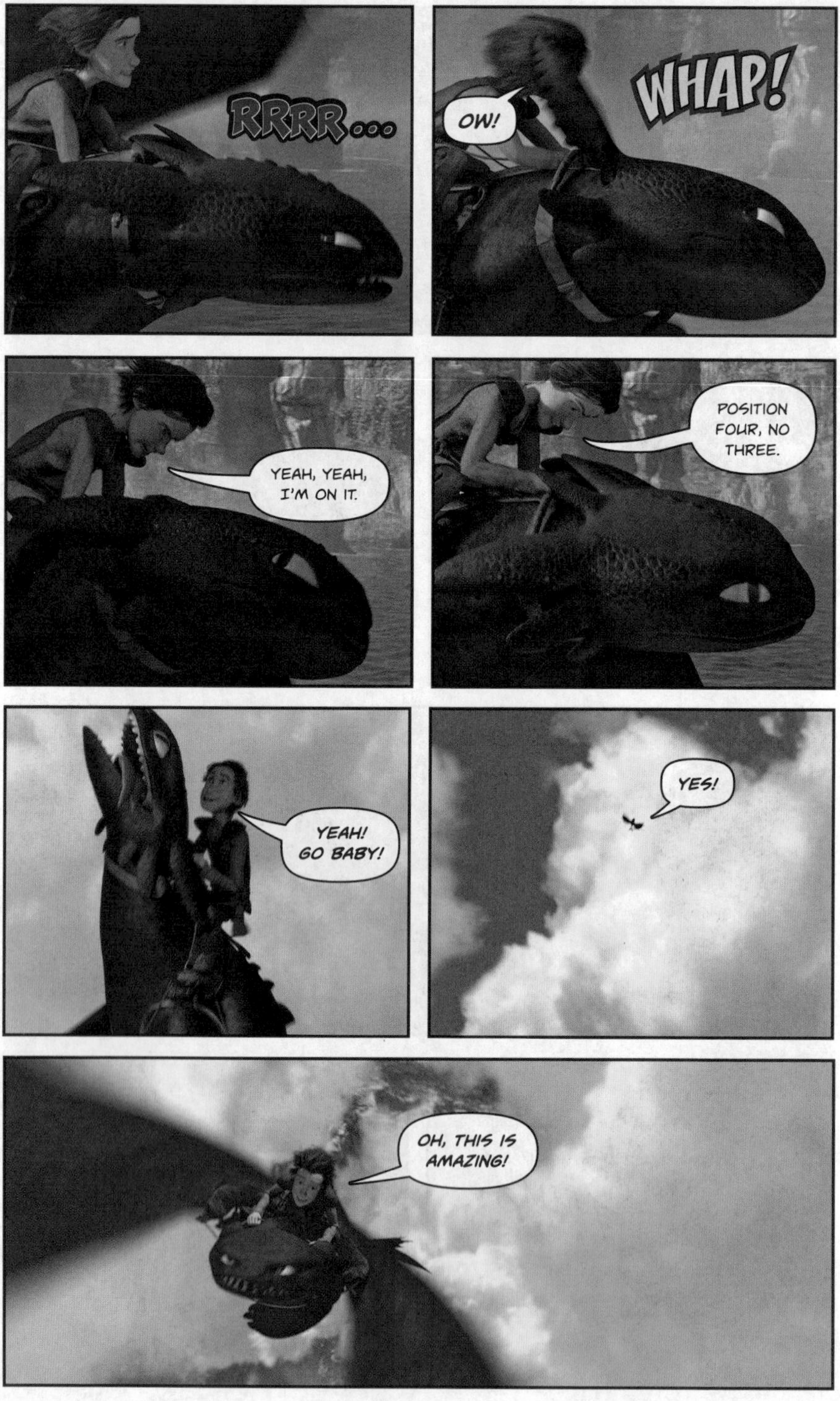
RRRR...
OW!
WHAP!
YEAH, YEAH, I'M ON IT.
POSITION FOUR, NO THREE.
YEAH! GO BABY!
YES!
OH, THIS IS AMAZING!

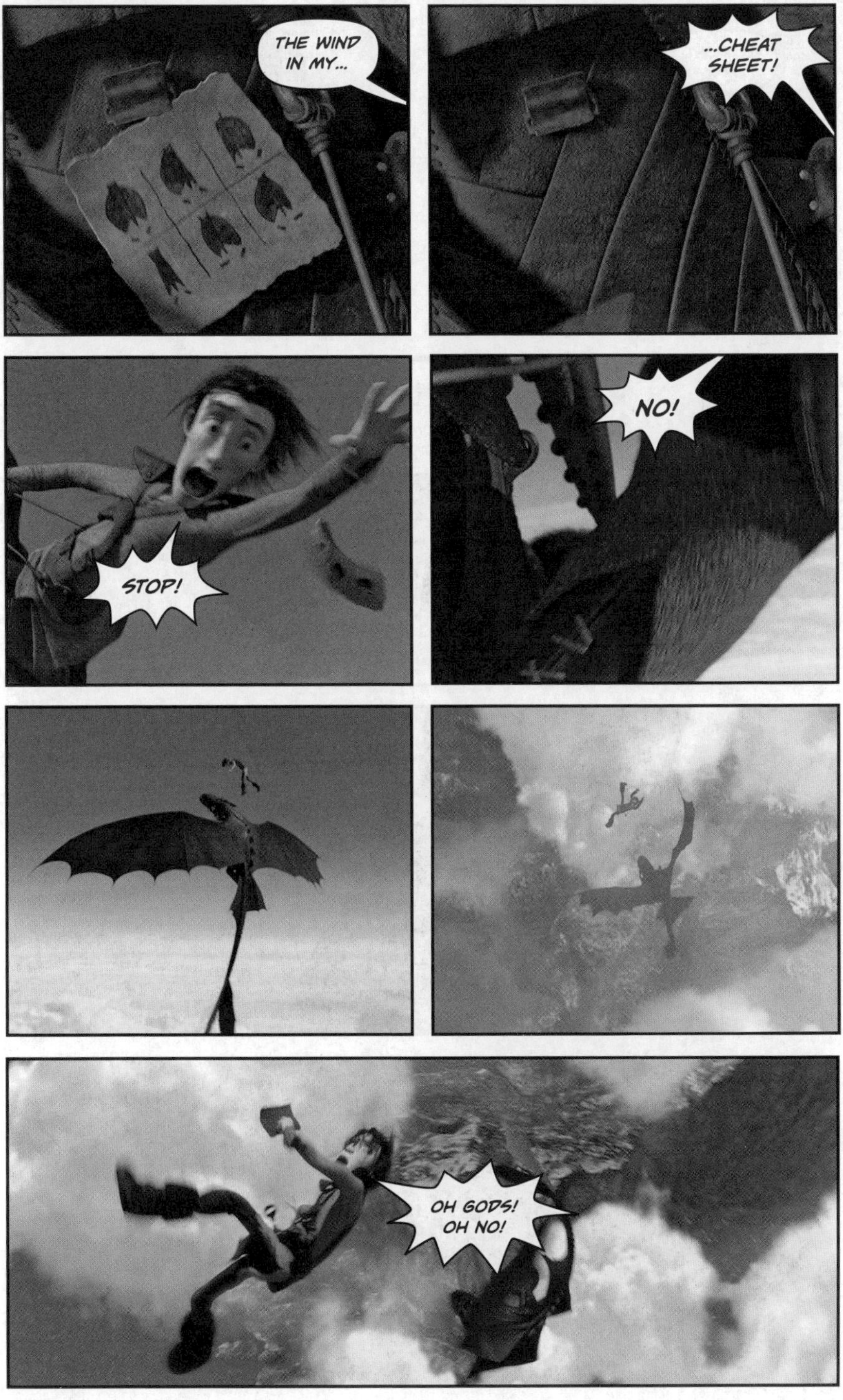
THE WIND IN MY...
...CHEAT SHEET!
STOP!
NO!
OH GODS! OH NO!

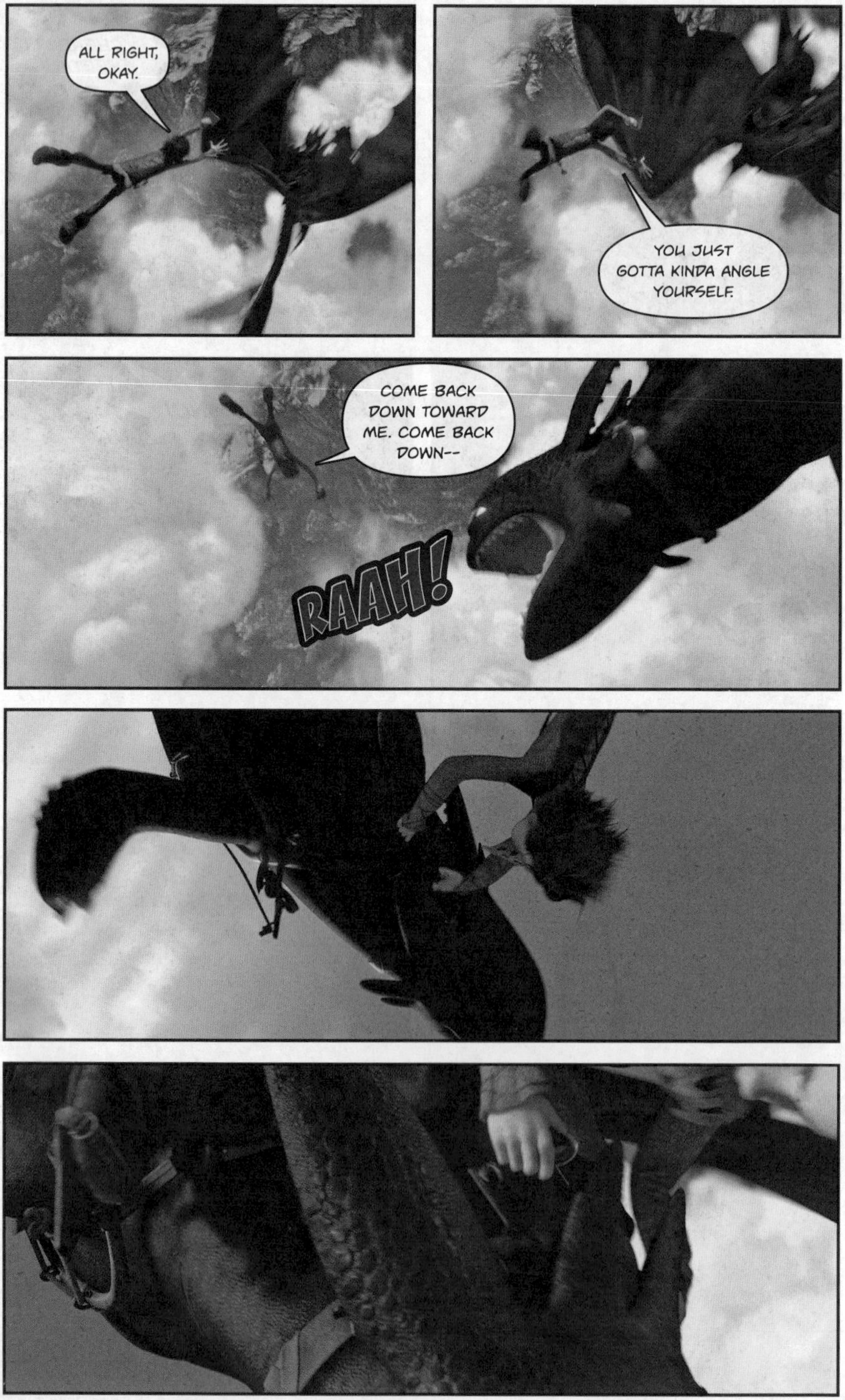
ALL RIGHT, OKAY.
YOU JUST GOTTA KINDA ANGLE YOURSELF.
COME BACK DOWN TOWARD ME. COME BACK DOWN--
RAAH!

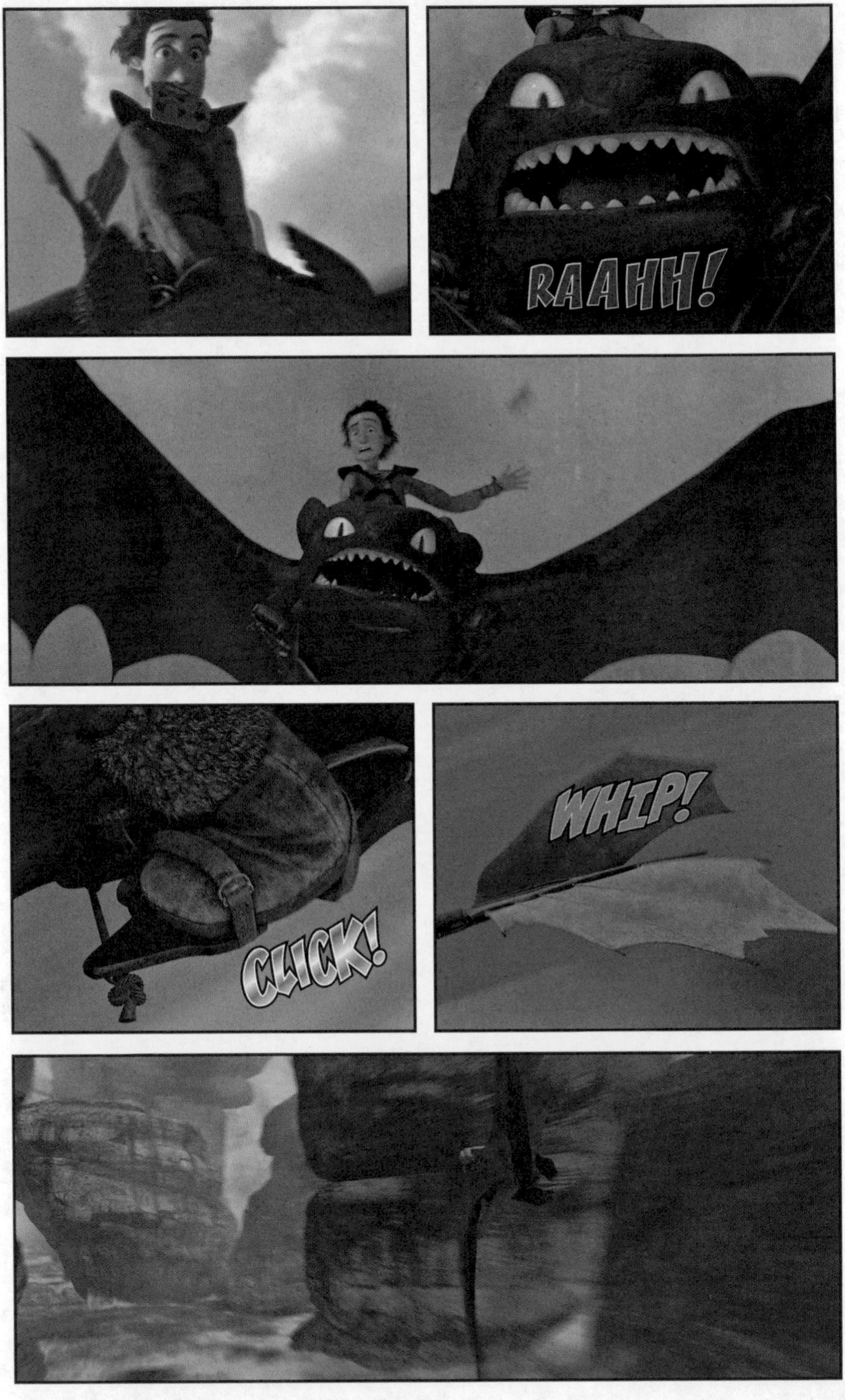
RAAHH!
CLICK!
WHIP!

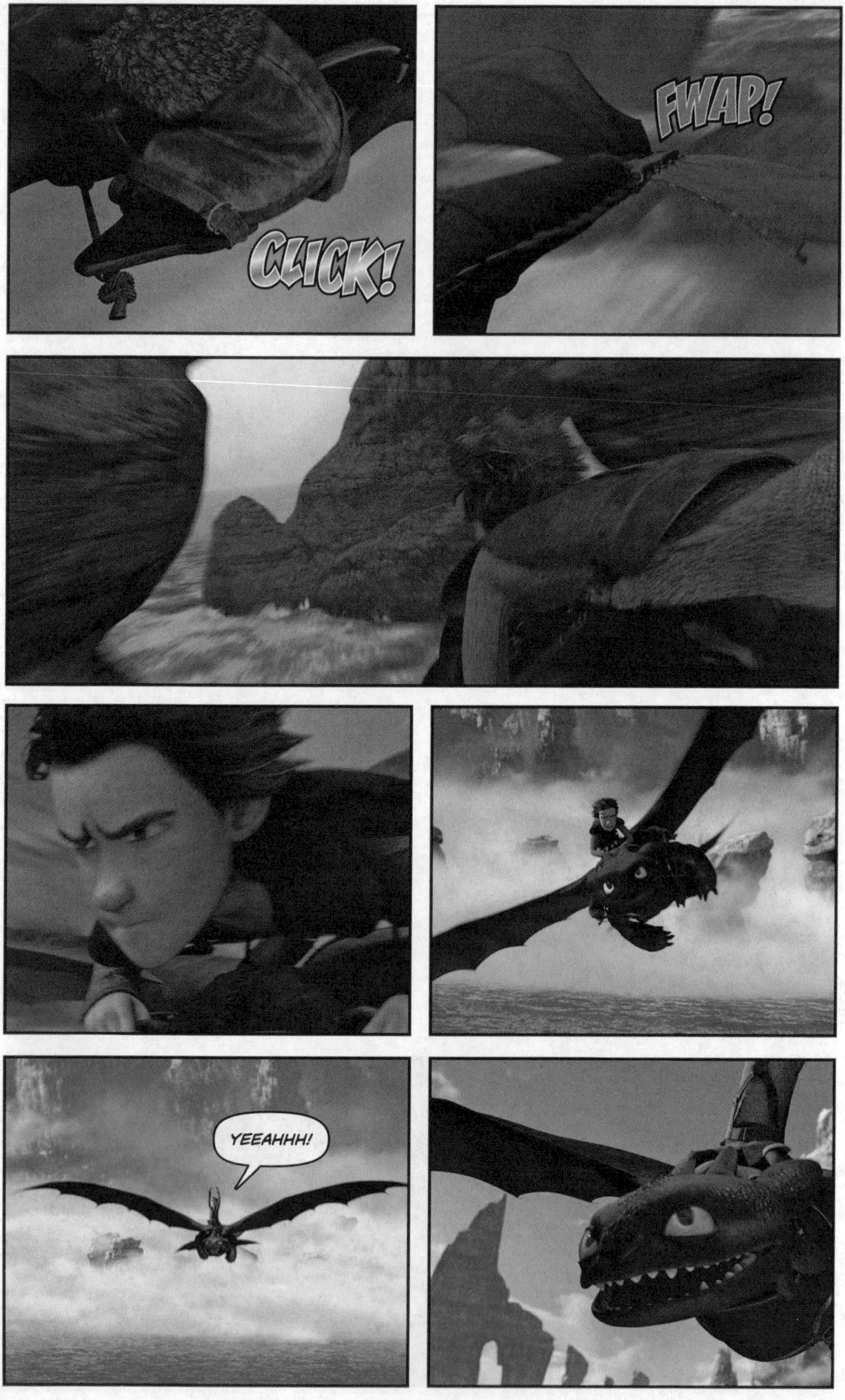
CLICK!
FWAP!
YEEAHHH!

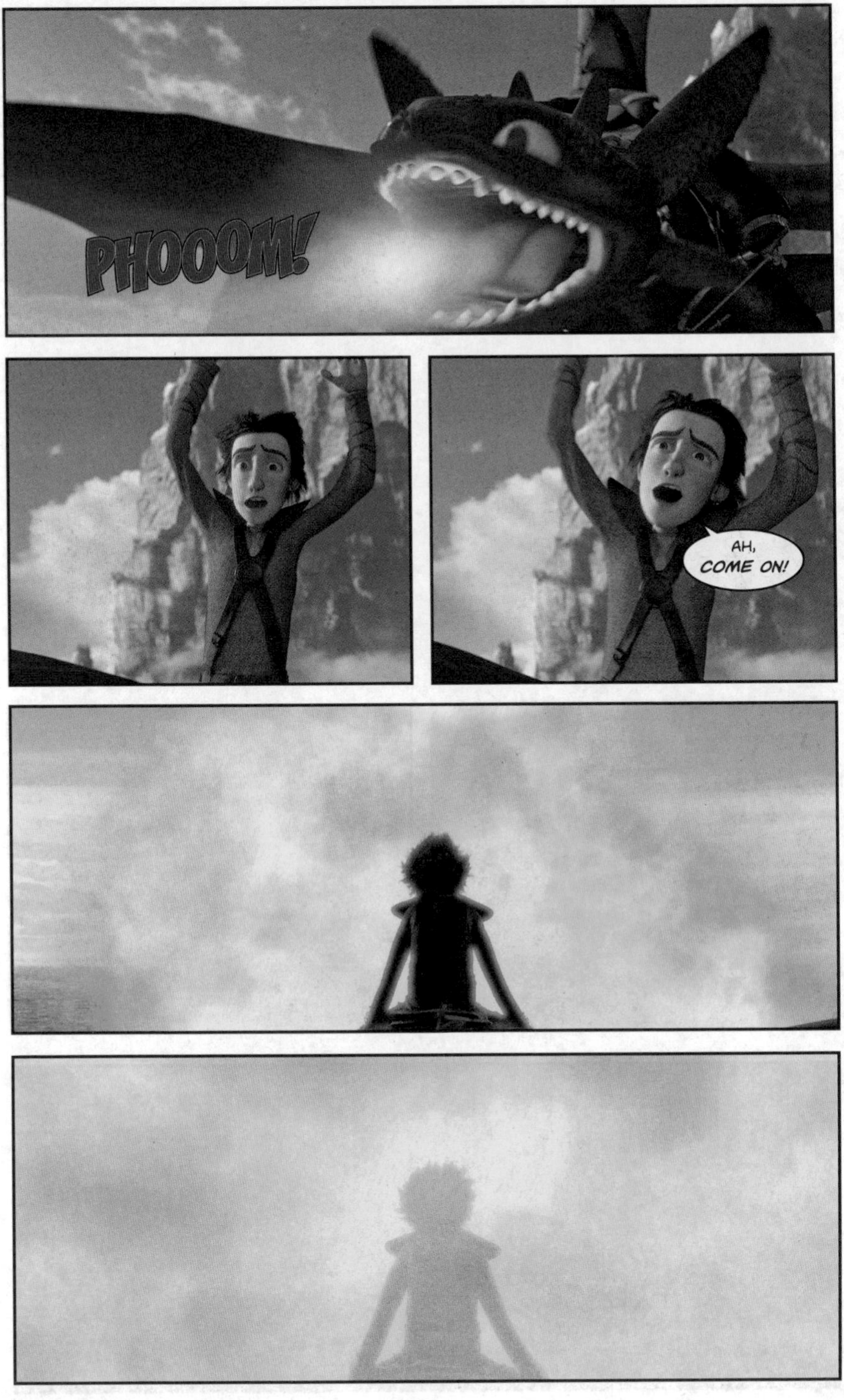
PHOOOM!
AH, COME ON!

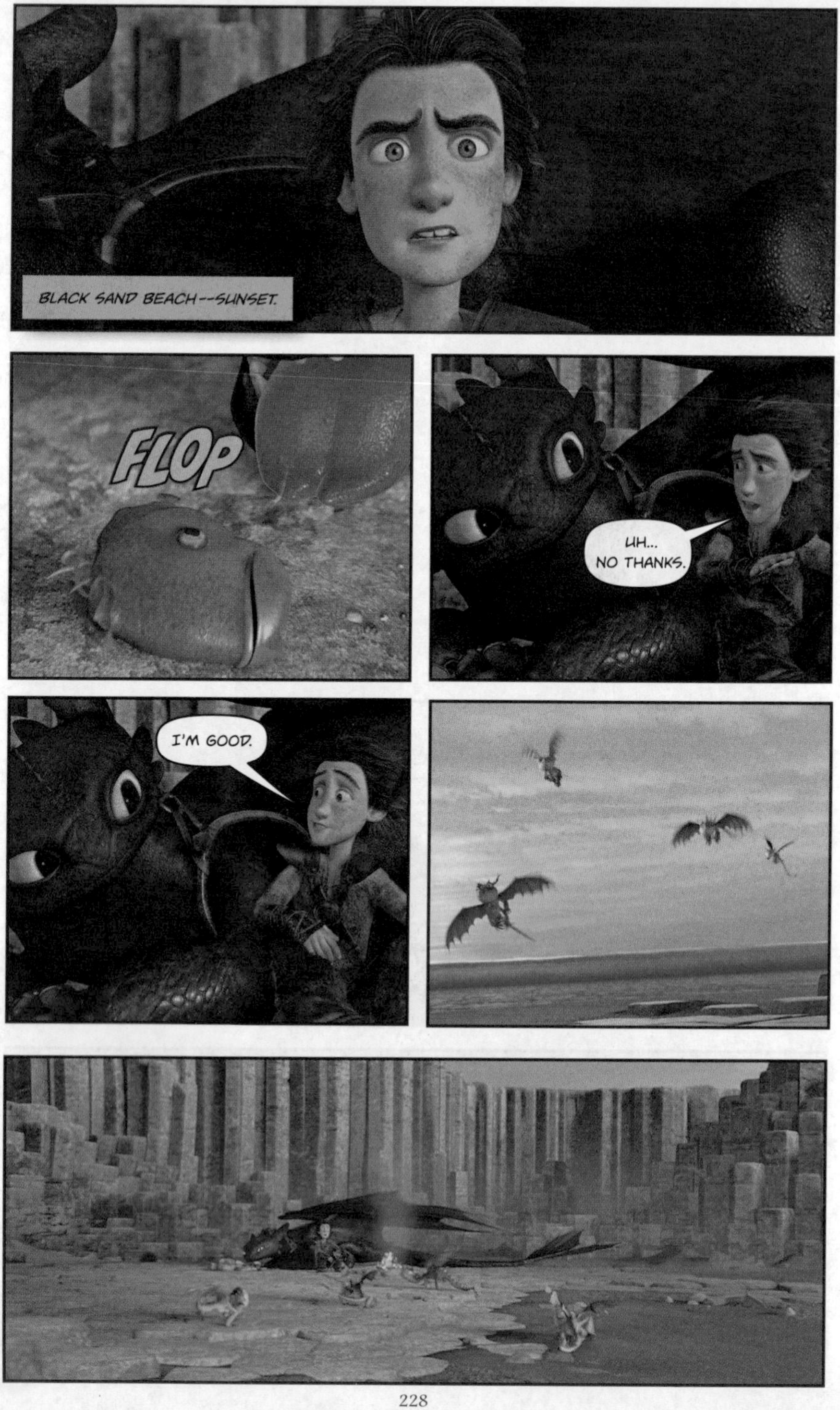
BLACK SAND BEACH--SUNSET.
FLOP
UH... NO THANKS.
I'M GOOD.

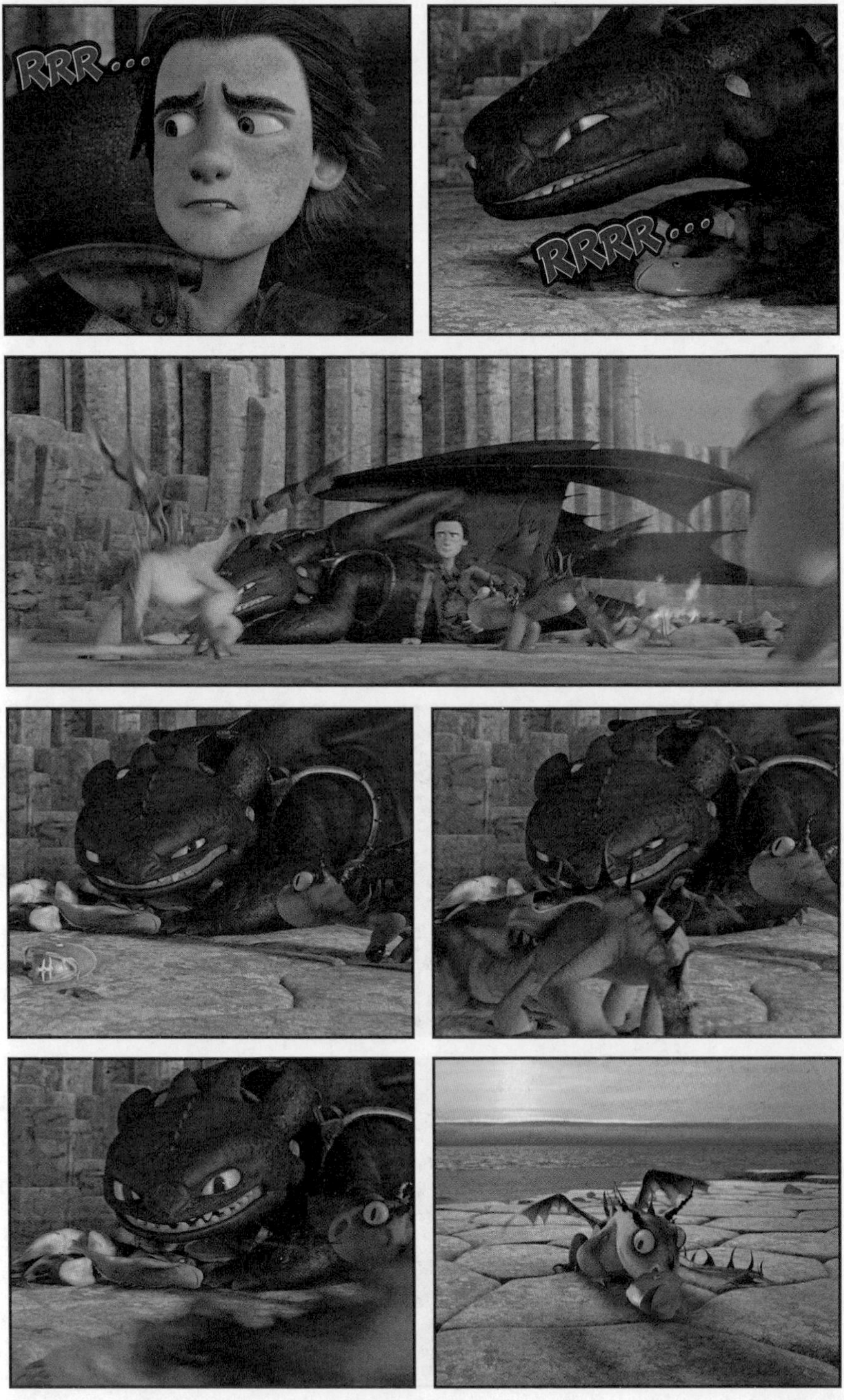
RRR...
RRRR...

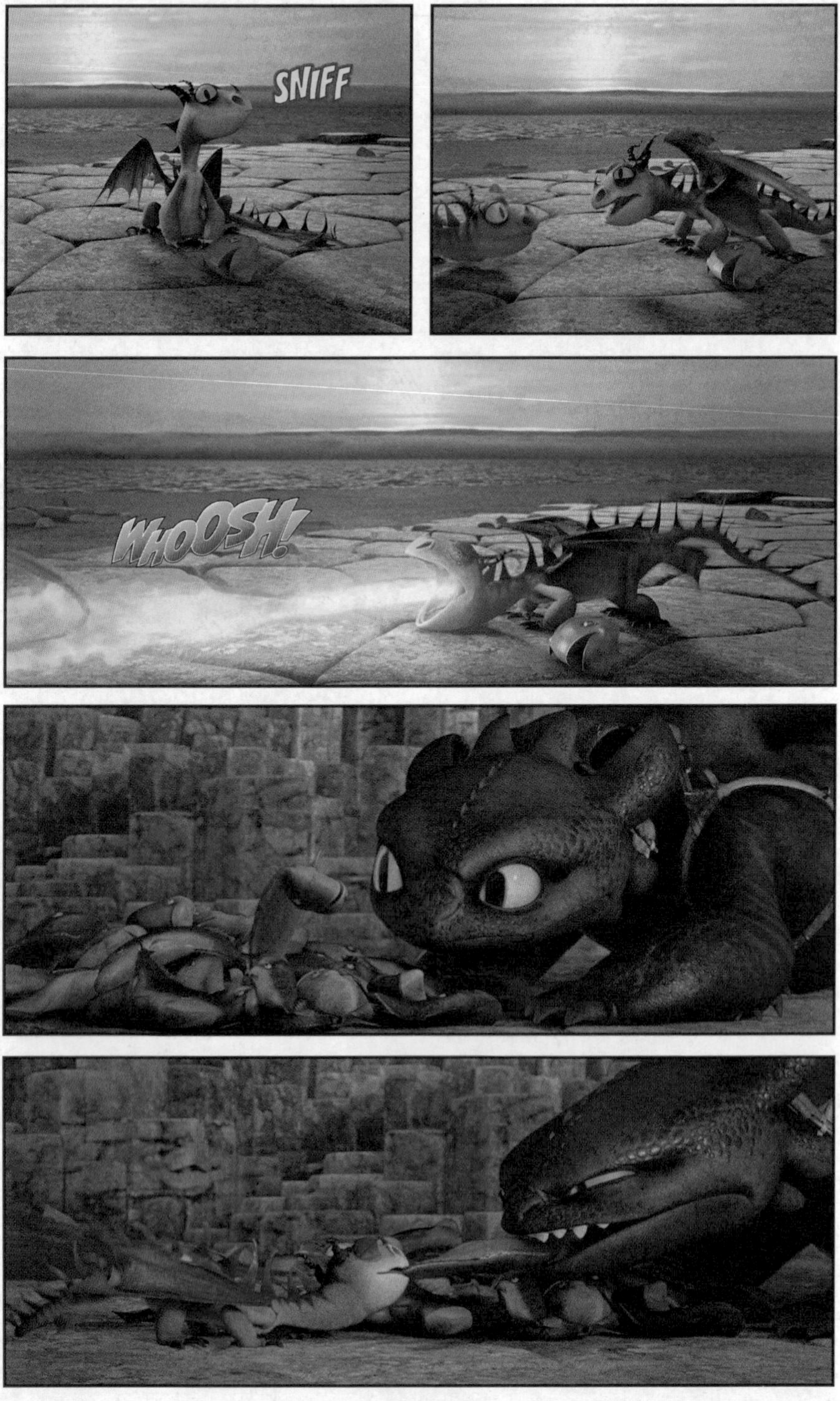
SNIFF
WHOOSH!

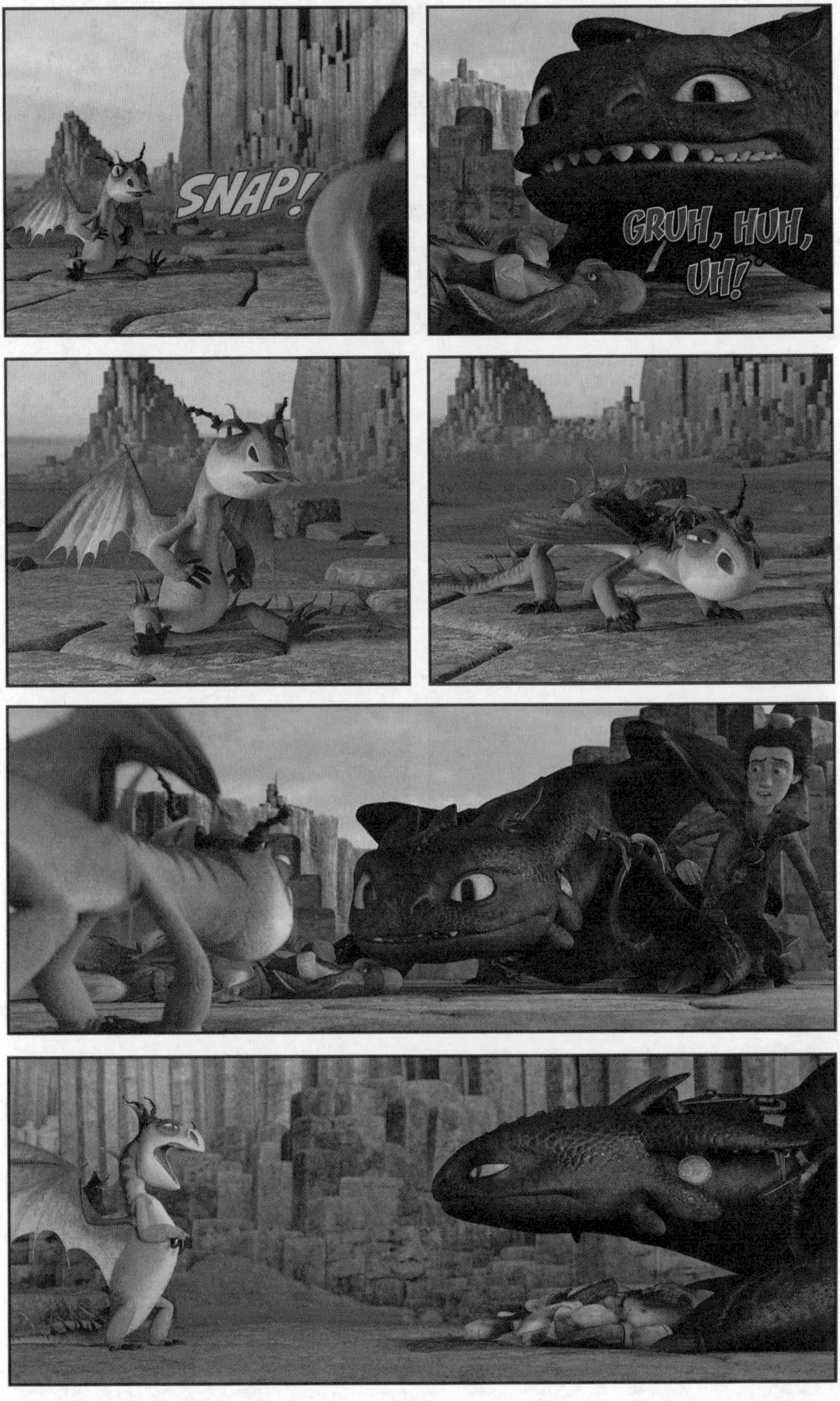
SNAP!
GRUH, HUH, UH!

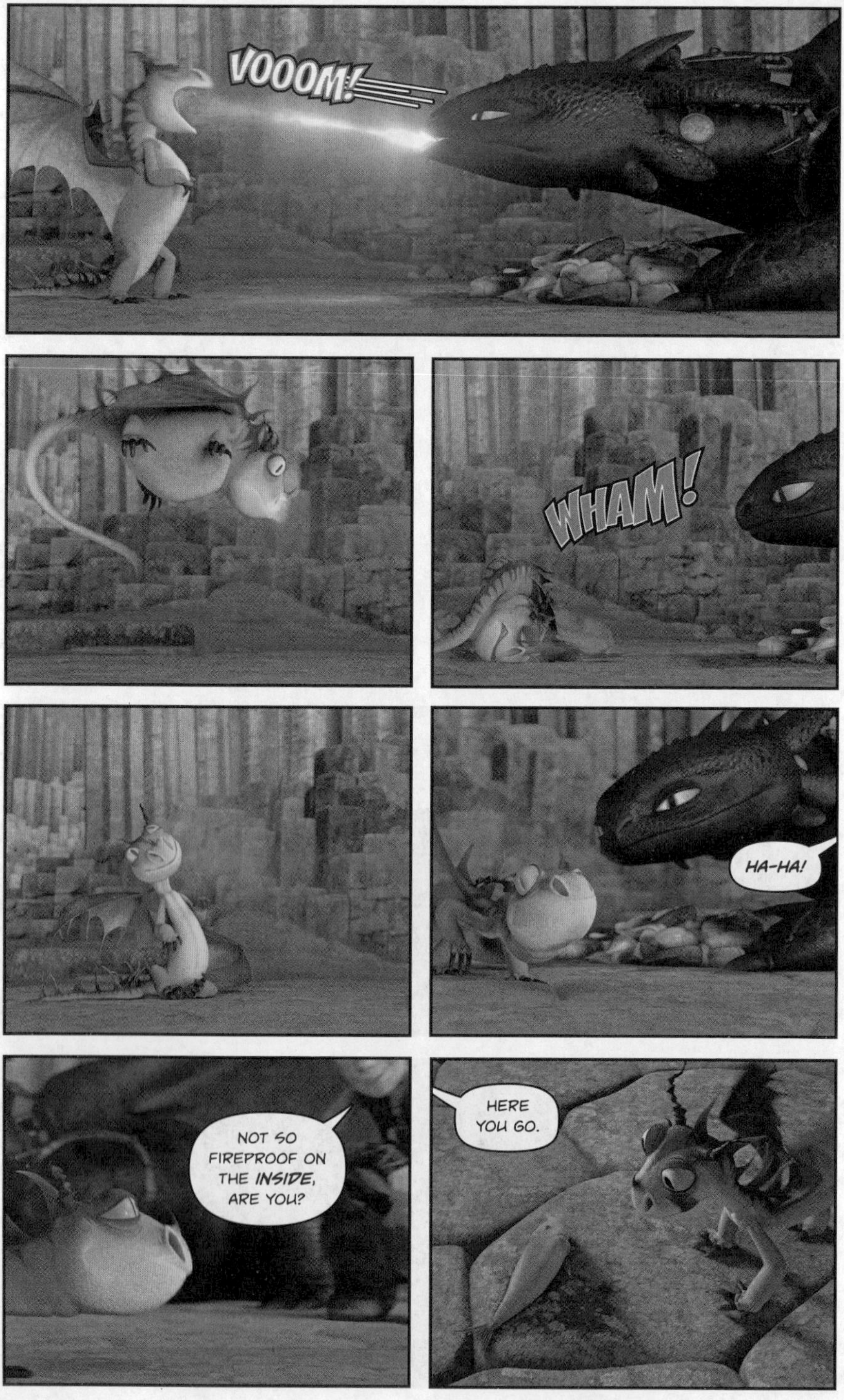
VOOOM!
WHAM!
HA-HA!
NOT SO FIREPROOF ON THE *INSIDE*, ARE YOU?
HERE YOU GO.

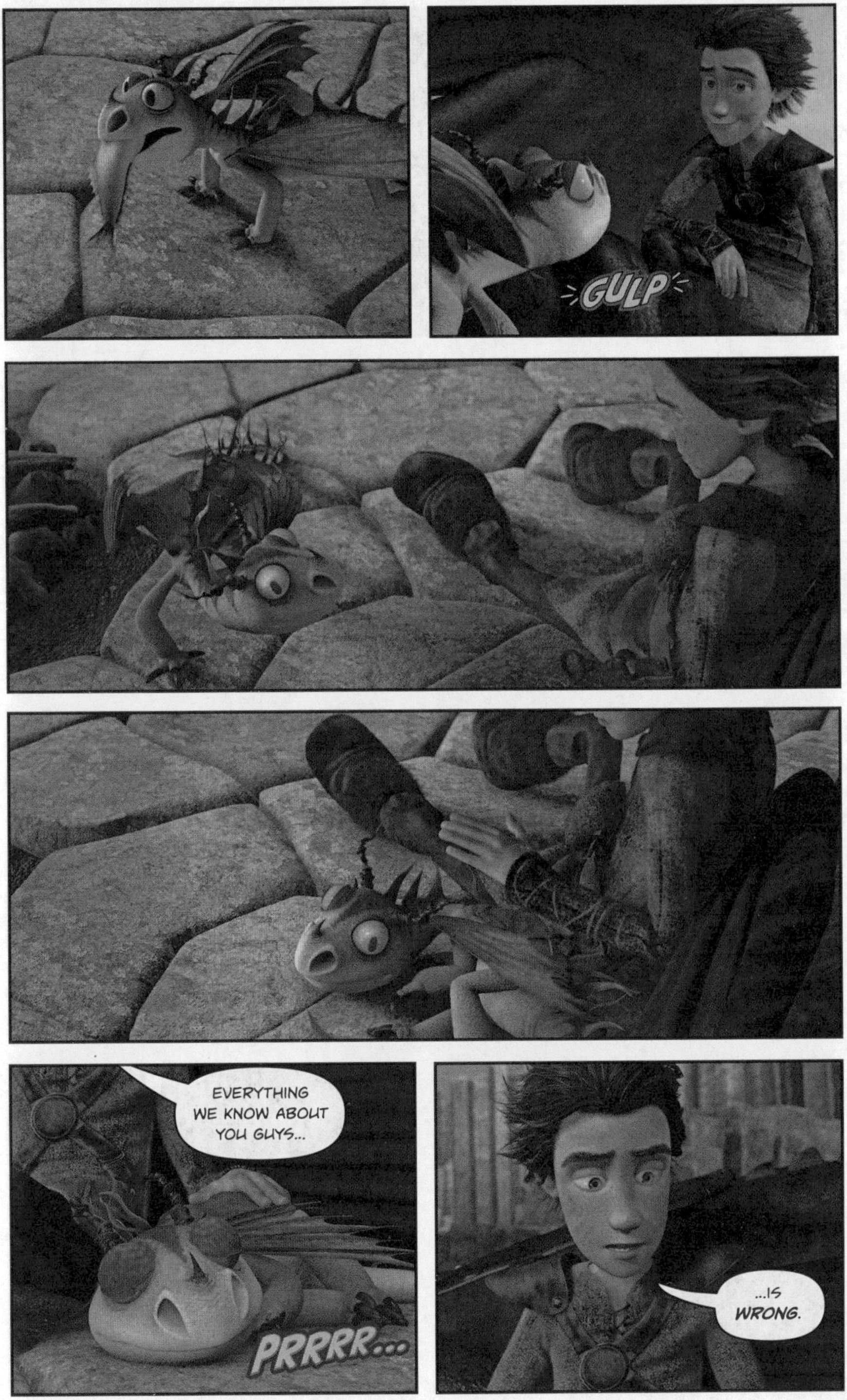
GULP
EVERYTHING WE KNOW ABOUT YOU GUYS...
PRRRR...
...IS WRONG.

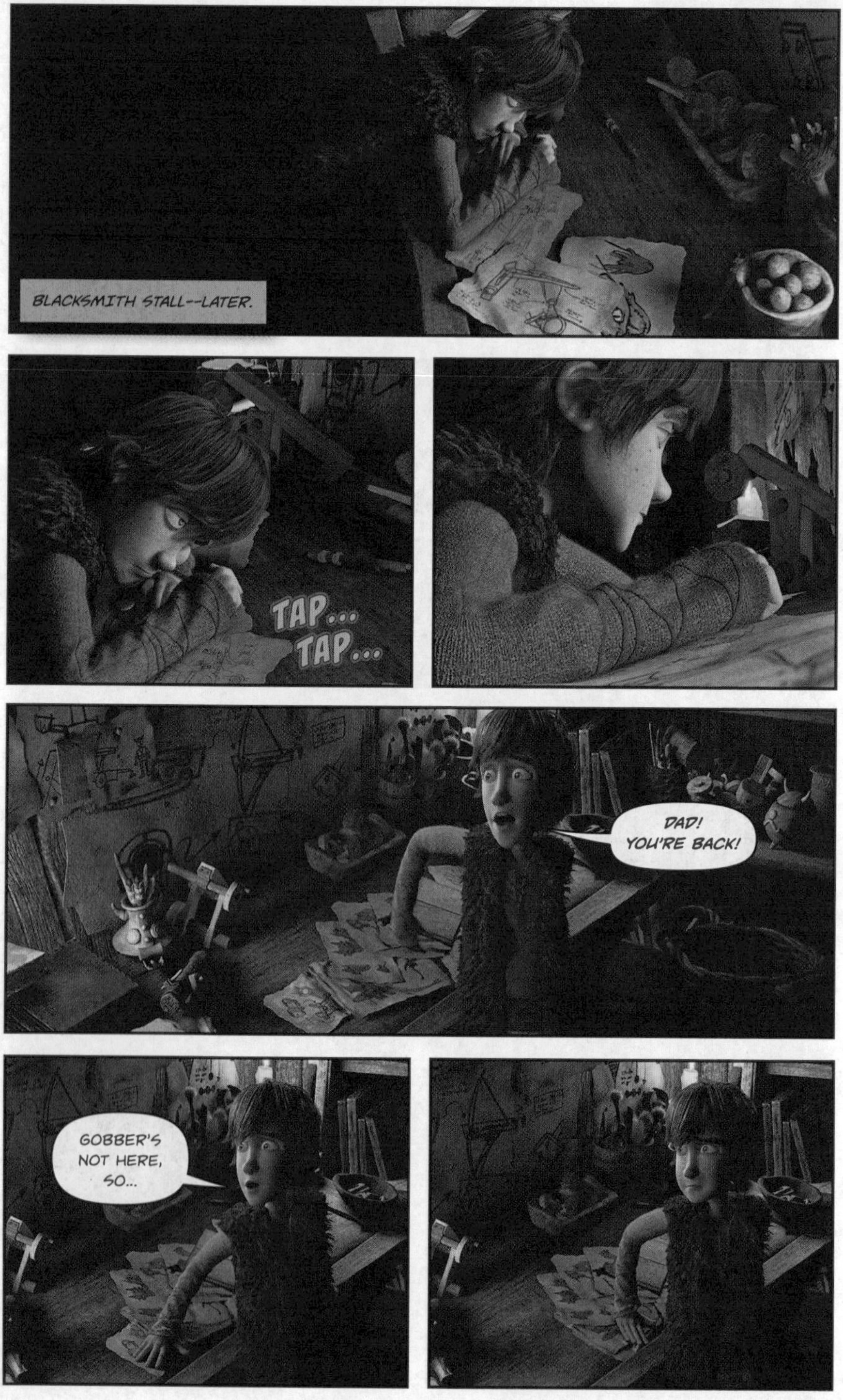
BLACKSMITH STALL--LATER.
TAP... TAP...
DAD! YOU'RE BACK!
GOBBER'S NOT HERE, SO...

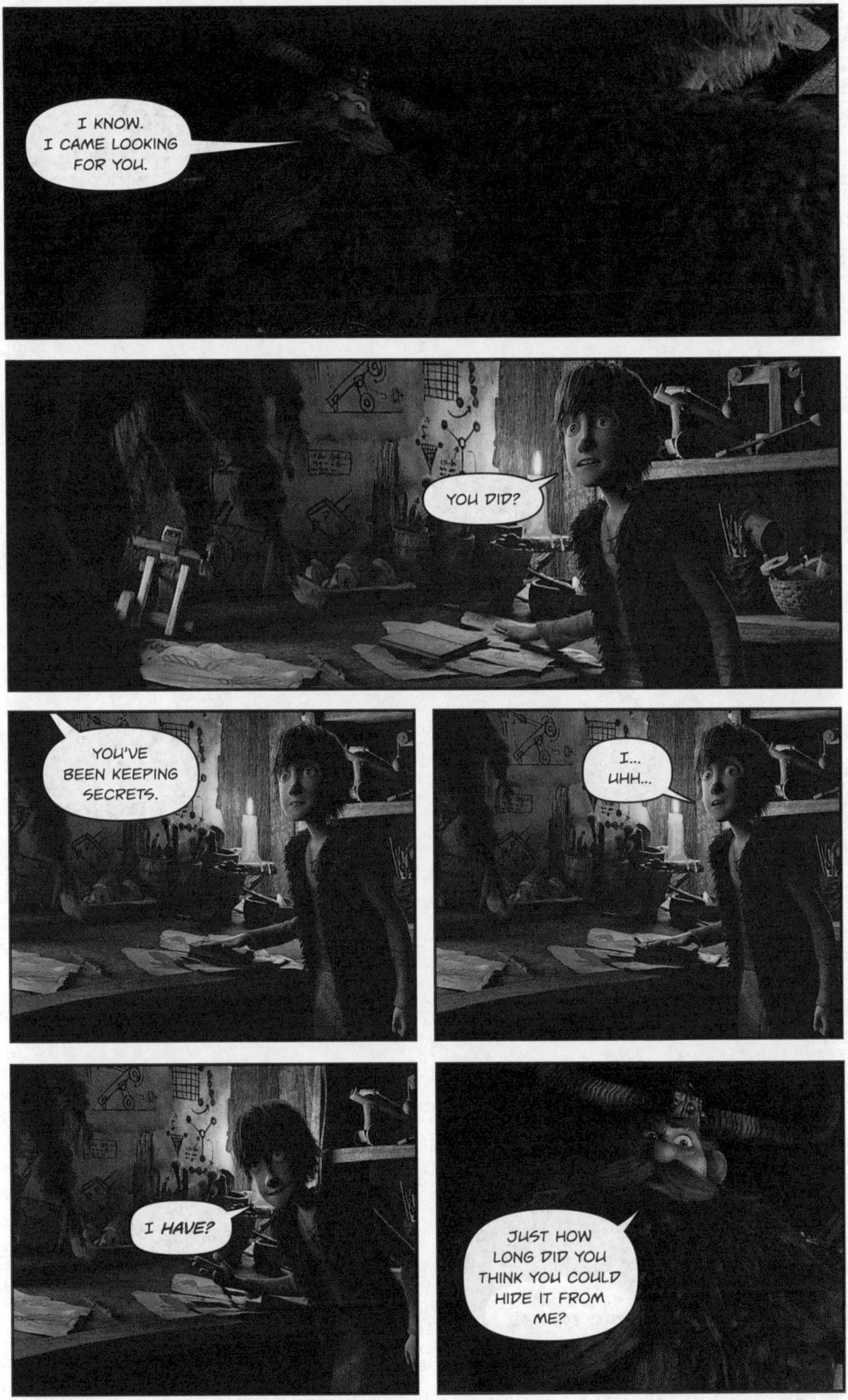
I KNOW. I CAME LOOKING FOR YOU.
YOU DID?
YOU'VE BEEN KEEPING SECRETS.
I... UHH...
I HAVE?
JUST HOW LONG DID YOU THINK YOU COULD HIDE IT FROM ME?

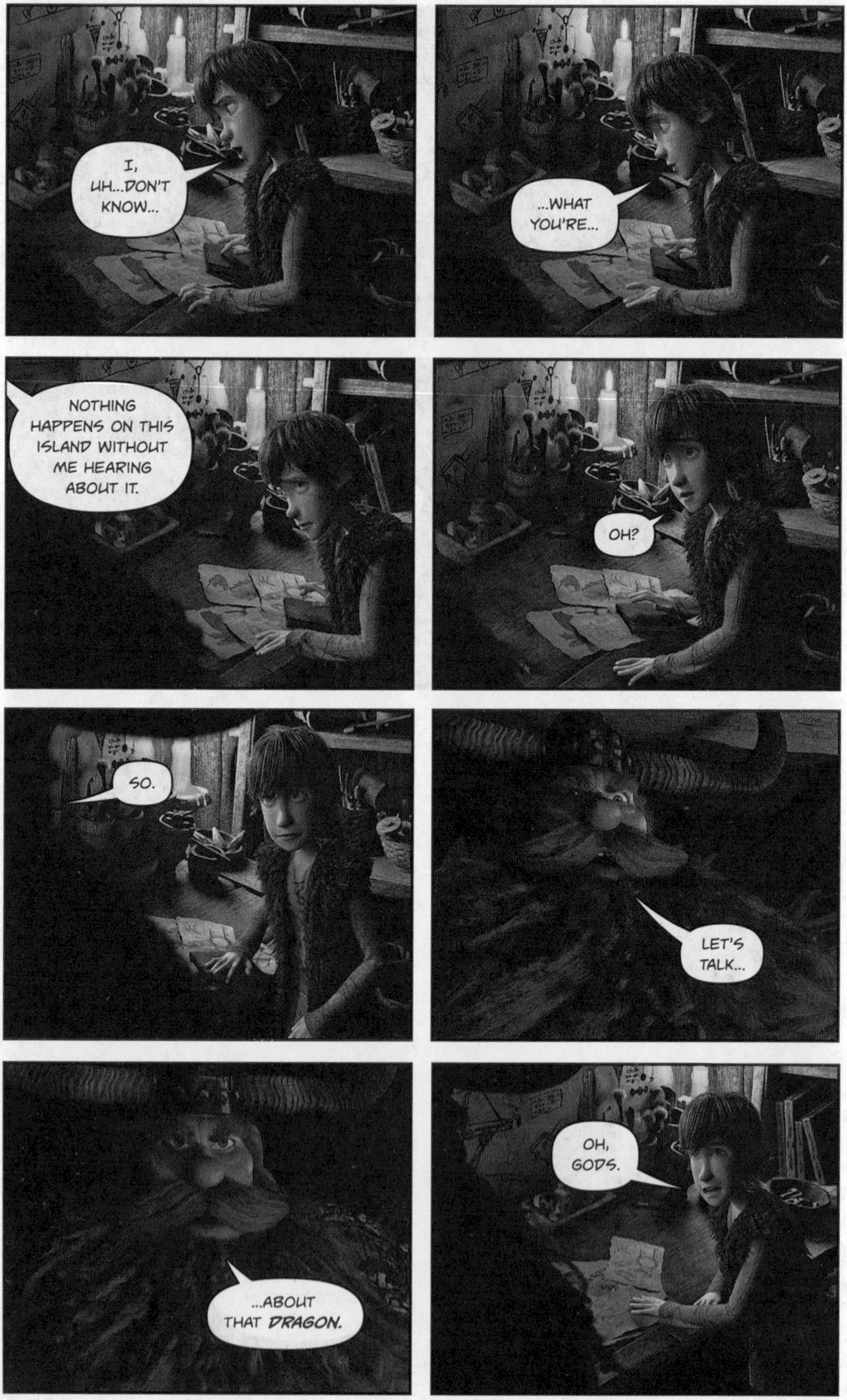
I, UH...DON'T KNOW...
...WHAT YOU'RE...
NOTHING HAPPENS ON THIS ISLAND WITHOUT ME HEARING ABOUT IT.
OH?
SO.
LET'S TALK...
...ABOUT THAT DRAGON.
OH, GODS.

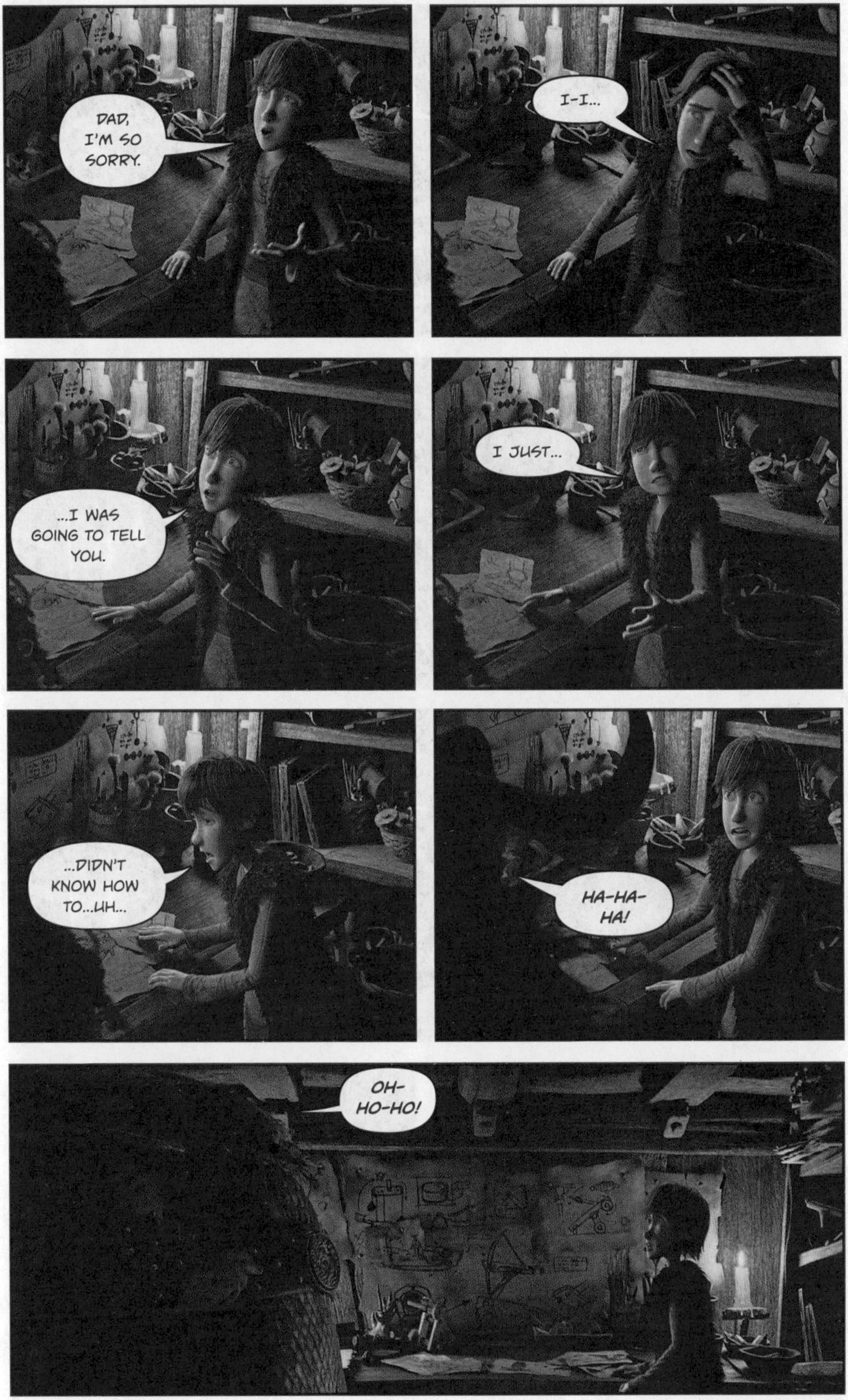
DAD, I'M SO SORRY.
I-I...
...I WAS GOING TO TELL YOU.
I JUST...
...DIDN'T KNOW HOW TO...UH...
HA-HA-HA!
OH-HO-HO!

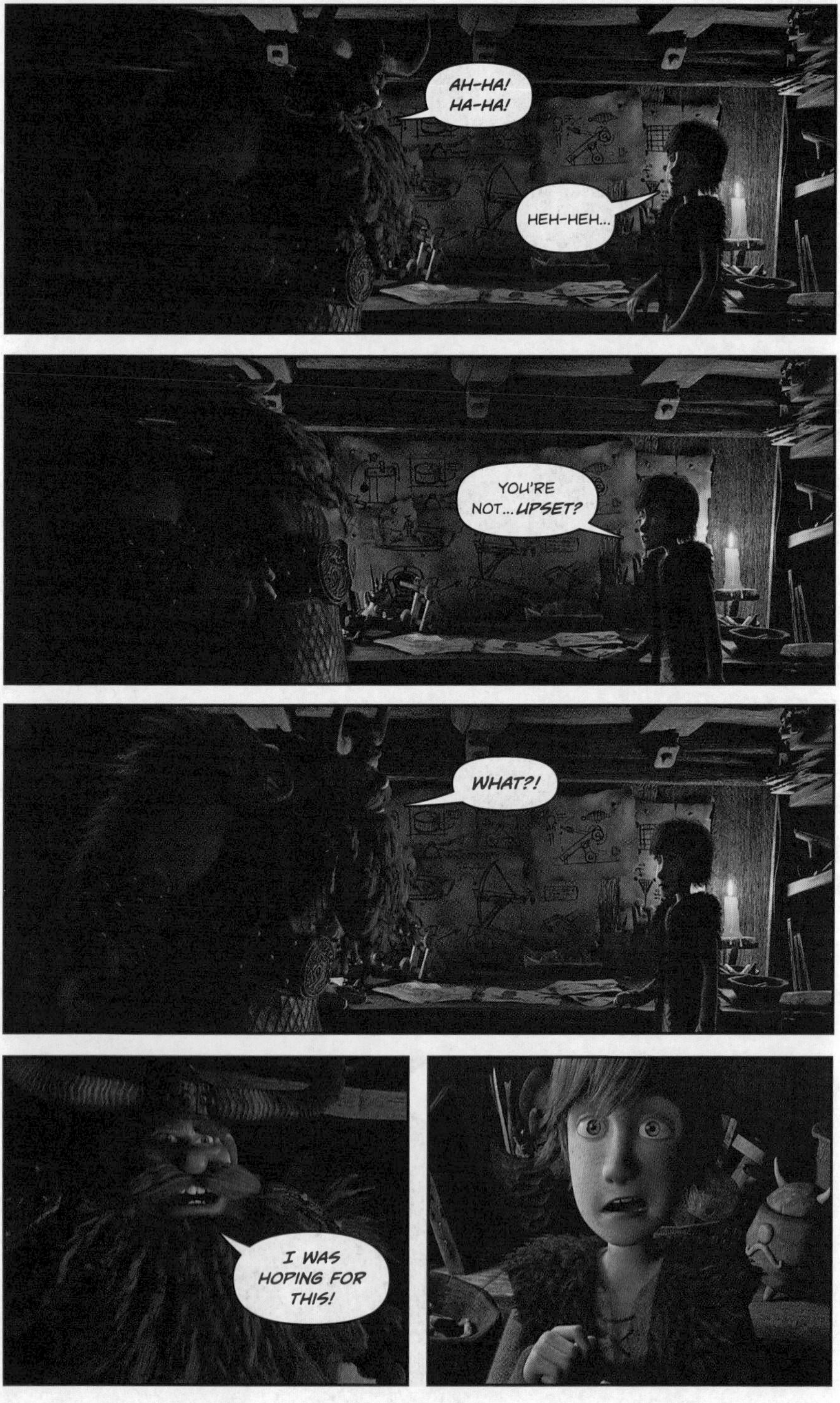
AH-HA! HA-HA!
HEH-HEH...
YOU'RE NOT...UPSET?
WHAT?!
I WAS HOPING FOR THIS!

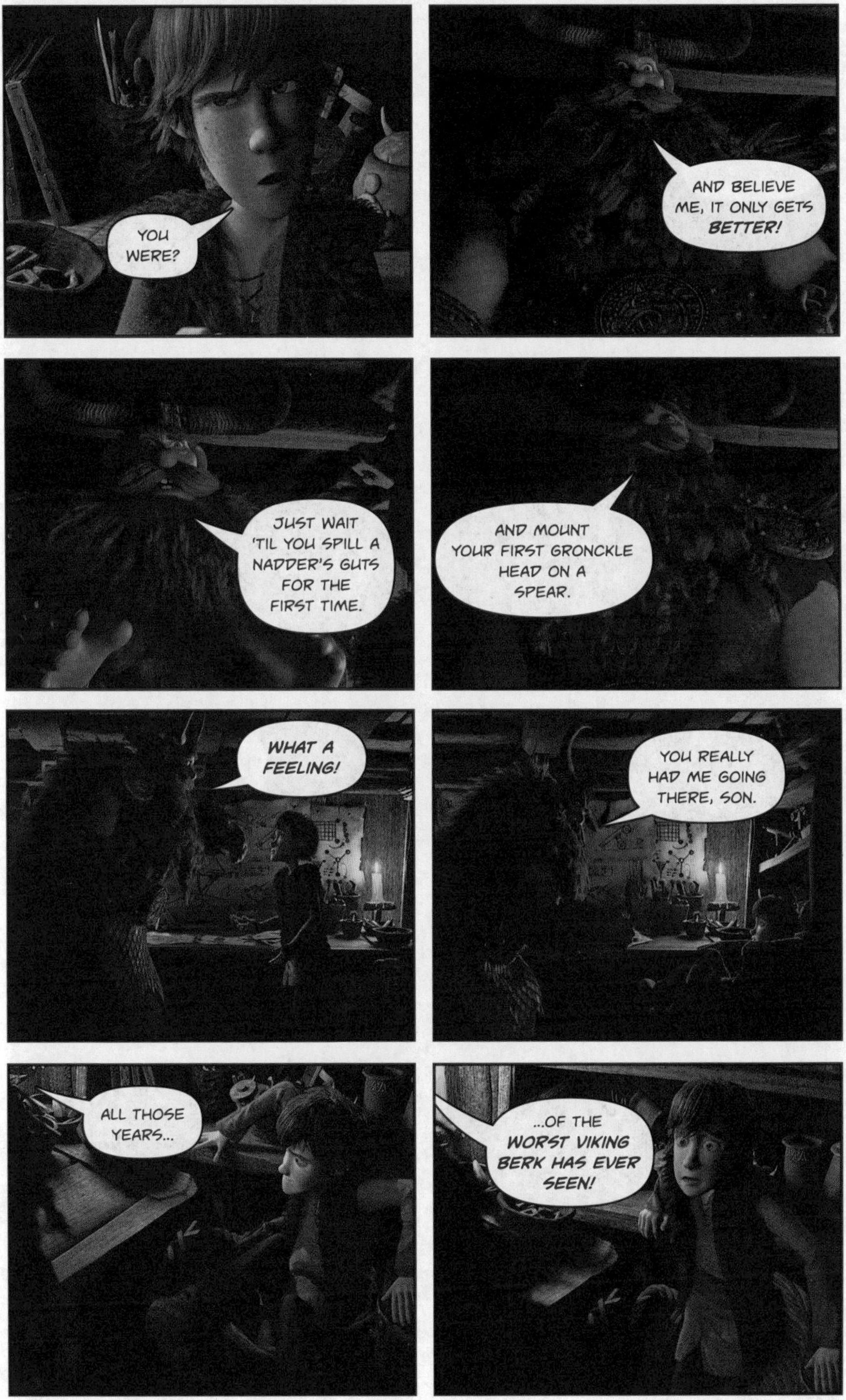
YOU WERE?
AND BELIEVE ME, IT ONLY GETS BETTER!
JUST WAIT 'TIL YOU SPILL A NADDER'S GUTS FOR THE FIRST TIME.
AND MOUNT YOUR FIRST GRONCKLE HEAD ON A SPEAR.
WHAT A FEELING!
YOU REALLY HAD ME GOING THERE, SON.
ALL THOSE YEARS...
...OF THE WORST VIKING BERK HAS EVER SEEN!

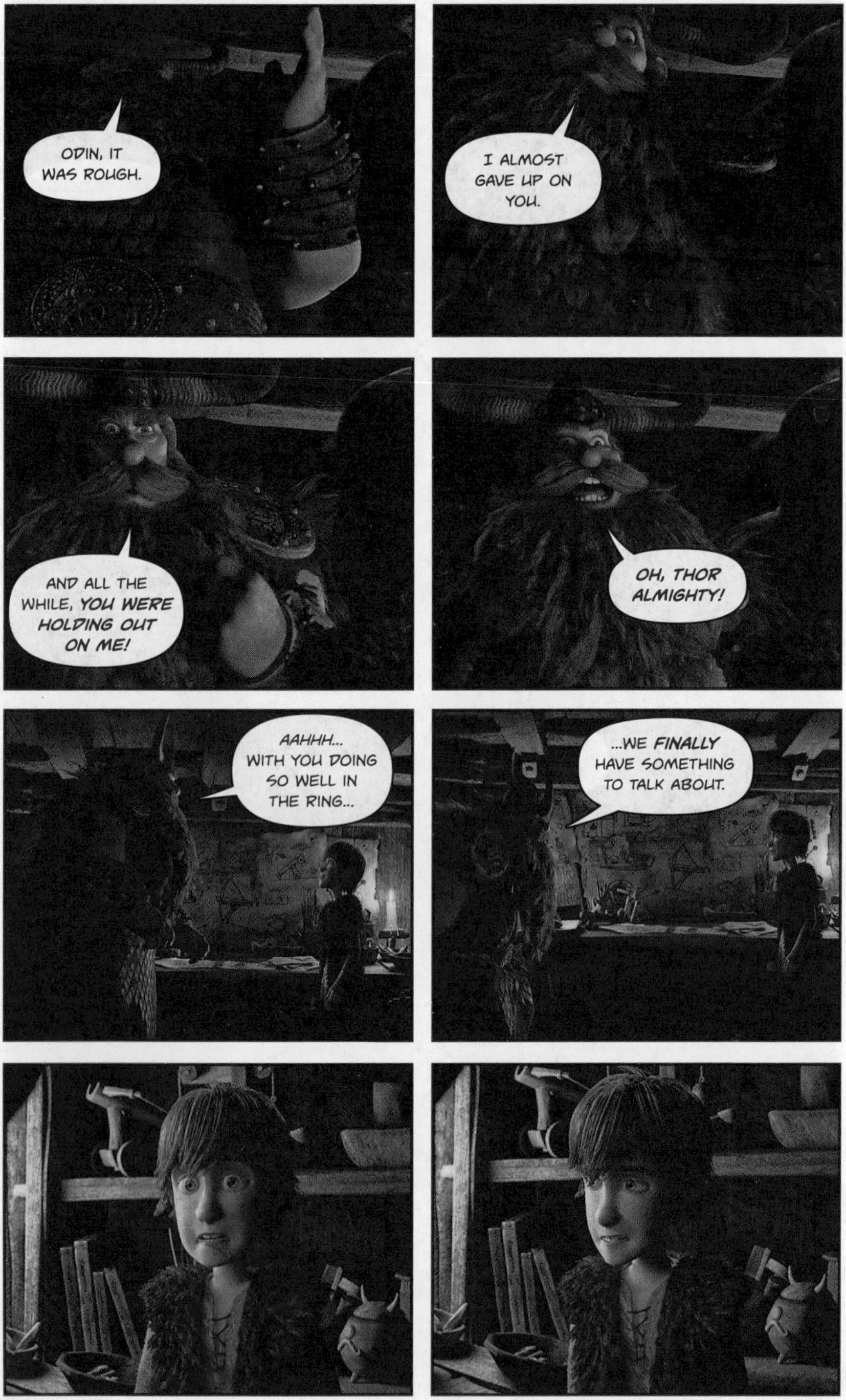
ODIN, IT WAS ROUGH.
I ALMOST GAVE UP ON YOU.
AND ALL THE WHILE, *YOU WERE HOLDING OUT ON ME!*
OH, THOR ALMIGHTY!
AAHHH... WITH YOU DOING SO WELL IN THE RING...
...WE *FINALLY* HAVE SOMETHING TO TALK ABOUT.

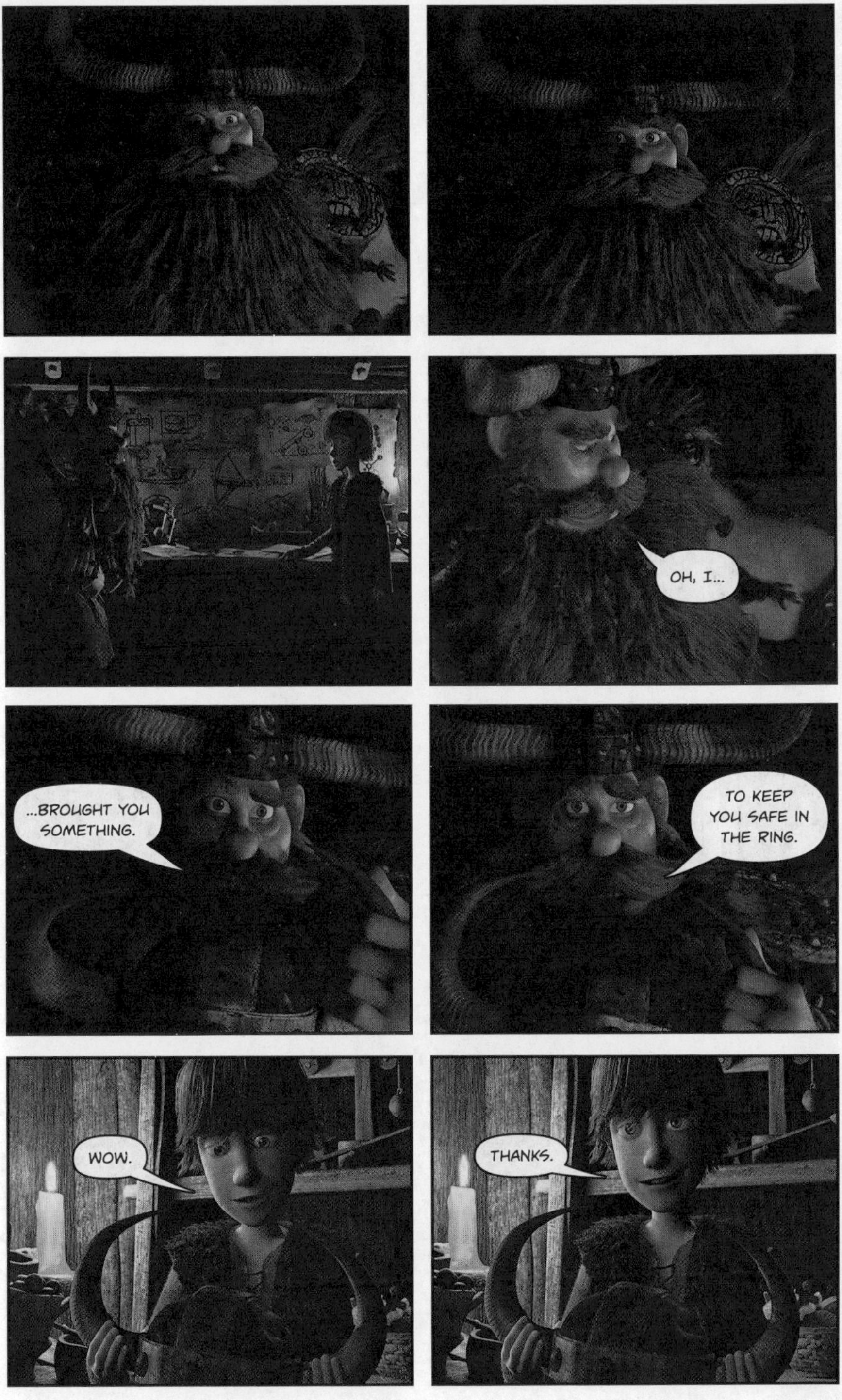
OH, I...
...BROUGHT YOU SOMETHING.
TO KEEP YOU SAFE IN THE RING.
WOW.
THANKS.

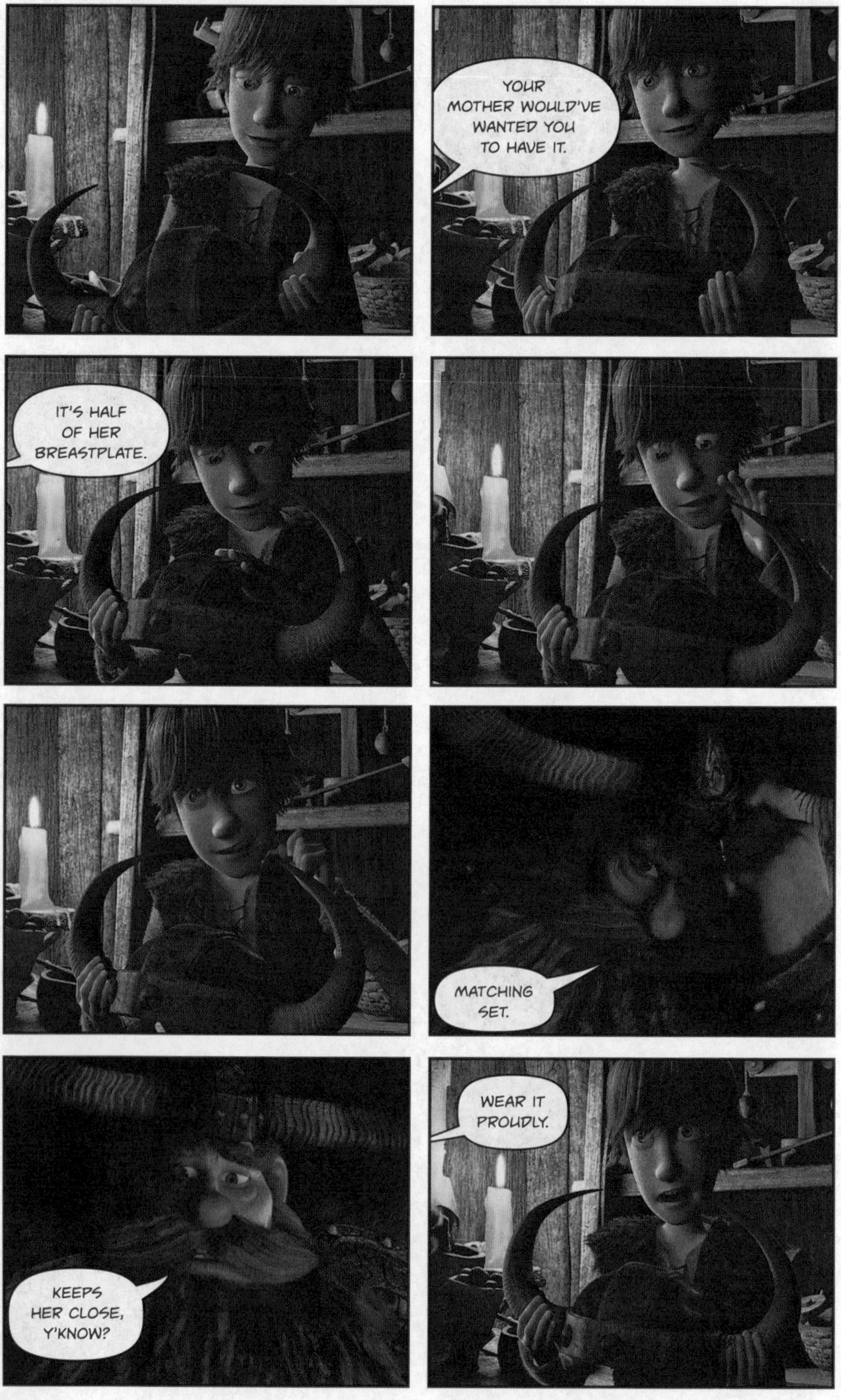
YOUR MOTHER WOULD'VE WANTED YOU TO HAVE IT.
IT'S HALF OF HER BREASTPLATE.
MATCHING SET.
KEEPS HER CLOSE, Y'KNOW?
WEAR IT PROUDLY.

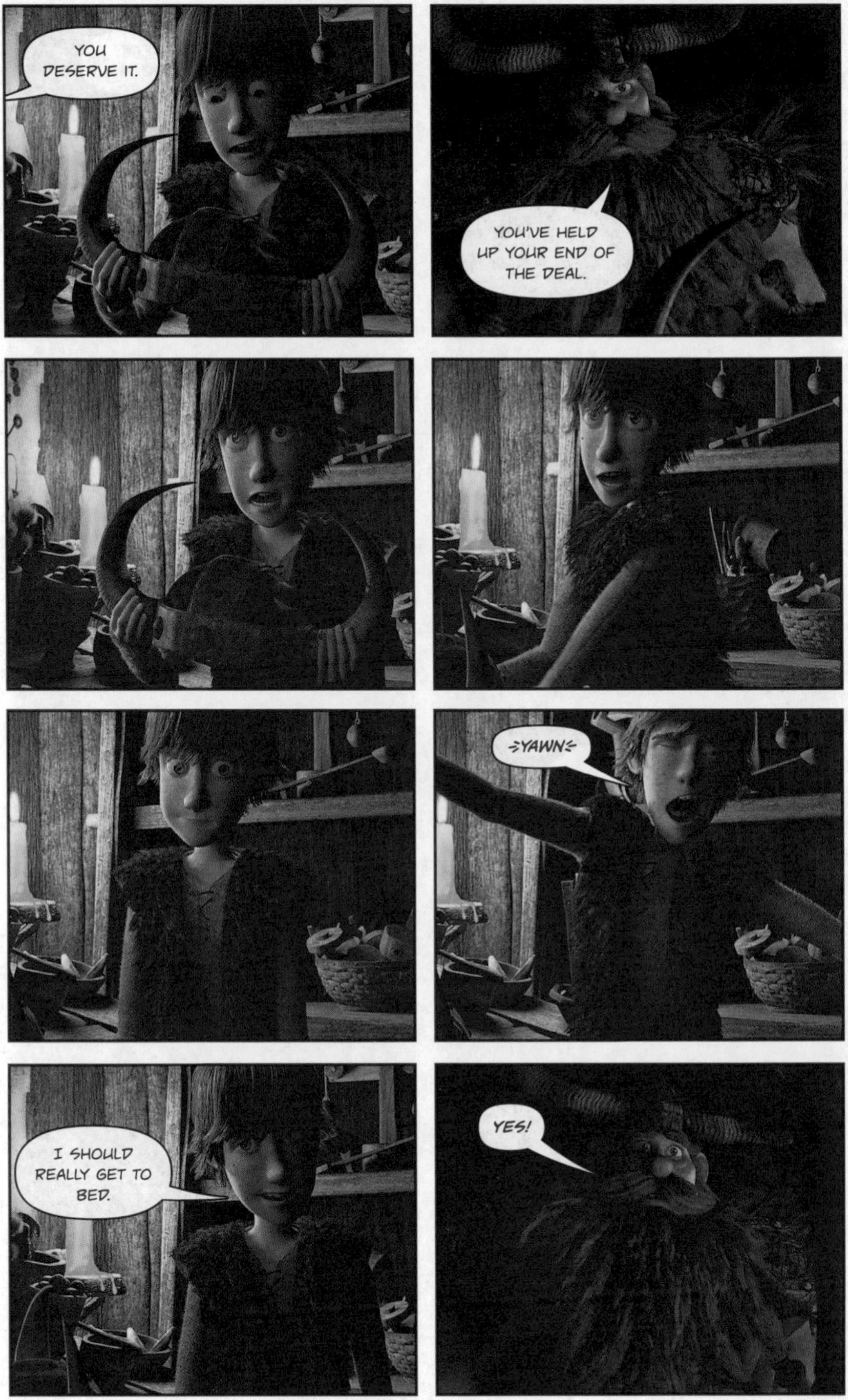
YOU DESERVE IT.
YOU'VE HELD UP YOUR END OF THE DEAL.
=YAWN=
I SHOULD REALLY GET TO BED.
YES!

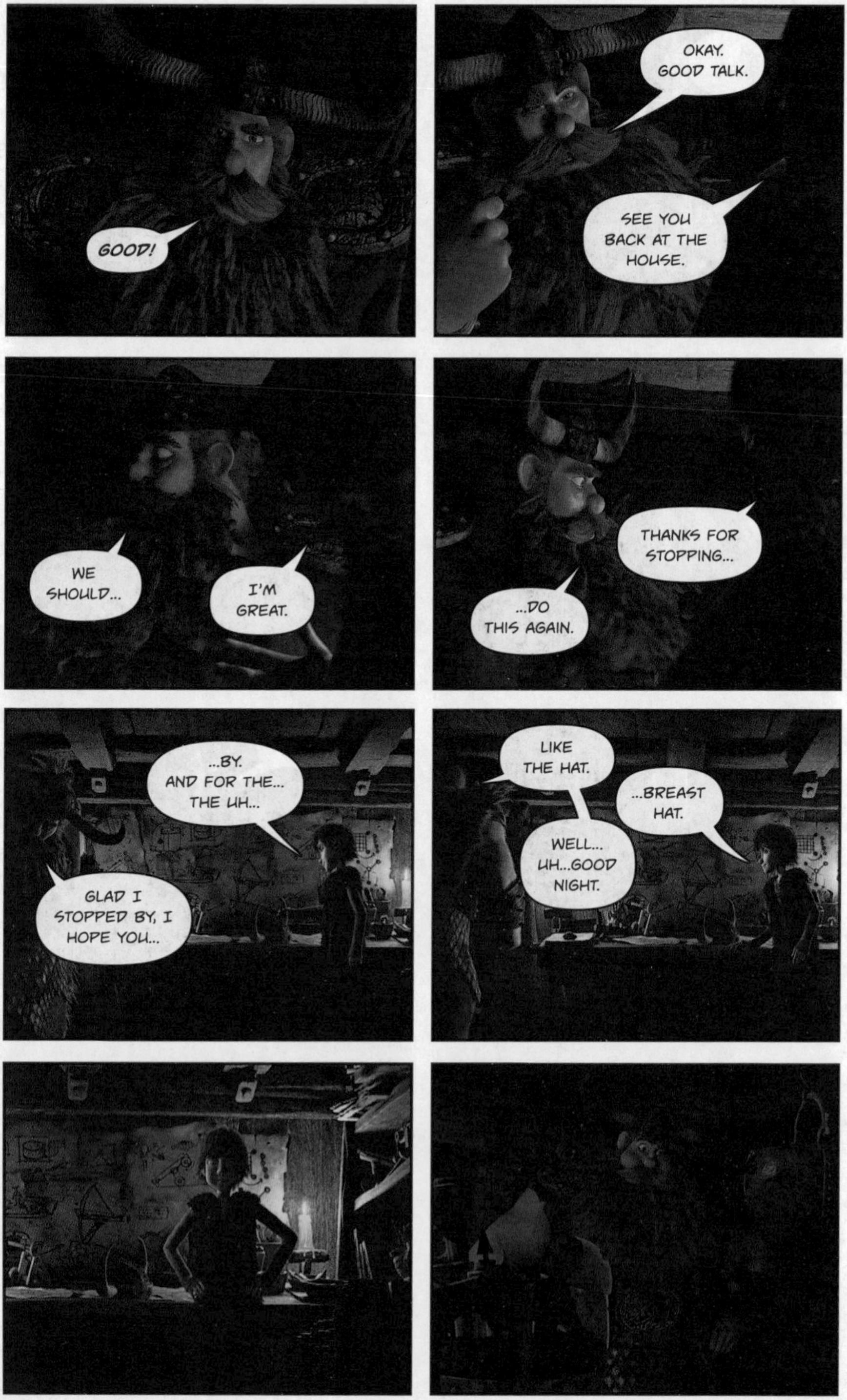
GOOD!
OKAY. GOOD TALK.
SEE YOU BACK AT THE HOUSE.
WE SHOULD...
I'M GREAT.
THANKS FOR STOPPING...
...DO THIS AGAIN.
GLAD I STOPPED BY, I HOPE YOU...
...BY. AND FOR THE... THE UH...
LIKE THE HAT.
...BREAST HAT.
WELL... UH...GOOD NIGHT.

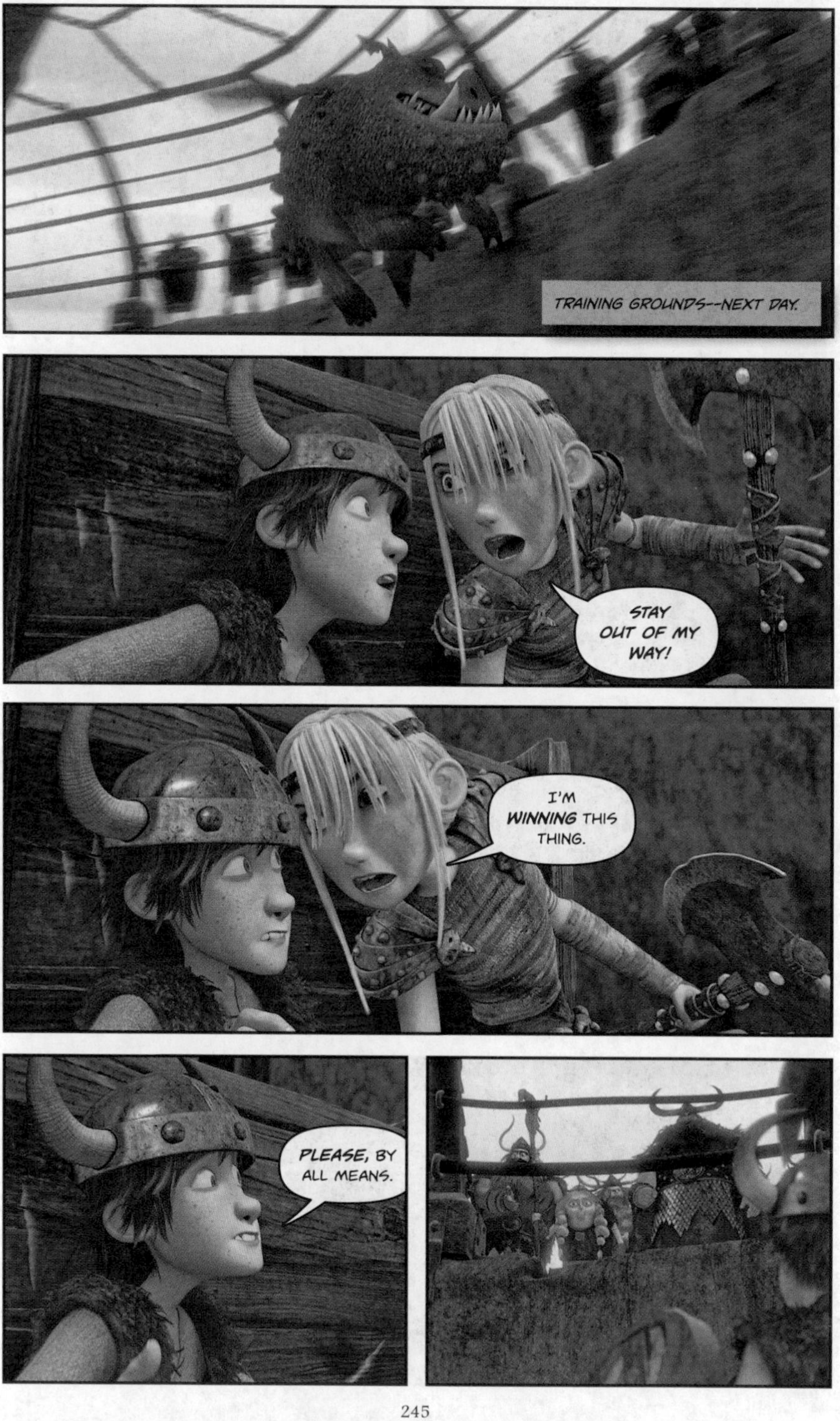
TRAINING GROUNDS--NEXT DAY.
STAY OUT OF MY WAY!
I'M WINNING THIS THING.
PLEASE, BY ALL MEANS.

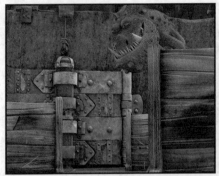

THIS TIME. THIS TIME FOR SURE.

AAAAAA AAAAA!...

246

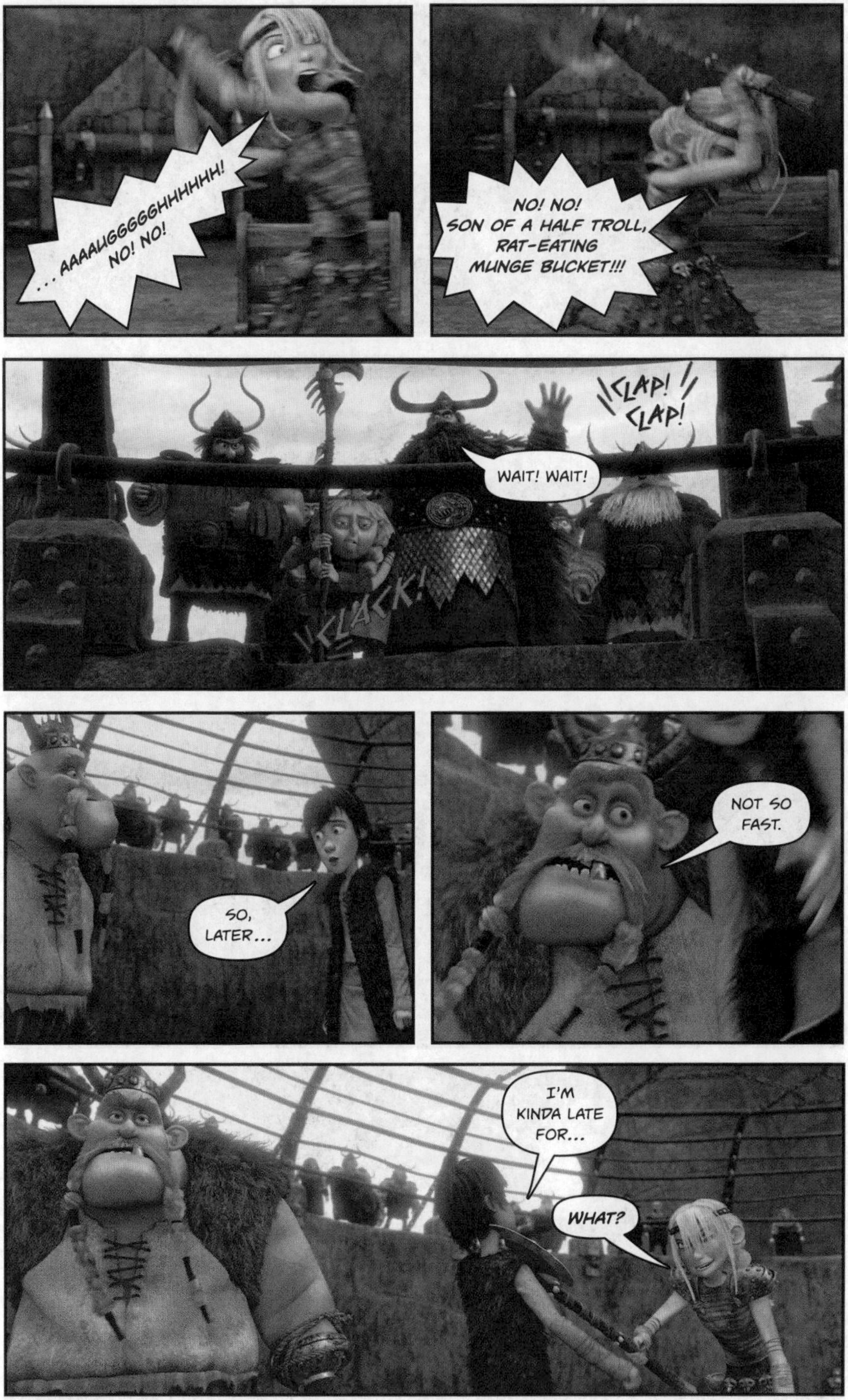

. . . AAAAUGGGGGHHHHHH! NO! NO!
NO! NO! SON OF A HALF TROLL, RAT-EATING MUNGE BUCKET!!!
CLAP! CLAP!
WAIT! WAIT!
CLACK!
SO, LATER...
NOT SO FAST.
I'M KINDA LATE FOR...
WHAT?

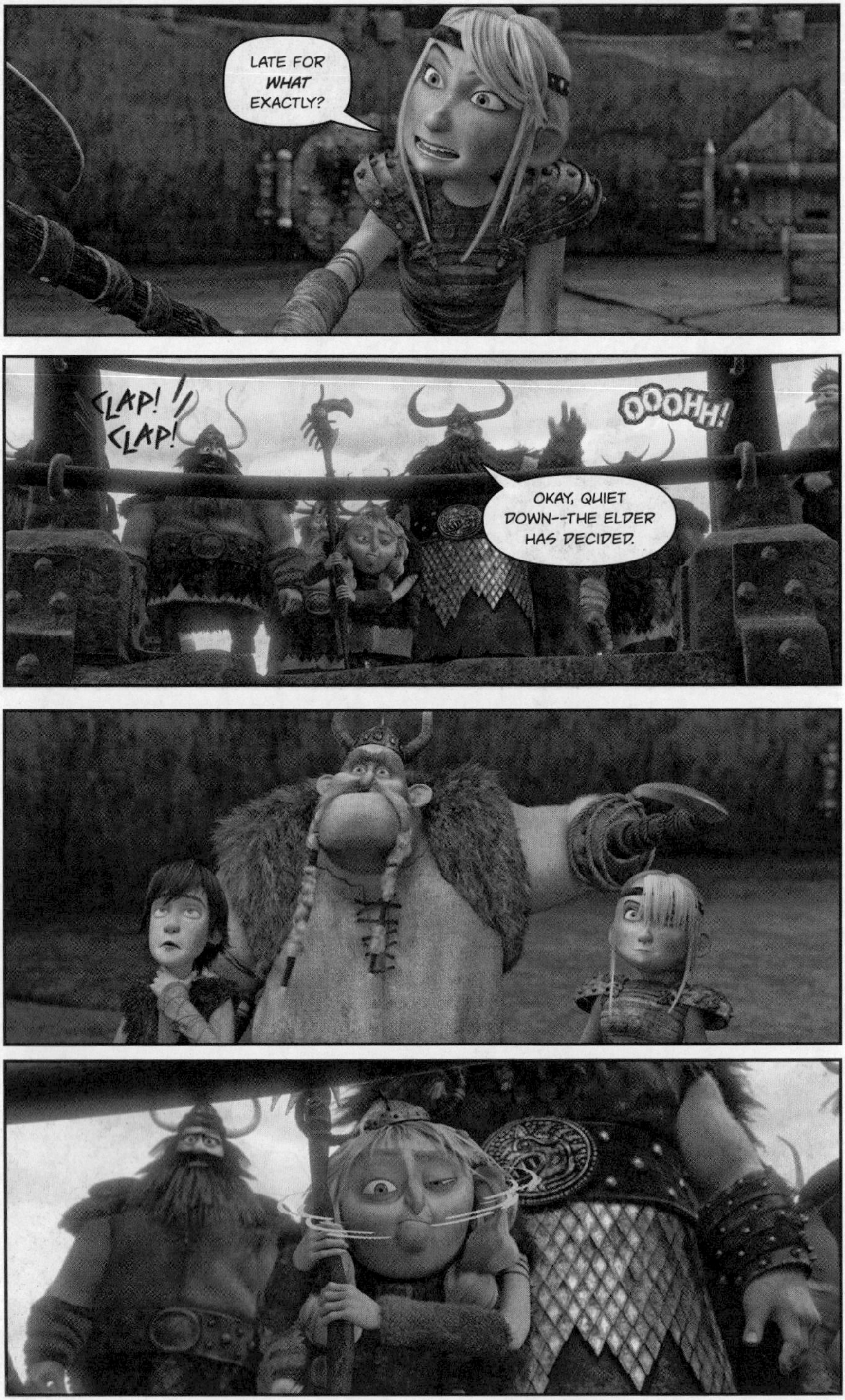
LATE FOR WHAT EXACTLY?
CLAP! CLAP!
OOOHH!
OKAY, QUIET DOWN--THE ELDER HAS DECIDED.

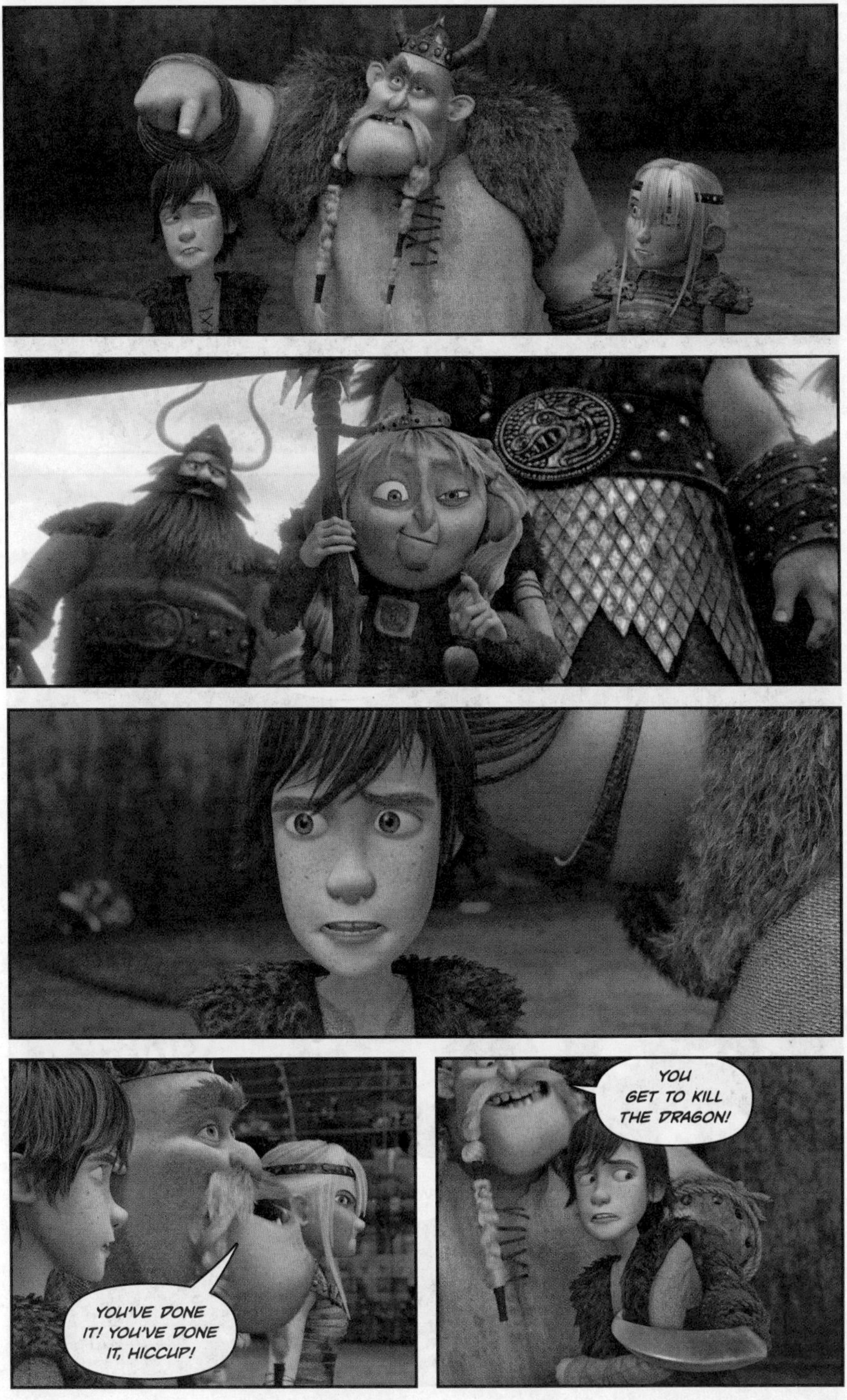
YOU'VE DONE IT! YOU'VE DONE IT, HICCUP!
YOU GET TO KILL THE DRAGON!

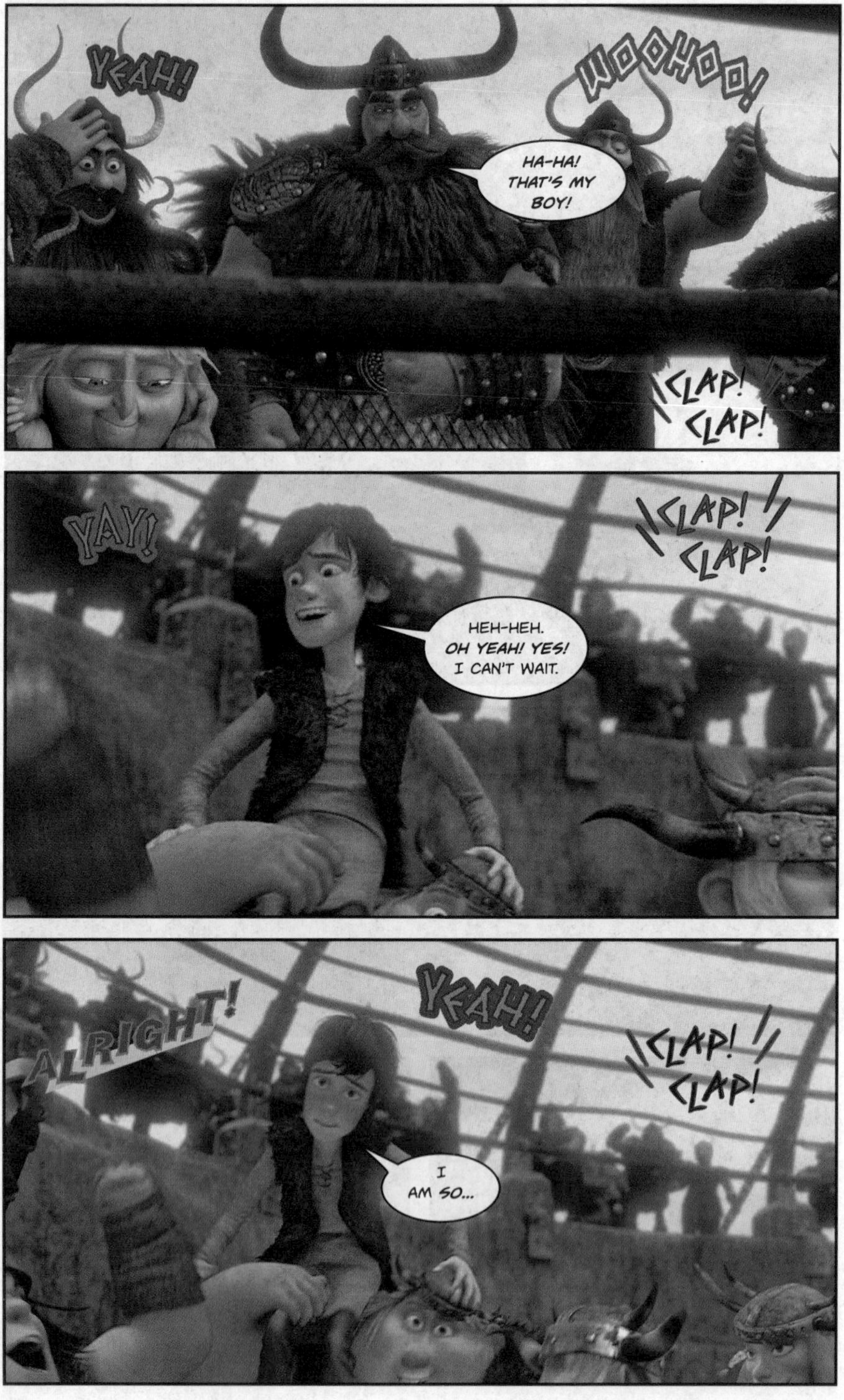
YEAH!
WOOHOO!
HA-HA! THAT'S MY BOY!
CLAP! CLAP!
YAY!
CLAP! CLAP!
HEH-HEH. OH YEAH! YES! I CAN'T WAIT.
ALRIGHT!
YEAH!
CLAP! CLAP!
I AM SO...

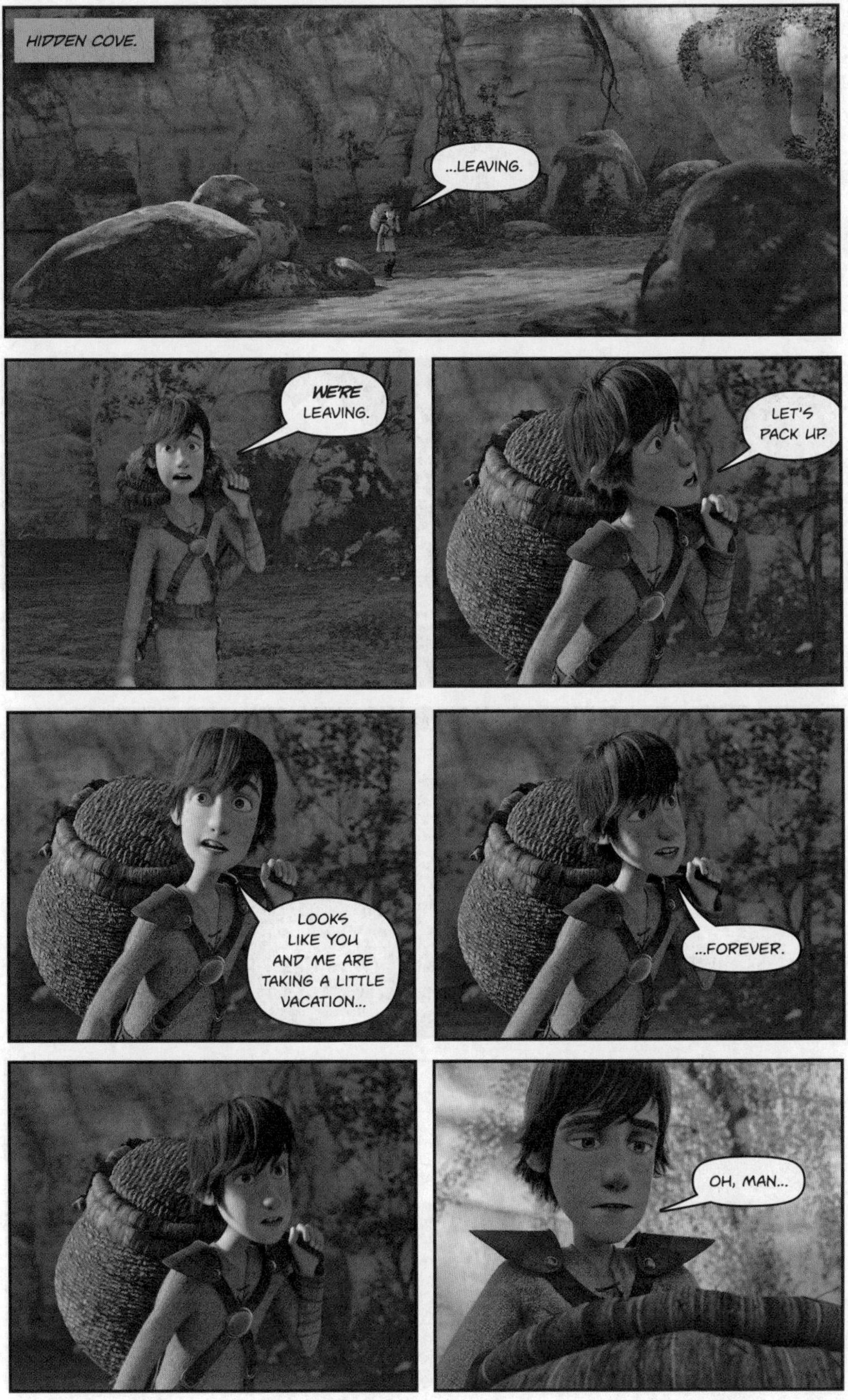
HIDDEN COVE.
...LEAVING.
WE'RE LEAVING.
LET'S PACK UP.
LOOKS LIKE YOU AND ME ARE TAKING A LITTLE VACATION...
...FOREVER.
OH, MAN...

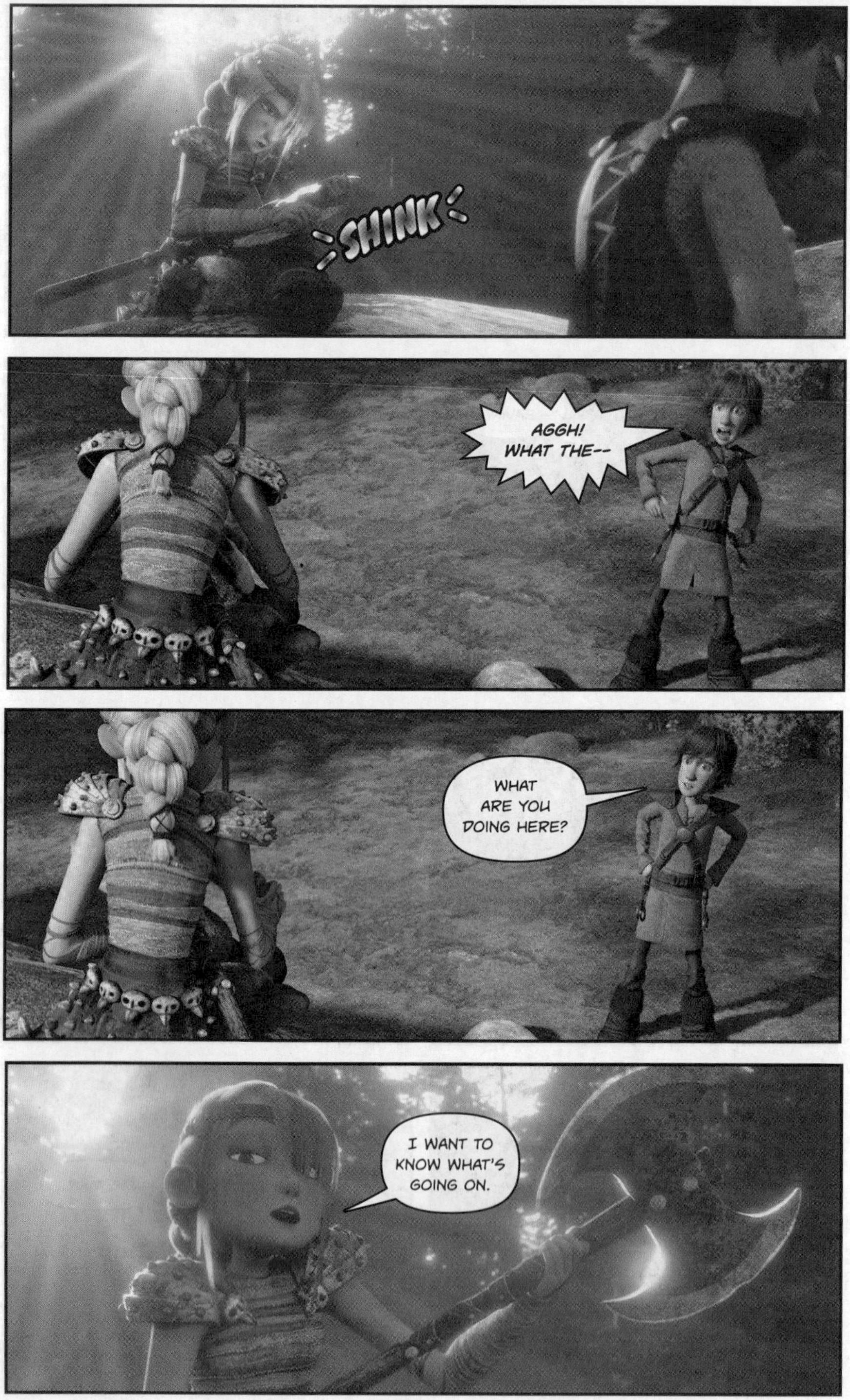
SHINK
AGGH! WHAT THE--
WHAT ARE YOU DOING HERE?
I WANT TO KNOW WHAT'S GOING ON.

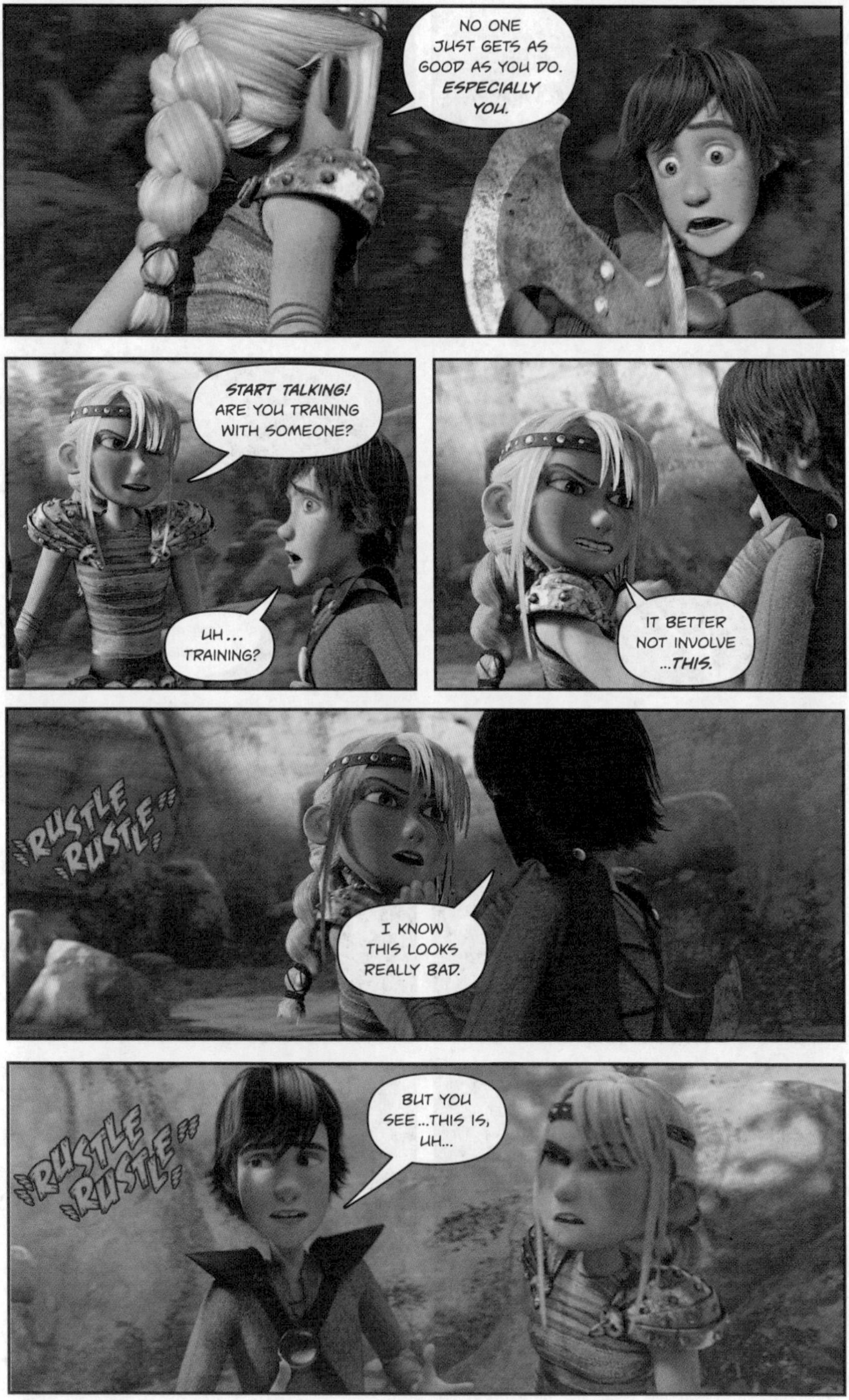
NO ONE JUST GETS AS GOOD AS YOU DO. ESPECIALLY YOU.
START TALKING! ARE YOU TRAINING WITH SOMEONE?
UH... TRAINING?
IT BETTER NOT INVOLVE ...THIS.
RUSTLE RUSTLE
I KNOW THIS LOOKS REALLY BAD.
RUSTLE RUSTLE
BUT YOU SEE...THIS IS, UH...

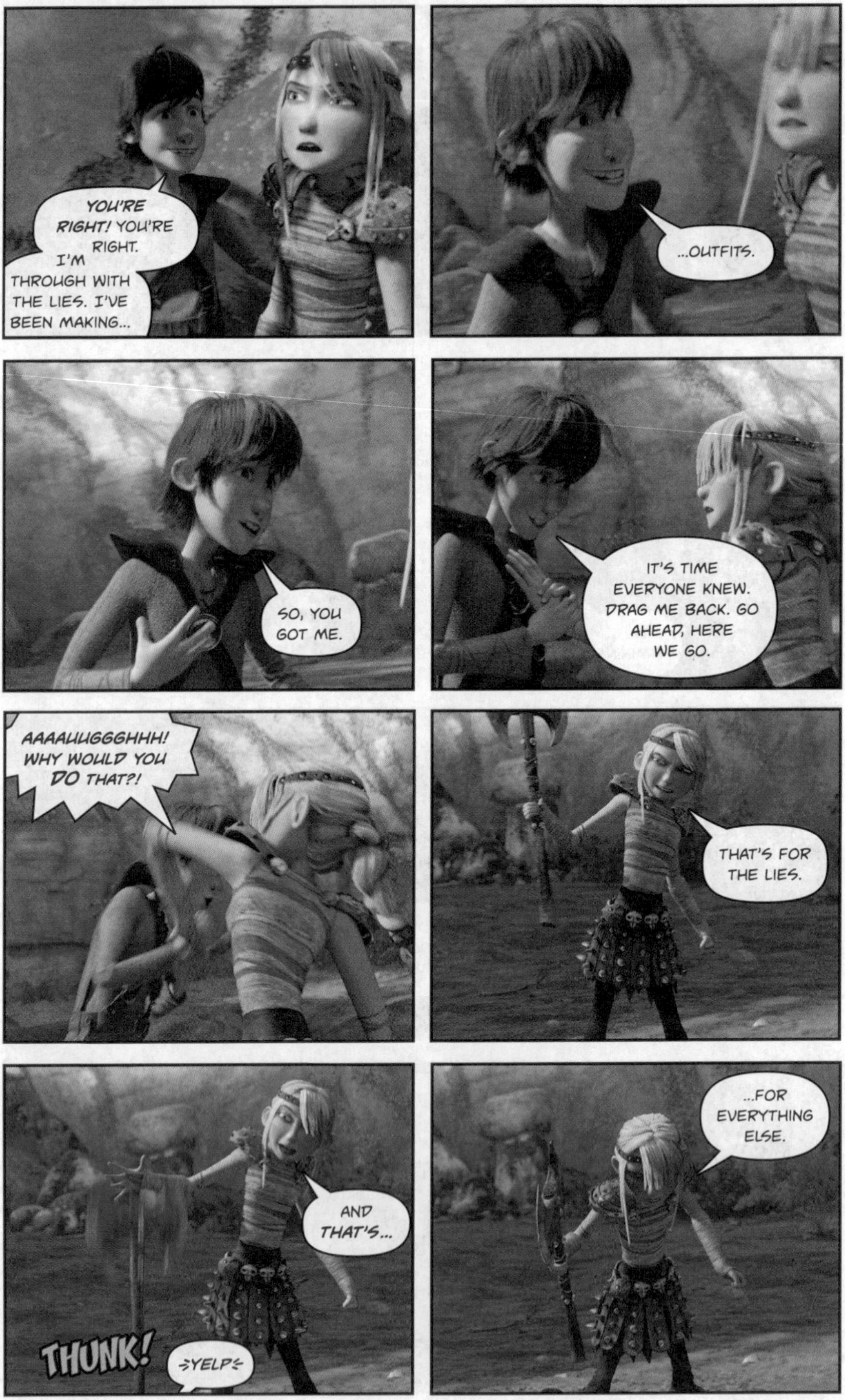
YOU'RE RIGHT! YOU'RE RIGHT.
I'M THROUGH WITH THE LIES. I'VE BEEN MAKING...
...OUTFITS.
SO, YOU GOT ME.
IT'S TIME EVERYONE KNEW. DRAG ME BACK. GO AHEAD, HERE WE GO.
AAAAUUGGGHHH! WHY WOULD YOU DO THAT?!
THAT'S FOR THE LIES.
AND THAT'S...
THUNK!
YELP
...FOR EVERYTHING ELSE.

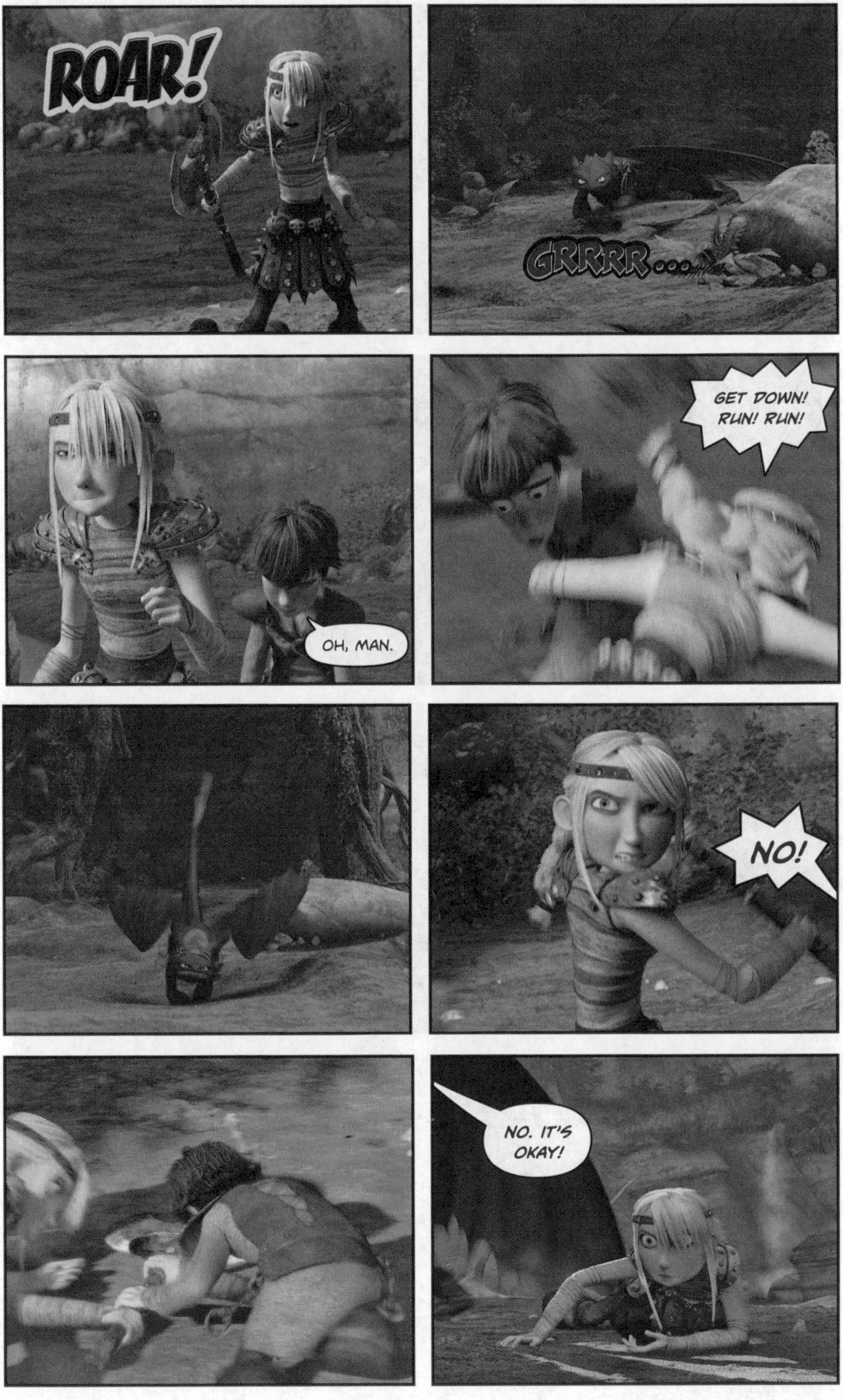
ROAR!
GRRRR...
OH, MAN.
GET DOWN! RUN! RUN!
NO!
NO. IT'S OKAY!

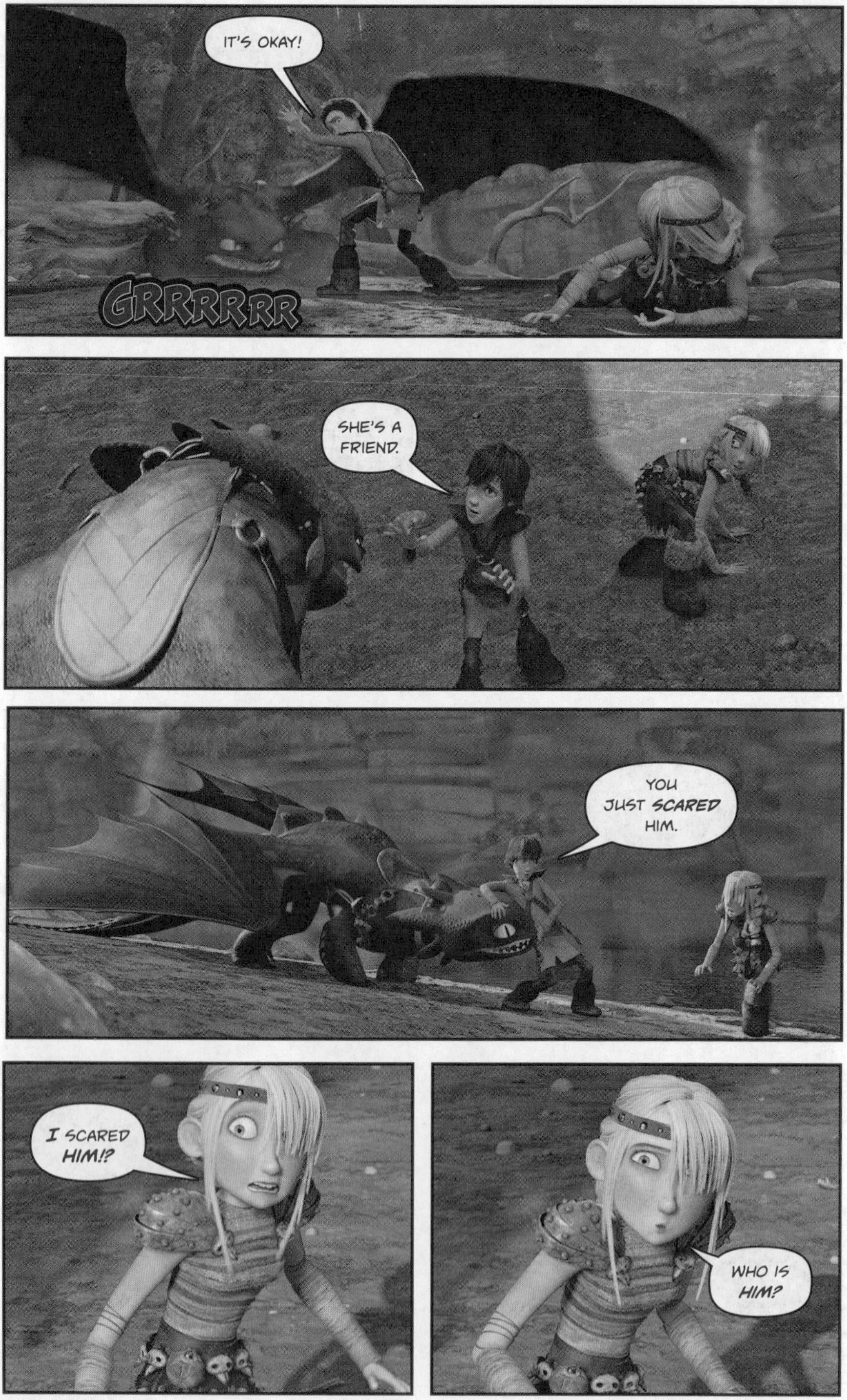
IT'S OKAY!
GRRRRRR
SHE'S A FRIEND.
YOU JUST **SCARED** HIM.
I SCARED **HIM!?**
WHO IS **HIM?**

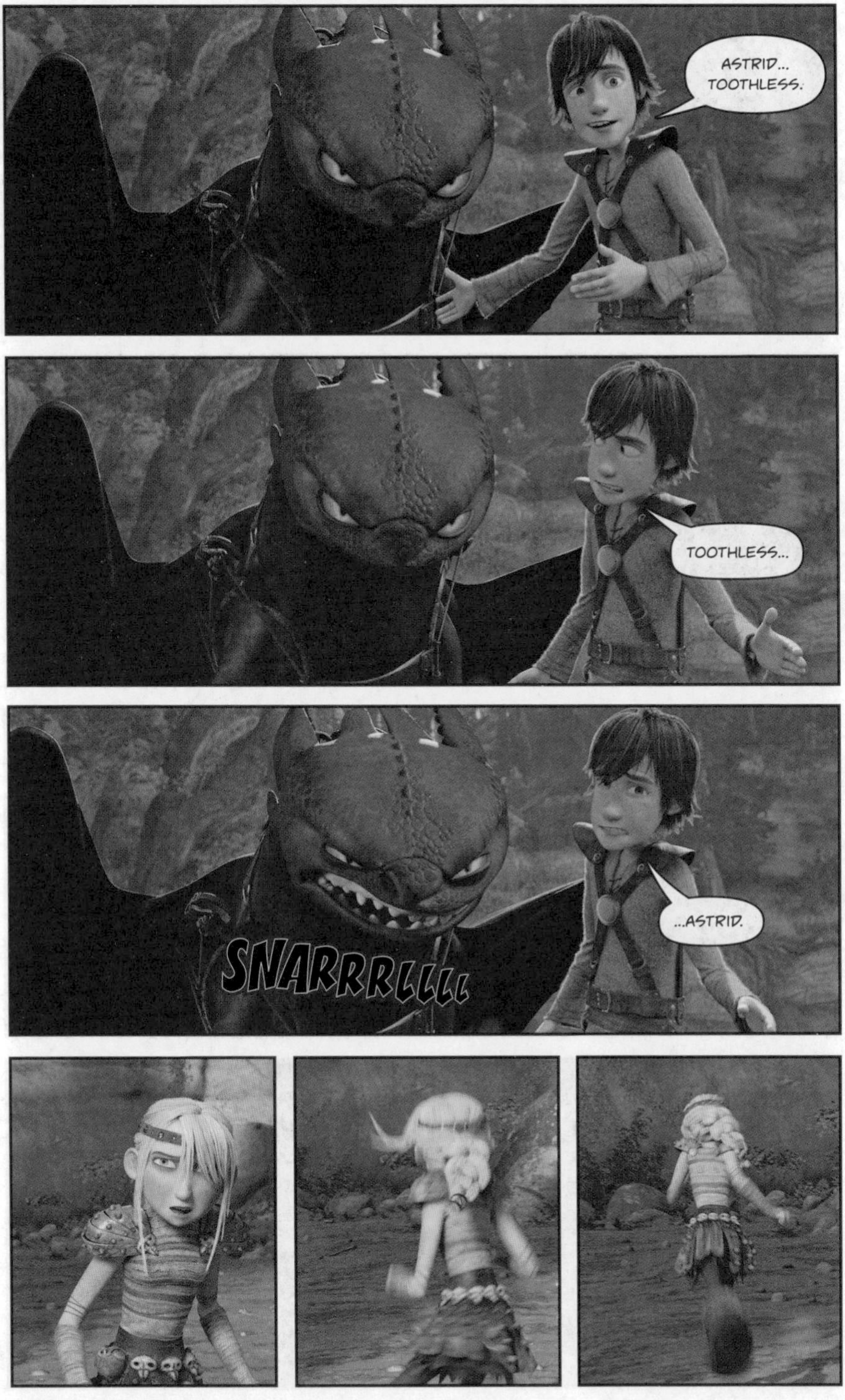
ASTRID...
TOOTHLESS.
TOOTHLESS...
...ASTRID.
SNARRRLLLL

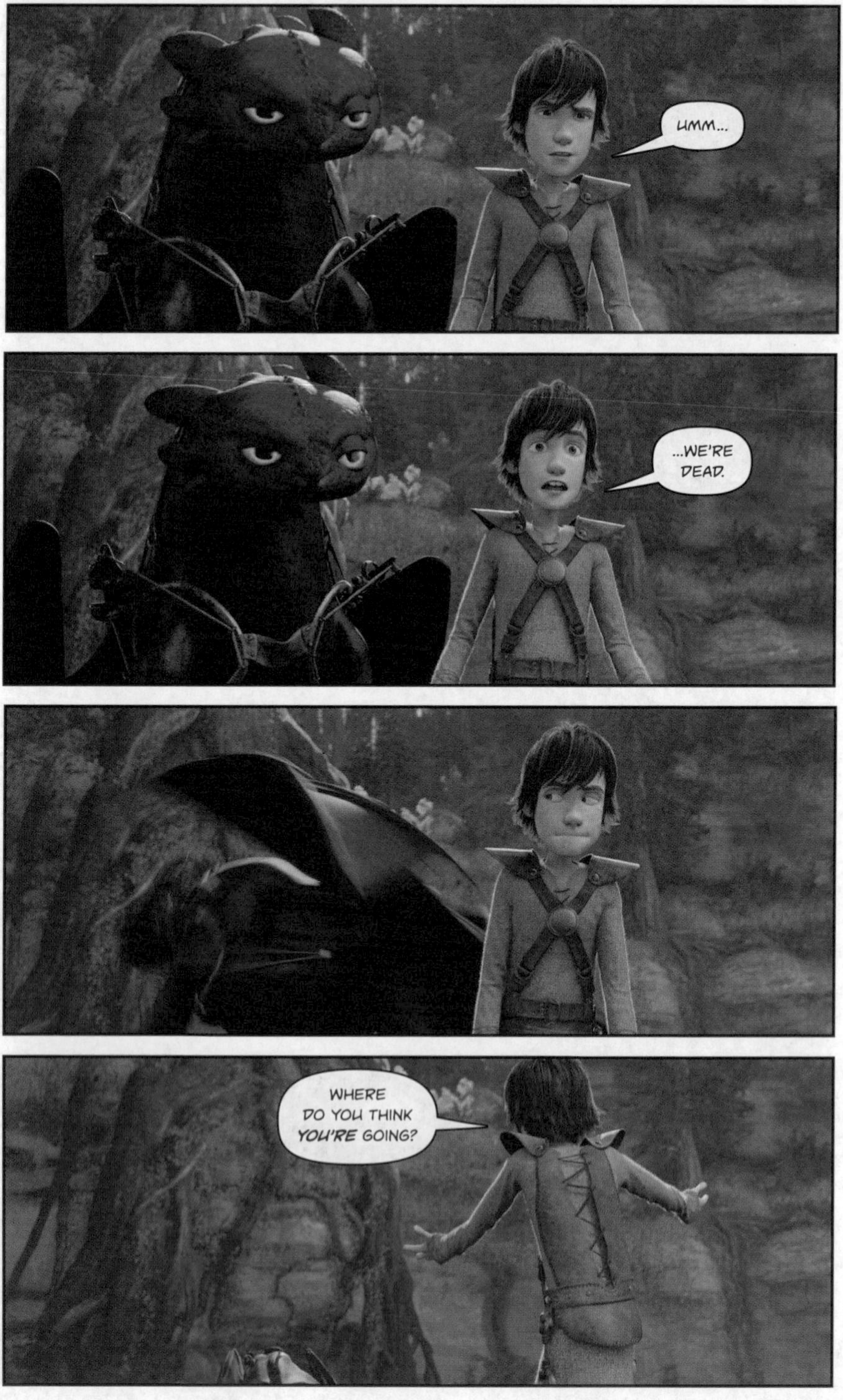
UMM...
...WE'RE DEAD.
WHERE DO YOU THINK YOU'RE GOING?

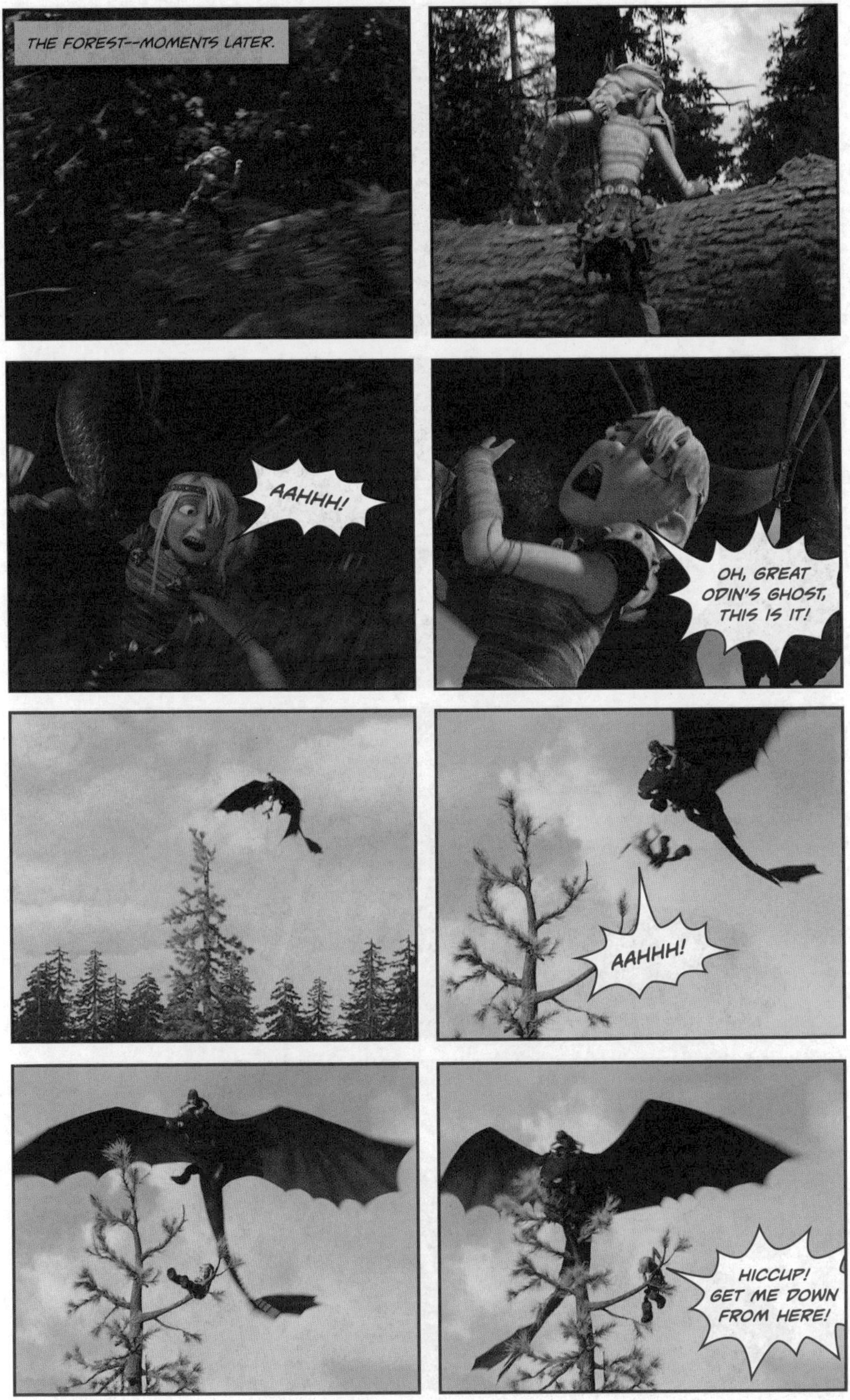
THE FOREST--MOMENTS LATER.
AAHHH!
OH, GREAT ODIN'S GHOST, THIS IS IT!
AAHHH!
HICCUP! GET ME DOWN FROM HERE!

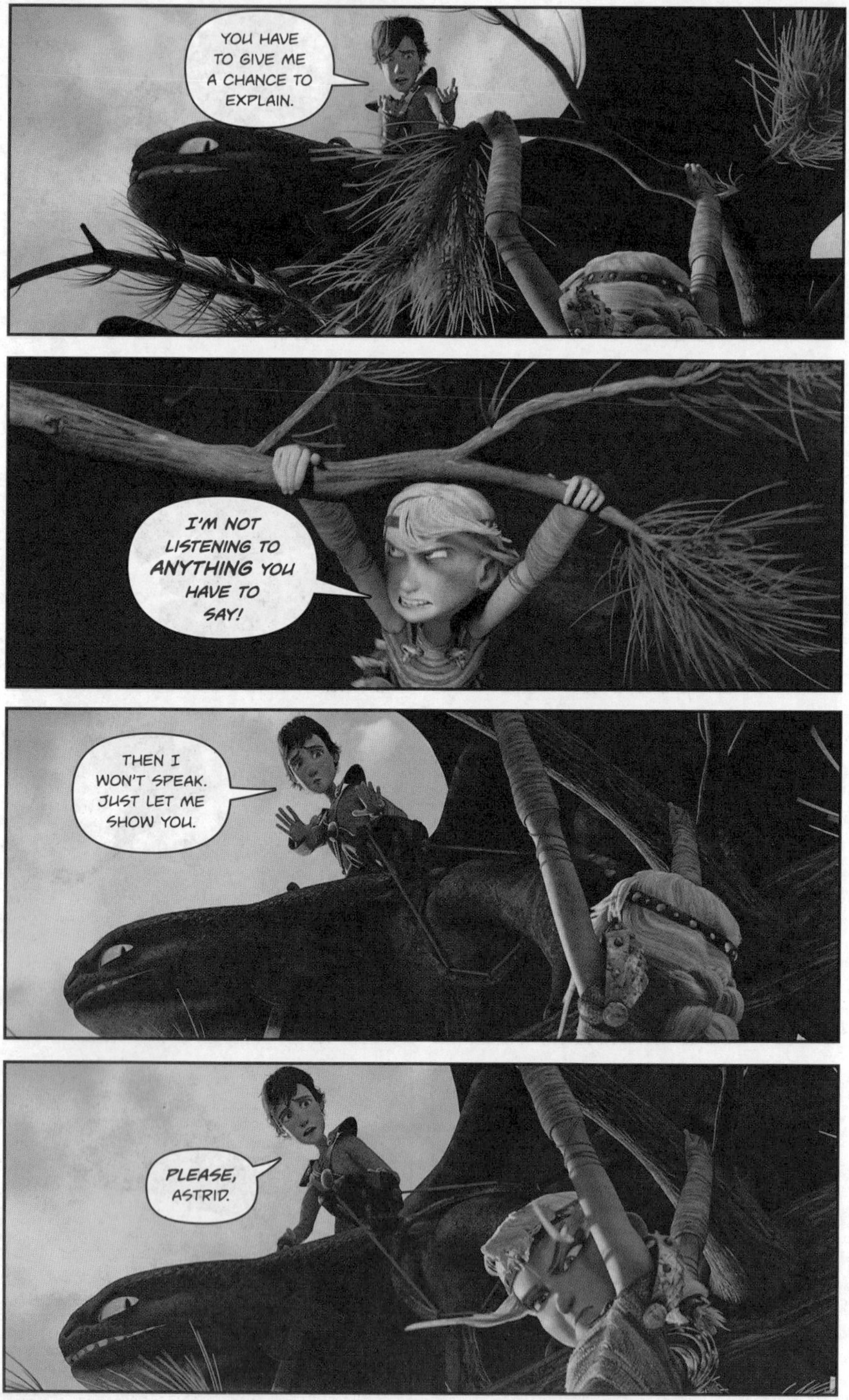
YOU HAVE TO GIVE ME A CHANCE TO EXPLAIN.
I'M NOT LISTENING TO ANYTHING YOU HAVE TO SAY!
THEN I WON'T SPEAK. JUST LET ME SHOW YOU.
PLEASE, ASTRID.

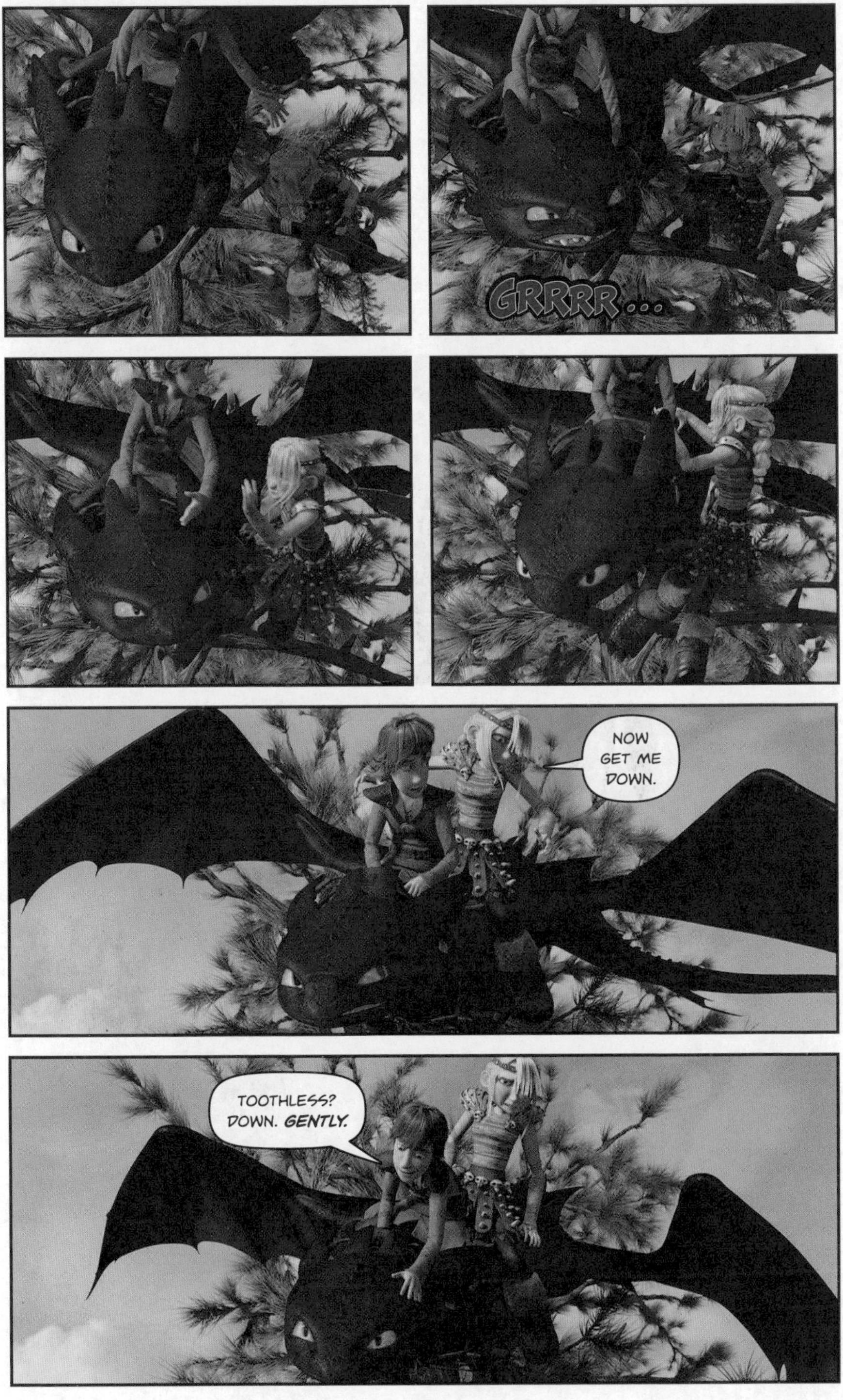
GRRRR...
NOW GET ME DOWN.
TOOTHLESS? DOWN. **GENTLY.**

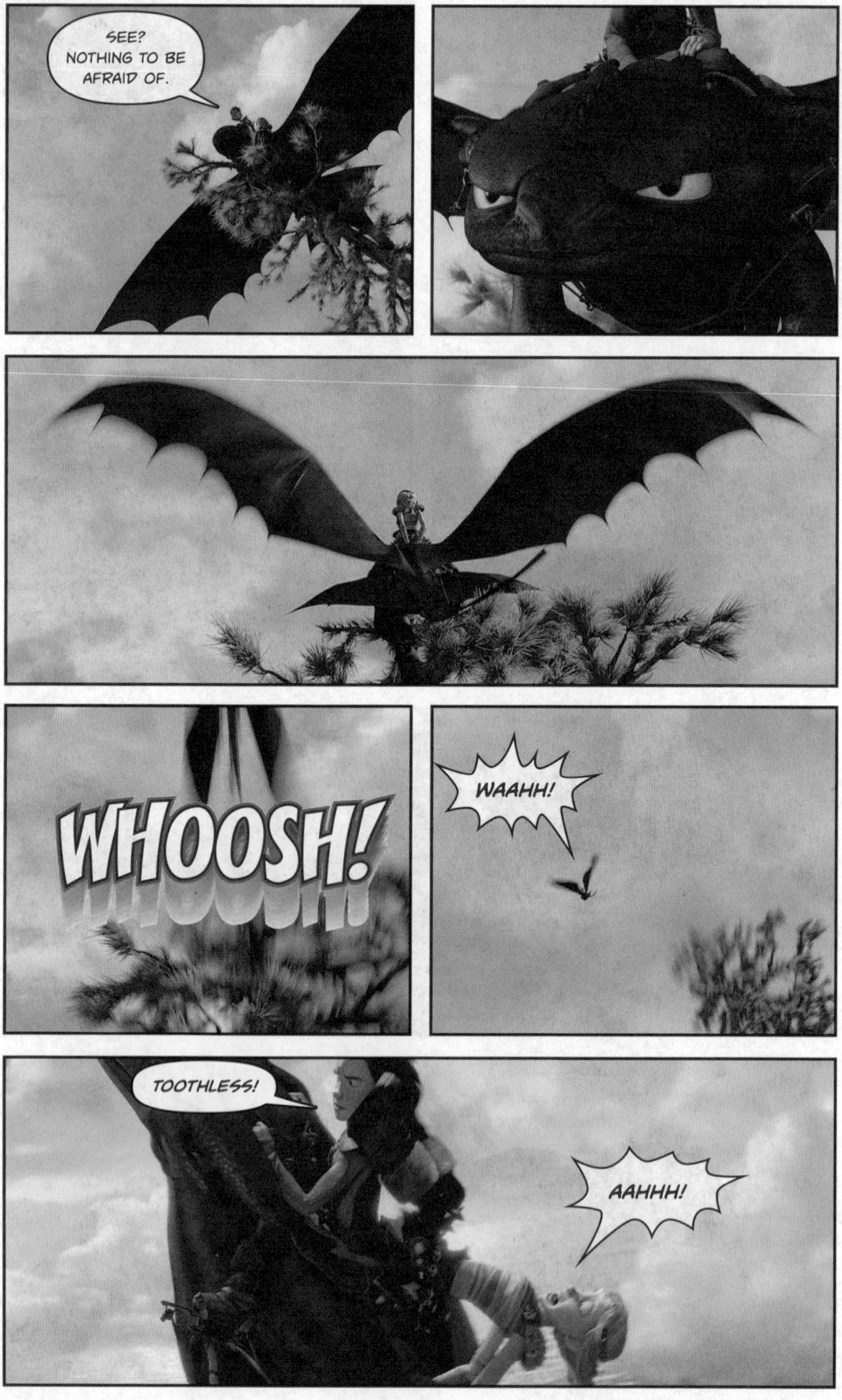
SEE? NOTHING TO BE AFRAID OF.
WHOOSH!
WAAHH!
TOOTHLESS!
AAHHH!

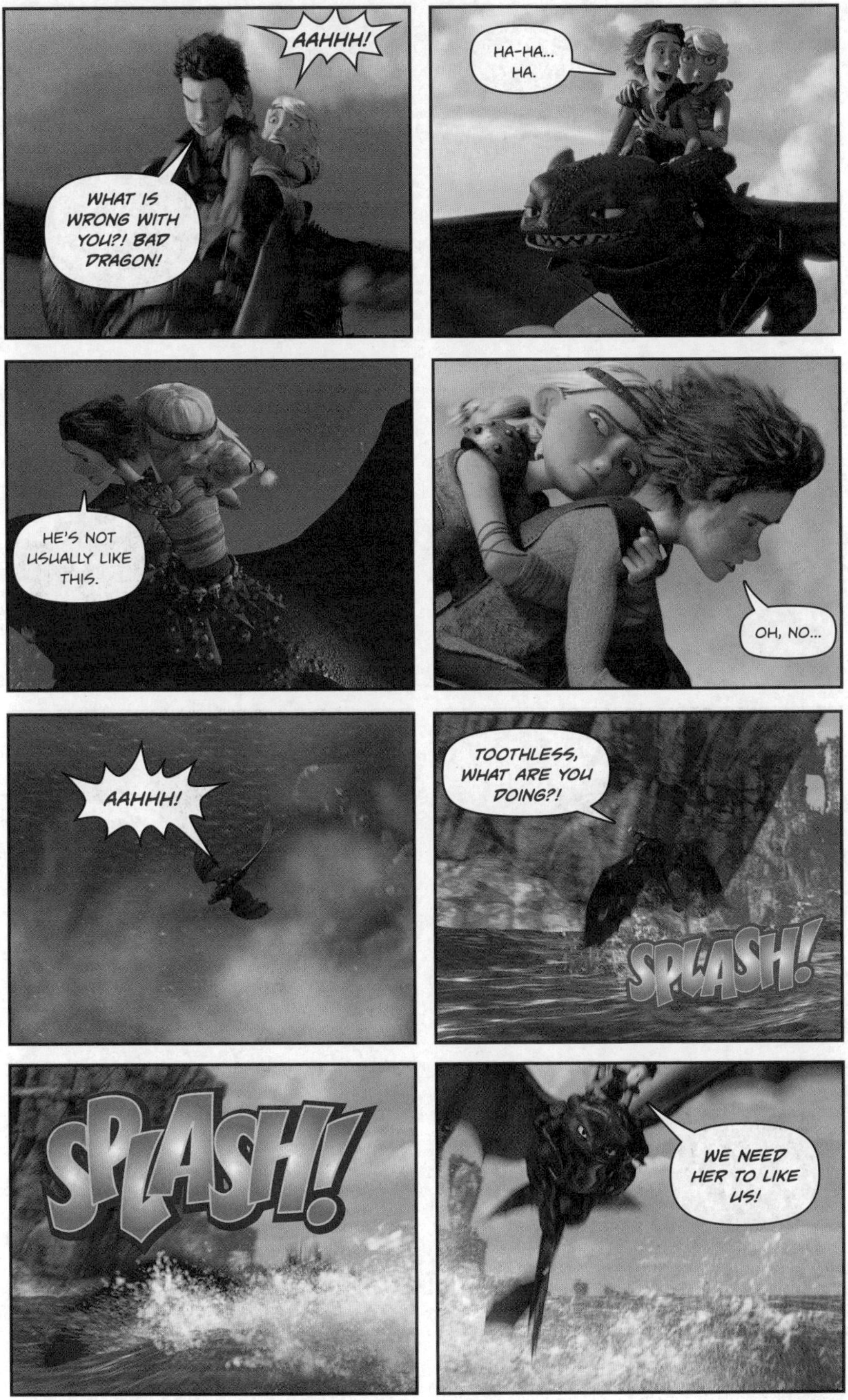
AAHHH!
WHAT IS WRONG WITH YOU?! BAD DRAGON!
HA-HA... HA.
HE'S NOT USUALLY LIKE THIS.
OH, NO...
AAHHH!
TOOTHLESS, WHAT ARE YOU DOING?!
SPLASH!
SPLASH!
WE NEED HER TO LIKE US!

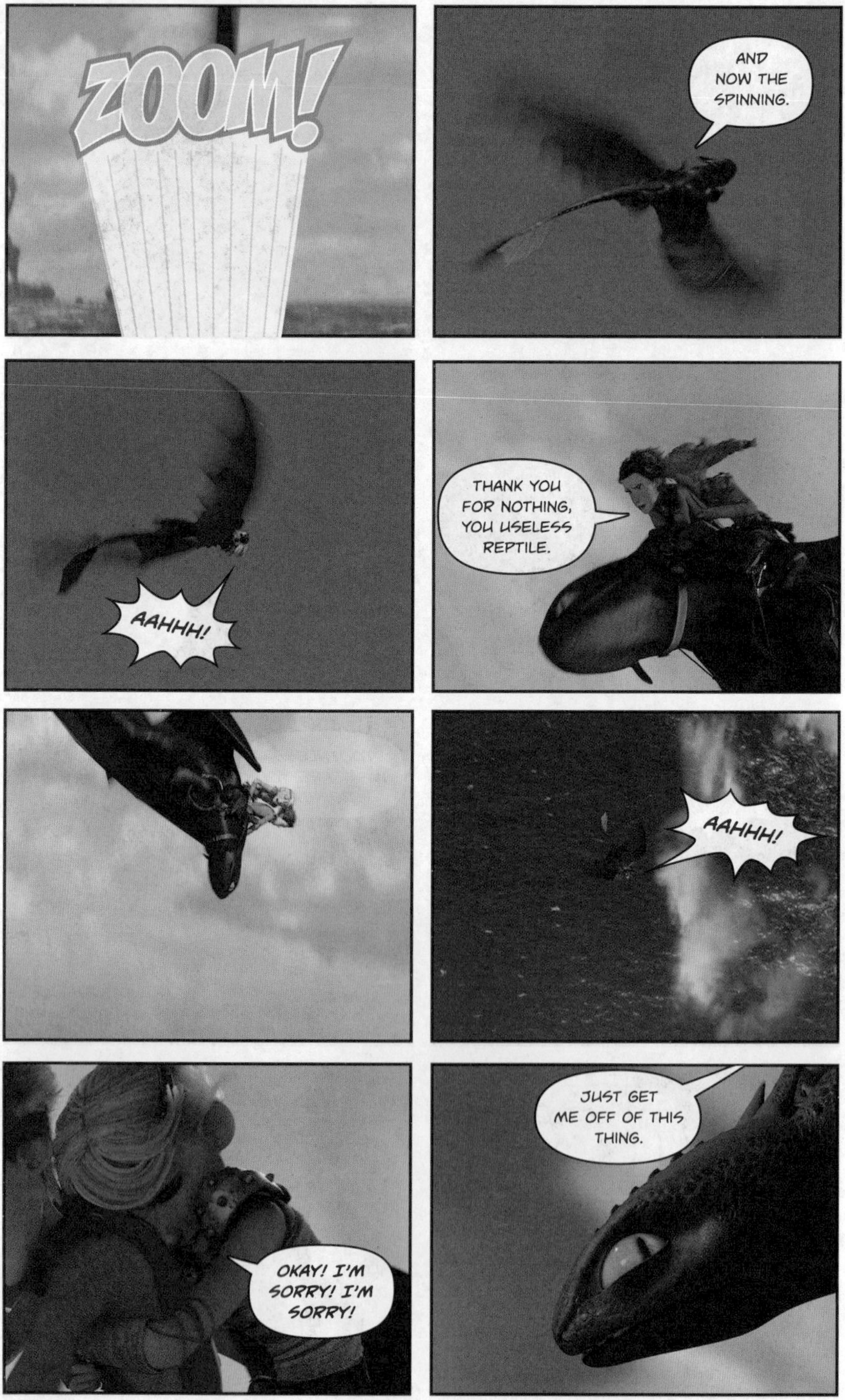
ZOOM!
AND NOW THE SPINNING.
AAHHH!
THANK YOU FOR NOTHING, YOU USELESS REPTILE.
AAHHH!
OKAY! I'M SORRY! I'M SORRY!
JUST GET ME OFF OF THIS THING.

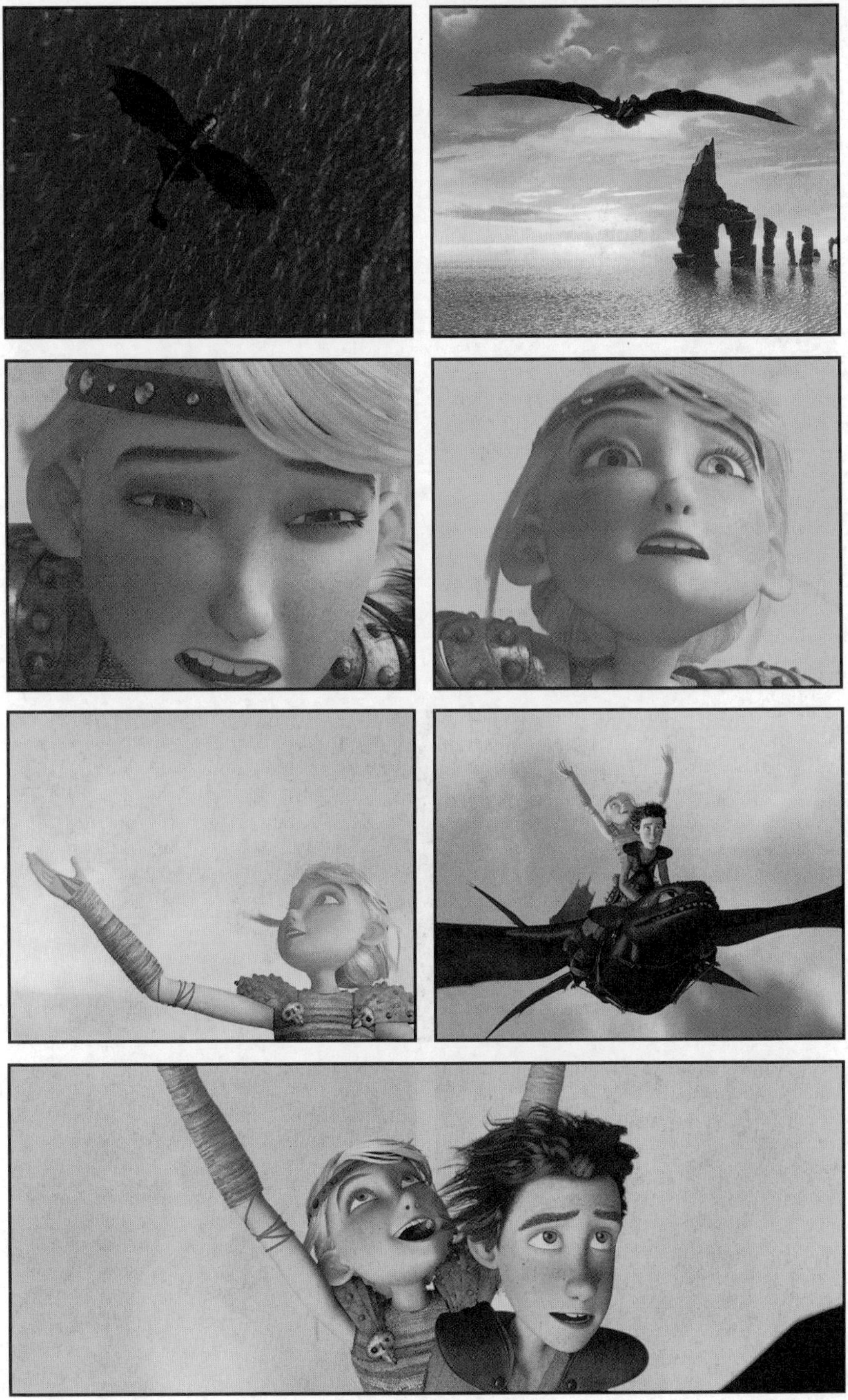

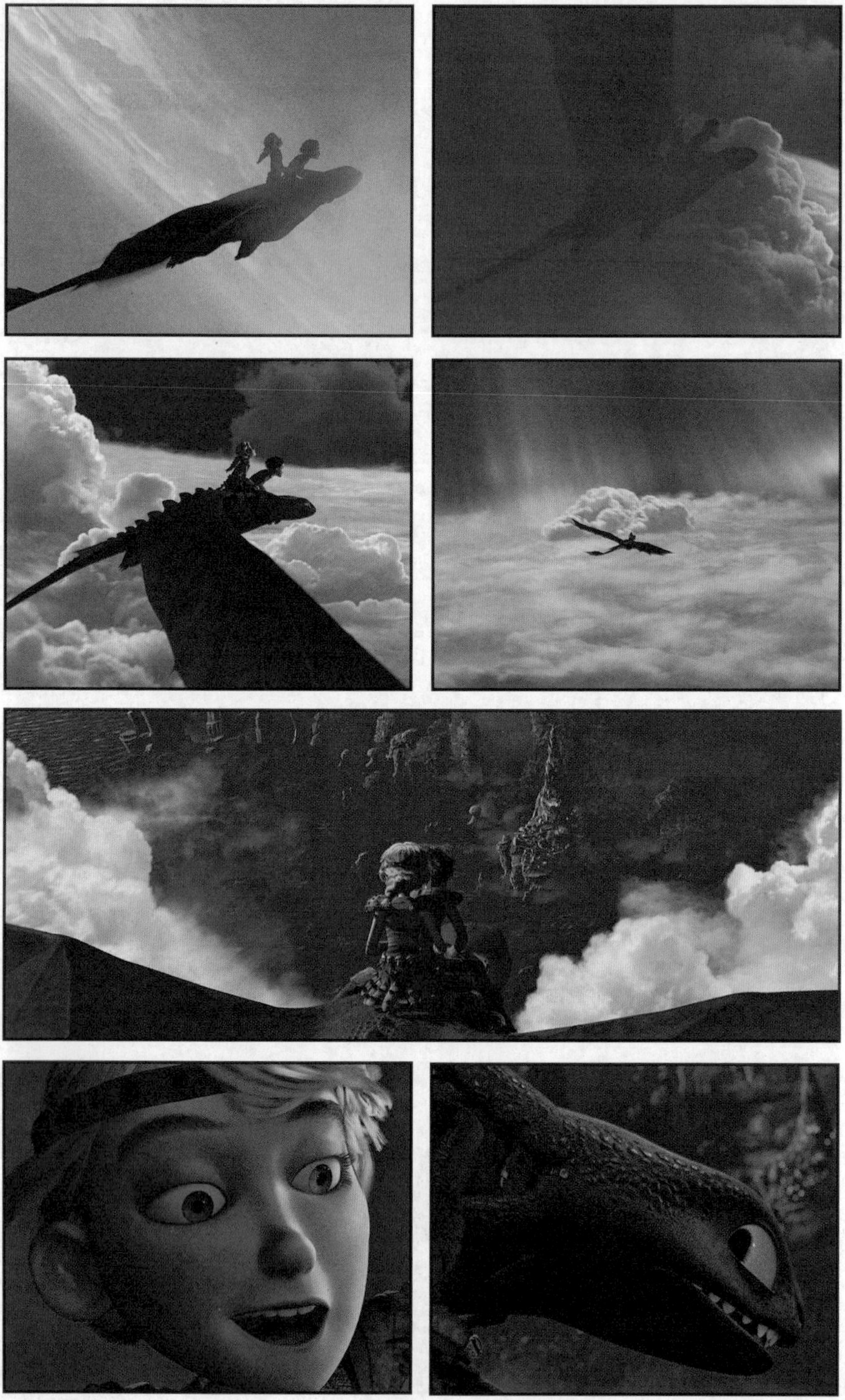

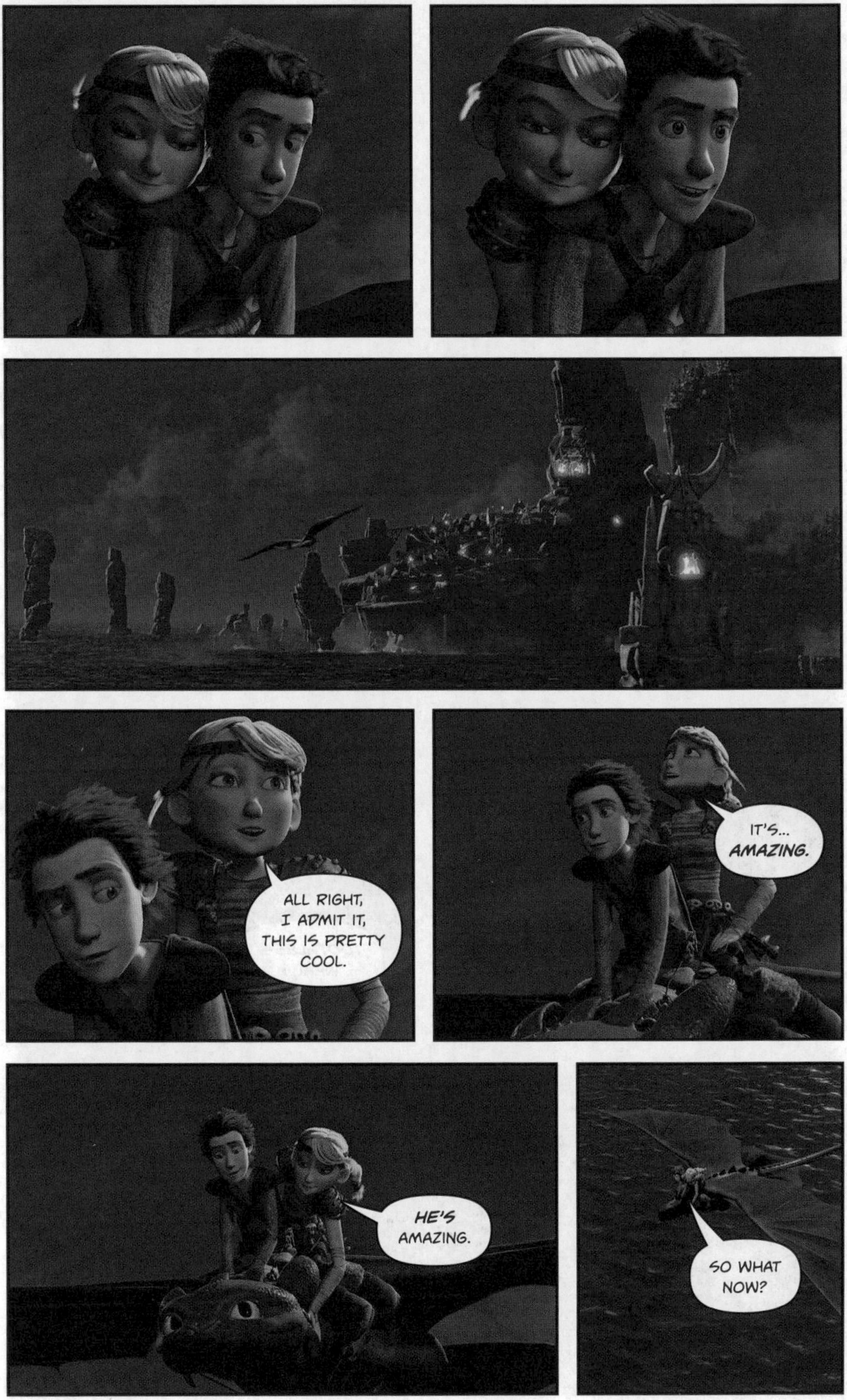
ALL RIGHT, I ADMIT IT, THIS IS PRETTY COOL.
IT'S... AMAZING.
HE'S AMAZING.
SO WHAT NOW?

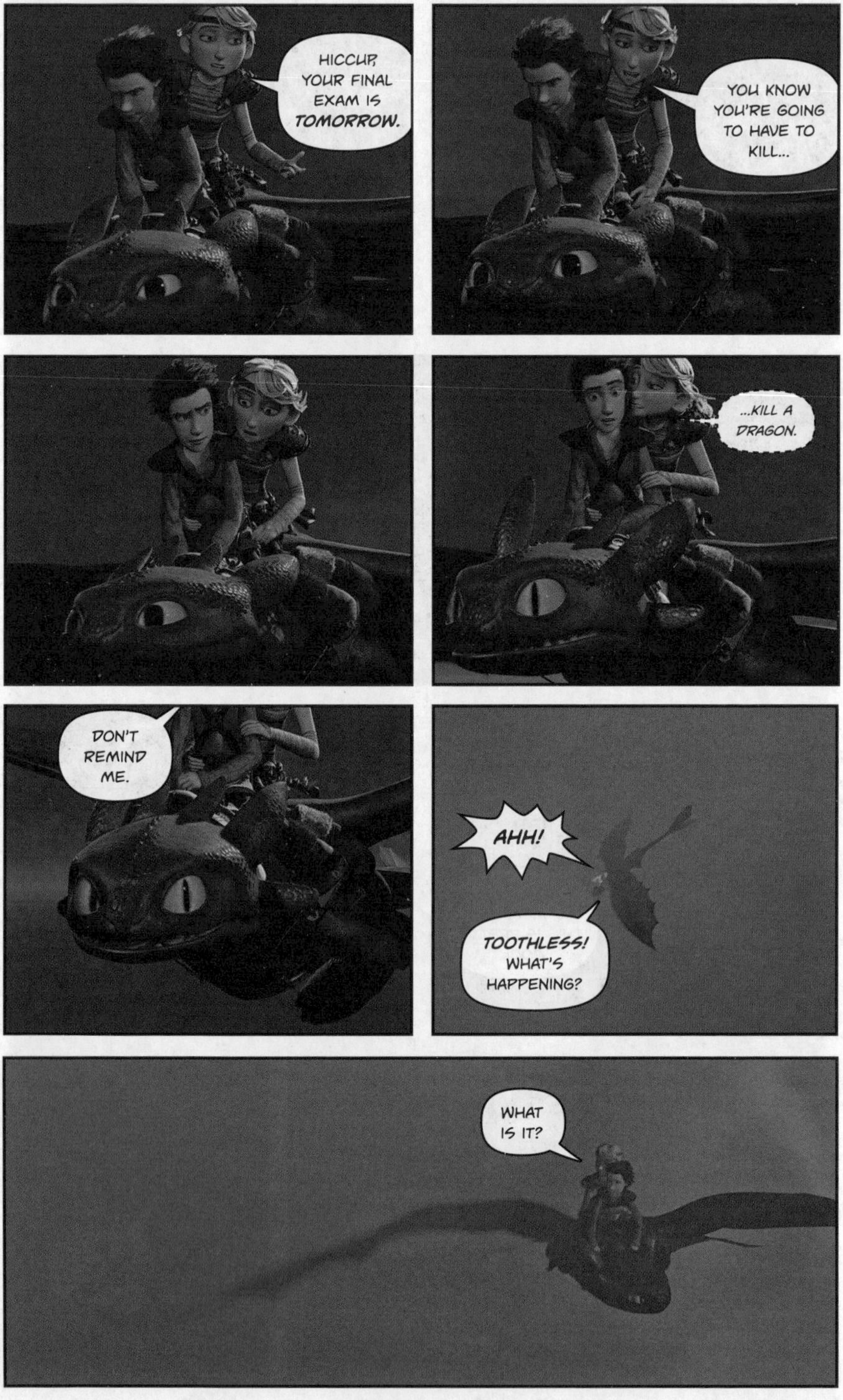
HICCUP, YOUR FINAL EXAM IS TOMORROW.
YOU KNOW YOU'RE GOING TO HAVE TO KILL...
...KILL A DRAGON.
DON'T REMIND ME.
AHH!
TOOTHLESS! WHAT'S HAPPENING?
WHAT IS IT?

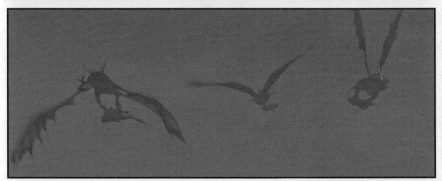

GET DOWN!

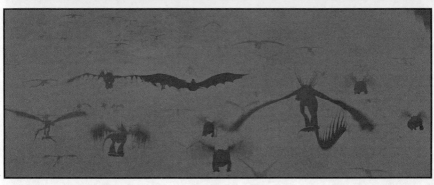

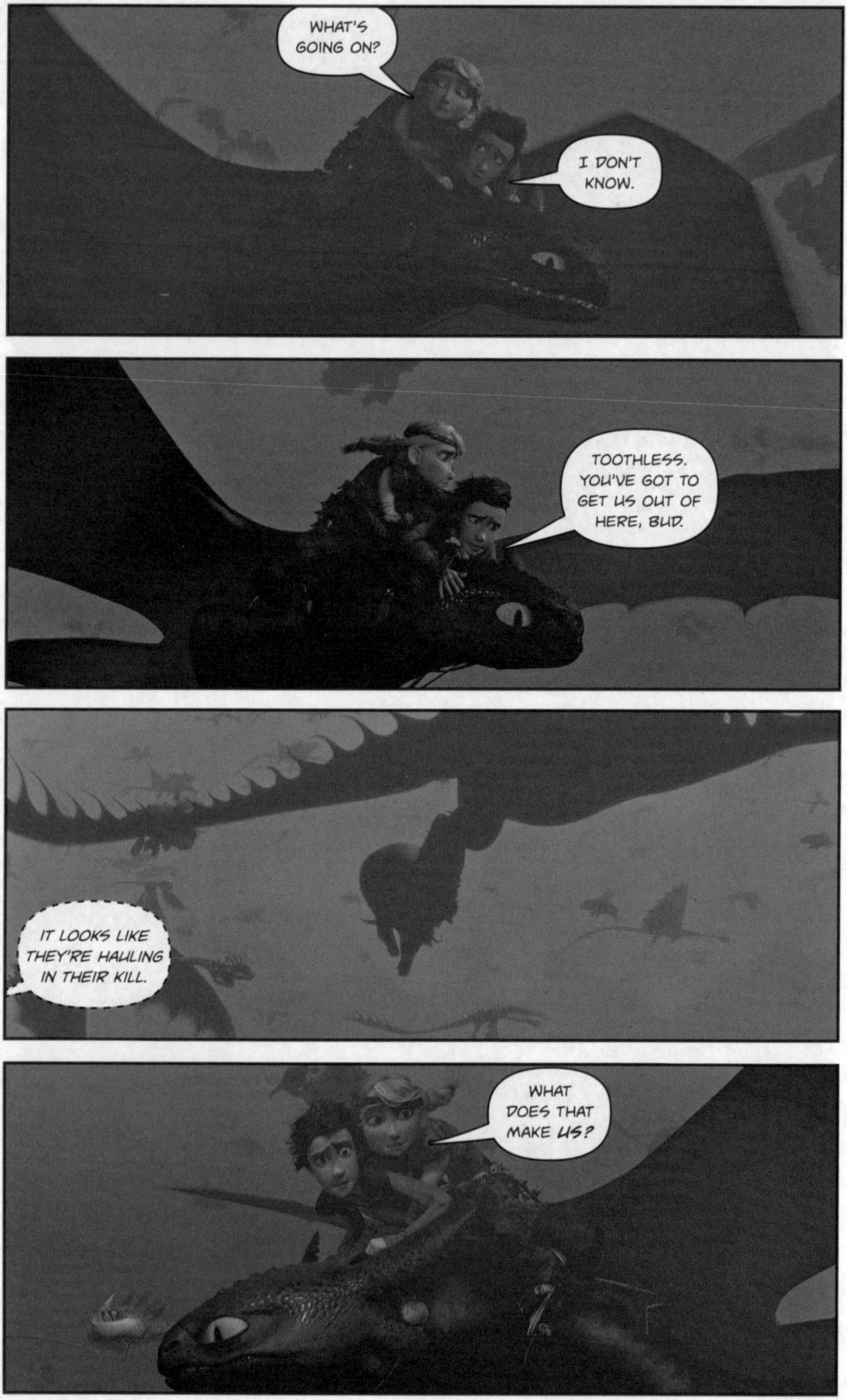
WHAT'S GOING ON?
I DON'T KNOW.
TOOTHLESS. YOU'VE GOT TO GET US OUT OF HERE, BUD.
IT LOOKS LIKE THEY'RE HAULING IN THEIR KILL.
WHAT DOES THAT MAKE *US*?

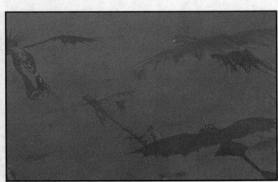

AHH...!

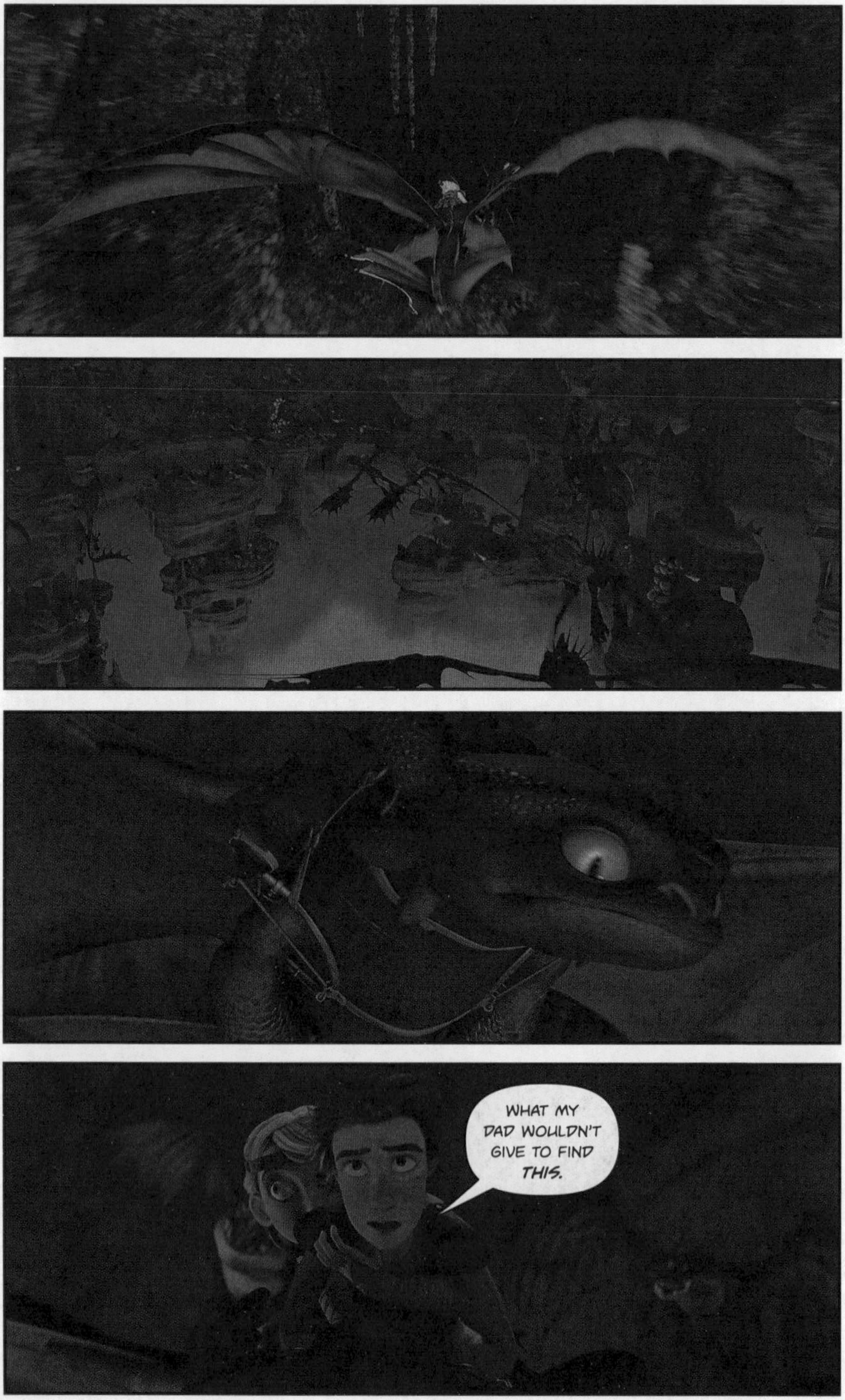
WHAT MY DAD WOULDN'T GIVE TO FIND THIS.

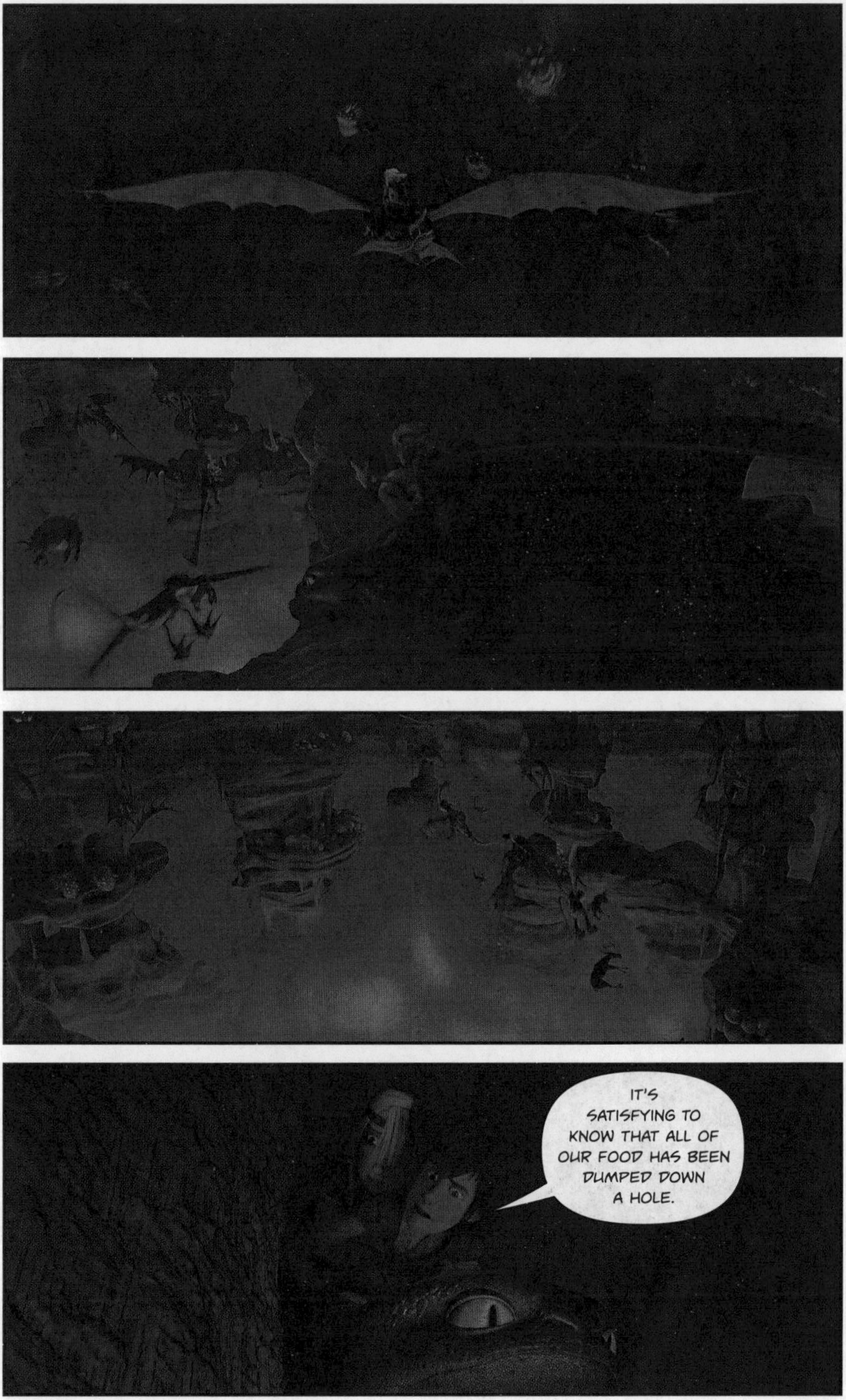
IT'S SATISFYING TO KNOW THAT ALL OF OUR FOOD HAS BEEN DUMPED DOWN A HOLE.

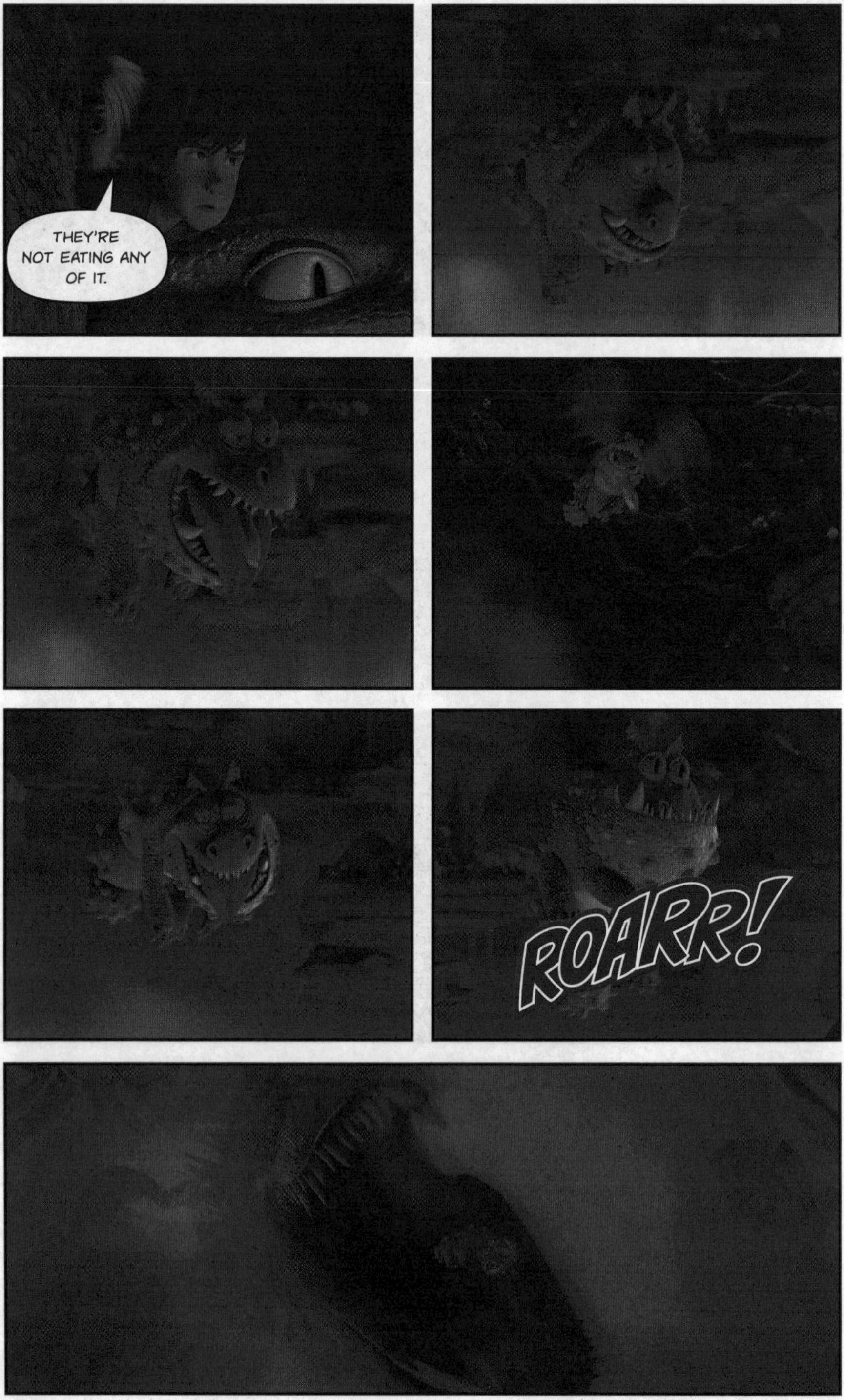
THEY'RE NOT EATING ANY OF IT.
ROARR!

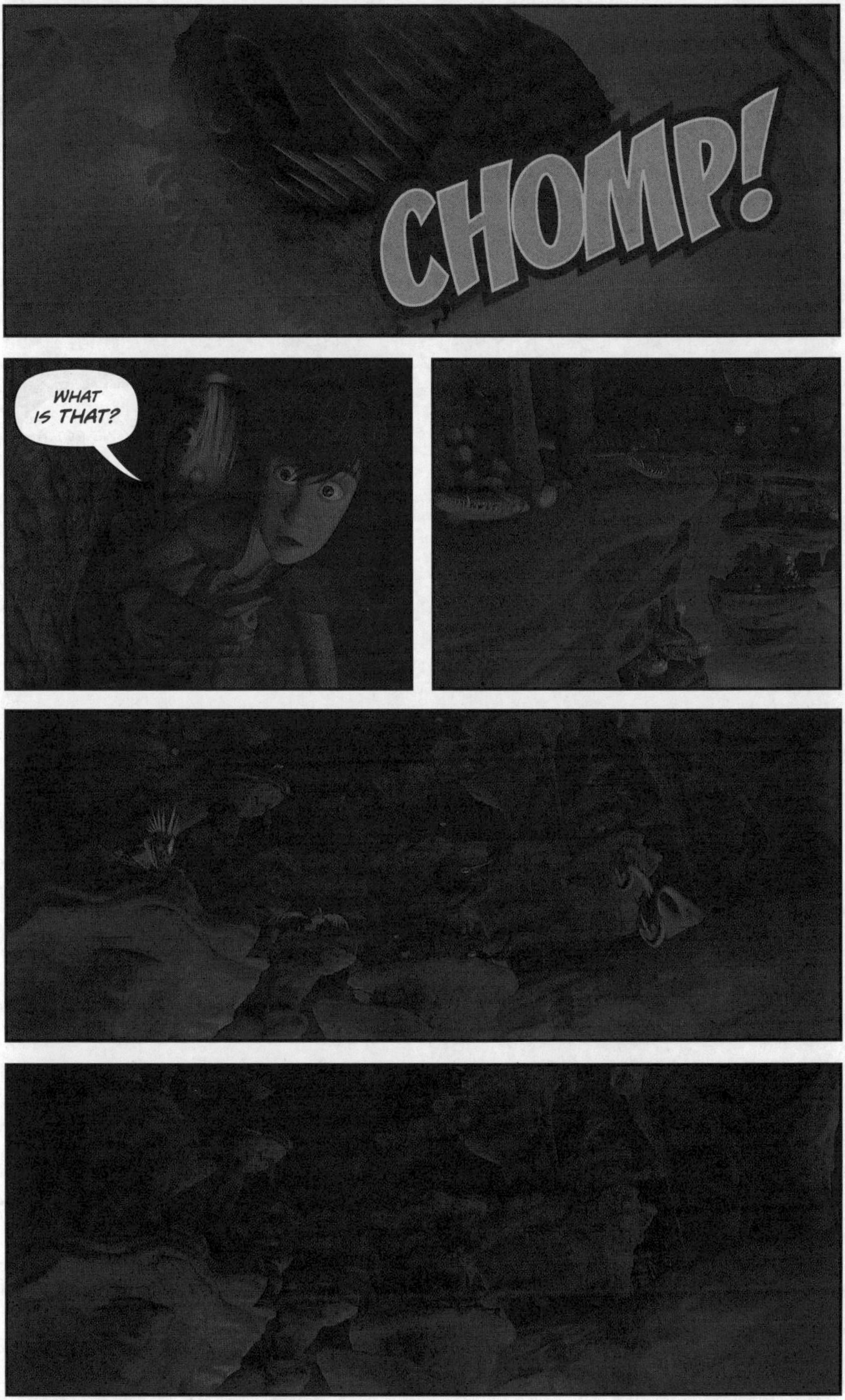
CHOMP!
WHAT IS THAT?

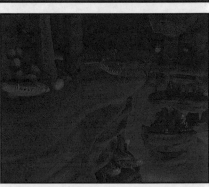

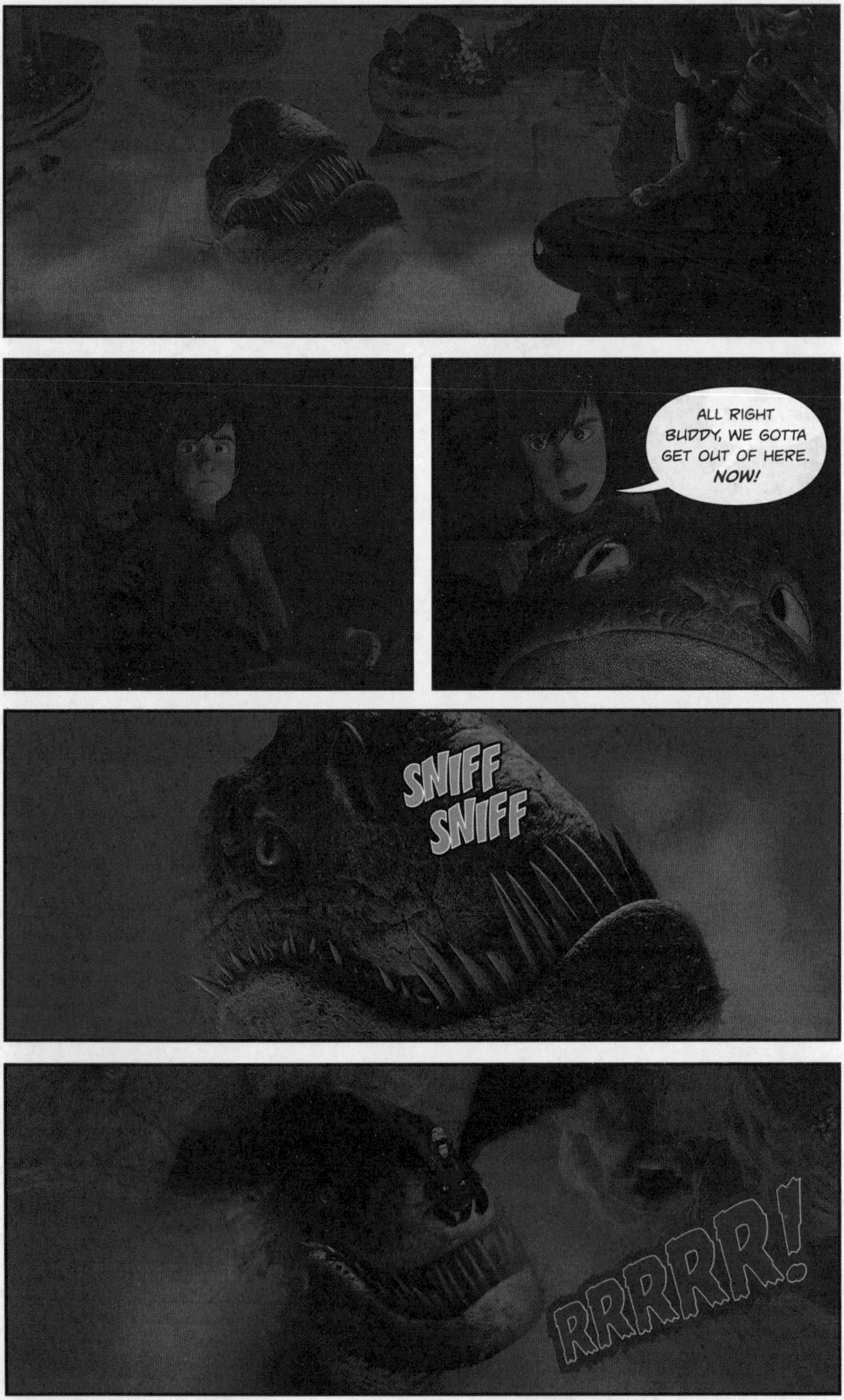
ALL RIGHT BUDDY, WE GOTTA GET OUT OF HERE. NOW!
SNIFF SNIFF
RRRRR!

RRAAAR!
CHOMP!

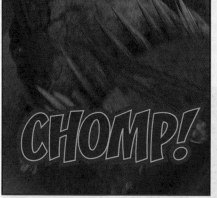

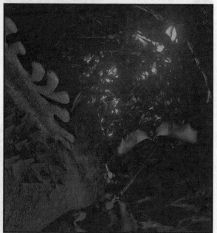

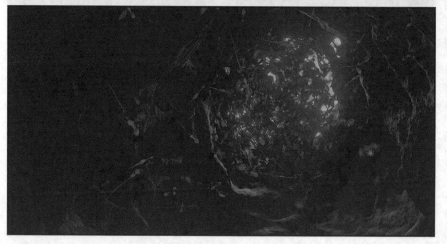

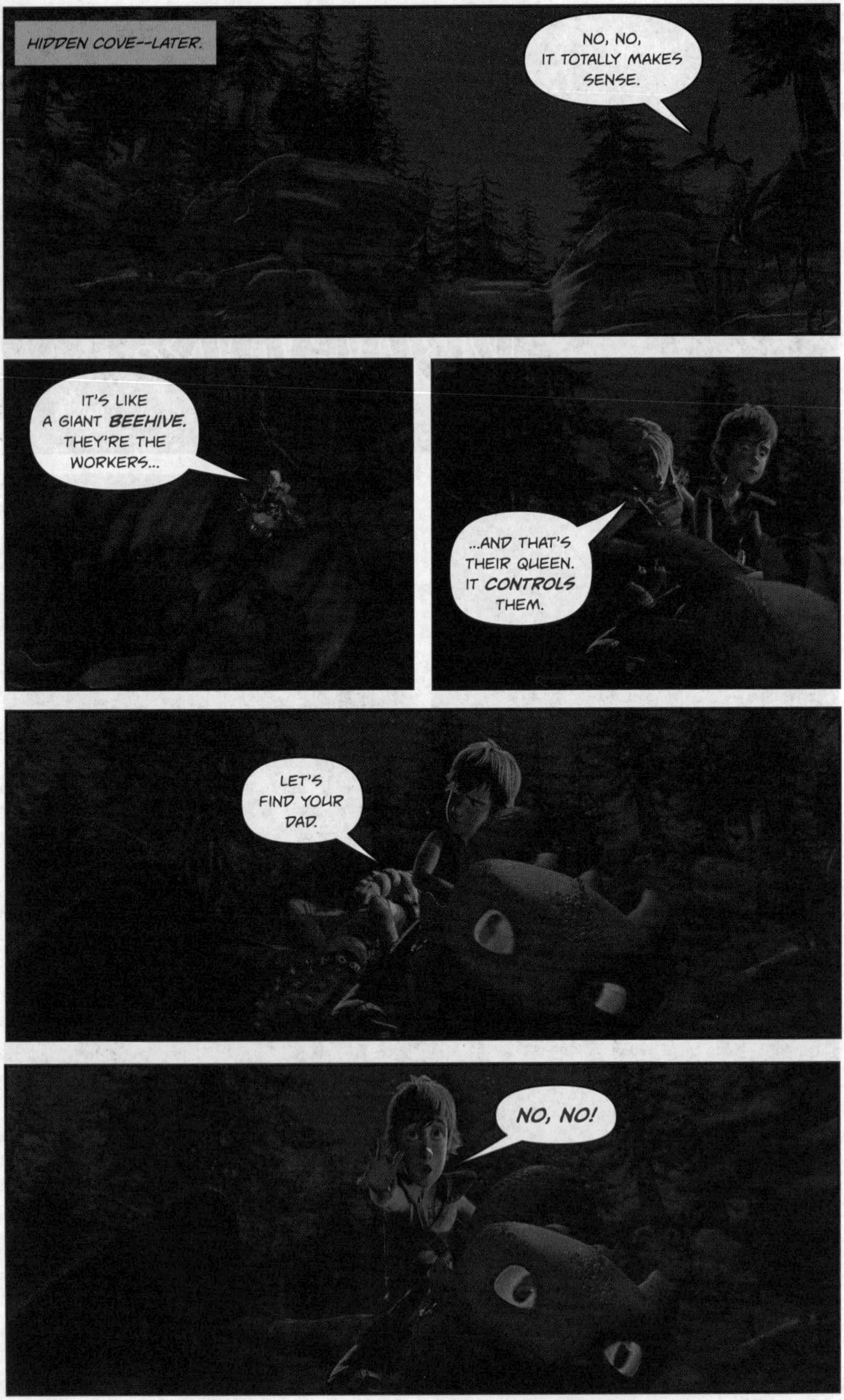
HIDDEN COVE--LATER.
NO, NO, IT TOTALLY MAKES SENSE.
IT'S LIKE A GIANT BEEHIVE. THEY'RE THE WORKERS...
...AND THAT'S THEIR QUEEN. IT CONTROLS THEM.
LET'S FIND YOUR DAD.
NO, NO!

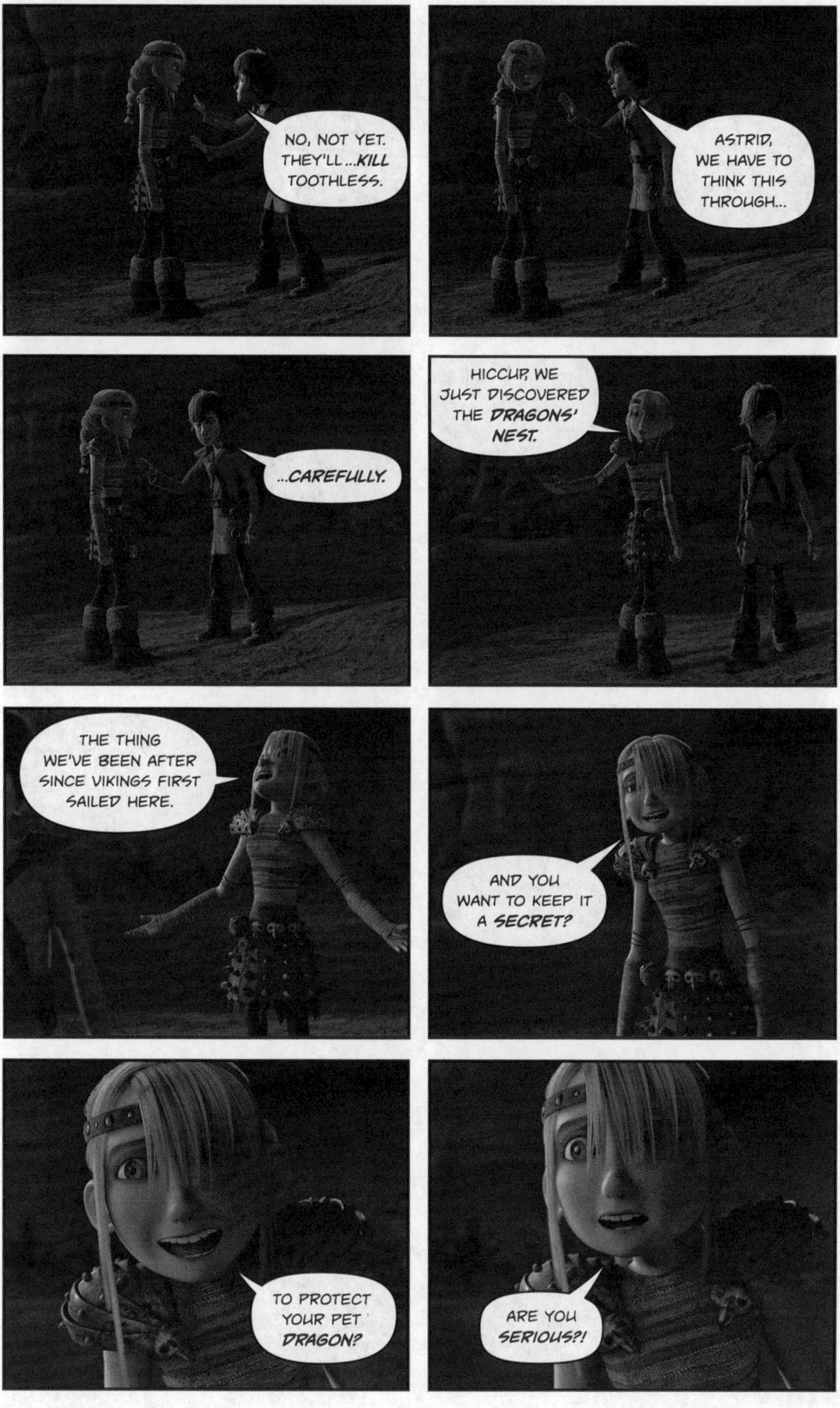
NO, NOT YET. THEY'LL ...KILL TOOTHLESS.
ASTRID, WE HAVE TO THINK THIS THROUGH...
...CAREFULLY.
HICCUP, WE JUST DISCOVERED THE DRAGONS' NEST.
THE THING WE'VE BEEN AFTER SINCE VIKINGS FIRST SAILED HERE.
AND YOU WANT TO KEEP IT A SECRET?
TO PROTECT YOUR PET DRAGON?
ARE YOU SERIOUS?!

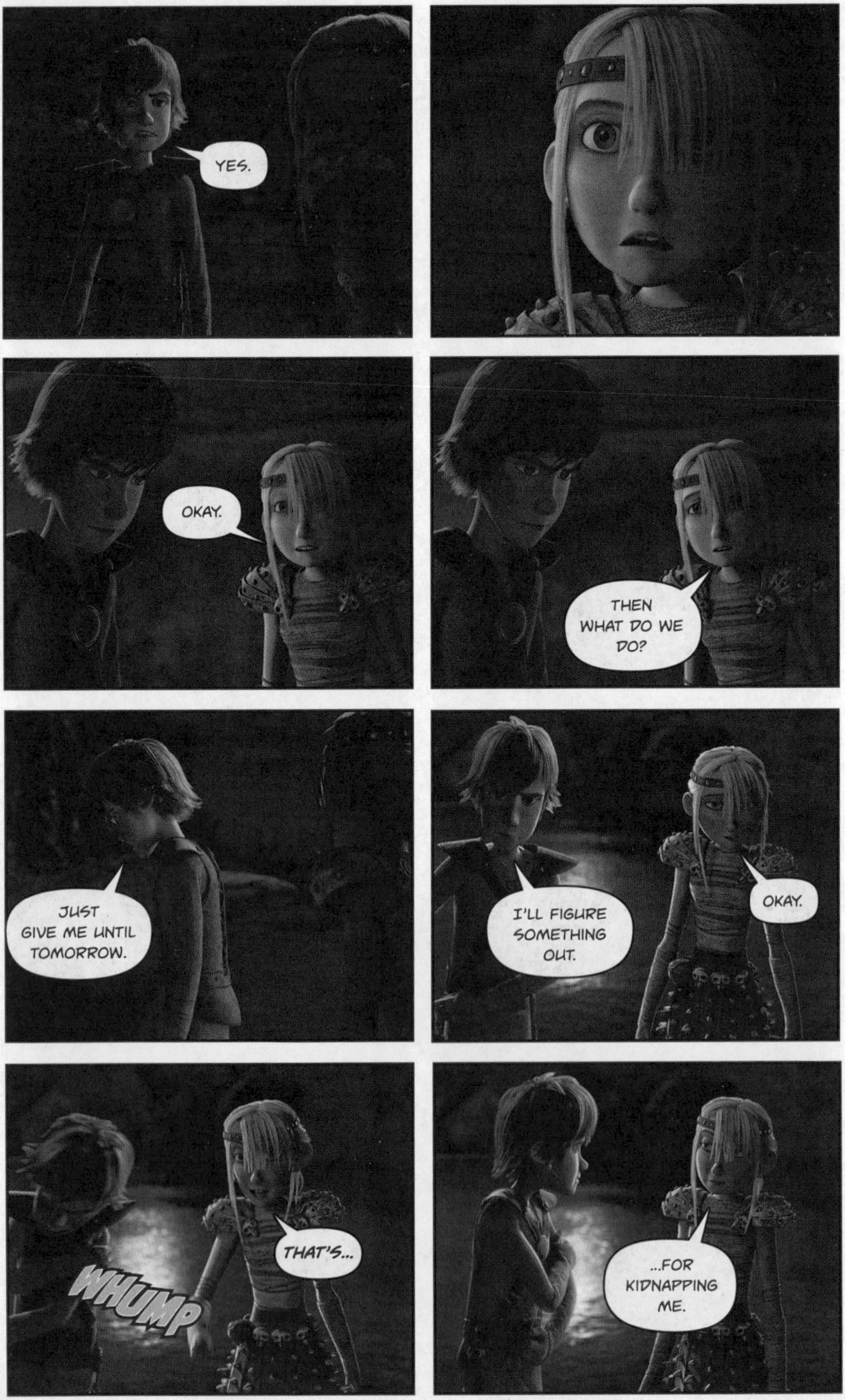

YES.
OKAY.
THEN WHAT DO WE DO?
JUST GIVE ME UNTIL TOMORROW.
I'LL FIGURE SOMETHING OUT.
OKAY.
WHUMP
THAT'S...
...FOR KIDNAPPING ME.

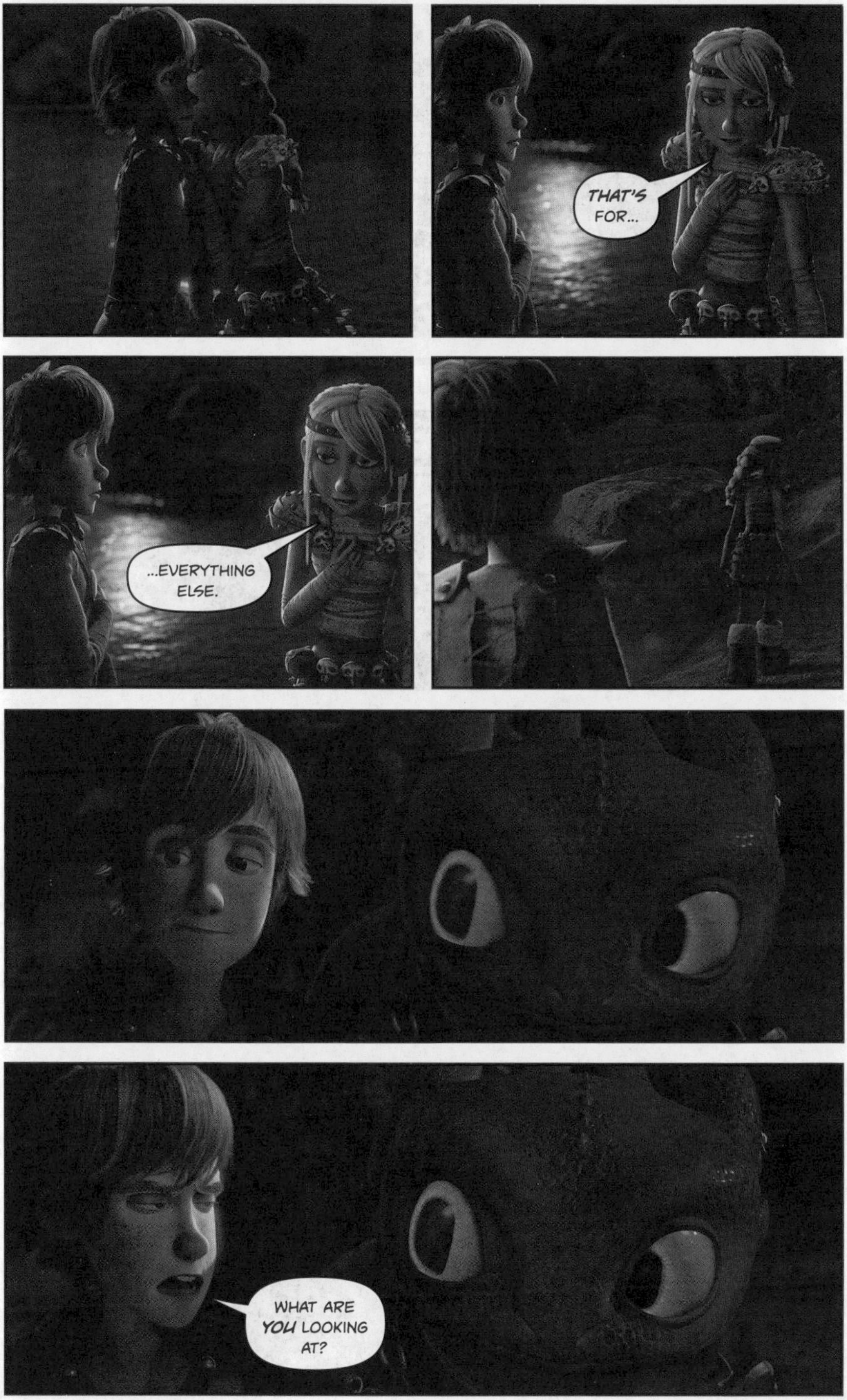
THAT'S FOR...
...EVERYTHING ELSE.
WHAT ARE YOU LOOKING AT?

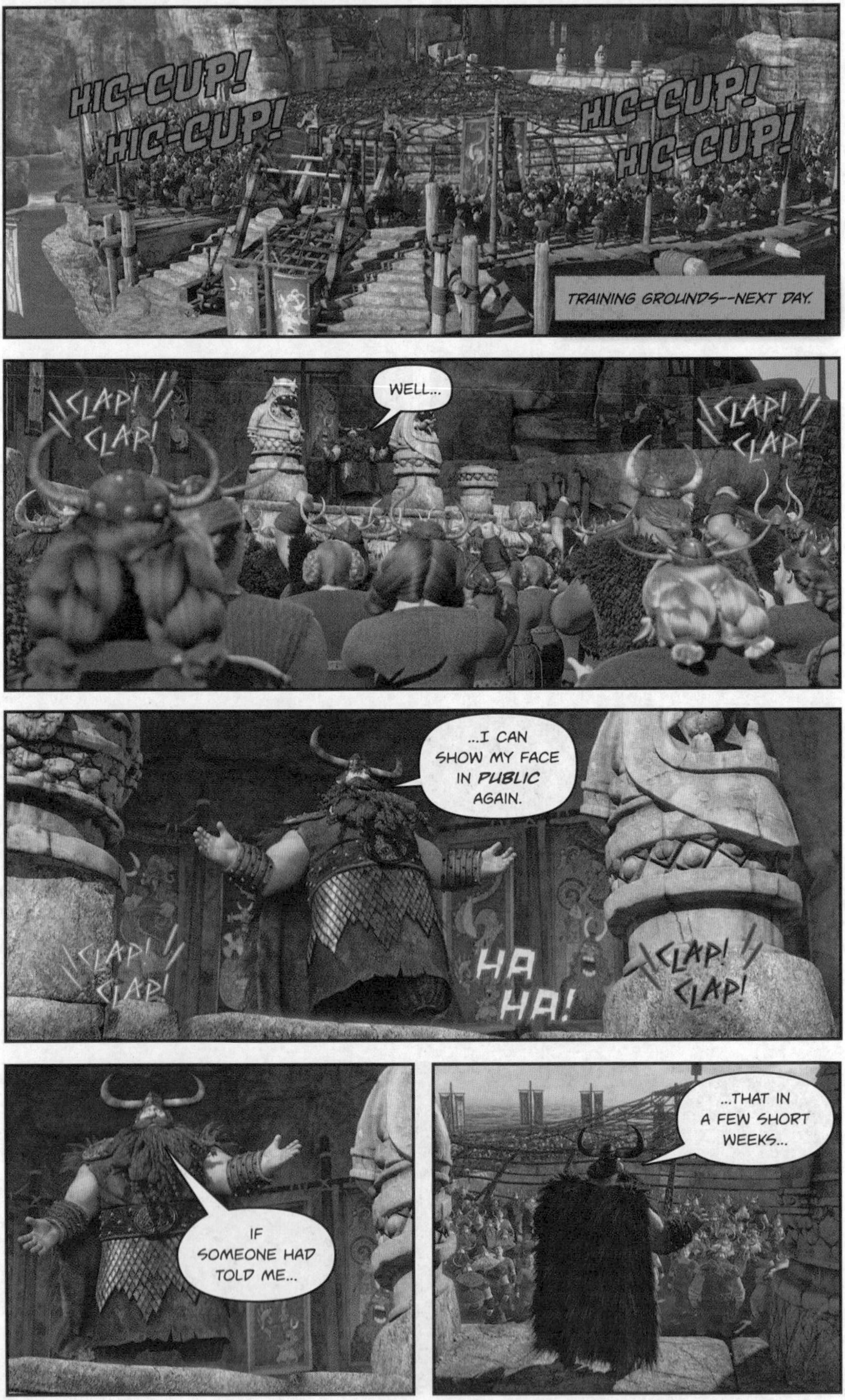
HIC-CUP! HIC-CUP!
HIC-CUP! HIC-CUP!
TRAINING GROUNDS--NEXT DAY.
CLAP! CLAP!
WELL...
CLAP! CLAP!
...I CAN SHOW MY FACE IN PUBLIC AGAIN.
CLAP! CLAP!
HA HA!
CLAP! CLAP!
IF SOMEONE HAD TOLD ME...
...THAT IN A FEW SHORT WEEKS...

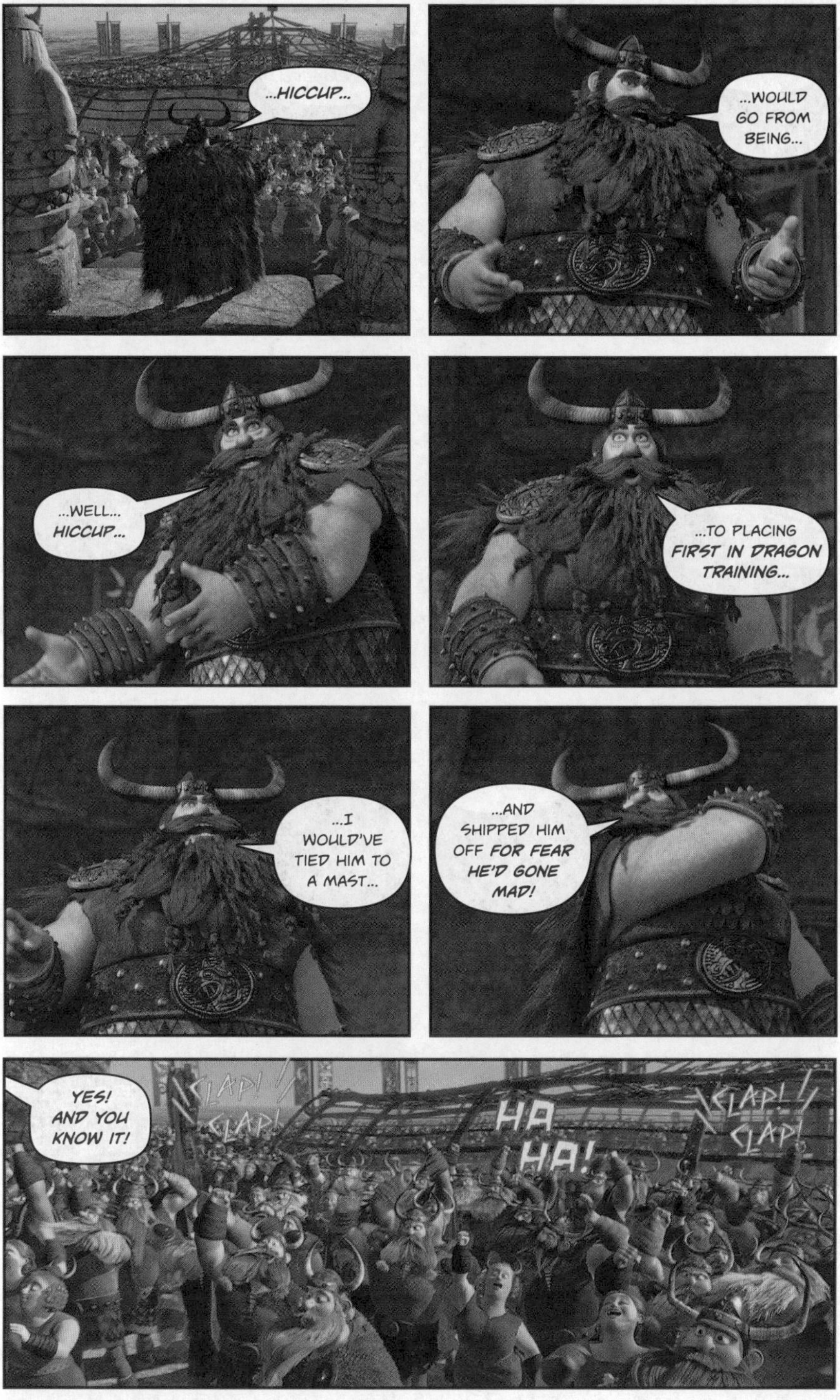
...HICCUP...
...WOULD GO FROM BEING...
...WELL... HICCUP...
...TO PLACING FIRST IN DRAGON TRAINING...
...I WOULD'VE TIED HIM TO A MAST...
...AND SHIPPED HIM OFF FOR FEAR HE'D GONE MAD!
YES! AND YOU KNOW IT!
CLAP! CLAP!
HA HA!
CLAP! CLAP!

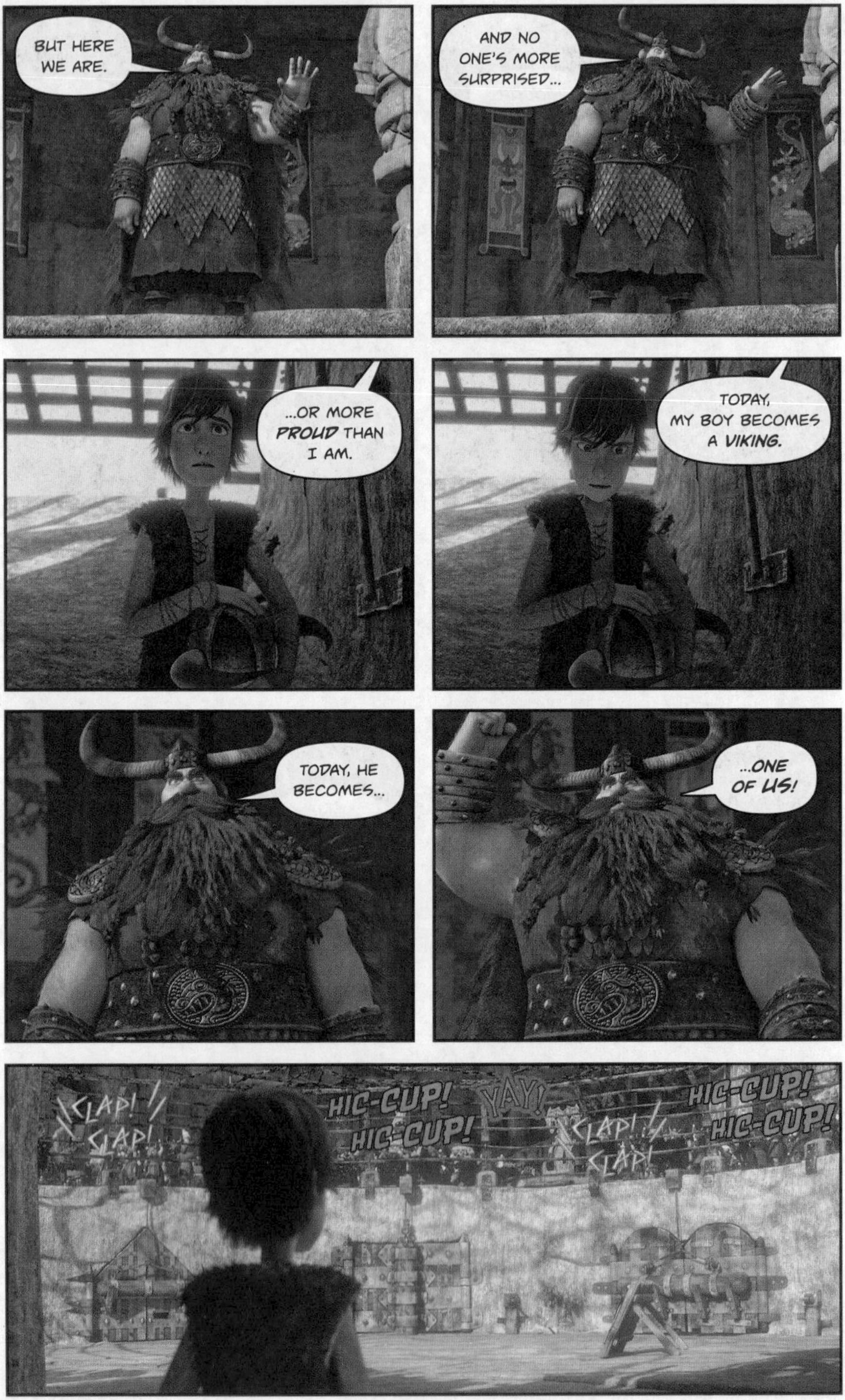
BUT HERE WE ARE.
AND NO ONE'S MORE SURPRISED...
...OR MORE PROUD THAN I AM.
TODAY, MY BOY BECOMES A VIKING.
TODAY, HE BECOMES...
...ONE OF US!
CLAP! CLAP!
HIC-CUP! HIC-CUP!
YAY!
CLAP! CLAP!
HIC-CUP! HIC-CUP!

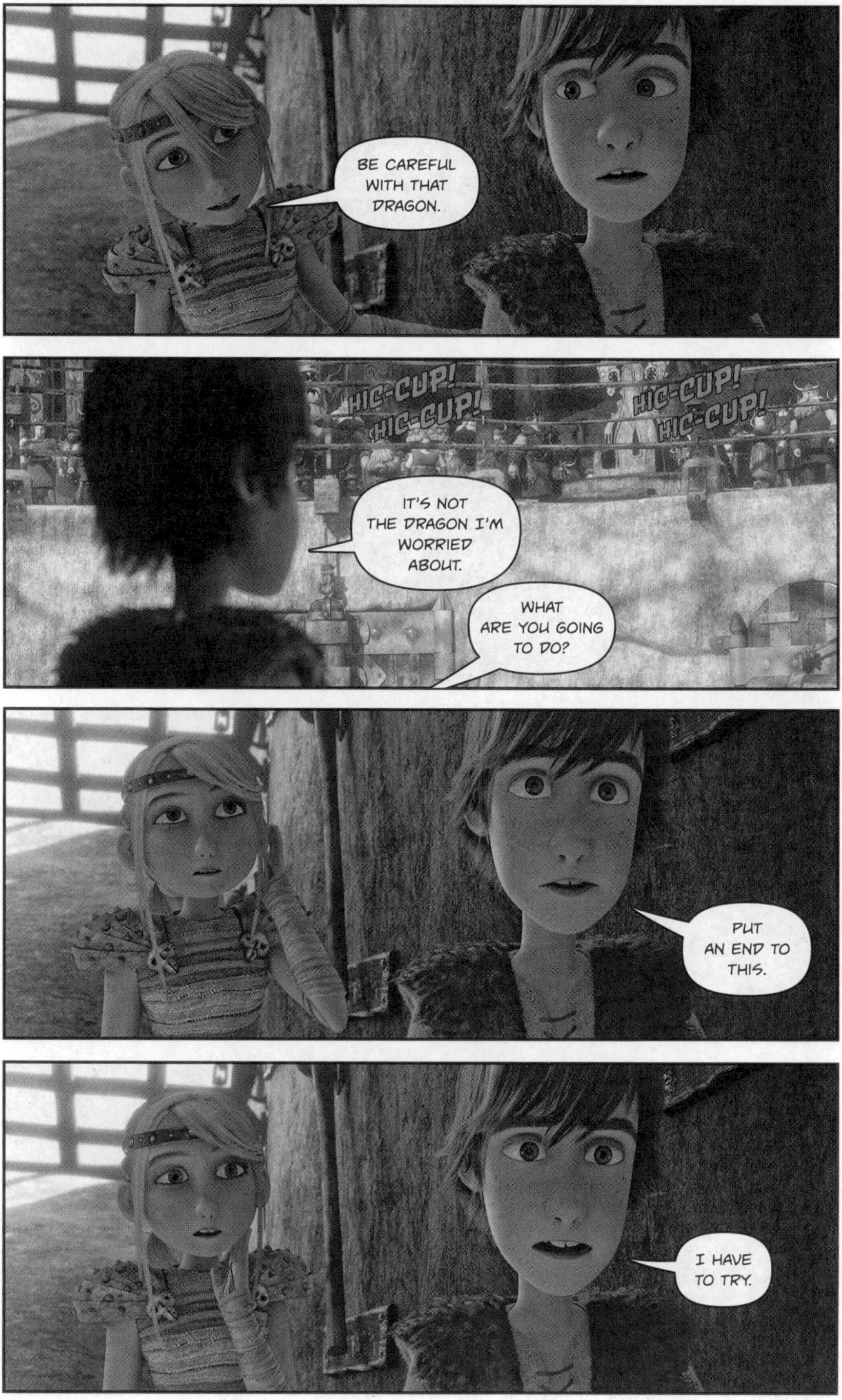
BE CAREFUL WITH THAT DRAGON.
HIC-CUP! HIC-CUP!
HIC-CUP! HIC-CUP!
IT'S NOT THE DRAGON I'M WORRIED ABOUT.
WHAT ARE YOU GOING TO DO?
PUT AN END TO THIS.
I HAVE TO TRY.

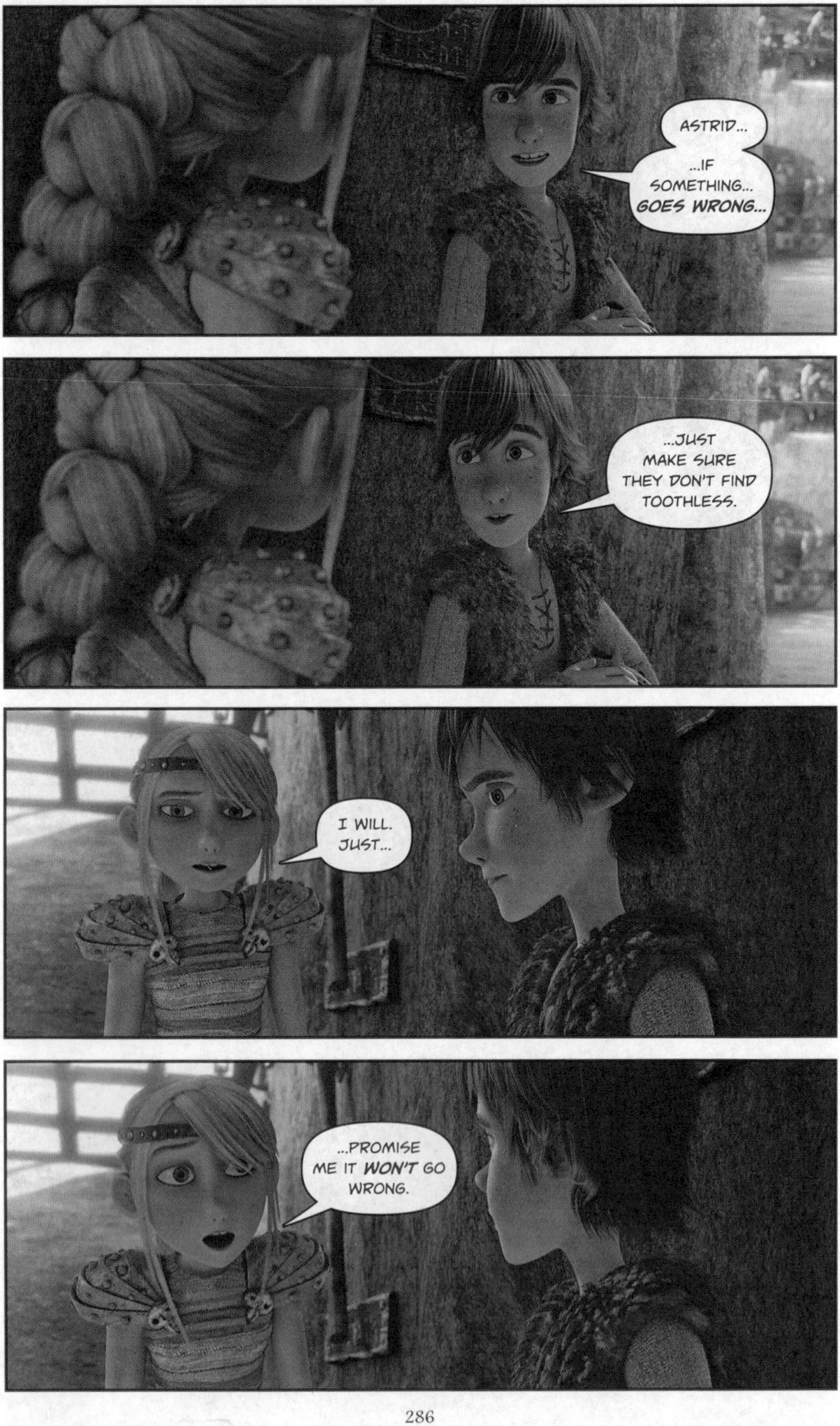
ASTRID...
...IF SOMETHING... **GOES WRONG...**
...JUST MAKE SURE THEY DON'T FIND TOOTHLESS.
I WILL. JUST...
...PROMISE ME IT ***WON'T*** GO WRONG.

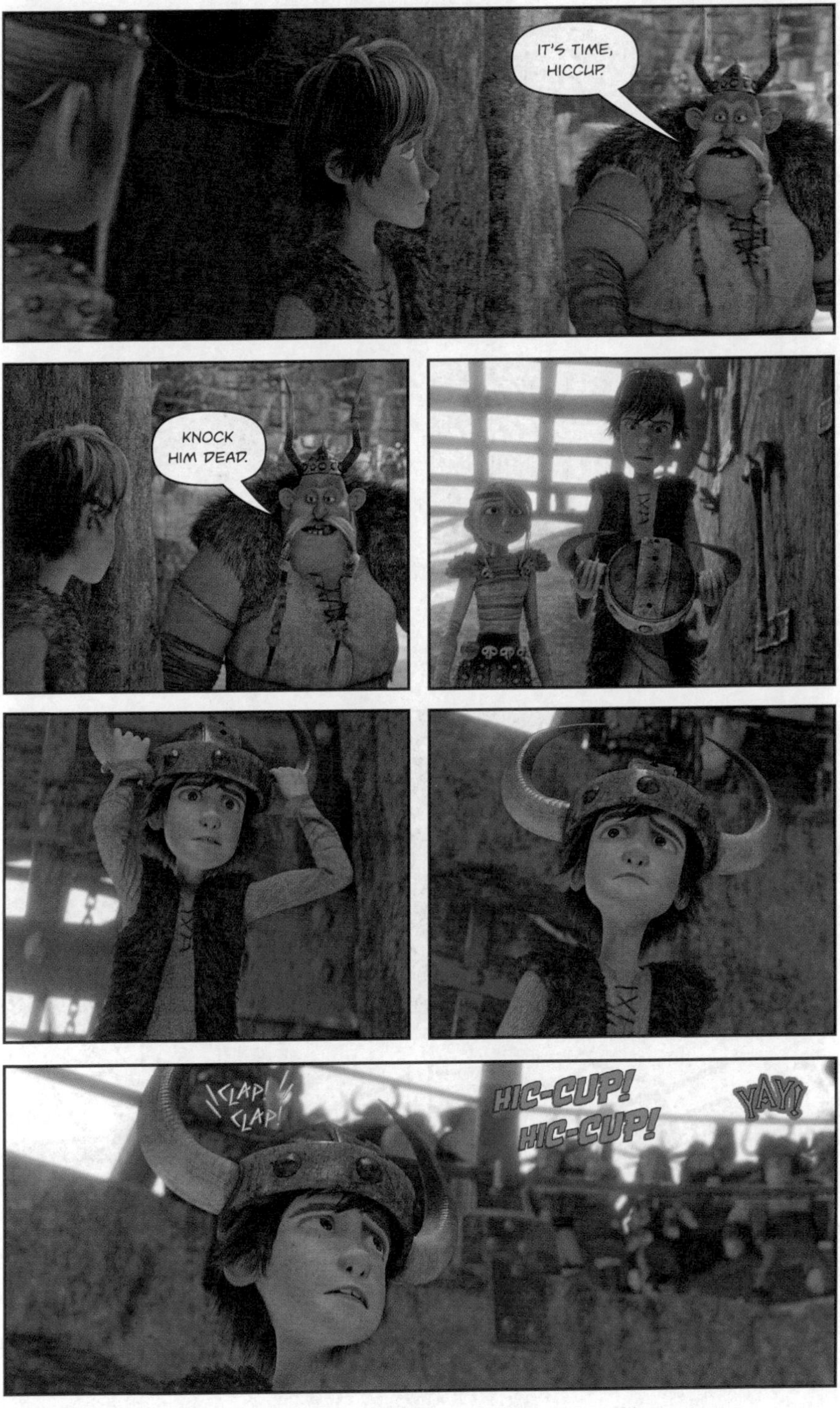
IT'S TIME, HICCUP.
KNOCK HIM DEAD.
CLAP! CLAP!
HIC-CUP! HIC-CUP!
YAY!

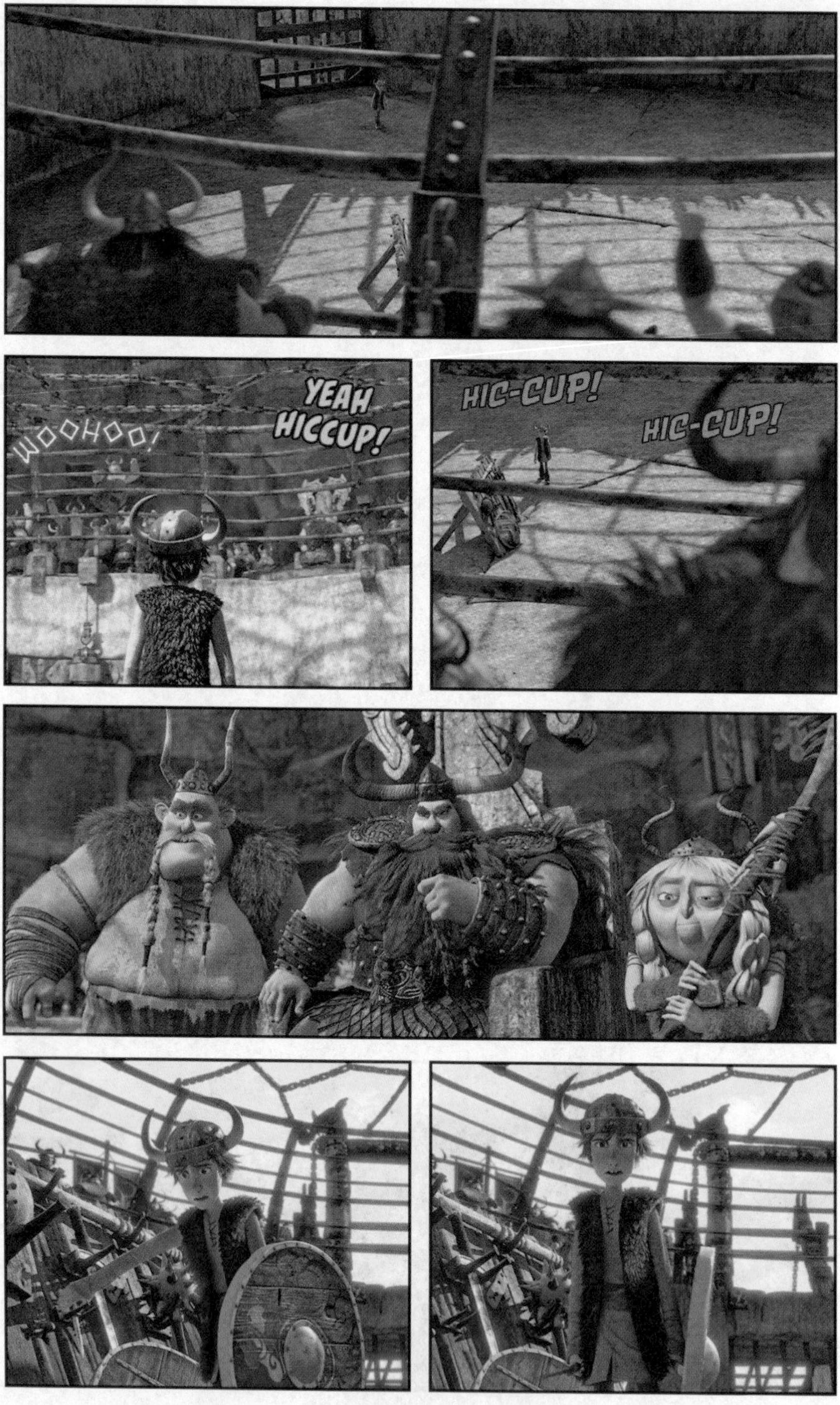
WOOHOO!
YEAH HICCUP!
HIC-CUP!
HIC-CUP!

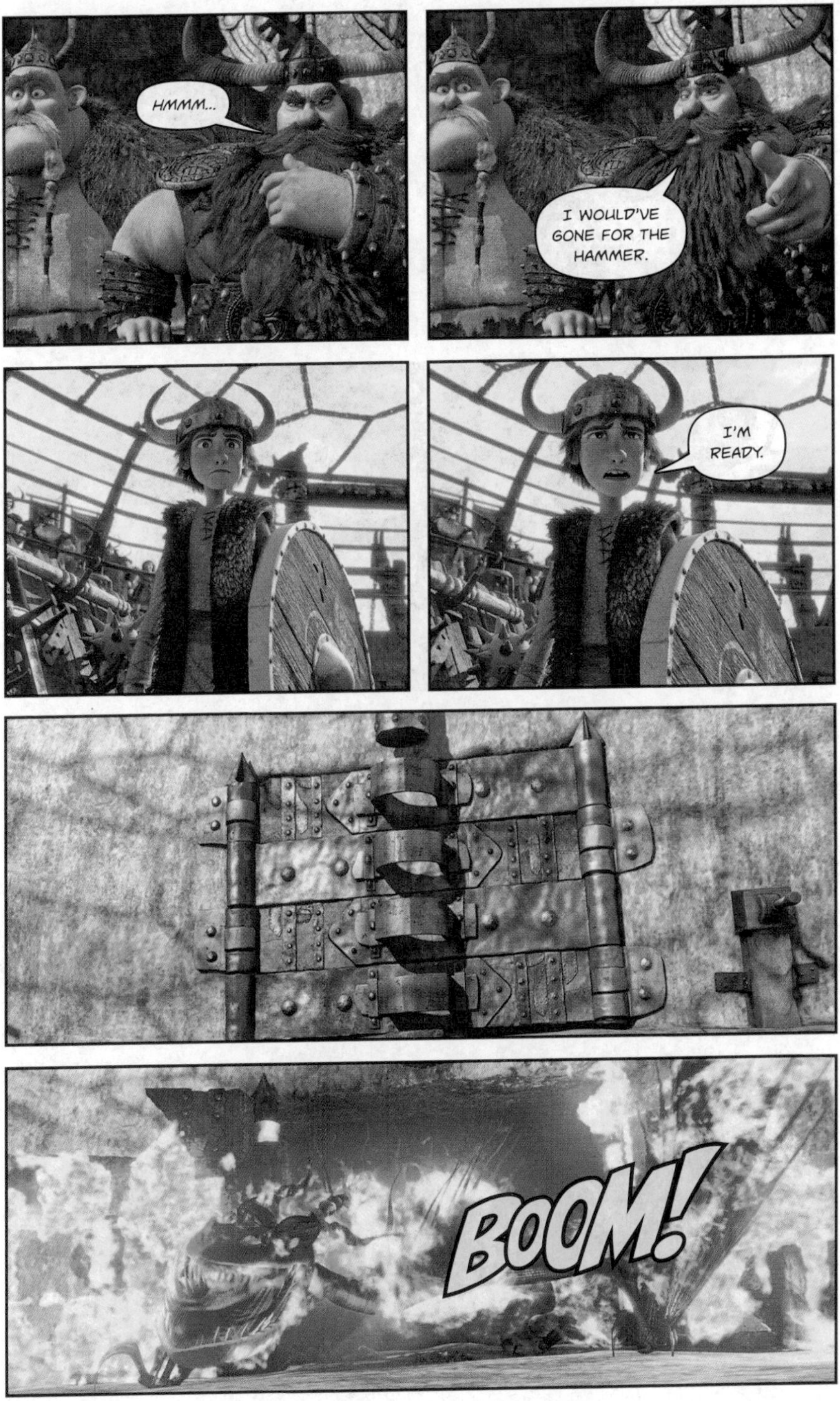
HMMM...
I WOULD'VE GONE FOR THE HAMMER.
I'M READY.
BOOM!

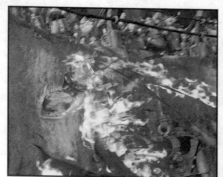

GO ON, HICCUP!

GIVE IT TO HIM!

290

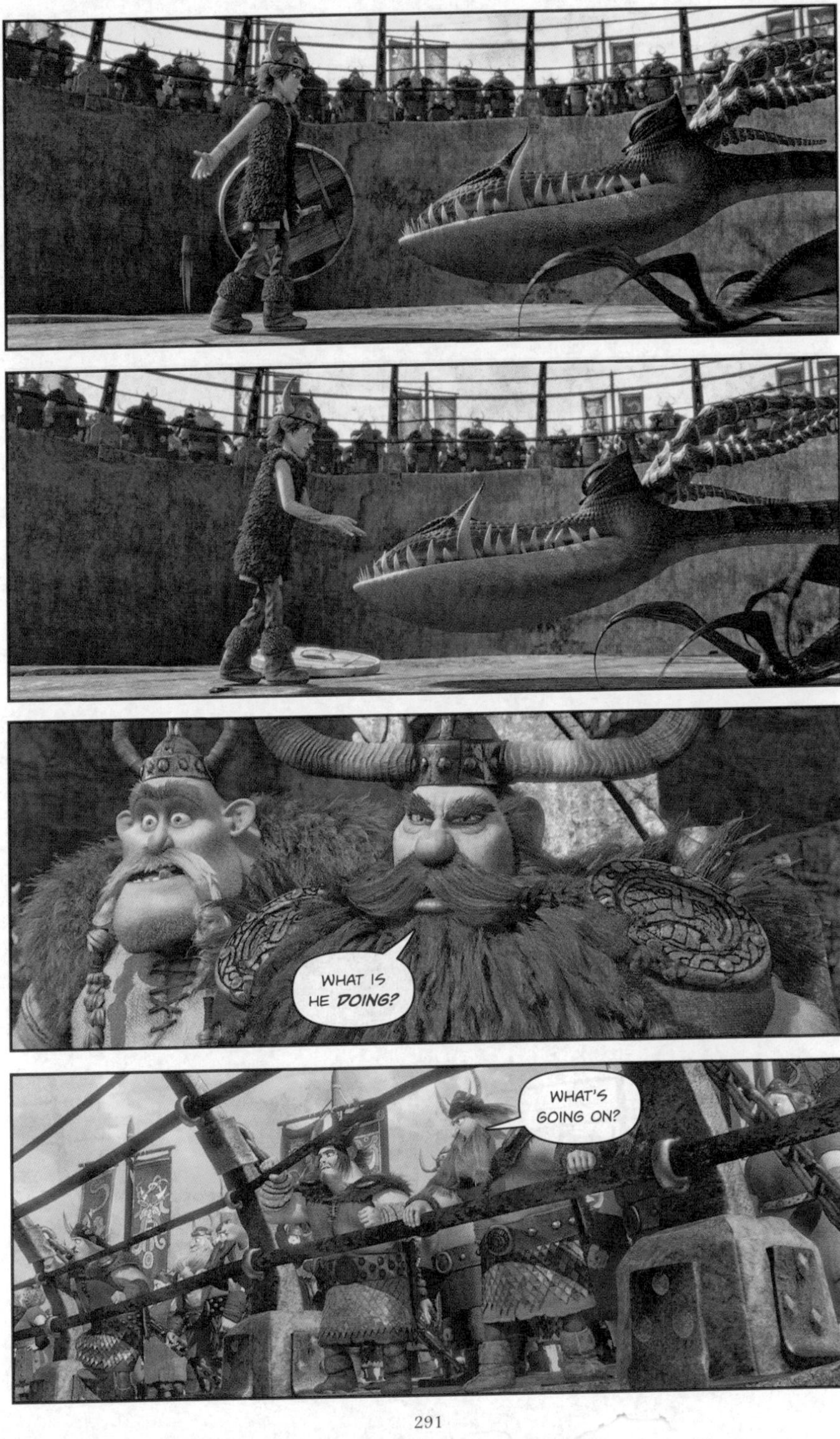
WHAT IS
HE DOING?
WHAT'S
GOING ON?

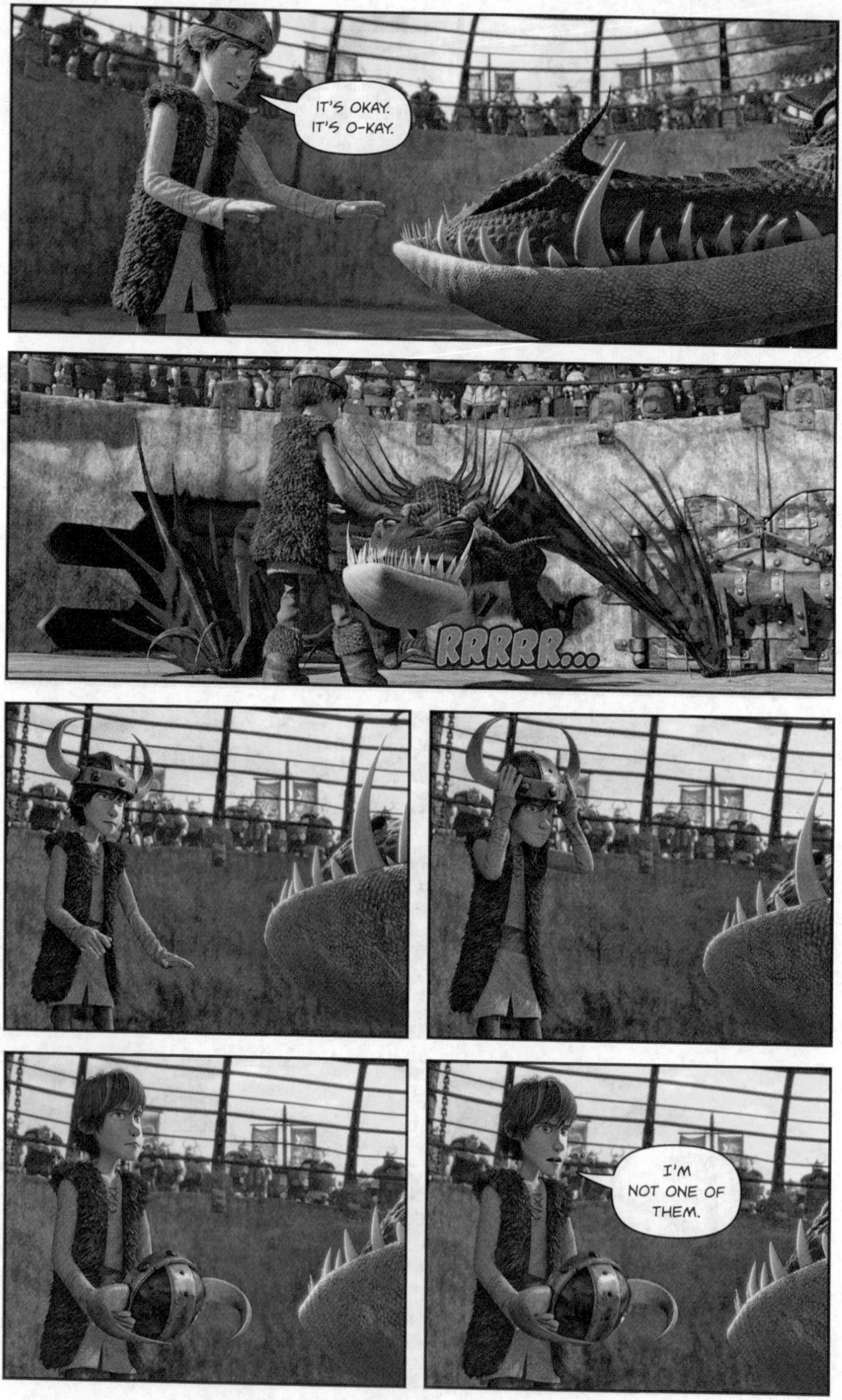
IT'S OKAY.
IT'S O-KAY.
RRRRR...
I'M
NOT ONE OF
THEM.

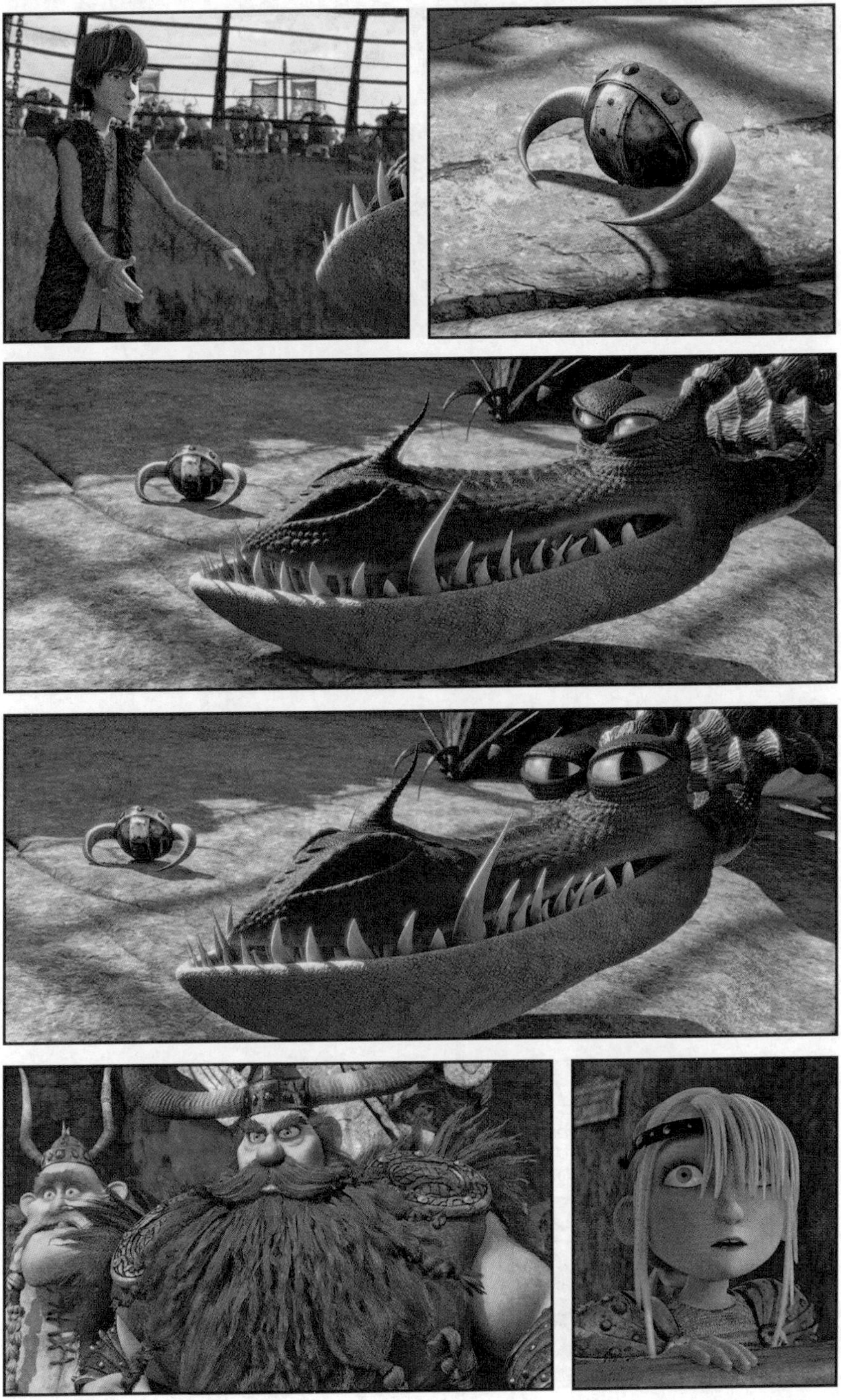

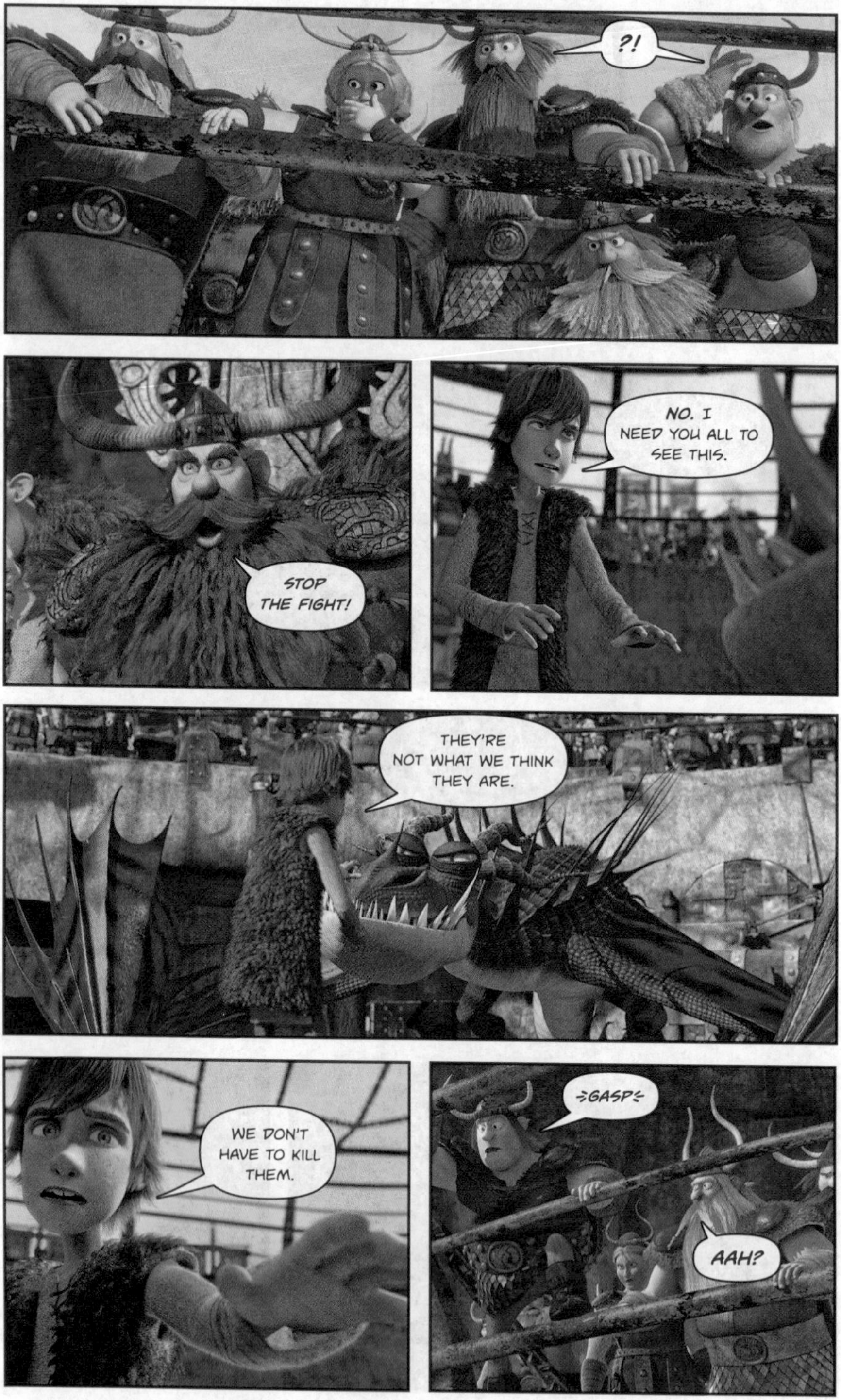
?!
STOP THE FIGHT!
NO. I NEED YOU ALL TO SEE THIS.
THEY'RE NOT WHAT WE THINK THEY ARE.
WE DON'T HAVE TO KILL THEM.
GASP
AAH?

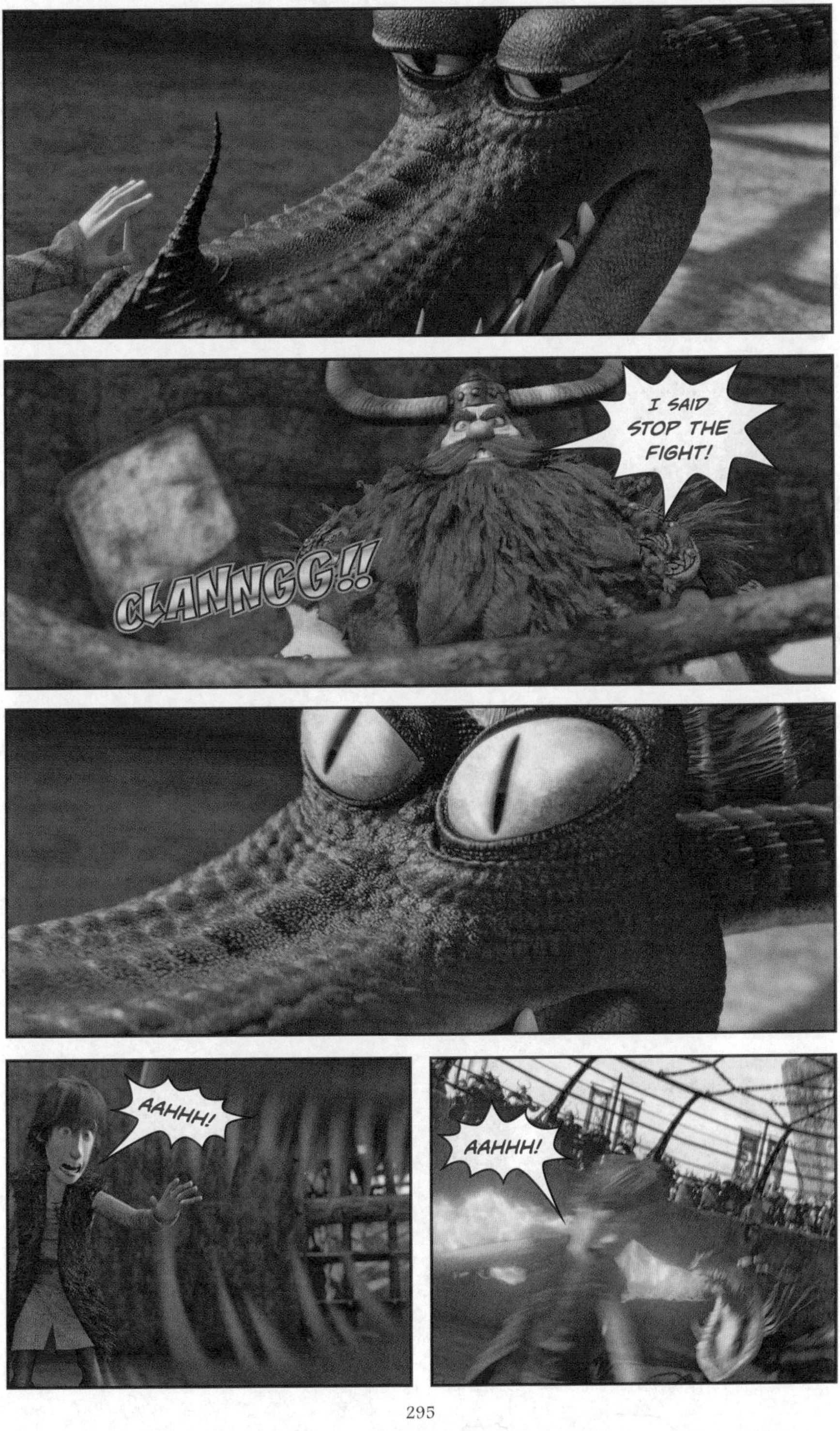
I SAID STOP THE FIGHT!
CLANNGG!!
AAHHH!
AAHHH!

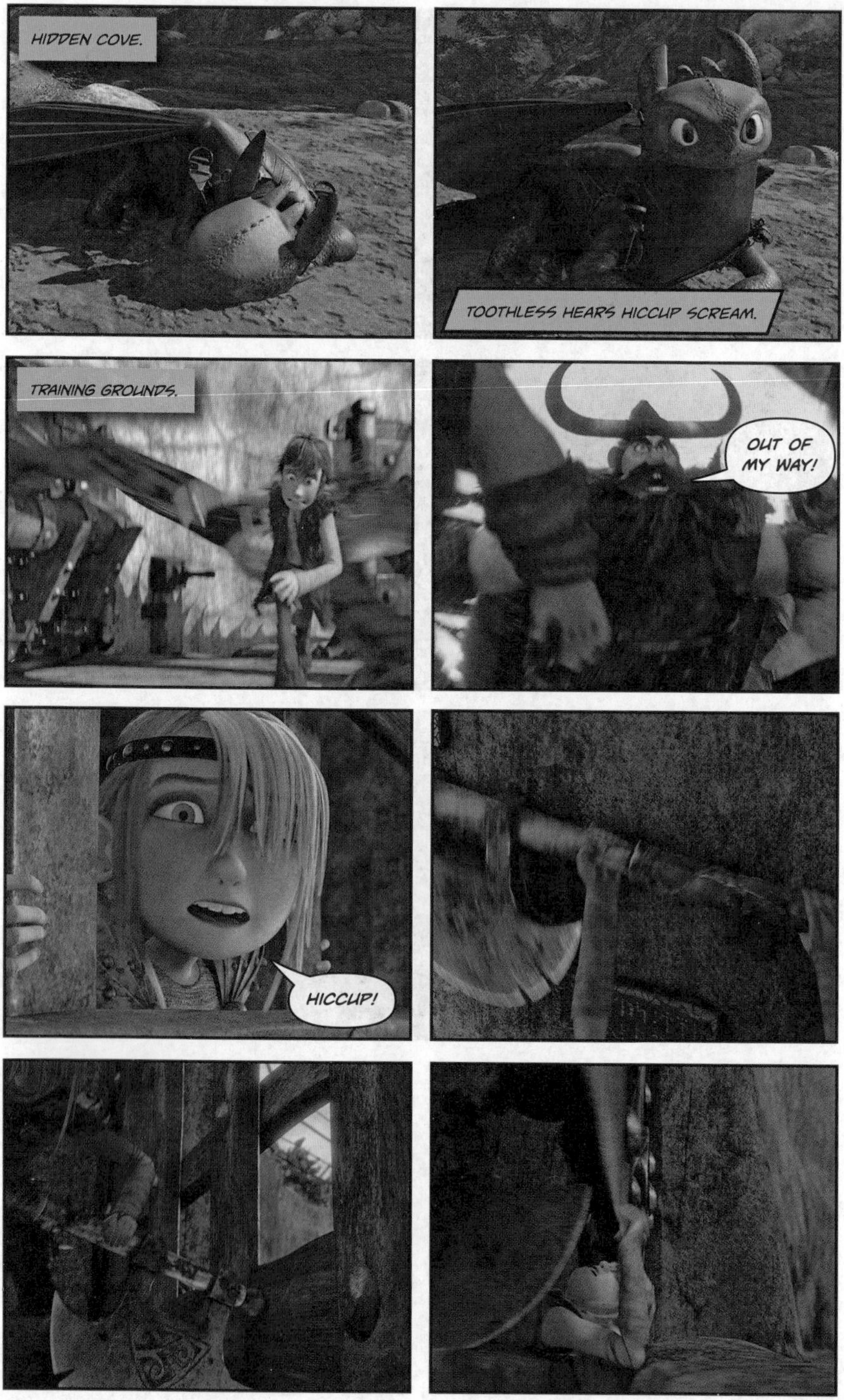
HIDDEN COVE.
TOOTHLESS HEARS HICCUP SCREAM.
TRAINING GROUNDS.
OUT OF MY WAY!
HICCUP!

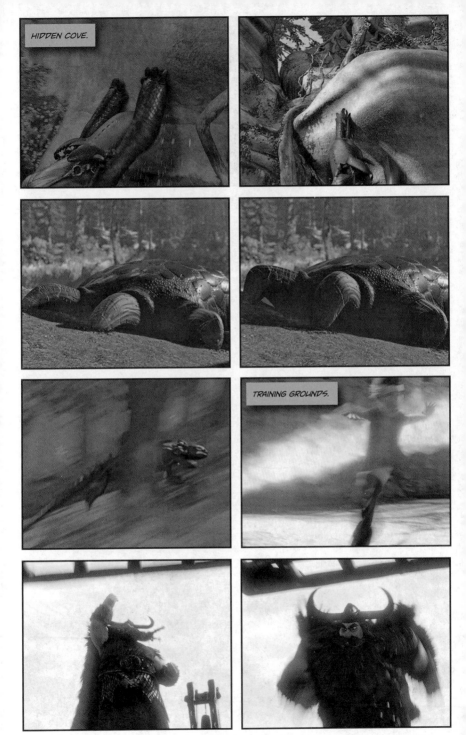

HIDDEN COVE.

TRAINING GROUNDS.

297

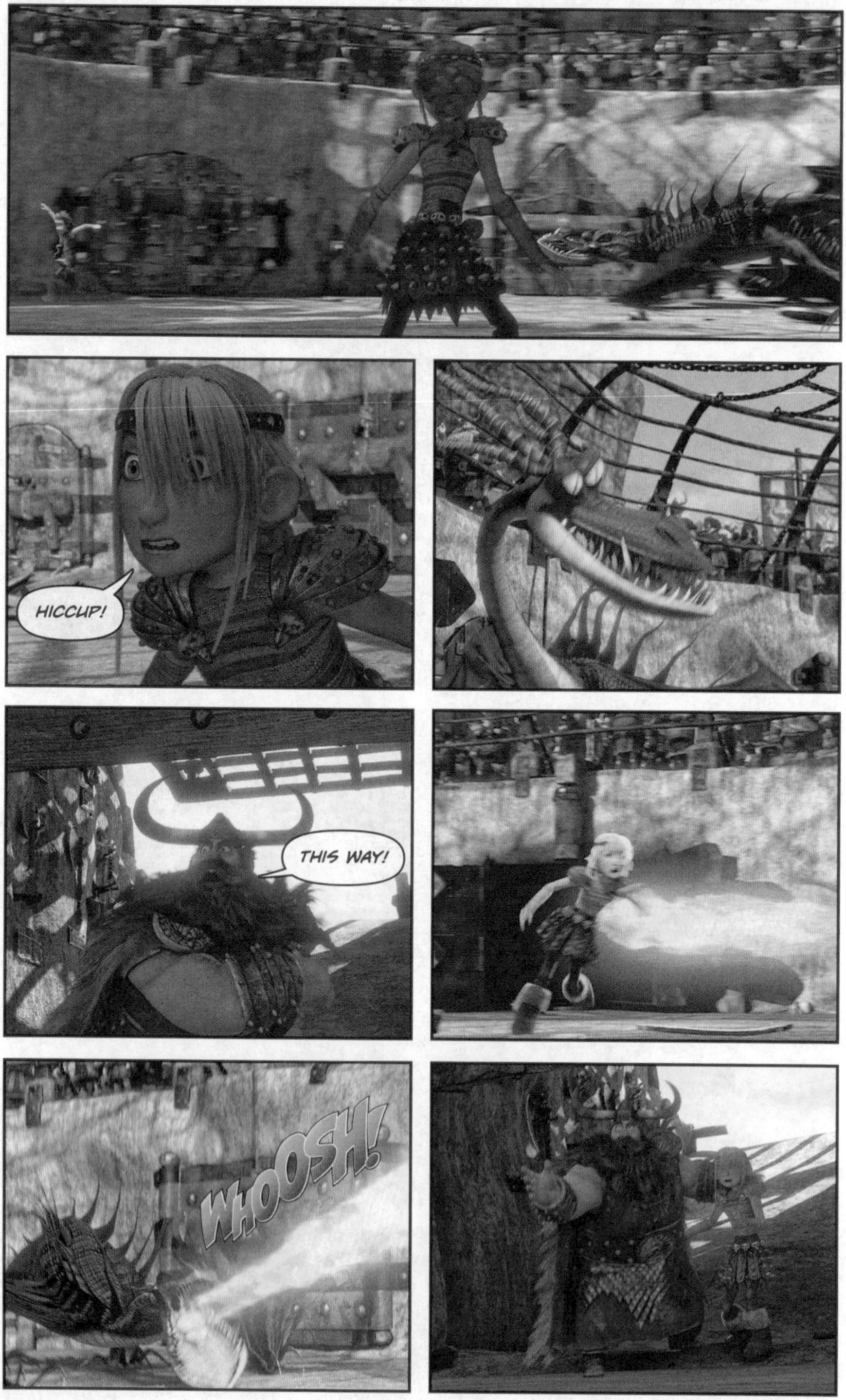
HICCUP!
THIS WAY!
WHOOSH!

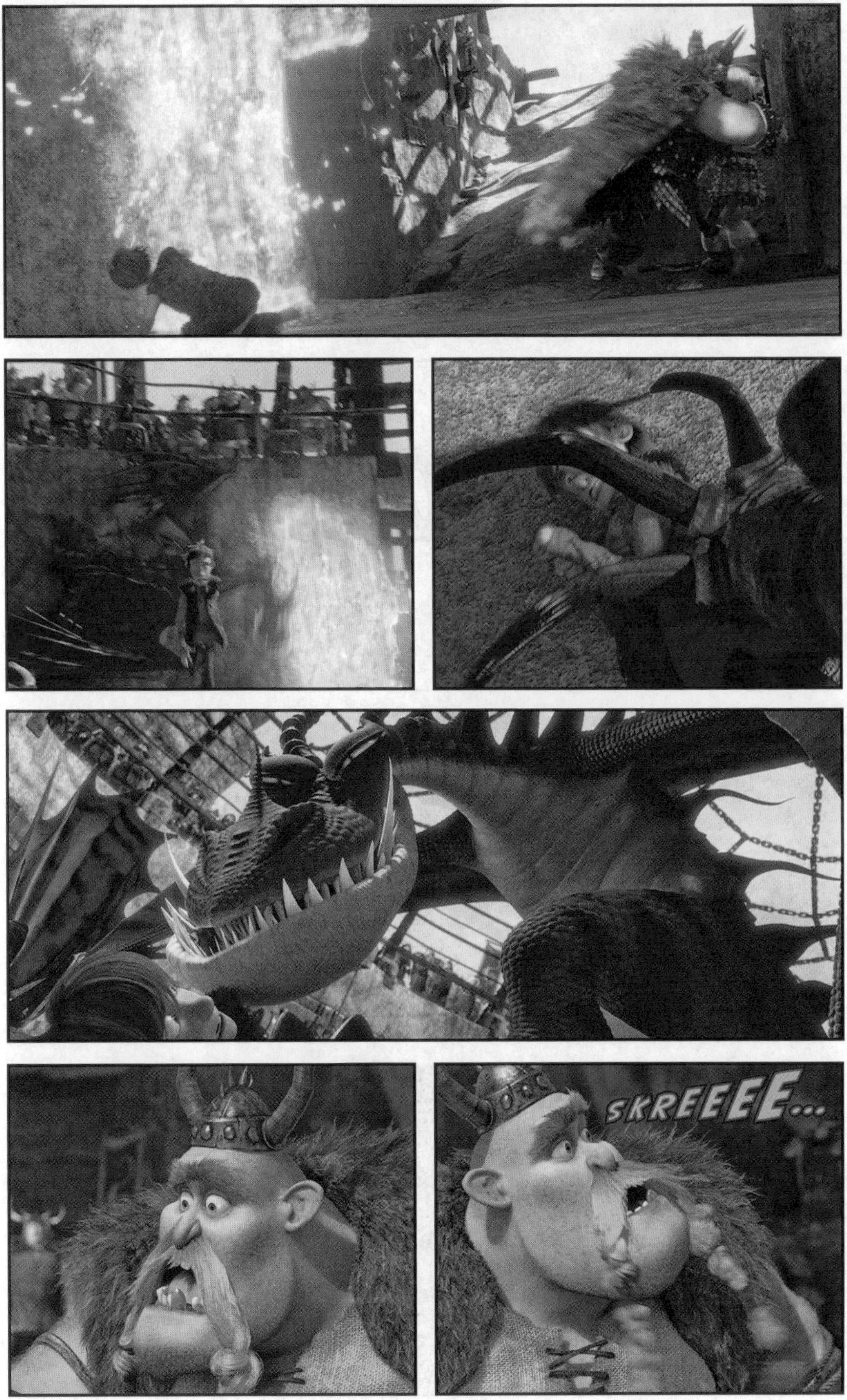
SKREEEE...

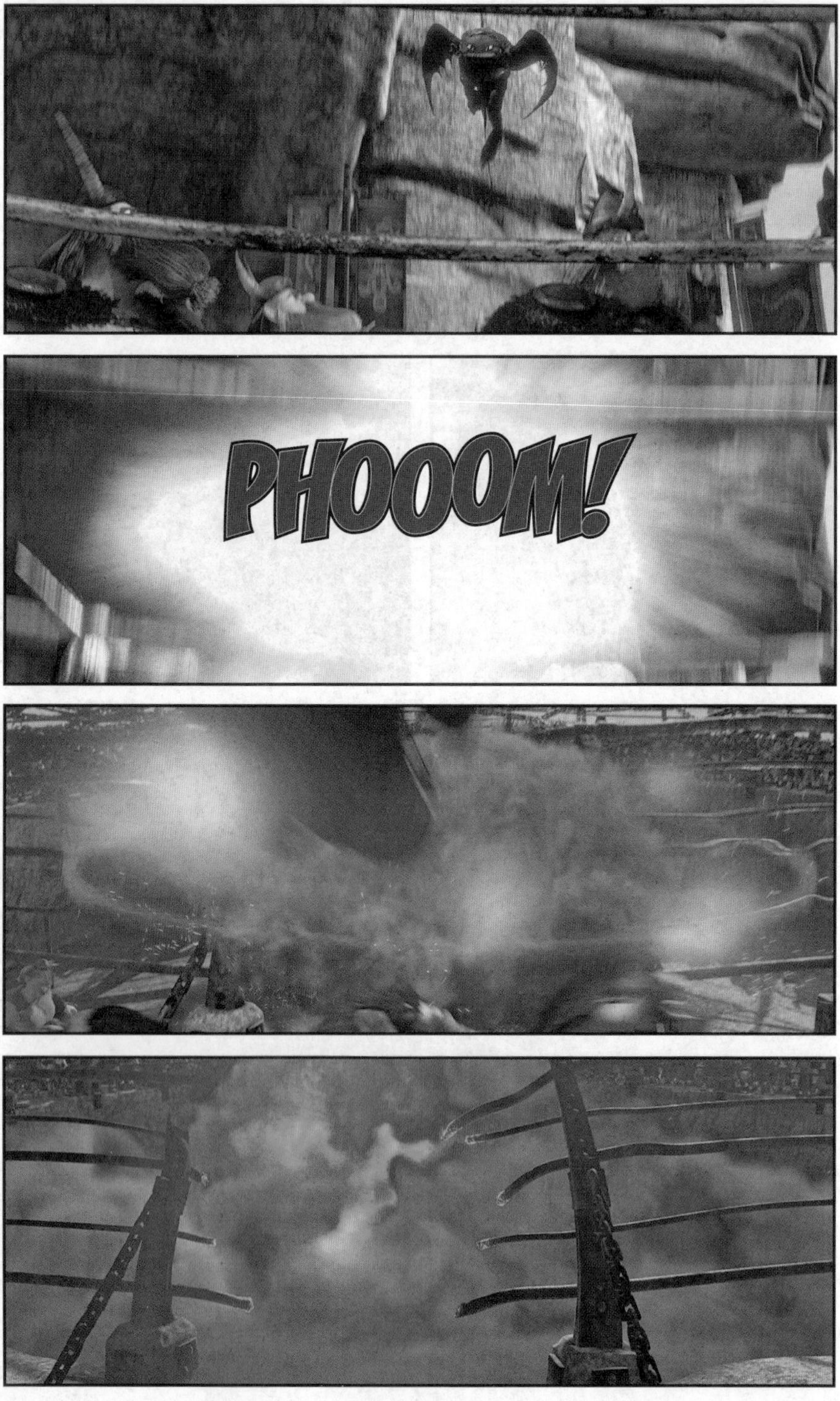
PHOOOM!

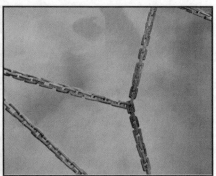

NIGHT FURY!

RRAAAR!

ROARR!

GRRRRRR

301

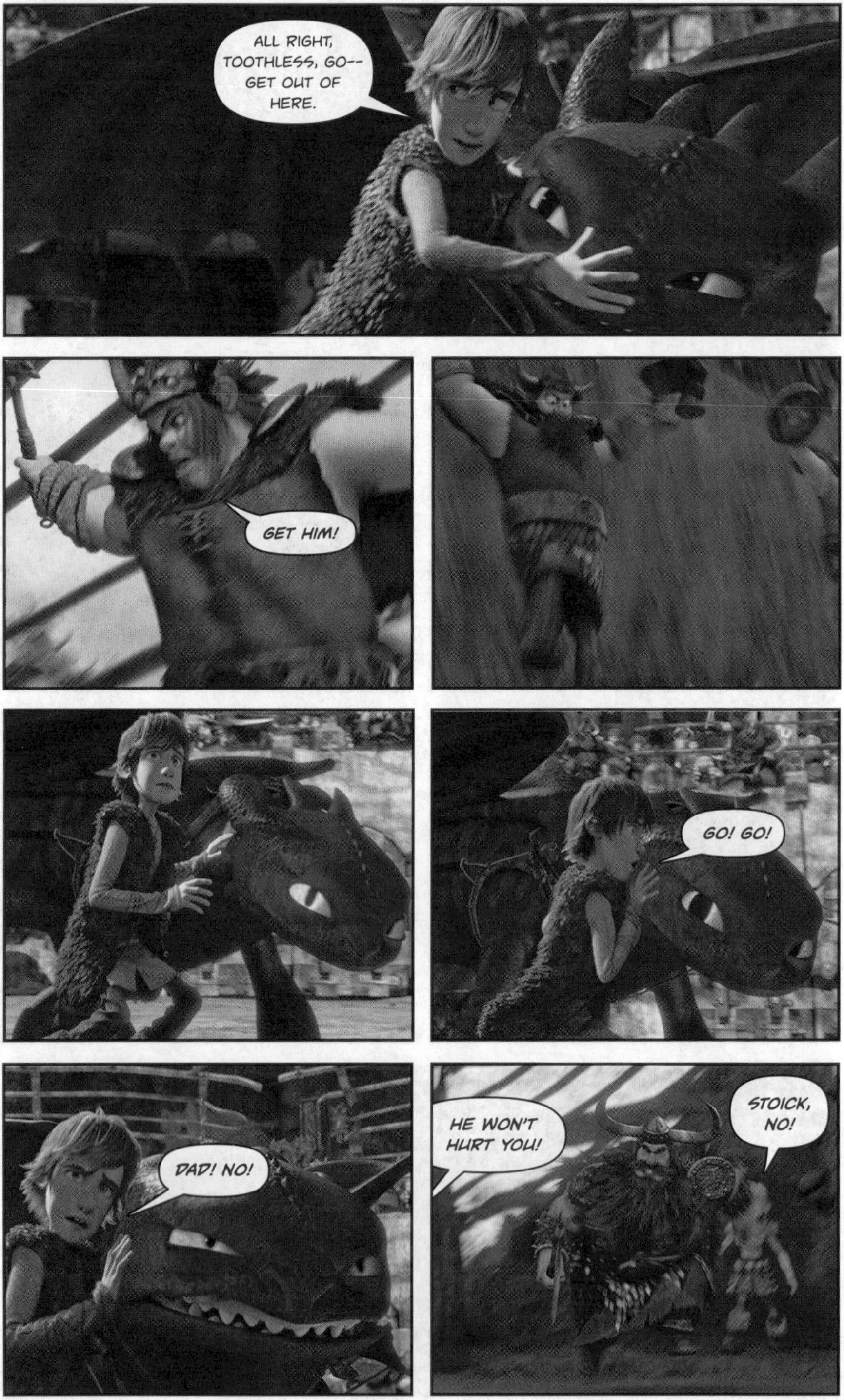
ALL RIGHT, TOOTHLESS, GO-- GET OUT OF HERE.
GET HIM!
GO! GO!
DAD! NO!
HE WON'T HURT YOU!
STOICK, NO!

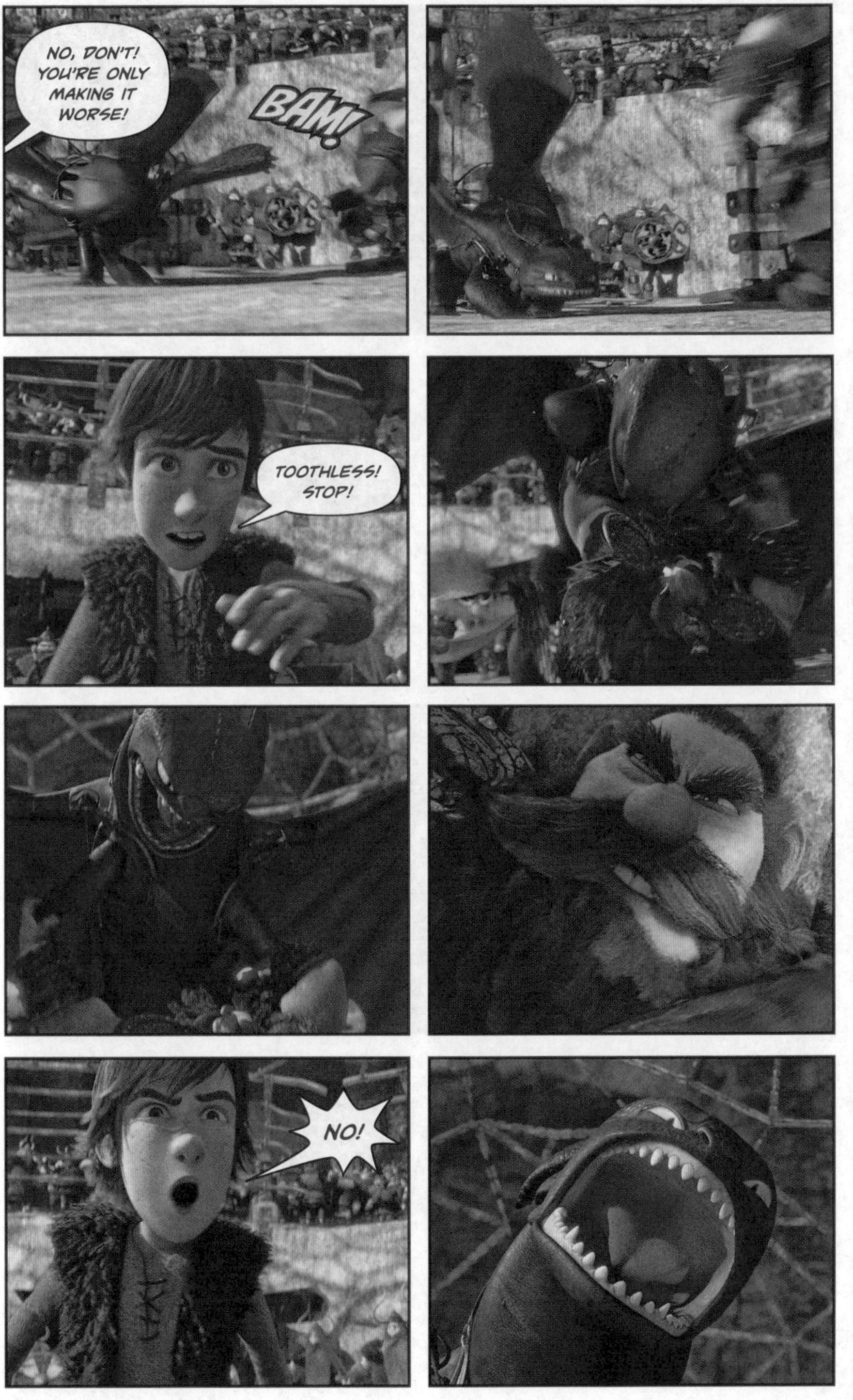
NO, DON'T! YOU'RE ONLY MAKING IT WORSE!
BAM!
TOOTHLESS! STOP!
NO!

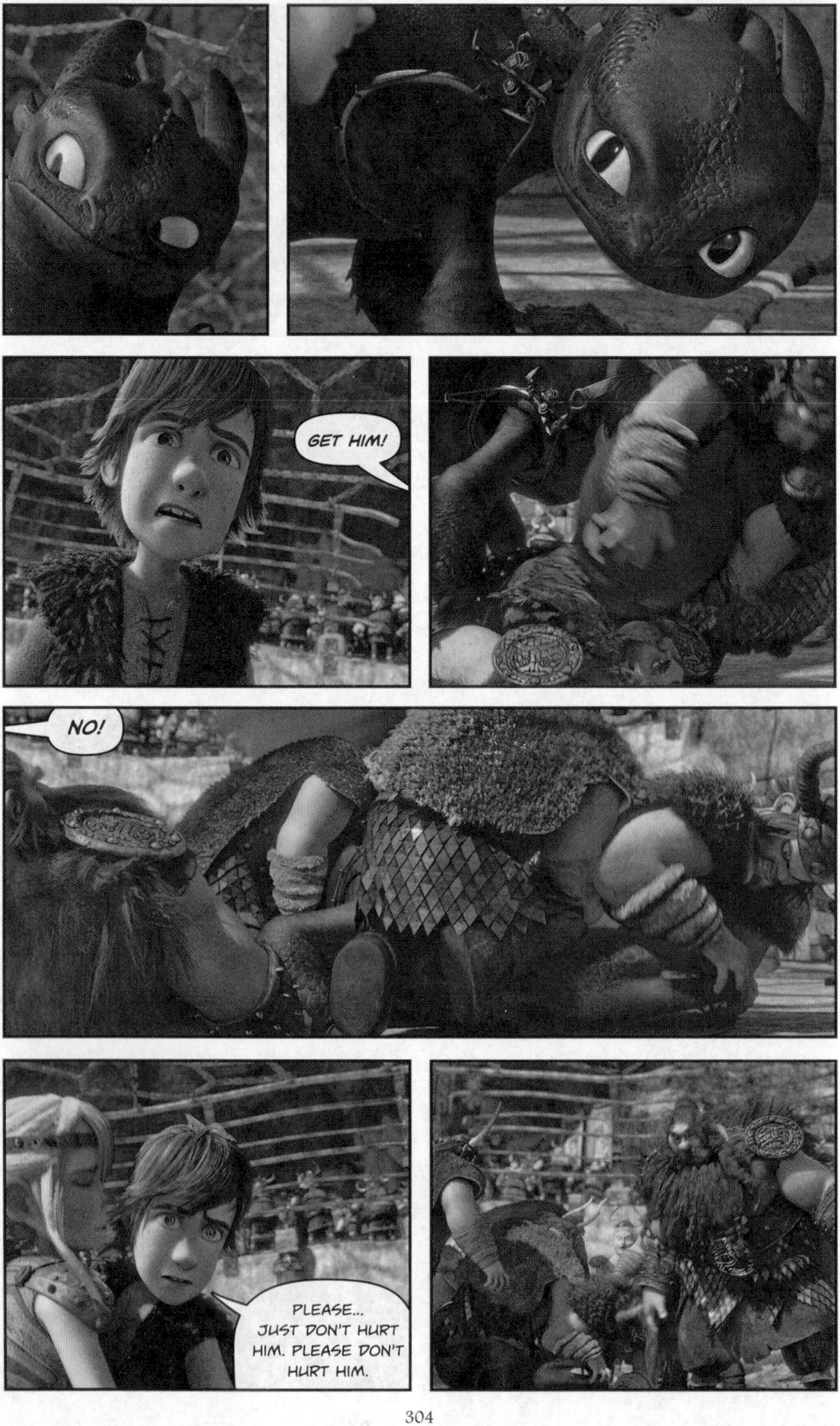
GET HIM!
NO!
PLEASE... JUST DON'T HURT HIM. PLEASE DON'T HURT HIM.

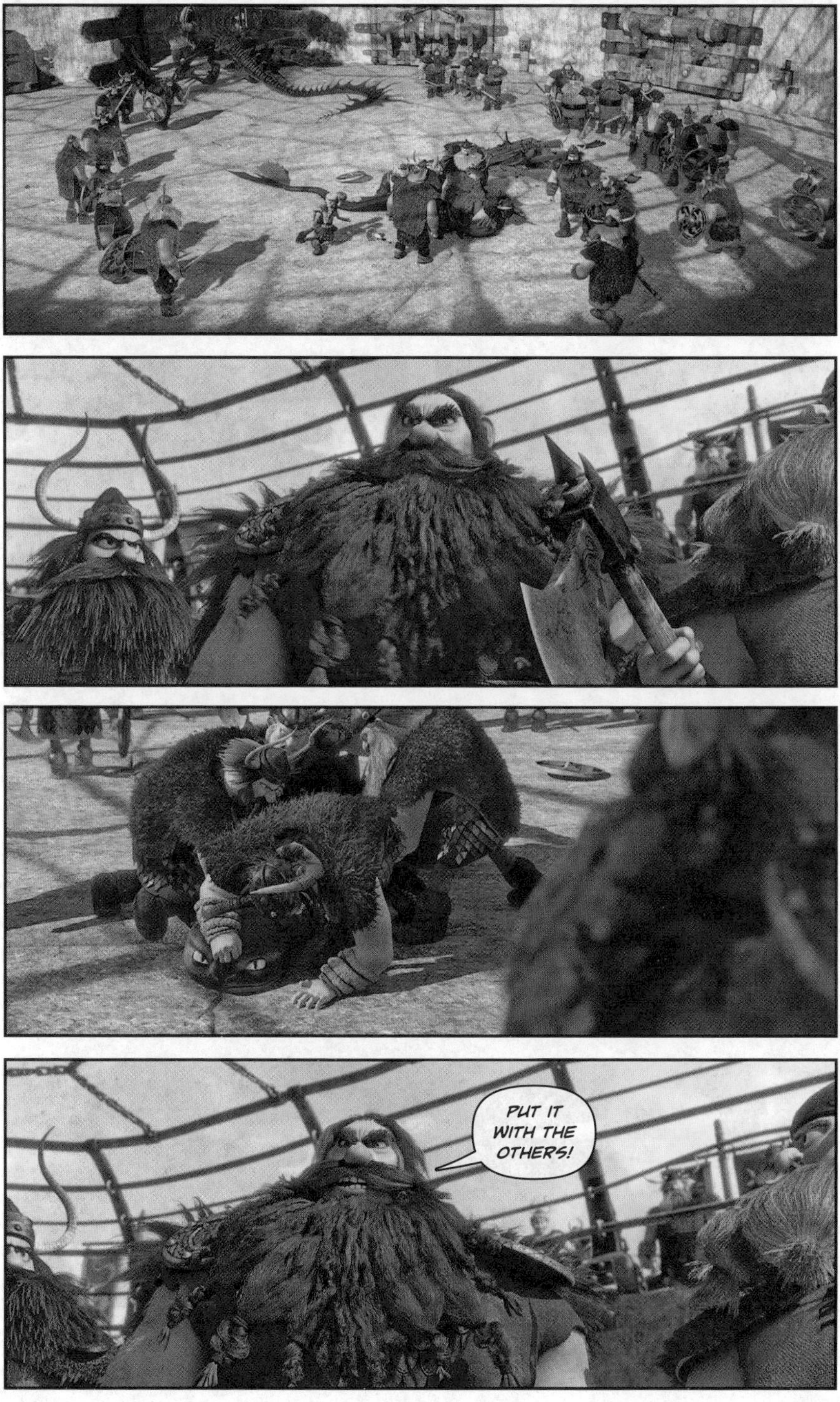
PUT IT WITH THE OTHERS!

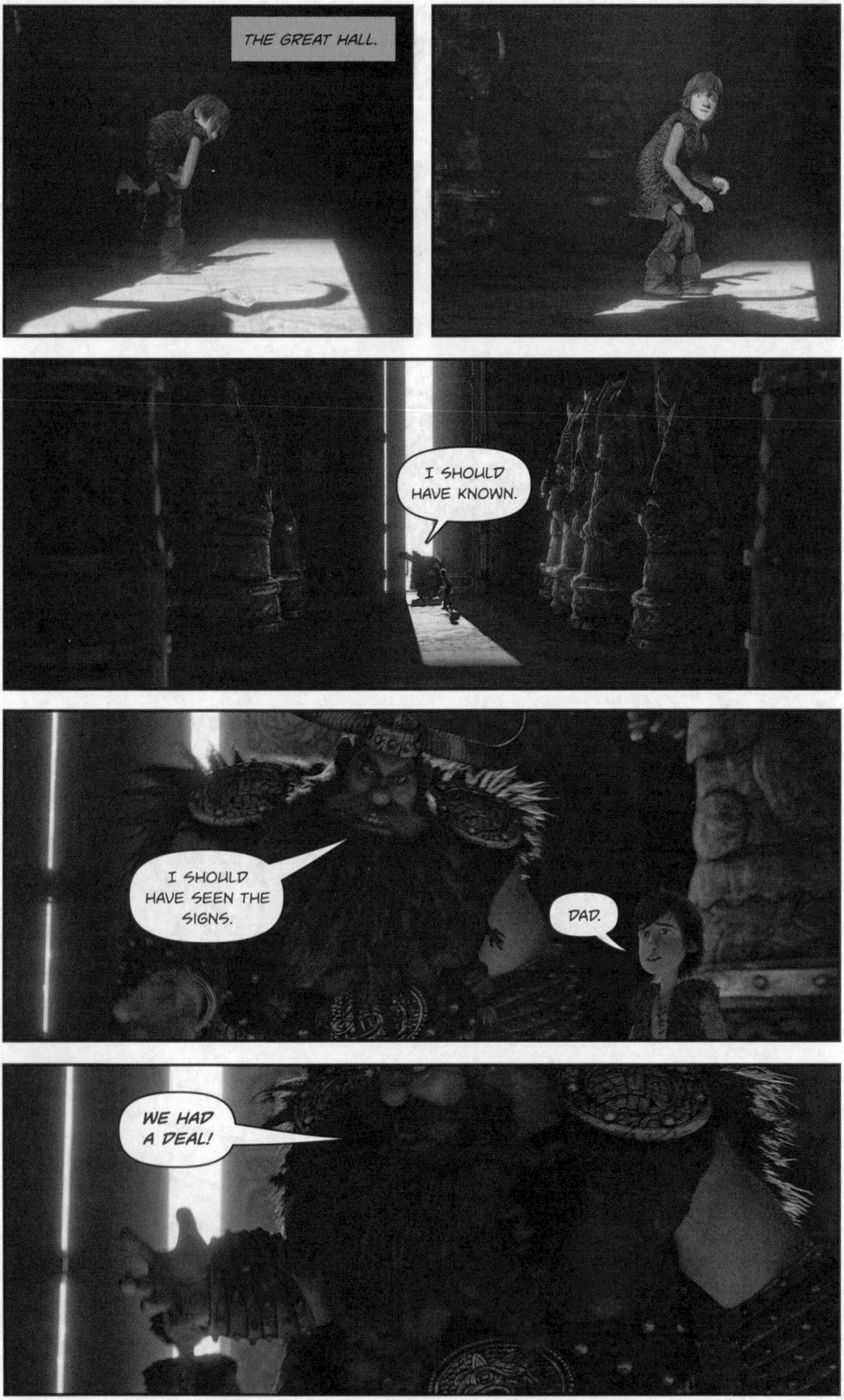
THE GREAT HALL.
I SHOULD HAVE KNOWN.
I SHOULD HAVE SEEN THE SIGNS.
DAD.
WE HAD A DEAL!

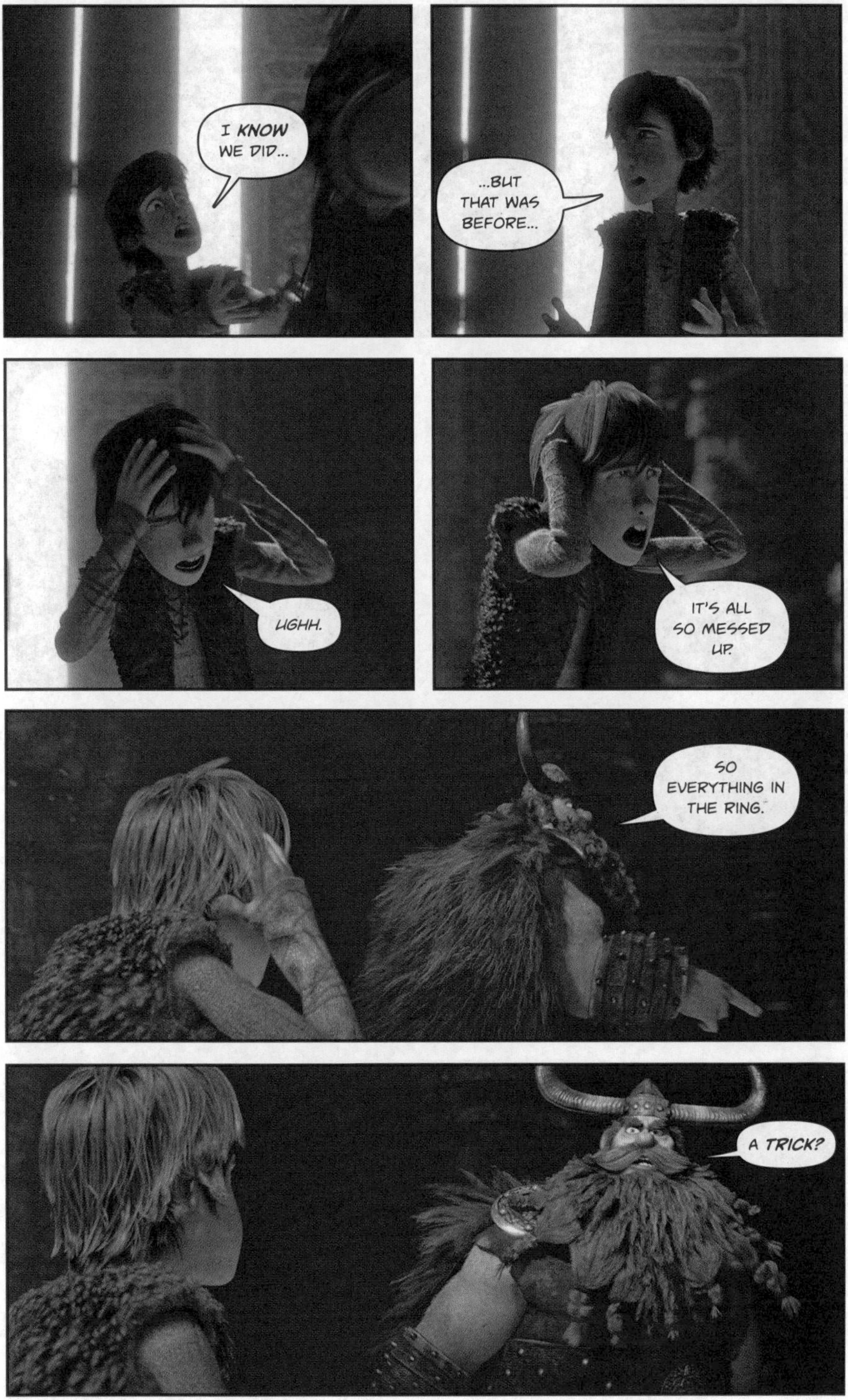
I KNOW WE DID...
...BUT THAT WAS BEFORE...
UGHH.
IT'S ALL SO MESSED UP.
SO EVERYTHING IN THE RING.
A TRICK?

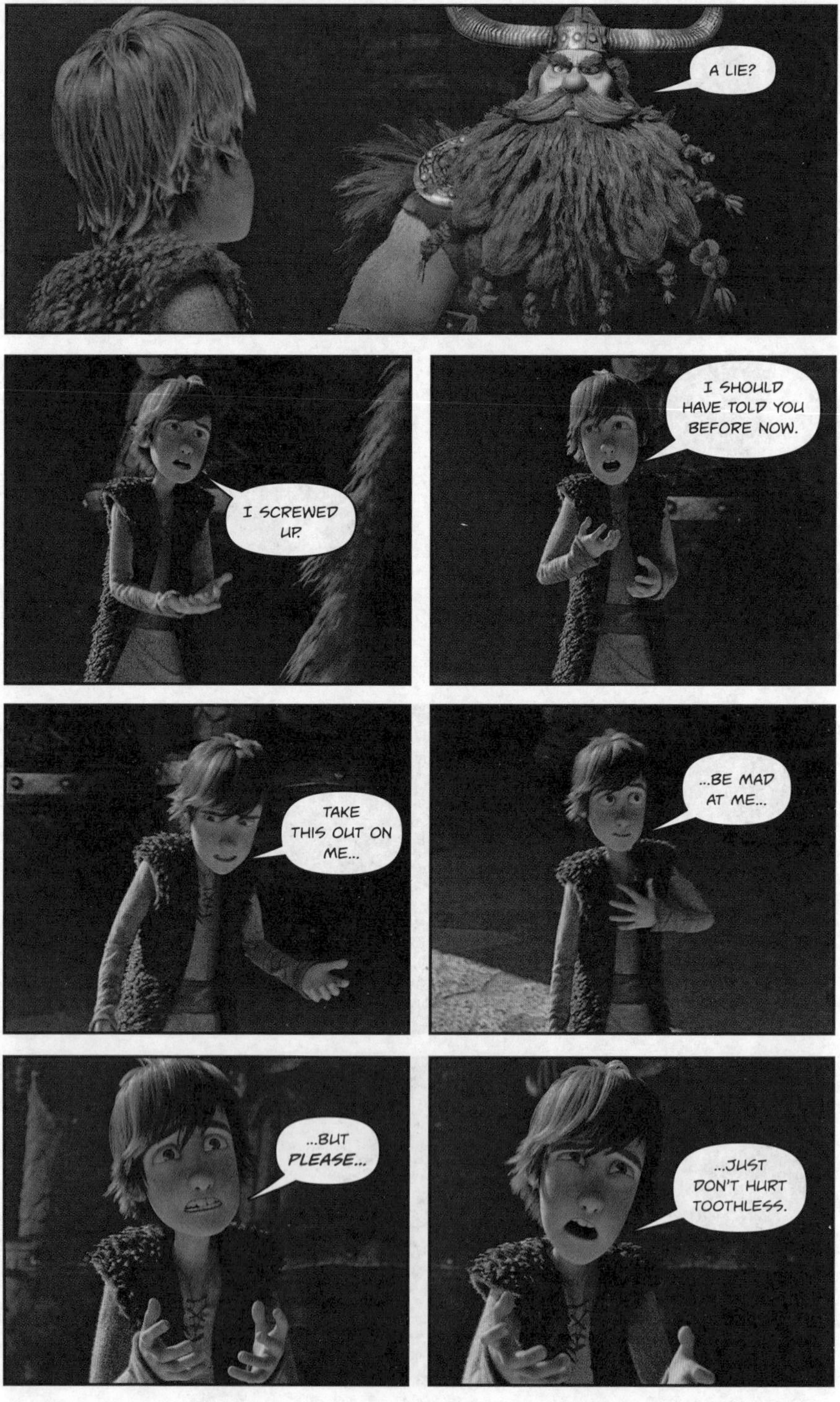
A LIE?
I SCREWED UP.
I SHOULD HAVE TOLD YOU BEFORE NOW.
TAKE THIS OUT ON ME...
...BE MAD AT ME...
...BUT PLEASE...
...JUST DON'T HURT TOOTHLESS.

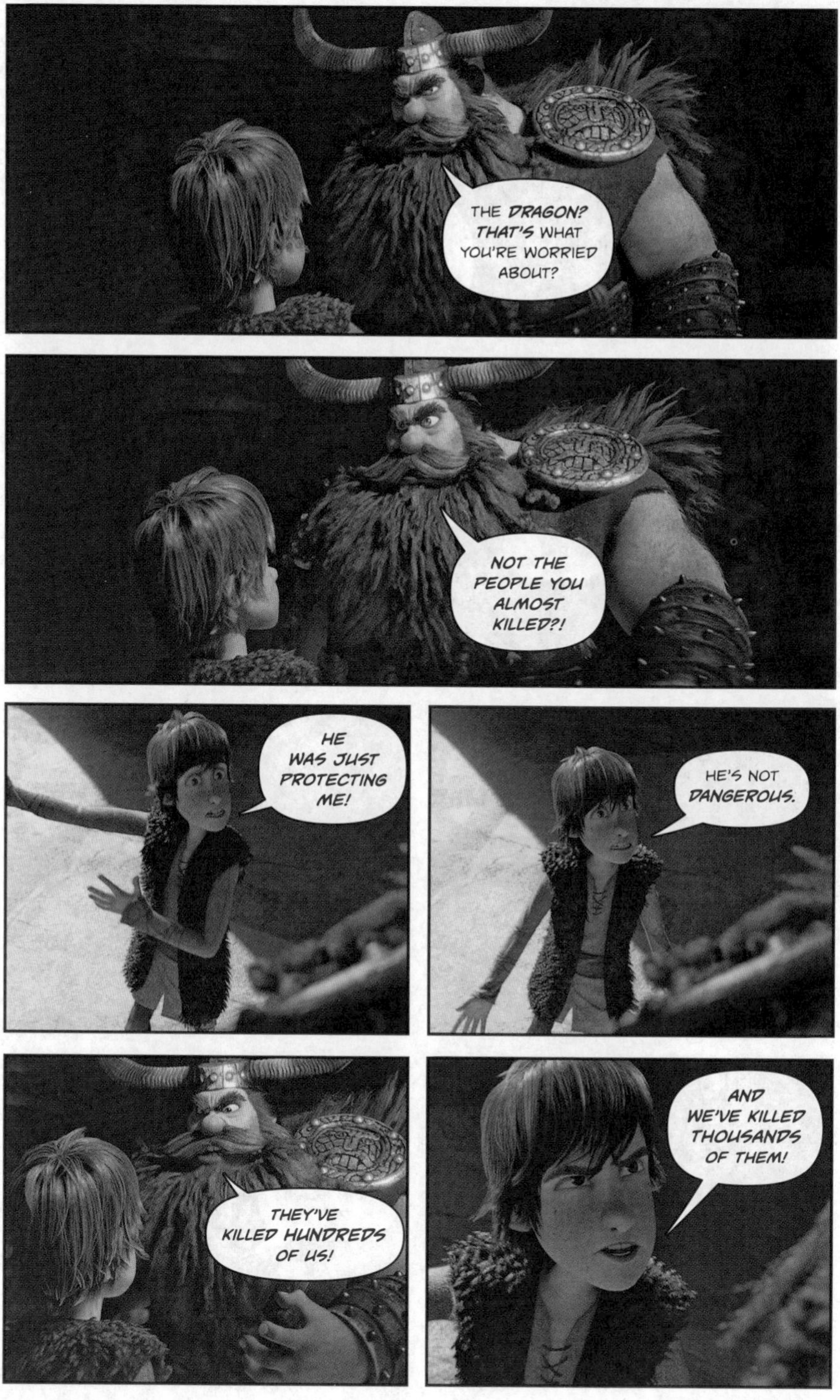
THE DRAGON? THAT'S WHAT YOU'RE WORRIED ABOUT?
NOT THE PEOPLE YOU ALMOST KILLED?!
HE WAS JUST PROTECTING ME!
HE'S NOT DANGEROUS.
THEY'VE KILLED HUNDREDS OF US!
AND WE'VE KILLED THOUSANDS OF THEM!

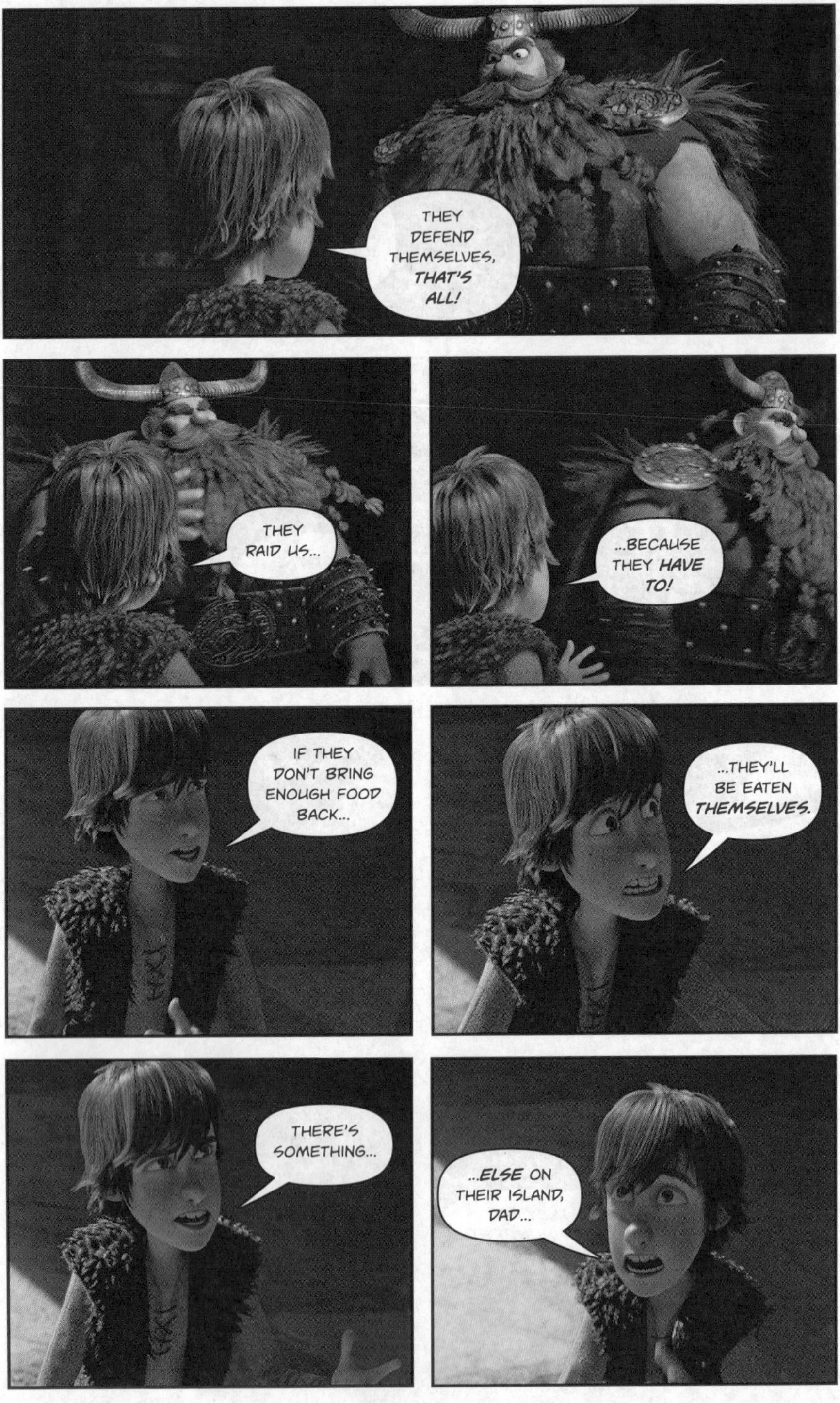
THEY DEFEND THEMSELVES, THAT'S ALL!
THEY RAID US...
...BECAUSE THEY HAVE TO!
IF THEY DON'T BRING ENOUGH FOOD BACK...
...THEY'LL BE EATEN THEMSELVES.
THERE'S SOMETHING...
...ELSE ON THEIR ISLAND, DAD...

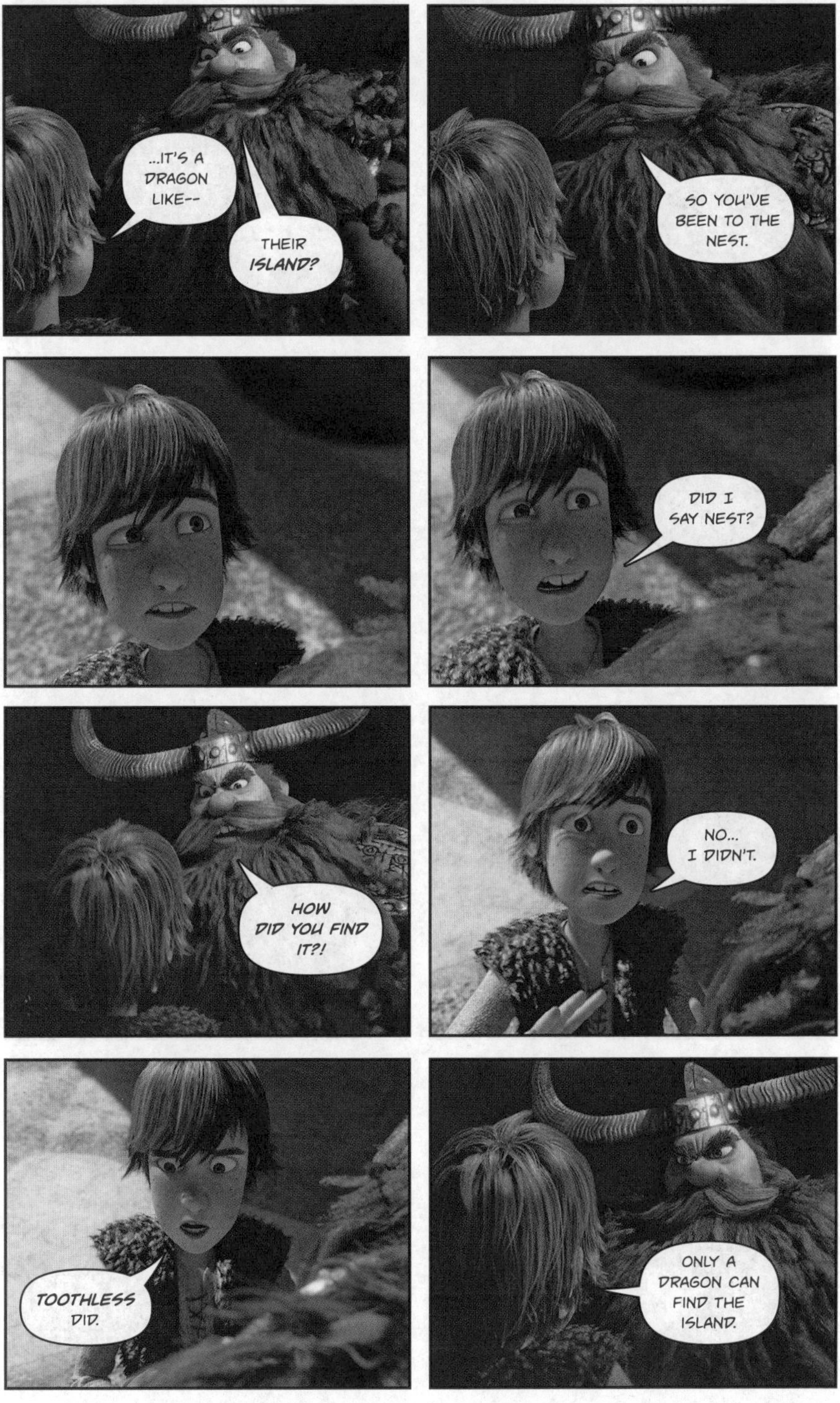
...IT'S A DRAGON LIKE--
THEIR ISLAND?
SO YOU'VE BEEN TO THE NEST.
DID I SAY NEST?
HOW DID YOU FIND IT?!
NO... I DIDN'T.
TOOTHLESS DID.
ONLY A DRAGON CAN FIND THE ISLAND.

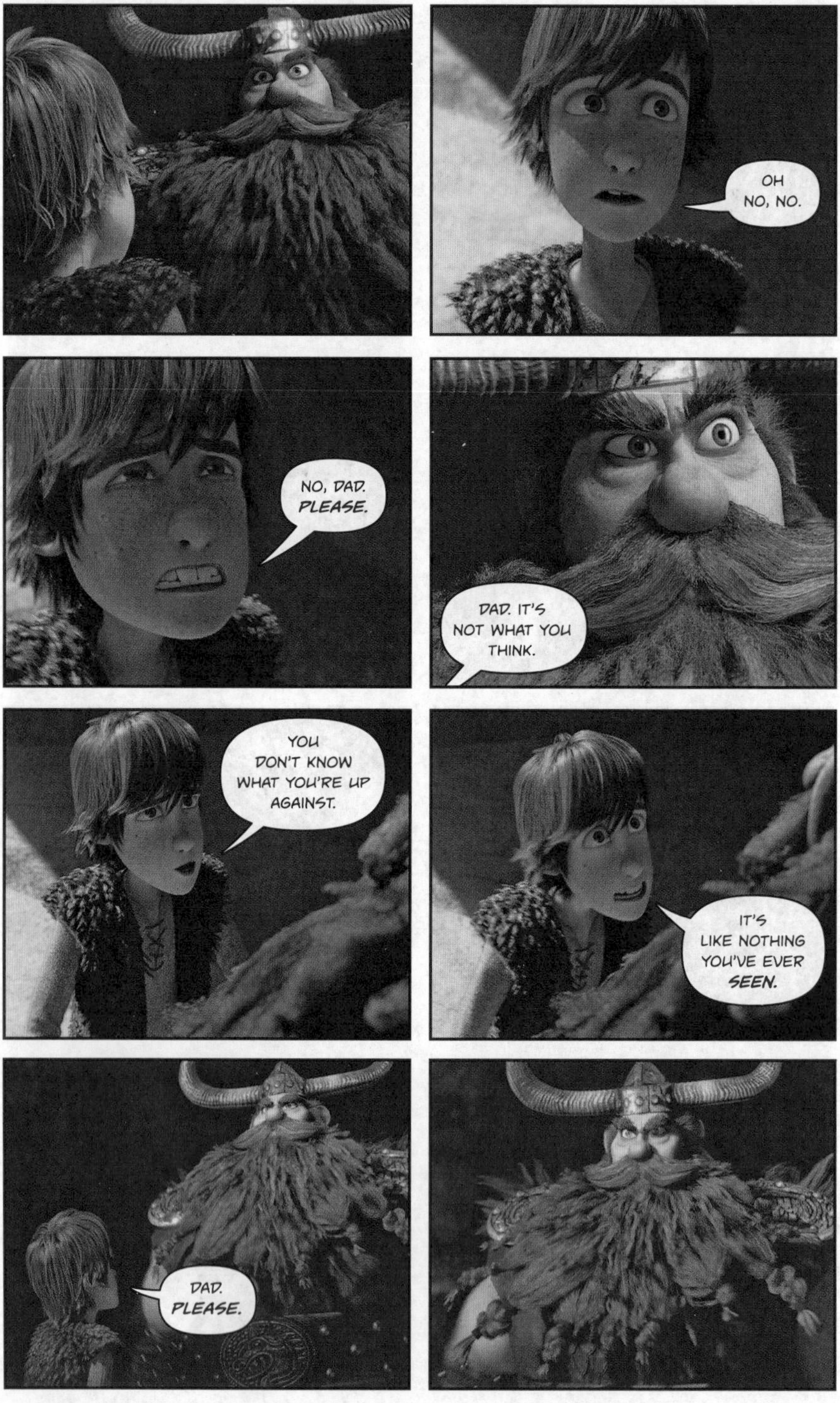
OH NO, NO.
NO, DAD. PLEASE.
DAD. IT'S NOT WHAT YOU THINK.
YOU DON'T KNOW WHAT YOU'RE UP AGAINST.
IT'S LIKE NOTHING YOU'VE EVER SEEN.
DAD. PLEASE.

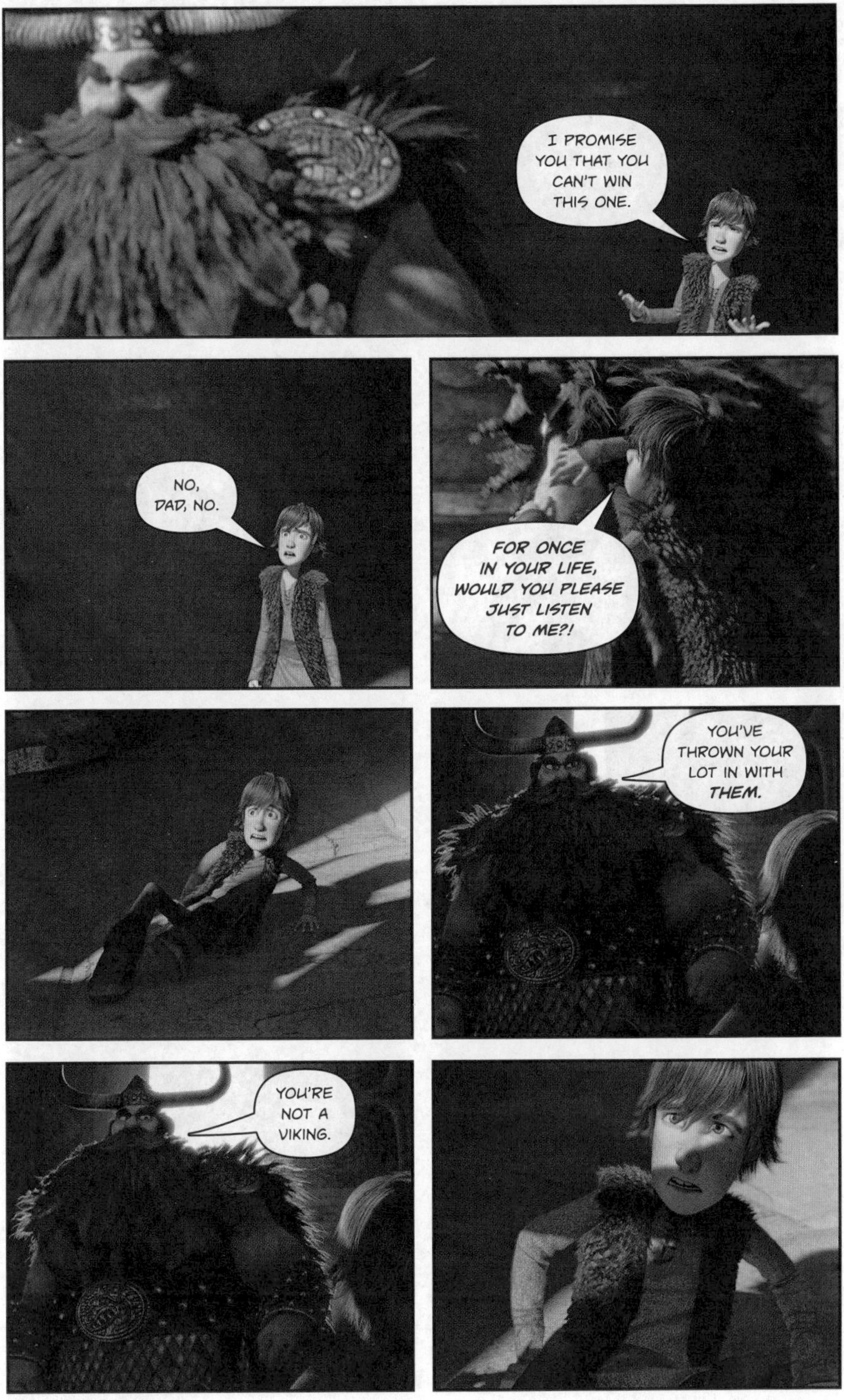
I PROMISE YOU THAT YOU CAN'T WIN THIS ONE.
NO, DAD, NO.
FOR ONCE IN YOUR LIFE, WOULD YOU PLEASE JUST LISTEN TO ME?!
YOU'VE THROWN YOUR LOT IN WITH *THEM.*
YOU'RE NOT A VIKING.

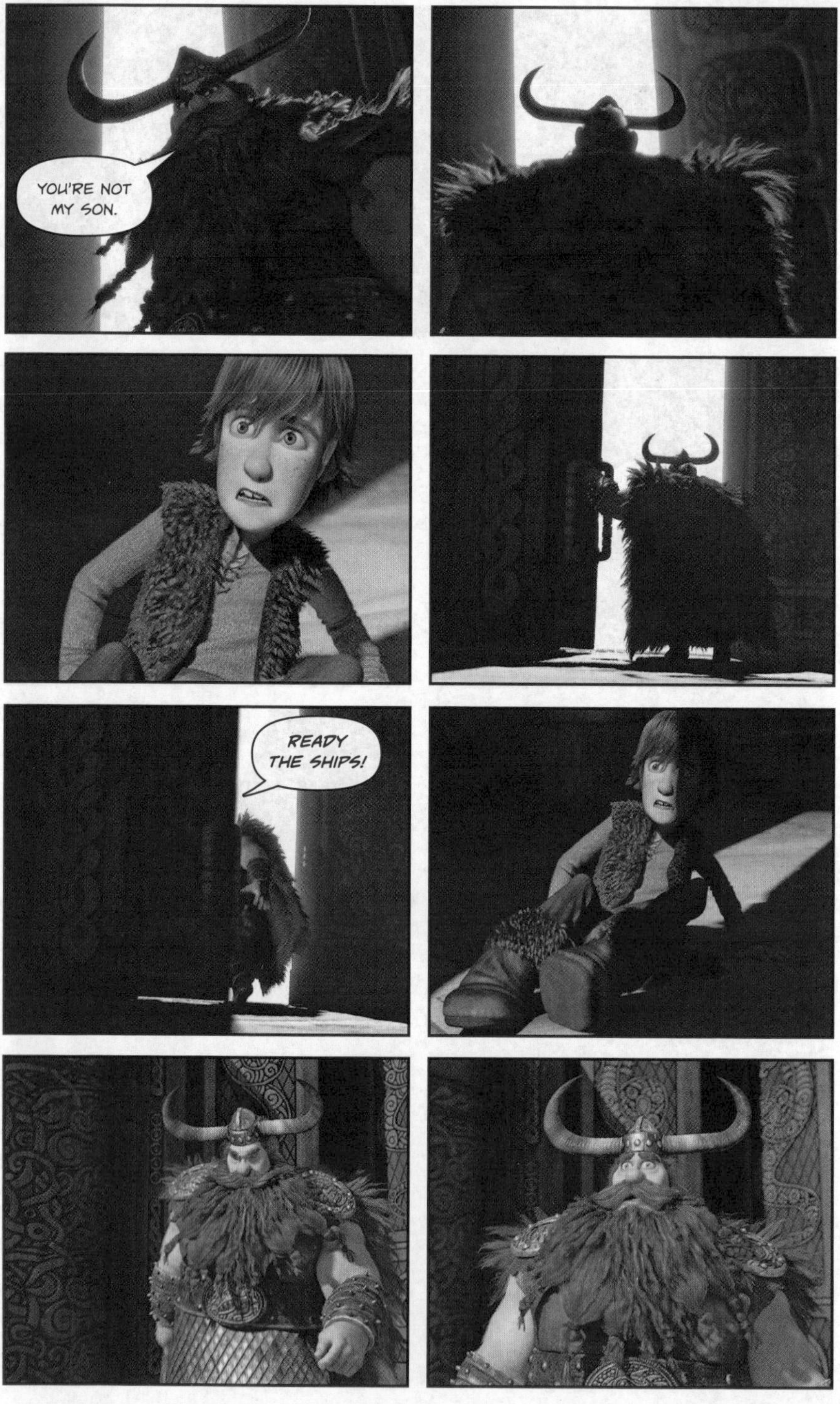
YOU'RE NOT MY SON.
READY THE SHIPS!

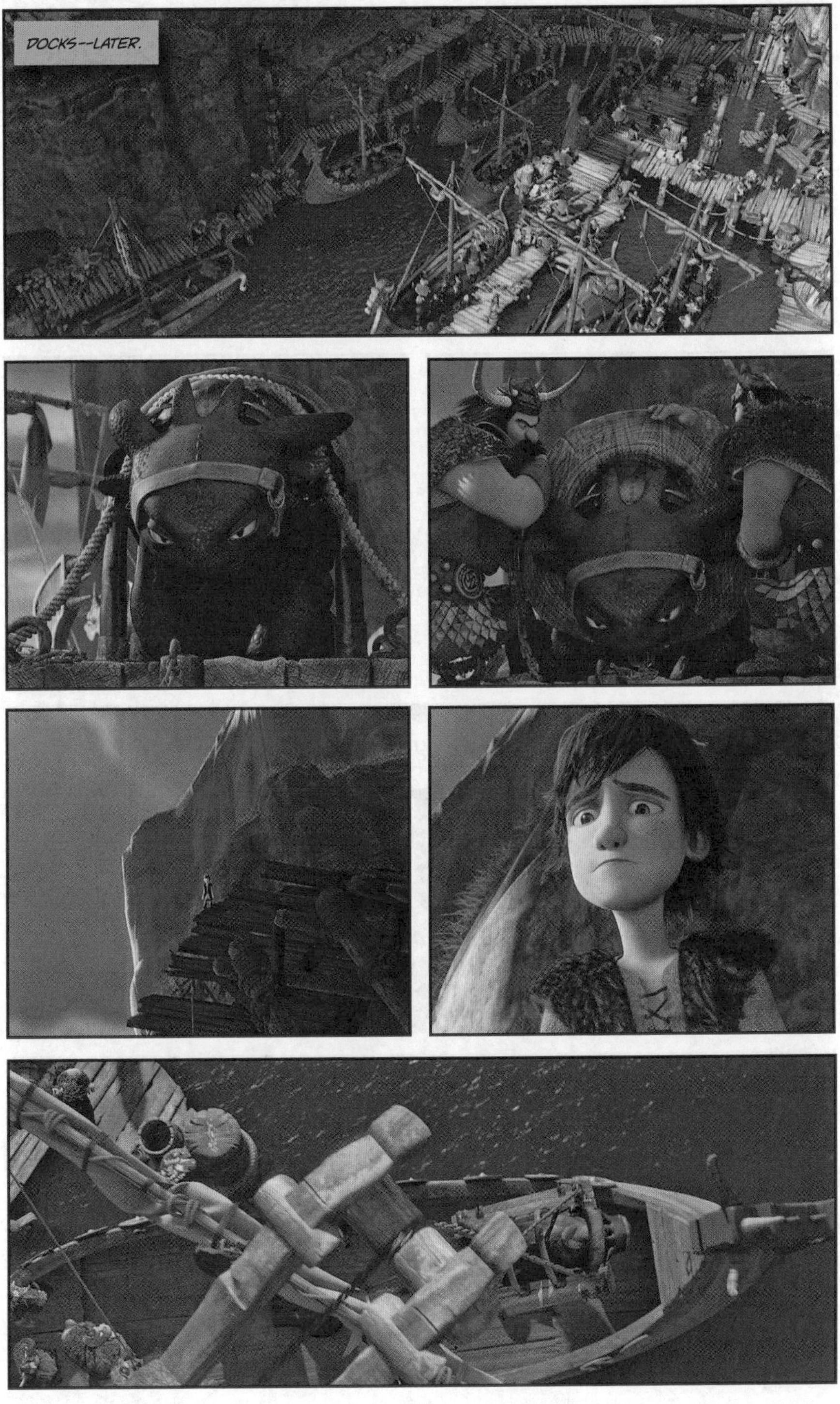
DOCKS--LATER.

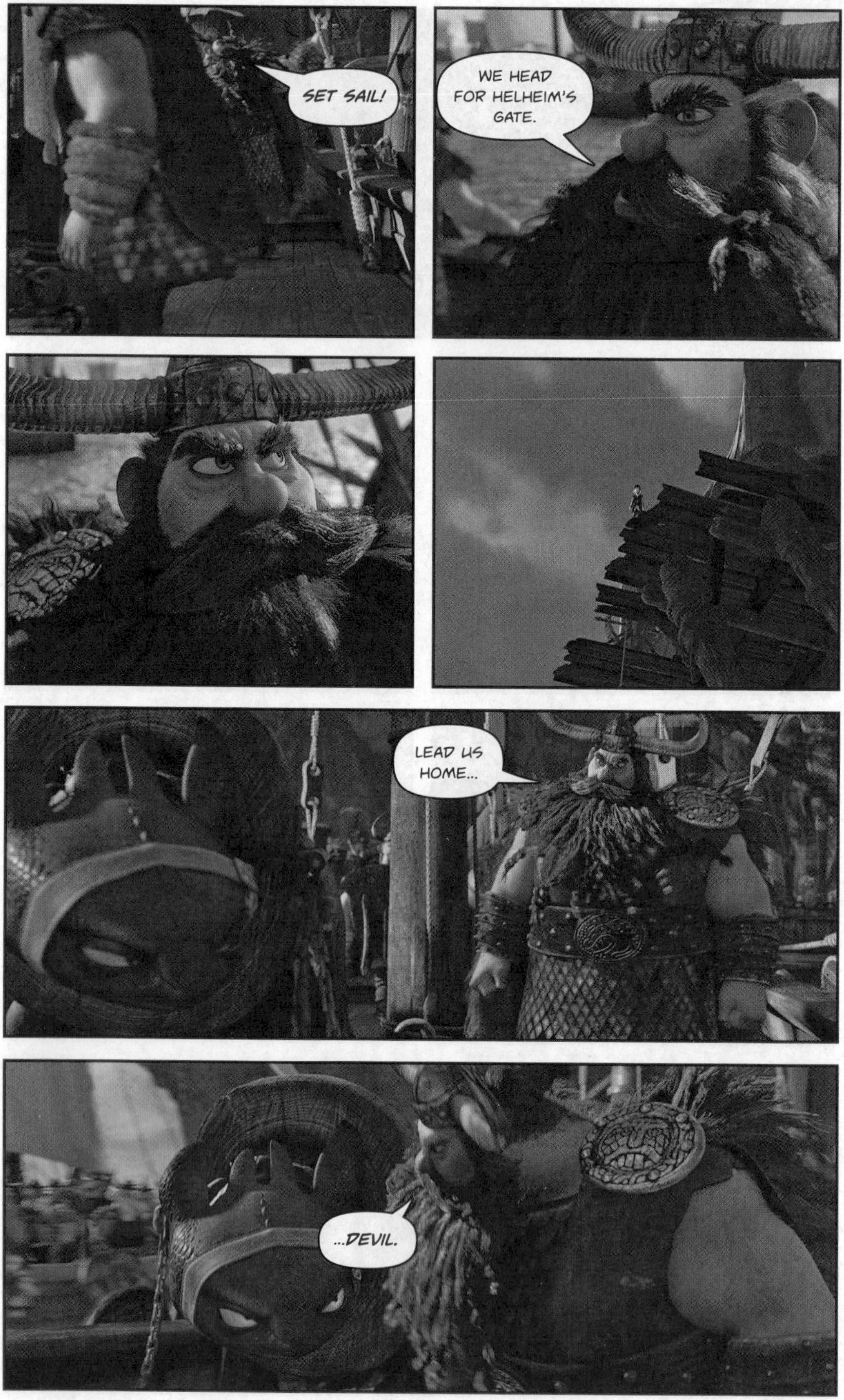
SET SAIL!
WE HEAD FOR HELHEIM'S GATE.
LEAD US HOME...
...DEVIL.

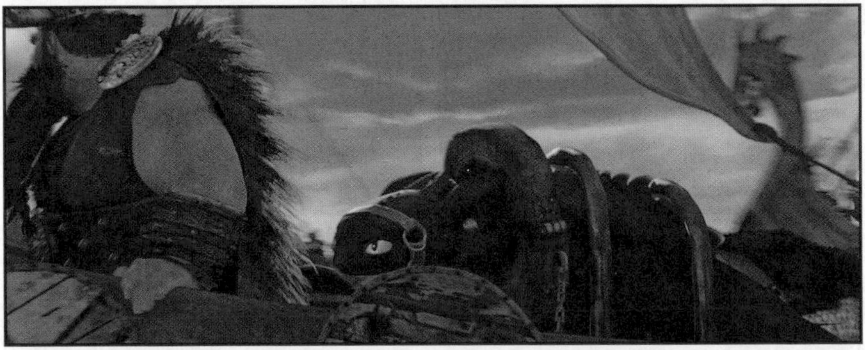

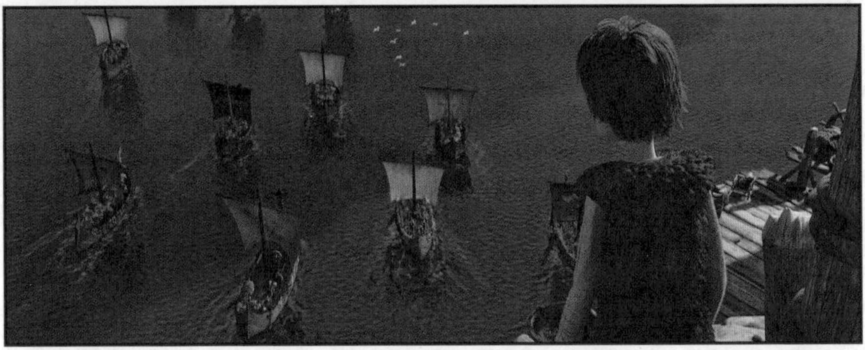

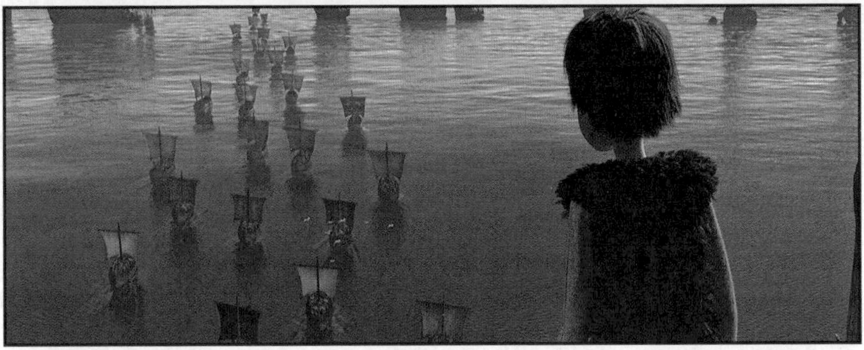

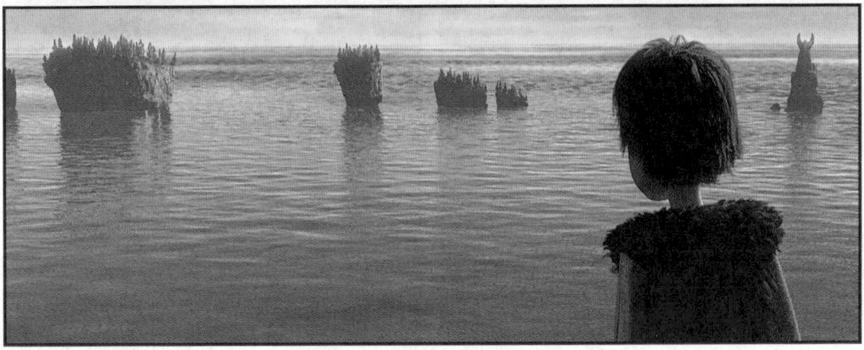

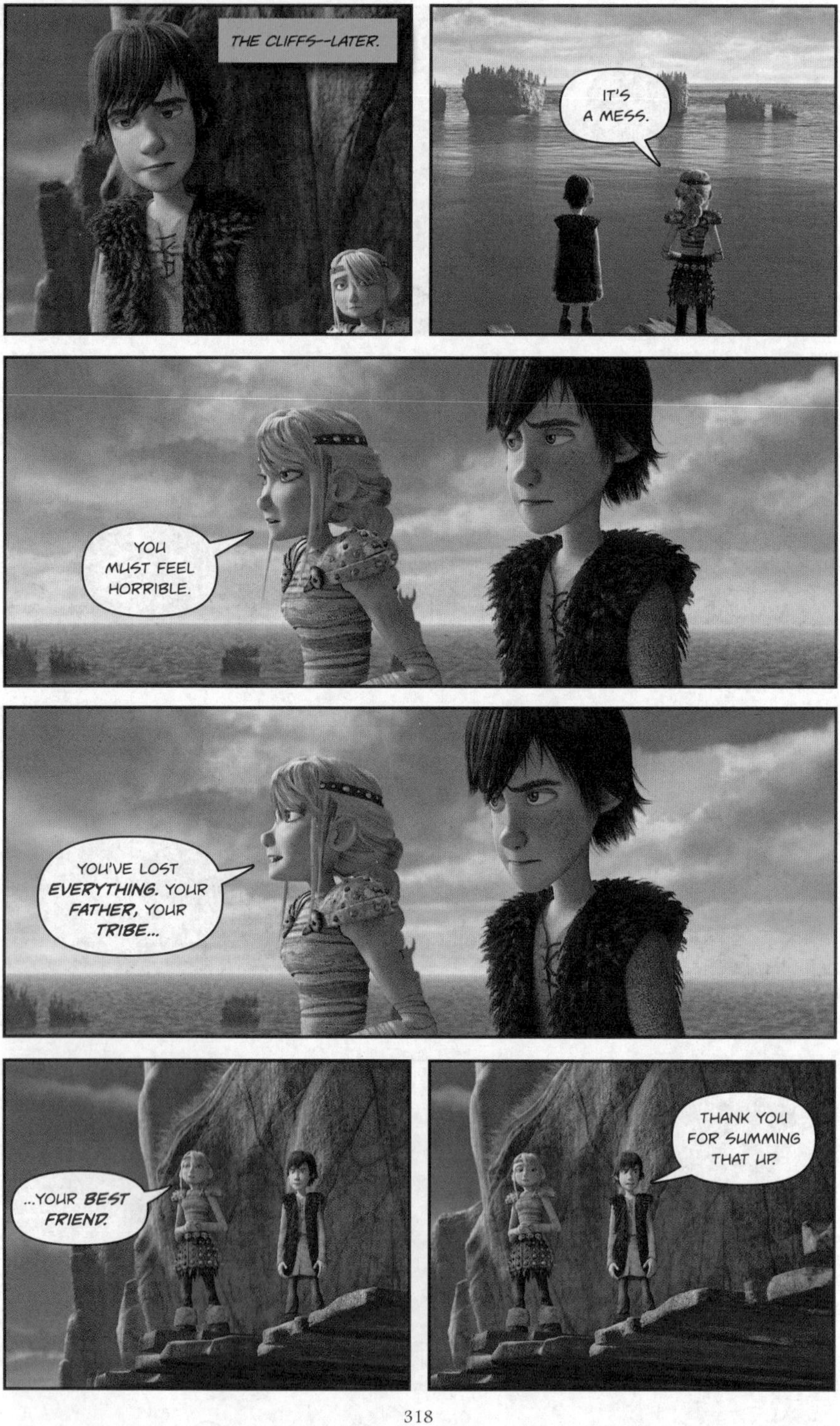
THE CLIFFS--LATER.
IT'S A MESS.
YOU MUST FEEL HORRIBLE.
YOU'VE LOST EVERYTHING. YOUR FATHER, YOUR TRIBE...
...YOUR BEST FRIEND.
THANK YOU FOR SUMMING THAT UP.

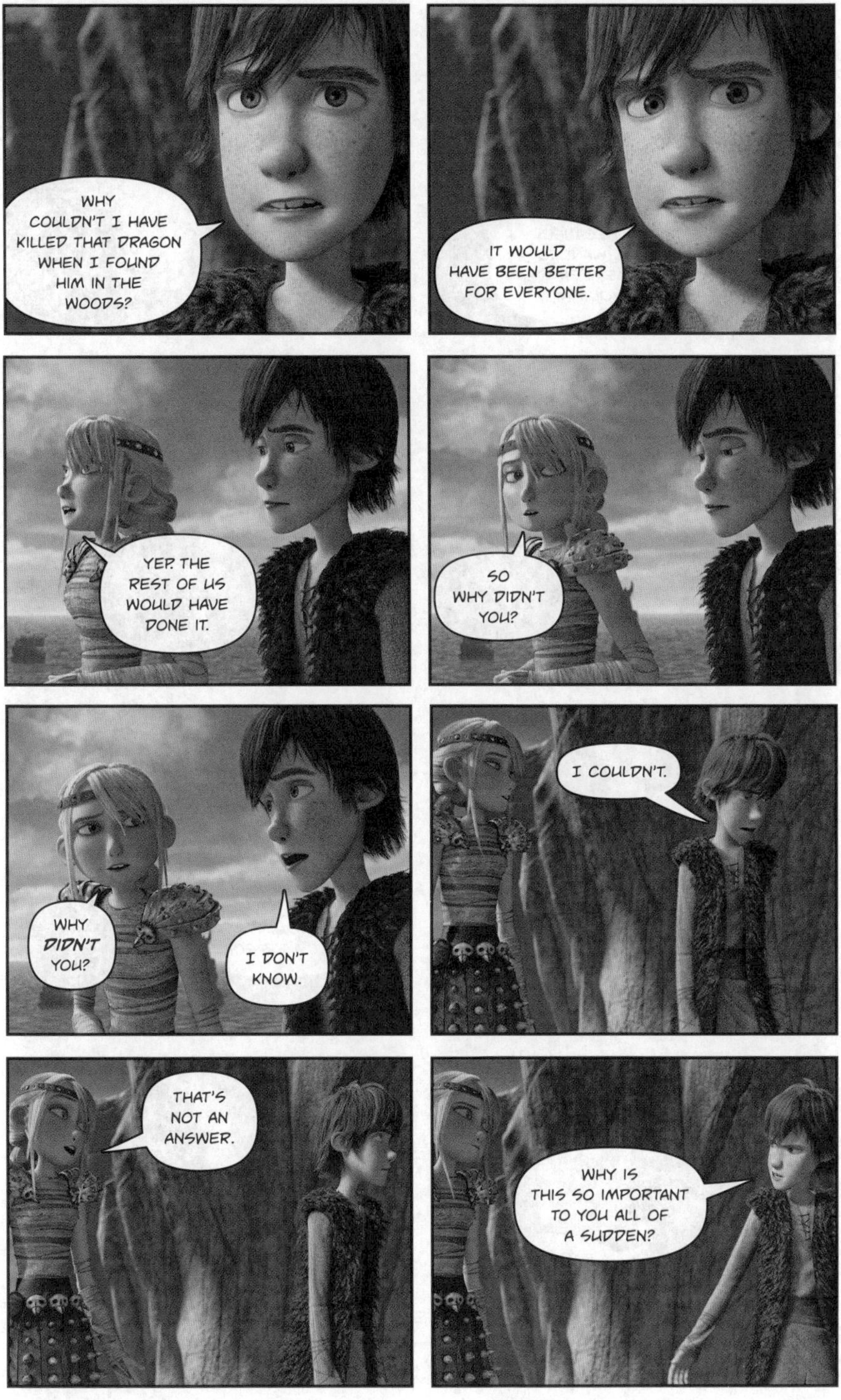
WHY COULDN'T I HAVE KILLED THAT DRAGON WHEN I FOUND HIM IN THE WOODS?
IT WOULD HAVE BEEN BETTER FOR EVERYONE.
YEP. THE REST OF US WOULD HAVE DONE IT.
SO WHY DIDN'T YOU?
WHY *DIDN'T* YOU?
I DON'T KNOW.
I COULDN'T.
THAT'S NOT AN ANSWER.
WHY IS THIS SO IMPORTANT TO YOU ALL OF A SUDDEN?

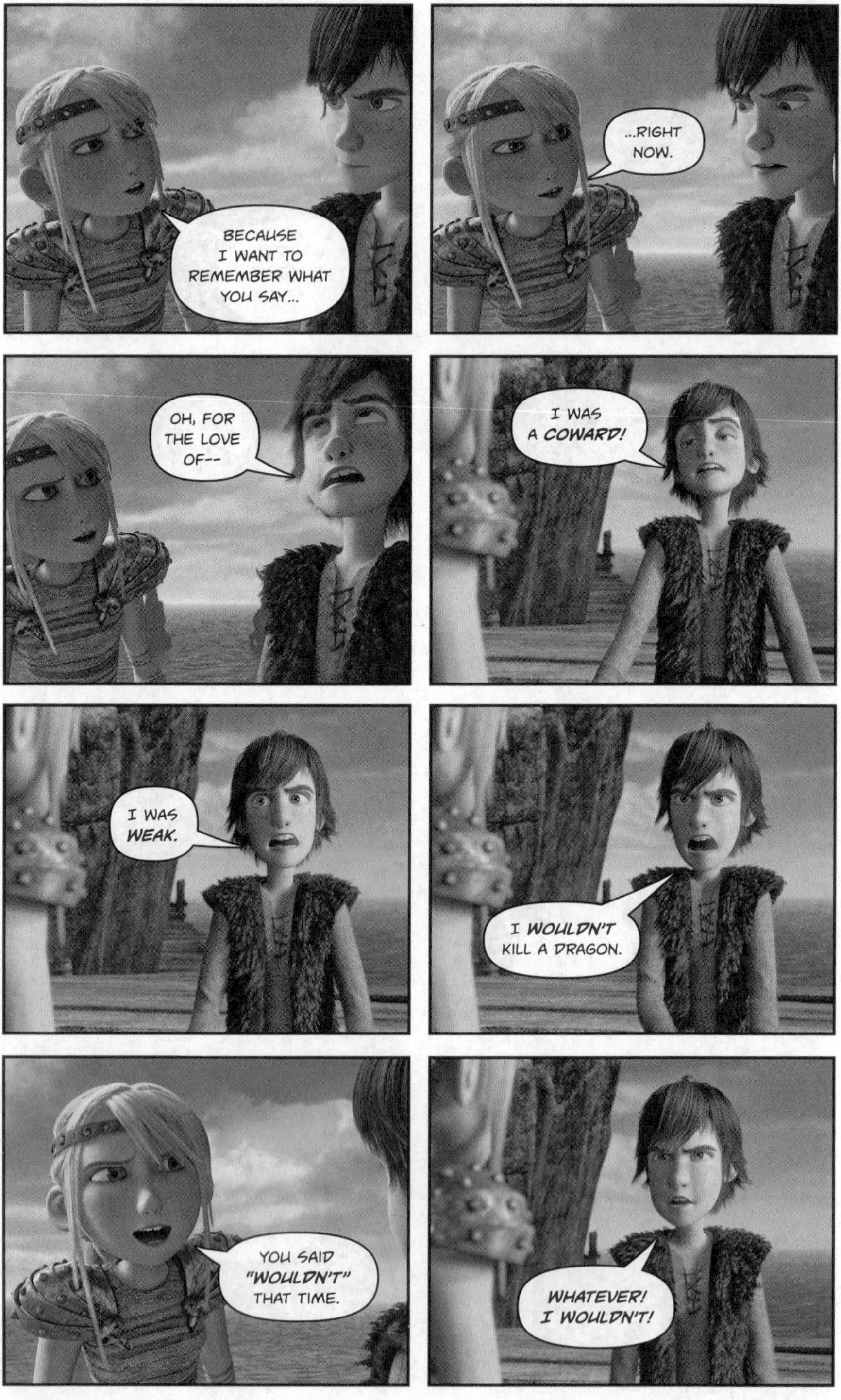
BECAUSE I WANT TO REMEMBER WHAT YOU SAY...
...RIGHT NOW.
OH, FOR THE LOVE OF--
I WAS A COWARD!
I WAS WEAK.
I WOULDN'T KILL A DRAGON.
YOU SAID "WOULDN'T" THAT TIME.
WHATEVER! I WOULDN'T!

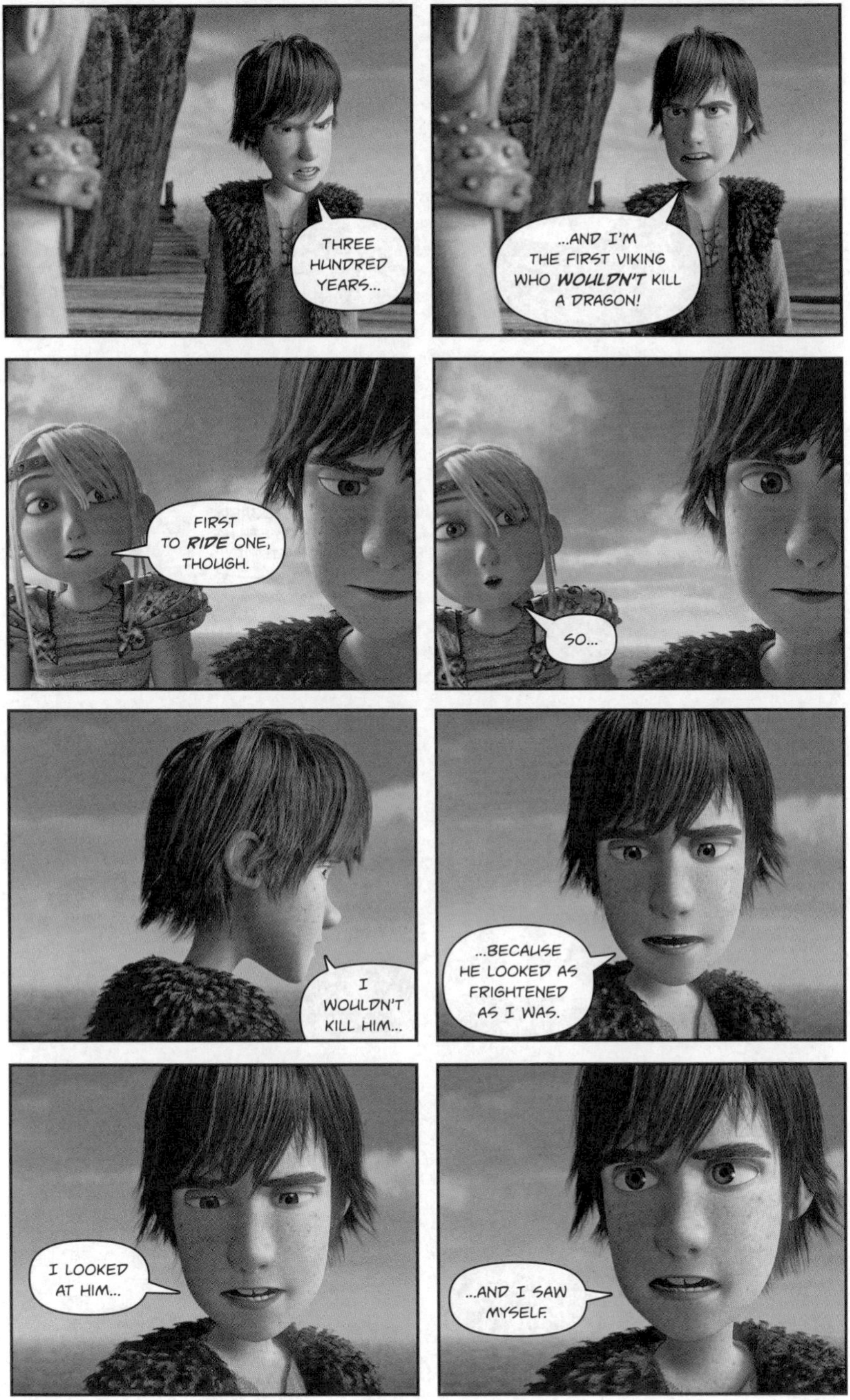
THREE HUNDRED YEARS...
...AND I'M THE FIRST VIKING WHO WOULDN'T KILL A DRAGON!
FIRST TO RIDE ONE, THOUGH.
SO...
I WOULDN'T KILL HIM...
...BECAUSE HE LOOKED AS FRIGHTENED AS I WAS.
I LOOKED AT HIM...
...AND I SAW MYSELF.

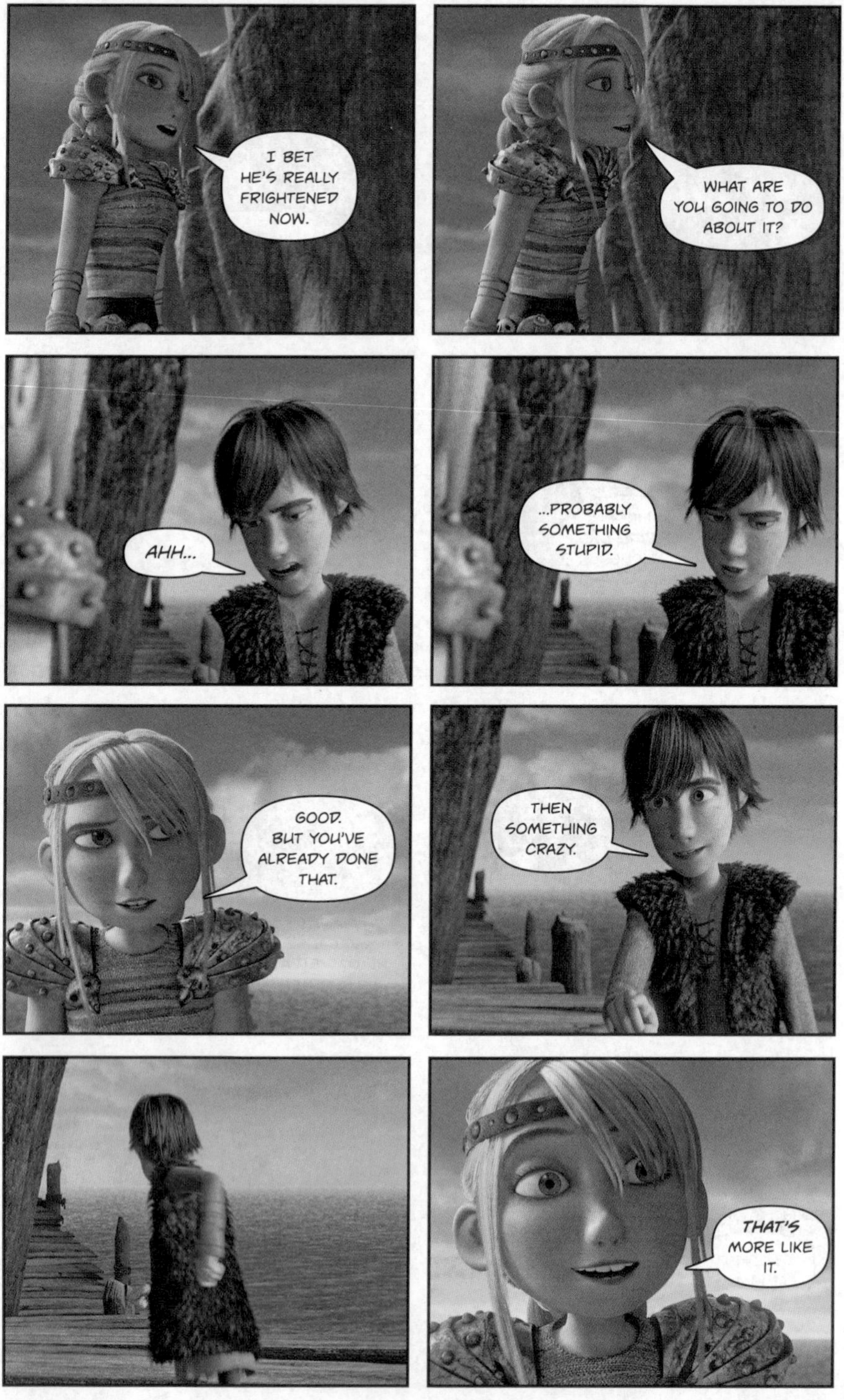
I BET HE'S REALLY FRIGHTENED NOW.
WHAT ARE YOU GOING TO DO ABOUT IT?
AHH...
...PROBABLY SOMETHING STUPID.
GOOD. BUT YOU'VE ALREADY DONE THAT.
THEN SOMETHING CRAZY.
THAT'S MORE LIKE IT.

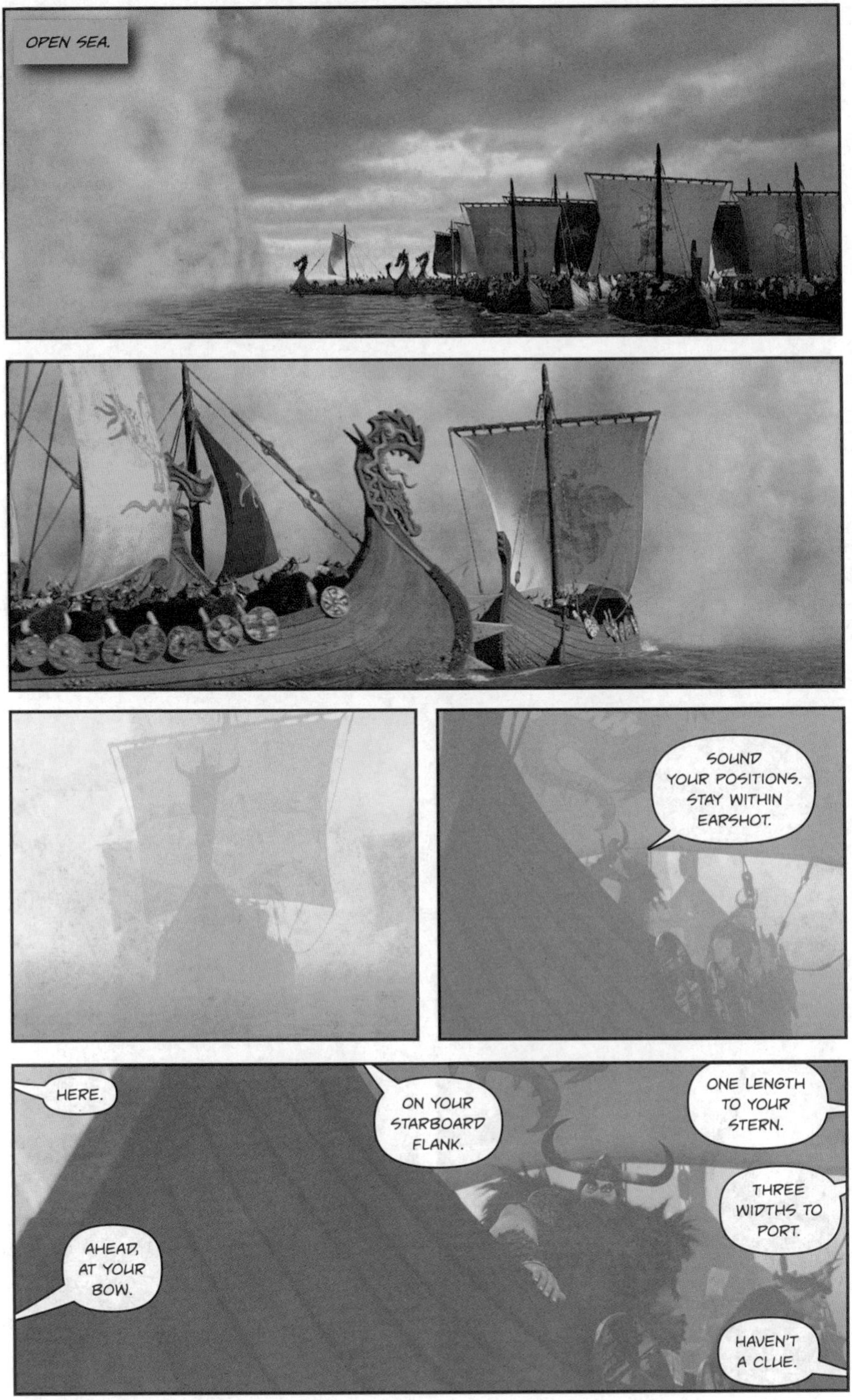
OPEN SEA.
SOUND YOUR POSITIONS. STAY WITHIN EARSHOT.
HERE.
ON YOUR STARBOARD FLANK.
ONE LENGTH TO YOUR STERN.
THREE WIDTHS TO PORT.
AHEAD, AT YOUR BOW.
HAVEN'T A CLUE.

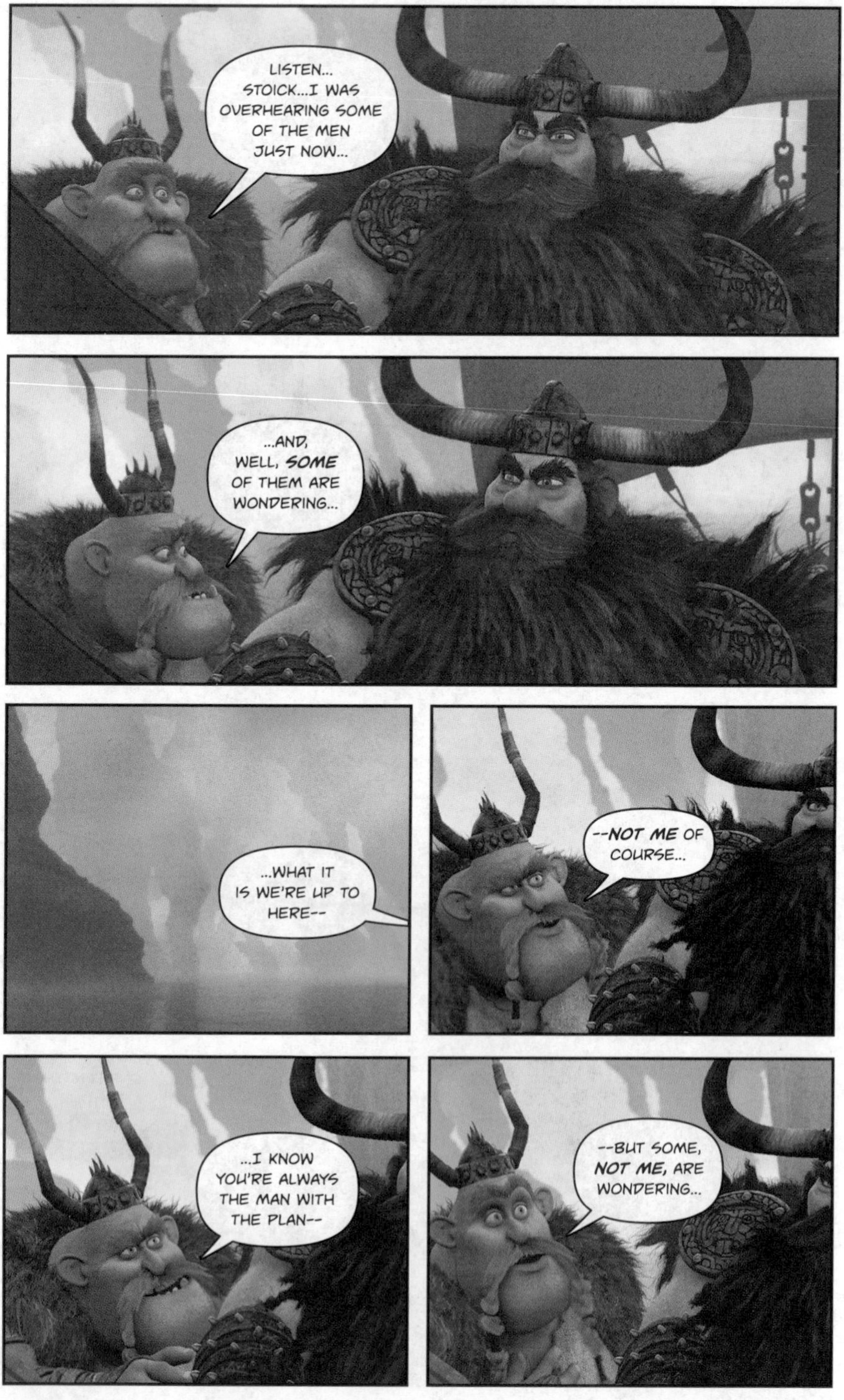
LISTEN... STOICK...I WAS OVERHEARING SOME OF THE MEN JUST NOW...
...AND, WELL, SOME OF THEM ARE WONDERING...
...WHAT IT IS WE'RE UP TO HERE--
--NOT ME OF COURSE...
...I KNOW YOU'RE ALWAYS THE MAN WITH THE PLAN--
--BUT SOME, NOT ME, ARE WONDERING...

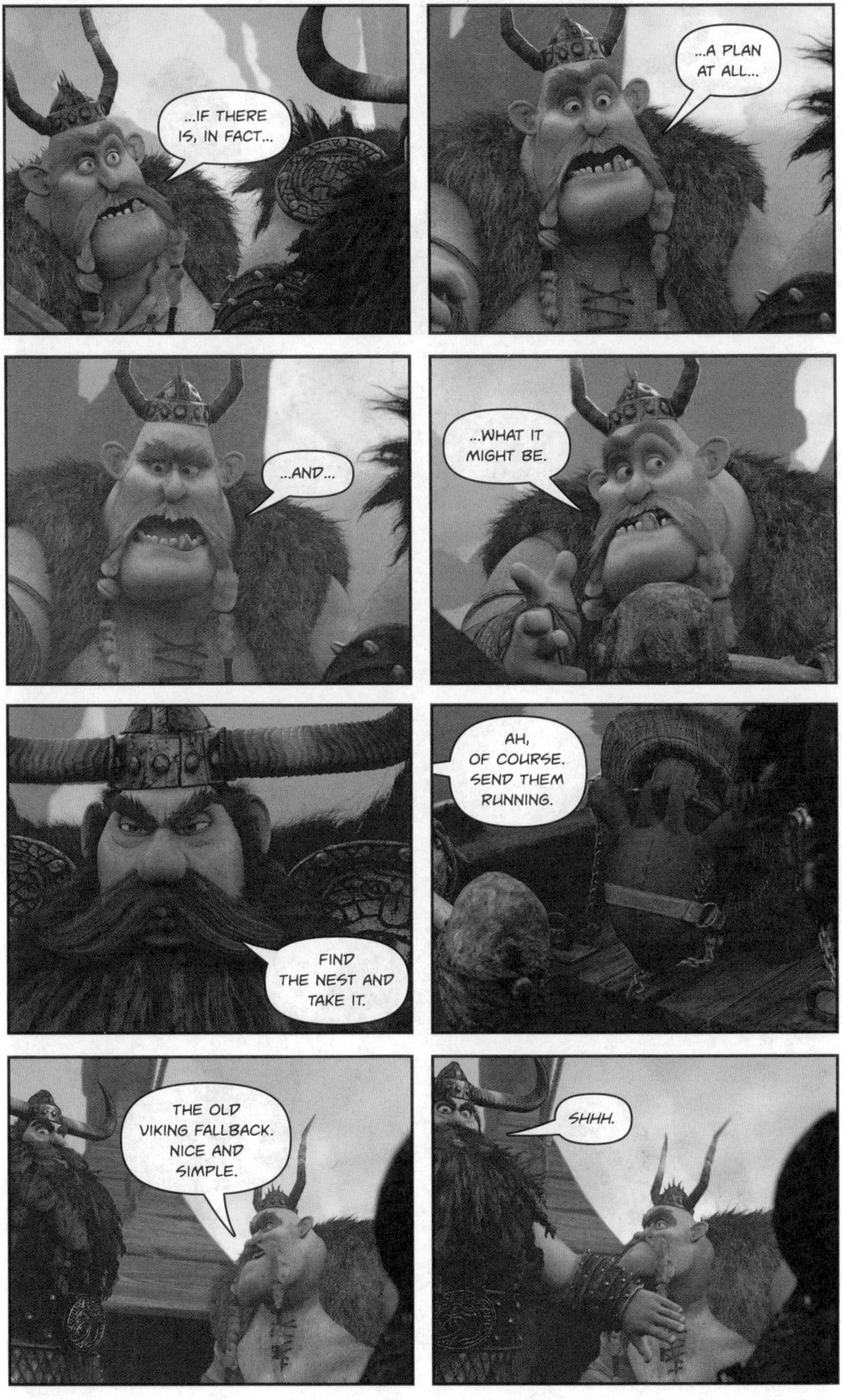
...IF THERE IS, IN FACT...
...A PLAN AT ALL...
...AND...
...WHAT IT MIGHT BE.
FIND THE NEST AND TAKE IT.
AH, OF COURSE. SEND THEM RUNNING.
THE OLD VIKING FALLBACK. NICE AND SIMPLE.
SHHH.

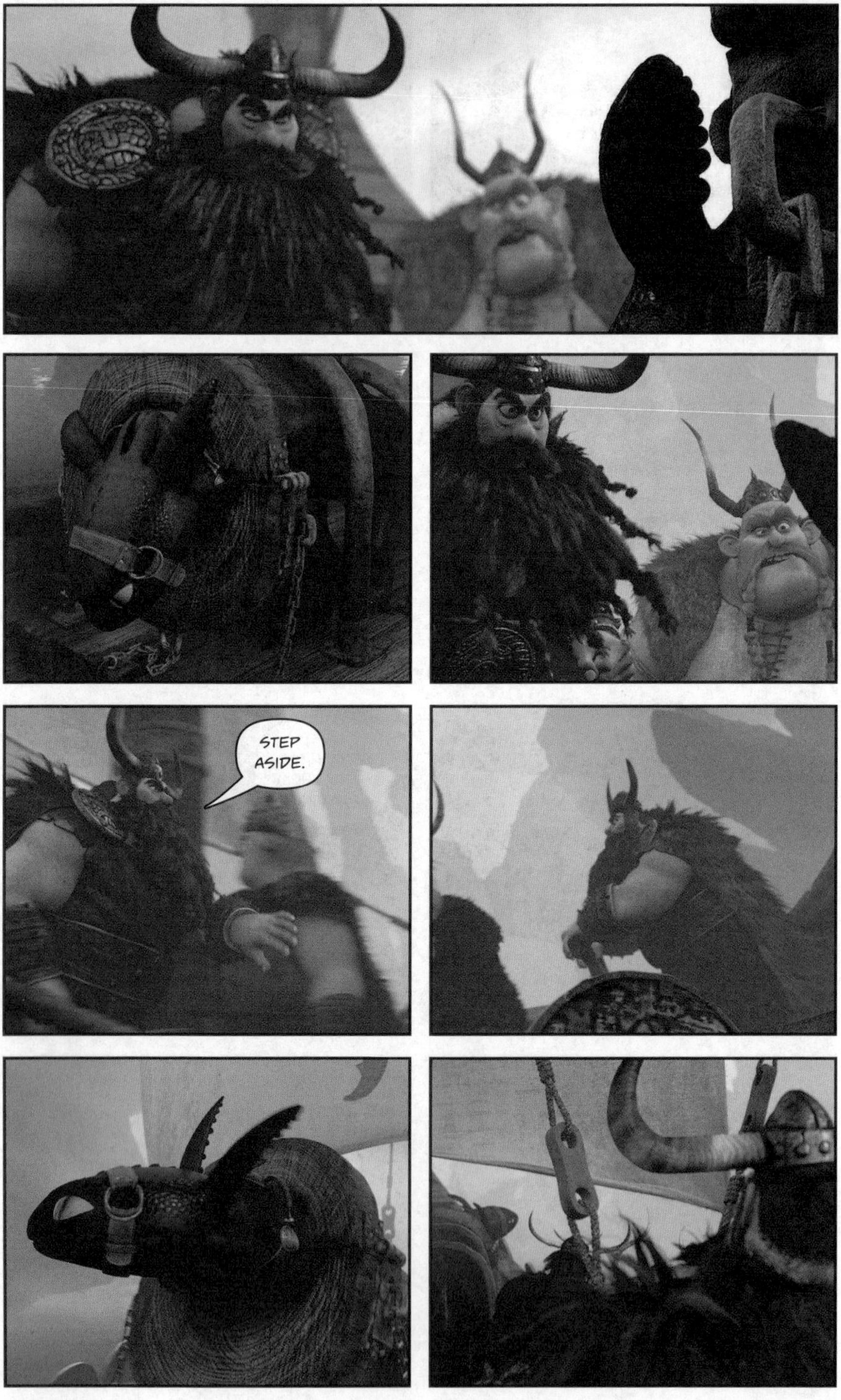
STEP ASIDE.

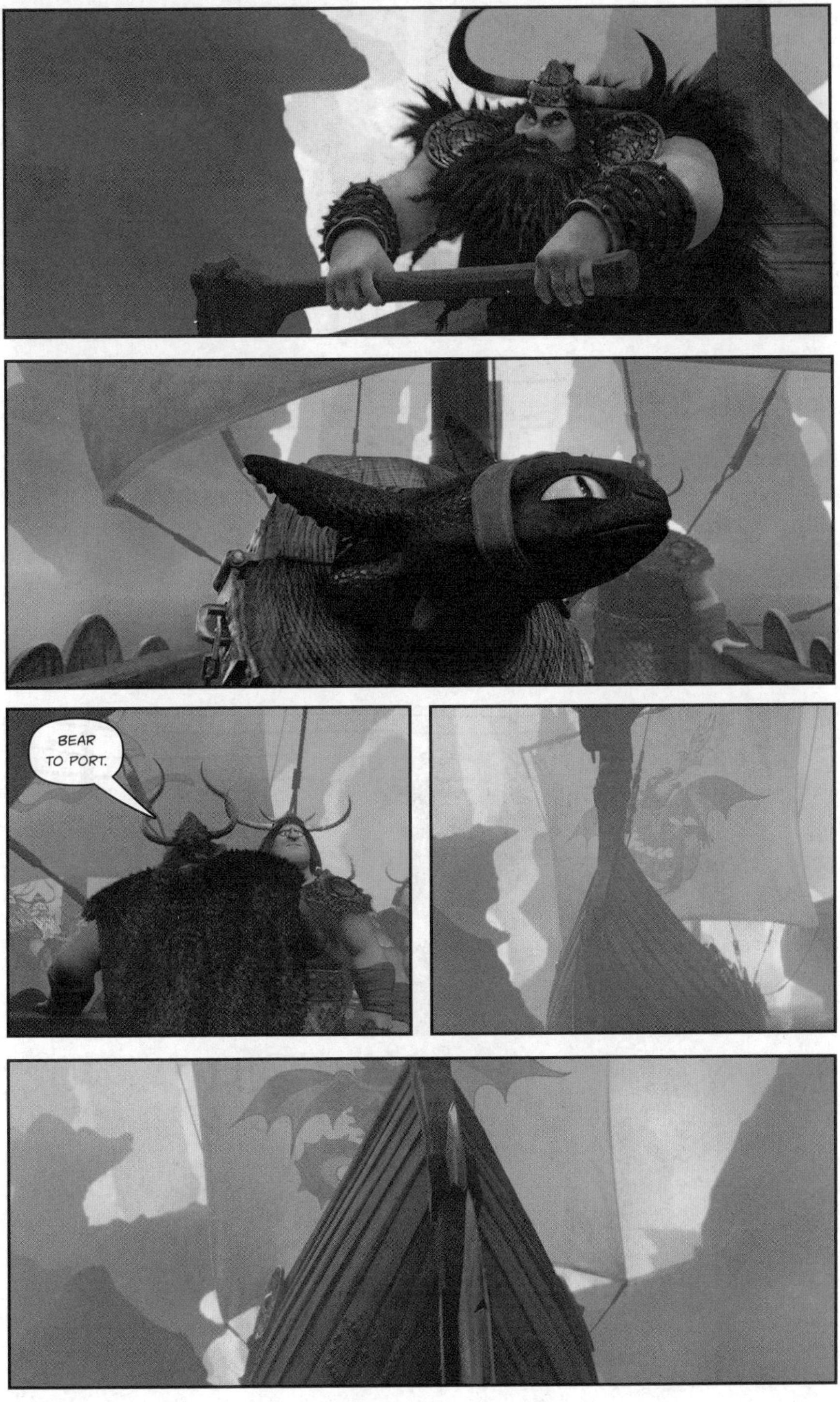
BEAR TO PORT.

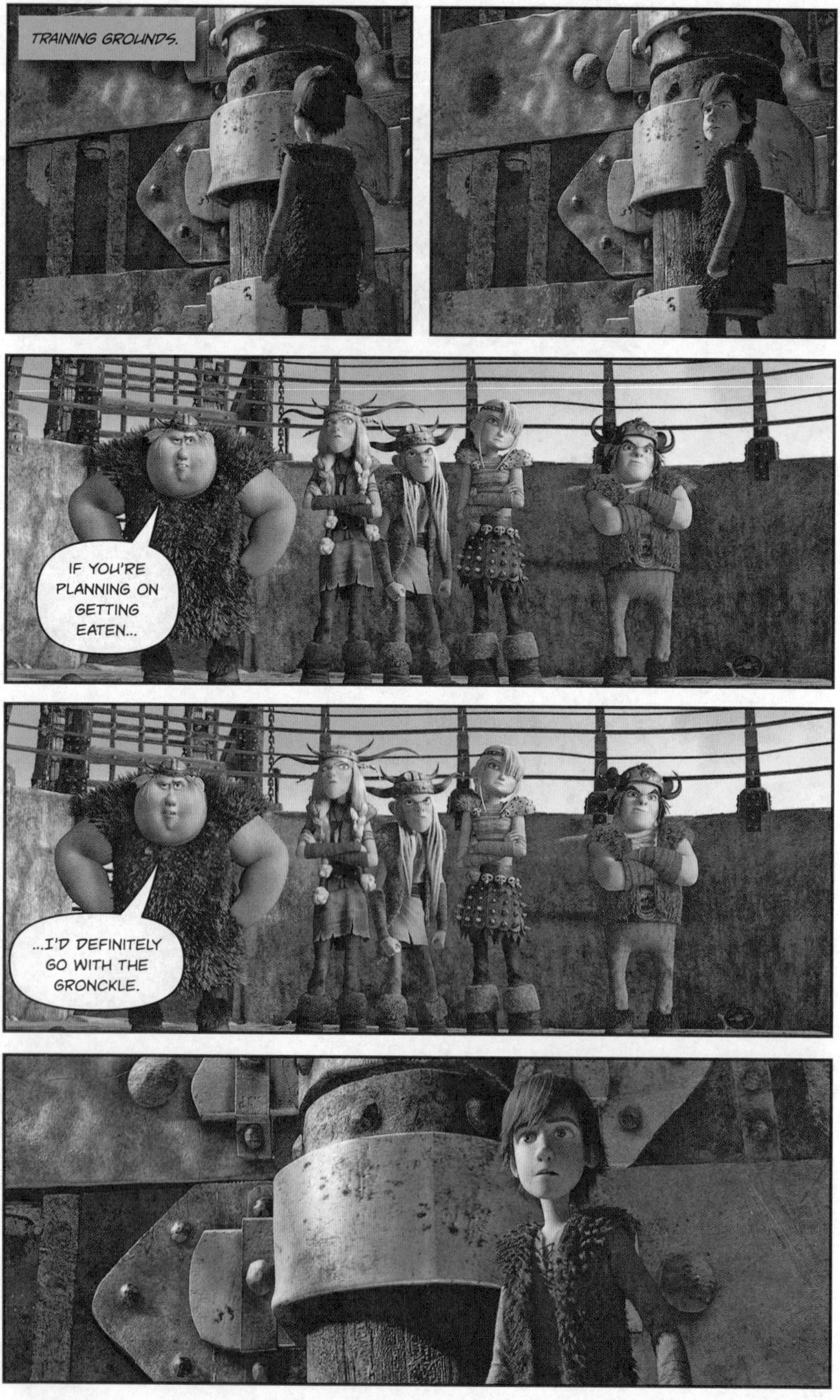
TRAINING GROUNDS.
IF YOU'RE PLANNING ON GETTING EATEN...
...I'D DEFINITELY GO WITH THE GRONCKLE.

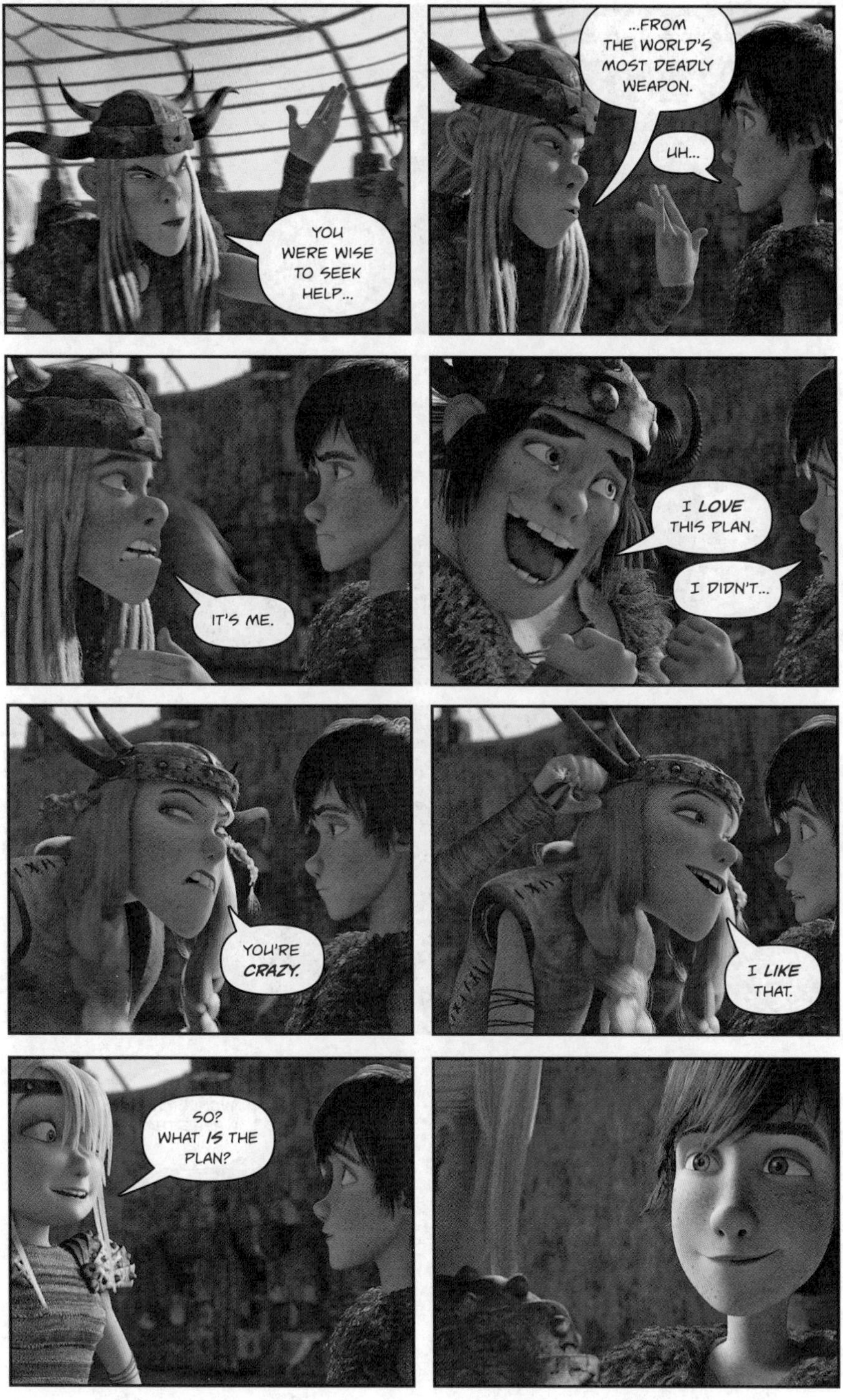
YOU WERE WISE TO SEEK HELP...
...FROM THE WORLD'S MOST DEADLY WEAPON.
UH...
IT'S ME.
I LOVE THIS PLAN.
I DIDN'T...
YOU'RE CRAZY.
I LIKE THAT.
SO? WHAT IS THE PLAN?

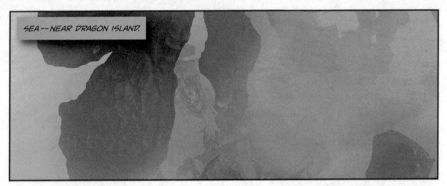

SEA--NEAR DRAGON ISLAND.

OH MY.

THAT'S NOT VERY ENCOURAGING.

AH.

I WAS WONDERING WHERE THAT WENT.

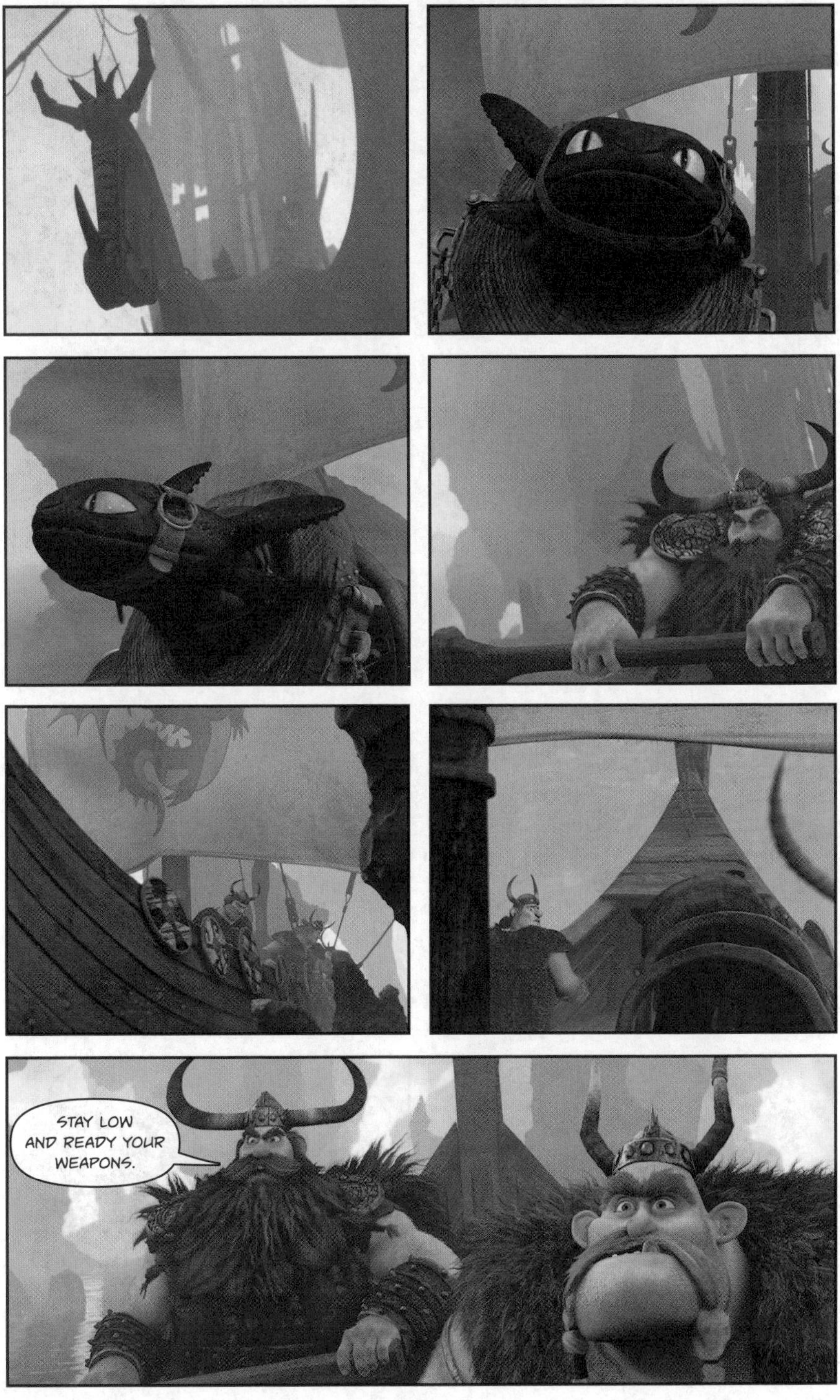
STAY LOW AND READY YOUR WEAPONS.

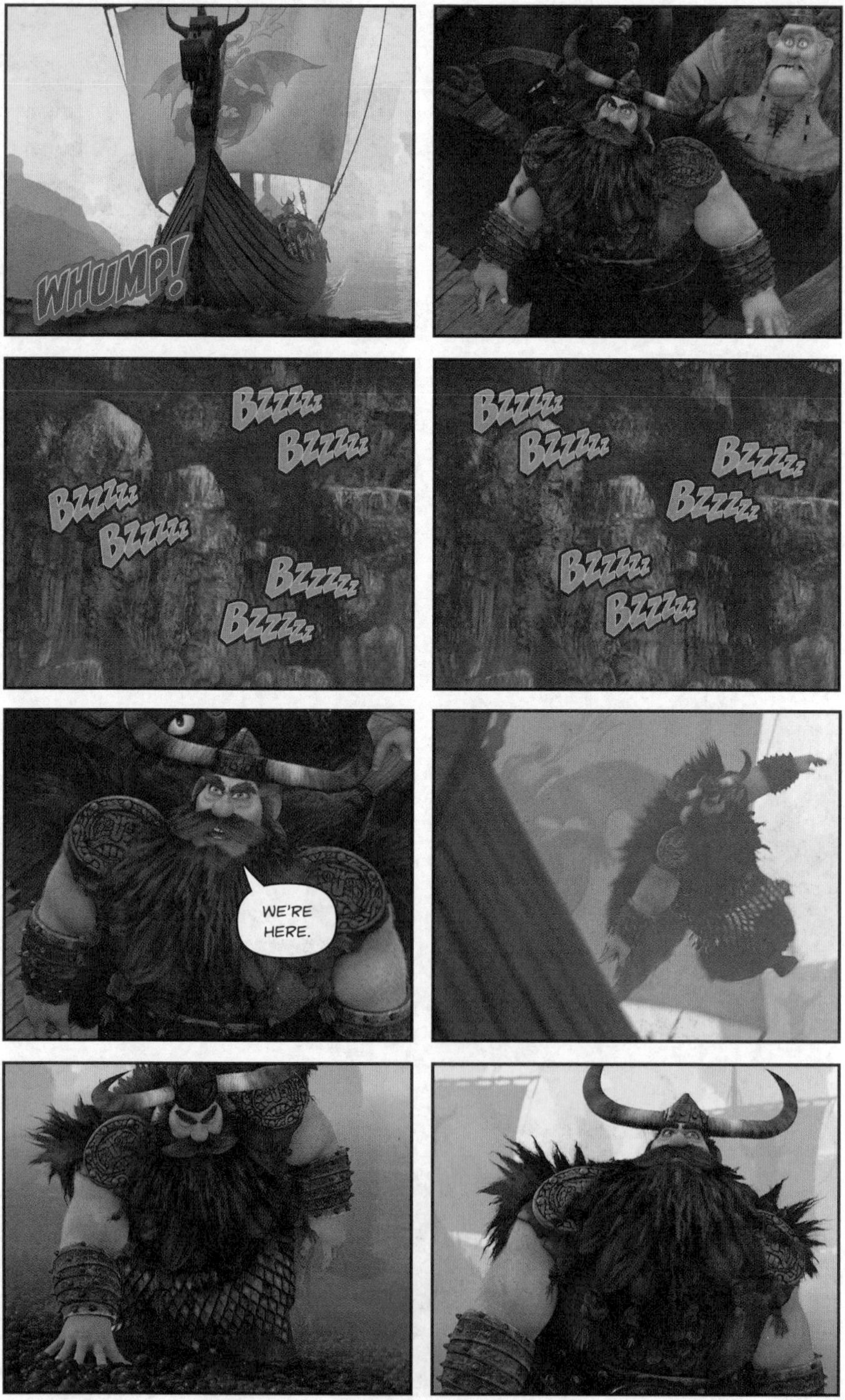
WHUMP!
Bzzzzz
Bzzzzz
Bzzzzz
Bzzzzz
Bzzzzz
Bzzzzz
Bzzzzz
Bzzzzz
Bzzzzz
Bzzzzz
Bzzzzz
Bzzzzz
WE'RE HERE.

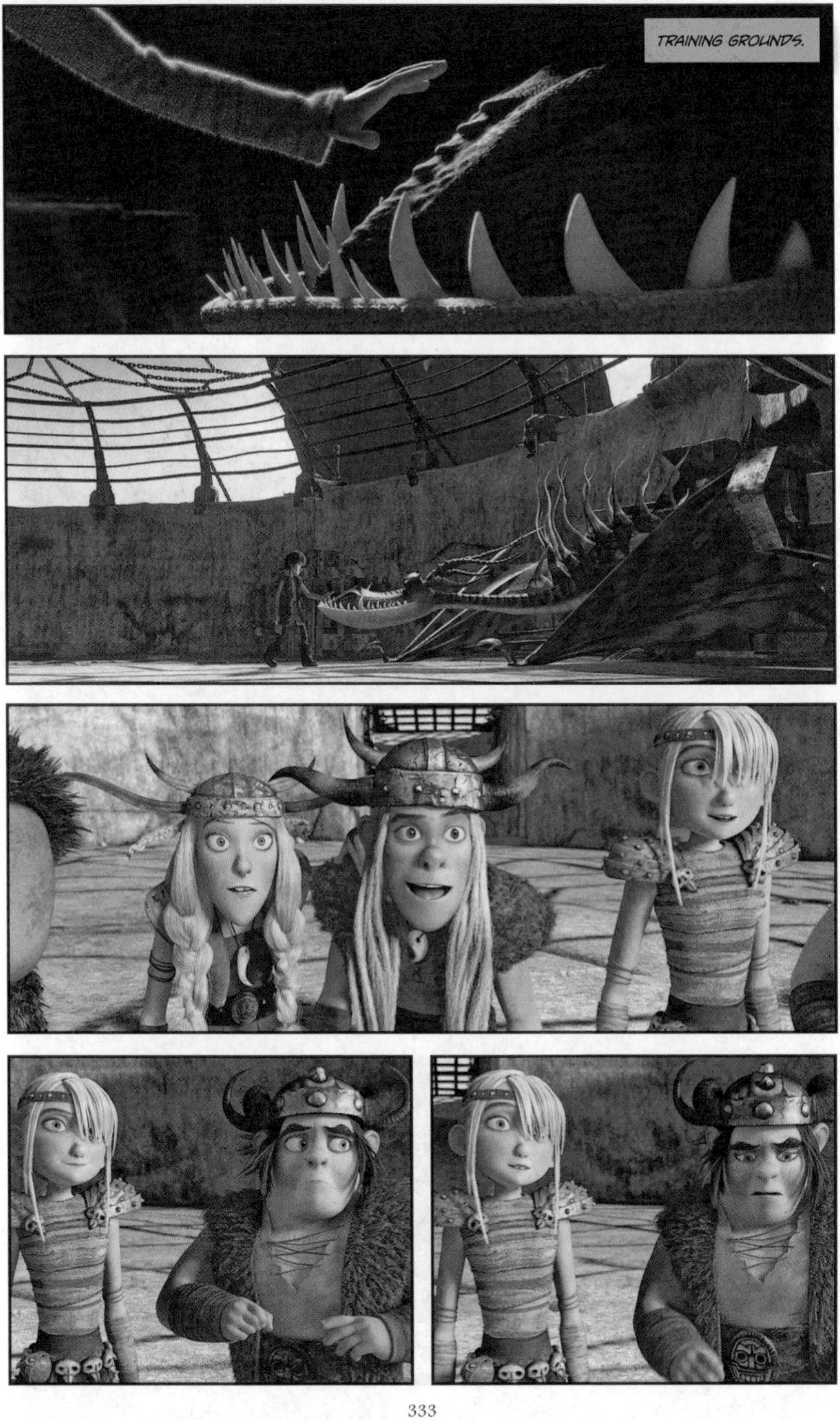
TRAINING GROUNDS.

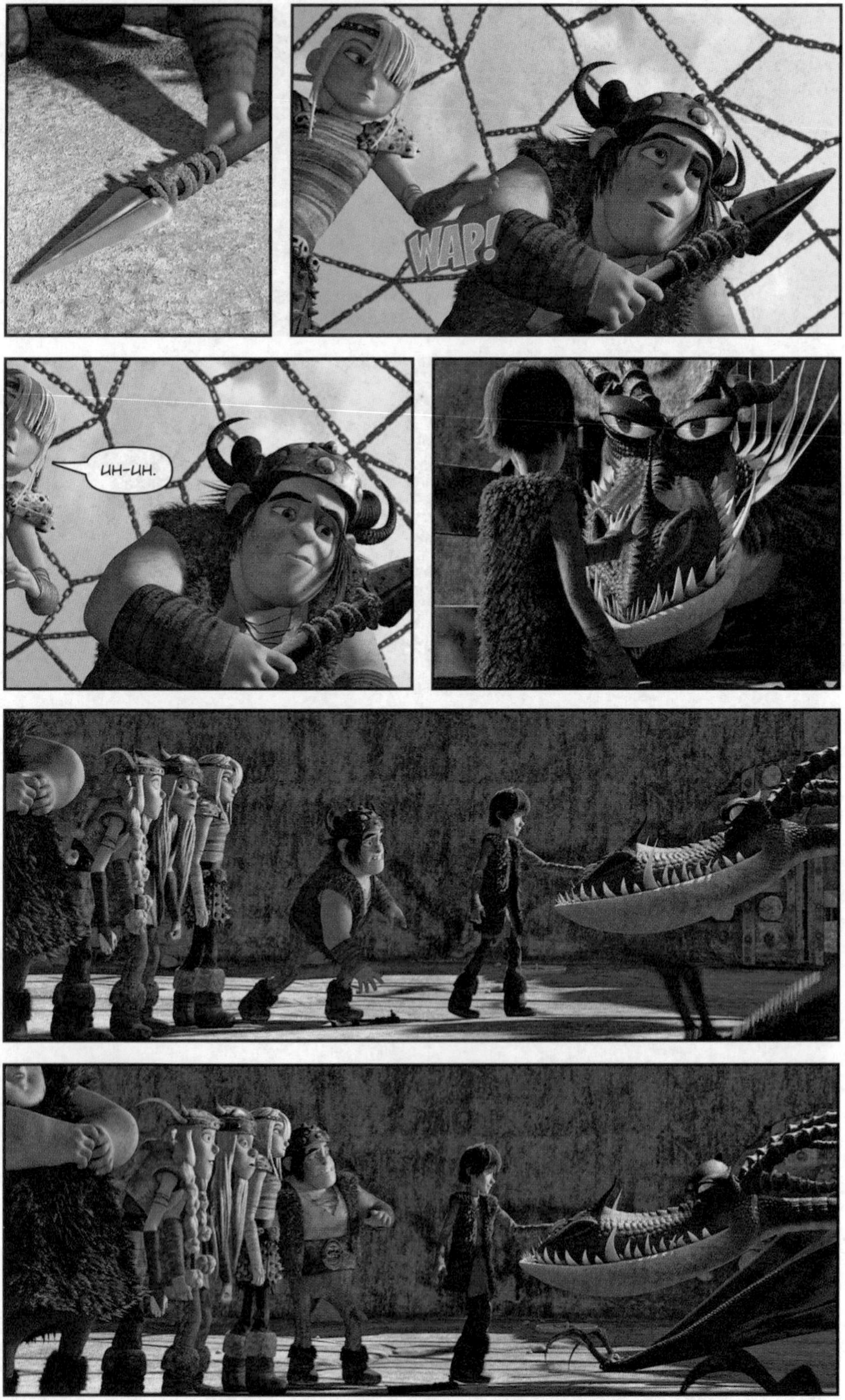
WAP!
UH-UH.

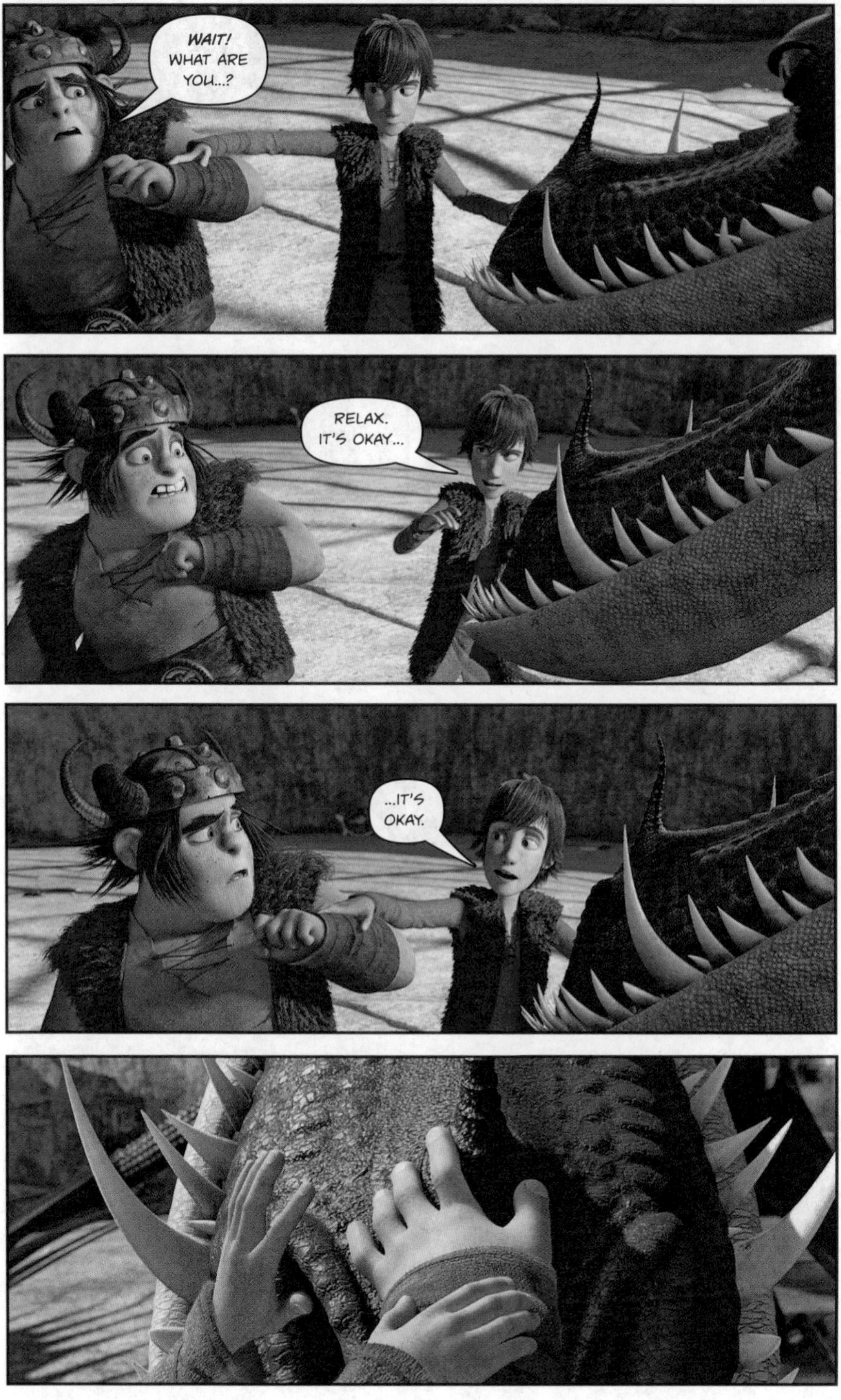
WAIT! WHAT ARE YOU...?
RELAX. IT'S OKAY...
...IT'S OKAY.

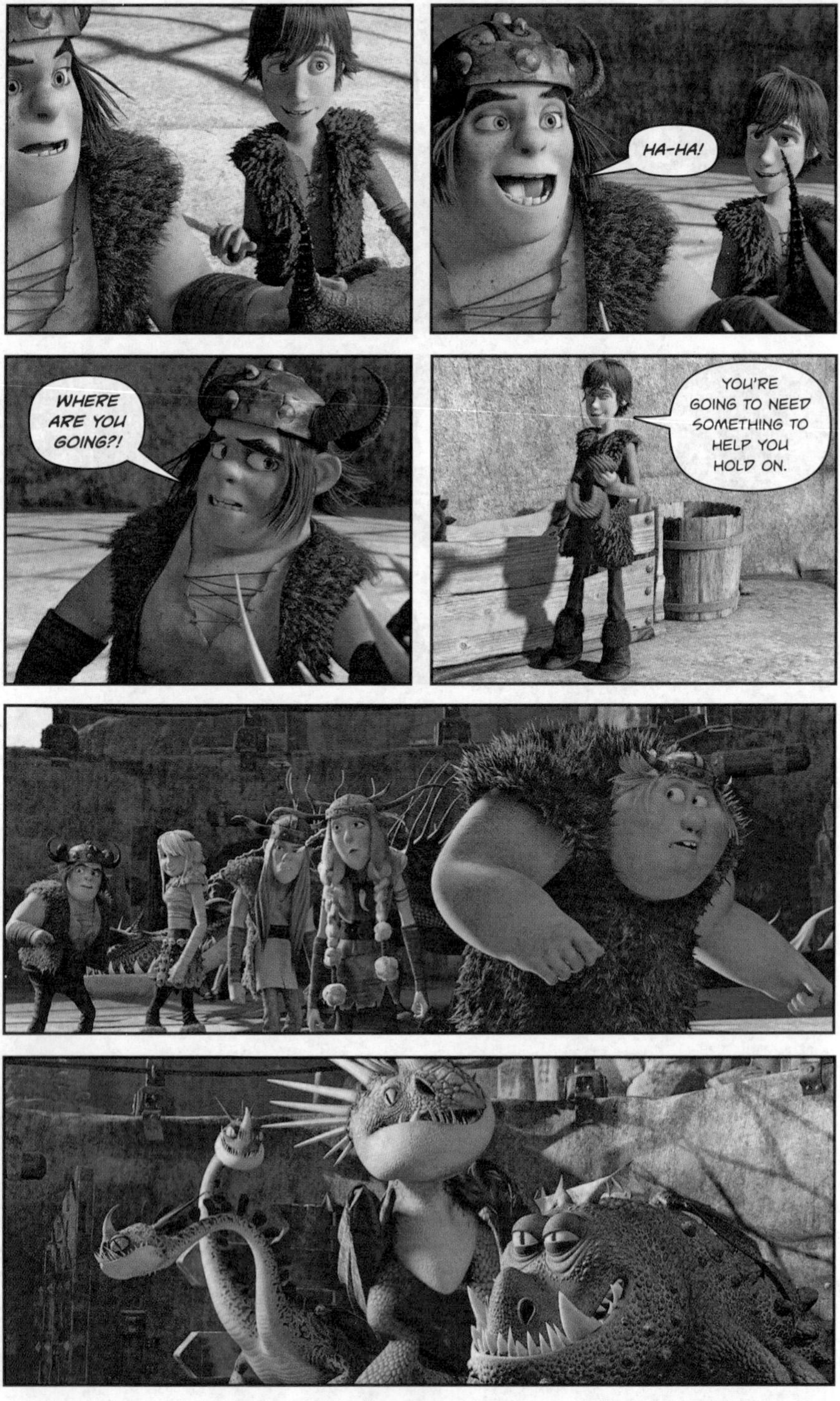
HA-HA!
WHERE ARE YOU GOING?!
YOU'RE GOING TO NEED SOMETHING TO HELP YOU HOLD ON.

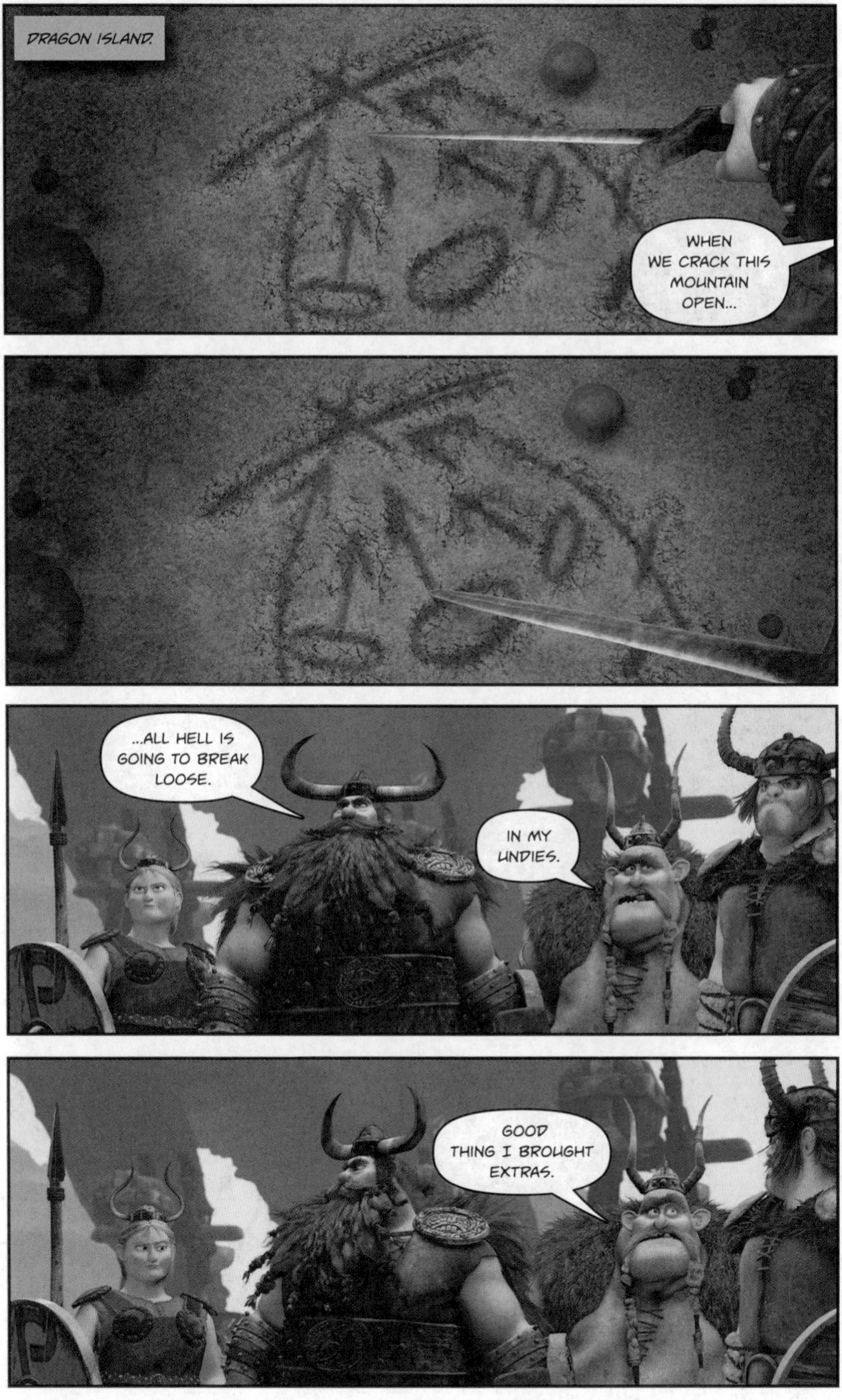
DRAGON ISLAND.
WHEN WE CRACK THIS MOUNTAIN OPEN...
...ALL HELL IS GOING TO BREAK LOOSE.
IN MY UNDIES.
GOOD THING I BROUGHT EXTRAS.

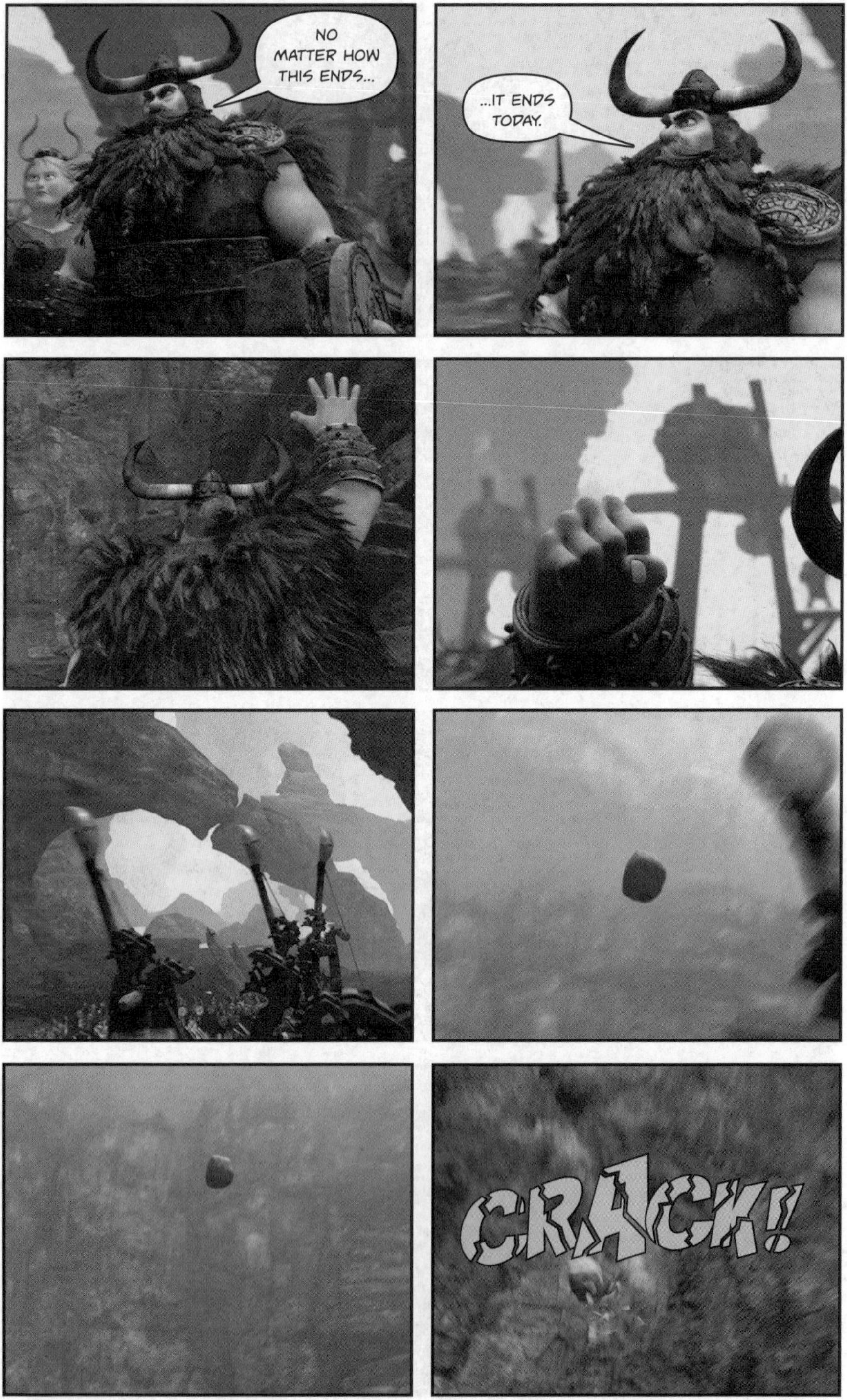
NO MATTER HOW THIS ENDS...
...IT ENDS TODAY.
CRACK!

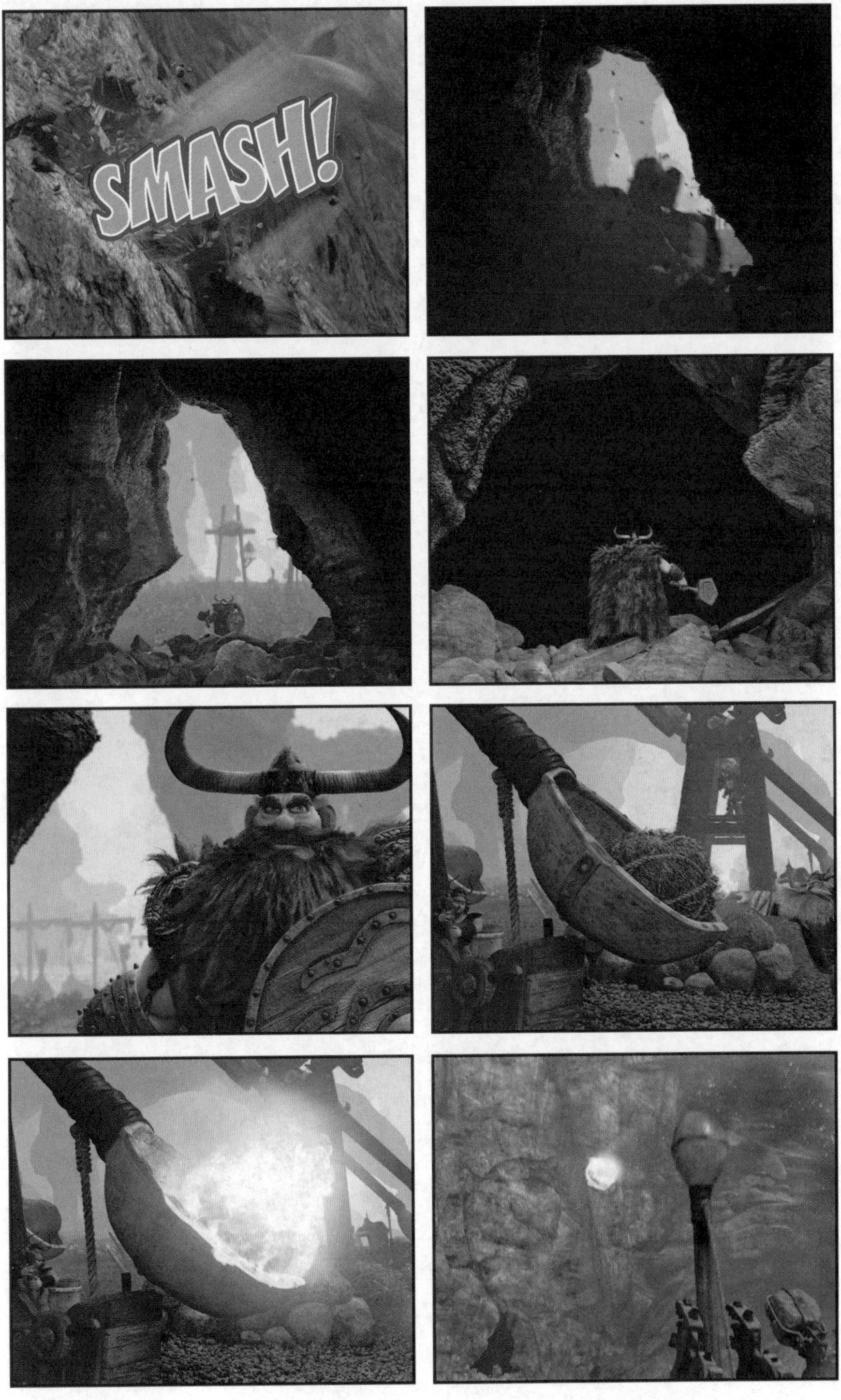
SMASH!

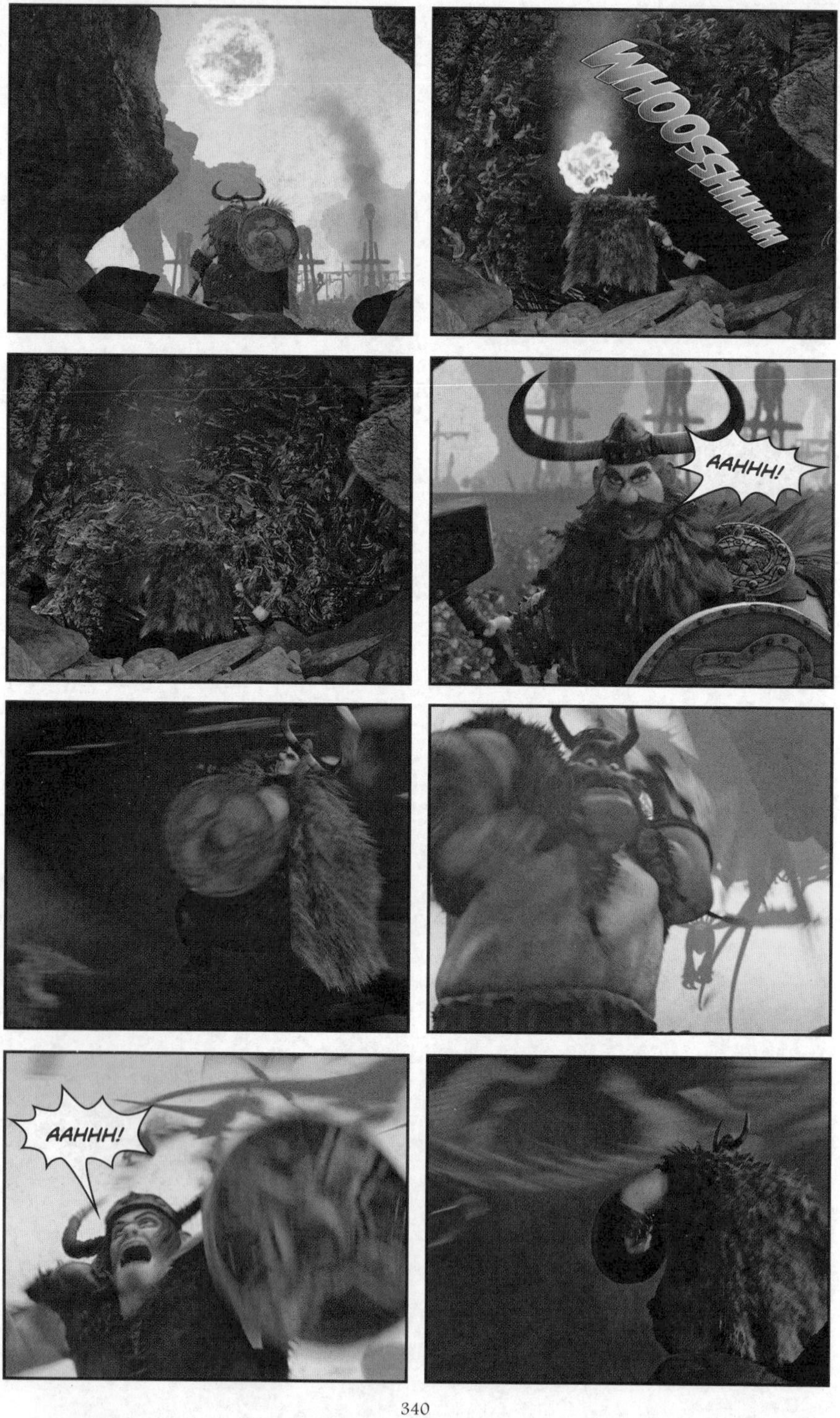
WHOOSSHHHHH
AAHHH!
AAHHH!

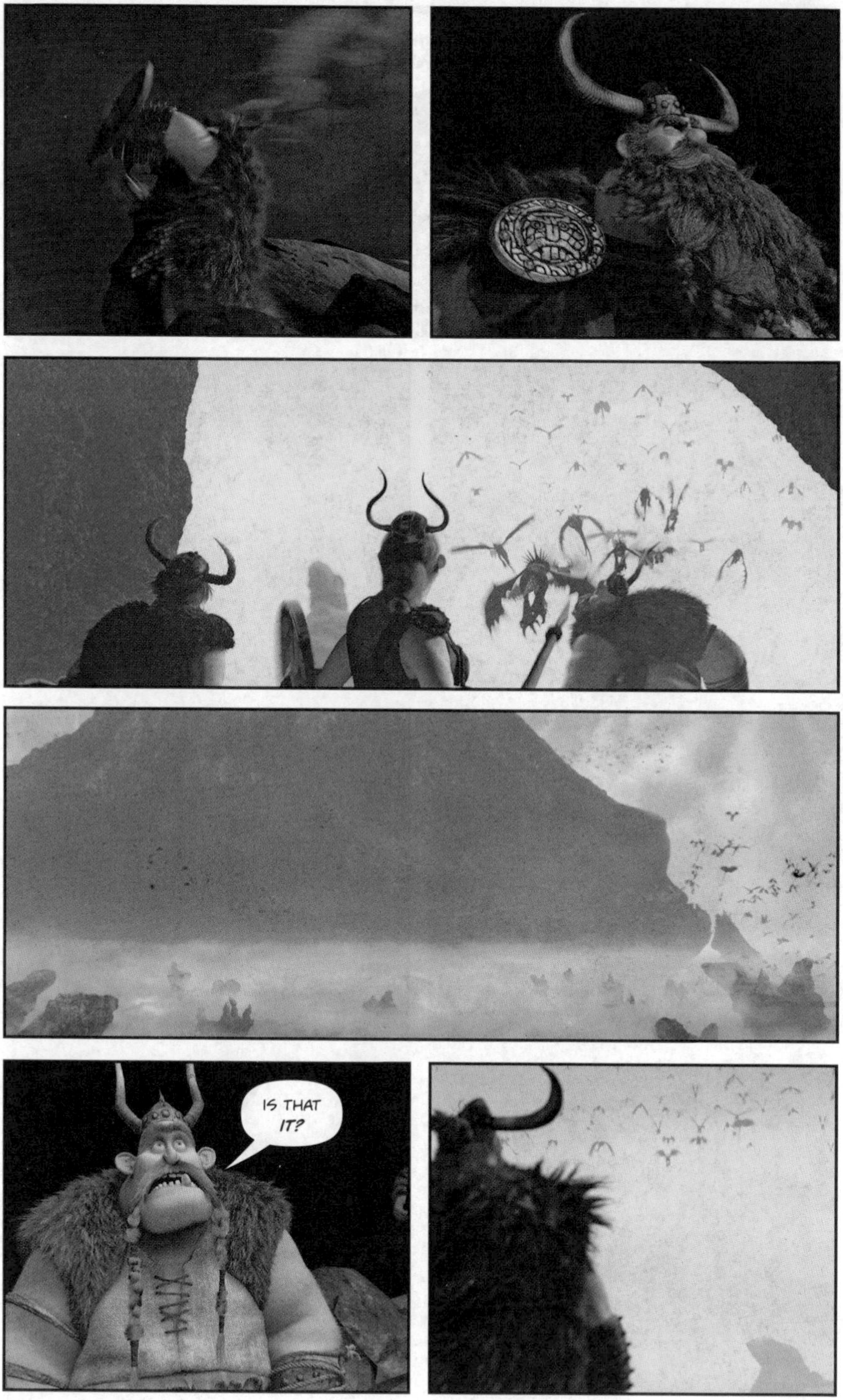
IS THAT IT?

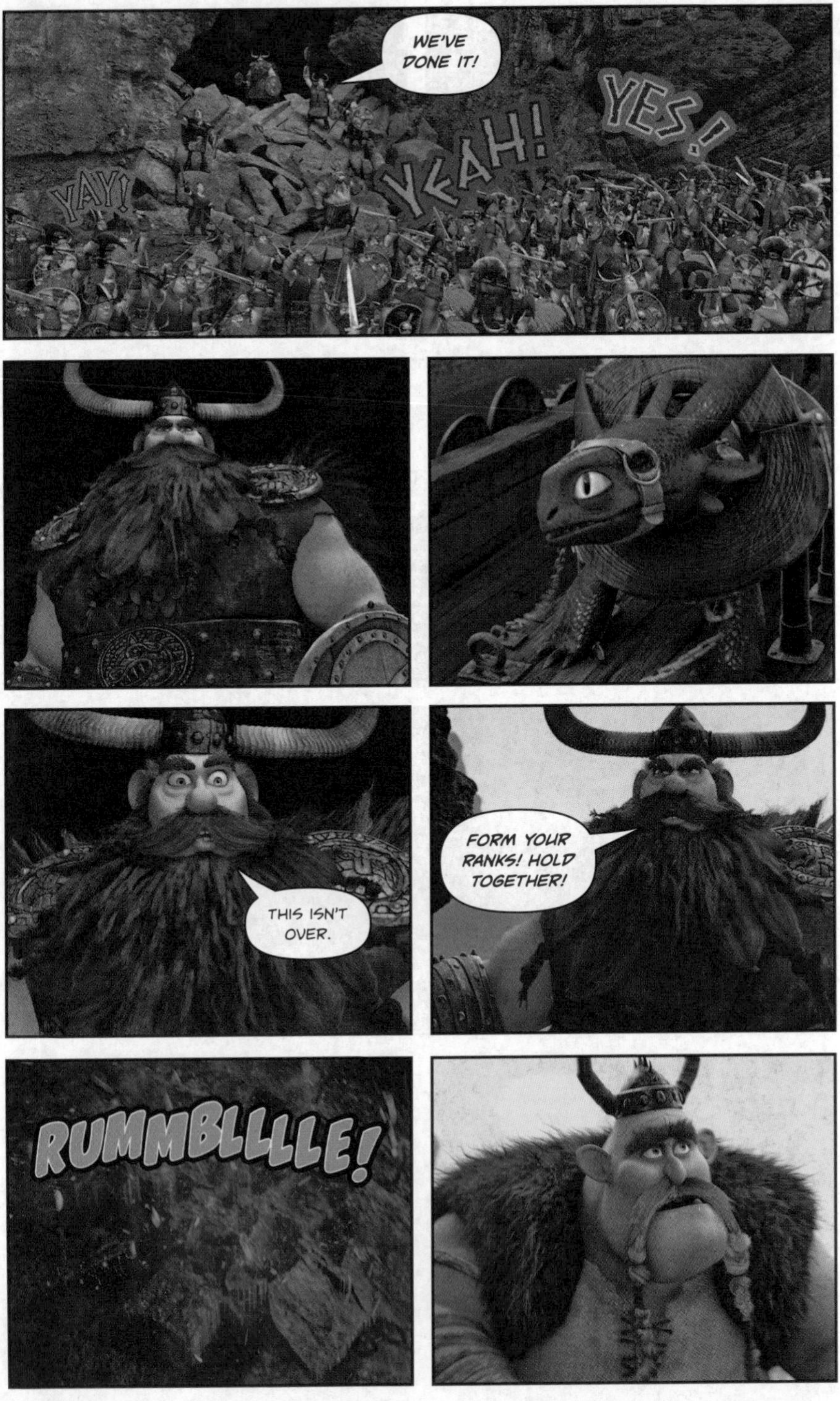

WE'VE DONE IT!
YAY!
YEAH!
YES!
THIS ISN'T OVER.
FORM YOUR RANKS! HOLD TOGETHER!
RUMMBLLLLE!

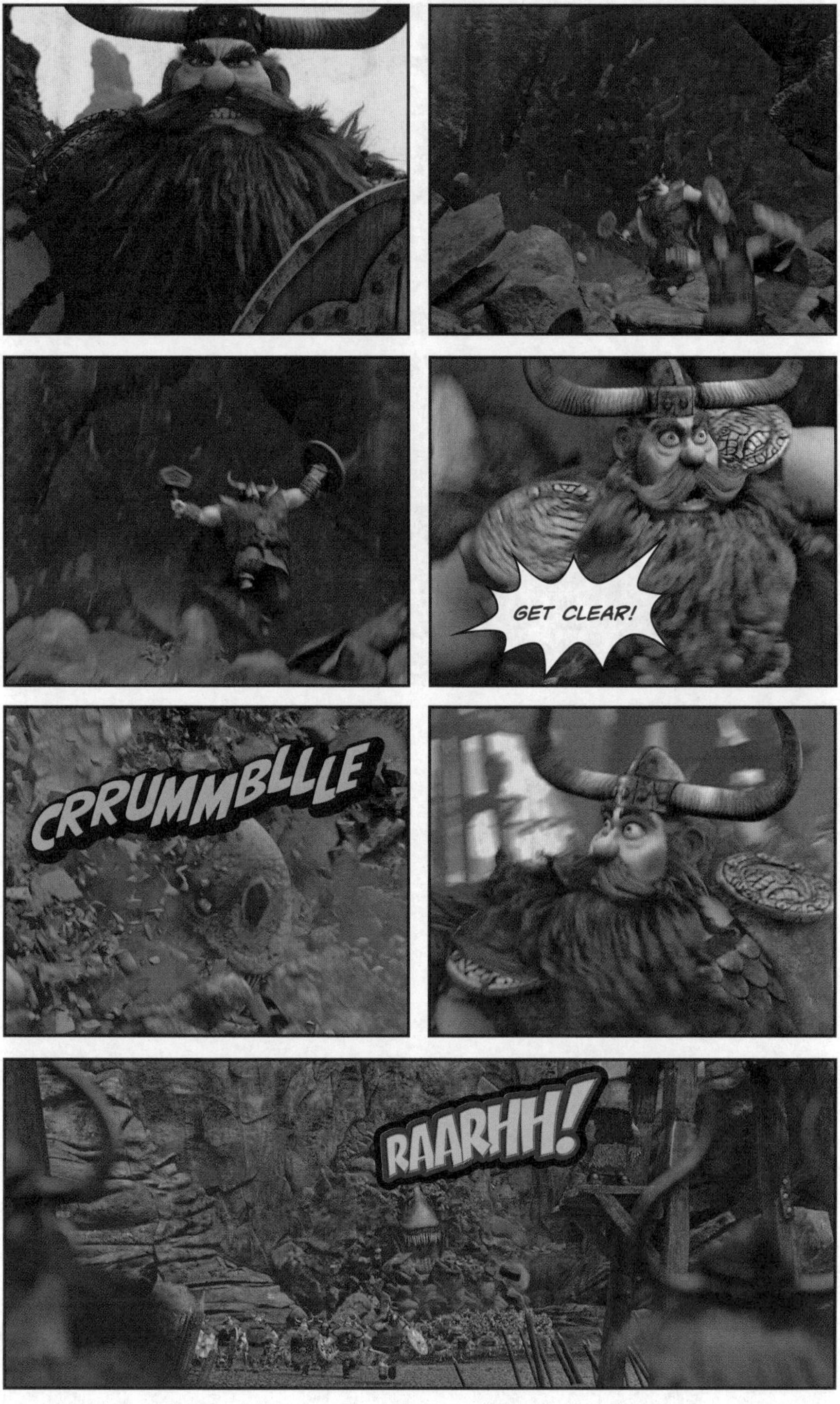
GET CLEAR!
CRRUMMBLLLE
RAARHH!

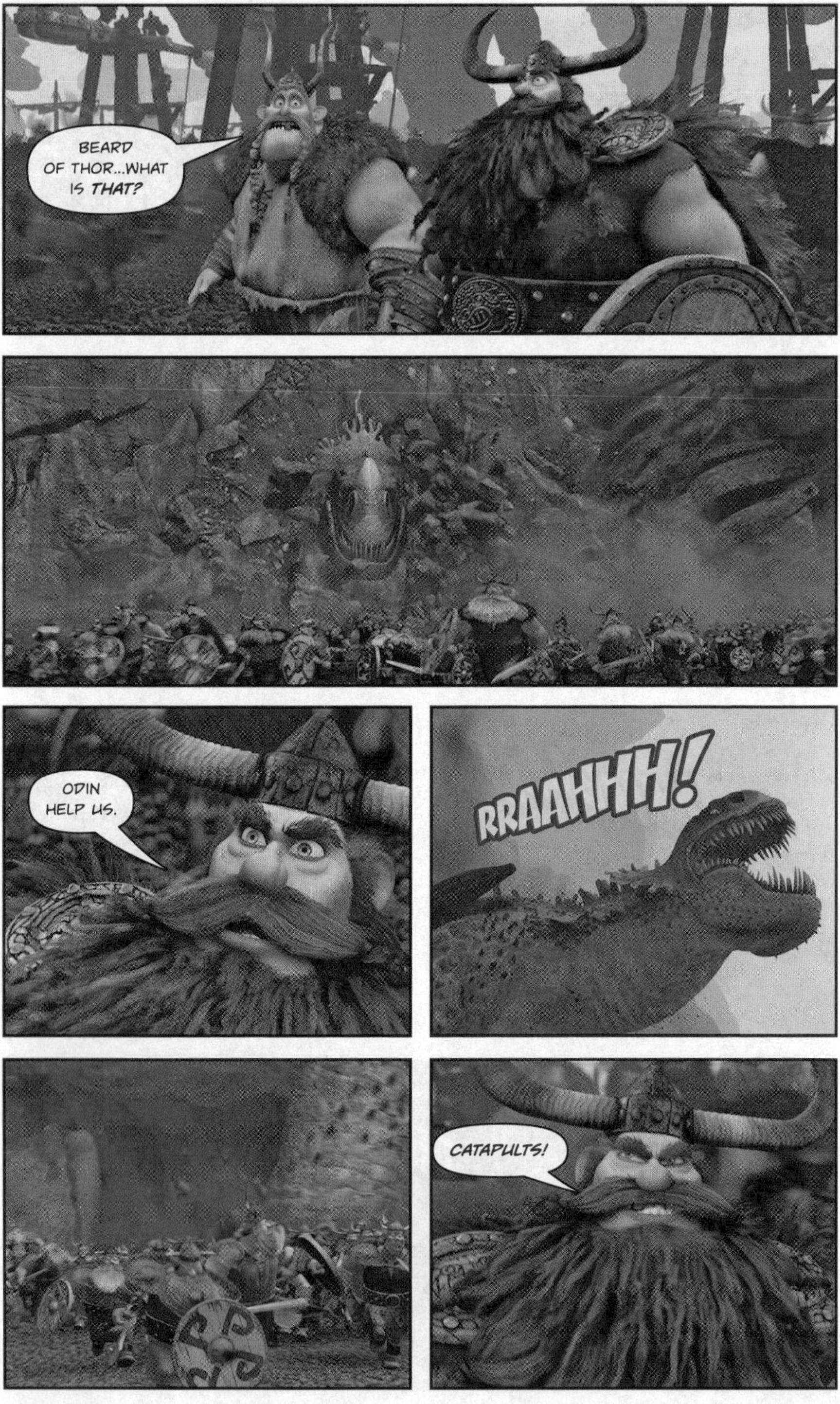
BEARD OF THOR...WHAT IS THAT?
ODIN HELP US.
RRAAHHH!
CATAPULTS!

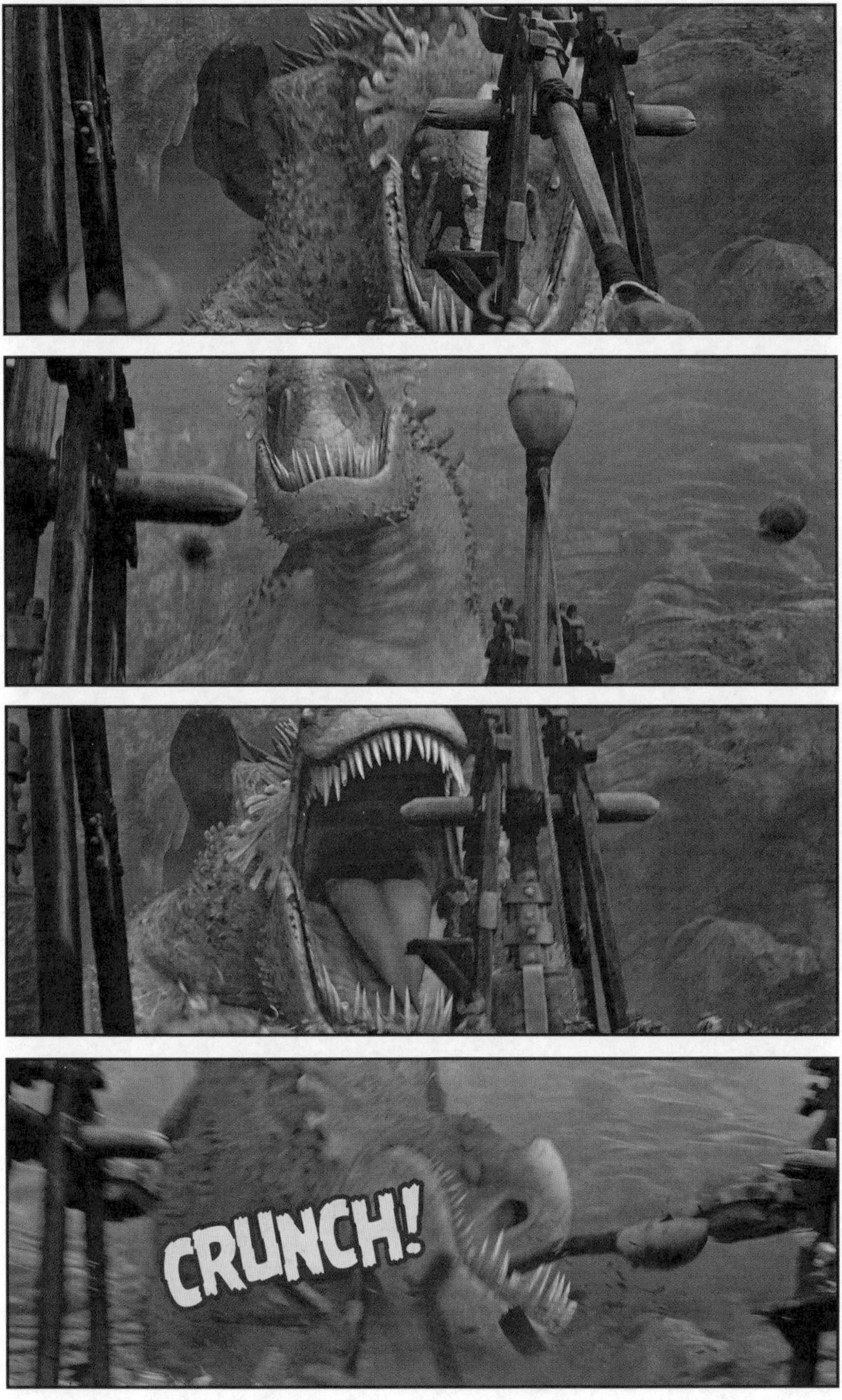
CRUNCH!

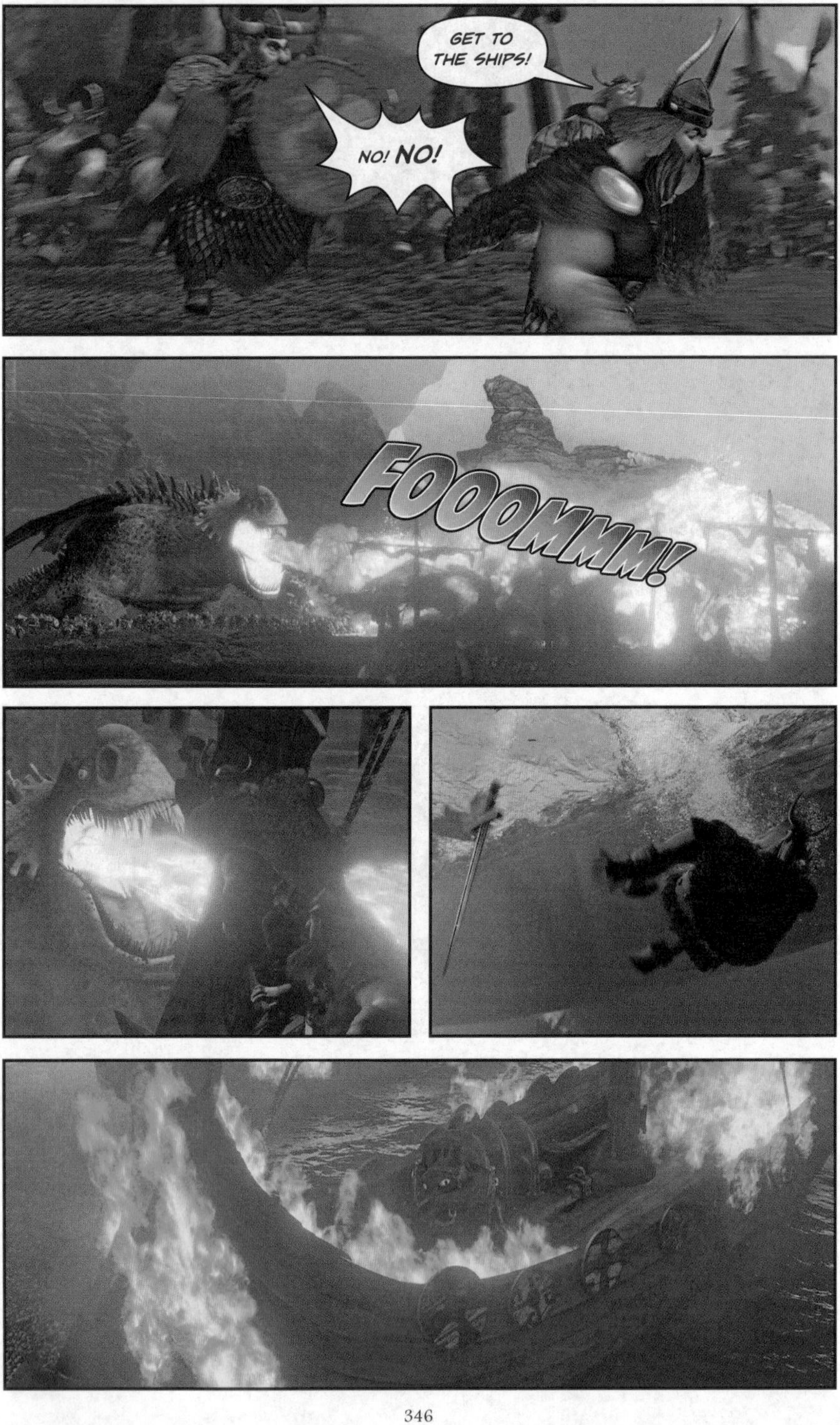
GET TO THE SHIPS!
NO! NO!
FOOOMMM!

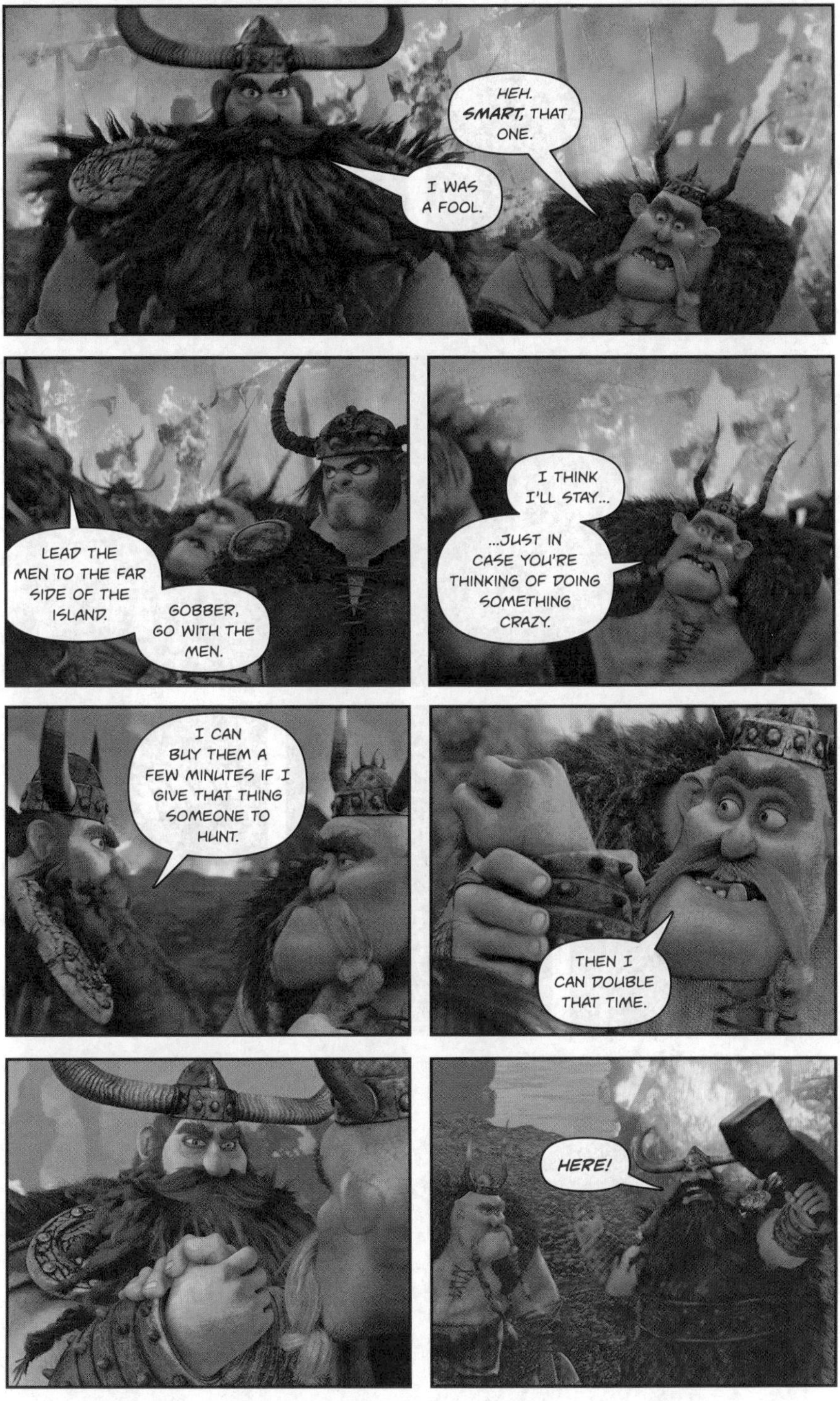
I WAS A FOOL.
HEH. SMART, THAT ONE.
LEAD THE MEN TO THE FAR SIDE OF THE ISLAND.
GOBBER, GO WITH THE MEN.
I THINK I'LL STAY...
...JUST IN CASE YOU'RE THINKING OF DOING SOMETHING CRAZY.
I CAN BUY THEM A FEW MINUTES IF I GIVE THAT THING SOMEONE TO HUNT.
THEN I CAN DOUBLE THAT TIME.
HERE!

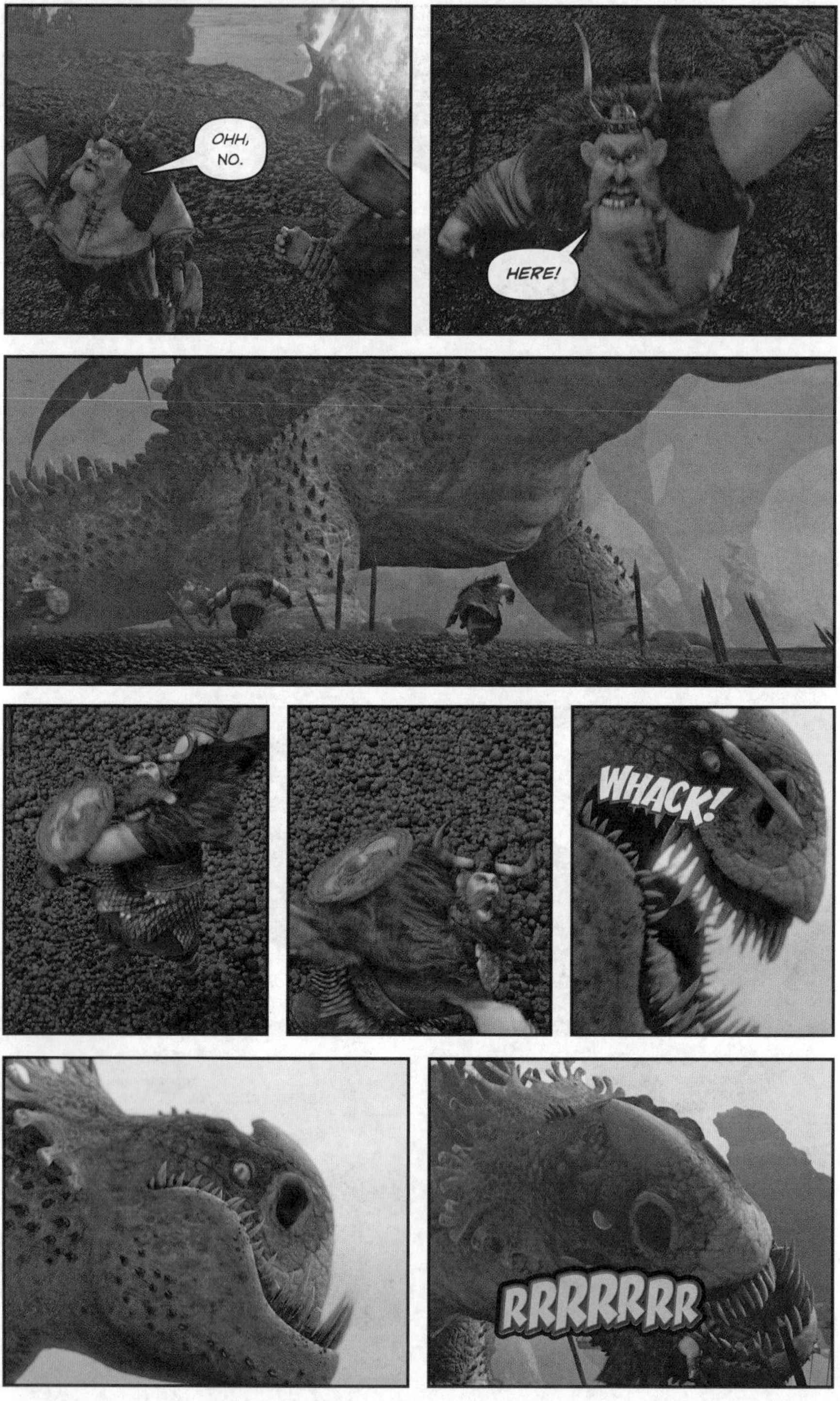
OHH, NO.
HERE!
WHACK!
RRRRRRR

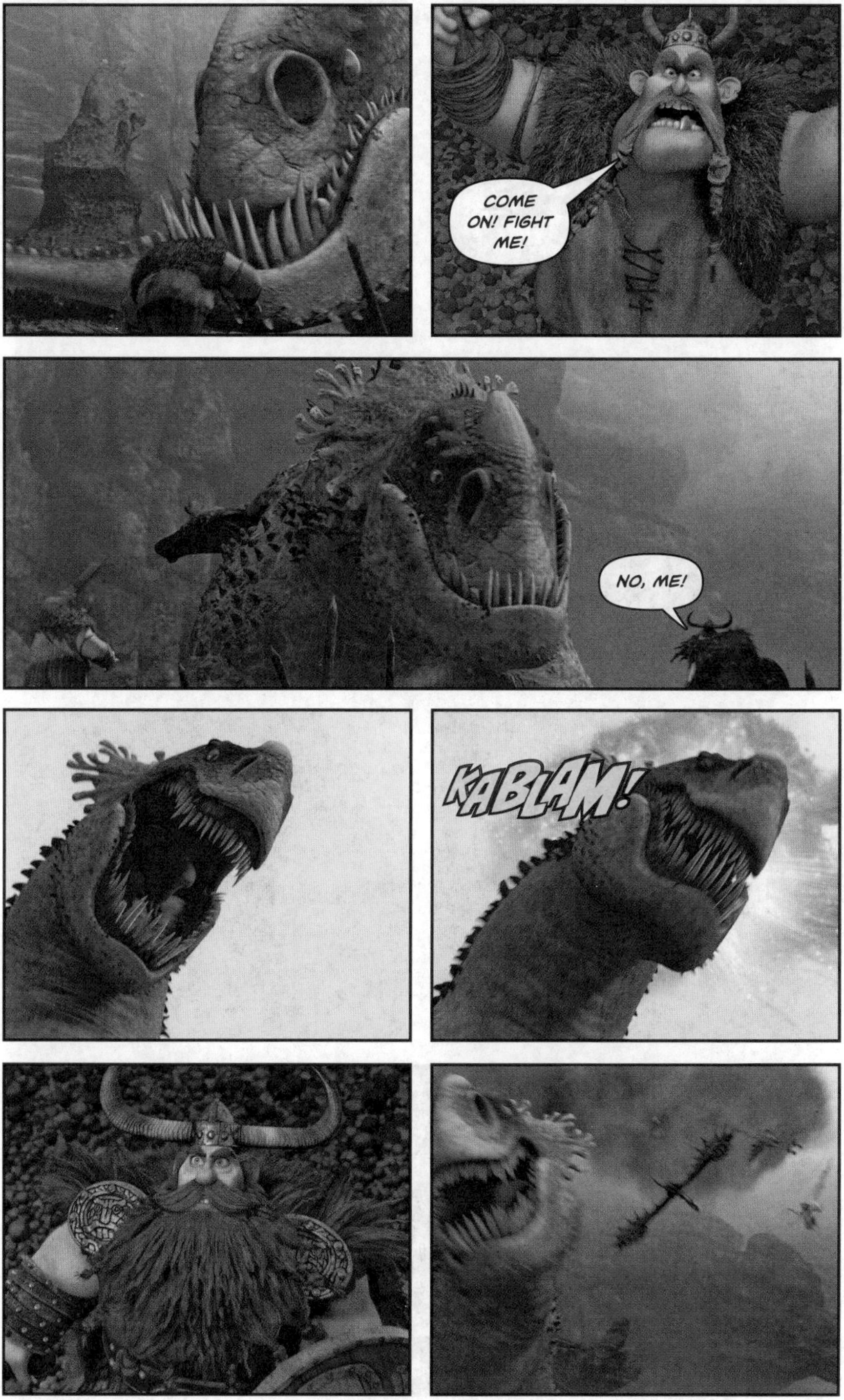
COME ON! FIGHT ME!
NO, ME!
KABLAM!

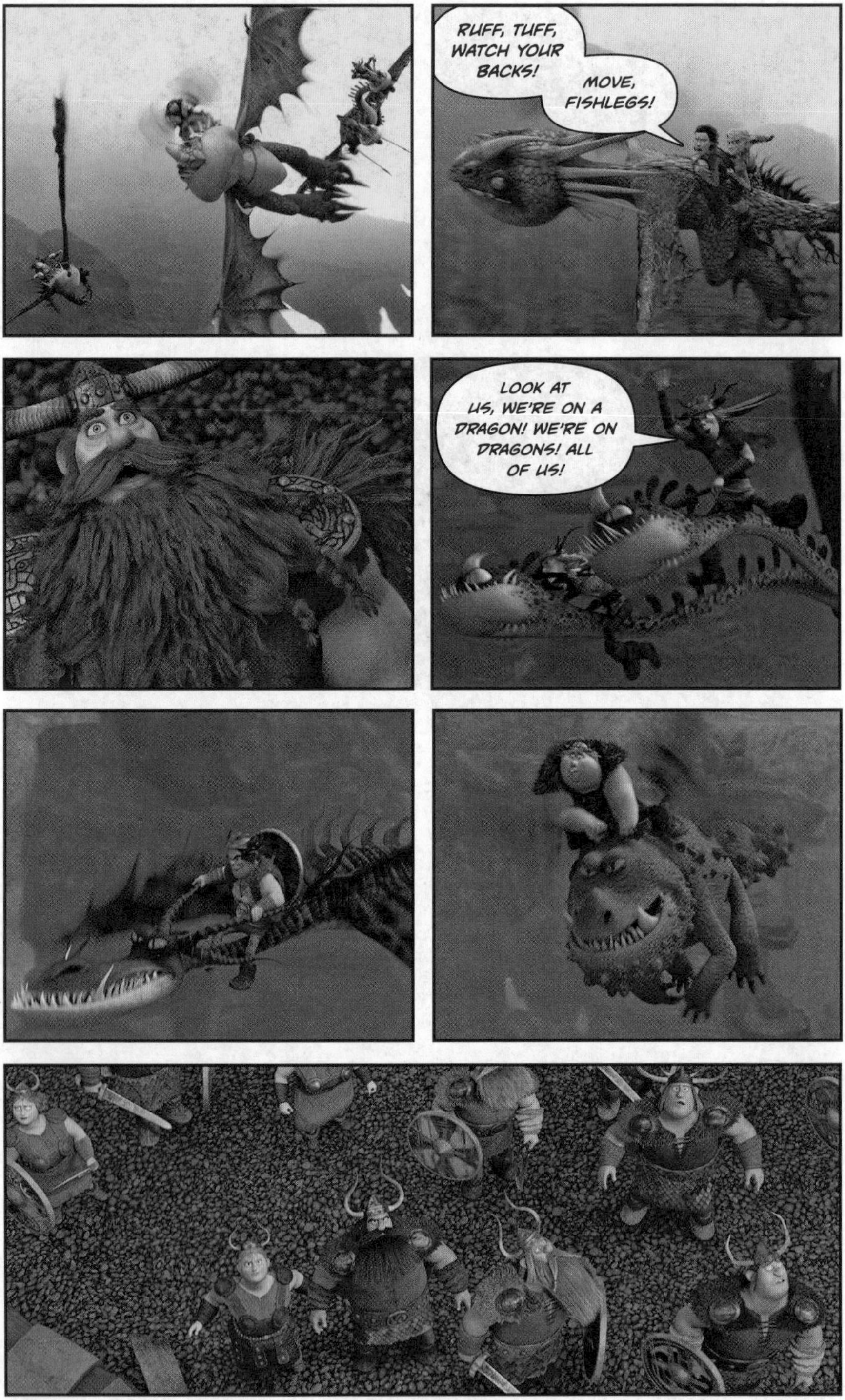
RUFF, TUFF, WATCH YOUR BACKS!
MOVE, FISHLEGS!
LOOK AT US, WE'RE ON A DRAGON! WE'RE ON DRAGONS! ALL OF US!

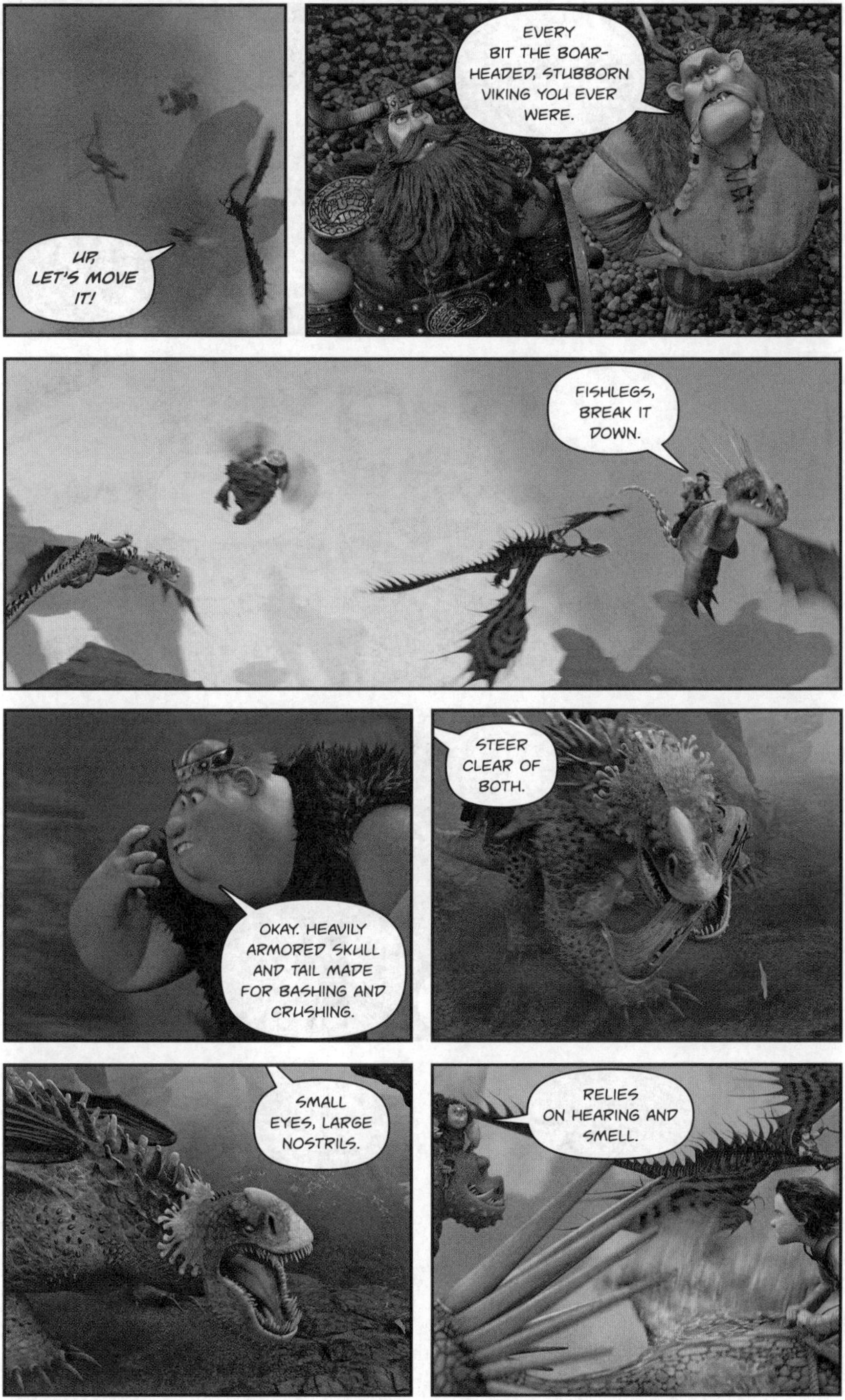
UP, LET'S MOVE IT!
EVERY BIT THE BOAR-HEADED, STUBBORN VIKING YOU EVER WERE.
FISHLEGS, BREAK IT DOWN.
OKAY. HEAVILY ARMORED SKULL AND TAIL MADE FOR BASHING AND CRUSHING.
STEER CLEAR OF BOTH.
SMALL EYES, LARGE NOSTRILS.
RELIES ON HEARING AND SMELL.

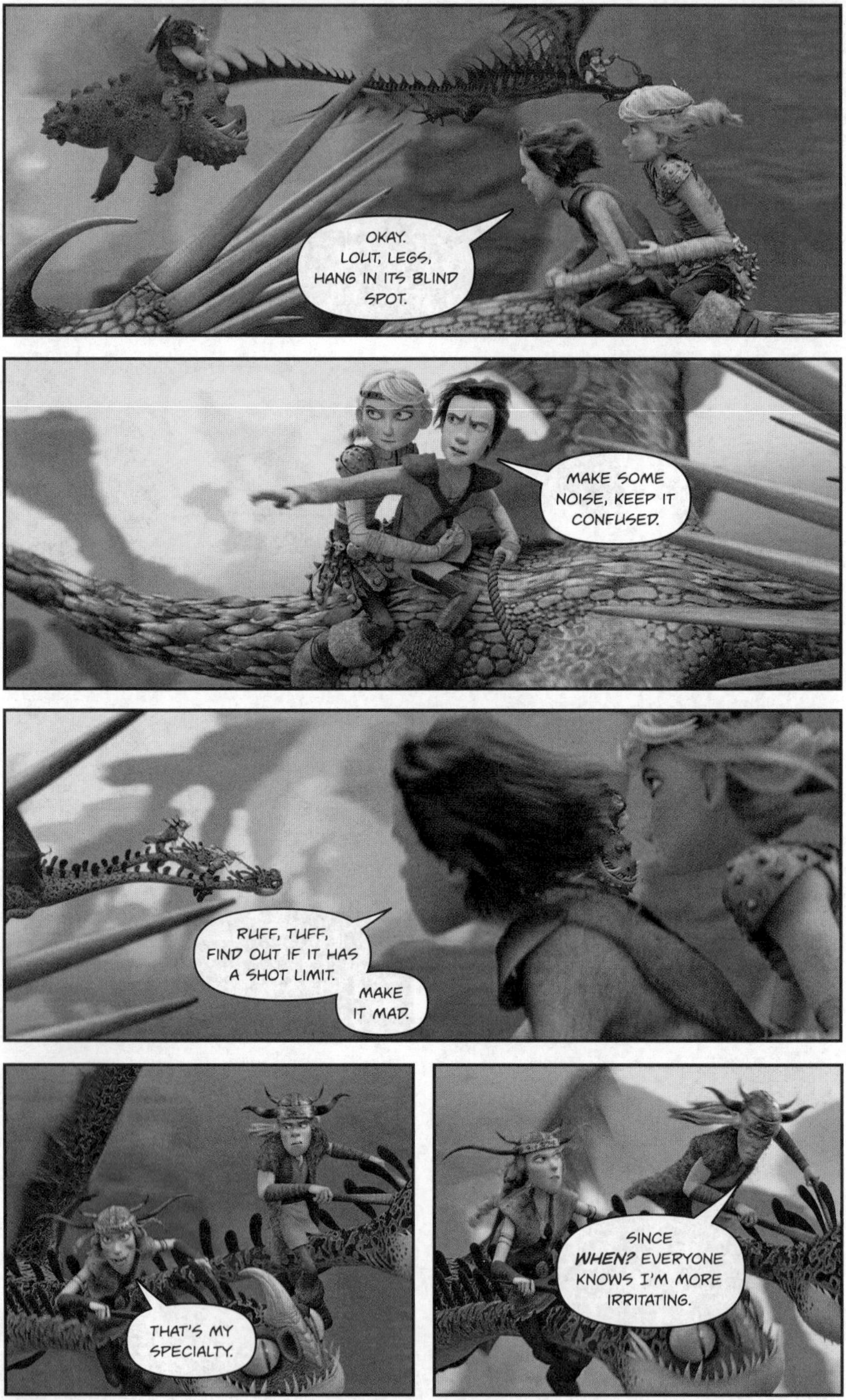
OKAY. LOUT, LEGS, HANG IN ITS BLIND SPOT.
MAKE SOME NOISE, KEEP IT CONFUSED.
RUFF, TUFF, FIND OUT IF IT HAS A SHOT LIMIT.
MAKE IT MAD.
THAT'S MY SPECIALTY.
SINCE *WHEN?* EVERYONE KNOWS I'M MORE IRRITATING.

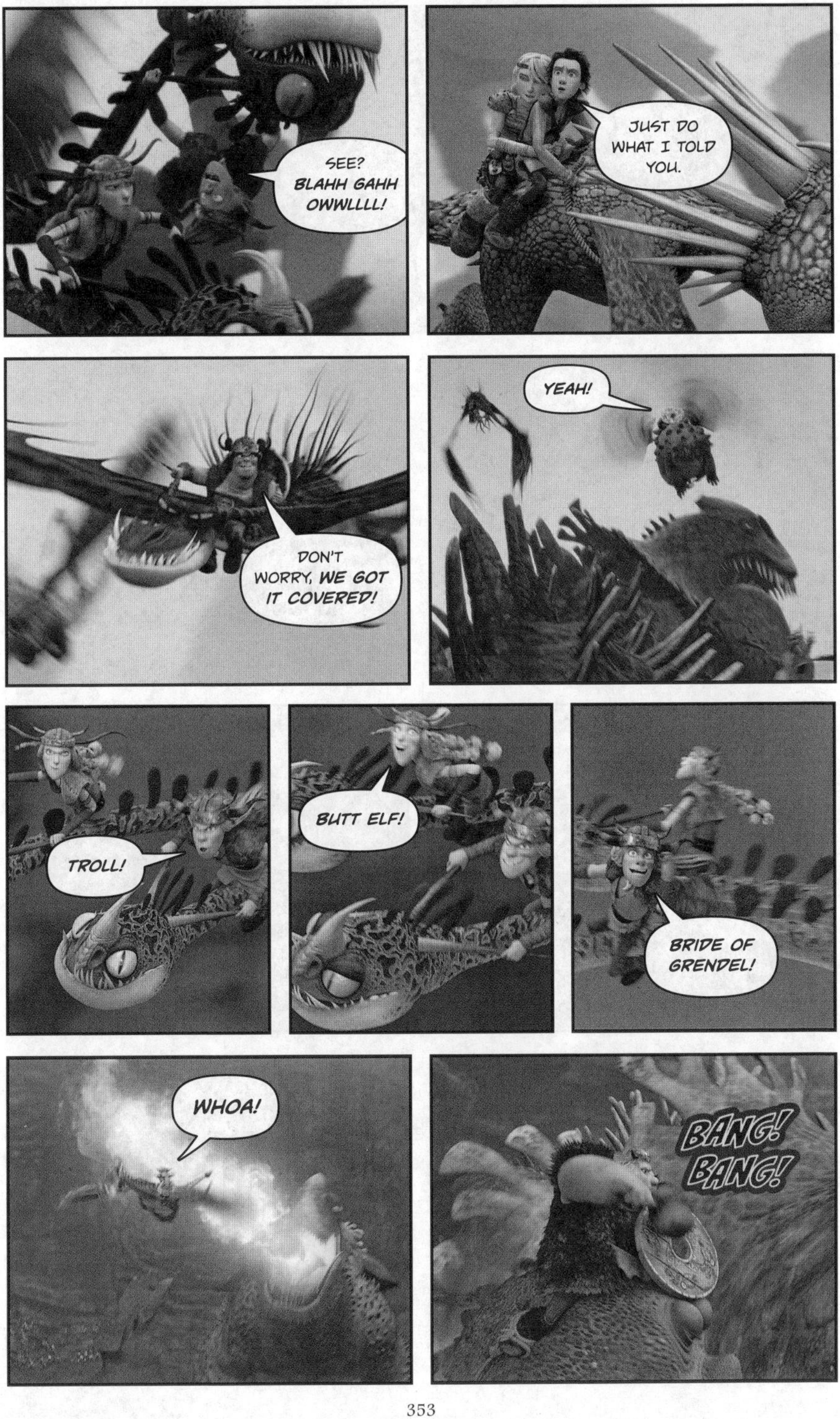
SEE? BLAHH GAHH OWLLLLL!
JUST DO WHAT I TOLD YOU.
DON'T WORRY, WE GOT IT COVERED!
YEAH!
TROLL!
BUTT ELF!
BRIDE OF GRENDEL!
WHOA!
BANG! BANG!

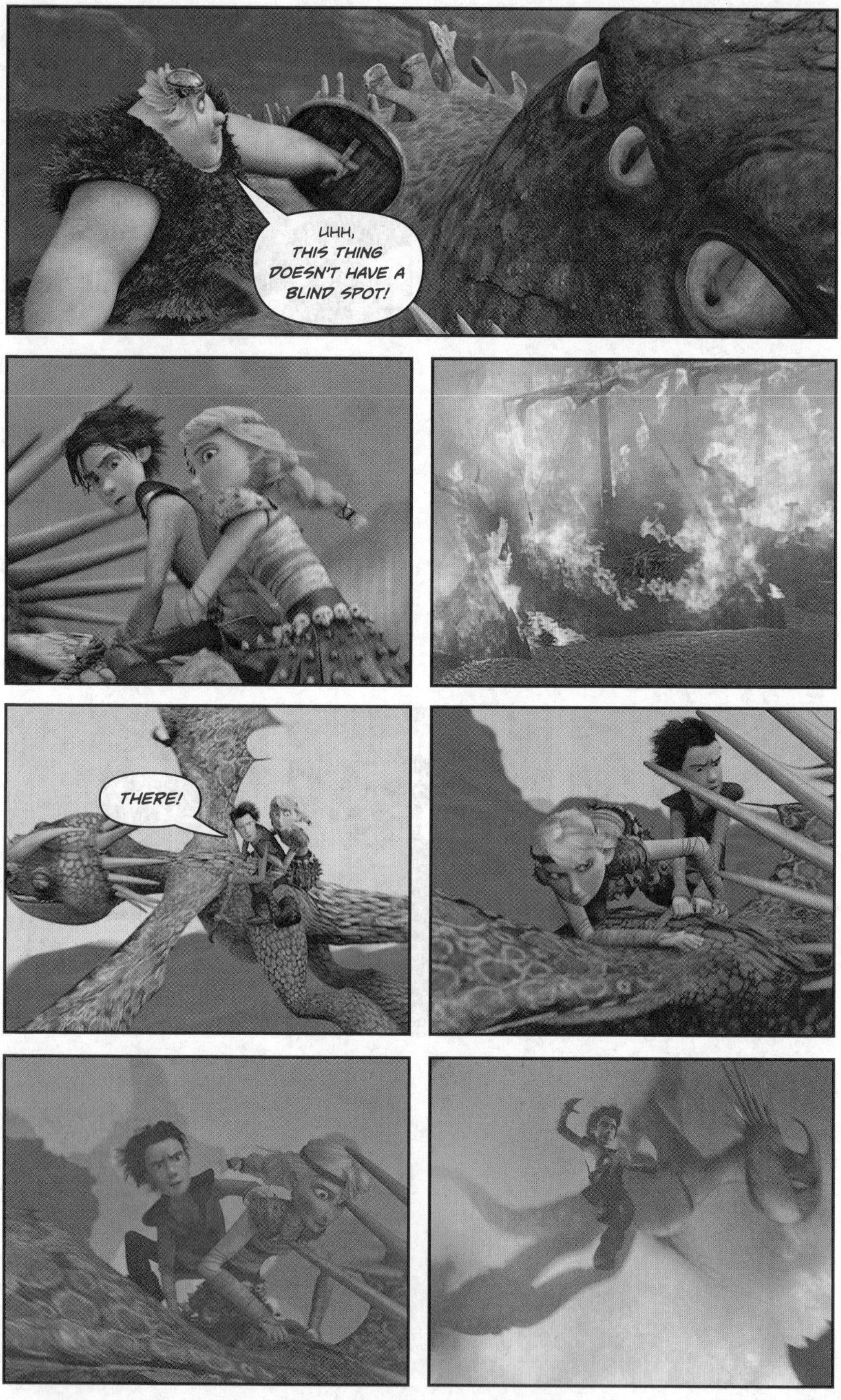
UHH, THIS THING DOESN'T HAVE A BLIND SPOT!
THERE!

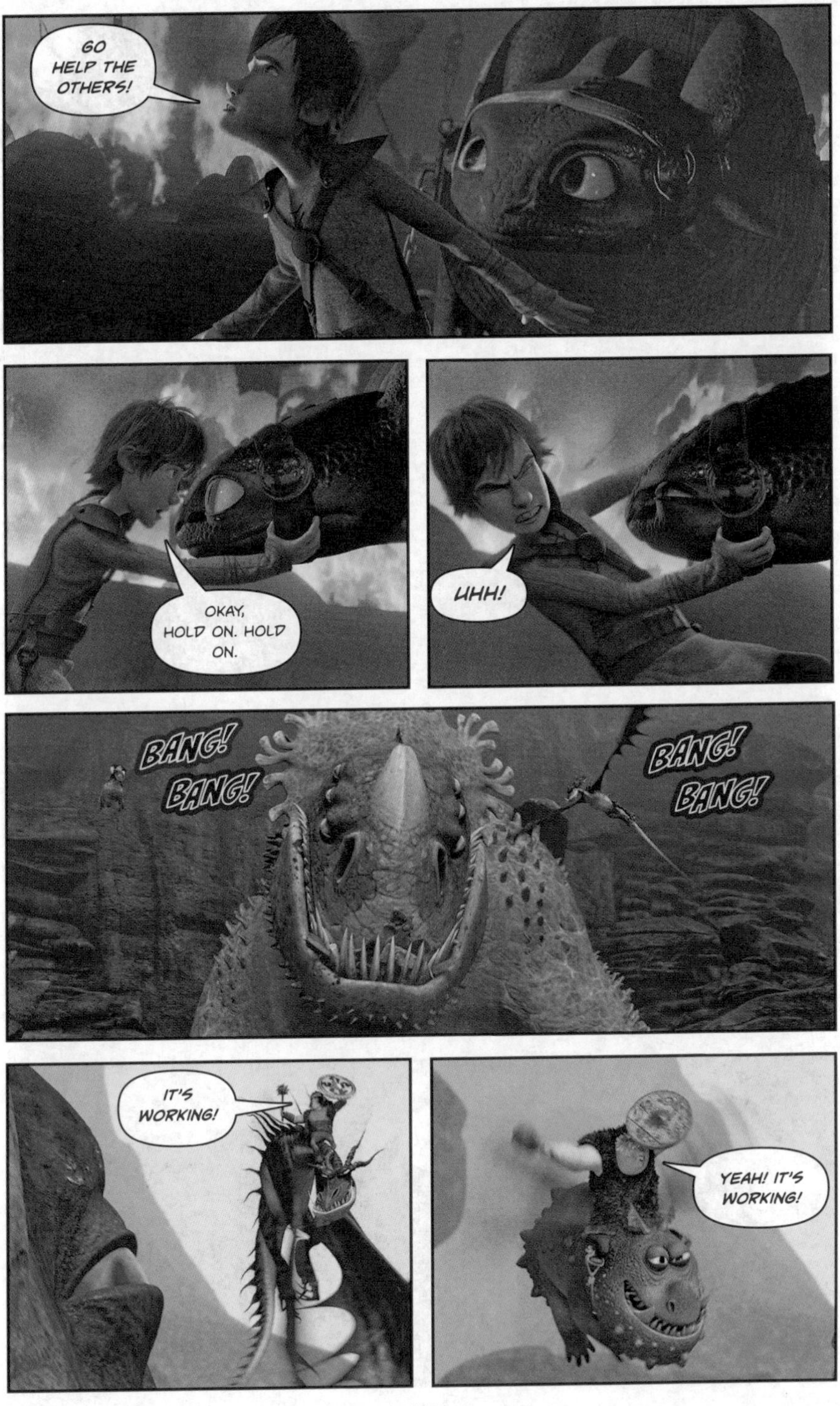
GO HELP THE OTHERS!
OKAY, HOLD ON. HOLD ON.
UHH!
BANG! BANG!
BANG! BANG!
IT'S WORKING!
YEAH! IT'S WORKING!

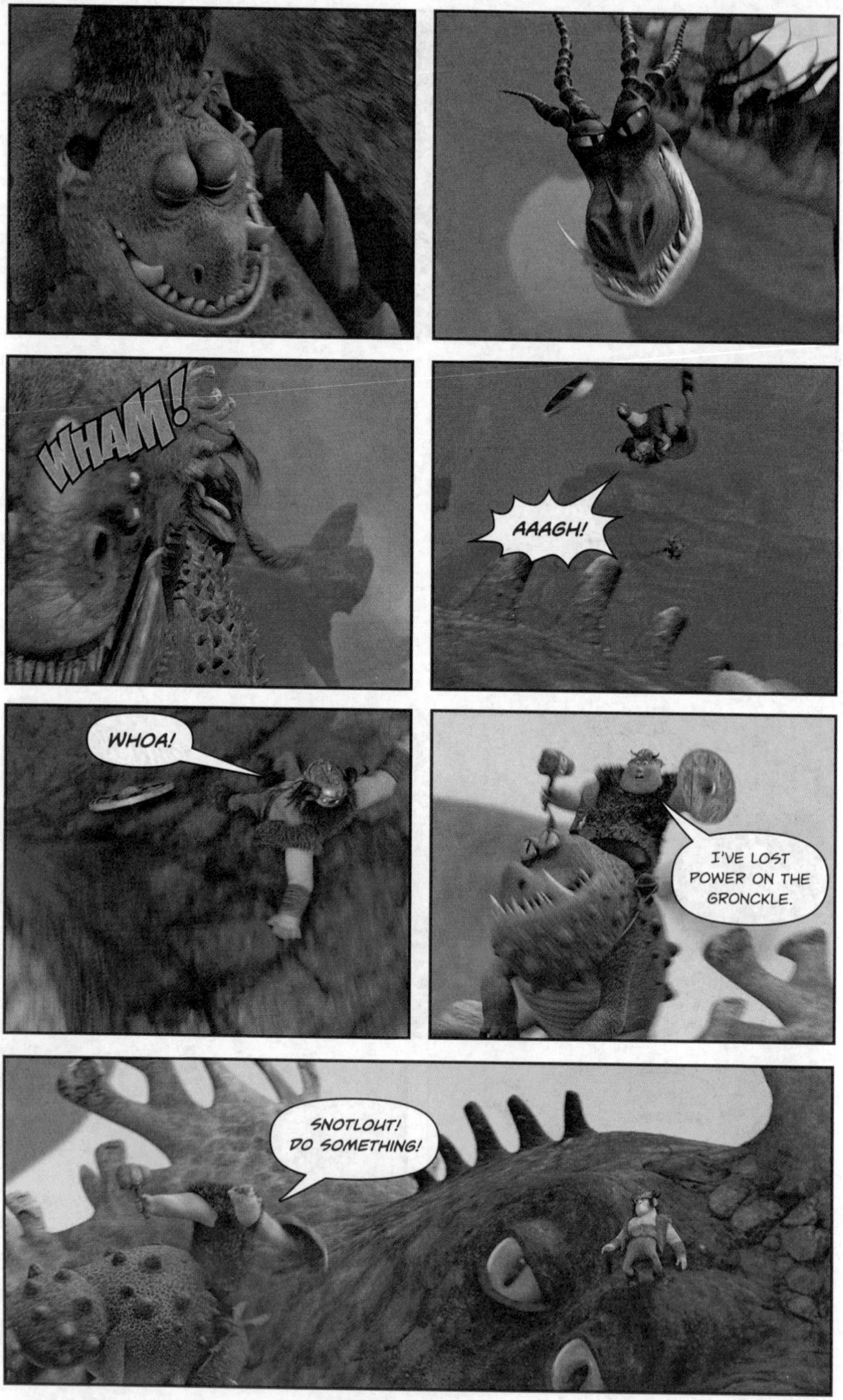
WHAM!
AAAGH!
WHOA!
I'VE LOST POWER ON THE GRONCKLE.
SNOTLOUT! DO SOMETHING!

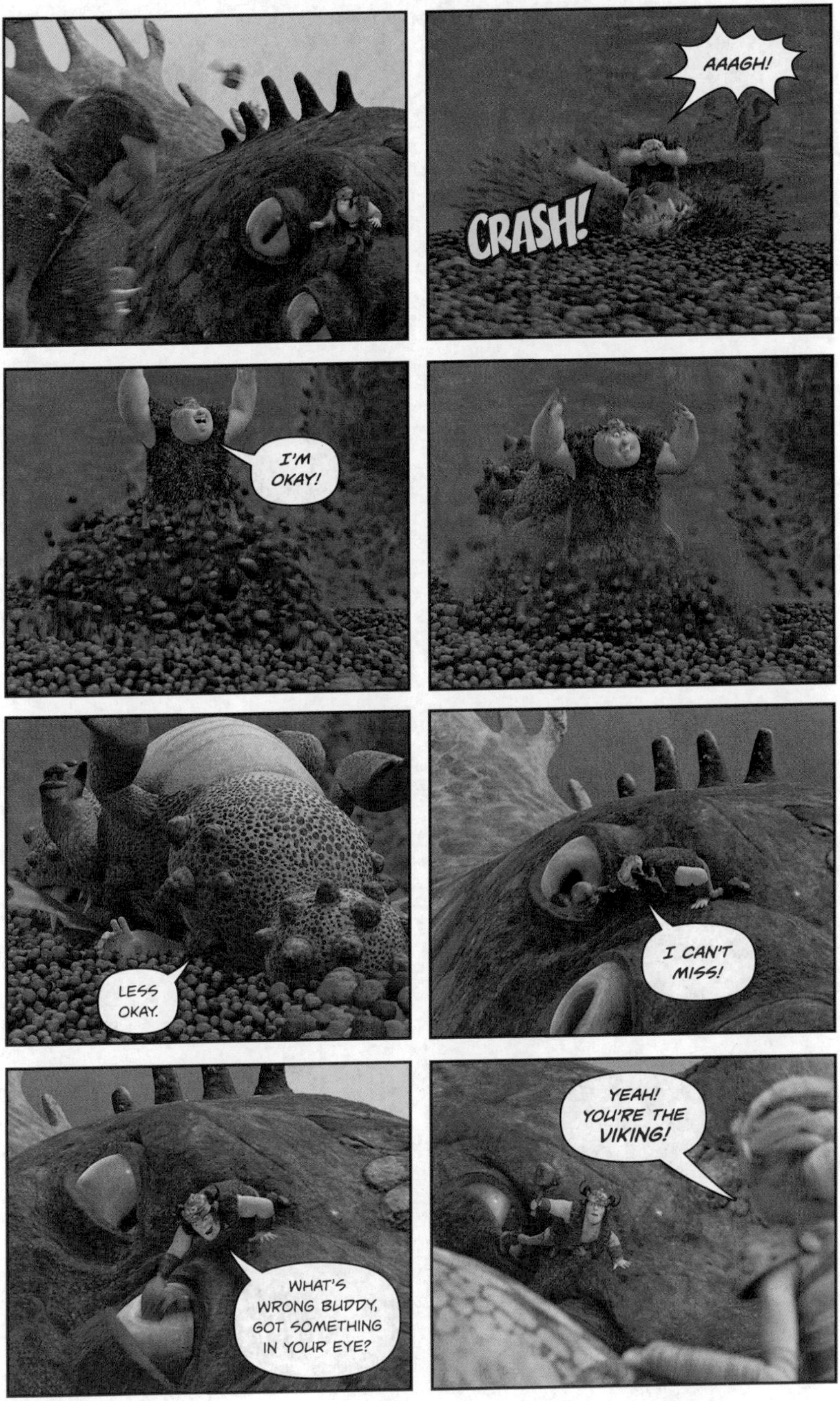
AAAGH!
CRASH!
I'M OKAY!
LESS OKAY.
I CAN'T MISS!
WHAT'S WRONG BUDDY, GOT SOMETHING IN YOUR EYE?
YEAH! YOU'RE THE VIKING!

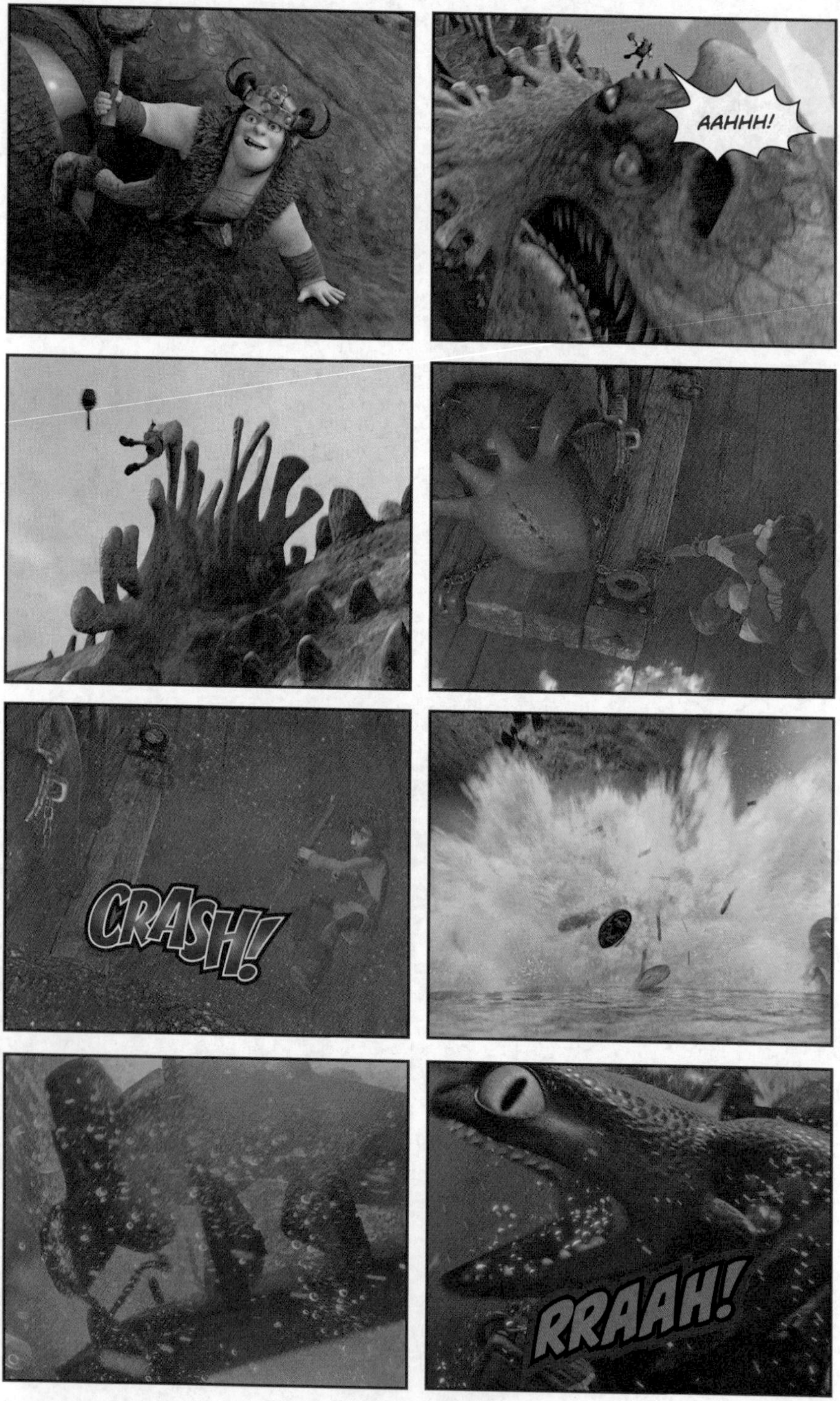
AAHHH!
CRASH!
RRAAH!

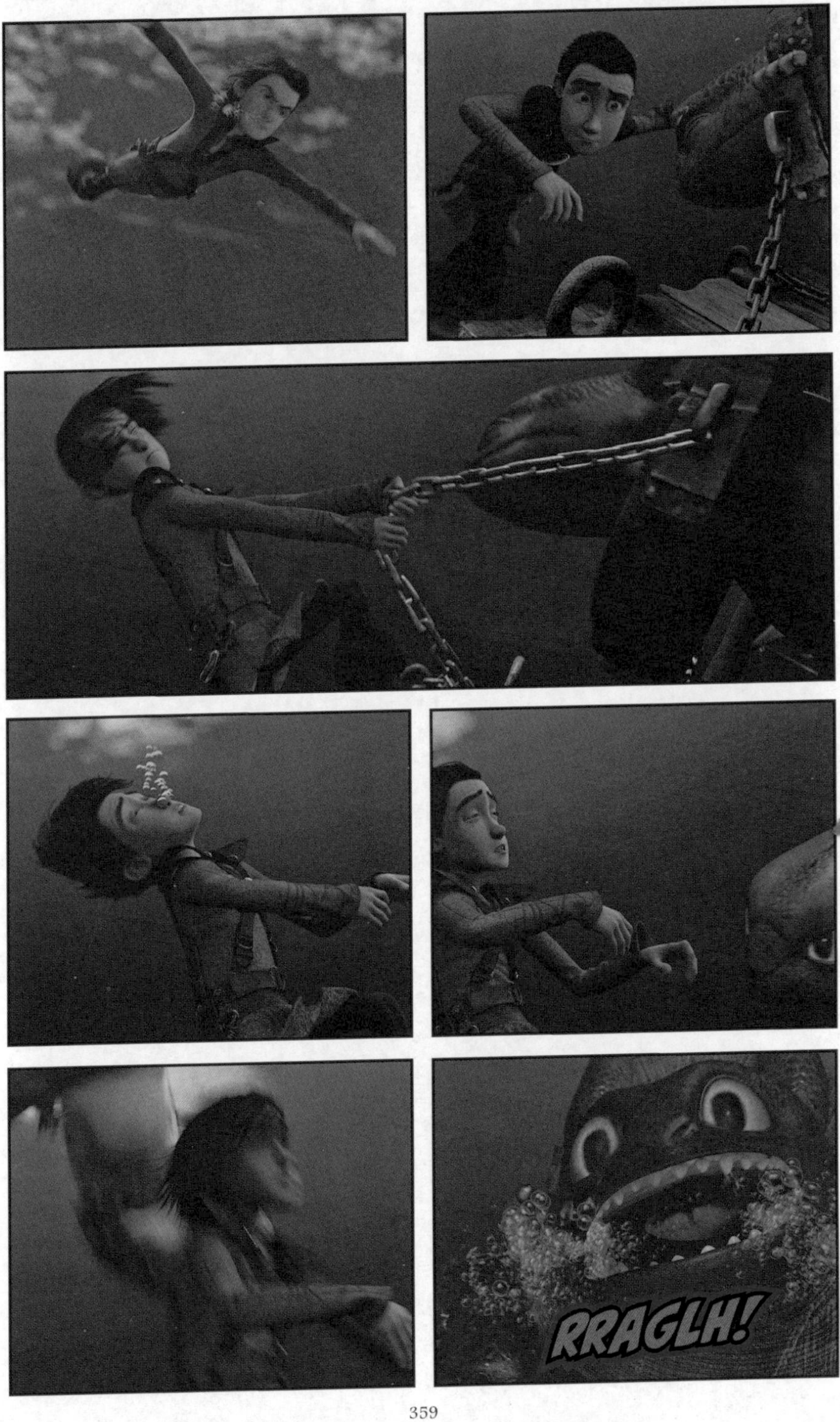
RRAGLH!

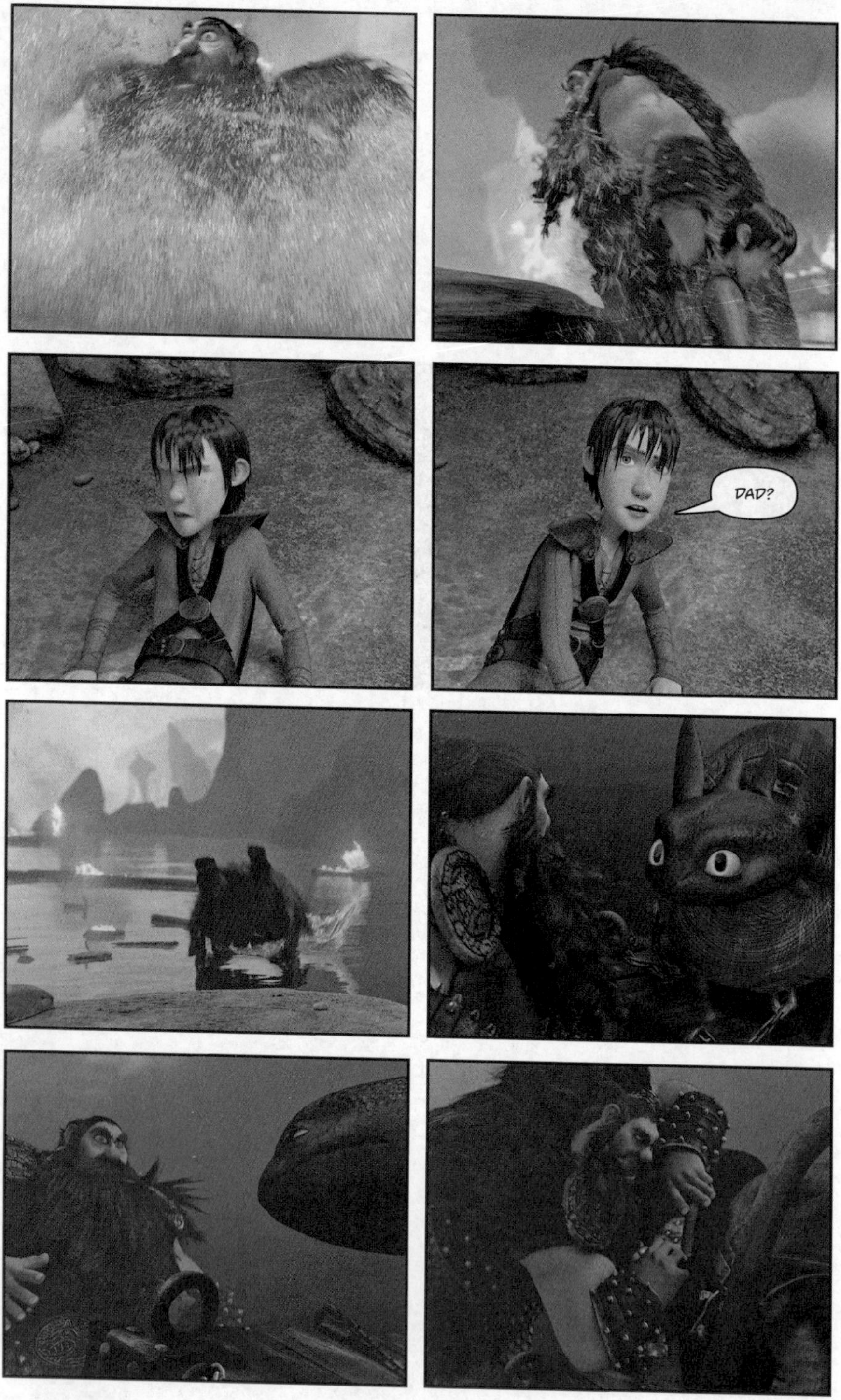
DAD?

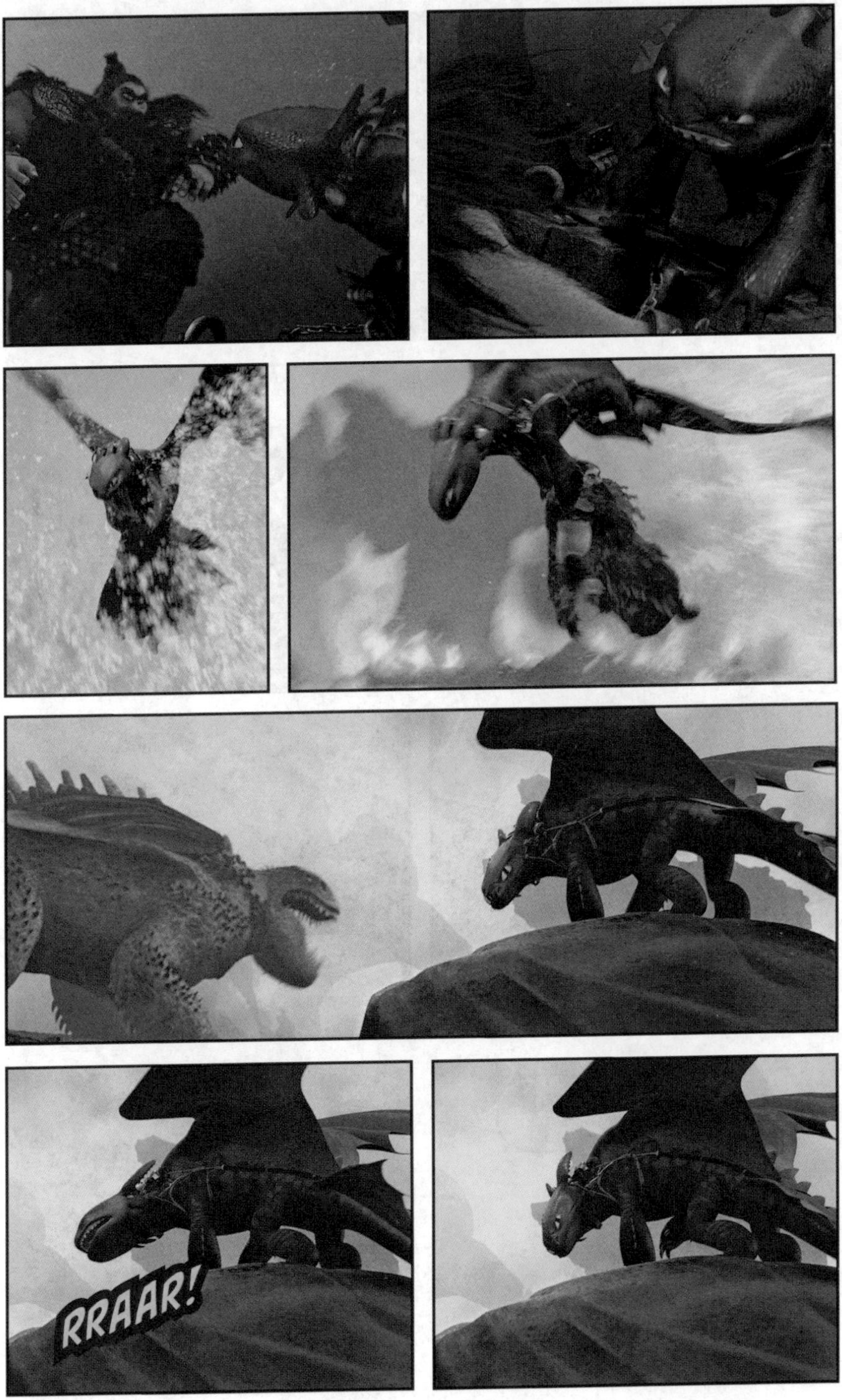
RRAAR!

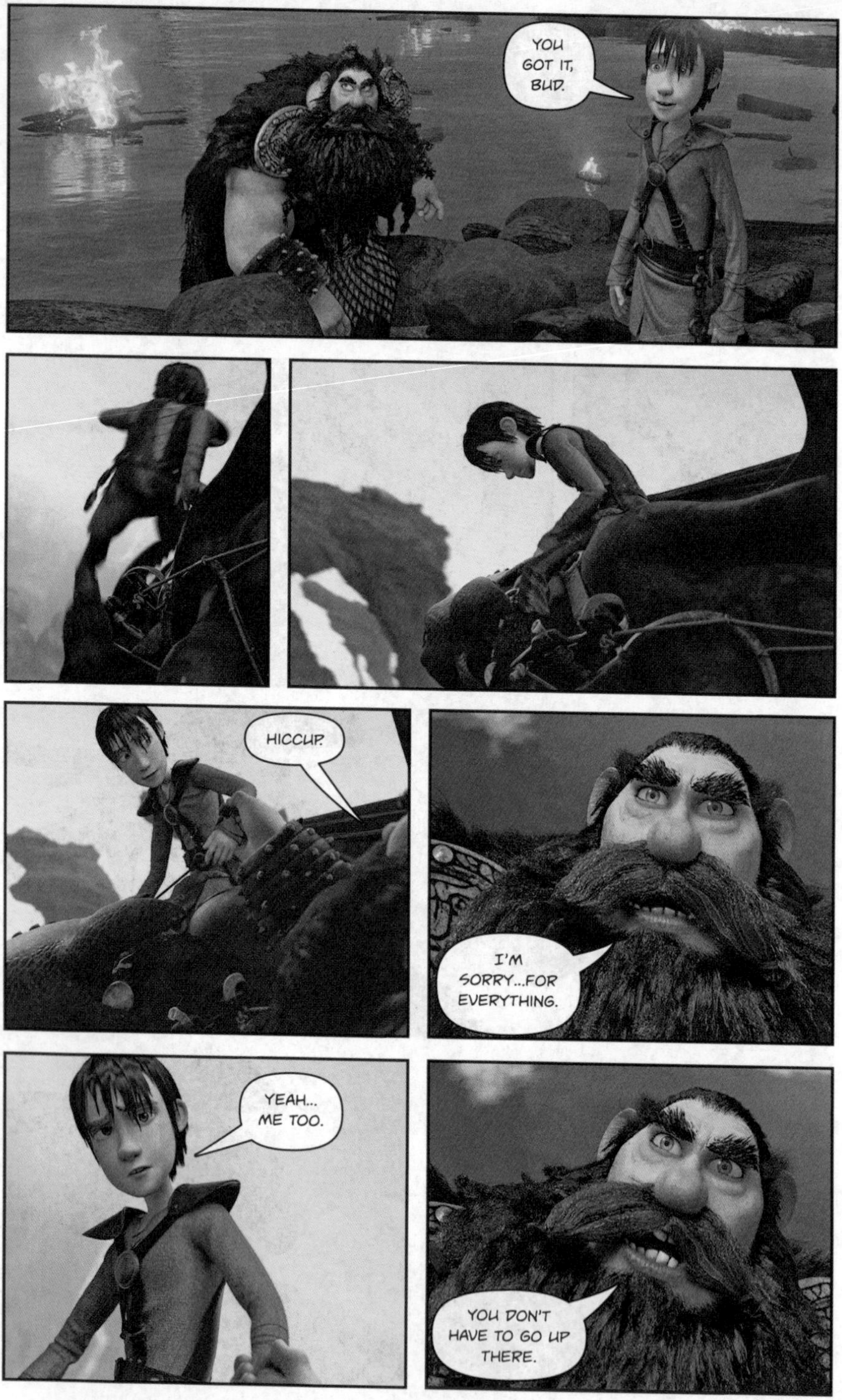
YOU GOT IT, BUD.
HICCUP.
I'M SORRY...FOR EVERYTHING.
YEAH... ME TOO.
YOU DON'T HAVE TO GO UP THERE.

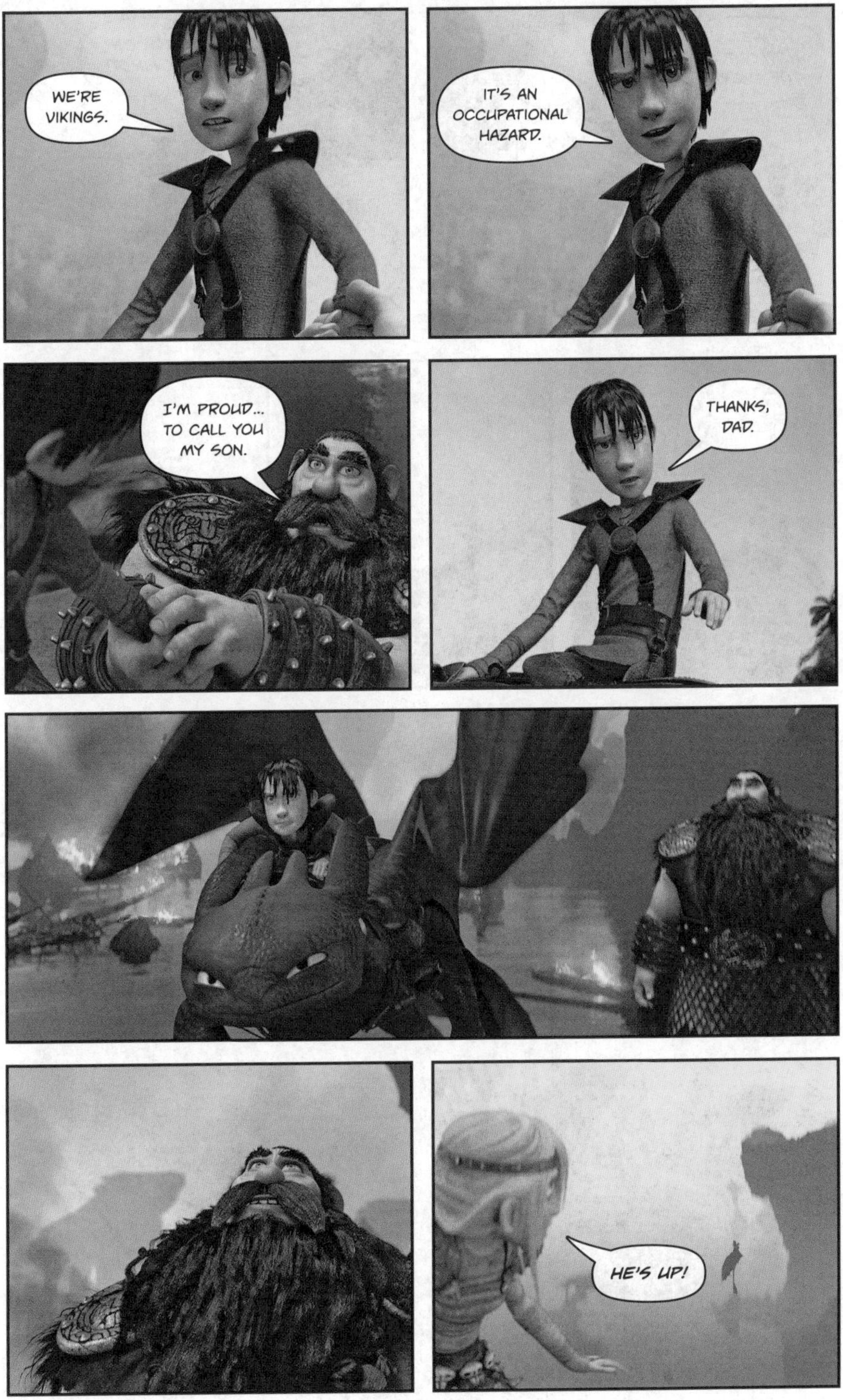
WE'RE VIKINGS.
IT'S AN OCCUPATIONAL HAZARD.
I'M PROUD... TO CALL YOU MY SON.
THANKS, DAD.
HE'S UP!

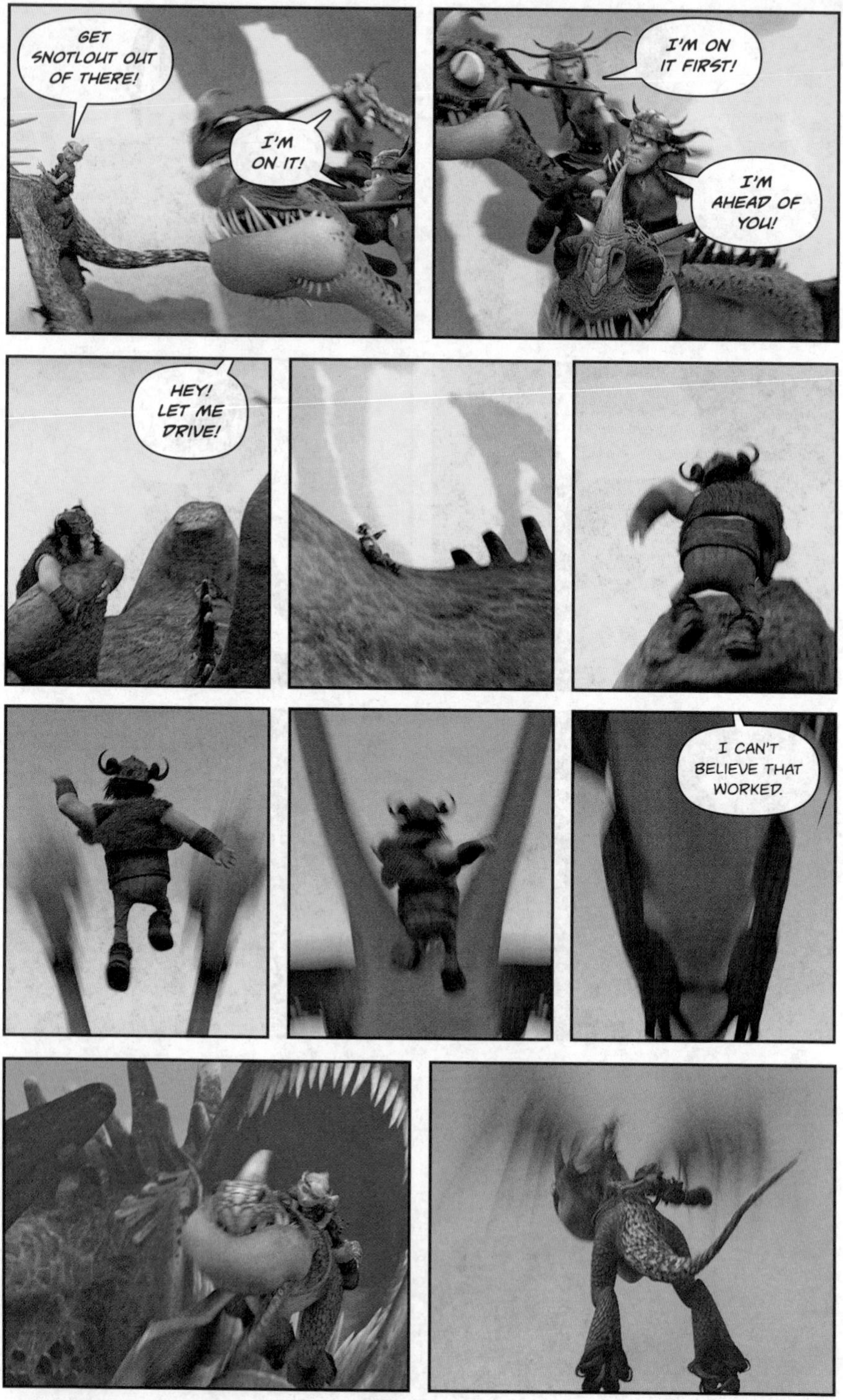
GET SNOTLOUT OUT OF THERE!
I'M ON IT!
I'M ON IT FIRST!
I'M AHEAD OF YOU!
HEY! LET ME DRIVE!
I CAN'T BELIEVE THAT WORKED.

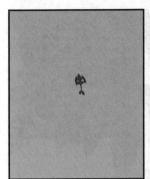

NIGHT FURY!

GET DOWN!

PHOOOM!

BOOM!

AAHHH!

DID YOU GET HER?

365

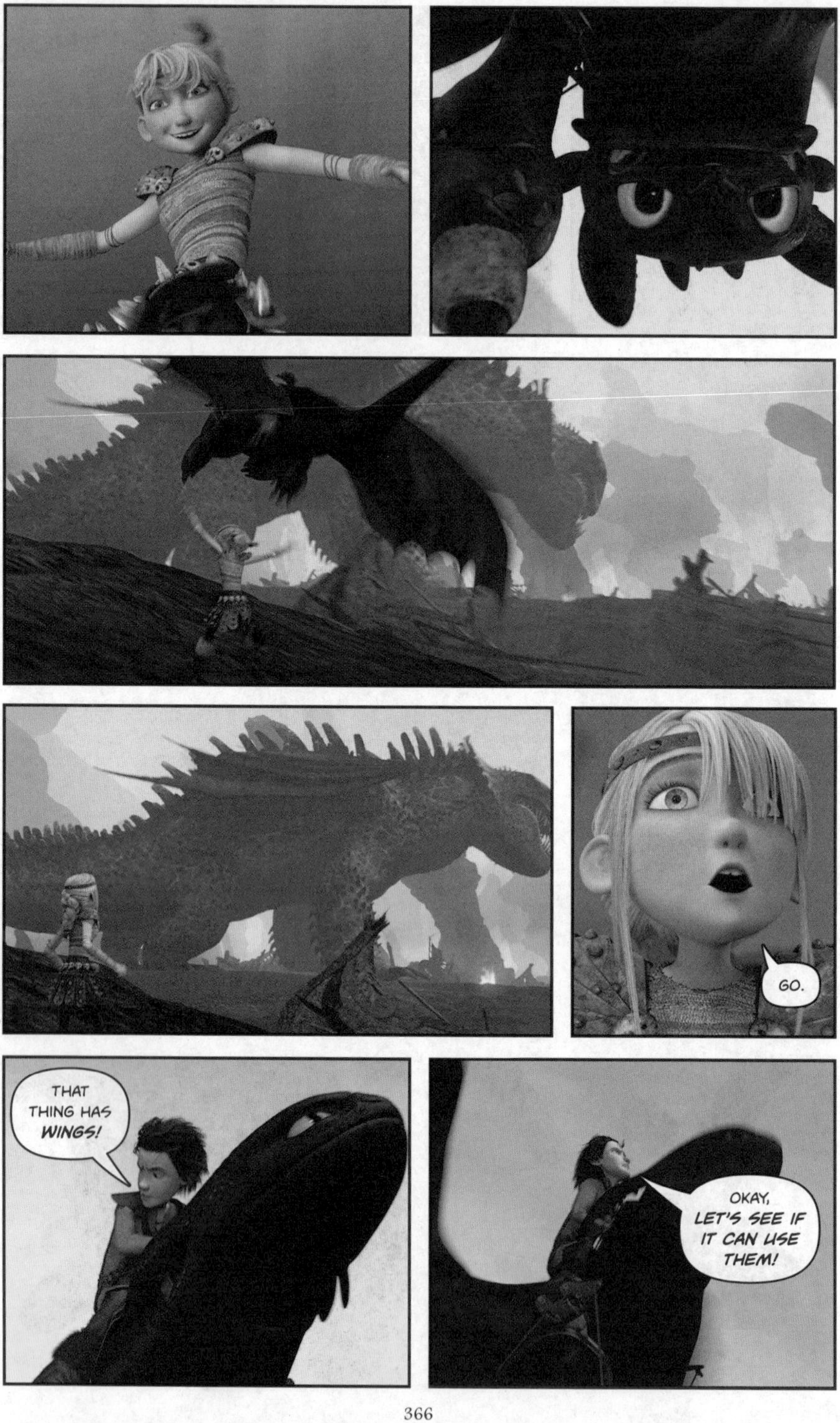
GO.
THAT THING HAS WINGS!
OKAY, LET'S SEE IF IT CAN USE THEM!

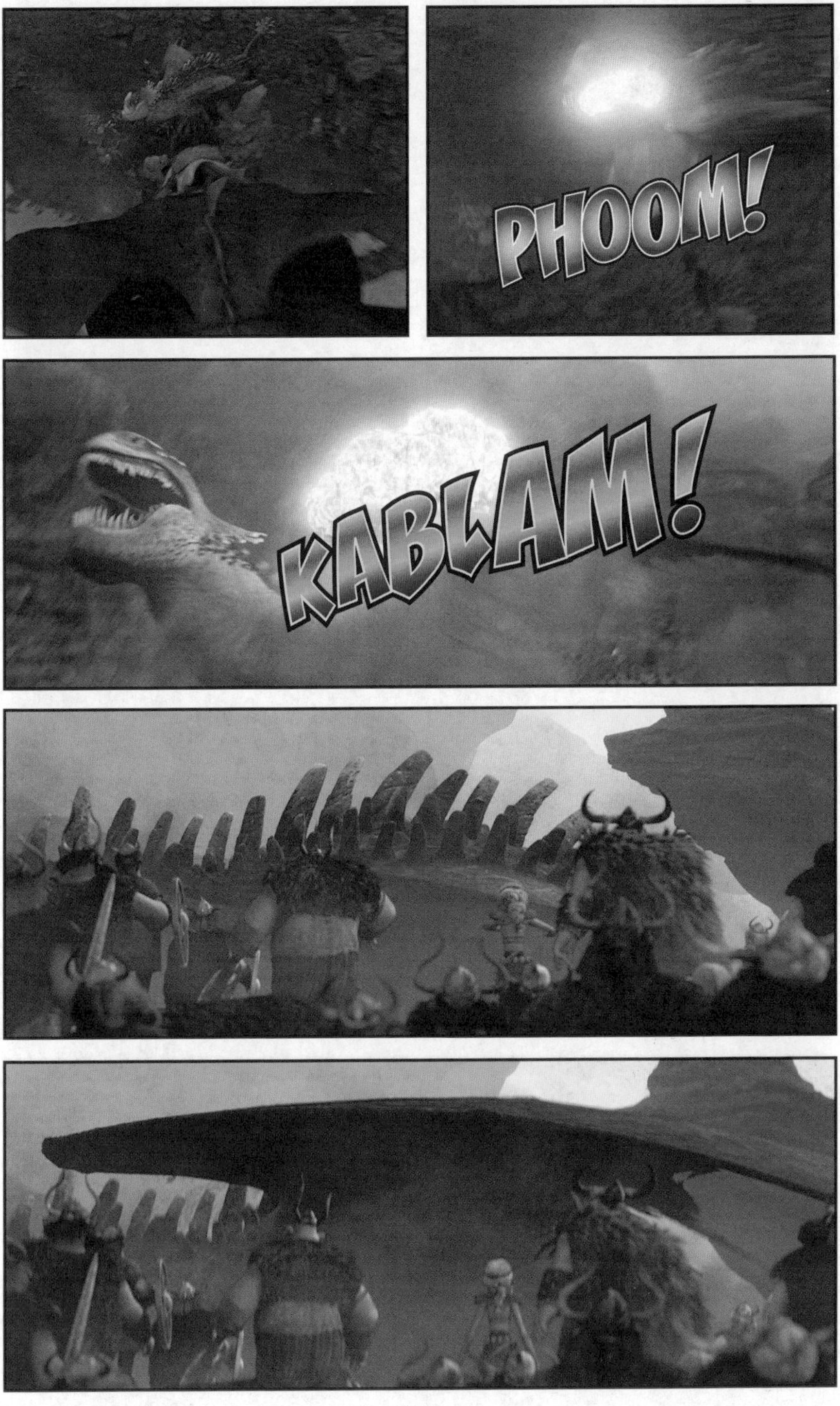
PHOOM!
KABLAM!

DO YOU THINK THAT DID IT?

WELL, HE CAN *FLY.*

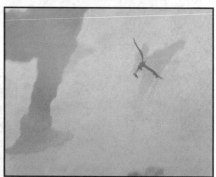

WOO!

YEAH!

YEAH!

OH YEAH!

368

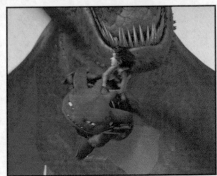

OKAY TOOTHLESS, TIME TO DISAPPEAR.

RRAAR!

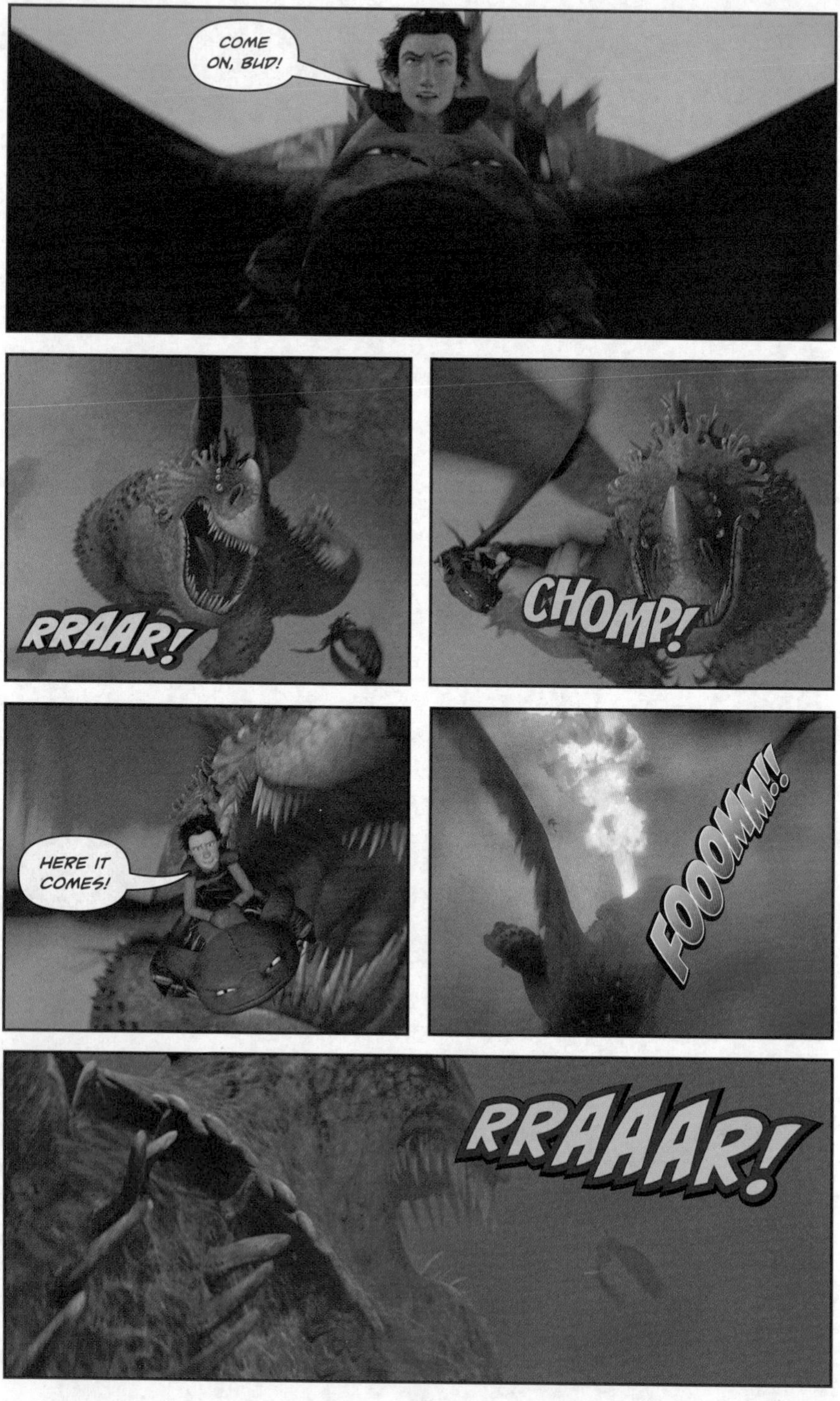
COME ON, BUD!
RRAAR!
CHOMP!
HERE IT COMES!
FOOOMM!!
RRAAAR!

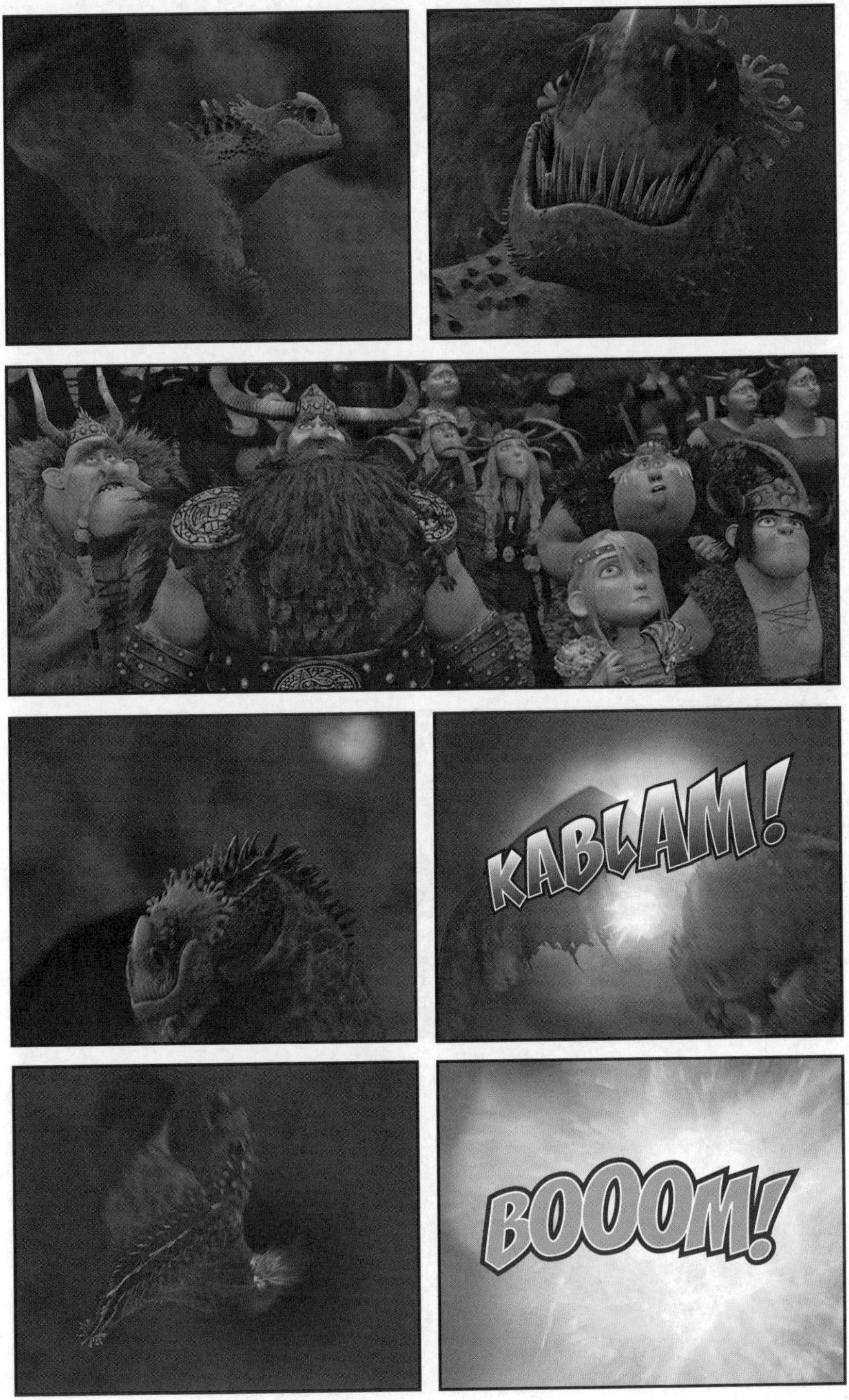
KABLAM!
BOOOM!

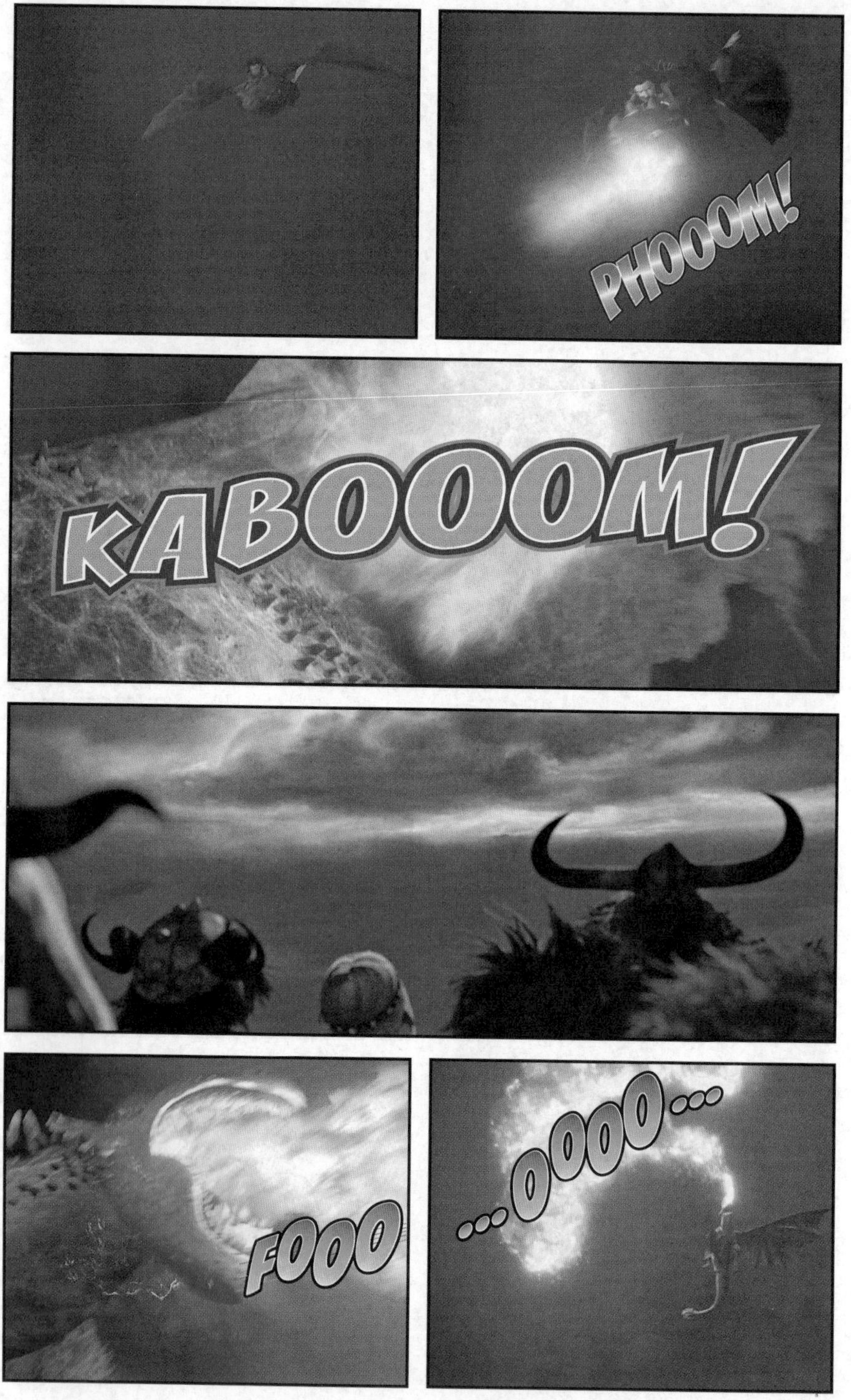
PHOOOM!
KABOOOM!
FOOO
...OOOO...

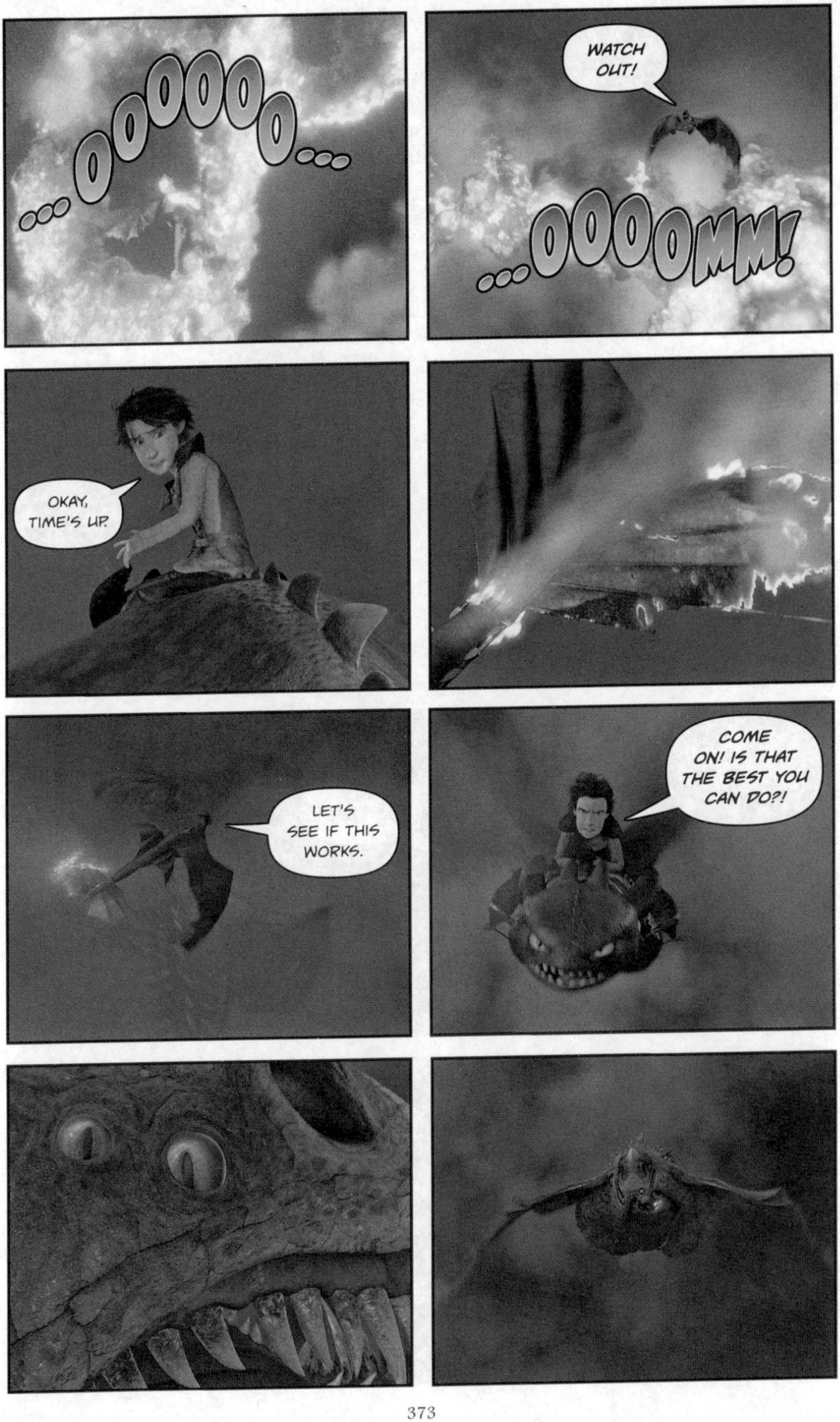
...OOOOOO...
WATCH OUT!
...OOOOMM!
OKAY, TIME'S UP.
LET'S SEE IF THIS WORKS.
COME ON! IS THAT THE BEST YOU CAN DO?!

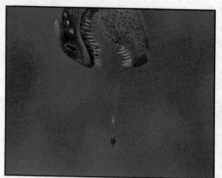

STAY WITH ME, BUDDY. WE'RE GOOD. JUST A LITTLE BIT LONGER.

HOLD, TOOTHLESS.

NOW!

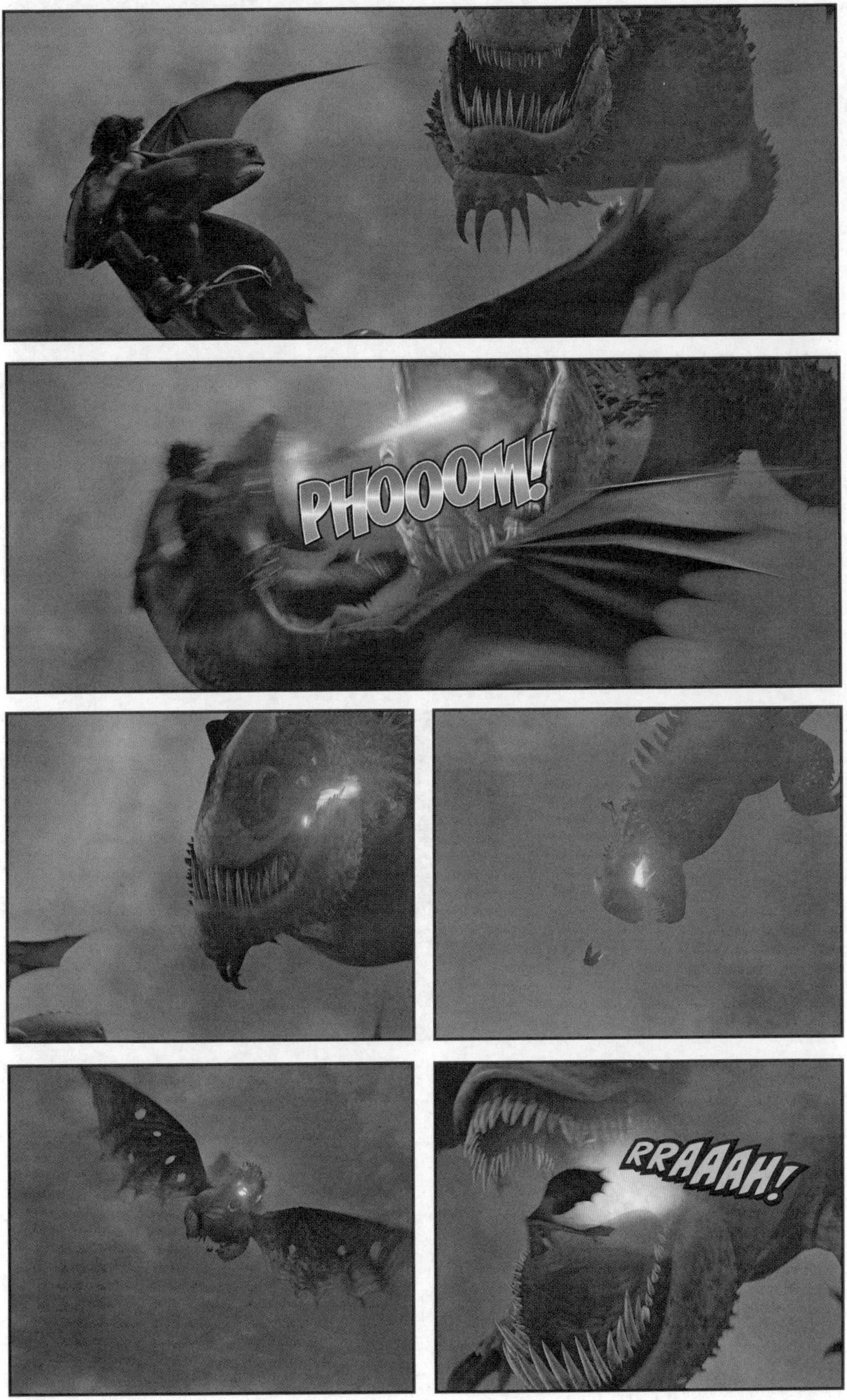
PHOOOM!
RRAAAH!

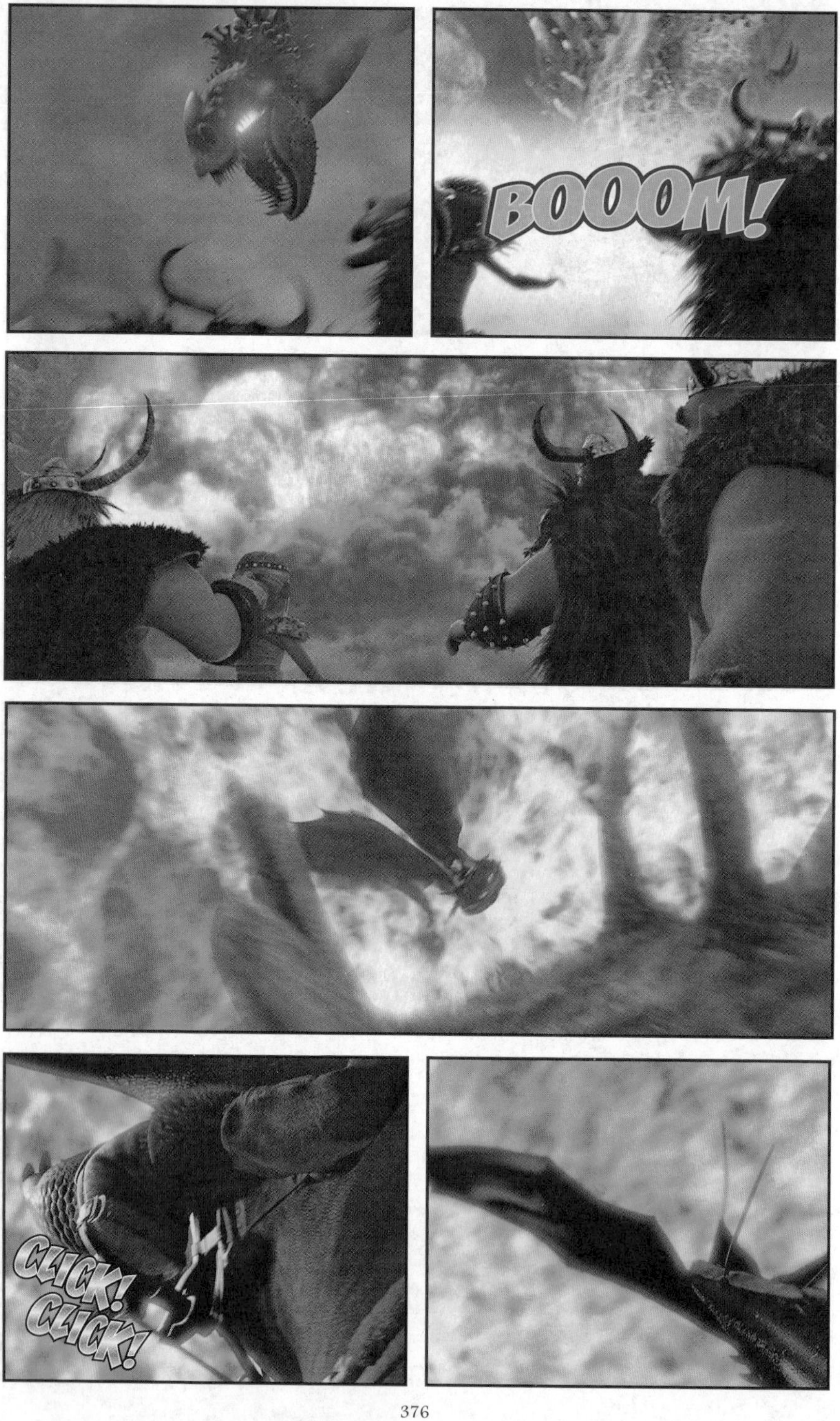
BOOOM!
CLICK!
CLICK!

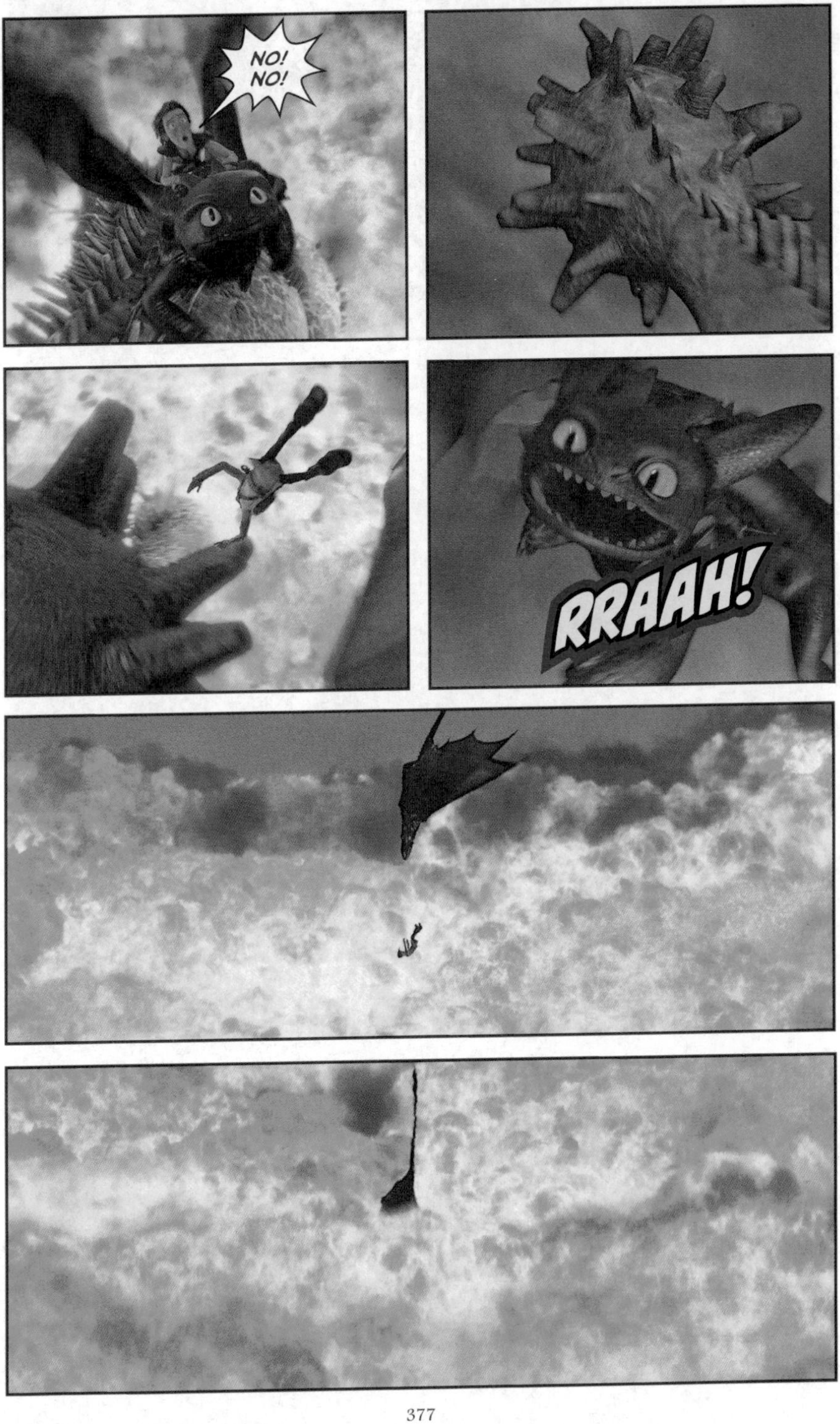
NO! NO!
RRAAH!

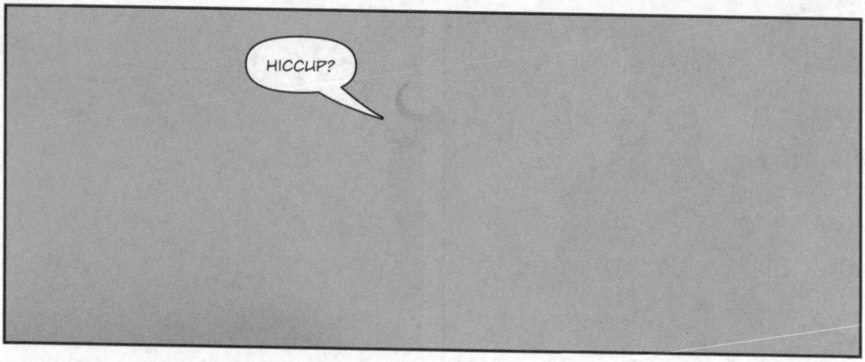
HICCUP?

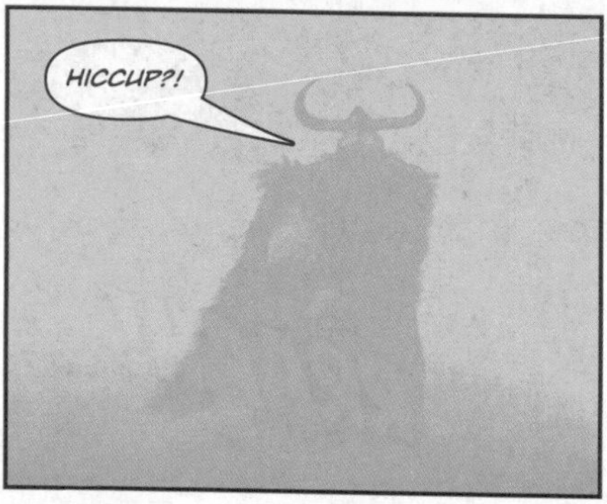
HICCUP?!

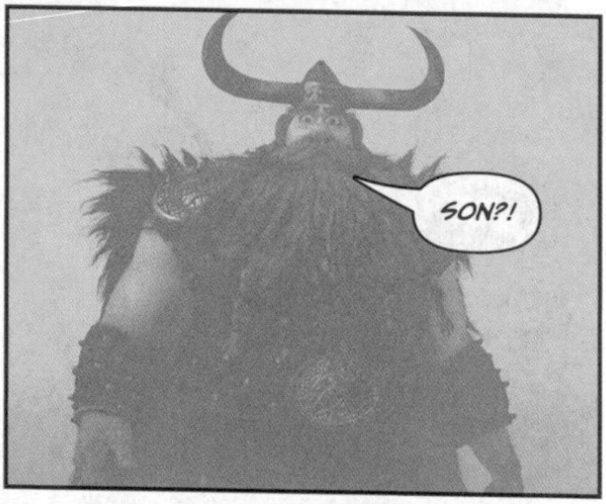
SON?!

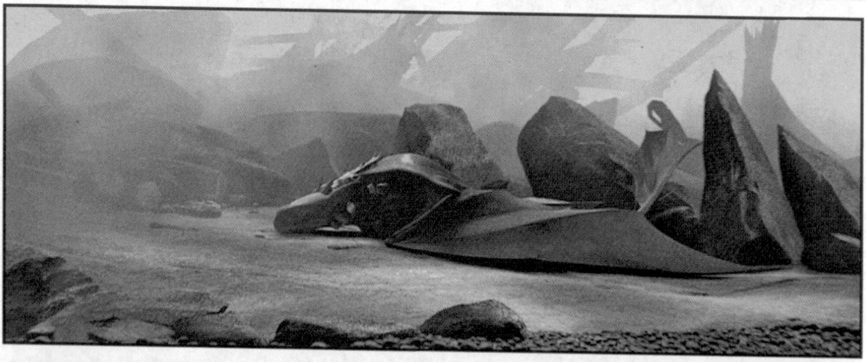

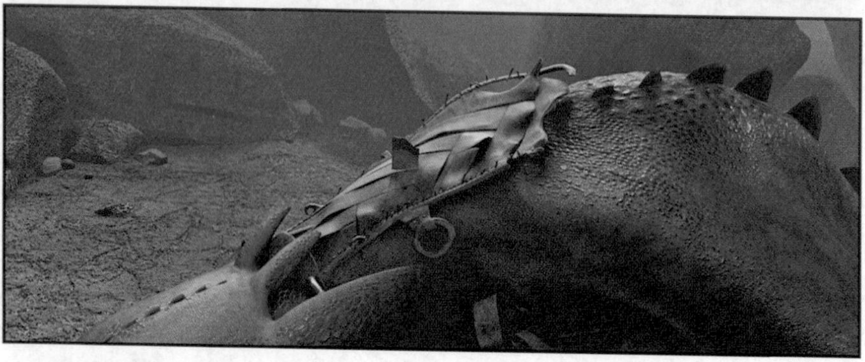

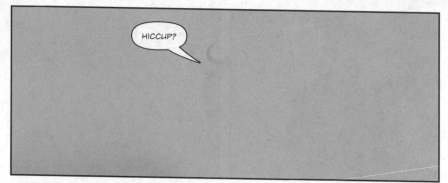

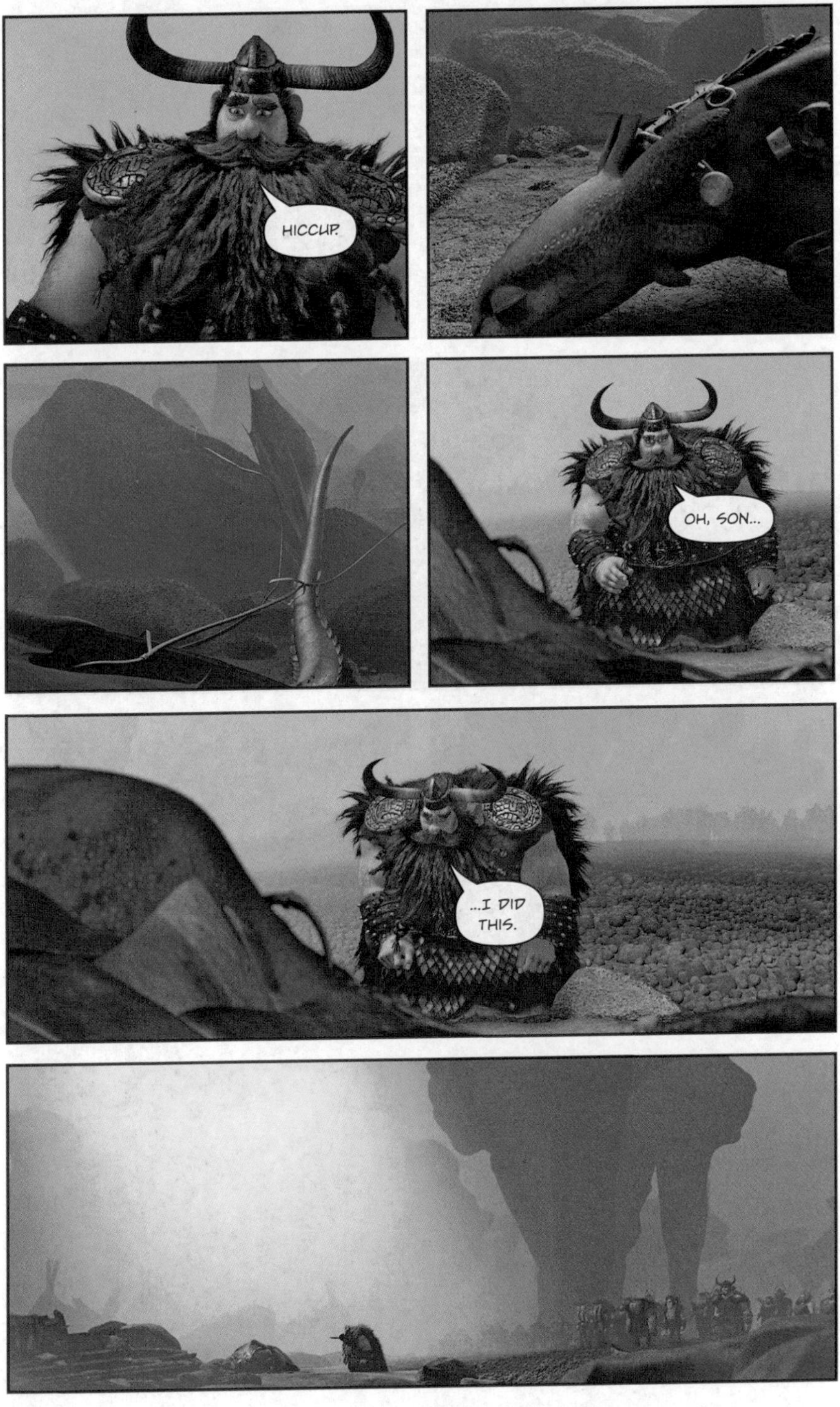
HICCUP.
OH, SON...
...I DID THIS.

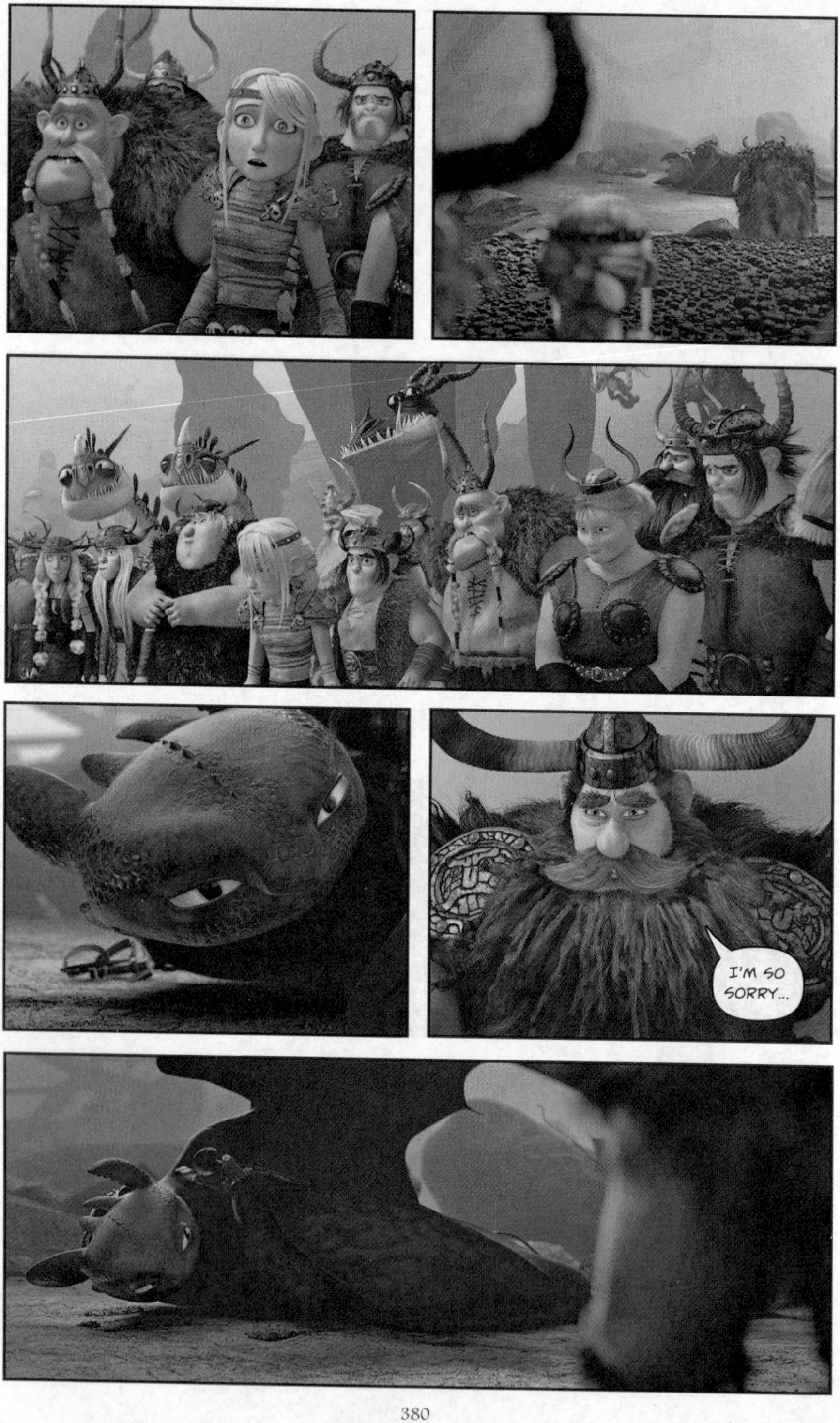
I'M SO SORRY...

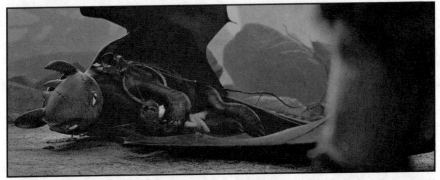

HICCUP!

HA-HA! HE'S ALIVE!

YOU BROUGHT HIM BACK ALIVE!

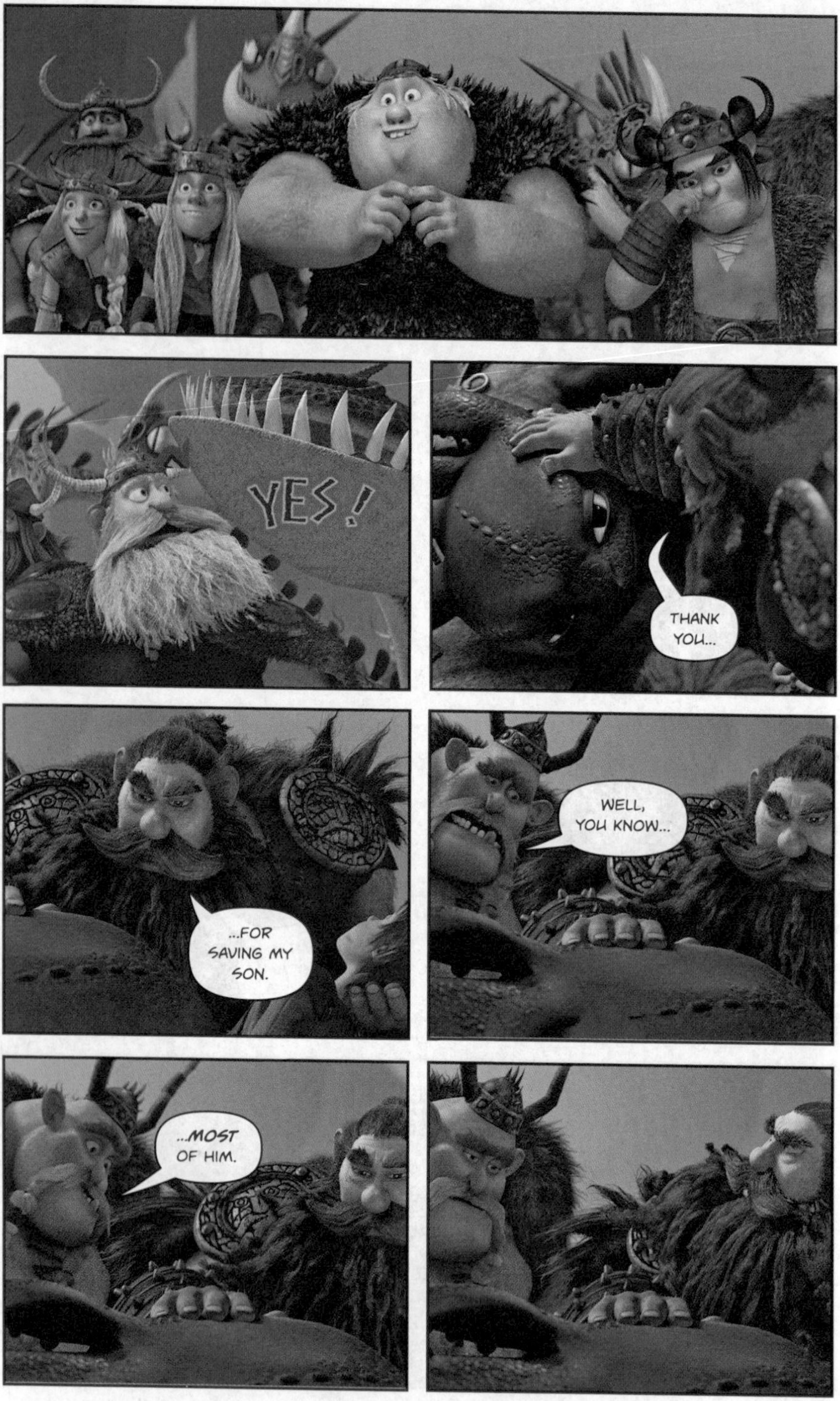
YES!
THANK YOU...
...FOR SAVING MY SON.
WELL, YOU KNOW...
...MOST OF HIM.

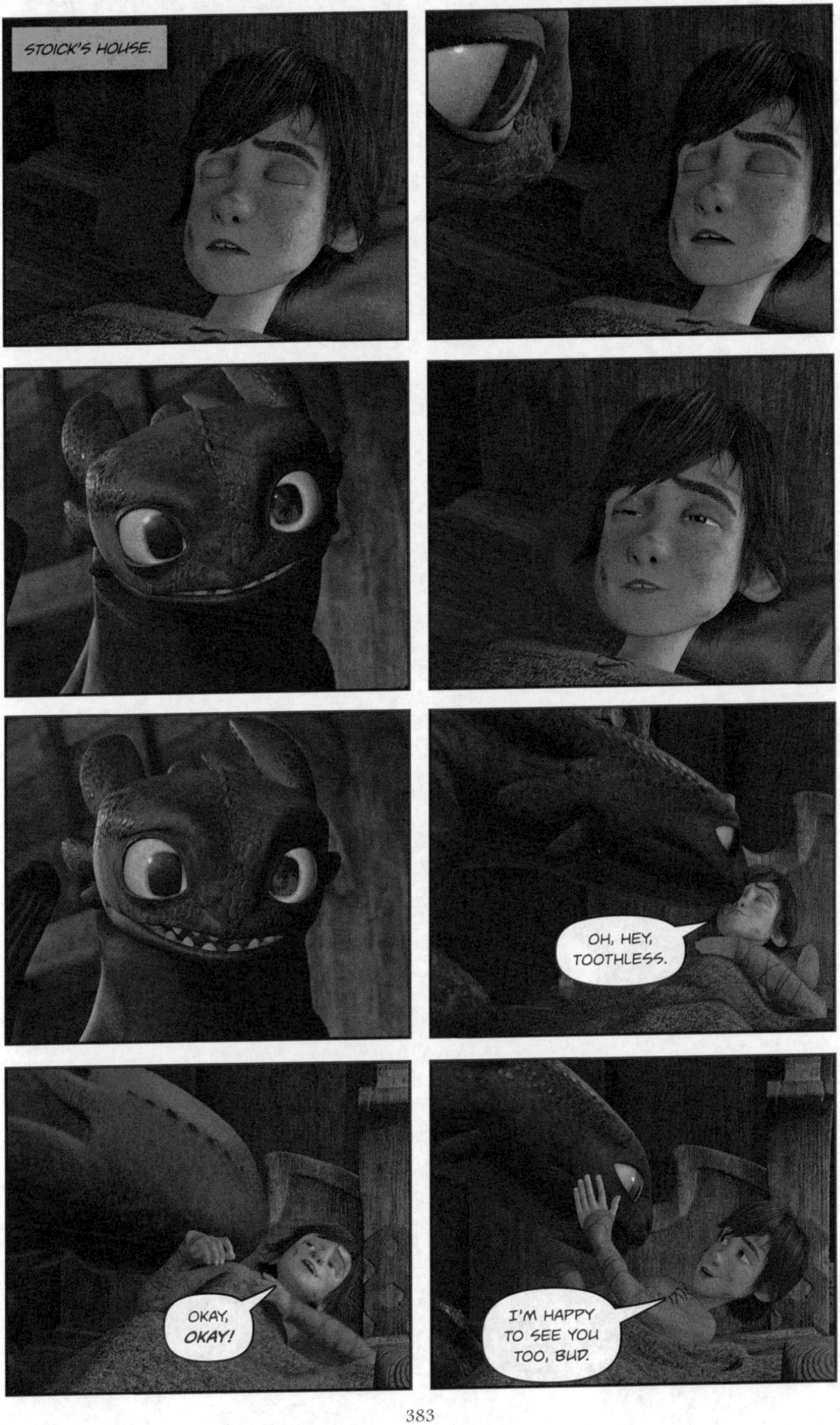
STOICK'S HOUSE.
OH, HEY, TOOTHLESS.
OKAY, OKAY!
I'M HAPPY TO SEE YOU TOO, BUD.

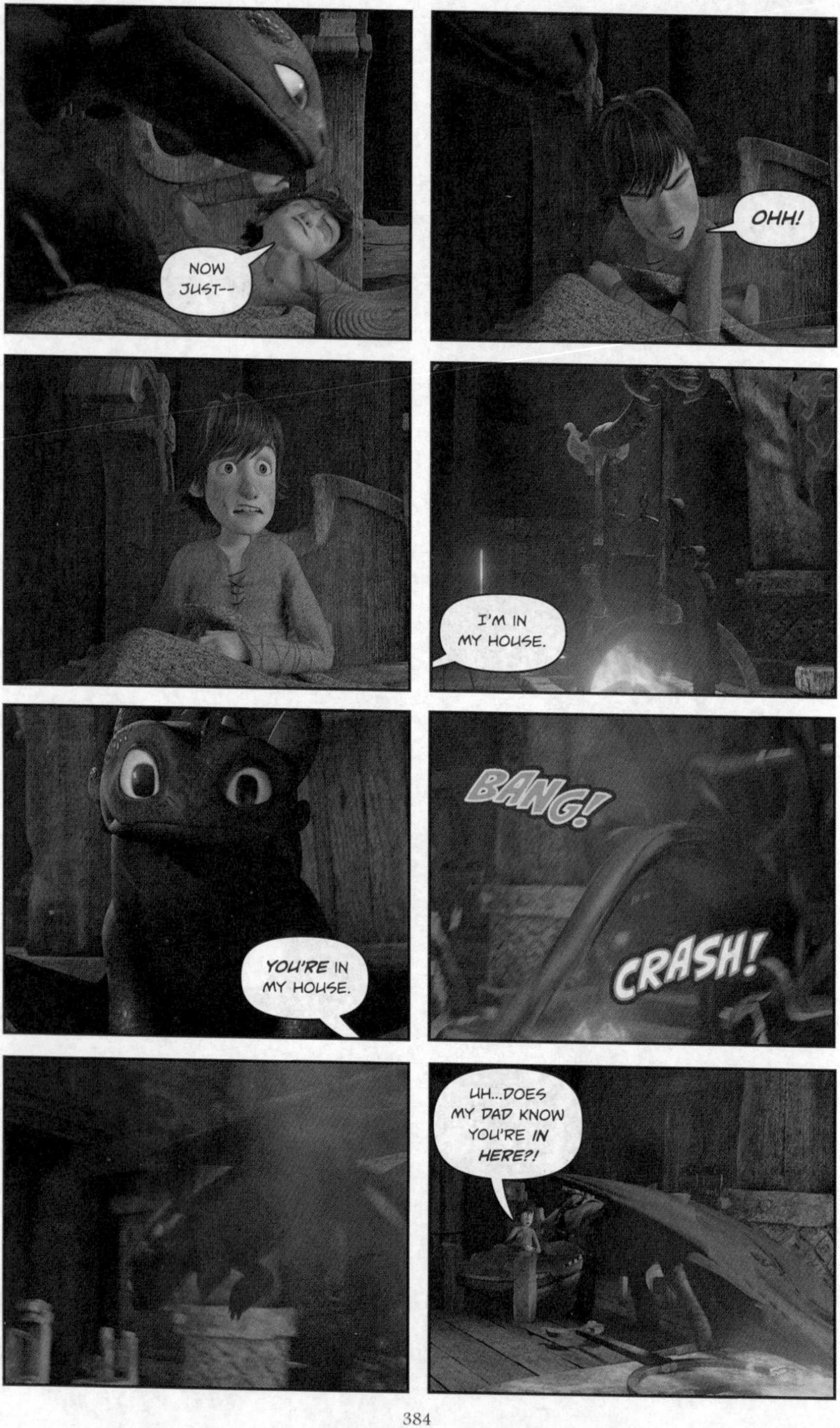
NOW JUST--
OHH!
I'M IN MY HOUSE.
YOU'RE IN MY HOUSE.
BANG!
CRASH!
UH...DOES MY DAD KNOW YOU'RE IN HERE?!

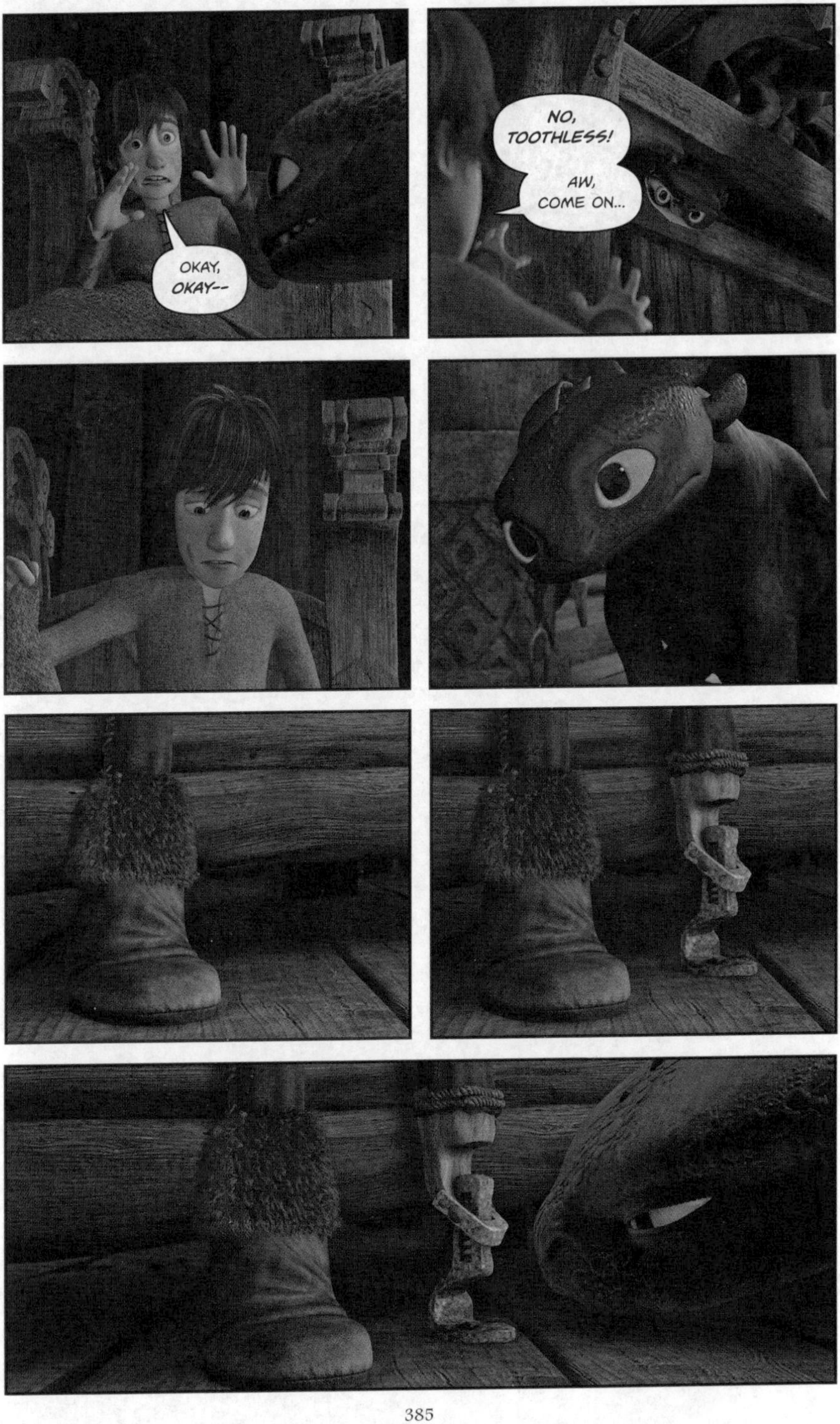
OKAY,
OKAY--
NO,
TOOTHLESS!
AW,
COME ON...

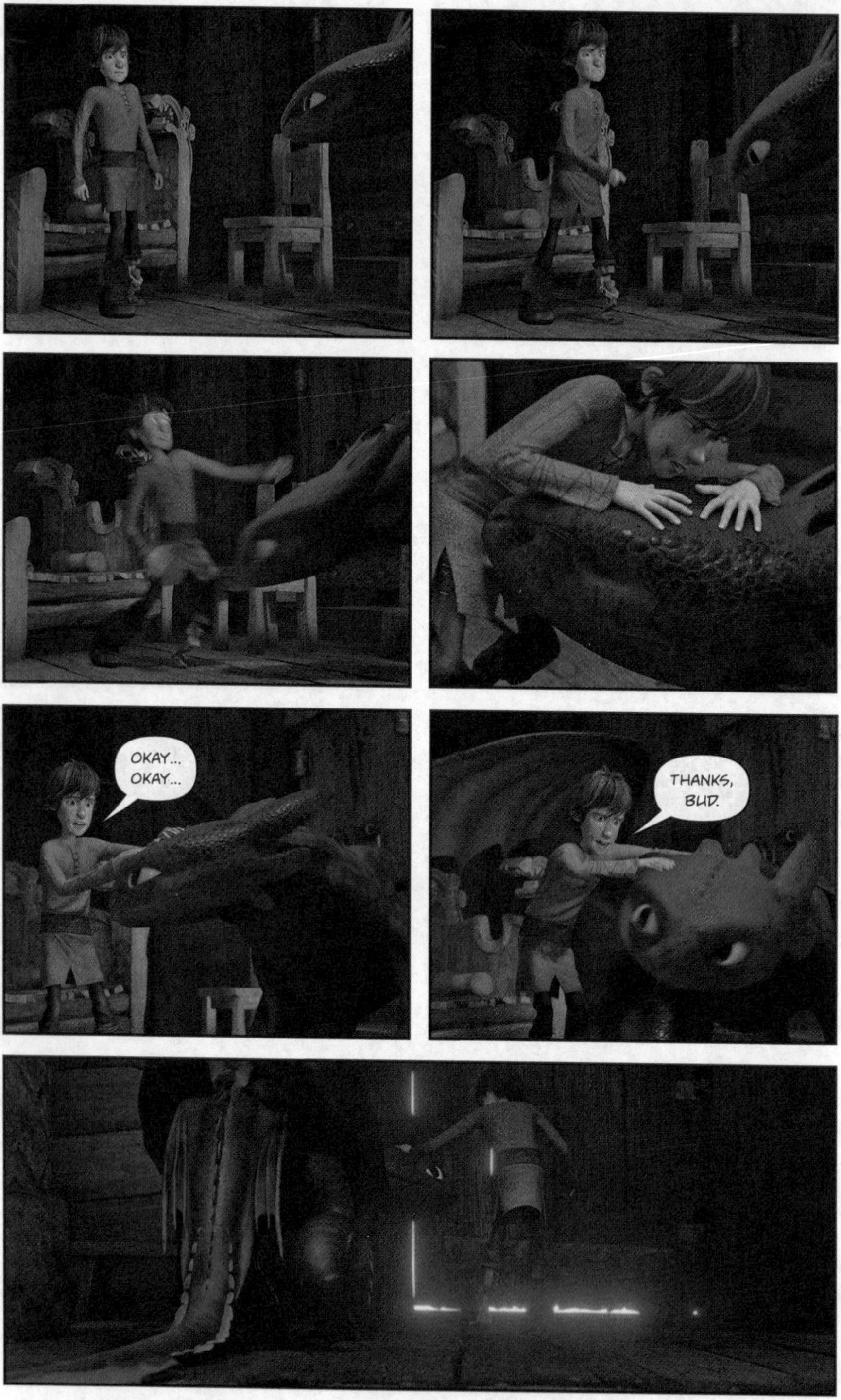
OKAY...
OKAY...
THANKS, BUD.

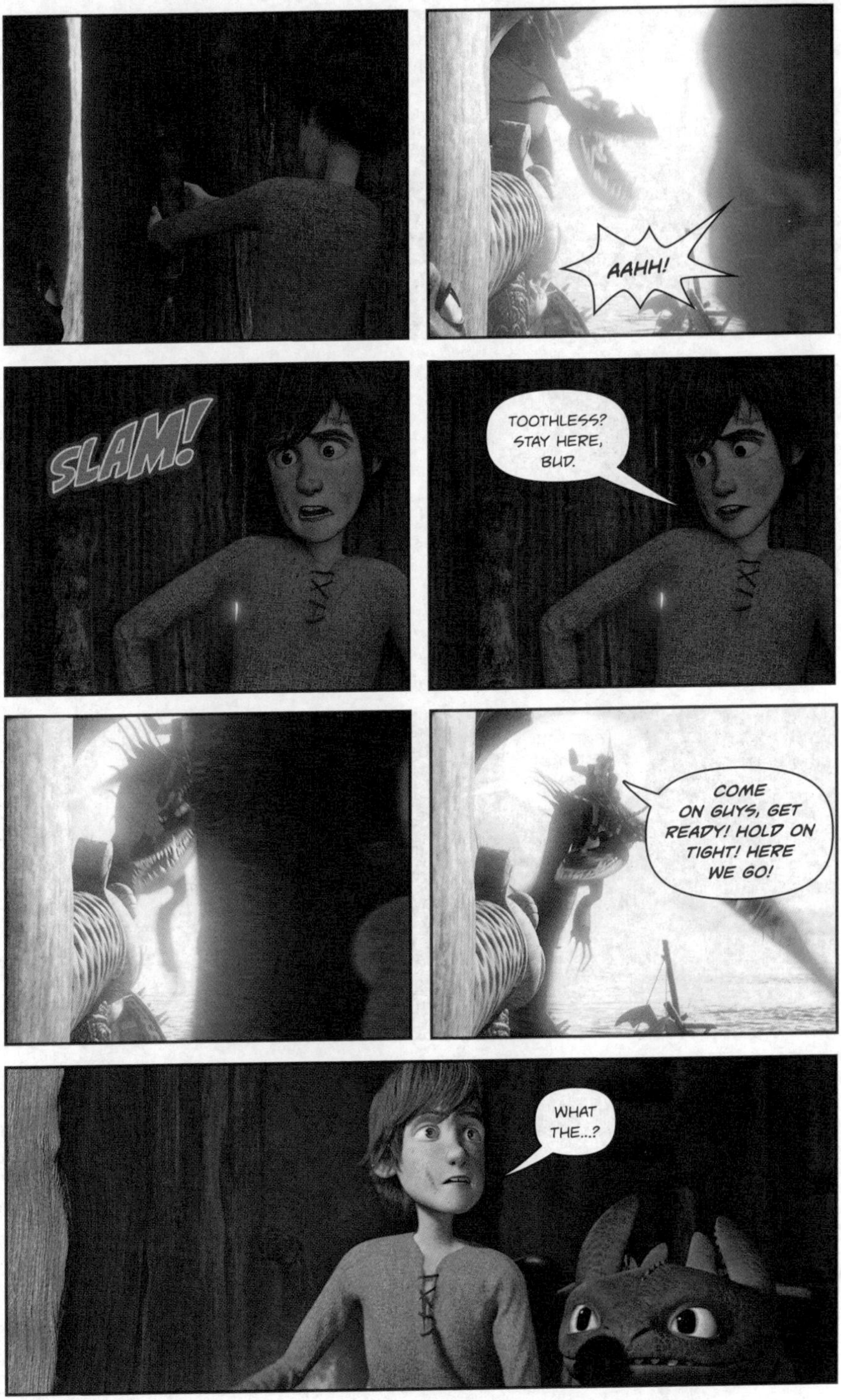
AAHH!
SLAM!
TOOTHLESS? STAY HERE, BUD.
COME ON GUYS, GET READY! HOLD ON TIGHT! HERE WE GO!
WHAT THE...?

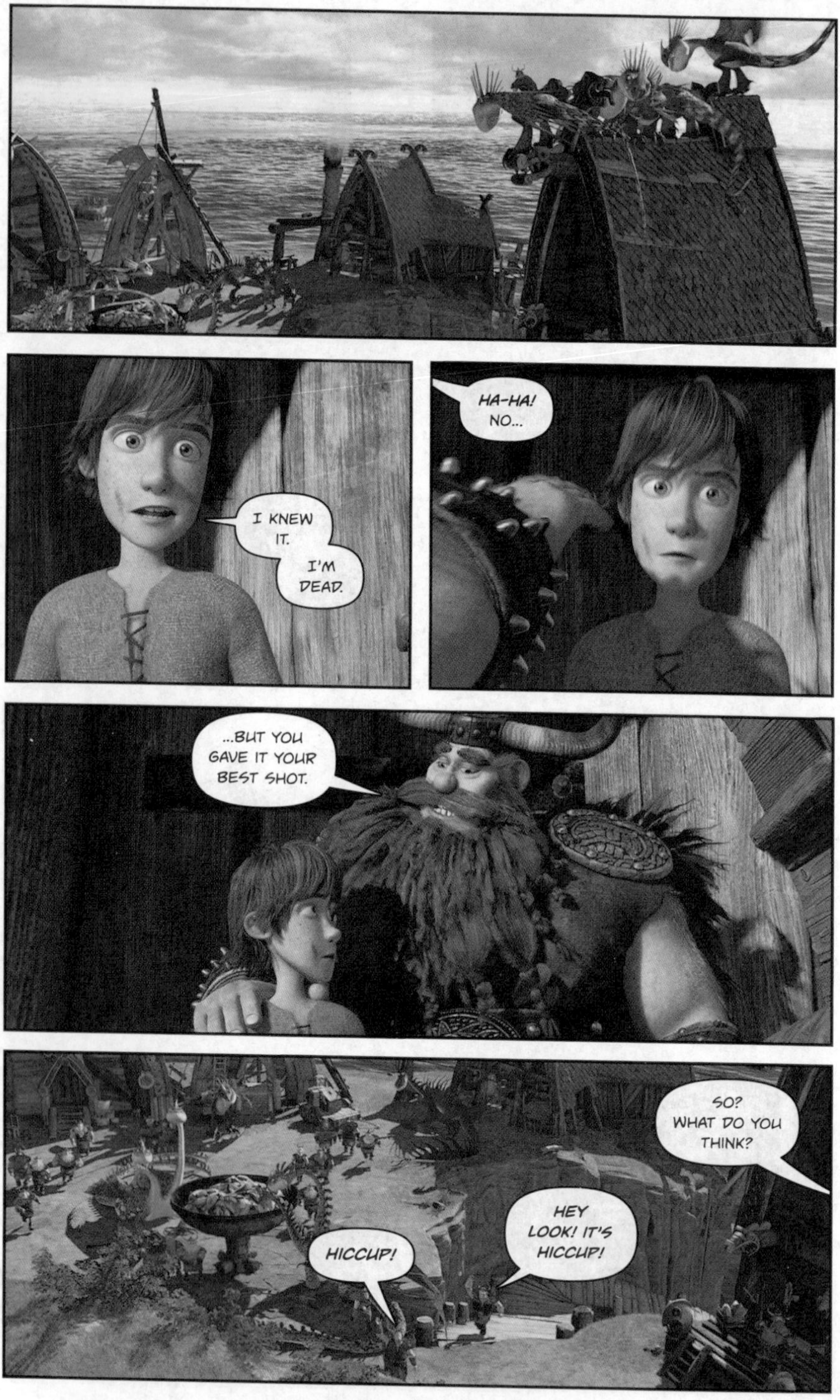
I KNEW IT.
I'M DEAD.
HA-HA! NO...
...BUT YOU GAVE IT YOUR BEST SHOT.
SO? WHAT DO YOU THINK?
HEY LOOK! IT'S HICCUP!
HICCUP!

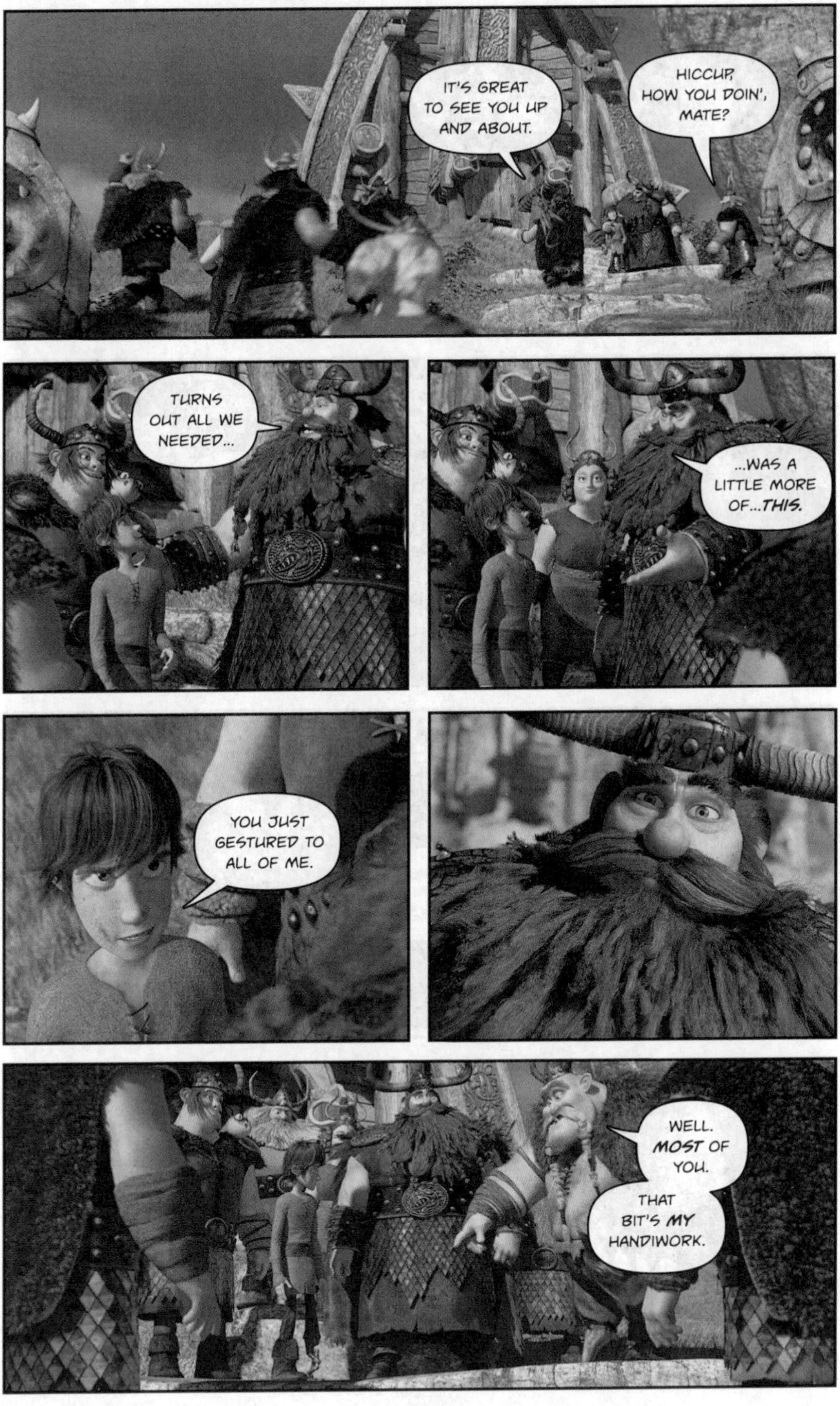
IT'S GREAT TO SEE YOU UP AND ABOUT.
HICCUP, HOW YOU DOIN', MATE?
TURNS OUT ALL WE NEEDED...
...WAS A LITTLE MORE OF...THIS.
YOU JUST GESTURED TO ALL OF ME.
WELL. MOST OF YOU.
THAT BIT'S MY HANDIWORK.

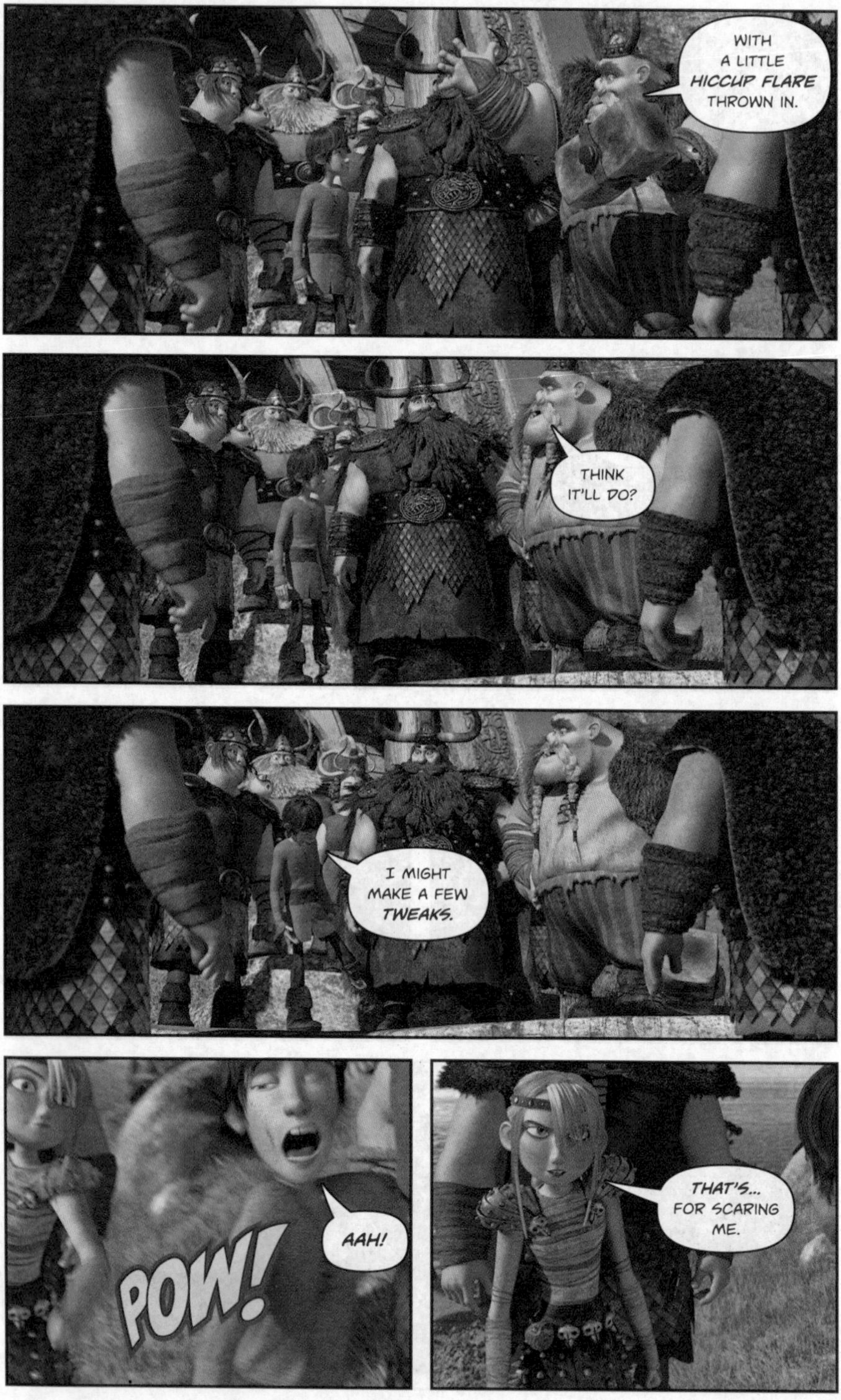
WITH A LITTLE HICCUP FLARE THROWN IN.
THINK IT'LL DO?
I MIGHT MAKE A FEW TWEAKS.
AAH!
POW!
THAT'S... FOR SCARING ME.

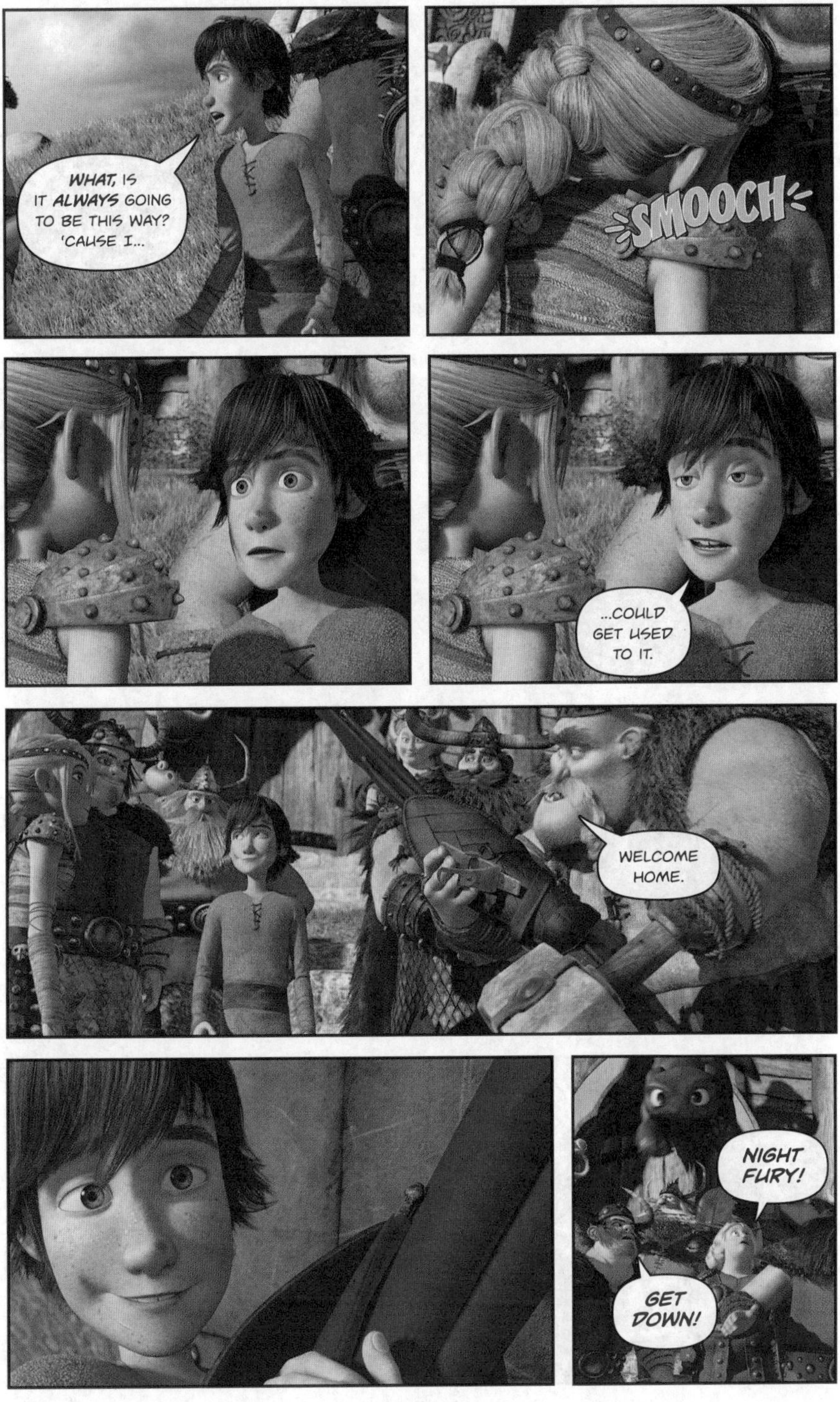
WHAT, IS IT ALWAYS GOING TO BE THIS WAY? 'CAUSE I...
SMOOCH
...COULD GET USED TO IT.
WELCOME HOME.
NIGHT FURY!
GET DOWN!

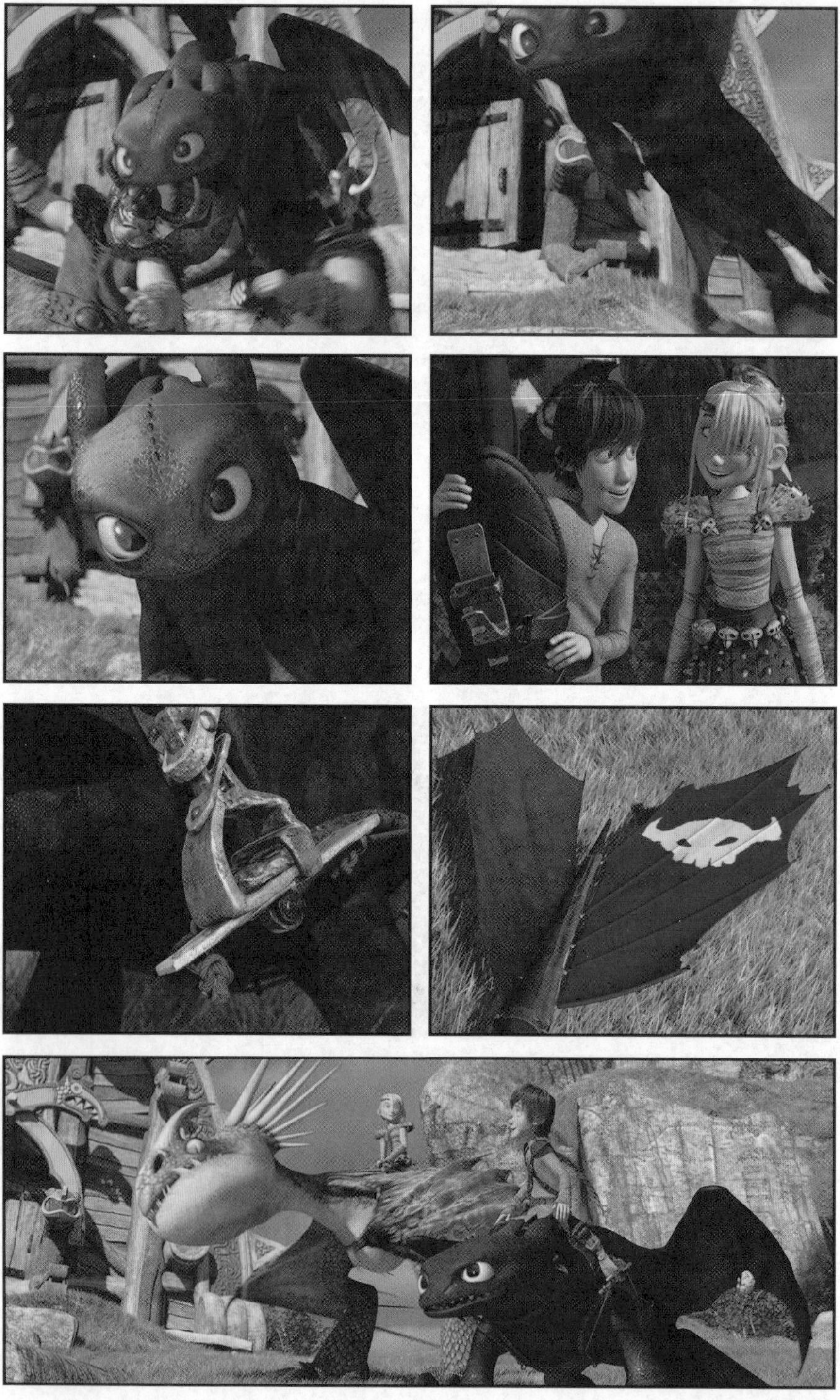

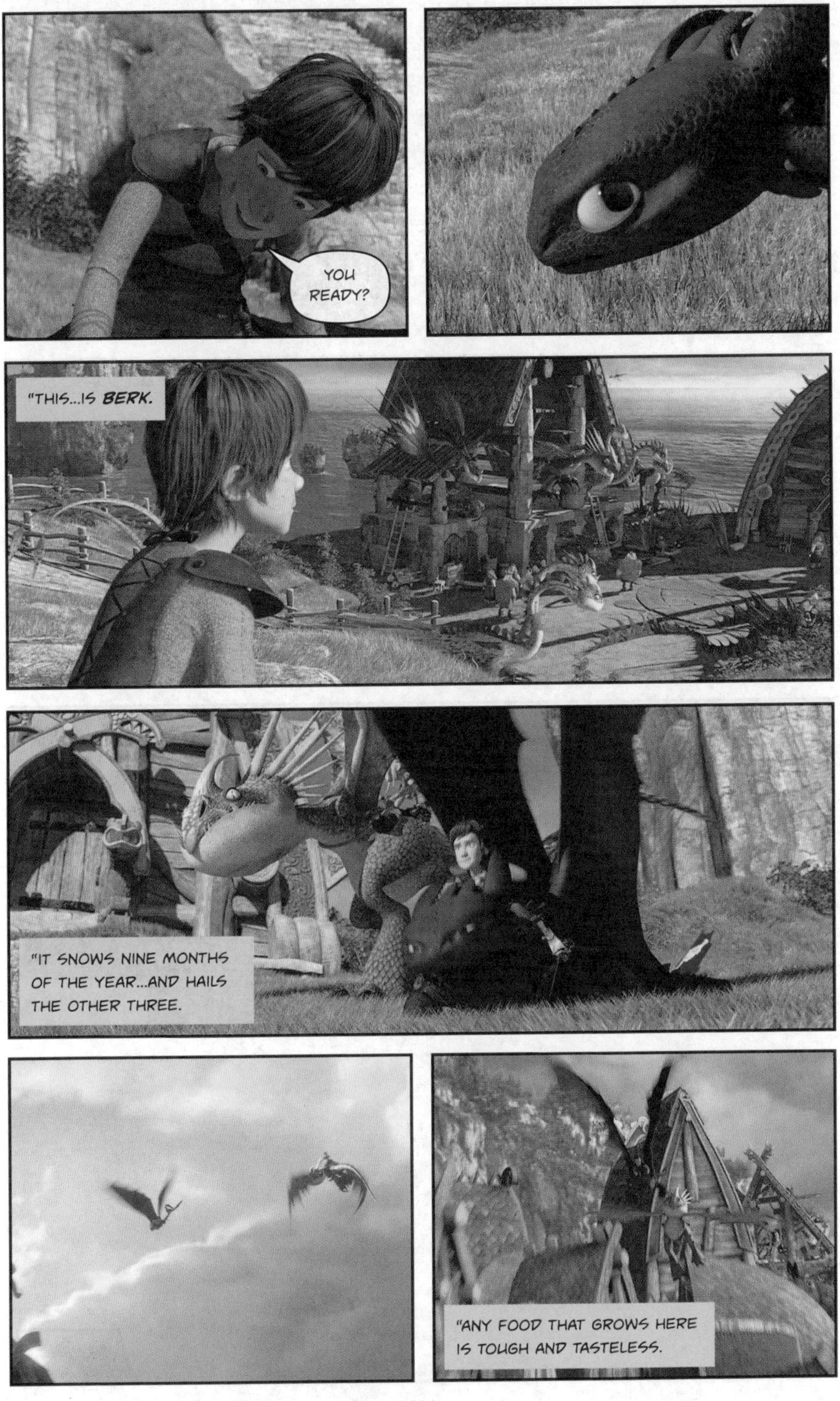
YOU READY?
"THIS...IS BERK.
"IT SNOWS NINE MONTHS OF THE YEAR...AND HAILS THE OTHER THREE.
"ANY FOOD THAT GROWS HERE IS TOUGH AND TASTELESS.

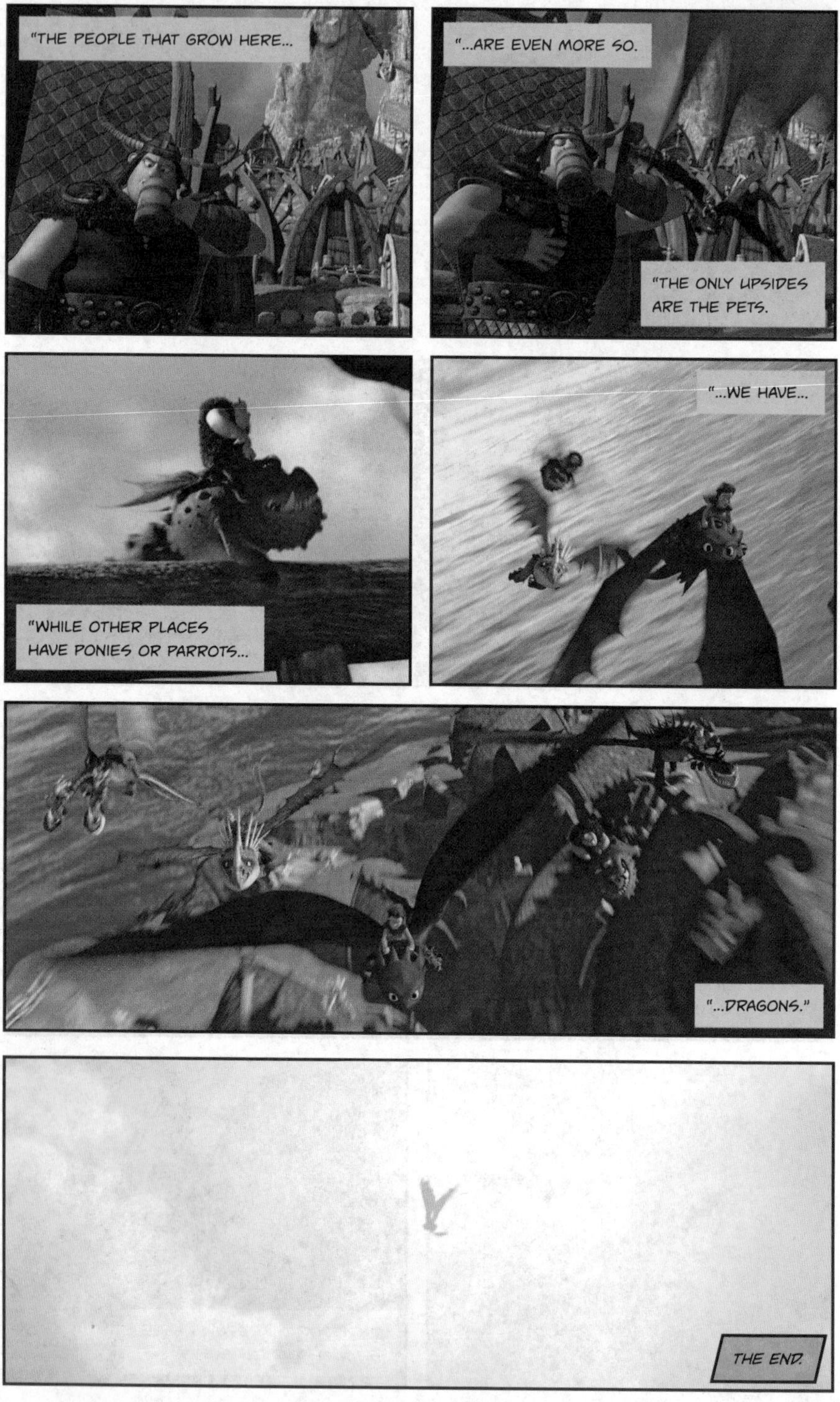
"THE PEOPLE THAT GROW HERE...
"...ARE EVEN MORE SO.
"THE ONLY UPSIDES ARE THE PETS.
"WHILE OTHER PLACES HAVE PONIES OR PARROTS...
"...WE HAVE...
"...DRAGONS."
THE END.